The Sh

Noël Coward was born in Teddington, Middlesex. He achieved fame with *The Vortex* (1924), in which he also appeared. Many other successful plays followed, including *Fallen Angels, Hay Fever, Private Lives* and *Blithe Spirit*. During the war he wrote screenplays such as *Brief Encounter* (1944) and *This Happy Breed* (1942). He later became a cabaret entertainer. He also published volumes of verse, a novel (*Pomp and Circumstance*) and two volumes of autobiography. He was knighted in 1970 and died three years later in Jamaica.

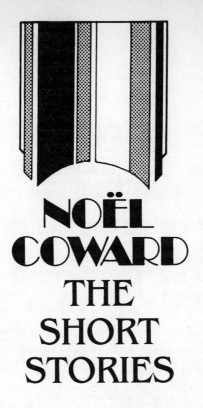

NOËL COWARD

THE SHORT STORIES

with a preface by Martin Tickner

Minerva

A Minerva Paperback

THE SHORT STORIES OF NÖEL COWARD
This collection first published in Great Britain 1985
by Methuen London Ltd.
This Minerva edition published 1991
Reprinted 1992
by Mandarin Paperbacks
Michelin House, 81 Fulham Road, London SW3 6RB

Minerva is an imprint of the Octopus Publishing Group,
a division of Reed International Books Limited.

This collection Copyright © 1985 by the Estate of the late Nöel Coward
Preface copyright © 1985 by Martin Tickner

'The Wooden Madonna', 'Traveller's Joy', 'Aunt Tittie', 'What Mad Pursuit?',
'Cheap Excursion', 'The Kindness of Mrs Radcliffe' and 'Nature Study'
first published in *To Step Aside* by William Heinemann Ltd in 1939

'A Richer Dust', 'Mr and Mrs Edgehill', 'Stop Me If You've Heard It',
'Ashes of Roses', 'This Time Tomorrow' and 'Star Quality'
first published in *Star Quality* by William Heinemann Ltd in 1951

'Mrs Capper's Birthday' (copyright © 1963 by Nöel Coward),
'Pretty Polly Barlow' and 'Me and the Girls' (both copyright © 1964
by Nöel Coward) first published in *Pretty Polly Barlow*
by William Heinemann Ltd in 1964

'Mrs Ebony' (originally published as 'Echo of Laughter'
– copyright © 1966 by Nöel Coward), 'Solali', 'Penny Dreadful' and
'Bon Voyage' first published in *Bon Voyage* (copyright © 1965, 1966
and 1967 by Nöel Coward) by William Heinemann Ltd in 1967

A CIP catalogue record for this title
is available from the British Library
ISBN 0 7493 9136 7

Printed and bound in Great Britain
by Cox & Wyman Ltd, Reading, Berks

CONTENTS

CONTENTS

PREFACE

Noël Coward was born on 16 December 1899 and had his first major success as a writer with the play *The Vortex* in 1924. This success was to continue through more than fifty plays and musicals as well as countless songs, films and performances until his death on 23 March 1973.

In his early writing career Noël had experimented with forms other than the plays and songs on which his reputation largely rests. However, it was not until the late 1930s that he started writing short stories in earnest. These were designed specifically for publication in *To Step Aside* (1939), the first of four collections, each taking its title from that of one of the stories included. The second collection, *Star Quality*, was published in 1951. This was followed in 1964 by *Pretty Polly Barlow* and, three years later, by *Bon Voyage*.

In 1962 *The Collected Short Stories of Noël Coward* gathered together all the stories in *To Step Aside* and *Star Quality*, with the exception of *The Wooden Madonna*. That story was included in a second volume of collected short stories, published in 1985, along with those in *Pretty Polly Barlow* and *Bon Voyage*.

This present book contains for the first time in one paperback volume (and in the case of many of the stories for the first time in *any* paperback volume) all the stories from the four collections.

For the 1962 *Collected Short Stories*, Noël contributed an Introduction the gist of which is as follows:

'Having been asked to write this preface re-introducing them (the short stories) to the reading public I decided, with a certain reluctance, to re-read them carefully and try to assess their worth as objectively as possible . . . I am happy to say I was most pleasantly surprised. These stories strike me as being neither outmoded nor inept, nor indeed so perfect that I feel I can never better them. In fact I enjoyed reading them very much and hope, before my day is done, to write several more.

The short story, like its cousin the one-act play, is regarded by some people with a certain irritated tolerance. It is not quite fish, flesh nor fowl, nor even, except in rare instances, good red herring. The rare instances, the good red herrings, have been provided by the masters of the craft such as de Maupassant, Maugham, Katherine Mansfield, O. Henry, Saki, etc. This is not to say that other writers have not occasionally produced masterpieces in this particular genre, but the great ones have remained constant and consistent and, as a general rule, have concentrated on this one form of creative activity rather than dally with any others. True, Somerset Maugham has written plays, novels and autobiographies, but I think that it is as a short story writer that he will chiefly be remembered. The same applies to de Maupassant and Saki, both of whom wrote excellent novels, but it was undoubtedly in the short story that their true genius shone.

In my own case, being primarily a dramatist, short stories have been an absorbing experiment in form, lying somewhere between a play and a novel. I found them fascinating to write, but far from easy. They demand perhaps a little less rigid self-discipline than a play, and a great deal more than a novel. In a novel there is room for divergencies and irrelevancies, in a play there is none; in a short story, just a little, but it must be strictly rationed. In a play the delineation of character must of course be limited to dialogue, and occasional dialogue at that. The author knows at the outset that all he has is two and a half hours of playing time at the most in which to develop his characters, unfold his plot and arrive at some sort of conclusive ending by eleven-fifteen. Naturally I am not suggesting that these arbitrary rules apply to some of our present-day playwrights to whom the idea of a plot or a conclusive ending at any time of night is beneath contempt. I am merely rambling on in my quaint old-fashioned way about how a play *should* be written and constructed. The same abyss of years lies between me and the sort of modern short story which begins in the middle of a sentence, wanders on for a while through a jungle of confused word-images and psychological abstractions, and comes to an end in the middle of another sentence. Like Mr Maugham, who is admittedly no chicken, I prefer my plays and stories and even novels to have a beginning, a middle and an end.'

Following the publication of that volume, the rest of the 1960s saw Noël turning more to prose, including the novel *Pomp and Circumstance*, although at the time he indicated that he was unlikely to pursue a new career as a novelist:

'The novel being done is a tremendous relief. I shall now, in my own good time, turn my attention to verse and perhaps short stories.'

There was no 'perhaps' about the stories, since between 1960 and 1966 he completed enough for the two later volumes. From reading Noël's diaries and autobiographies it is apparent that he found the form of the short story to be a relaxation between writing plays and composing songs.

Noël's stories could be said to have gone in a complete geographic circle. In his 1939 notes for *Past Conditional* (his incomplete third volume of autobiography), he wrote:

'Rented beach shack at Mokolaela (Honolulu). Lived in it completely alone and happy as a clam . . . I drove into town once a week for supplies and managed to write nearly all of *To Step Aside*. A very very peaceful and happy interlude . . . Went Switzerland April 25th. Finished off *To Step Aside* at the Beau Rivage in Lausanne.'

It was, of course, in Switzerland, not far from Lausanne, that Noël made one of his two bases (the other being Jamaica) in the later years of his life. A large number of the later stories in the present book were conceived there and the hotel in *Mrs Ebony* is certainly not a million miles from the Beau Rivage where Noël was also to set his trilogy of plays in which he made his last stage appearances, *Suite in Three Keys*.

MARTIN TICKNER

THE
WOODEN
MADONNA

Aubrey Dakers relaxed, a trifle self-consciously, in a pink cane chair outside the Café Bienvenue. He crossed one neatly creased trouser leg over the other and regarded his suede shoes whimsically for a moment and then, lighting a cigarette, gave himself up to enjoyment of the scene before him. His enjoyment was tempered with irritation. He had a slight headache from the train and the air was colder than he had anticipated, also it looked suspiciously as though it might rain during the next hour or so; however the sun was out for the time being and there was quite a lot to look at. On the other side of the water, mountains towered up into the sky, a number of small waterfalls lay on them like feathers and, in the distance, the higher peaks were still covered with snow. Little white streamers with black funnels bustled about the lake while immediately before him, beneath the blossoming chestnut trees, promenaded a series of highly characteristic types. By the newspaper kiosk for instance there was a group of young men, three of them wore bottle green capes and hats with feathers at the back, the fourth was more mundane in an ordinary Homburg and a buttoned-up mackintosh that looked quite like a cardboard box. Two artificial-looking children, dressed in red and

1

blue respectively, galloped along the pavement bowling hoops; a gray man with an umbrella waited furtively by the ticket office at the head of the little wooden pier, obviously a secret agent. Seated at a table on Aubrey's right were two English ladies, one very grand in black, wearing several gold chains and brooches and a patrician hat mounted high on bundles of gray hair; the other, small and servile, waited on her eagerly, pouring tea, offering patisserie, wriggling a little, like a dog waiting to have a ball thrown for it. "How funny," thought Aubrey, "if the Grand one really did throw a ball and sent her scampering off yapping under people's feet!" Pleased with this fantasy he smiled and then, observing a waiter looking at him, ordered a cup of coffee rather crossly.

Aubrey Dakers at the age of twenty-seven was in the enviable position of having written a successful play and in the less enviable position of having eventually to follow it up with another. If not another play, a novel, or at least a book of short stories. His play *Animal Grab* had already run for over a year in London and showed every sign of continuing indefinitely. It had been hailed enthusiastically by the critics. He had been described as "A new star in the theatrical firmament." "A second Somerset Maugham." "A second Noël Coward." "A second Oscar Wilde" and "A new playwright of considerable promise." This last had been in *The Times* and, as was right and proper, headed the list of press comments outside the theater. The extraordinary part of the whole thing was that Aubrey had never really intended to write a play at all, nor indeed to write anything. He had been perfectly content running a little antique shop with Maurice Macgrath in Ebury Street, which had been reasonably successful for six years and they had been happy as larks together. Aubrey remembered with a pang of nostalgia those early days, before they had actually opened the shop, when the whole thing was still in the air so to speak. That fateful Easter Monday when Maurice had suddenly come up from his parents' home in Kent and broken the glorious news. "My dear!" Aubrey could still recapture the thrill in his voice, "I've got the money!—Uncle Vernon's promised it and got round father and everything and we're to start looking for premises right away—isn't it absolutely heavenly?"

Then those lovely spring days motoring over the countryside, in Maurice's sister's Talbot, ransacking every antique shop they could find and often returning long after dark with the rumble seat crammed with oddments. The bigger stuff they bought was of course impossible to convey in the Talbot so this was all sent to be stored in Norman's studio, where, Norman being away in Capri for the winter, it could stay in the charge of Norman's housekeeper until May at least. Before May, however, they had found the shop in Ebury Street, fallen in love with it on sight and taken it recklessly on a twelve-year lease. Aubrey sighed. There had been anxious hours during those first few months. Then had come the sale of the Queen Anne set, broken chair and all, and then, almost as though Fate had suddenly determined to bewilder them with success, the bread trough and the Dutch candelabra were bought on the same day. You could never forget moments like that. The evening of celebration they'd had! Dinner at the Berkeley Grill and front-row stalls for the ballet.

After that the business had climbed steadily. They had always thought it would once they had a good start, and it did. During the ensuing years dinners at the Berkeley and stalls for the ballet became almost commonplace. But alas, even for amiable harmless lives like those of Aubrey and Maurice the laws of change are inexorable. In the year nineteen thirty-six the blow fell or, to be more accurate, a series of blows, beginning with Lady Brophy opening an elaborate interior decorating establishment five doors away from them. Lady Brophy was idle and rich, and with the heedless extravagance of the amateur, altered her window display completely every few weeks. She seldom arrived at her shop before noon, and then in a Rolls Royce, when Aubrey and Maurice had been at their post since nine o'clock as usual. Lady Brophy was undoubtedly the first blow. The drop in business within a few weeks of her arrival was only too apparent. The second blow was Maurice getting flu and then pneumonia and being sent to Sainte Maxime to convalesce where he first met Ivan. The third blow was a small but effective fire in the basement of the shop which demolished a Sheraton chair, two gate-legged tables, one good, the other so-so, a Jacobean corner cupboard, a set of Victorian engravings, two painted ostrich eggs circa 1850 and a really precious Spanish four-poster bed that Maurice had bought at an auction in Sevenoaks. The final and ultimately most decisive blow was Maurice's return to London with Ivan.

Ivan was more thoroughly Russian than any Russian Aubrey had ever seen. He was tall, melancholy, intellectual, given to spectacular outbursts of temperament and connected with the film business. Not, of course, in an active commercial way but on the experimental side. He was ardently at work upon a color film of shapes and sounds only, for which, he asserted positively, one of the principal companies in Hollywood was eagerly waiting. Aubrey often reproached himself for having been so nice to Ivan. If only he had known then what he knew later he would probably have been able to have nipped the whole thing in the bud, but then of course he could never have believed, unless it had been hammered into his brain by brutal reality, that Maurice could be so silly and, above all, so deceitful—but still there it was. Maurice suddenly announced that he wanted to give up the shop and lead a different sort of life entirely. You could have knocked Aubrey down with a feather. Maurice began the scene just as they were dressing to go to a first night at the Old Vic. Of course they hadn't gone. Even now Aubrey could hardly think of that awful evening without trembling. They had stayed in the flat, half dressed, just as they were and had the whole thing out. It had finally transpired that the root of the whole trouble was that Maurice was dissatisfied with himself. That, of course, was typical of Maurice—suddenly to be dissatisfied with himself when there was so much extra work to be done on account of the fire and a lot of new stuff to be bought. In vain Aubrey had remonstrated with him. In vain he had reiterated that what you are you are, and all the wishing in the world won't make you any different. Maurice had argued back that deep in his subconscious mind he had always had a conviction that what he was he wasn't really, that is to say at least not nearly so much as Aubrey was and that Ivan with his brilliant mind and wonderful view of life was the only person in the world who could really understand and help him; also, he added, he was an expert horseman. A few hours later they had gone out and had a chicken sandwich upstairs at the Café de Paris, both of them quite calm, purged of all emotion, but miserably aware that whatever the future might have in store for them, something very precious and important had been lost irretrievably.

That had all happened two and a half years ago. They had sold the shop jointly. Stock, lease, goodwill and everything. Aubrey had felt himself unable, even in the face of Maurice's pleading, to carry it on by himself or even with Norman, who had been quite keen to come in. The whole thing was over and that was that. Much better make a clean cut and embark on something new.

Maurice had, in due course, departed for America with Ivan, but there had apparently been some sort of hitch over the color film, for Aubrey had received a brief postcard from him some months later saying that he had obtained a position as assistant in Gump's Oriental Store in San Francisco and was very happy.

To embark on something new proved to be difficult for Aubrey for the simple reason that he had not the remotest idea what to embark on. He had a small amount of money saved from his share of the shop, and in order to husband this as carefully as possible he rejoined his family and stayed with them unenthusiastically for several months. He might have been less apathetic and devitalized had he but known at the time that those months at home with his parents, two unmarried sisters, a young brother and an elder brother with a wife and child, were the turning point in his life. *Animal Grab*, the comedy that had so entranced London and brought him such staggering success, had actually been written at his sister-in-law's request, for the local Amateur Dramatic Society to perform at the Town Hall for Christmas. There it had been seen, quite by chance, by

Thornton Heatherly, who happened to be staying in the neighborhood and was taken to it. Thornton Heatherly, an enterprising young man with a harelip, had been running a small repertory theater at Hounslow for nearly two years at a loss although with a certain amount of critical réclame and *Animal Grab* impressed him, not so much by its wit or craftsmanship or story, but by its unabashed family appeal. There was a persistent vogue of family plays of all sorts in London. *Animal Grab* was as authentic and definitely noisier than most, in addition to which it had two surefire characters in it. A vague, lovable mother who always forgot people's names and a comedy cook who repeatedly gave notice.

Thornton Heatherly drove over to see Aubrey the next day, bought a year's option on the play with a minimum advance on account of royalties, and exactly eight weeks later, after a triumphant fortnight at Hounslow, it became the smash hit of the London season.

Since then Aubrey had had a busy time adjusting himself to his new circumstances. First he took the upper part of a small house in South Eaton Place, which he furnished bit by bit with impeccable taste, until, finally, for sheer perfection of Victorian atmosphere, it rivaled even Norman's famous flat in Clebe Place. Then he gradually acquired, with expensive clothes to go with it, a manner of cynical detachment, which was most effective and came in handy as an opening gambit when meeting strangers. "How extraordinary," they would exclaim. "One would never imagine that the author of *Animal Grab* looked in the least like you," to which he would reply with a light sophisticated smile and a certain disarming honesty—"Actually the play is based on my own family which only goes to prove how wickedly deceptive appearances can be!" Everyone, in the face of such amused candor, found him charming and he was invited everywhere. It was, of course, inevitable that the more intellectual of his friends shouldn't much care for *Animal Grab*. While having to admit its authenticity they were scornful of its excessive naïveté. Vivian Melrose, who contributed abstract poems and, occasionally, even more abstract dramatic criticisms to *The Weekly Revue* and ran a leftist bookshop in Marylebone summed it up very pungently, *"Animal Grab,"* he said, "makes Puberty seem like Senile Decay!" Aubrey was smart enough to quote this with a wry laugh on several occasions, but in his heart he felt that Vivian had really gone a little too far. However, fortified by his weekly royalty checks, the sale of the amateur rights, the sale of the film rights and serialization in the *Evening Standard,* he could afford to ignore such gibes to a certain extent, but nevertheless a slight sting remained. He had signed an optional contract with Thornton Heatherly for the next two plays he wrote but as yet he had been unable to put pen to paper. After endless conversations with his intimate friends, such as Norman, and Elvira James, who was a literary agent and knew a thing or two, he had decided that his next effort should not be a play at all. He would first of all write a book of short stories, some of which need not be more than light sketches, in order to form an easy flexible style and then try his hand at a novel. He felt a strong urge—as indeed who doesn't?—to write a really good modern novel. Elvira and he had discussed this project very thoroughly. "To begin with," she had said, "it must not be about a family, either your own or anybody else's. The vogue for family life, although running strong at the moment, will not last for ever and there will be a reaction, mark my words." Aubrey agreed with her wholeheartedly, for truth to tell, family feeling, although charmingly expressed in *Animal Grab*, was not, and never had been, his strong point. "Then," went on Elvira relentlessly, "there must be no character in your book who is absentminded, your heroine must never say 'Come on, old Weasel, let's have another set,' and no old gentleman, father, uncle, vicar or professor must be called 'Boffles'!" Aubrey, recognizing the innate wisdom of this, promised. "Away with you," said Elvira, "go away and take notes, watch people, travel, look at Somerset Maugham!" This conversation had taken place a week ago and here he was alone in Switzerland having looked at Somerset Maugham steadfastly since leaving Victoria.

It must not be imagined that Aubrey intended to imitate anybody's particular style, he was far too intelligent for that, but he realized that a careful study of expert methods must in the long run be of some use to a beginner, and Aubrey had no illusions whatever as to his status as a writer. He only knew now, after the violent change that had occurred in his life during the last eighteen months, that he wanted, really wanted, to write. His notes, since leaving England, while not exactly copious, at least showed praiseworthy determination. "Old Lady on platform in wheelchair, probably French Duchess." "Man in dining car with elderly woman obviously German." He had had later to cross out German and put Scotch as he happened to hear them talking in the corridor. "The French countryside seen from a railway carriage looks strangely unfinished." That wasn't bad. "Indian Colonel and wife going to take cure in Wiesbaden suddenly have terrible row and he kills her in tunnel." This had been suggested by two disagreeable people at the next table to him at dinner in the Wagon restaurant.

Sitting outside this café in the afternoon sunshine his mind felt pleasantly alert. It had certainly been a good idea, this little continental jaunt; here he could sit, for hours if need be, just watching and listening and absorbing atmosphere. Later, of course, in the bar of the hotel or in the lounge after dinner, he would get into conversation with various people and draw them out subtly to talk about themselves, to tell him their stories. His knowledge of French being only adequate he hoped that should they wish to lay bare their lives in that language that they would not speak too rapidly. Of German he knew not a word, so whatever he gathered would have to be in English, slow French or by signs.

At this moment in his reflections his attention was caught by the seedy-looking man whom he had noticed before buying a ticket for the boat. Something in the way he was standing, or rather leaning against the railing, struck a familiar chord in his mind. He reminded him of somebody, that's what it was, but who? He scrutinized him carefully, the gray suit, the umbrella, the straggling moustache, the air of depressed resignation. Then he remembered—he was exactly like a commoner, foreign edition of Uncle Philip. Aubrey sighed with relief at having identified him; there is nothing so annoying as being tantalized by a resemblance. Uncle Philip! It might make quite an interesting little story if Uncle Philip, after all those years of marriage, suddenly left Aunt Freda and came here to live in some awful little pension with a French prostitute. Or perhaps not live with her, just meet her every afternoon here at the pier. His eyes would light up when she stepped off the boat (she worked in a café in a town on the other side of the lake and only had a few hours off), and they would walk away together under the chestnut trees, he timidly holding her arm. Then they would go to some sordid bedroom in the town somewhere and he, lying with her arms round him, would suddenly think of his life, those years at Exeter with Aunt Freda, and laugh madly. Aubrey looked at the Swiss Uncle Philip again; he was reading a newspaper now very intently. Perhaps, after all, he was a secret agent as he had at first thought and was waiting for the boat to take him down the lake to the town on the other side of the frontier, where he would sit in a bar with two men in bowler hats and talk very ostentatiously about his son who was ill in Zurich, which would give them to understand that Karl had received the papers satisfactorily in Amsterdam.

At this moment a bell rang loudly and a steamer sidled up to the pier. The man folded his paper, waved his hand and was immediately joined by a large woman in green and three children who had been sitting on a seat. They all went onto the boat together, the children making a good deal of noise. Aubrey sighed. Just another family.

While Aubrey was having his bath before dinner he visualized, on Somerset Maugham lines, the evening before him. A cocktail in the bar, then a table in the corner of the dining room commanding an excellent view of all the other tables. A distinguished-looking man, slightly gray at the temples eating alone at a table by the window, high cheekbones, skin yellowed by malaria and tropical suns.

Then later, in the lounge, "Perhaps you would do me the honor of taking a glass of brandy with me." Aubrey agreeing with an assured smile, noting the while those drawn lines of pain round the finely cut mouth, those hollow, rather haunted eyes. "One can at least say of this hotel that the brandy is of unparalleled excellence!" That slightly foreign accent, Russian perhaps or even Danish! Then the story—bit by bit, gradually unfolding—"I wonder if you ever knew the Baroness Fugler? A strange woman, dead now poor thing; I ran across her brother once in the Ukraine, that was just after the war, then later on, seven years to be exact, I ran across him again in Hankow; I happened to be there on business. He was probably the most brilliant scientist of his time. Has it ever occurred to you to reflect upon the strange passions that lie dormant in the minds of the most upright men?" The lounge emptying, still that level unemotional voice retailing the extraordinary, almost macabre, history of the Baroness Fugler's brother, the scandal in Hong Kong, the ruining of his career, his half-caste wife and finally the denouement.

Aubrey, at last rising. "Thank you so much—what a wonderful story. And what happened to the woman?" Then the sudden bitter chuckle, "The woman, my friend—happens to be my wife!"

2

Aubrey, immaculately dressed in a dinner jacket, descended to the bar, where he was discouraged to find no one whatever except the barman, who was totting up figures and absently eating potato salad. Aubrey suspected that there must be garlic in the potato salad as it smelt very strong. It was a rather dingy little bar, dimly lit, although modern in decoration to the extent that everything that looked as though it ought to be round was square or vice versa and there was a lot of red about. Aubrey hoisted himself on to a square stool and ordered a dry Martini and a packet of Player's. The barman, although quite willing to be pleasant, was not discursive and turned on the radio. Aubrey sipped his Martini and listened, a trifle wistfully, to an Italian tenor singing "Santa Lucia," and when that was over "La Donna E Mobile." Presently several people came in together, they were elderly and without glamour, and they stood silently by the bar as though they were waiting for some catastrophe. The barman glanced at the clock and then switched the radio to another station. A tremendous shriek ensued which he modulated until it became a German voice announcing the news. Aubrey could only pick out a word or two here and there such as "Einmal," "Americanische," "Freundschaft" and "Mussolini," so he ordered another dry Martini in a whisper. At the end of the news, which lasted half an hour, everybody bowed to the barman and filed out. Just as Aubrey was preparing to give up the whole thing and go and have dinner, a bald man of about fifty came in. He was obviously English and although not quite as sinister and distinguished as Aubrey would have wished, he was better than nobody. Aubrey noted the details of his appearance with swift professional accuracy. A long nose, eyes rather close together, a jutting underlip, slight jowl, as though at some time in his life someone had seized his face with both hands and pulled it downward. His clothes were quite good and his figure podgy without being exactly fat. He said "Good evening" in a voice that wasn't quite cockney but might have been a long while ago. Aubrey replied with alacrity and offered him a drink, whereupon the man said, "That's very nice of you, my name's Edmundson," as though the thought of accepting a drink from anyone who didn't know his name was Edmundson was not to be tolerated for a moment. Aubrey said that his name was Dakers and they shook hands cordially.

Mr. Edmundson was more than ready to talk, and before a quarter of an hour had passed Aubrey had docketed a number of facts. Mr. Edmundson was fifty-four and was in the silk business although he intended to retire shortly and let his son, who was married and had two children, a boy and a girl, take over for him. He also had two daughters both unmarried. One, however, was engaged to a nice young fellow in the Air Force, this was Sylvia the younger. The elder, Blanche, was having her voice trained with the object of becoming an opera singer. It was apparently a fine voice and very high indeed, and both Mr. and Mrs. Edmundson were at a loss to imagine where she had got it from as neither of them had any musical talent whatsoever. She was very good-looking too, although not so striking as Sylvia, who was the sort of girl people turn round to stare at in restaurants. Mr. Edmundson produced a snapshot from his note-case showing both girls with arms entwined against a sundial with somebody's foot and calf in the left-hand corner. "That's Mrs. Edmundson's foot," he said gaily, "she didn't get out of the way in time." Aubrey looked at the photograph with his head on one side and gave a little cluck of admiration. "They *are* nice-looking girls," he said as convincingly as he could. Thus encouraged, Mr. Edmundson went on about them a good deal more. Sylvia was the dashing one of the two and in many ways an absolute little minx; whatever she set her heart on she got, she was that sort of character; in fact, a few years ago when she was just beginning to be grown up, both he and Mrs. Edmundson had frequently been worried about her. Blanche, on the other hand, despite her musical gift, was more balanced and quiet, which was very odd really, because you would have thought it would have been just the other way round. Aubrey agreed that it certainly was most peculiar but there just wasn't any way of accounting for things like that. "This is my son Leonard," said Mr. Edmundson, pro-

9

ducing another snapshot with the deftness of a card manipulator. "He's different again." Aubrey looked at it and admitted that he was. Leonard was short and sturdy with an under-slung jaw and eyebrows that went straight across his forehead in a black bar. On his lap he was holding, rather self-consciously, a mad baby. Mr. Edmundson discoursed for a long while upon Leonard's flair for engineering which apparently fell little short of genius. Ever since he was a tiny boy he had been unable to see a watch or a clockwork engine or a musical box without tearing it to pieces immediately, and when he was sixteen he had completely dismembered his new motorcycle on the front lawn within three hours of having received it.

During dinner, Mr. Edmundson having suggested that as they were both alone it would be pleasant to share a table, he explained that the reason he had come to Switzerland was to see a specialist on diseases of the bladder who had been recommended to him by a well-known doctor in Tonbridge. It appeared that for nearly a year past there had been a certain divergence of opinion as to whether he was forming a stone or not, and both he and his wife had decided, after mature consideration, that by far the wisest thing to do was to get an expert opinion once and for all. The Swiss specialist, who wasn't really Swiss but Austrian, had declared that as far as he could discover there were no indications of a stone having been formed or even beginning to form, but that in order to be on the safe side Mr. Edmundson must lead a perfectly normal life for ten days eating and drinking all that was habitual to him, which of course accounted for the three dry Martinis he had had in the bar, and then further tests would be made and we should see what we should see.

After dinner, in the lounge where they took their coffee, Mr. Edmundson reverted to his domestic affairs, discussing, at length, Blanche's prospects in Grand Opera; the problematical happiness of Sylvia when married to an aviator who might be killed at any minute; the advisability of forcing Leonard into the silk business where he would be certain of an assured income, or allowing him to continue with his experimental engineering; and last, but by no means least, whether Mrs. Edmundson's peculiar lassitude for the past few months was really caused by her teeth, which had been suggested, or whether it could be accounted for by those well-known biological changes that occur in all women of a certain age. He personally was in favor of the teeth theory and agreed with the doctor that she ought to have every man jack of them pulled out, and a nice set of artificial ones put in. The idea of this, however, somehow repelled Mrs. Edmundson, and so at the moment things were more or less at a deadlock.

Leaving them at a deadlock, Aubrey, increasingly aware that

his head was splitting, almost abruptly said good night and departed, on leaden feet, to his room.

The next morning, round about half-past ten, Aubrey was sun-
ning himself on his balcony, breathing in gratefully the fresh mountain air and enjoying the romantic tranquil beauty of the view. The
lake was calm and blue and without a ripple except for the occasional passing of a steamer and a few little colored rowing boats
sculling about close to the shore. Fleecy clouds lay around the
peaks of the mountains and the morning was so still that the cow
bells in the high pastures could be heard quite clearly. Presently Mr.
Edmundson appeared on the next balcony about four feet away from
him. "What a bit of luck," he said cheerfully. "I had no idea we were
next-door neighbors." Conversation, or rather monologue, set in immediately. "I've had a postcard from Leonard's wife," he went on.
"The younger child, the boy, woke up yesterday morning covered
with spots and they're very worried, of course. I don't suppose it's
anything serious, but you never know, do you? Anyhow, they sent for
the doctor at once and kept the little girl away from school in case it
might turn out to be something catching, and they're going to telegraph me during the day."

Aubrey endured this for a few minutes and then rose with a
great air of decision. Mr. Edmunson, with the swiftness of a cat who
perceives that the most enjoyable mouse it has met for weeks is
about to vanish down a hole, pounced. "I thought we might take a
little excursion on the lake; those skiffs are no trouble to handle."

Aubrey, shaken by the suggestion, replied that there would be
nothing he would have liked better but that he was being called for
by some friends who were driving him up to the mountains for lunch.

"Never mind," said Mr. Edmundson, "we're sure to meet later."

Aubrey lay on his bed for a while, shattered. He had been looking forward to a stroll through the town by himself and later a quiet
lunch either on the hotel terrace or at a café down by the lake. Now,
having committed himself to a drive in the mountains with his mythical friends, he was almost bound to be caught out. Why, oh why
hadn't he been smart enough to think of a less concrete excuse?
Suddenly he jumped up. The thing to do was to finish dressing and
get out of the hotel immediately before Mr. Edmundson got downstairs. Once in the town he could keep a careful lookout and dart
into a shop or something if he saw him coming. Fortunately, he had
already bathed and shaved and in less than ten minutes he tiptoed
out of his room. The coast was clear. He ran lightly down the stairs
rather than use the lift which might take too long to come up. He
was detained for a moment in the lounge by the hotel manager inquiring if he had slept well, but contrived to shake him off and sped

through the palm garden on to the terrace. Mr. Edmundson rose from a chair at the top of the steps. "No sign of your friend's car yet," he said. "Why not sit down and have a Tom Collins?"

"I'm afraid I can't," said Aubrey hurriedly. "I promised to meet them in the town and I'm late as it is."

"I'll come with you." Mr. Edmundson squared his shoulders. "I feel like a brisk walk."

Halfway to the town Aubrey gave an elaborate glance at his wristwatch. "I'm afraid I shall have to run," he said. "I promised to meet them at 11:15 and it's now twenty to twelve."

"Do us both good," said Mr. Edmundson and broke into a trot. In the main square, which Aubrey had chosen at random as being the place where his friends were meeting him, there was, not unnaturally, no sign of them. Mr. Edmundson suggested sitting down outside a café and waiting. "They've probably been held up on the road," he said.

"I'm afraid," murmured Aubrey weakly, "that they're much more likely to have thought I wasn't coming and gone off without me."

"In that case," said Mr. Edmundson with a comforting smile, "we can take a little drive on our own and have lunch in the country somewhere."

During lunch, in a chalet restaurant high up on the side of a mountain, Mr. Edmundson spoke frankly of his early life. He had not, he said, always known the security, independence and comparative luxury that he enjoyed now, far from it. His childhood, most of which had been spent in a small house just off the Kennington Road, had been poverty-stricken in the extreme. Many a time he remembered having to climb a lamp-post in order to get a brief glimpse of a cricket match at the Oval, and many a time also he had been chased by the police for this and like misdemeanors; indeed on one occasion—

Aubrey listened and went on listening in a sort of desperate apathy. There was nothing else to do, no escape whatever. Incidents of Mr. Edmundson's life washed over him in a never-ending stream; his experiences in the war during which he hadn't got so much as a flesh wound in three years; his apprenticeship to the silk trade as a minor office clerk in Birmingham; his steady climb for several years until he arrived at being first a traveler and then manager of a department in a big shop in South London; his first meeting with the now Mrs. Edmundson at a dance in Maida Vale; his marriage; his honeymoon at Torquay; the birth of Blanche. By the time the doctor had arrived to deliver Mrs. Edmundson of Sylvia it had become quite chilly in the chalet restaurant and the shadows of the mountains were beginning to draw out over the lake. In the taxi driving back to the town Sylvia was safely delivered and Leonard well on the way.

Finally, having reached his room and shut and locked the door Aubrey flung himself down on the bed in a state of collapse. His whole body felt saturated with boredom and his limbs ached as though he had been running. Through the awful deadness of his despair he heard Mr. Edmundson in the next room humming a tune. Aubrey buried his head in the pillow and groaned.

3

Aubrey came down into the bar before dinner resolute and calm. He had had a hot bath, two aspirin, thought things out very carefully and made his decision. Consequently he was able to meet Mr. Edmundson's jocular salutation with equanimity. "I am leaving tomorrow evening," he said, graciously accepting a dry Martini. "For Venice."

Mr. Edmundson looked suitably disappointed. "What a shame," he said. "I thought you were staying for a week at least; in fact I was looking forward to being able to travel as far as Paris with you if my test turns out to be all right on Tuesday. You did say you were going to Paris from here, you know," he said reproachfully.

"I've changed my mind," said Aubrey. "I'm sick of Switzerland and I've always wanted to see Venice."

"Nice time of year for it anyhow," said Mr. Edmundson raising his glass. "Here goes."

The one thing that Aubrey had realized in the two hours' respite before dinner was that no compromise was possible. He couldn't very well stay on in the same hotel as Mr. Edmundson and refuse to eat with him or speak to him. That would be unkind and discourteous and hurt his feelings mortally. Aubrey shrank from rudeness and there was a confiding quality about Mr. Edmundson, a trusting belief that he was being good company which it would be dreadfully cruel to shatter. It was all Aubrey's own fault anyhow for having encouraged him in the first place. The only thing was to put up with things as they were for this evening and, he supposed, most of the next day and leave thankfully on the Rapide the next night. He had already arranged about his ticket and sleeper with the porter.

Mr. Edmundson banished melancholy by shrugging his shoulders, shooting his cuffs and giving a jolly laugh. "Anyway," he said, "it's all right about the baby's spots! I had a telegram this evening. The doctor said it was nothing but a rash, which only goes to show that there's no sense in being fussy until you know you've got something to be really fussy about. But that's typical of Nora, that's Leonard's wife, she's like that over everything, fuss, fuss, fuss. Sometimes I don't know how Len stands it and that's a fact; fortunately his

13

head's screwed on the right way; it takes more than a few spots on baby's bottom to upset *his* apple-cart!"

Mr. Edmundson continued to be gay through dinner. He ordered a bottle of Swiss wine just to celebrate, "Hail and Farewell you know!" After dinner they went to the Kursaal and sat through an old and rather dull German movie. Mr. Edmundson seemed to enjoy it enormously and actually laughed once or twice, which irritated Aubrey, as he knew Mr. Edmundson understood German as little as he did. In the foyer on the way out a man in a bowler hat with a very foreign accent asked Mr. Edmundson for a light. "Right you are, me old cock robin," said Mr. Edmundson, and slapped him on the back. Aubrey hung his head in shame.

The next morning Aubrey woke with a great sense of relief, only one more day, one more lunch, one more dinner and then escape. He was careful, while dressing, not to venture out on to the balcony and, with amazing luck, managed to get out of the hotel and into town without seeing Mr. Edmundson at all. He chose a table, partially screened by a flowering shrub, outside the "Bienvenue," where he had sat the first afternoon of his arrival. It seemed incredible that it was only the day before yesterday—he felt as though he'd been living with Mr. Edmundson for weeks. The scene before him was as light and varied as ever, but he found after a while that he was looking at it with different eyes. A lot of the charm, the glitter of potential adventure had faded. He felt like some passionate virgin who had just had her first love affair and discovered it to have been both uncomfortable and dull. Rather pleased with this simile he jotted it down on the back of an envelope that he happened to have in his pocket. For instance, now, with this new, cynical disillusionment, he was certain that the man walking by with the pretty girl in a yellow beret was *not* her lover and had *not* just broken his leave in order to fly from Brussels to see her. Nor was the heavily made-up woman encased in black satin and wearing high-heeled white shoes the depraved Madame of a Brothel who had amassed a fortune out of the White Slave Traffic. Nor even was the ferrety-looking man in the gray raincoat carrying a violin case a secret agent. He was just a family man with five children. The made-up woman was probably the mother of six and the man and the girl were brother and sister and bored to tears with each other.

Elvira was wrong and so, damn it, was Somerset Maugham. The prospect of going through life alone in hotels and running the risk of meeting a series of Mr. Edmundsons was too awful to be contemplated. If that was the only way to gain material and inspiration he'd rather go back to antiques or write another play about his own family.

It depressed him to think that a man could live for fifty-four years like Mr. Edmundson and have nothing of the faintest interest happen to him at all beyond a problematical stone in the bladder. Of course he fully realized that a great writer with technique, humanity, warmth and vivid insight, such as Arnold Bennett, could make Mr. Edmundson an appealing hero for several hundred pages, but he himself felt that even though, in the far future, he should become a successful author, that sort of thing would, most emphatically, not be his line. He sipped a cup of delicious chocolate, with a large blob of cream on the top and anticipated the pleasures of Venice. He would sit on the terrace of a hotel on the Grand Canal and watch the sun setting over the lagoon, if it did, and the gondolas drifting by, and he wouldn't speak a word to anyone at all in any circumstances whatever unless they looked so madly attractive that he couldn't restrain himself.

He finished his chocolate, paid for it, scanned the horizon carefully and got up. There was an antique shop in a side street that he had noticed on his way to the café with some rather nice things in the window, and he thought he might go in and poke about a bit. He gave a little sigh. If only Maurice hadn't been so tiresome and were here with him, what fun it would be. But still, if Maurice hadn't been tiresome he would never have written *Animal Grab* and wouldn't be here at all, so there was no sense in being wistful about that. He turned up the little side street and shot back into an archway while Mr. Edmundson, fortunately looking the other way, passed within a few inches of him. Aubrey giggled with relief at his escape and fairly scampered off to the antique shop. The man in the shop greeted him politely. His English was very bad and Aubrey was certain he had heard his voice and seen his face before. He routed about for nearly an hour, not finding anything of interest apart from a very lovely Italian mirror that would have made Maurice's mouth water and some bits of rather fakey-looking *cinque-cento* jewelry. He bought a pair of malachite earrings for sixteen francs for Elvira, and was on his way out when his eye was caught by a small wooden Madonna. It was probably not older than eighteenth century or the beginning of the nineteenth and had once been painted in bright colors, but most of the paint had either faded or been rubbed off, giving the figure a pale almost ethereal quality. It was obviously of no particular value but certainly quite charming and might make a nice present for someone. He asked the man the price and was astonished to hear that it was two hundred francs. The man went off into a long rigmarole about it being very old and having belonged to the famous Marchesa something or other, but Aubrey, who wouldn't have paid more than ten shillings for it at most, cut him short with a polite bow and went out. On his way back to the hotel he suddenly remembered where he had seen the man before and gave a little gasp of remembered embarrassment. It was the man who

15

had asked for a light in the foyer of the cinema last night, and to whom Mr. Edmundson with agonizing heartiness had said, "Right you are, me old cock robin!"

As he was walking through the lounge the underwaiter who generally served their coffee after dinner stopped him with information that his uncle was waiting for him in the bar. Aubrey laughed, repressing a shudder at the thought. "That's not my uncle," he said, "that's Mr. Edmundson." The waiter bowed politely and Aubrey went up to his room to wash.

At lunch Mr. Edmundson seemed a little less animated than usual. Aubrey, feeling that he could afford to be magnanimous as there were only a few hours to go, explained that the reason he hadn't seen him during the morning was that he had to get up early to go to Cook's about his passport and do a little shopping in town. He told him about the antique shop and also, with a little edge of malice, about recognizing the man. "You remember," he said, "the one you nearly knocked down in the Kursaal last night." Mr. Edmundson had the grace to look rather startled for a moment and then gave a shamefaced laugh. "I think I was a bit over the odds last night," he said. "That Swiss wine and the brandy after dinner." Then he changed the subject.

4

Mr. Edmundson insisted on coming with Aubrey to the station, merrily waving aside all protests. In the hotel bus his conversation was more domestic than ever. Apparently an aunt of Mrs. Edmundson's, hitherto concealed from Aubrey, had been living with them for nearly two years and was nothing more nor less than a damned nuisance. One of those whining women, always on the grumble and always causing trouble with the servants. They'd had altogether five parlormaids since she'd been in the house and now the present one was leaving, having told Mrs. Edmundson candidly that she just couldn't stand it and that was a fact. When the bus reached the station Mr. Edmundson was seriously considering whether or not it wouldn't be better and cheaper in the long run to set up the aunt on her own in a little flat in some seaside resort such as Herne Bay or Broadstairs. "After all," he said, "it isn't as if she's all that old, seventy-three's getting on I grant you, but she's in full possession of all her faculties, a bloody sight too full if you ask me, and she could live her own life and do what she pleased and grumble to her heart's content."

When Aubrey had got himself and his bags into his sleeper there were still a few minutes to spare before the train went, which Mr. Edmundson utilized by sitting on the bed and reverting briefly to the subject of Mrs. Edmundson's teeth. At last a whistle blew and he jumped up. "Well, bye-bye, old man," he said. "It's been jolly nice to have known you." Then, to Aubrey's embarrassment, he plunged his hand into the pocket of his coat and produced a small brown paper package. "I've bought you this this afternoon in the town just as a little souvenir. I know you like that sort of thing. No—" he held up his hand—"don't start thanking me, it isn't anything at all, just look at it every now and then and think of me and be good." The train started to move, and he dashed down the corridor and out on to the platform. Aubrey, feeling guilty and ashamed, opened the package and was appalled to discover that it was the little wooden Madonna he had seen in the antique shop that morning. He turned it over in his hands; the head had been broken off at some time or other and been stuck on again. Two hundred Swiss francs! That was about ten pounds! He closed his eyes and felt himself blushing with mortification at the cruel thoughts he had harbored against Mr. Edmundson. Poor Mr. Edmundson. Pathetic Mr. Edmundson. That was the worst of bores, they always turned out to have hearts of gold; it was awful. He undressed pensively and went to bed. In the night he was half wakened by the figure of a man stretching across to his luggage on the rack. Drowsily he realized that the train must be at the Italian Frontier.

"Nothing to declare," he muttered.

The man went away and he went to sleep again.

The next day, about a half an hour before the train was due to arrive in Venice, he unwrapped the Madonna again, which had been lying on the rack, and was in the act of putting it into his suitcase among his dirty washing when the head fell off and rolled under the seat. This tickled him enormously; he sat down and laughed until he cried. It really was too sad—poor Mr. Edmundson. He retrieved the head and tried to fix it on again, but it wouldn't stick without glue. The body was hollow and he shook it upside down just to see whether or not any priceless jewels might have been concealed inside, but it was quite empty. People like Mr. Edmundson, he reflected, are born unlucky, they can't even give a present without it being a failure.

Mr. Edmundson, on leaving the station, walked briskly down to the lake side and turned into the Bienvenue Café. It wasn't very crowded, but the air was smoky and thick and the radio was turned on full. He sat down and ordered a beer and an evening paper. Two men in bowler hats were seated at a table opposite to him playing dominoes, one of them was the proprietor of the antique shop. After a little while he looked across at Mr. Edmundson and raised his eyebrows inquiringly. Mr. Edmundson looked casually round the room, nodded briefly and went on reading his paper.

TRAVELER'S JOY

Leroy Street started high up in the social scale, just off Vernon Square where the Boots' Cash Chemists was, and the Kardomah Café and the new Regal Cinema, but it deteriorated just about in the middle, where the houses, although the same size as those further up, seemed to lose caste subtly, like respectable women who are beginning to take a drink. Toward the end of the street all pretensions died, and it wandered inconclusively in squalor out into the waste land behind the town among slag heaps, piles of rubbish, broken bits of Ford cars rusting in the weather, and marshy ponds lying stagnant by the side of the canal.

The Theatre Royal was in the High Street, and although it backed practically on to the garden of Number Fourteen, you had to walk right up into Vernon Square and round and down again before you got to it. Herbert Darrell could actually see into his "combined" on the first floor if he turned his head while he was making up. It irritated him sometimes to see Miss Bramble fussing about among his things; he had to repress an impulse to yell at her from the dressing-room window, but, he told himself, these sudden bursts of annoyance were only liver, and so he controlled himself and took an extra sip of Guinness as a nerve soother. He generally had a little rule by which he limited himself to only one glass before the first act. It was a game he played, resisting small temptations, and he had it all laid out beautifully. Two or three gulps before starting to make up, two or three more after the foundation had been put on (Numbers Five, Three and Nine, Leichner always, although it was not so good now as before the War), then a nice long draft before he put on his eyes and mouth, leaving just a little at the bottom of the glass to give a final tickle to the gullet before going down on to the stage.

Not having much imagination, the signs of age in his face depressed him rarely. On the whole it seemed to him to look much the same as it always had. Of course there were more lines and the eyes were a bit puffy underneath, but there was still a glint in them all right. He sometimes winked archly in the glass just to prove it and also, when dressing alone, he occasionally indulged in the "Passion" face. This was one of his triumphs of the past. A slight projection of the head, half-closed eyes swimming with desire, and an almost imperceptible dilating of the nostrils. In the garden scene in *Lady Mary's Love Affair* in nineteen hundred and four, that particular expression had caused a considerable sensation. He had been hailed, for a time, as one of the great lovers of the stage. Now, in nineteen thirty-four, he still used it, but with a deliberate slackening of intensity, a gallant middle-aged mellowness. He was no fool, he often told himself, none of that painful mutton-dressed-as-lamb business for him! Why, he had voluntarily given up playing Juveniles years ago when he was a bare forty-five.

Just before the end of the performance every night, during his wait in the last act, he usually gave way to a little misty retrospection. Misty, owing to the fact that his fourth Guinness was standing at his elbow. It was pleasant to review the past without anger or bitterness, although God knows he had cause enough for bitterness; the Theater going to the dogs as it was and all these inexperienced muttering young actors playing leadings parts in the West End. But he was all right, pretty contented on the whole, generally in work and with enough money saved to tide him over the bleak periods between tours. Just every now and then, quite unaccountably, in the middle of the night, or riding along on the top of a bus, awareness of failure plunged at him like a sword; twisting in his consciousness cruelly as though it had been lying in wait to murder his self-respect and puncture and wound his pleasure in himself. These searing moments were fortunately rare and passed away as swiftly as they came. There was always something to do, some amiable method of passing the time. Life was full of small opportunities of enjoyment; the sudden meeting of an old friend on a train call for instance, the hurried furtive Guinness in a pub opposite the station with one eye on the clock.

19

Hashing over the past lightly enough not to rumple the dust of illusion, which, more and more as the years advanced, was settling deeper upon it. Every gay episode was, by now, overcolored into vivid relief, magnified beyond all proportion of its actual happening. Every bad moment was trodden into the lower darkness. Short runs. Bad press notices. The losing of jobs after perhaps a week's rehearsal. "I'm afraid, Mr. Darrell, you are really not quite suited to this part." Agonies such as these had been too swift and sudden to be dodged immediately; egos, however strong and truculent, must be allowed a little time to summon their forces, and the moments between the actual shock and the soothing palliative of a drink were frequently unbearably long, little gray eternities stretching from the stage door to the nearest pub, with the head averted so that passersby should not catch the glimmer of unmanly, mortified tears. These happenings lay low in his mind, fathoms deep, like strange twisted creatures that inhabit the depths of the sea; blind and unbelieved and only horrible when some unforeseen tidal disturbance brings them to the surface. In these awful moments Herbert Darrell turned tail and ran, stumbling, panic-stricken and breathless until exhaustion outstripped the pursuit and he could relax with some acquaintance, not even a friend was necessary, and preen his draggled feathers; fluffing them out bravely and crowing a little, weakly at first, until the second or third drink gurgled smoothly into his stomach and drowned his fears.

His digs in Leroy Street were really very good. Better and cleaner than Mrs. Blockley's in Nottingham that everyone went on so much about. They were cheaper too. Mrs. Blockley was too bloody grand, and even if the Martin Harveys had stayed there once there was no need to make such a song and dance about it. Here, at Number Fourteen there were no star memories. No eminent ghosts in Shakespearean tights leered down from the mantelpiece. There were, in point of fact, very few photographs, which was a relief. Only one group of Miss Bramble's mother and father and elder sister, and a tinted enlargement of Miss Bramble herself as a girl. A very pretty girl she must have been too, sitting down on a sofa with her humped back cunningly obscured by a jagged cloud of pink tulle. It was only a very slight hump, anyhow, poor thing. Herbert Darrell regarded her with a pity that he was careful not to let her see, his manner to her being occasionally quite brusque in consequence. She must be, he thought, round about the middle-forties now. Her eyes and skin were still young and her mouth, at certain moments, attractive but overfull, with a lift of the upper lip which might have denoted sensuality in anyone else, but Miss Bramble, poor dear, what chance had she had for that sort of thing with her deformed back and little spindly legs. He wondered if she minded. Minded as much as he would have under the circumstances. His imagination balked at the idea of himself, Herbert Darrell, not being physically attractive. It was difficult to conceive a life utterly devoid of "That sort of thing." Poor Miss Bramble!

When remembering his past loves he allowed his face to slide into a whimsical smile. Women, many of them nameless, held out their arms to him across the years. He could still recapture the sensation of their smooth bodies in his arms; hear the echo of their small whimpering cries under his lips. A procession of incompletely identified bedrooms passed slowly before his mind's eye, like rather foggy lantern slides projected on to a screen. Dressing tables. Wardrobes. Chintz curtains. Lace curtains. Silk and velvet curtains. Small tables. Scent bottles. Little feminine clocks ticking away complacently, unmoved by desire or fulfillment or ecstasy. Beds of all shapes and sizes. Doubles. Singles. With canopies. Without canopies. One with a little naked Cupid dangling a light just above his head. Another with a gilt bird catching up mauve taffeta in its claws. That must have been Julia Deacon's, either hers or Marion Cressal's. Funny how he always got those two muddled up. They had both been high spots, definite triumphs for him. Both well kept and difficult to attain. Then there was Minnie. Here his mind shied in the darkness because he had married Minnie and memories of her were clearer and less glamorous. The first two years had been all right. Quite a nice little flat they had had in New Cavendish Street. He had been playing *Captain Draycott* then, his last success in the West End. Then things had begun to slide, gradually at first, then three failures on top of one another, forcing him out into the provinces with the tour of *Captain Draycott,* starting with the number one towns and finishing, the following year, with an undignified scamper through the number threes. Penarth had been the worst, he remembered. So near Cardiff and yet so far. The reason that it had been the worst had been because of Minnie. It was in Penarth that he had seen her strongly and clearly for the first time as a bitch. His memory lifted its skirts over this bad patch and hurried convulsively, like an old lady picking her way barefoot across a shingly beach. The digs just near the pier. Billy Jenner's party at the hotel on the Thursday night to celebrate his having fixed a job at Wyndham's for the autumn. Then suddenly feeling ill and going home early and hearing Minnie's "Oh Christ!" as he turned the handle of the bedroom door.

Herbert Darrell turned over heavily in Miss Bramble's combined room-bed and went to sleep.

On Sunday morning the alarm clock dragged Miss Bramble out of a deep tranquil dream at seven o'clock precisely, and she lay for a while blinking at the ceiling and trying to locate a pain somewhere in her inside. Not a physical pain; not even a pain at all really, more a sensation of loss, vague and undefined, as though someone she loved had died and she couldn't quite remember who it was. Sleep still pulled at her eyes, and she turned her head sharply on the pillow; staring at the room until the worn familiarity of everything in it wakened her to reality and sent the last clinging vestiges of her dream sliding back into the night. The acorn knob on the end of the blind cord rapped intermittently against the wainscotting because the window was open a little at the top, and the chintz strip on her dressing table twitched irritably in the draft. She had left the top off her box of Houbigant powder and the edges of stiff paper sticking up inside it looked like a face, somebody lying down asleep, or perhaps dead. A beam of light shooting from behind the blind caught the bristles of her hairbrush showing a few fuzzy hairs with a surprisingly blond glint on them, and she noticed, with a pang, that the small framed photograph of her mother had fallen over on its face. This got her out of bed with a jerk, and when she had set it upright again and caught sight of herself in the glass, full and complete memory of last night struck at her savagely. Just as a flash of lightning sears against the sky every detail of a landscape, she saw, in an instant, the bright wallpaper of the "combined" room and the heavy blue-and-white stripes of Mr. Darrell's pajamas.

Still looking in the glass she put out her hand to steady herself and noted, mechanically, a red flush creeping up from under her Celanese nightgown and suffusing her face. Then she sat down suddenly on the dressing-table chair and felt sick. After a little she went over to the bed again and sat on the edge of that, feeling the linoleum ice cold under her bare toes. The bland Woolworth clock announced six minutes past seven. At a quarter to eight he was to be called, with a cup of tea and a boiled egg, because the company was going on to Derby and the train went at nine. At a quarter to eight she would be in that room again. She would open the door, after a discreet knock, and walk in as though nothing had happened at all. Just as last night she had walked in in answer to his bell bringing him nothing but her starved and stunted little body, this morning she would bring him a cup of tea and a boiled egg.

She got up from the bed and started to dress feverishly; the cold water splashed over the edge of the basin as she poured it out of the jug and she whimpered a little, making a clucking noise with her tongue against her teeth. A lot of things went wrong with her dressing. Her hair pulled and wouldn't stay up properly. She put her blouse on inside out and had to struggle out of it and into it again, and the button came off one of her strap shoes. Her face looked redder than ever in the glass, and even when she had rubbed in a lot of Icilma vanishing cream and dabbed it generously with the puff, it still flamed shamefully. Finally she got herself downstairs to the kitchen with her loose shoe strap flapping on every step.

At twenty minutes to eight she absentmindedly ate one of the bits of toast she had made and had to do another piece hurriedly. He liked his egg done four minutes, and she stood over the gas-stove watching it bobbing about in the saucepan jumping up and down again and rolling over and over impudently as though it were mocking her. Nellie wouldn't arrive to do the rooms until nine-thirty, if then, it being Sunday she would have the house to herself for a bit when he'd gone, when the taxi had rattled him out of her life together with his two fiber suitcases, his bulgy Gladstone bag and his dark blue Aquascutum mackintosh with the grease marks on the inside of the collar. She glanced at it hanging up in the hall as she passed along with the tray. It looked tired and depressed, and one of the little sockets at the side was broken causing the belt to hang down on to the floor like a snake.

She mounted the stairs slowly and carefully; the geyser snorted at her as she passed the bathroom door and one of the stair-rods rattled loose as her feet touched it, nearly tripping her up. At last she stood outside his door waiting for a moment for the courage to knock, and listening to the beating of her heart, the only sound in the silent house. It was lucky there weren't any other lodgers this week. She couldn't have borne that; other rooms to enter, other breakfasts to get. It was very silly, she felt, just to go on standing there outside the door letting his tea and his egg get cold; she balanced the tray in her right hand and lifted her left to knock, then she lowered it again and with a little shiver, sat down on the top step of the stairs putting the tray carefully down beside her. The blind of the landing window was not drawn, and she could see out across the roofs to where the spire of St. Catherine's stood up against the gray sky. It was raining a little. She remembered the very first time she had seen that view, from the small room at the top of the house which she had always had when she came to stay with Aunt Alice. She was fifteen then and Aunt Alice, although rather grim and domineering, had been very kind on the whole. Now she was dead and lying in St. Catherine's churchyard, possibly tormented by the knowledge that her clean, respectable boardinghouse had dwindled slowly, in the hands of her niece, from gentility and social pride into theatrical lodgings. Miss Bramble often thought of this. She often regretted the hard circumstances and lack of stamina which had caused her to deal so shabbily with Aunt Alice's bequest. Theatrical people, according to Aunt Alice, were a worthless lot, possessing little or no moral sense and seldom any religion whatsoever. Miss Bramble wondered dimly what Aunt Alice would say if she knew that her favorite niece, deformity or no deformity, had become so lost to all sense of what was right and proper as to allow herself to be seduced, at the age of forty-four, by an elderly actor in the second floor back. Again she shivered, this time with the sudden chill of clear realization that she wanted him again, that every nerve in her body was tingling with an agony of desire. She recaptured, behind her closed eyes, the strength of his arms round her; the roughness of his face against her neck and the weight of his body crushing her down deep into an ecstasy sweeter than any she had ever dreamed. It was the "being in love" of all the people in the world. The essence of every love scene from every movie and play she had ever been to, concentrated miraculously in her. And now, now the moment had gone, no more of it, no more of it ever again in her life probably. The ordinary way of things would continue; shopping, cooking, washing up, welcoming lodgers, saying "good-bye" to lodgers. . . . This very afternoon Mabel Hodge was coming and a new couple, Mr. and Mrs. Burrell, whom she had never had before. They were all in the same show at the Royal, *Disappearance,* direct from the Shaftesbury Theatre, London. The Burrells would have the ground floor front with sitting room, and Mabel Hodge, the "combined." She had had it several times before; her silly face had greeted Miss Bramble many a morning when she had gone in with her glass of hot water—"It must be fraightfully, fraightfully hot, Miss Bramble dear, with just the teeniest slaice of lemon"—She remembered thinking once that Mabel Hodge's face was like one of the fancy cakes in Jones's window in the High Street, one that had been there for a long time until the sugar had melted a bit at the edges, and being ashamed of herself afterward for being so uncharitable. It was because of Mabel Hodge that she had had a gas-fire put in. She had always grumbled so about the cold, and Nellie letting the fire out, and one thing and another. . . .

Once more a surge of pain engulfed her. The gas-fire had been on last night. In the first moment of putting the light out it hadn't been noticeable at all, and then, gradually, the warm glow of it had spread, throwing a vast shadow of the armchair against the wall. She had opened her eyes to that shadow just once or twice and then closed them again.

The Town Hall clock struck the quarter and, a few seconds later, the clock downstairs did the same, a feeble little noise it made with a convulsive whirr before and after as though it had a cold. Miss Bramble rose to her feet, picked up the tray and walked into the "combined" forgetting, in the sudden urgency of her decision, to knock at all.

Herbert Darrell was lying on his back with his head turned away toward the wall. His mouth was open and he was breathing stertorously; the top button of his pajama jacket was undone, and a tangle of wispy, grayish hairs rose and fell languidly with the movement of his chest. Miss Bramble put the tray on the table and jerked the blind; the cord escaped her fingers and it went flying up with a tremendous clatter, whirling round and round itself at the top.

Herbert Darrell moved uneasily and opened his eyes, and he had said "good morning" huskily before she could detect any memory in them. She said quite firmly, but in somebody else's voice, that she was sorry that she was a bit late but that the fire had refused to light properly. He sat up at this, and then she saw him frown and look at her suddenly, blinking. No kind intentions, not all the practiced graces of the world could have concealed that expression in time. It was the look she was waiting for and when it came, cutting straight through her heart and out through her hump at the back, she greeted it with an excellent smile. "I'll go and light the geyser," she said, and went jauntily out of the room.

AUNT
TITTIE

Once upon a time in a small fishing village in Cornwall there lived a devout and angry clergyman named Clement Shore. He was an ex-missionary and had a face almost entirely encircled by whiskers, like a frilled ham. His wife, Mary, was small and weary, and gave birth to three daughters, Christina, Titania, and lastly Amanda, with whose birth she struggled too long and sadly, and died, exhausted by the effort. Amanda was my mother. On Christmas day 1881, Grandfather Clement himself died and my Aunt Christina then aged sixteen, having arranged for what furniture there was to be sold, and the lease of the house taken over, traveled to London with several tin trunks, a fox terrier named Roland and her two younger sisters aged respectively thirteen and eleven. They were met, dismally, at Paddington by their father's spinster sister Ernesta, a gray woman of about fifty, who led them, without protest, to Lupus Street, Pimlico, where with a certain grim efficiency she ran a lodging house for bachelors. Once installed they automatically became insignificant but important cogwheels in the smooth running machinery of the house, which was very high and respectable. The three of them shared a small bedroom with Roland, from whom they refused to be parted, and lived two years of polite slavery until in the spring of 1883 Christina suddenly married James Rogers, Ernesta Shore's first-floor-front tenant, and went with him to a small house in Camberwell, taking with her Titania and Amanda.

James Rogers was a good man and a piano tuner at the time of his marriage, later he developed into a traveling agent for his firm, so that during my childhood in the house I didn't see much of him, but he was mild-tempered and kind when he did happen to be at home and only drank occasionally, and then without exuberance.

Aunt Christina was formidable, even when young, and ruled him firmly until the day of his death. She was less successful however with Aunt Titania and my mother. Aunt Titania stayed the course for about a year and then eloped to Manchester with a young music hall comedian, Jumbo Potter, with whom she lived in sin for three years to the bitter shame of Aunt Christina. At the end of this liaison she went on to the stage herself in company with three other girls. They called themselves "The Four Rosebuds" and danced and sang through the music halls of England. Meanwhile my mother, Amanda, continued to live in Camberwell, helping with the housework and behaving very well until 1888, when Titania reappeared in London, swathed in the glamour of the Theater, and invited her to a theatrical supper party at the Monico. Amanda climbed out of her bedroom window and over the yard fence in order to get there and never returned. Titania on being questioned later by Christina stated that the last she'd seen of Amanda, she was seated on the knee of an Argentine with a paper fireman's cap on her head, blowing a squeaker. Titania's recollections were naturally somewhat vague as she had been drinking a good deal and left the party early on the strength of an unpremeditated reunion with Jumbo Potter. Christina anxiously pursued her enquiries, but could discover nothing about the Argentine; nobody knew his name, he had apparently drifted into the party, entirely uninvited. Finally when two days had elapsed and she was about to go to the police, a telegram arrived from Amanda saying that she was at Ostend and that it was lovely and that nobody was to worry about her and that she was writing. A few weeks later she did write, briefly, this time from Brussels, she said she was staying with a friend, Madame Vaudrin, who was very nice and there were lots of other girls in the house, and it was all great fun, and nobody was to worry about her as she was very, very happy.

For five years after that, neither Titania nor Christina heard from her at all until suddenly just before Christmas 1893, she appeared at Christina's house in Camberwell in a carriage and pair. She was dressed superbly and caused a great sensation in the neighborhood. Christina received her coldly but finally melted when Amanda offered to pay off all the installments on the new drawing-room set and gave her a check for twenty-five pounds as well. Titania by this time had married Jumbo Potter and Amanda gave a family Christmas dinner party at the Grosvenor Hotel where she was staying, and as a *bonne bouche* at the end of the meal, produced an Indian Prince who gave everybody jewelry. She stayed in London for six weeks and then went to Paris, still with her Prince, and spent a riotous month or two, until finally she accompanied him to Marseilles where he took ship for India leaving her sobbing picturesquely on the dock with a cabuchon emerald and a return ticket for Paris. It was while she was on the platform awaiting the Paris train that she met my father, Sir Douglas Kane-Jones. He was a prosperous-looking man of about fifty, returning on leave from Delhi to visit his wife and family in Exeter. However he postponed his homecoming for three weeks in order to enjoy Paris with Amanda. Finally they parted, apparently without much heartbreak, he for England, and she for Warsaw, whither she had been invited by a Russian girl she had met in Brussels, Nadia Kolenska. Nadia had been living luxuriously in Warsaw for a year as the guest of a young attaché to the French Embassy. Upon arrival in Warsaw, Amanda was provided with a charming suite of rooms and several admirers, and was enjoying herself greatly when to her profound irritation, she discovered she was going to have a child.

She and Nadia, I believe, did everything they could think of to get rid of it but without success, and so Amanda decided to continue to enjoy life for as long as she could and then return to England. Unfortunately, however, she left it rather late, and on a frozen morning in January, I was born in a railway carriage somewhere between Warsaw and Berlin. The reason for my abrupt arrival several weeks earlier than expected was the sudden jolting of the train while my mother was on her way back from the lavatory to her compartment. She fell violently over a valise that someone had left in the corridor, and two hours later, much to everyone's embarrassment and discomfort, I was born and laid in the luggage rack wrapped in a plaid traveling rug.

A week later Aunt Christina arrived in Berlin in response to a telegram, just in time to see my mother die in a hospital ward. With her usual prompt efficiency she collected all my mother's personal effects, which were considerable, and having ascertained that there were no savings in any bank, took me back to England with her and ensconced me in her own bedroom in her new house, Number 17, Cranberry Avenue, Kennington.

2

My life until my Uncle James Rogers' death in 1904 was as eventful for me as it is for most children who are learning to walk and talk and become aware of things. A few incidents remain in my memory. Notably, a meeting with my Aunt Titania when I was about three. She smelt strongly of scent and her hair was bright yellow. She bounced me gaily on her knee until I was sick, after which, she seemed to lose interest in me. I remember also, when I was a little older, my Uncle Jim came into my room late at night. I awoke just in time to see him go over to the mantelpiece and throw two green china vases onto the floor. I cried a lot because I was frightened, Aunt Christina cried too and finally soothed me to sleep again by singing hymns softly and saying prayers.

When I was five I was sent to a kindergarten on weekdays, and a Sunday School on Sunday afternoons. A Miss Brace kept the kindergarten. She wore shirt blouses with puffed sleeves, and tartan skirts. Her hair was done up over a pad. Twice a week we had drawing lessons and were allowed to use colored chalks. I didn't care for any of the other children, and disliked the little girls particularly because they used to squabble during playtime, and pull each other's hair, and cry at the least thing.

I enjoyed the Sunday School much more because we used to stand in a circle and sing hymns, and the teacher had a large illustrated Bible which had a picture of God the Father throwing a hen out of Heaven, and another one of Jesus, with his apostles, sitting at a large table and eating india-rubber rolls. Everybody had beards and white nightgowns, and looked very funny.

When I was nine, Uncle Jim died. All the blinds in the house were pulled down, and we walked about softly as though he were only asleep and we were afraid of waking him. Iris, the servant, who had only been with us for two weeks, trailed up and down the stairs miserably with woebegone tears streaking her face. Perhaps she cried as a natural compliment to bereavement, however remote from herself, or perhaps she was merely frightened. Even the cat seemed depressed and lay under the sofa for hours at a time in a sort of coma. Aunt Christina took me in to see Uncle Jim lying in bed covered with a sheet up to his chin, his eyes were closed, and his face was yellow like tallow, his nose looked as though someone had pinched it. Aunt Christina walked firmly up to the bed, and having straightened the end of the sheet, bent down and kissed him on the forehead so suddenly that I'm sure he would have jumped if he had been alive. Outside in the street a barrel organ was playing and there were some children yelling a little way off, but these sounds seemed faint and unreal as though I were listening to them from inside a box.

I went to the funeral with Aunt Christina and Aunt Titania in a closed carriage which smelt strongly of horses and leather. On the way Aunt Titania wanted to smoke a cigarette but Aunt Christina was very angry and wouldn't let her. I sat with my back to the horse and watched them arguing about it, sitting side by side joggling slightly as the carriage wheels bumped over the road. Finally Aunt Christina sniffed loudly and shut her mouth in a thin line and refused to say another word, whereupon Aunt Titania leaned a little forward and looked grandly out of the window until we reached the Cemetery. I stood under a tree with her while the actual burial was going on and she gave me some peppermints out of her muff. When we got home again we all had tea and Iris made some dripping toast, but the atmosphere was strained. After tea I went down to the kitchen to help Iris with the washing up and we listened to the voices upstairs getting angrier and angrier until finally the front door slammed so loudly that all the crockery shook on the dresser. Presently we heard Aunt Christina playing hymns and I didn't see Aunt Titania again for many years.

Soon after this I went to a day school in Stockwell, it wasn't very far away and I used to go there in a bus and walk home. There was an enormous horse chestnut tree just inside the school gate and we used to collect the chestnuts and put them on strings and play conkers. They were rich shiny brown when we first picked them up, like the piano in our front room, but afterward the shine wore off and they weren't nearly so nice. I hated the Headmaster who was stout and had a very hearty laugh. He insisted on everybody playing football and used to keep goal himself, shouting loudly as he jumped about. One of the undermasters was freckled and kind and used to pinch my behind in the locker room when I was changing. Much as I disliked school, I disliked coming home in the evenings still more, my heart used to sink as I stood outside the front door and watched Aunt Christina wobbling toward me through the colored glass. She generally let me in without saying a word and I used to go straight upstairs to my bedroom and read and do my homework until supper time, because Iris left at six and there was nobody to talk to. Aunt Christina always said grace before and after meals, and regularly, when we'd cleared away the supper things and piled them up in the kitchen, she used to play hymns and make me sing them with her. Sundays were particularly awful because I had to go to Church morning and evening, as well as to Sunday School in the afternoons. The Vicar was very skinny and while I listened to his throaty voice screeching out the sermon I used to amuse myself by counting how many times his Adam's Apple bobbed up and down behind his white collar. The woman who always sat next to us had bad feet and the whole pew smelt of her.

I used to ask Aunt Christina about my mother but all she'd say was that Satan had got her because she was wicked, and whenever I asked about my father she said he was dead and that she had never known him.

At the beginning of 1906 when I was eleven, things became even gloomier. Aunt Christina bought a whole lot of modeling wax and made a figure of Jesus lying down, then she put red ink on it to look like blood, but it soaked in. It wasn't a very good figure anyhow; the face was horrid and the arms much too long, but she used to kiss it and croon over it. Once she tried to make me kiss it but I wouldn't, so she turned me out into the yard. I stayed all night in the shed and caught cold. After that she wouldn't speak to me for days, I was unhappy and made plans about running away, but I hadn't any money and there was nowhere to run.

One evening in April, I came home from school and she was in bed with a terrible headache; the next morning when I went into her room, she was gasping and saying she couldn't breathe, so I ran out and fetched a doctor. He said she had pneumonia and that we must have a nurse, so we did, and the nurse rattled about the house and clicked her tongue against her teeth a good deal and washed everything she could. Three days later Mr. Wendell, the Vicar, came and stayed up in Aunt Christina's room for a time, and a short while after he'd gone the nurse came running downstairs and said I was to fetch the doctor. Just as I was leaving the house to fetch him, I met him at the gate on his way in. He went upstairs quickly and an hour later he and the nurse came down and told me my aunt had passed away.

He asked me for Aunt Titania's address, so we looked through Aunt Christina's davenport and found it and sent her a telegram. Late that afternoon Uncle Jumbo Potter arrived and interviewed the nurse, and then took me round to the doctor's house, and he talked to him for ages while I sat in the waiting room, and looked at the people who had come to be cured; one little boy with a bandage round his head was whimpering and his mother tried to comfort him by telling him stories. Presently Uncle Jumbo came out and took me home with him in a cab. He lived in rooms near Victoria Station. He told me that Aunt Titania wasn't living with him anymore and that she was in Paris singing at a place called the Café Bardac, and that he was going to send me to her the next day. That night I went with him to Shoreditch where he was doing his turn at the Empire. I sat in his dressing room and watched him make up and then he took me down onto the stage and let me stand at the side with the stage manager. Uncle Jumbo was a great favorite and the audience cheered and clapped the moment he walked onto the stage. He wore a very small bowler hat and loose trousers and had a large red false nose. His songs were very quick indeed until it came to the chorus, when he slowed down and let the audience join in too. The last thing he did was a dance in which his trousers kept nearly falling off all the time. At the end he had to go before the curtain and make a speech before they'd let him go. He took me upstairs with him and undressed, still very out of breath. He sat down quite naked and smoked a cigarette,

31

and I watched the hair on his chest glistening with sweat as he breathed. He asked me if I liked his turn and I said I loved it and he said, "Damned hard lot down here, can't get a bloody smile out of 'em, pardon me." After he'd taken his makeup off and powdered his face and dressed we went to a bar just opposite the Theater and he drank beer with two gentlemen and a woman with a white fur, then we went home first in a tram and then on a bus. I went to sleep in the bus. When we got to his rooms he gave me a glass of soda water and made up a bed for me on the sofa.

The next morning Uncle Jumbo took me back to Aunt Christina's house. The nurse was still there, and Mrs. Harrison from next door, who kissed me a lot and told me to be a brave little man and asked me if I would like to come upstairs and see my dear Auntie, but Uncle Jumbo wouldn't let me, he said he didn't hold with kids looking at corpses because it was morbid. He helped me pack my clothes and then we got a cab and drove back to his rooms. In the afternoon he went out and left me alone and I amused myself by looking at some magazines and a large album of photographs and press cuttings about Aunt Titania and Uncle Jumbo. When he came back he had a friend with him, Mrs. Rice, who he said would take me to the station, as the train went at eight o'clock and he would be in the Theater. Mrs. Rice was pretty and laughed a lot. We all made toast, and had tea round the fire. Mrs. Rice sat on Uncle's knee for a little and he winked at me playfully over her shoulder and said, "You tell your Aunt Tittie how pretty Mrs. Rice is, won't you?" whereupon she got up and said, "Leave off, Jumbo, you ought to be ashamed" and looked quite cross for a minute. Uncle Jumbo went off to the Theater at 5:30; he gave me five pounds and my ticket and said he had telegraphed to Aunt Tittie to meet me at the station. He kissed me quite affectionately and said, "Fancy me being fatherly!" Then he laughed loudly, tickled Mrs. Rice under the arms, and went down the stairs whistling. When he'd gone Mrs. Rice and I went back and sat by the fire. She asked me a lot of questions about Aunt Titania but as I hadn't seen her since Uncle Jim's funeral I couldn't answer them very well. After a while she went to the cupboard and poured herself a whiskey and soda, and while she was sipping it she told me all about her husband who used to beat her and one night he tied her to the bed in their rooms in Huddersfield and kept on throwing the wet sponge at her until her nightgown was soaking wet and the landlady came in and stopped him. She said she'd met Uncle Jumbo in Blackpool in the summer and that they used to go out after the show and sit on the sand dunes in the moonlight, and then her husband found out and there was an awful row, and Jumbo knocked her husband down on the pier and brought her to London on the Sunday and she hadn't seen her husband since, but she believed he was still on tour in *Miss Mittens* and hoped to God he'd stay in it and not come worrying her. She had several more whiskies and sodas before it was time to go and showed me a scar on her thigh where a collie bit her during her honeymoon in Llandudno. I looked at it politely and then she pulled her skirts down and said I was a bad boy and how old was I anyhow? I said I was eleven and she laughed and asked me if it made me feel naughty to see a pretty girl's bare leg. I said no and she said "Get along with you. I must put some powder on my nose." After a minute she came out of the bedroom, put her hat on and said we must go. We took a cab to the station on account of my trunk and Mrs. Rice told the porter to register through to Paris. She bought me some buns and chocolate and two magazines and put me in the train and waited to tell the guard to keep his eye on me before she kissed me and said good-bye. I waved to her all the way up the platform until she was out of sight and then sat back in my corner feeling very grown up and excited and waiting for the train to start.

That journey to Paris was momentous for me. I was alone and free for the first time, my going was in no way saddened by memories of people I'd left behind. I had left no one behind whom I could possibly miss; my school friendships were casual and I had definitely grown to hate poor Aunt Christina during the last few years of her life. I pressed my face against the cold glass of the carriage window and searched for country shapes in the darkness, trees and hills and hedges, and felt as though I should burst with joy. There were two other people in the carriage with me; a man and a woman who slept, sitting up, with their mouths open. When we reached Newhaven, the guard came and led me to the gangway of the ship and gave me in charge of one of the men on board who offered me a ham sandwich and showed me a place in the saloon where I could put my feet up and go to sleep, but I couldn't begin to sleep until the ship started although I was dead tired, so I went up on deck and watched the lights of the town receding, and the red and green harbor lamps reflected in the water and I looked up at the clouds scurrying across the moon, and, suddenly, like a blow in the face, loneliness struck me down. I was chilled through and through with it—I wondered what I should do if when I got to Paris Aunt Titania was dead too. I tried very hard not to cry but it was no use, I had a pretty bad fit of hysteria and everyone crowded round me and patted me and tried to comfort me with eatables, until finally one kind woman took me in charge completely and gave me some brandy which made me choke but pulled me together. Then she put me to sleep in her private cabin and I didn't wake up until we got to Dieppe. I was all right from then on, the woman's name was Roylat and she was on her way to Ceylon to visit her son who was a rubber planter. I had some tea with her in the station buffet at Dieppe and traveled with her to Paris, sleeping most of the way.

When we arrived at the Gare St. Lazare Aunt Titania was waiting at the barrier wearing a sealskin coat and a bright red hat with a veil floating from it. I said good-bye to Mrs. Roylat who kissed me, bowed to Aunt Titania and disappeared after her luggage. Aunt Titania and I had to go and sit in the Customs room for three-quarters of a hour until my trunk came in. She was pleased to see me but very cross with Jumbo for having sent me by night instead of day. She said it was damned thoughtless of him because he knew perfectly well that she never got to bed before four o'clock in the morning and to have to get up again at six-thirty was too much of a good thing; then she hugged me and said it wasn't my fault and that we were going to have jolly times together.

At last, when the Customs man had marked my trunk, we got a cab and drove out into Paris. It had been raining and the streets were wet and shiny. The shutters on most of the shops were just being put up and waiters in their vests and trousers were polishing the tables outside the cafés. We drove across the river and along the quai Voltaire with the trees all glistening and freshly green; our cab horse nearly fell down on the slippery road as we turned up the rue Bonaparte. Aunt Tittie talked all the way about everything she'd been doing and her contract at the Café Bardac which they'd renewed for another month. She asked me if Aunt Christina had left me any money and I said I didn't know, but I gave her a letter that Jumbo had told me to give her. She pursed up her lips when she read it and then said, "It looks like I shall have to find a job for you, duckie, you'd better come along with me and see Monsieur Claude but there's no hurry, we'll talk about that later on." Finally the cab drew up before a very high house, and a little man in a shirt and trousers ran out and helped the driver down with my trunk. Aunt Tittie said something to him in French and took me up four flights of dark stairs and opened the door into a sitting room which had a large bedroom opening out of it on one side with a feather mattress on the bed that looked like a pink balloon, and a tiny room on the other side which she said I was to have. There were lots of colored bows on the furniture and hundreds of photographs, lots of them fixed to the blue-striped wallpaper with ordinary pins. There was a small alcove in her bedroom with a washhand stand in it and a gas-ring, and on the sitting-room table was a tray with some dirty glasses on it and a saucer full of cigarette ends. Aunt Tittie took off her hat and coat and threw them on the sofa, then she ran her fingers through her hair and said, "Well, here we are. Home Sweet Home with a vengeance." Then she went out onto the landing and screamed: "Louise!" very loudly and came in again and sat down. "We'll have some coffee and rolls," she said, "then we'll go to bed until lunch time, how does that suit you?" I said it suited me very well and we lapsed into silence until Louise came. Louise was about seventeen with a pallid face, a dirty pink dress turned up under an apron, and green felt slippers, her hair was bristling with curl-papers. Aunt Tittie had a long conversation with her in French and then the little man came clambering upstairs with my trunk and put it in my room. Then Louise and he both disappeared and I was left alone again with Aunt Tittie. I felt rather strange and oddly enough a little homesick, not really homesickness for that dreary house in Kennington, but a longing for something familiar. Aunt Tittie must have sensed that I wasn't feeling too happy because she put her arm round me and hugged me. "It's funny, isn't it?" she said, "you arriving suddenly like this? You must tell me all about poor Aunt Christina and what you've been learning at school and everything, and you haven't got any cause to worry about anything because you're going to be company for me and I shall love having you here." Then she held me close to her for a moment and surprisingly burst out crying, she fumbled for her handkerchief in her belt and went into the bedroom and shut the door. I didn't know what to do quite, so I started to unpack my trunk. Presently Louise returned with a tray of coffee and rolls and butter; she plumped it down on the table and screamed something at Aunt Tittie through the door and went out again. I sat at the table and waited until Aunt Tittie came out of the bedroom in a long blue quilted satin dressing gown, with her hair down. She looked quite cheerful again. "I can't think what made me burst out like that," she said as she seated herself at the table. "It came over me all of a sudden about you being all alone in the world and your poor mother dying in childbirth and now Christina. We're the only ones left out of the whole lot and that's a fact. Two lumps?" She poured out coffee for us both and talked volubly all the time, a stream of scattered remarks, beginnings of stories, references to people I'd never heard of, all jumbled together incoherently, but somehow all seeming to fit into a sort of pattern.

She must have been about forty then, her hair had been redyed so often that it was entirely metallic, as bright as new brass fire irons. Her face was pretty with a slightly retroussé nose and wide-set blue-gray eyes, her mouth was generous and large and gay when she laughed. She talked of Jumbo a good deal, irritably, but with underlying tenderness. I suspect that she always loved him more than anyone else. She asked me if I'd seen Mrs. Rice and said that she was sorry for any man that got tangled up with a clinging vine of that sort. After breakfast, and when she'd smoked two or three cigarettes, she said she was going to bed until one o'clock and that I could do what I liked, but that she strongly advised me to go to bed too as I was probably more tired after my journey than I thought I was.

I went into my little room and when I'd finished unpacking I sat and looked out of the window for a while. It was at the back of the house looking down into a courtyard, the sun was shining into the rooms on the other side of the court, in one of them I saw an old woman in a blue dressing gown working a sewing machine, the whirr of it sounded very loud, and every now and then there was the noise of rattling crockery far down on the ground floor, and somebody singing.

There were lots of gray roofs and chimney pots and several birds flying about and perching on the telegraph wires, which stretched right across into the next street and then were hidden by a tall many-windowed building that looked like some sort of factory. I felt very drowsy and quite happy so I went and lay down on the bed and the next thing I knew was that it was lunch time and Aunt Tittie was shaking me gently and telling me to get up. She was still in her dressing gown, but her head was done up in a towel because she'd just washed her hair.

We had hot chicken and vegetables and salad for lunch and fresh crusty bread and coffee. When we'd finished Aunt Tittie stretched herself out on the sofa and moved her legs so as to make room for me on the end of it.

"Now we'd better talk a bit," she said. "I had a good think while I was washing my head and if you'll listen carefully I'll tell you just how things stand and then we'll decide what's best to be done." I settled myself more comfortably and handed her the matches off the table which she was reaching out for. "To begin with," she said, "I haven't got any money except what I earn, but we can both live on that if we're careful anyhow for a bit, until you start to make a little on your own. I know I ought to send you to school really but I can't, it's none too easy living in this damned town, because you've got to look smart and have nice clothes otherwise nobody will take any notice of you. Now I've got an idea which I'll have to talk over with Mattie Gibbons, she's my partner. We do a parasol dance, and then she does her skipping rope specialty which is fine, then I sing a ballad, one verse and chorus in English and the second verse and chorus in French and then we do a number together called 'How Would You Like a Rose Like Me?' and go round to all the tables giving the men paper roses out of a basket. My idea was that you should be dressed up as a little dandy with a silk hat and a cane and gloves, you know the sort of thing, and flirt with us during the parasol dance and bring on our props for us all through the act. If Mattie agrees we'll ask Monsieur Claude about it. I think he'll say yes because he's a bit keen on me if you know what I mean and you ought to get about fifteen francs a week which would be a help to begin with. Would you like that?"

I said eagerly that I'd love it better than anything in the world and flung my arms round her neck and kissed her and she said, "Here wait a minute, it isn't settled yet, we've got to talk to Mattie and Monsieur Claude and arrange hundreds of things. I shall have to tell you a whole lot you're really too young to know, before I let you loose in the Café Bardac; to start with how much do you know?" This was a rather difficult question to answer so I sat looking at her without saying anything. "You know about men and women having babies and all that, don't you?" she said with an obvious effort.

I said "Yes," and blushed.

"Well, that's a good start anyway," she said. "Now then—" she stopped short and blushed herself, and then giggled nervously. "Oh, my God, I don't know how the hell to begin and that's a fact, well—" she pulled herself together. "Take the plunge, that's always been my motto, so here goes." She crushed out her cigarette and sat up and spoke very fast. "Now listen, Julian, it's a strange world, and it's not a bit of good pretending it isn't. You're only a kid and you ought to have a nice home and go to a nice school and learn history and geography and what not and get to know all about everything gradually, so it wouldn't be a shock to you, but as it happens you haven't got a home at all, you're alone except for me and Christ knows I'm no Fairy Godmother, but I've got to tell you everything I can so that you don't go and get upset by things and led away through not realizing what it's all about. To begin with, dear, you're a bastard, which sounds awful but isn't so bad really, it only means that your mother wasn't married to your father, they just had an affair and that was that, no obligations on either side and then you were born and your mother died and nobody knew who your father was anyhow except by rumor and what Nadia Kolenska, who was your mother's friend, wrote to your Aunt Christina. You were brought up on the money that your mother's jewels fetched when your Aunt Christina sold them, and now she's dead too and here you are, alone in Paris with your Aunt Tittie who's not a 'good' woman by any manner of means, but she's all you've got so you'd better make the best of her." Here she leant back and the cushion fell over the end of the sofa onto the floor, so I picked it up and put it behind her head and sat down again.

"When I say I'm not a good woman," she went on, "I mean I'm not what your Aunt Christina would call good. I take life as I find it and get as much as I can out of it. I always have been like that, it's me all over and I can't help it, tho' many's the row I've had with Christina because she never would see that what was good for her, wasn't necessarily good for me. I'm more like your mother I think really, only not quite so reckless.

"Now if you're going to live with me here, there's a lot of goings on you'll have to open your eyes to wide and then shut 'em tight and not worry, and you mustn't be upset by Mattie's swearing, her flow of language is something fierce when she gets going, but she's a really good friend and you'll like her. As far as the Café Bardac goes you'll have to look out and not be surprised by anything, it's none too refined there after one in the morning. People of all sorts and sizes come and drink at the bar, and sometimes there's a fight and you'll get a good laugh every now and again to see the way those old tarts shriek and yell and carry on. You know what tarts are, don't you?"

I said I wasn't sure, but I thought I did.

"Well," she continued, "they're women who have affairs with men professionally, if you know what I mean. They take 'em home and cuddle up with 'em and the men pay them for it, though when you've had a look at some of them you'll wonder how the hell they get as much as fourpence. But they're quite decent sorts, most of them. Then there are young men who dance around and get paid by the women, they're called 'macros' and aren't much use to anyone except that they dance well and keep the rich old American ladies happy. Then there are lots of boys and young men who make up their faces like women, they're tarts too, only male ones as you might say. Heaps of men like cuddling up with them much better than women, though I should think personally it must feel rather silly, but after all that's their look-out and no business of mine. They're awfully funny sometimes, you'd die laughing to see them have a row. They scream and slap one another. There's one at the Bardac called Birdie, always in trouble, that one, but he's awfully sweet so long as he doesn't get drunk. If any of the old men ever come up and ask you to drink or go out with them don't you do it, and if they catch hold of you and start getting familiar just wriggle away politely and come and tell me. I'll let 'em have it all right. It's a queer world and no mistake, and you'd much better get to know all you can about it as soon as may be and then you can stand on your own feet and not give a damn for anyone."

She finished up with rather a rush and then looked at me anxiously. I felt slightly bewildered but I said I'd try to remember all she'd told me and not be surprised at anything whatever happened; then we talked about other things. She asked me to tell her the details of Aunt Christina's death which I did and she sighed and shook her head sadly and looked for a moment as if she were going to cry, but fortunately just then there was a loud banging on the door and Mattie Gibbons came in. She was shorter and plumper than Aunt Tittie and very dark, she had a gray dress with gray laced-up boots which showed when she sat down, and a bright green blouse with a small diamond watch pinned on it, her hat was gray felt with a blue bird on it. She was very nice to me and shook hands politely and said she didn't know I was going to be such a big boy. She had a deep husky voice, and I liked her at once.

Aunt Tittie said they wanted to talk privately for a while and would I like to go out for a walk. I said I would, and after she'd warned me about looking to the left first when crossing the road, and told me to mark well the number of the house and street so that I wouldn't get lost, she kissed me and waved me out of the door. I felt my way carefully down the dark stairs and when I got to the front door it wouldn't open. After I'd struggled with it for a long time, a woman put her head out of a door and screamed something at me and then there was a click and the door opened of its own accord. The street was very narrow and filled with traffic. I walked down it slowly looking into all the shop windows; pastry-cooks with the most beautiful-looking cakes I'd ever seen; several artists' shops with easels and paints and boxes of colored pastels, and wooden jointed figures in strange positions; and a toy shop with hundreds of cheap toys jumbled up in cardboard boxes. There were also grocers and greengrocers and one big shop filled with old furniture and china. This was on the corner and half of it faced the river. I crossed over carefully and walked along the other side past all the little boxes on the parapet filled with books and colored prints and thousands of back numbers of magazines, very tattered and dusty and tied together in bundles with string.

There were lots of people fingering the books and hurrying along the pavement, nearly all the men had long beards and some of them went into round iron places covered with advertisements on the outside, and then came out again doing up their trousers. I was very puzzled by this so I peeped into one of them and saw what it was. After that it amused me a lot, looking at the different kinds of feet standing round underneath.

I crossed over a bridge and leant on the stone rail, the water was very green and there were several steamers puffing up and down, occasionally a larger one would come along and its funnel would bend in half as it went under the bridge. The river divided a little way further up, leaving an island in the middle with houses on it coming out almost into a point, and there were trees everywhere all along the edges. Everything looked much clearer and cleaner than London and the shadows of the houses stretched right across the road, sharp and definite.

I felt excited and adventurous and went across to the other side and walked for a long way under the trees; every now and then a noisy yellow tram came along. The lines were more like railway lines than tram lines, and grass was growing between them. By the time I got back to the house the sun was setting and all the windows along the quai looked as though they were on fire.

That evening Mattie came round at about nine o'clock and we all three of us went and had dinner at a café. Our table was right on the pavement and there was a little red-shaded lamp on it. Mattie and Aunt Tittie were very gay and talked very fast in French to the people that they knew and in English to each other and to me. Aunt

Tittie told me what lots of things were in French and said I'd better learn to speak it as quickly as I could as it was very useful. They had had a long talk about me being a "dandy" in their turn and Mattie was pleased with the idea; they said they'd take me that night to the Café Bardac with them and interview Monsieur Claude right away.

After dinner we walked along the boulevard to another café where we had coffee in glasses and they had brandy as well, then we went home and Aunt Tittie made me lie down for an hour while she dressed. She said that as I was going to be up late I'd better get as much rest as possible. At about half-past eleven Mattie called for us, she and Aunt Tittie were both in sparkling evening dresses and cloaks and then we all got into a cab and drove a long way through brightly lighted streets. In the cab Aunt Tittie gave me a latchkey and some money and made me repeat the address over and over again, and said that I should always have to come home by myself, even when I was actually acting in the turn with them, because they generally had to stay on and talk to people sometimes nearly all night. She told me how much the cab would cost and then very slowly and clearly what I was to say to the driver. When I repeated it she and Mattie both laughed and said I spoke French like a native. Mattie said she wondered if it was all right to let me wander about Paris alone at night, and Aunt Tittie said I was very sensible for my age and that it was much better for me to get used to managing for myself and learn independence.

When we arrived at the Café Bardac nobody was there but a lot of waiters and a man behind the bar. We all went upstairs and sat in a small dressing room which Mattie and Aunt Tittie shared. Their dresses were hanging up on pegs and there were two chairs, two mirrors on a shelf, and a very small washbasin in the corner with a jug without a handle standing on the floor by the side of it.

Mattie took a bottle out of the cupboard and they both had a drink. Presently Aunt Tittie went downstairs to see Monsieur Claude and left me to talk to Mattie.

Mattie asked me if I didn't feel strange and I said yes but that I was enjoying it. She said, "It's a bloody awful life this really, you know, but it has its funny moments. This café's not so bad as some I've been in. I was dancing with a troupe in Antwerp once and they made us dress in a lavatory on the third floor, and the smell was enough to knock you down I give you my word; this is a little peep at Paradise compared to that and no error!"

Then she took out the bottle again and had another swig and said would I like a taste. I said "yes" and she said "My God, here I go corrupting you already," but she let me have a sip and laughed when I made a face. "It's raw gin, ducks, and don't let anybody ever tell you it's water, but it does make you feel fine, all ready to go out and fight someone, and believe me or believe me not you need that feeling in this Pavilion d'Amour!"

Aunt Tittie came back, looking very pleased and said Monsieur Claude wanted to see me, so down we went onto the next floor into a little room with a desk in it and a lot of photographs of naked women stuck on the walls. Monsieur Claude was fat and excitable; he kissed me on both cheeks and then held me by the shoulders and pushed me away from him and looked at me carefully, talking all the time very quickly in French. Then he whispered a lot to Aunt Tittie, gave her a smacking kiss on the lips and ushered us out into the passage. Just as I went through the door, he fumbled in his pocket and gave me three francs. Aunt Tittie was frightfully pleased and said didn't I think he was a dear. "Kind as can be, you know, of course he gets a bit excited now and again but he's never downright nasty except when he's had a couple, which isn't often, thank God."

We went upstairs to the dressing room again and told Mattie all about it. I was to get ten francs a week to begin with and fifteen later on if I was good. Mattie said the mean old bastard might have come across with a bit more, but Aunt Tittie reminded her that after all he did have to think of his business. We all three went downstairs after a little while. Aunt Tittie introduced me to the barman. He spoke English and gave me a high stool to sit on in a corner behind the bar where I could watch all the people. I sat there for ages until my eyes prickled with the smoke. Every now and then Mattie or Aunt Tittie would come and see if I was all right, then they came down dressed as shepherdesses with bare legs and after they'd had a little port at the bar they did their parasol dance. Nobody seemed to watch it very much, but they all applauded and cheered when it was finished. I watched their turn all through and then felt so tired that I decided to go home, so I went upstairs to the dressing room to fetch my hat. I knocked and went in thinking Aunt Tittie and Mattie were downstairs, but they weren't—at least Aunt Tittie wasn't. She was in there with Monsieur Claude. She was sitting on his knee with hardly any clothes on at all and he was kissing her. They both had their eyes closed and neither of them saw me, so I closed the door again very quietly and went out without my hat. I got a cab quite easily and he drove me home and when I paid him, had a long conversation with me which I didn't understand, so I bowed and said *bon soir* and he drove away.

I lay in bed for a long while without sleeping. I felt strange, as though none of the things that were happening to me were real. I wondered whether Aunt Tittie liked being kissed by fat Monsieur Claude, and then all the faces of the people I'd seen at the café seemed to go across my eyes very fast until they were all blurred and I fell asleep. I woke up just for a second in the early morning; a cold gray light was showing through the shutters and I heard Aunt Tittie's voice in the next room. Then her bedroom door slammed and I turned over and went to sleep again.

3

When I first appeared with Aunt Titania and Mattie Gibbons at the Café Bardac in Paris, I had a great personal success; all the tarts made a tremendous fuss of me and said I was *très gentil* and *très beau gars* and gave me sweet cakes, and Monsieur Claude raised my salary from ten francs to fifteen francs a week, quite soon. When the engagement came to an end Mattie and Aunt Tittie had a row and parted company. I think the row somehow concerned Monsieur Claude and it was terrible while it lasted. Aunt Tittie cried a lot and said Mattie was a dirty double-faced bitch and Mattie just sat there laughing until Aunt Tittie completely lost control and threw a vermouth bottle at her, which missed her and went flying through the open door into my bedroom and broke the looking glass over my washbasin. After that Mattie stopped laughing and chased Aunt Tittie round the table, swearing loudly. They were both drunk and I got rather frightened so I ran outside and sat on the stairs with my fingers in my ears. Presently Mattie came rushing out and fell over me; she smacked my face and went on downstairs screaming. I heard her wrestling with the front door and swearing at it, finally she got it open and slammed it behind her so hard that a large bit of plaster fell off the ceiling into a slop pail on the landing. When I went back into the sitting room Aunt Tittie was lying on the sofa crying; her hair was down and her nose was bleeding, making stains all down the front of her dress. When I came in she got up and stumbled into her bedroom where I heard her being very sick. I shut my door and locked it and opened the shutters to see what the day looked like. It was raining hard and the gutters were gurgling loudly so I went back to bed and slept.

Soon after this Aunt Tittie and I packed up everything and went to Ostend. We appeared at a Café Concert in a side street which led down to the Plage. Aunt Tittie did three songs and I learnt a speech in French to introduce her. Everybody used to laugh and clap when I came on with my silk hat and cane and white gloves. Aunt Tittie thought it would be a good thing if I wore a monocle, but I couldn't keep it in my eye until we stuck it in with spirit gum, then it was a great success. We stayed there for six weeks and I used to play about on the Plage during the day.

We lived in a cheap hotel kept by a very thin woman called Madame Blücher; she was half German and sometimes made chocolate cakes with whipped cream on them which were delicious. She had a lot of sons and used to show me photographs of them. One was a sailor and he was photographed holding an anchor and sticking his chest out. He had the biggest behind I've ever seen.

When we'd finished our engagement in Ostend we went to Brussels and were out of work for nearly five weeks. We used to go and sit in the waiting room of an agent's office with lots of other people wanting a job. The walls were plastered with posters of celebrated stars very vividly colored and there was a signed photograph of Sarah Bernhardt looking like a sheep in white lace.

We had to move out of the hotel we were in and go to a still cheaper one. Aunt Tittie got more and more depressed, but one day she met an Austrian officer in some café or other and came home late looking much more cheerful. He was very handsome and took us both to dinner at an open-air restaurant one night; he joked with me a lot and pinched my ear which hurt, but I pretended I liked it. After dinner he put me in a cab and told it to go to the hotel, and gave me the money to pay it, but I stopped the driver when we'd got round the corner and paid him a little and walked home; it was further than I thought but I was three francs to the good. About a week after this Aunt Tittie got a contract to go to Antwerp for three weeks. After that we went to Amsterdam and then back again to Brussels, where we stayed for two months and played for some part of the time at the Mercedes Music-hall.

It was strange at first, doing our turn on an actual stage, but I liked it much better. It wasn't really a proper theater because the audience sat at tables, but it had footlights and scenery and a drop curtain.

Aunt Tittie taught me a song which I did dressed as a pierrot while she changed her dress. It was called "Keep Off the Grass" and was out of a musical comedy in England. Nobody seemed to pay very much attention to it but I enjoyed doing it enormously.

After this we got a long contract and traveled all over France playing a week in each place, ending up with Lyons and Nice and Marseilles and then we went over to Algiers where we stayed for three weeks. There was a conjuror on the bill with us who took a great fancy to me. He asked me to have supper with him one night and we sat in a café with lots of Arabs wearing fezzes. I think he was half an Arab himself. Then we went for a drive along by the sea and he said I was "very nice boy" and "very pretty and had naughty eyes." He held my hand for a little and I knew what was coming so I said I felt very sick and started retching. He took me back to the hotel at once. His turn came on after ours and I always used to wait and watch it; he did card tricks and shot pigeons out of a gun and then to finish up with he used to walk down to the front of the stage and say very solemnly, *"Mesdames, Messieurs, maintenant je vous monterai un experiment très, très difficile, un experience de vie,"* whereupon he would take off his coat and shirt and stand stripped to the waist in dead silence for a moment, then, with great deliberation, he'd take a sharp pointed dagger from a table, test it and bend it slightly with his long thin fingers, and then proceed, amid a breathless hush from the audience, to carve out his left nipple. It was very realistically done even to a dark stream of blood which ran down over his ribs. Then suddenly, with a quick jerk, he'd throw the dagger away, whip out a handkerchief, and staunch the blood and cry "Voilà" and the curtain fell. He had, I think, a small rubber squeezer filled with red solution concealed in his hand, and then having made up his own nipple with flesh color, he stuck a false red one over the top of it. It always brought forth thunders of applause.

After Algiers we went on to Tunis which was very much the same except that the weather was warmer. Then we had a week's engagement in Genoa which was a great failure—all the young Italian men made such a noise that we couldn't make ourselves heard, so we worked our way to Paris by slow degrees, playing in Geneva and Montreux on the way.

We tried to get the same rooms we'd had before but they were occupied, so we went to a small hotel behind the Invalides and stayed for a few weeks until Aunt Tittie fixed up an autumn contract. Then to fill in the time we went and stayed at a farm near Bordeaux with an old friend of Aunt Tittie's, Madame Brinault. She had been a dancer and had married and retired; she was fat and kind and had three grown-up stepdaughters and a stepson, who looked after the vines. They were all very vivacious and talked at the top of their voices all through meals. They had a monkey which bit every now and then but could be very affectionate when it liked. We used to fish in the pond for eels and small mud fish, and walk all along the vines and pinch the grapes to see if they were coming along all right.

We stayed there for six weeks, and it did us a lot of good. Aunt Tittie got quite fat from drinking so much milk and cream and she let her hair go for the whole time without dyeing it so that it looked very odd, yellow at the ends and brownish-gray at the roots.

We spent most of the next year in Germany playing in Frankfurt, Hamburg, Dresden, Nuremberg, Munich, Hanover, Heidelberg and Berlin, where Aunt Tittie met Arthur Wheeler, an acrobat, and fell violently in love with him. We stayed on there for several months, playing sometimes in suburban halls and sometimes in cafés in Potsdam and Berlin itself. Arthur Wheeler was a thick-set bad-tempered little man and he used to beat Aunt Tittie often, but I don't think she minded. He came with us in the summer to a place called Achenzee in the Tyrol and we stayed in a pension hotel and used to go out for picnics on the lake. He taught me to swim and dive. The lake water was ice cold even with the hot sun on it, but I got used to it and often swam seven or eight times a day. Wheeler used to lie on the grass by the side of the water with a towel tied round his middle, and do acrobatics, frequently with such violence that the towel would fall off and Aunt Tittie would laugh until she cried and say: "That's it, Arthur, give the poor Germans a treat!"

Every evening we used to sit outside the pension and have dinner. The tables were set almost in the road and processions of German families would march by, very hot and tired from their climbing. Even the young men had fat stomachs and they all wore shorts, and embroidered braces and small hats.

Every evening at about six o'clock we had beer at an open-air restaurant just by the water. We liked watching the steamer come puffing across the lake and then stop at the pier and land the passengers.

One evening when Wheeler had paid for the beer and we were about to walk back to the pension, he suddenly stood stock-still, clutched Aunt Tittie's arm and said: "Jumping Jesus, that's my wife!"

I looked up and saw a thin woman in a brown dress walking down the pier and staring fixedly at us. We all stood where we were until she came up to us. She looked very angry and was biting her lips nervously.

"Arthur," she said, "I want to talk to you." Her voice was grating and hard, and completely determined.

Arthur Wheeler started to bluster a bit: "Now look here, Amy—" he began, but she cut him short by taking his arm and leading him to the other end of the garden where they sat down at a table. I looked at Aunt Tittie who was very white, she hadn't said a word.

"Shall we go back to the pension?" I said. She shook her head. "No, we'll stay here," so we sat down again at the table we'd just got up from, and waited. The steamer gave a sudden hoot of its siren which made me jump, then it went churning away up the lake. It was twilight and the mountains looked jagged against the sky as though they had been cut out of black paper. On the other side of the lake lights were already twinkling in the villages. The steamer hooted again a good way off and a flock of birds flew chattering out of the big trees behind the restaurant. I looked at Aunt Tittie. She was staring straight in front of her and her face was set and still except for two little pulses twitching at her temples.

Presently Mrs. Wheeler came over to us. Aunt Tittie stood up.

"Arthur's leaving with me on the first boat tomorrow morning," said Mrs. Wheeler. "He's going back to your hotel now to pack his things. I've engaged a room here for us for tonight."

"Oh," said Aunt Tittie. "That will be nice, won't it?"

45

"If you haven't any money," went on Mrs. Wheeler, "I'm sure Arthur'll give you enough to get you back to wherever you came from."

Aunt Tittie gave a little gasp. "Thank you for nothing," she said, her voice sounded high and strained. "I don't want Arthur's money and you know it."

"You're a low woman," said Mrs. Wheeler. "I don't wish to exchange words with you."

"I'm not so low as to live on a man's earnings for fifteen years and not give him anything in return."

"Your sort couldn't hold a man fifteen years," said Mrs. Wheeler.

"I wouldn't want to hold anyone who didn't want to stay," said Aunt Tittie. "He loves me more than he does you, otherwise he wouldn't be here, would he? And you can put that in your pipe and smoke it."

Mrs. Wheeler trembled. "You're nothing but a low class prostitute," she said hoarsely, whereupon Aunt Tittie gave her a ringing slap on the face which knocked her hat on the side and left a pink stain on her cheek.

Arthur came running up looking very frightened. "Leave off you two, for Christ's sake," he said. "Everyone's looking at you."

"I'm sorry I hit her," said Aunt Tittie. "I never did know when to control myself. Come on home, Arthur, and pack your bag." She turned and walked away. Arthur followed her rather uncertainly and I came last. I looked back at Mrs. Wheeler who was standing quite still where we'd left her with her hat still on one side. I know she was crying because the lamp by the gate showed wet streaks on her face.

We all walked back to the pension in silence. When we got there I stayed outside and let them go in by themselves. I went and sat on the wall by the lake. The water was completely still and lay along the shore like a glass sheet. Presently Arthur Wheeler came out of the house carrying his suitcase, he waved to me halfheartedly and then walked away quickly.

When I went back into the pension, Aunt Tittie was sitting at the window with her head buried in her arms, sobbing. She didn't take any notice of me so I sat on the bed and said nothing. Presently she pulled herself together and got up and looked in the glass. "I'm a pretty sight and no mistake," she said huskily, and tried to smile, then she put on her hat and went out. I watched her from the window wandering along in the opposite direction from the village. I waited up until she came back at about half-past ten. She seemed glad I was there and made a great effort to be cheerful. She took off her hat and fluffed out her hair and we made tea on the gas-ring and ate biscuits with it.

She talked a lot but didn't mention Arthur once. She said she'd been thinking things out and had decided to go to Vienna; she said she knew an agent there called Max Steiner and that we'd probably get work right away. She said Vienna was a lovely place and she was longing to see it again, she'd been there once before with Mattie several years ago. When I said good night she suddenly hugged me very tight and said: "Well, dear, we're on our ownsome again now, so let's enjoy it!"

After this, poor Aunt Tittie was terribly dispirited and unhappy for weeks. We went to Vienna and found that Max Steiner was away so we trudged around to several other agents until we had no more money left. Then I got a job in the Prater Amusement Park at a Houp-la Booth. I had to jerk the hoops onto a stick after the people had thrown them and then sling them back to the proprietor who was a brass-throated fat little man but quite kind. I made enough money that way to get us food, and Aunt Tittie managed to pay for our rooms in a very dirty little hotel by picking up men every once in a while, but it wasn't really too easy for her because there were so many young and attractive professionals who knew the best cafés and resented intrusion on their beats. I used to be dreadfully tired when I got home every night and I got awful blisters on my feet from standing about all day.

In October, Aunt Tittie met a very rich old man who took her to Budapest. When she'd been gone about a week she telegraphed me some money to come at once so I gave a day's notice to the Houp-la Booth and went. Aunt Tittie met me at the station in a smart motor-car; she was well-dressed and looked much happier. She said she had a small flat overlooking the river and that if only her old man could live for a little longer we'd be on velvet, but that he was very, very old indeed, and she was afraid he couldn't keep through the winter. We laughed a lot and were delighted to be together again. Her flat really was quite nice and I slept in a little servant's room at the back. There was a Hungarian cook who came in by the day and we did the housework ourselves. The old man didn't trouble us much, he only came to dinner two or three times a week and then didn't stay very late. I used to go out when he came and walk in the town, which was beautiful, and sit about in cafés drinking coffee and listening to the Tziganes.

After we'd been there a few weeks Aunt Tittie met an old friend of hers from Paris in the Hungaria Hotel. He was a Frenchman, and was running a small café on the other side of the river. He came to tea at the flat two days later and we did our turn for him and he said he would engage us. Aunt Tittie was really looking very well just then and had a lot of nice clothes. We started work the following Monday and stayed there the whole winter, we changed our songs every fortnight, and saved quite a lot of money.

In April, Aunt Tittie's old man had to go and do a cure at Baden-Baden. He decided to go quite suddenly and wrote a letter to her saying good-bye and enclosing enough money to pay the last month's rent and a bit over besides. We were both very relieved really and never saw him again. A year later we read in the paper that he had died.

We left Budapest in May and went back to Vienna where we stayed a few days, then went to Prague where we played in an open-air café for six weeks. Then we came back to Paris with enough money to keep us for the summer at least, if we lived cheaply.

That autumn we started again on our travels, we got return engagements in some of the towns we had played before. I was now fourteen and getting very tall. For the next two years our lives went along pretty evenly. We met Arthur Wheeler once in Nice on the Pro-menade des Anglais; he looked spruce and well and was wearing a straw hat, which he lifted politely, but Aunt Tittie cut him dead, and as we were leaving the next day we didn't see him again. In the sum-mer of 1911 we were back in Paris. Aunt Tittie wasn't well and complained of pains inside. We didn't work for a few weeks and then went away.

In the January following, I had my seventeenth birthday. It came on a Sunday and we were traveling to Spain where we'd neither of us been before. We got out at Bayonne and bought a bottle of champagne and had a celebration all to ourselves in the compart-ment. We finished the bottle between us and I got drunk for the first time in my life and went shouting up and down the corridor. Aunt Tit-tie was too weak with laughter to stop me.

We played in a Café Chantant in San Sebastian; it had only just opened and was new and gaudy and smelt of paint. The proprietor was a fat Belgian Jew who wore an enormous diamond and sapphire ring on his little finger. We had been recommended to him by Demaire, our agent in Paris, as a novelty. He didn't seem to think we were very novel and was rude to Aunt Tittie when she asked for the band to play more quietly, but it mattered little as hardly anybody came to the café anyhow and we were paid our salary and dismissed after the first week. We played in several different places in Spain but without much success. The Spaniards were polite and applauded our turn perfunctorily and that was all; there was no enthusiasm, and when Aunt Tittie went from table to table singing "How Would You Like a Little Rose Like Me?" they generally sat quite silently and looked at her, and very seldom even held out their hands for the paper roses, so poor Aunt Tittie had to put them down on the table and go on to the next one. It was very discouraging for her; of course, she was be-ginning to look rather old, and her smile lacked the gaiety it used to have.

When we got to Barcelona we played in a very dirty music hall which was a bit better because the floor of the auditorium was uncarpeted wood and the people stamped their feet instead of clapping, which made a tremendous noise and made everything we did seem like a triumphant success. We went to a big bullfight one afternoon which upset us both horribly. Aunt Tittie cried all the way back to the hotel, thinking about the horses, and how they trotted into the ring so amicably with a bandage over one eye to prevent them from seeing the bull coming. Some of them screamed dreadfully when they were gored and the memory of it haunted us for days.

We sat outside a café on the way home and had Ochata which is an iced sweet drink made of nuts, and looks like very thick milk. Aunt Tittie kept on bursting into tears and then laughing at herself hysterically, altogether she was in such a state that she had to have some brandy and lie down before the show. Two nights after that when we had finished our turn and I was waiting outside the dressing room under the stage, while Aunt Tittie dressed, there was suddenly a terrific crash up above and a loud scream and the orchestra stopped dead. I rushed up on to the stage to see what had happened. Everyone was running about and yelling. One of the big limelight lamps had exploded and fallen down and set fire to the curtains, which were blazing.

A conjuror who had been doing his turn when the thing fell came rushing past me and knocked me against the wall; his wife, who was his assistant, was shut up in his magic cabinet in the middle of the stage and was hammering on the inside of it to be let out. The stage manager ran toward it to open it, but before he could reach it a whole length of blazing curtain fell right across it.

I ran quickly downstairs to fetch Aunt Tittie and met her coming up in her dressing gown with grease all over her face. We heard the conjuror's wife shrieking horribly as the cabinet started to burn, but there was no chance of rescuing her because by this time the whole stage was blazing. We tried to beat our way through the thick smoke to the stage door. Aunt Tittie was choking and a stagehand, mad with fright, knocked her down and stumbled right over her; one of his boots cut her face. I helped her up and we finally got out into the alley. There was a terrific crash behind us as part of the roof fell in. Aunt Tittie gave a little gasp and collapsed, so I grabbed her under the arms and dragged her along the alley with her heels scraping over the cobblestones. There were hundreds of people running about screaming and I was terrified that we'd be thrown down and trampled to death. When I got Aunt Tittie out of the alley into the street I suddenly thought of the conjuror's wife trapped inside that cabinet, and I laid Aunt Tittie on the ground and was violently sick in the gutter.

When I'd finished, I sat down on the curb by her side. Then I noticed that her face was bleeding, so I dabbed it with my handkerchief and she opened her eyes. The fire engines had arrived by this time. I could hear them in the next street. A man came up and we both helped Aunt Tittie to her feet; she stood swaying for a moment with our arms supporting her and then gave a scream and clutched her side and fainted again. I didn't know what to do, the man couldn't speak French or English, and I only knew a few words of Spanish. He helped me carry her along to the street corner and I signed to him to wait with her while I got a taxi. I ran very fast but couldn't see one anywhere. Suddenly I saw a motor ambulance coming out of a side street, I stopped it and directed it back to where I'd left Aunt Tittie. The two ambulance men lifted her into it and I said good-bye to the strange man and thanked him very much, and he raised his bowler hat and bowed and we drove away to the hospital leaving him standing there.

When we arrived at the hospital they took Aunt Tittie into the emergency ward and I sat by her for ages before anyone came near us. She came to after a little and started to cry; she said she had a terrible pain in her stomach at the side! Her voice sounded very weak and husky. There were lots of other people lying on beds and groaning. One man's face was almost black and all the hair on the top of his head was burnt away leaving mottled red patches. He kept on giving little squeaks like a rabbit, and clutching at the sheet with his hands which were dreadfully burned.

Presently two Sisters of Mercy came in and went round to all the beds and tried to make people a little more comfortable. Finally two doctors came with several nurses; and they went from bed to bed and talked a lot, in low voices. When they got to us I stood up and explained in French about Aunt Tittie's pain. Fortunately one of them understood all right and felt her stomach with his fingers, then he sent one of the nurses away and she came back in a few minutes with a stretcher on wheels. We all got Aunt Tittie on to it and I walked behind it with the doctor through miles of passages.

Eventually we got to a very quiet ward with only a few beds occupied. A Sister of Mercy was sitting reading at a table with a shaded lamp on it. She got up when we came in. Then the doctor took me downstairs to the waiting room and said that he was afraid Aunt Tittie had a very bad appendix but that he was going to give her a thorough examination and make sure and that I'd better go home and come back in the morning. I said I'd rather stay in case Aunt Tittie wanted me, so he said "very well" and left me. I lay on a bench all night and slept part of the time. In the early morning two cleaners came in and clattered about with pails. I got up and found my way to the main entrance and finally found a nurse who spoke a little

French. She said it was too early to find out anything and that I'd better have some coffee and come back, so I went out into the street and found a café that was just opening and drank some coffee and ate a roll. When I got back I met the doctor coming down the steps, he took me into an office and a Sister of Mercy took down particulars about Aunt Titania which I gave her in French, and the doctor translated into Spanish. When that was done he told me that the only chance of saving Aunt Tittie's life was to operate immediately. I asked if I could see her and he said no, that she was almost unconscious and that if I was agreeable he would operate right away. I said he'd better do what he thought best and that I'd wait, so I went back to the waiting room. A lot of people had come in, several were relatives of people who had been in the fire, most of them moaned and wailed and made a great noise. About three hours later a nurse came and called out my name. I stood up, and she took me into the office again. After a minute or two the doctor came in looking very serious. He told me that there was scarcely any hope of Aunt Tittie living, as when they operated they discovered that the appendix had burst. He said she hadn't come to yet from the anesthetic, but that I could see her when she did. I asked when that would be and he said he couldn't tell for certain, but that I'd better wait. They let me stay in the office which was nicer than the waiting room, and the Sister of Mercy gave me some dry biscuits out of a tin on her desk. She had a round face, and glasses, and peered at me through them sympathetically. Presently a nurse appeared and signed to me to follow her. We went several floors in a lift. There was a wheel stretcher in it with a man lying on it and an orderly standing by the side. The man didn't move at all and his head was covered with bandages.

This time Aunt Tittie was in a private room which was very dim and there was a screen round the head of the bed and another near the door. When I went in I could hardly see for a minute; the nurse drew up a chair and I sat down by the bed. Aunt Tittie was lying quite still with her eyes closed. Her face was dead white and she had a nightdress on of thick flannel which was buttoned up to the chin. She looked terribly, terribly tired and every now and then her mouth gave a little twitch. I felt a longing to put my arms round her and hold her tight and tell her how much I loved her, but when I thought about that I wanted to cry, so I looked away for a moment and tried to control myself. Presently she opened her eyes and moved her head to one side; she saw me and said "Hello, dearie," in a whisper. Then she frowned and closed her eyes again. I took her hand which was outside the coverlet, and held it. It felt dry and hot. After a little while she moved again and tried to speak, her hand clutched mine very hard and then relaxed. I put my head down close to hers and she said: "Take care of yourself." I started crying then, hopelessly, but I was careful not to make any noise and her eyes were still shut so she couldn't see. Suddenly she gave a little moan and the nurse came out from behind the screen and motioned me to go out of the room. I disengaged my hand from Aunt Tittie's very gently; she didn't seem to notice, and I went out into the passage. There was a window at the end and I stood and looked out across the hospital grounds to the town. It was a very windy day and there was a flagstaff upon the hill with the flag standing straight out from it looking as though it were made of wood. Every now and then it fluttered and subsided for a moment and then blew out straight again.

I waited about all day in the hospital, but they wouldn't let me in to see Aunt Tittie again, because they said she was unconscious, and in the evening at about seven o'clock she died. I went back to the hotel and lay on my bed, trying to be sensible and think things out, but I wasn't very successful and finally gave way and cried for a long time until I dropped off to sleep. When I woke up it was about eleven o'clock and I felt better, but I couldn't sleep any more so I went out and wandered about the town. I walked right down to the harbor and watched the ships. There was a big liner, standing a little way out, all the decks were brilliantly lighted and I could hear music faintly. I suddenly realized that I hadn't had anything to eat all day, so I went into a restaurant which was filled with sailors, and had a plate of stew and some coffee, everything was very greasy and I couldn't eat much of it.

The next day I went through all Aunt Tittie's things and discovered that she had twenty sovereigns locked in her jewel case, also a brooch with diamonds and two rings, one with very small rose diamonds, and the other plain gold. I myself had fourteen pounds saved, mostly in francs. I went back to the hospital and interviewed the doctor about the operation and funeral expenses. He was very kind, and when I told him how much I had, said that he wouldn't charge for the operation. In spite of this, however, I had to pay out a good deal and when the whole business was over I had about seventeen pounds left. Aunt Tittie was buried two days later. An English clergyman appeared and did it all. He was officious, and kept on asking me questions about her. I bought a bunch of flowers and put them on the grave, and I went back and packed up everything and bought a ticket for Paris.

The Paris train was crowded, and I sat in the corridor all night and thought about Aunt Tittie, until my heart nearly burst with loneliness and I pressed my head against the window and longed to be dead, too.

WHAT
MAD
PURSUIT?

Evan Lorrimer's celebrity value was unquestionably high. In the course of twenty years he had written no less than eleven novels; a volume of war poems, tinged with whimsical bitterness; one play which had been much praised by the London critics and run nearly two months; a critical survey of the life and times of Madame de Staël entitled *The Life and Times of Madame de Staël*; sundry essays and short stories for the more literary weeklies; and an autobiography. The autobiography had been on the whole the least successful of his works, but he in no way regretted having written it. For years he had been aware that incidents, journeys, and personal experiences had been accumulating in his mind until it had come to a point when he could no longer feel free to pursue his historical researches. He felt himself to be congested, or, to put it more crudely, constipated, and that unless he could get rid of this agglomeration of trivia, his real genius, which was writing graphically of the past in terms of the present, would atrophy. The autobiography, therefore, was a sort of cathartic and as such achieved its object. Hardly had the corrected and revised manuscript been delivered to the publishers before he was at work again, drafting out with renewed energy and clarity of thought his great novel of the Restoration, *A London Lady*. There was no doubt in his mind that if *My Steps Have Faltered*, which was the title of the autobiography, had not been written when it was, *A London Lady* would never have been written at all. The success of *A London Lady* transcended by far everything else he had ever written. It went into several editions within the first few weeks of its publication. It was elected, without one dissentient vote, as the Book Society's choice for the month of February. The most important moving picture company in Hollywood acquired the film rights of it at an even higher price than they had paid for *The Life of Saint Paul*, which had been awarded the Pulitzer Prize for the year before, and in addition to all this, its sales in America surpassed those of England a hundredfold before it had been out six weeks. It was on the suggestion of Evan's New York publishers, Neuman Bloch, that he had agreed to do a short lecture tour in the States. He had been naturally apprehensive of the idea at first, but after a certain amount of coaxing, and tempted by the prospect of visiting America for the first time in such singularly advantageous circumstances—full expenses there and back, a tour of only eight weeks visiting the principal towns, and a guaranteed fee for each lecture that appeared to be little short of fantastic—he gathered his courage together, made exhaustive notes on the subjects on which he intended to speak, and set sail on the *Queen Mary*.

Now it would be foolish to deny that Evan Lorrimer enjoyed publicity. Everyone enjoys publicity to a certain degree. It is always pleasant to feel that your name is of sufficient interest to the world to merit a prominent position in the daily newspapers. For many years past, Evan had been privately gratified to read such phrases as "Of course Evan Lorrimer was there, suave and well-groomed as usual," or "That inveterate first-nighter, Evan Lorrimer, arrived a few minutes before the curtain rose and was seen chatting laughingly to Lady Millicent Cawthorne in the foyer," or "Evan Lorrimer whose new novel, *A London Lady*, has caused such a sensation, was the guest of honor at the Pen and Pencil Club on Sunday evening." Such allusions, guileless and dignified, are immensely agreeable. Unimportant perhaps in their essence, but in their implication very important indeed. Just as millions of little coral animals in so many years construct a barrier reef against the sea, so can these small accolades, over a period of time, build, if not quite a barrier reef, at least a fortification against the waves of oblivion. Evan felt this very strongly. His reviews he read as a matter of course, regarding them rightly as part of the business. Naturally he was pleased when they were good and pained when they were bad, but the gossip columns were different. They were both unprejudiced and uncritical; they contented themselves with the simple statement that he was here or there with so-and-so, or accompanied by such-and-such, and by their repetitious banality did more to consolidate his reputation than all the carefully phrased opinions of the literati put together. But Evan, well used as he was to being photographed and interviewed and occasionally signing a few autograph books, was certainly unprepared for the violence of his reception in New York. From the moment the ship paused at Quarantine turmoil engulfed him. He was belabored with questions by over a dozen reporters at the same time, photographed waving to mythical friends by no less than fifteen cameras simultaneously, hurried on to the dock where he was met by Neuman Bloch, Mrs. Bloch, the firm's publicity agent, several more reporters and, most surprisingly, a man who had been at school with him and whom he hadn't clapped eyes on for twenty-six years. In the flurry of Customs examination, interviews, and the effort to sustain a reasonably intelligent flow of conversation with the Blochs, he was completely unable to recall the man's name; however it didn't matter, for after wringing his hand warmly, and standing by his side in silence for a few minutes, he disappeared into the crowd and Evan never saw him again.

Evan Lorrimer at the age of forty-seven was, both in appearance and behavior, a model of what an eminent Englishman of letters should be. He was five-foot-ten, his figure was spare but well-proportioned, he had slim, expressive hands, dark hair graying slightly at the temples, deep-set gray eyes, a small, neat moustache and an urbane smile. Perhaps his greatest asset was his voice which was rich in tone and, at times, almost caressing, particularly when, with his slyly humorous gift of phrase, he was describing somebody a trifle maliciously. Lady Cynthia Cawthorne who, in Lowndes Square had achieved the nearest approach to a London salon since Lady Blessington, was wont to say, with her loud infectious laugh, that had she only been younger she'd have married Evan Lorrimer out of hand if only to hear him repeat over and over again his famous description of being taken, at the age of fifteen, to the Musée Grevin by Marcel Proust.

Evan, like so many people who have attained fame and fortune by their own unaided efforts, was a firm self-disciplinarian. He apportioned his time with meticulous care: so many hours for writing, so many for reading. He ate and drank in moderation and indulged in only enough exercise to keep himself fit. He contrived, although naturally of a highly strung, nervous temperament, to maintain an agreeable poise both physically and mentally and to derive a great deal of enjoyment from life, admittedly without often scaling the heights of rapture, but also without plumbing the depths of despair. This self-adjustment, this admirable balance, was dependent upon one absolute necessity and that necessity was sleep. Eight solid hours per night minimum, with a possible snooze during the day, was his deadline. Without that he was lost, his whole organism disintegrated. He became jumpy and irascible, unable to concentrate. In fact on one occasion, owing to an emotional upheaval when the pangs of not sufficiently requited love gnawed at his vitals for nearly four months, he became actively ill and had to retire to a nursing home. Realizing this one weakness, this Achilles heel, he arranged his life accordingly.

At home, in his small house in Chesham Place, his two servants had been trained to a mouselike efficiency. Until he was called in the morning the house was wrapped in the silence of death. The knocker had been taken off the front door, and both bells, front and back, muffled down to the merest tinkle; the telephone by his bed was switched off nightly and rang in the basement, and even there, after a series of dogged experiments by Albert his valet, it had been reduced to nothing more than a purr. Naturally, taking all this into consideration, the first few nights in New York were a torture to him. He had, of course, been warned that the sharpness of the climate and the champagne quality of the air would enable him to do with less sleep than he was accustomed to in the older, more stagnant atmosphere of England, and although he discovered this to be true to a certain extent, he was unable to repress a slight feeling of panic. If only, he reflected, he could get away into the country for two or three days, to relax, to give himself time to adjust himself, he might come to view the so much swifter tempo of American life with more equanimity.

It was on the fourth day after his arrival, toward the end of a strenuously literary cocktail party given in his honor by the Neuman Blochs, that he met Louise Steinhauser. He was introduced to her by his hostess and immediately taken out onto the terrace to look at the view. This had already happened to him five times, and although he had been deeply impressed by the view the first two times, it was now beginning to pall a little; however Louise was adamant. "Look at it," she said in a husky, rather intense voice. "Isn't it horrible?"

Evan gave a slight start of surprise. Louise went on: "Every time I look at New York from a height like this, I positively shudder. All those millions of people cooped up in those vast buildings give me such a feeling of claustrophobia that I think I'm going mad. If I didn't live out in the country most of the time I really should go mad. My husband, poor darling, comes in every day of course, and we have an apartment at the Pierre—you can just see it from here behind that tower that looks like a pencil with india rubber on top—but really I hardly ever use it unless I happen to come in for a late party or an opening night or something, and even then I often drive down home afterward, however late it is."

"How far away is your home in the country?" enquired Evan.

"About an hour in the automobile; at night of course, it's much quicker and I can't begin to tell you how lovely it is to arrive at about two in the morning and smell the sea—my house is right on the sea—and just go to sleep in that wonderful silence—you'd think you were miles away from anywhere, and yet it's actually only a little way from New York. There are no houses near us, we're completely isolated— You really must come down for a weekend, except that I warn you there isn't a thing to do except lie about and relax. Bonwit, that's my husband, plays golf occasionally or a little tennis, but I don't play anything. I find at my age—I shall be forty-four next month, imagine!"—she laughed disarmingly, "I never try to hide my age, it's so silly, after all what *does* it matter. Anyhow, as I was saying, at my age I find that all I want are my comforts, nice books, a few real friends, not just acquaintances, and good food. I'm afraid that's all I can offer you, peace and good food, but if you would like to slip away from all this," she indicated the remainder of the cocktail party milling about inside with a wave of her hand, "and really lead the simple life for a couple of days, you don't even have to bring dinner clothes if you don't want to. Please come, both Bonwit and I would be absolutely enchanted."

Evan had been looking at her carefully while she was talking, carefully and critically. Being a writer, he was naturally observant, his mind was trained to perceive small indicative details. Being a celebrity he was also cautious. He noted Louise's clothes first; they were obviously expensive, the ruby and diamond clip in her small cloche hat could only have come from Cartier. Her pearls might or might not be real, but the clasp most certainly was. In addition to these external advantages he liked her. She was vivacious, humorous and friendly. She also seemed to have a sensible appreciation of the values of life.

"You're most kind," he said. "There's nothing I should like better."

"Now isn't that lovely," cried Louise. "How long are you going to be here?"

"Alas, only until next Wednesday, then I have to lecture in Chicago."

"I suppose you're booked up for this next weekend?"

Evan shook his head. He had been tentatively invited to the Neuman Blochs' house at Ossining, but he hadn't definitely accepted. "I was supposed to go to the Blochs'," he said, "but I can get out of it."

"Then that's settled," said Louise gaily. "I'm coming in on Saturday to go to *Starlight*, that's a musical comedy that Lester Gaige is in. He's one of my greatest friends, you'll adore him. Why don't you dine with me and come too, and we'll all three drive down afterward.

57

He's the only person I've invited for this weekend. I daren't have a lot of people when he comes because he insists on being quiet. He says he gives out so much at every performance during the week that he's damned if he'll give a special performance on Sundays. He really is divine, and he certainly won't bother you because he does nothing but sleep."

As they rejoined the cocktail party, Evan felt that the much-vaunted American hospitality was a very genuine and touching trait.

2

Lester Gaige was certainly amusing. At first, watching him on the stage, Evan had been unsure as to whether or not he was going to like him; he seemed to be too debonair, almost arrogant in the manner in which he moved through the bewildering intricacies of *Starlight*. True, he danced beautifully, sang, with no voice but compelling charm, and dominated by sheer force of personality every scene he was in; but there was something about him, a mocking veneer that made you a trifle uneasy as to what you might discover underneath. However, in the car driving down to the country, he was much more human. His clothes were inclined to be eccentric. He had on suede shoes, thin silk socks, very pale gray flannel trousers of exquisite cut, a bois de rose sweater with a turtleneck, a tweed sports jacket of extravagant heartiness and a fur-lined overcoat with an astrakhan collar. In addition he wore a small beret basque and a pair of the largest horn-rimmed glasses Evan had ever seen. The conversation between him and Louise was stimulating if a little local in allusion. They referred to so many people in such a short space of time that Evan became quite confused; but he sat back in the corner of the luxurious Packard and gave himself up to being agreeably soothed and entertained. It was obvious that Louise and Lester had been intimate friends for several years; their talk, generally in a gaily reminiscent vein, jumped from London to Paris, from Antibes back to New York, from New York to Venice and from Venice to California. "That amazing party of Irene's when Broddie got blind and had that awful scene with Carola." "That terrible night in Salzburg when Nada refused to go home and finally disappeared into the mountains with Sonny Boy for three days." Occasionally Evan, not wishing to appear out of it, ventured a question as to who So-and-so was, and was immediately rewarded by a vivid, if not always entirely kind, description of So-and-so's life, activities, and morals. On the whole he enjoyed himself very much. To begin with, they had all three had a Scotch Highball (ridiculous expression) in Lester's dressing room before they started and then another at 21 where they had had to stop for a moment because Lester had to give some message to Ed Bolingbroke, who had been apparently too drunk to understand it, then, not long after they had crossed the Fifty-ninth Street Bridge, Lester had produced a bottle of Scotch from his overcoat pocket, and they had all had a little extra swig to keep them warm. It was necessary to keep warm for the night was bitterly cold; there had been a blizzard the day before and the snow was several inches thick and freezing over.

When they finally reached the Steinhauser home Evan got out of the car, stretched his cramped legs and gave an exclamation of pleasure. It really was most attractive. A large low white house built on three sides of a square and looking out over Long Island Sound. It was a clear moonlight night and far away on the Connecticut coast lights twinkled across the water. Behind the house was nothing but snow, and a few bleak winter trees. Above all, there was silence, complete and soul-satisfying silence, broken only by the soft lap of the waves on the shore.

Inside, the house was the acme of comfort, a large fire was blazing away in a wide open fireplace in the main living room; before it was set a table laid for supper. A pleasant, colored butler in a white coat met them at the front door. Evan sighed a deep sigh of relief. This was even better than he had imagined.

They sat up until very late over the fire talking. The supper had been delicious, a simple but tasty dish of spaghetti, tomatoes and eggs, a well-mixed green salad with cream cheese and Bar le Duc and further Scotch Highballs. Evan had had two since his arrival and although he was far from intoxicated he felt enjoyably mellow. Lester, who was really a great deal more intelligent than one would expect a musical comedy actor to be, displayed a flattering interest in Evan's work. He had read *A London Lady,* and been thrilled with it, he was also one of the few people who had read and enjoyed *My Steps Have Faltered.* Evan dismissed his praise of this with a deprecatory laugh, but he was pleased none the less. Louise was a good hostess and more than that, Evan decided, an extremely good sort. She talked with vivacity and her sense of humor was true and keen. She appeared to be one of those rare types, a rich woman who is completely unaffected by her wealth. She was downright, honest, and withal very attractive. She alluded to her husband frequently, and it was apparent that although they might not quite see eye to eye over certain things, she was deeply attached to him. They had a son at Harvard to whom they were both obviously devoted. Louise showed Evan a photograph of him dressed in the strange robotish armor of an American footballer. He was a husky, fine-looking lad. Lester was highly enthusiastic about him. "That boy is fantastic," he said, "you'd never believe it to look at him, but he paints the most remarkable watercolors! He gave me one when I was playing Boston in *And So What.*

It's a seascape, rather Japanesey in quality, almost like a Foujita."
Evan looked again at the photograph, slightly puzzled. Really Americans were most surprising. It was difficult to imagine that six feet of
brawn and muscle painting demure seascapes, and even more difficult to understand how Lester Gaige playing in *And So What* in Boston could ever have heard of Foujita. Perhaps there was something to
be said after all for that American culture that Europeans referred to
with such disdain.

It wasn't until nearly four o'clock that Louise suddenly jumped
up from the sofa on which she had been lying and cried: "Really this
is terrible—I bring you down here to rest and keep you up to all
hours talking. We simply *must* go to bed." She led the way through
the hall and along a little passage. "I've given you the quietest room
in the house," she said over her shoulder, "it's on the ground floor
and you'll have to share a bathroom with Lester. I would have given
you a room upstairs with a bath to yourself but it isn't nearly so shut
away and you might be disturbed by Bonwit getting up early or the
servants or something." She opened the door leading into a charmingly furnished bedroom. "This is Lester's," she said, "you're along
here." They passed along another little passage and there was Evan's
room. It was large, with two beds and decorated in a pale, restful
green. In addition to the two beds there was a chaise longue piled with
cushions in front of the fire which, although it must have been lit
hours ago, was still burning cozily. Evan smiled with pleasure. "What a
perfect room," he said gratefully. Louise gave the fire a poke. "I know
how English people loathe central heating," she said, "and I've told
them to have a fire for you all the time you're here, but if you'll take my
advice you'll have the heat on a little bit as well, because the weather's
really freezing."

After Louise had said good night and gone up to bed, and Lester and Evan had smoked one more cigarette and exchanged the
usual politenesses as to which of them should use the bathroom
first, Evan, at last alone, opened the window, and, cold as it was,
stood for a moment looking up at the stars and listening to the
silence. He sniffed the icy air into his lungs, and with a sigh of utter
contentment climbed into bed and was asleep in five minutes.

3

Evan woke at ten-thirty, which was rather early considering how late
he had gone to bed. He counted up in his mind, four-thirty to ten-
thirty, only six hours, but still it didn't matter, he could easily make
up for it that night. He lay there idly looking at the reflection of the
sea on the ceiling and contemplating, with a slight sinking of the
heart, his lecture on Monday night. It was drawing very near and he

was naturally nervous, but still he had certainly been wise to give himself this breathing space immediately before it. He planned to go over his notes sometime during the day. He was aware, of course, that he spoke well and that his subject "History and the Modern Novel" was pretty certain to interest his American audience. He intended to start with the middle ages, the period of his first two novels, then jump to French eighteenth century, bringing in his *Porcelaine Courtesan, Madame Is Indisposed* and *The Sansculotte,* then to the Directoire and *Madame de Staël,* leaving the Restoration and *A London Lady* to the last. He was determined, in spite of the cautious advice of Neuman Bloch, to deliver a few well-deserved slaps at some of the more successful American writers who so impertinently twisted European history to their own ends. Evan detested slang and the use of present-day idiom in describing the past. Not that he was a believer in the "Odd's Boddikins" "Pish Tushery" school of historical writing; he himself eschewed that with the greatest contempt, but he did believe in being factually accurate insofar as was possible, and in using pure English. Had not the exquisite literacy of *A London Lady* been one of the principal reasons for its success with the Book Society? And not only the Book Society, with the reviewers of both continents and with the general public. One of Evan's most comforting convictions was that the general public had a good deal more discrimination and taste than it was given credit for, and that all this careless, slipshod, *soi disant* modern style with its vulgarity of phrase and cheap Americanisms would, in a very little while, be consigned to the oblivion it so richly deserved.

At this point in his reflections he broke off to wonder whether or not he should ring for some fruit juice and coffee. He remembered from last night that the only entrance to his room was through Lester's and the bathroom and it would be inconsiderate to wake Lester if he were still sleeping. Evan, with a little sigh not entirely free from irritation, decided to go and see. He tiptoed out into the passage and into the bathroom and opened the door leading to Lester's room very quietly. Lester *was* still sleeping in a pair of pastel blue silk pajamas with his head buried in the pillow. Evan stood there regarding him uncertainly for a moment. It would, of course, be unkind to wake him, and yet on the other hand he might possibly sleep until lunch time and Evan would have to wait nearly three hours for his coffee. He retired into the bathroom, closing the door softly after him, and pondered the situation. Presently, renouncing indecision once and for all, he flushed the toilet and then listened carefully with his ear to the door. He was rewarded by hearing a few grunts and then the creaking of the bed. Quick as a flash he darted across to the lavatory basin and turned the tap on full, once embarked he intended taking no chances. After a few moments he opened the door again and peeped in. Lester was sitting up looking, he was glad to observe, quite amiable. Evan coughed apologetically. "I'm awfully sorry," he said, "I'm afraid I woke you up. I'd no idea the tap would make such a row."

"It wasn't the tap," said Lester without rancor, "It was the Lulu."

"How does one get coffee, do you suppose?"

"Let's ring," said Lester. "We can either have it here or put on our dressing gowns and go into the sun porch—which do you prefer?"

"I don't mind a bit." Evan, his plan having succeeded so easily, was feeling a little guilty and determined to be amenable at all costs.

"I think the sun porch is nicer." Lester jumped out of bed, rang the bell and went into the bathroom to brush his teeth.

While they were breakfasting on the sun porch, an agreeable glass-enclosed room at the side of the house commanding a wide view of the sea and the drive, Bonwit Steinhauser appeared in elaborate plus fours. He was a red-faced, rather dull-looking man, with a large body that had once been muscular but was now just fat. He said "good morning" affably, and after a little desultory conversation went away. When he had gone Lester pushed his coffee cup out of his way and leant across the table almost furtively.

"You know I like Bonwit," he whispered as though by such a confession he was straining credulity to the utmost. "There's something really awfully kind about him. Of course everyone says he's a bore and I suppose he is in a way, but when he's had a few drinks, my dear!" He did one of his characteristic gestures of pawing the air with his right hand. "He can be terribly, terribly funny! I shall never forget when I was up here one weekend with Ida Wesley, she's dead as a doornail now, poor sweet, and Bonwit, who shall be nameless, got so fried—" Here he broke off abruptly and said: "My God!" Evan turned round to see what had startled him and saw a car coming slowly up the drive. He jumped to his feet. Lester got up too, and, after looking out carefully a moment gave a laugh. "It's all right," he said, "it's only Irene and Suki and Dwight and Luella—I thought for a minute it was strangers."

"Are they coming for lunch?" asked Evan apprehensively.

"I expect so," replied Lester, sitting down again. "But you'll love Irene, she's divine, but *divine*—you've heard her sing, haven't you?"

Evan shook his head.

"You've never heard Irene Marlow sing!" Lester was horrified. "You haven't lived that's all, you just haven't lived! We'll make her sing after lunch. Suki's with her fortunately, he always plays with her. It really is the most lovely voice and there's somebody with an amazing sense of humor! I mean, she really gets herself, which is more than you can say for most prima donnas, and if you could hear her when she's in a real rage with Dwight, that's Dwight Macadoo who shall be nameless. My God! it's wonderful—bang goes the Italian accent and out pops Iowa!"

"We'd better go and dress, hadn't we?" suggested Evan, feeling unequal to greeting a famous Iowan prima donna in his pajamas.

"You go and dress," said Lester. "And you might turn on a bath for me when you've finished. I'll go and deal with the visiting firemen."

Evan retired to his room, shattered. It was really appalling luck that these people should have selected today of all days to come to lunch. How cross Louise would be. But still, he comforted himself, she'd be sure to get rid of them all as soon as possible.

When he emerged, bathed, shaved and dressed in perfectly cut English country clothes he found everybody in the large living room. Apparently, while he had been dressing, some more people had arrived. Bonwit was mixing cocktails behind a little bar in the far corner of the room. There was no sign of Louise.

Seeing Evan come in, Lester, who was sitting on the sofa with a fattish little man and two women, jumped up. "This is my friend," he cried, "I don't think you know my friend! who shall be nameless," he added with a light laugh. Evan smiled sheepishly, he was unused to being nameless, but Lester came over and took him affectionately by the arm. "I must introduce you to everybody," he said. "We'd better begin right here and work round the whole Goddamned circle." He raised his voice. "Listen, everybody—this is Evan Lorrimer, one of the greatest living English novelists, he's my friend and I'm mad about him!" He turned enquiringly to Evan. "Aren't I, honey?"

Evan summoned up enough poise to give a little smile and say, "I hope so," whereupon Lester, holding him firmly by the arm, walked him round the room. A slight hush fell while this tour was in progress. Evan shook hands with everyone and responded pleasantly to their assurances of how glad they were to know him, but he was unable to catch more than a few names as he went along, and finally sat down feeling rather confused, in the place on the sofa that Lester had vacated. The fattish little man, he discovered, was Otis Meer, who wrote a famous gossip column for one of the daily papers, and the two women were Irene Marlow and Luella Rosen. Irene was flamboyant, but attractively so, she was dressed in a scarlet sports suit, with a vivid green scarf, her brown hair was done in clusters of curls and her hat—it couldn't have been anyone else's—was on the mantelpiece. Luella Rosen was sharp and black, like a little Jewish bird, she also was wearing sports clothes, but of a more somber hue.

Irene smiled, generously exposing a lot of dazzlingly white teeth. "Lester had been telling us all about you," she said—her voice had a trace of a foreign accent—"and you've no idea how thrilled we are to meet you. I haven't read your book yet, but I've got it."

"Mr. Lorrimer has written dozens of books, dear," said Luella.

Irene sat back and closed her eyes in mock despair. "Isn't Luella horrible?" she said. "I'm never allowed to get away with a thing—anyway, I meant your last one, and I know it couldn't matter to you whether I've read it or not; but I really am longing to, particularly now that I've met you." She winked at Evan, a gay, confiding little wink and nudged him with her elbow. Luella gave a staccato laugh. "Irene's our pet moron," she said. "She's never read a book in her life except *Stories of the Operas*. She's just an Iowa girl who's made good, aren't you, darling?"

"Listen, lamb pie," said Irene, "you leave Iowa out of this. What's the matter with Iowa, anyway?"

"Nothing apart from Julia de Martineau," said Otis Meer, and went into a gale of laughter. Irene and Luella laughed too. Evan was naturally unaware of the piquancy of the joke. At this point an exceedingly handsome man came up and handed him an "old-fashioned."

"This is my dream prince," said Irene. "Dwight, you know Mr. Evan Lorrimer, don't you?"

"We've met already," said Evan, nodding to Dwight who nodded back with a grin and sat down on the floor at their feet, balancing his own drink carefully in his right hand as he did so. "Where the hell's Louise?" he asked.

"Louise has never been known to be on time for anything," said Luella.

Irene turned to Evan. "Isn't Louise a darling? You know she's one of the few really genuine people in the world. I can't bear people who aren't genuine, can you?" Evan made a gesture of agreement and she went on. "Being a writer must be just as bad as being a singer in some ways, having to meet people all the time and look pleased when they say nice things about your books."

"Tough," said Luella. "My heart goes out to you both." She got up and went over to the bar.

"You mustn't pay any attention to Luella," said Irene, comfortingly, observing that Evan looked a trifle nonplussed. "She always goes on like that, she's actually got the kindest heart in the world, sometimes I really don't know what I'd do without her, she's one of our few really genuine friends, isn't she, Dwight?" Dwight looked up and nodded and then stared abstractedly into the fire. At this moment, Louise came into the room with a scream.

"I'm so terribly sorry, everybody—" she wailed. "I overslept." While she was swamped with greetings, Evan looked at her in horror. She seemed to be a totally different person. Could this be the same woman whose friendly tranquillity and wise, philosophical outlook had so charmed him last night? Could she have known all these people were coming or was she merely masking her dismay at their appearance and trying to carry everything off with a high hand? If so, she was certainly doing it very convincingly. She seemed to be wholeheartedly delighted to see them. Her eye lighted on him and she came over with her arms round a red-haired women in black and a small fair man. "My dear," she said, "you really must forgive me—I do hope you slept all right—" She broke off and turned to the red-haired woman. "He's a sleep maniac just like me," she said. Then to Evan again: "You have met everyone, haven't you, and been given a drink and everything?" Evan held up his glass in silent acknowledgment, he was bereft of words, whereupon she snatched it out of his hand. "You must have another at once," she cried. "That looks disgusting," and led him vivaciously to the bar.

During the next half an hour, which Evan spent leaning against the bar, he managed to sort out people a little in his mind. The red-haired woman in black was the Countess Brancati, she had been a Chicago debutante a few years back and had married into the Italian aristocracy. The thin gray man by the window talking to Luella Rosen was her husband. The little fair man was Oswald Roach, commonly known as Ossie. Ossie was a cabaret artist whose speciality was to sing rather bawdy monologues to his own improvisations on the ukulele. The source of this information was Bonwit, who, although sweating copiously from the efforts of mixing different sorts of drinks for everybody, was willing, almost grateful, for an opportunity to talk. "Who is the thin boy with the pale face?" Evan asked him. Bonwit shook the cocktail shaker violently. "That's Suki," he said with obvious distaste. "He's a Russian fairy who plays the piano for Irene, he's all right until he gets tight, then he goes cuckoo."

Evan was regarding this phenomenon with interest, when there was a loud commotion in the hall, and two enormous Alsatians sprang into the room followed by a neatly-dressed girl in jodhpurs and a fur coat. "I came just as I was," she said, as Louise advanced to kiss her. "I was riding this morning and Shirley couldn't wait, she's gone into the kitchen to see about food for Chico and Zeppo." She indicated the Alsatians who were running round the room wagging their tails and barking. "I do hope you didn't mind us bringing them, but we couldn't leave them all alone in the apartment for the whole day." Louise gaily assured her that she didn't mind a bit and brought her over to the bar. "Here's someone who's been dying to meet you," she said to Evan. "Leonie Crane, she's written three plays herself, she's one of my closest friends and she's read everything you've ever written." Leonie Crane blushed charmingly and wrung Evan's hand with considerable force. "Not quite all," she said in a well-modulated deep voice. "Louise always exaggerates, but I think *A Lady of London* was swell. Shirley and I read it in Capri in the summer."

"*A London Lady*," Evan corrected her gently and she blushed again. "That's typical of me," she said. "I'm so vague that Shirley says she wonders how I've lived as long as I have without being run over—Hallo, Bonny," she leant over the bar and patted Bonwit's wet hand. "What about a little hard liquor—I'm dying!"

Leonie was undeniably attractive, she radiated health and a sort of jolly schoolboyish vitality; her canary-colored silk shirt was open at the neck and her curly brown hair was cut close to her head. She was a little shy and tried to conceal it with a certain lazy gaucherie. Evan found her most sympathetic, and they talked for several minutes and then Shirley appeared. Leonie presented her to Evan with brusque matter-of-fact despatch.

"This is Evan Lorrimer, Shirley—Shirley Benedict." They shook hands. Shirley was on the same lines as Leonie but older and a little more heavily built. She had jet black hair, clear blue eyes, and was wearing a perfectly plain gray flannel coat and skirt. She wore no jewelry except a pair of pearl button earrings. Both girls were singularly free from trifling adornments.

Presently Lester reappeared dressed in an entirely new color scheme so far as tie and sweater went, but with the same strong, garish sports coat that he had worn the night before. He kissed Leonie and Shirley affectionately, and told Evan that they were both angels and that when he'd got to know them a little better he'd worship them. They all four had an old-fashioned on the strength of this prophecy and Evan began to feel a little drunk. It was not part of his usual routine to drink three tumblers of practically neat whiskey in the middle of the day on an empty stomach, but he had now become sufficiently light-headed not to care. After all, there was no sense in just sitting about in corners looking sulky, just because some rather odd people had happened to come over for lunch. It would be both disagreeable and silly. Everyone seemed disposed to be most gay and friendly, why not relax and enjoy himself. Comforted by this successful disposal of his conscience, he agreed with cheerful resignation when Louise suggested that they should all go over to the Hughes-Hitchcocks for one more tiny drink before lunch. He had not the remotest idea who the Hughes-Hitchcocks were, but it was apparent from the enthusiastic assent of everyone present and from Lester's glowing description of them that they were an entrancing young married couple who lived only just down the road. Evan accepted an offer to go in Leonie's car and together with her and Shirley and Lester—the Alsatians were left behind—he went.

Lester's assurance that the Hughes-Hitchcocks lived only just down the road proved to be inaccurate. Evan, wedged between Shirley, who was driving, and Leonie in a small Dusenberg roadster, with Lester on his lap, suffered cramp and terror simultaneously for a full half an hour's fast going. Shirley drove well, there was no doubt about that, if she had not they would all have been dead within the first five minutes; but it was the sort of driving that is liable to react unfavorably on the nerves of anyone who happens to drive himself. Evan had driven for years. He owned a sedate Studebaker in faraway green England and frequently conveyed himself back and forth through the country in it, but not at a pace like this, not at seventy miles an hour over an ice-covered road that had frozen so hard that it was like glass. The fact that he was also unaccustomed to a right-hand drive added considerably to his agony. His instinct time and time again was to seize the wheel and swerve over to the left side to avoid what seemed to be imminent destruction. Fortunately, however, he restrained himself and sat in frozen misery until at last they turned into a large driveway under tall trees.

On the terrace outside the Hughes-Hitchcocks' house, which was a vast gray structure built on the lines of a French château, stood several cars. It was obviously quite a large party. Once inside, his legs felt so shaky after Lester's weight and the rigors of the drive, that he accepted with alacrity the first drink that was offered to him, which was a dry Martini in a glass larger than the cocktail glasses he was used to. After a little he relaxed sufficiently to look about him. There were at least twenty people in the room apart from his own party which was arriving in groups. His host, a good-looking hearty young man, brought up a fair girl whom he introduced as Mrs. Martin. Evan, as he shook hands with her, was unable to avoid noticing that she was in an advanced stage of pregnancy. She seemed quite unembarrassed over the situation and looked at him with vague brown eyes. He observed that her fragile young hand was clasping a highball. "Don't be frightened," she said with a simper, "it's not due until Wednesday, and if it doesn't come then I'm going to have a cesarean." Evan felt at a loss to know how to reply to such compelling candor, so he smiled wanly. She gave a slight hiccup and said: "Excuse me." Evan fidgeted awkwardly.

"Is that necessary?" he asked, and then flushed to the roots of his hair at the thought that she might imagine he was referring to the hiccup, but she either hadn't noticed or was too drunk to care. "Not necessary," she replied with a little difficulty, "not exactly necessary, but nice work if you can get it," then she drifted away. Presently Lester came up and they went over and sat down together in a window seat. "It's always like this in this house," he said. "Thousands of people milling around—I can't think how they stand it. They're such simple people themselves too, and grand fun, you know, there's no chichi about them, that's what I like and Hughsie—"

here Lester chuckled—"Hughsie's a riot, my dear, if you get Hughsie alone sometimes and get him to tell you some of his experiences in the Navy, he'll slay you; of course he's settled down now, and mind you he adores Sonia, and they've got two of the most enchanting children you've ever seen, but still what's bred in the bone comes out in the what have you. . . ."

At this moment Otis Meer joined them. "Christ," he whispered to Lester, "Charlie Schofield's still trailing around with that bitch. I thought they were all washed up weeks ago."

"You should know," replied Lester, "if anybody should."

Evan asked for this interesting couple to be pointed out to him.

"That man over by the fireplace, the tall one with the blonde. He's Charlie Schofield, one of our richest playboys. She's Anita Hay, she used to be in 'The Vanities.' Otis hates her," he added, Evan thought rather unnecessarily.

"She's one of these high-hatting dames," said Otis. "She'd high-hat her own father if she knew who he was."

"Is she invited everywhere with Mr. Schofield?" enquired Evan, who was puzzled by the social aspects of the situation.

"If she's not he just takes her," replied Lester laconically. "He's been crazy about her for years."

Presently Louise came up with Luella Rosen. "I must apologize for dragging you over here," she said to Evan, "but I absolutely promised we'd come, and they're such darlings really, but I'd no idea there was going to be this crowd—have another drink and we'll go in five minutes."

"Can I drive back with you?" asked Evan wistfully.

"Of course," said Louise. "We'll meet in the hall in about five minutes."

During the next hour Evan was forced to the conclusion that the time sense, in the wealthier strata of American society, was lacking. Louise showed no indication of wanting to leave. Almost immediately after she had promised to meet Evan in the hall in five minutes, she sat down with Mr. Hughes-Hitchcock and began to play backgammon; her laugh rang out several times and Evan wondered bleakly if "Hughsie" were retailing some of his experiences in the Navy.

Lester had disappeared. Otis Meer, Ossie and the Russian pianist were sitting in a corner engrossed in an intense conversation. Irene Marlow was entertaining a large group of people with a description of her first meeting with Geraldine Farrar—a few disjointed sentences came to Evan's ear—"That vast empty stage—" "My clothes were dreadful, after all I was completely unknown then, just an ambitious little girl from Iowa—" "She said with that lovely gracious smile of hers 'My child—'" What Miss Farrar had said was lost to Evan for at that moment Charles Schofield came and spoke to him.

"We haven't been formally introduced," he said amiably, "but I think you know a great friend of mine, the Prince of Wales?" Evan, endeavoring not to betray surprise, nodded casually. "Of course," he said, "although I fear I don't know him very well." Actually he had met the Prince of Wales twice, once at a charity ball at Grosvenor House and once at a supper party at Lady Cynthia Cawthorne's. On both occasions he had been presented and the Prince had been charming, if a trifle vague; neither conversation could truthfully be said to have established any degree of intimacy.

"He's a grand guy," went on Charlie Schofield, "absolutely genuine. I've played polo with him a lot. Do you play polo?"

"No—I don't ride well enough."

"It's a grand game," said Charlie. "I used to play on Boots Leavenworth's team—you know Boots Leavenworth, of course?"

Evan did not know the Earl of Leavenworth except by repute, but he felt it would sound churlish to go on denying everything. "Rather," he said, "he's awfully nice."

"I suppose you don't know what's happened about him and Daphne?"

"I think things are much the same," hazarded Evan.

"You mean Rollo's still holding out?"

"When I left England," said Evan boldly, "Rollo was still holding out."

"God!" said Charlie with vehemence. "Aren't people extraordinary! You'd think after all that business at Cannes last summer he'd have the decency to face facts and come out into the open. As a matter of fact, I've always thought he was a bit of a bastard, outwardly amusing enough you know, but something shifty about him. As a matter of fact poor Tiger's the one I'm sorry for, aren't you?"

"Desperately," said Evan.

"Where is Tiger now?"

"I don't know." Evan wildly racked his brains for an appropriate place for Tiger to be. "Africa, I think."

"Jesus!" cried Charlie aghast, "you don't mean to say he's thrown his hand in and left poor Iris to cope with everything?"

The strain was beginning to tell on Evan. He took refuge in evasion. "Rumors," he said weakly. "One hears rumors, you know how people gossip!"

Fortunately at this moment Shirley and Leonie came up and asked him if he'd like to play Ping-Pong. "We can't play at all," said Shirley, "we're terrible, but it's good exercise." Evan smiled affably at Charlie and went with them into an enormous room glassed in on three sides, furnished only with a Ping-Pong table, a few garden chairs and some large plants in pots. It was hotter than a Turkish bath. On the way he confided to them that he didn't play, but would be enchanted to watch them. He sat down, lit a cigarette and they started. They hadn't been playing a minute before he realized how wise he had been to refuse. They played like lightning, grimly, with an agility and concentration that was nothing short of ferocious. He watched them amazed. These two attractive young women, smashing and banging, occasionally muttering the score breathlessly through clenched teeth. Sometimes Leonie gave a savage grunt when she missed a shot, like a prizefighter receiving a blow in the solar plexus. Presently, they having finished one game and changed round and started another, Evan began to feel drowsy. The hypnotic effect of following the little white ball back and forth and the monotonous click of the wooden bats lulled him into a sort of coma. Vague thoughts drifted thorugh his mind. He wondered who Rollo was and why he was probably holding out, and what Tiger might have left poor Iris to cope with—Poor Iris—Poor Tiger—Evan slept.

4

At ten minutes past four precisely the Steinhauser party rose from the lunch table and Evan went to his bedroom and shut the door. Lunch had not started until after three. There had been a certain amount of delay while Louise and Lester were rounding everybody up at the Hughes-Hitchcocks'. Then several arguments as to whom should drive back with whom. Evan, with commendable tenacity, considering that he had just been awakened from a deep sleep, had clung to Louise like a leech despite all efforts of Shirley and Leonie to persuade him to go back with them, and finally succeeded in being brought home at a more reasonable speed in Louise's Packard. Lunch had been rather a scramble and consisted principally of clam chowder which he detested and veal cutlets which, not surprisingly, were so overdone as to be almost uneatable. Evan, whose head was splitting, took two aspirin, divested himself of his shoes, trousers and coat, put on his dressing gown and lay thankfully on the bed pulling the eiderdown up to his chin. If he could get a real sleep now, he reflected, not just a doze in a chair, and get up at about seven and bathe and change, everyone would have assuredly gone. They must all have dinner engagements in New York, and he would be able to dine peaceably with Louise and Bonwit and Lester, allow a polite hour or so for conversation, and go to bed firmly at ten-thirty. The warmth of the eiderdown stole round him, his legs began to congeal pleasantly with a prickling sensation, the throbbing of his head gradually diminished and he fell asleep.

About an hour later he felt himself being dragged to con-

sciousness by somebody shaking him rhythmically. With intense reluctance he opened his eyes and beheld Lester bending over him. He
moaned slightly and tried to evade that inexorable hand.

"You must wake up now, honey," said Lester. "You've had over
an hour and Irene's going to sing." Evan's mind, still webbed with
sleep, tried unsuccessfully to grapple with this announcement.
"Who's Irene?" he muttered.

"Don't be silly," said Lester. "Irene Marlow; she's mad about
you, she says she won't so much as open her trap unless you're
there—we've been trying to persuade her for twenty minutes—she
says she'll sing for you or not at all—come on." He flicked the eiderdown off the bed and pulled Evan into a sitting posture. It was no use
trying to go to sleep again now, even if Lester had allowed him to.
Once wakened up like that he was done for. He went drearily into the
bathroom and sponged his face, then came back and put on his
trousers, coat and shoes. Lester, while he did so, lay on the chaise
longue and discoursed enthusiastically upon the quality of Irene's
voice, her passion for Dwight Macadoo and the fact that leaving all
her success and glamour aside she was really completely genuine.
"It's amazing about that boy," he said apropos of Dwight. "Really
amazing—she's absolutely nuts about him and although he may be
the biggest thing since *Ben Hur* I must say I think he's just plain
dumb! Of course, you can't expect him to be anything else really, he
was only a cowboy in Arizona when she met him, galloping about on
a horse all day in 'chaps,' and rounding up all those Goddamned
steers—who shall be nameless—well, anyway, she met him out on
Grace Burton's ranch and gave her all if you know when I mean, and
since that she's taken him everywhere—mind you, I'm not saying he
isn't sweet, he is, but he just doesn't matter."

Lester led the way into the living room. The party was sitting
round expectantly. Irene was standing by the piano while Suki, with a
cigarette dangling from his lips, was playing a few introductory
chords. When Lester and Evan came in everybody said "Shhh" loudly.
They sank down onto the floor by the door, Irene flashed Evan a
charming smile and started off on "Vissi d'Arte." She sang beautifully. Evan, whose understanding of music was superficial to say the
best of it, recognized at once that the quality of her voice and the
charm with which she exploited it was of a very high order indeed.
When she had finished "Tosca" everyone gave little groans and cries
of pleasure, and someone called for "Bohème." Irene sang "Bohème";
then Ossie implored her to sing the waltz from *The Countess Maritza*.
She started this and forgot the words halfway through, so she
stopped and sang three songs of Debussy in French, and then some
Schumann in German. Evan, being by the door in a draft, wished
that she'd stop, the floor was beginning to feel very hard and he was

afraid of catching cold. Irene, blissfully unaware that even one of her audience wasn't enjoying her performance to the utmost, went on singing for over an hour. When she finally left the piano and sat down, amid ecstasies of admiration, Evan rose stiffly and went over to the bar. Otis was leaning against it with Shirley and Leonie, Bonwit was still behind it.

"Isn't that the most glorious voice you've ever heard?" cried Ossie. "Frankly I'd rather listen to Irene than Jeritza, Ponselle and Flagstad all together in a lump." Evan, repressing a shudder at the thought of Jeritza, Ponselle and Flagstad all together in a lump, agreed wholeheartedly and asked Bonwit for a drink.

"Martini, old-fashioned, Daiquiri, rye and ginger ale, Scotch highball, pay your dime and take your choice," said Bonwit cheerfully. Evan decided on a highball, not that he wished to drink any more for the pleasure of it, but he was chilled by the draft from the door. Bonwit mixed him a strong one, and after a while he began to feel more cheerful. Louise came over. Evan noticed that she looked very flushed, and dragged Ossie away from the bar. "Darling Ossie, you must," she insisted, "everybody's screaming for you— Lester's gone to get your ukulele, you left it in the hall." Ossie, after some more persuasion, sat down in the middle of the room with his ukulele which Lester had handed to him, and began to tune it. Otis shouted out: "Do 'The Duchess,'" and Irene cried, "No, not 'The Duchess,' do 'Mrs. Rabbit.'" Louise cried, "No, not 'Mrs. Rabbit,' do 'Ella Goes to Court.'" Several other people made several other suggestions, and there was pandemonium for a few moments. Shirley whispered to Evan, "I do hope he does 'Ella Goes to Court,' you'll adore it, it's all about Queen Mary."

Ossie silenced the clamor by striking some loud chords; then he sang "Mrs. Rabbit." "Mrs. Rabbit" was a description, half-sung and half-spoken, of the honeymoon night of an elderly lady from Pittsburgh. It was certainly amusing, while leaving little to the imagination. Ossie's rendering of it was expert. He paused, raised his eyebrows, lowered and raised his voice, and pointed every line with brilliantly professional technique. Everyone in the room shouted and wept with laughter. When he had finished with a vivid account of the death of Mrs. Rabbit from sheer excitement, the clamor started again. This time he sang "The Duchess." It was rather on the same lines as "Mrs. Rabbit" although the locale was different. It described a widow from Detroit who married an English Duke and had an affair with a Gondolier during their honeymoon in Venice. Evan permitted himself to smile tolerantly at Ossie's somewhat stereotyped version of an English Duke. Finally, when he had sung several other songs, all of which varied only in the degree of their pornography, he consented to do "Ella Goes to Court." Evan having finished his highball and noticing another close to his elbow, took it hurriedly and braced himself for the worst. "Ella Goes to Court" was, if anything, bawdier than the others had been. It was a fanciful description of a middle-aged meat packer's wife from Chicago who, owing to the efforts of an impecunious English Countess, is taken to a Court at Buckingham Palace and becomes intimately attached to a Gentleman-in-Waiting on her way to the Throne Room. The whole song was inexpressibly vulgar, and to an Englishman shocking beyond words. Fortunately the references to the Royal Family were comparatively innocuous; if they had not been Evan would undoubtedly have left the room, but still, as it was, the whole thing with its sly implications, its frequent descents to barroom crudeness, and above all the ignorance and inaccuracy with which Ossie endeavored to create his atmosphere, irritated Evan profoundly. Aware that several people were covertly watching him to see how he would take this exhibition, he debated rapidly in his mind whether to look as disgusted as he really felt or to pretend to enjoy it. He took another gulp of his highball and forced an appreciative smile on his face. "Do you know," said Leonie when Ossie had finished and the enthusiasm had died down, "that's the favorite song of the Prince of Wales. Ossie had to sing it for him over and over again when he was at the Café de Paris in London." Evan was about to reply with some tartness that that could only possibly be another imaginative flight of Ossie's when a diversion was caused by the noisy entrance of four newcomers. "My God!" cried Lester. "It's Carola!" There was a general surge towards a smartly dressed woman with bright eyes and still brighter hair who walked in a little ahead of the others. Lester kissed her, Louise kissed her, everybody kissed her except Evan, who was formally introduced a little later by Otis Meer.

Her name was Carola Binney and she was, according to Leonie and Shirley, the most famous and gifted comedienne on the New York stage. Evan vaguely remembered having heard of her at some time or other. She certainly possessed abundant vitality and seemed to be on the most intimate terms with everybody present. The people with her, Evan learned, were Bob and Gloria Hockbridge who were scenario writers from Hollywood, and Don Lucas. There was probably no one in the world, even Evan, who had not heard of Don Lucas. Evan looked at him and really experienced quite a thrill. He was even handsomer in real life than he was on the screen. His young finely modeled face healthily tanned by the sun; his wide shoulders and long curling lashes; his lazy, irresistible charm. There it all was. "It was exactly," thought Evan, "as tho' some clear-eyed, vital young God from the wider spaces of Olympus had suddenly walked into a nightclub." Lester brought him over. "This is Don Lucas," he said exultantly. "He's just a struggling boy who's trying to make a name for himself and got sidetracked by somebody once saying he was good-looking."

"Nuts, Les!" said the clear-eyed Olympian as he shook hands. "Glad to know you, Mr. Lorrimer."

Lester, Don and Evan drifted over to the bar where Bonwit, after greeting Don, gave them each a highball. Evan tried to refuse but Lester insisted. "Phooey!" he cried, placing his arm round Evan's shoulders. "This is a party and life's just one big glorious adventure—which shall be nameless!"

Don, it appeared, was on a three weeks' vacation from Hollywood; he had just completed one picture, *The Loves of Cardinal Richelieu*, and was going back on Thursday to start another which was to be called *Tumult*, and was based on Tolstoi's *War and Peace*. The Hockbridges were writing it and had apparently done a swell job. Evan glanced across at the Hockbridges. Mr. Hockbridge was a plump bald man in the early forties, while his wife was much younger, possibly not more than twenty-five, with enormous wide blue eyes and platinum blonde hair done in the style of Joan of Arc. Evan tried to imagine them sitting down together and writing the story of *War and Peace* and gave up. After three strong whiskeys and sodas such fantasy was beyond him.

Don, within the first few minutes of their conversation, pressed him warmly to come and stay with him when he lectured in Los Angeles. "It's a very simple house," he said. "None of that Spanish crap—all loggias and whatnot, but I can let you have a car and an English valet." "Simple house!" Lester gave a shriek. "It's about as simple as Chartres Cathedral. It's the most gorgeous place in California." He turned to Evan. "You really must go," he went on. "Seriously, I mean it—it's an experience, if you know what I mean, and when I say experience, well!—" He laughed and dug Don in the ribs.

"It would be grand to have you if you'd come," he said. "You mustn't pay any attention to the way Les goes on—we happened to have a party when he was there and Oh boy!" He shook his handsome head and sighed as though shattered by the memory of it. "But if you came you wouldn't be disturbed. I shall be working all day anyhow—you could do exactly as you liked."

Evan thanked him very much, and said it sounded delightful. Lester went off into further eulogies about the magnificence of Don's house but was interrupted by Louise who came up and placed one arm around Don's waist and the other around Evan's.

"We're all going over to the Grouper Wendelmanns' for just ten minutes," she said. "Carola's longing to see their house; I must say it's unbelievable what they've done with it." Evan gently disentangled himself. "I don't think I'll come if you don't mind," he said. "I've got to go over my notes for my lecture tomorrow night."

There was a shocked silence for a moment, then Louise gave a wail of distress. "Oh my dear," she cried, "please come, just for a few minutes. The Grouper Wendelmanns will be so bitterly disappointed, they're pining to meet you and they're such darlings."

Evan shook his head. "I'd really rather not," he said firmly.

"Then I won't go either," said Lester.

"Neither will I," said Louise. "We'll none of us go."

Don Lucas patted Evan's shoulder encouragingly. "Come on," he coaxed. "Be a sport."

"They're divine people," said Lester. "They really are, you'll love them, and old Bernadine's a riot; she's Jane Grouper Wendelmann's mother, you know; you can't go back to Europe without having seen Bernadine Grouper."

"Only for just ten minutes," said Louise. "I shall really feel terribly badly if you don't go—it's quite near, just down the road and the house really is lovely, the most perfect taste, they've spent millions on it—"

"Don't worry him if he'd rather not," said Don. "Let's all have another drink."

Evan, touched by the sympathy in Don's voice and embarrassed by Lester's and Louise's obvious disappointment, gave in. "Very well," he said, "but I really must get back in time to go over my notes before dinner."

Louise's face lit up with pleasure. "Of course you shall," she cried. "You're an angel—the four of us shall go in my car—come on everybody."

5

It was nearly an hour's drive to the Grouper Wendelmanns' house, and in the car Lester suggested playing a word game to pass the time. Evan didn't care for word games, but as he couldn't very well sit in morose silence he capitulated with as good a grace as possible. They played "Who Am I?" and "Twenty Questions" and "Shedding Light." Evan acquitted himself favorably and, owing to his superior knowledge of history, won reverent praise for his erudition in "Twenty Questions."

"Shedding Light" bewildered him, but he was glad to see that it bewildered Don Lucas even more. As a matter of fact everything bewildered Don Lucas; his contributions consisted mainly of the names of obscure baseball players and movie directors, but he persevered with naïf charm in the face of the most waspish comments from Lester. Suddenly the games were interrupted by the chauffeur taking a wrong turning and arriving, after a few minutes of violent bumping, on to the edge of a swamp. Louise, who had been too occupied in trying to think of a Spanish seventeenth-century painter beginning with M to notice, leant forward, slid back the glass window and shouted a lot of instructions, most of which Lester contradicted. "We ought to have turned to the left by the bridge, I know we ought," she said.

"If we'd done that we should have arrived at the Witherspoons'," said Lester. "And God forbid that we should do that."

"Nonsense," cried Louise. "The Witherspoons are right over on the other side near the Caldicotts."

"If," said Lester with a trace of irritation, "we had gone up that turning just past the Obermeyers' gate and then on over the hill we should have got into the highway and been able to turn right at the crossroads."

"Left," said Louise. "If you turn right at the crossroads, you come straight to the golf course, and that's miles away, just next to the Schaeffers'."

"You'd better back," said Lester to the chauffeur. "And when you get into the main road again stop at the first petrol station and ask."

Presently after some more bumping and a frightening moment when the frozen surface of the ground nearly caused the car to skid into a ditch, they emerged again onto the main road. About a quarter of an hour later, having followed the instructions of a Negro at a petrol station, and gone back the way they had come for a few miles, they turned up a small lane and arrived at the Grouper Wendelmanns'. The rest of their party had naturally arrived some time before and everybody was playing skittles in a luxurious skittle alley with a bathing pool on one side of it and a bar on the other. Mr. and Mrs. Grouper Wendelmann came forward to meet them both grasping large wooden balls. They were a good-looking young couple in bathing costume. "This is wonderful," cried Mrs. Grouper Wendelmann. "We thought you were dead, we're just going to finish this game, have one more drink and then go in the pool—go and talk to mother, she's stinking!"

Mr. Grouper Wendelmann led them to the bar where the members of his own house party were sitting on high stools apparently having relinquished the joys of the alley and the pool to the invaders. Old Mrs. Grouper, elaborately coiffed and wearing a maroon tea gown and a dog collar of pearls, greeted Evan warmly. "You may or may not know it," she said in a harsh, bass voice, "but you're my favorite man!"

Evan bowed politely and tried to withdraw his hand, but she tightened her grasp and pulled him toward her. "That book of yours," she said portentously, and cast a furtive look over her shoulder as though she were about to impart some scurrilous secret, "is great literature— No, it's no use saying it isn't because I know—Henry James used to be an intimate friend of mine and I knew poor Edith Wharton too, and believe me," her voice sank to a hoarse whisper, "I *know*." She relaxed Evan's hand so suddenly that he nearly fell over backward. At that moment his host gave him an "old-fashioned" with one hand and piloted him with the other up to an emaciated dark woman in a flowered dinner dress.

"Alice," he said, "you English ought to get together—this is a countryman of yours—Mr. Lorrimer—Lady Kettering." Lady Kettering shook hands with him wearily and gave an absent smile. "How do you do," she said. The sound of an English voice comforted Evan, he hoisted himself on to a vacant stool next to her. Mr. Grouper Wendelmann, having done his duty as a host, left them. "What a lovely house," said Evan. Lady Kettering looked at him in surprise and then glanced round as though she were seeing it all for the first time. "I suppose it is," she replied, "if you like this sort of thing."

Evan felt a little crushed. "Of course I haven't seen much of it, I've only just arrived."

"I've been here for three months," said Lady Kettering, "and I must say it's beginning to get me down. I'm going to Palm Beach next week. I think Palm Beach is bloody, don't you?"

"I've never been there," said Evan.

"Well, take my advice and don't go. It's filled with the most frightening people."

"I shan't be able to anyhow," said Evan. "I'm over here to do a lecture tour."

"How horrible," said Lady Kettering. "Whatever for?"

"My publishers were very insistent that I should." Evan was slightly nettled. "And after all I think it will be interesting to see something of America. This is my first visit."

"You ought to go to Mexico," said Lady Kettering. "That's where you ought to go."

"I'm afraid I shan't have time."

"That's the one thing you don't need in Mexico— Time doesn't exist—it's heaven.

"Why don't you go to Mexico instead of Palm Beach?"

"I've promised to join the Edelstons' yacht and go on a cruise in the Bahamas," said Lady Kettering. "Do you knew the Edelstons?"

"No," replied Evan.

"Well take my advice," she said, "and give them a wide berth. They're bloody."

At this moment Don Lucas came and prised Evan gently off his stool. "Come and swim," he said.

The idea of swimming on a Sunday evening in mid-February seemed fantastic to Evan. "I don't think I will."

"Come on, be a sport."

"I'd rather watch you."

"Nuts to that," cried Don. "Everybody's going to swim, it'll be swell."

Evan allowed himself to be led over to the pool, inwardly vowing that no power on earth would get him into the water. Leonie and Shirley were giving an exhibition of fancy diving from the highest board, while Louise, Lester, Carola Binney, Irene Marlow and Ossie, who were already in bathing suits, sat around the edge and applauded. "Isn't that amazing?" cried Lester as Leonie did a spectacular jackknife. "I'd give anything in the world to be able to dive like that, but everything, if you know what I mean!"

Don took Evan firmly into a richly appointed men's dressing room and handed him a pair of trunks. "Now undress," he ordered.

Once more Evan protested. "Really I'd rather not—"

"What the hell—" said Don. "The water's warm and we'll all have fun—come on, be a pal—"

"Honestly—" began Evan.

"Now listen here," Don sat down on a bench and looked at Evan reproachfully, "this is a party and we're all having a good time and you're just bent on spoiling the whole shooting match."

"Why should you be so anxious for me to swim?" asked Evan almost petulantly.

"Because I like you," said Don with a disarming smile. "I liked you from the word go and you like me too, don't you? Come on, be frank and admit it."

"Of course I like you," said Evan. "I like you very much."

"Very well then," said Don triumphantly. "Do we swim or don't we?"

"You do and I don't."

"You wouldn't like me to get tough now, would you?" said Don in a wheedling voice, but with an undertone of menace. "I could, you know!"

"I'm sure you could, but I fail to see—"

"Come on now, quit stalling." Don advanced toward him and forcibly removed his coat. For one moment Evan contemplated screaming for help, but visualizing the ridiculous scene that would ensue he contented himself with struggling silently in Don's grasp. "Please let me go," he muttered breathlessly, "and don't be so silly."

Don had succeeded in slipping Evan's braces off and was endeavoring to unbutton his shirt when Lester came in. "Boys, boys," he cried admonishingly, "do try to remember that this is Sunday—which shall be nameless," and went into gales of laughter. Don released Evan immediately.

"This guy's a big sissy," he said. "He won't swim."

"I don't blame him," said Lester. "The water's like bouilla-baisse. It's got more things in it than Macy's window."

"To hell with that, I'm going to swim if it kills me."

"It probably will on top of all that liquor." Lester went over and took a packet of cigarettes out of the pocket of his coat which was hanging on a peg. Then he came and sat on the bench next to Evan who, with a flushed face, was adjusting his clothes. "Relax, honey," he said, "Don always goes on like this when he's had a few drinks. Have a Camel?"

Evan took a cigarette, meanwhile Don was tearing off his clothes with ferocious speed. When he was completely naked he stood over Lester and Evan with arms folded and regarded them with scorn. Lester looked up at him. "It's all right, Puss," he said, "we've seen all that and it's gorgeous, now go jump in the pool and sober up."

"I don't know what's the matter with you guys," he grumbled, and went toward the door.

"You'd better put on some trunks," said Lester, "or have I gone too far?"

Don came slowly back and put on a pair of trunks. "Funny, hey?" he said bitterly and went out. A moment later they heard a loud splash and a shriek of laughter.

"What about another little drinkie?" said Lester.

6

About an hour later Evan found himself in a car sitting between Carola Binney and Luella Rosen whom he hadn't spoken to since before lunch. Don and Lester were squeezed together in the front seat next to Dwight Macadoo who was driving. The car apparently belonged to Irene Marlow. Evan had had two more "old-fashioneds" since his struggle with Don and was drunk, but in a detached sort of way. He had lost all capacity for resistance. From now on, he decided, he would drink when he was told to, eat when he was told to and go where he was taken. There was no sense in fighting against over-whelming odds. He lay back, quite contentedly, with his head on Luella's shoulder listened to Carola describing a man called Benny Schultz who had directed a play she had tried out in Boston last September—

"Never again—" she was saying vehemently, "would I let that rat come within three blocks of me—My God—you've no idea what I went through—he comes prancing into my dressing room on the opening night after the first Act—the first Act! believe it or not, and starts giving me notes—'Listen, Benny,' I said, 'you may have directed *Crazy Guilt* and *Mother's Day* and *The Wings of a Dove,* and you may have made Martha Cadman the actress she is, and Claudia Bitmore the actress she certainly isn't, but you're not coming to my room on an opening night and start telling me that my tempo was too fast and that I struck a wrong note by taking my hat off at my first entrance. To begin with I had to take that Godawful hat off which I never wanted to wear anyway because the elastic band at the back was slipping, and if I hadn't it would have shot up into the air and got a laugh in the middle of my scene with Edgar; in the second place if you had engaged a supporting company for me who could act and a leading man who had some idea of playing comedy, and at least knew his lines, I wouldn't have had to rush through like a fire engine in order to carry that bunch of art-theater hams and put the play over, and in the third place I should like to remind you that I was a star on Broadway when you were selling papers on the East Side, and I knew more about acting than you when I was five, playing the fit-ups with *The Two Orphans*. And what's more, if you think I'm going to tear myself to shreds trying to get laughs in the supper scene in the pitch dark—well, you're crazy—'" She paused for a moment, Luella gave a barely audible grunt.

"You've got to have light to play comedy," she went on, "and all the phony highbrow directors in the world won't convince me otherwise."

"For all that I think Benny's pretty good," said Luella.

"He's all right with Shakespeare. I give you that," said Carola. "His *Macbeth* was fine, what you could see of it, but comedy never— look at the flop he had with *Some Take It Straight*."

"*Some Take It Straight* was the worst play I ever sat through," Luella admitted.

"It needn't have been," cried Carola. "I read the original script. They wanted me to do it with Will Farrow, it really wasn't bad apart from needing a little fixing here and there—then that rat got hold of it and bitched it entirely."

Lester let the window down. "What's Carola yelling about?" he enquired.

"Benny Schultz," said Luella.

"I wouldn't trust him an inch, not an inch," said Lester. "Look what he did to *Macbeth*."

"Are we nearly home?" asked Evan.

"We're not going home—we're going to Maisie's."

Evan lifted his head from Luella's shoulder. "Who's she?" he asked sleepily.

"She's divine," replied Lester. "You'll worship her—I mean she's a real person, isn't she, Luella?"

"It depends what you call real," said Luella. "Personally she drives me mad."

At this point the car turned into a gateway and drew up before a low, rather rambling white-walled house. Everyone got out and stamped their feet on the frozen snow to keep warm, while they waited for the door to be opened, which it presently was by a large forbidding-looking Swedish woman who regarded them suspiciously. Lester embraced her. "It's all right, Hilda," he said, "it's only us."

She stood aside and they all trooped in, shedding their coats in the hall. Lester led the way into a sort of studio paneled in pitch pine with wide bow windows and an immense log fire. The room was luxuriously furnished in a style that Evan supposed was early American. Anyhow in spite of its being extremely overheated, its simplicity was a relief after the other houses he had visited. He felt as though he had been going from house to house all his life. A grizzled woman with fine eyes and wearing a riding habit greeted them brusquely and introduced the other people in the room. There were two girls called Peggy and Althea, one fat and the other thin, a very pale young man in green Chinese pajamas called George Tremlett, and a statuesque Frenchwoman with raven hair who appeared to be dressed as a Bavarian peasant. The only two members of their own party present were Leonie and Shirley who were lying on the floor playing with a Siamese cat. There was a large table of drinks along one of the windows. Don Lucas made a beeline for it. "Donny wants some fire water," he said. "Donny wants to get stinking."

"You were stinking at the Grouper Wendelmanns'," said Luella.

"Isn't he beautiful?" said the Frenchwoman.

When everyone had helped themselves to drinks Evan found himself sitting on a small upright sofa with George Tremlett.

"You arrived in the middle of a blazing row," whispered George with a giggle. "Suzanne and Shirley haven't spoken for two years and suddenly in she walked with Leonie—"

"Which is Suzanne?"

"The dark woman, Suzanne Closanges. She writes poetry either in French or English, she doesn't care which, and she lives here with Maisie."

"Maisie who?" asked Evan.

"Maisie Todd, of course," said George with slight irritation. "This is Maisie Todd's house—I did it."

"How do you mean 'did it'?"

"Designed it," George almost squealed. "I'm George Tremlett."

"How do you do?" said Evan.

"It was lovely doing this house," went on George, "because I had an absolutely free hand—Maisie's like that—we had the grandest time driving all over New England and finding bits and pieces here and there. I found this very sofa we're sitting on tucked away in a fisherman's bedroom at Cape Cod."

"How extraordinary," said Evan—he felt overpoweringly sleepy.

Leonie came over with the Siamese cat and placed it on Evan's lap. "Isn't he adorable?" she said. "I gave him to Maisie for a Christmas present in 1933 and he's grown out of all knowledge."

The cat arched its back, dug its claws into Evan's leg and with a loud snarl hurled itself to the floor. "They're very fierce," went on Leonie picking it up again by the nape of its neck so that it hung spitting and kicking in the air. "And the older they grow the fiercer they get, but Dante isn't fierce though he's older than hell—are you, my darling?" she added affectionately, kissing it on the side of the head. The cat gave a sharp wriggle and scratched her cheek, from her eye, which it missed by a fraction, to her chin. She screamed with pain and dropped it onto a table where it knocked over and smashed a photograph of a lady in fencing costume framed in glass, jumped down and disappeared behind a writing desk. Evan started to his feet, everyone came crowding over.

"The son of a bitch," wailed Leonie. "He's maimed me for life." With that she burst into tears. Maisie Todd took charge with fine efficiency. She produced a large white handkerchief to staunch the blood, dispatched George to fetch some iodine from her bathroom. Shirley flung her arms round Leonie and kissed her wildly. "Don't darling, don't cry," she besought her. "For God's sake don't cry, you know I can't bear it."

"There's nothing to cry about," said Maisie, "it's only a scratch."

"It may only be a scratch," cried Shirley, "but it's terribly deep and it's bleeding."

"Don't fuss," said Maisie.

"It's all very fine for you to say don't fuss," Shirley said furiously, "but it might very easily have blinded her—you oughtn't to keep an animal like that in the house, it should be destroyed."

"Leonie gave it to Maisie herself before she knew you," put in Suzanne with a little laugh.

"Mind your own business," snapped Shirley.

Leonie dabbed her eyes and her cheeks alternately with the blood-stained handkerchief.

"For God's sake shut up, everybody. I'm all right now, it was only the shock."

"Drink this, darling," said Lester, handing her his glass.

"We should never have come—I knew something awful would happen," said Shirley.

"There is nothing to prevent you going." Suzanne spoke with icy dignity. There was a horrified silence for a moment. Shirley left Leonie and went very close to Suzanne.

"How dare you," she said softly. Evan noticed that she was trembling with passion. "How dare you speak to me like that—"

Maisie intervened. "Now listen, Shirley," she began. Shirley pushed her aside. "I've always disliked you, Suzanne, from the first moment I set eyes on you, and I wish to say here and now that you're nothing but a fifth-rate gold digger sponging on Maisie the way you do and making her pay to publish your lousy French poems, and you're not even French at that—you're Belgian!"

Suzanne gave a gasp of fury, slapped Shirley hard in the face and rushed from the room, cannoning into George Tremlett who was coming in with the iodine and knocking the bottle out of his hand on to the floor. "Oh, dear!" he cried sinking on to his knees. "All over the best Hook rug in the house!"

From then onward everybody talked at once. Maisie dashed out of the room after Suzanne, Leonie started to cry again. The two girls, Althea and Peggy, who had been watching the whole scene from a corner, decided after a rapid conversation to follow Maisie and Suzanne, which they did, slamming the door after them. George was moaning over the Hook rug and trying to rub out the iodine stains with a silk scarf. Lester joined Luella and Carola by the fireplace. Carola was protesting violently at Suzanne's behavior, while Luella smiled cynically. Lester, genuinely distressed, was sympathizing with Shirley and Leonie, while Don added to the din by strolling over to the piano with Dwight Macadoo and playing "Smoke Gets in Your Eyes" with one hand. Presently he desisted. "This piano stinks," he said. "No tone—where's the radio?" Before he could find it Luella, to Evan's intense relief, suggested that they should all go, and led the way firmly into the hall. While they were struggling into their coats and wraps the large Swedish woman watched them silently with a baleful expression. The freezing night air struck Evan like a blow between the eyes; he staggered slightly. Don quickly lifted him off the ground and deposited him in the car with infinite tenderness.

"You were wrong about that swim," he said affectionately. "It was swell, made me feel like a million dollars. Now we'll go home and have a little drinkie."

7

They had no sooner got inside the Steinhausers' front door when Irene came rushing out of the living room. "Where the hell have you been?" she cried angrily to Dwight. "I looked for you all over and when I came out you'd gone off in my car."

"Now don't be mad at me, darling—" began Dwight.

"Mad at you! I've never been madder in my life—come in here." She dragged him into the library and banged the door.

"Well," said Lester, "isn't she the cutest thing—My dear!" He waved his hand benevolently after them. "These prima donnas—who shall be nameless—"

Louise appeared with a great cry and flung her arms round Evan. He was dimly aware that she had changed into a long flowing tea gown. "*There* you are," she said. "I couldn't think what had happened to you—you must be starving." Still holding him tightly she pulled him into the living room which had undergone a startling change. All the furniture had been pushed out onto the sun porch with the exception of the chairs which were arranged round the walls. An enormous buffet loaded with hams, turkeys, salads, bowls of fruit, bowls of cream, two large cakes and piles of plates, stood along one side of the room. Another smaller table for drinks was joined onto the bar behind which Bonwit was still officiating, assisted by a Japanese in a white coat. There were at least fifty people in the room and the noise was deafening. Evan, dazed as he was, distinguished the Grouper Wendelmanns, Lady Kettering, and several of the people he had seen at the Hughes-Hitchcocks', including the young expectant mother who was sitting on the floor with her back against one of the piano legs, and a large plate of variegated food on her lap, apparently in a stupor, while Suki played an unending series of complicated syncopation in her ear.

Louise led Evan to the table and gave him a plate on which she piled, with professional speed, a turkey leg, Virginia ham, baked beans, a fish cake, potato salad, lettuce, a wedge of Camembert cheese and a large slice of strange-looking brown bread. "There," she said, "now sit down quietly, and eat, you poor dear." With that she whisked away from him and rushed across to Carola and Luella. He looked round for a vacant chair but there wasn't one, so he stayed where he was and ate standing against the table. The food was certainly good although there was far too much of it on his plate. He was about to slide the cheese and one of the slices of ham into an empty bowl that had held salad when he was arrested by Charlie Schofield putting his hand on his shoulder. He jumped guiltily as though he'd been caught in the act of doing something nefarious.

"I told Alice Kettering what you said about Tiger being in Africa," said Charlie, "and she's in an awful state—she was crazy about him for years you know."

Before Evan could reply Don came up and forced a glass into his hand. "I promised you a little drinkie," he said genially, "and a little drinkie you're going to have."

A big woman in yellow put her arm through Charlie Schofield's and led him away. Evan saw out of the corner of his eye that Lady Kettering was drifting toward him. He retreated onto the sun porch followed by Don looking very puzzled.

"What's the idea?"

"Just somebody I don't want to talk to," said Evan with as much nonchalance as he could muster.

"Listen, Pal," said Don. "If there's anyone you don't like just you tip me off and I'll sock 'em."

Evan, shuddering inwardly at the thought of Don socking Lady Kettering, muttered that it was of no importance really, and leant against the window. Outside the moon had come up and the sea shone eerily in its light like gray silk; far away in the distance a light-house flashed. It all looked so remote and quiet that Evan felt inclined to weep. Don squeezed his arm reassuringly. "You know I like you," he said, "I like you better than any Englishman I've ever met. Most Englishmen are high-hat, you know, kind of snooty, but you're not high-hat at all, you're a good sport."

"Thank you," said Evan dimly.

"I hope you weren't sore at me for trying to make you go in the pool," Don went on. "I wouldn't like to have you sore at me. It isn't often I get a chance to talk to anyone really intelligent—not that you're only just intelligent, you're brilliant, otherwise you wouldn't be able to write all those Goddamned books, would you now?"

"Well," began Evan, feeling that some reply was demanded.

"Now don't argue." Don's voice was fierce. "Of course you're brilliant and you know you are, don't you?"

Evan smiled. "I wouldn't exactly say—"

Don patted his hand tolerantly. "Of course you do—everybody knows when they're brilliant, they'd be damned fools if they didn't. Jesus, the way you played that question game in the car—if that wasn't brilliant I should like to know what is. But what I mean to say is this: I'm just a simple sort of guy, really, without any brains at all—I've got looks, I grant you that otherwise I shouldn't be where I am today should I? But no brains, not a one. Why, the idea of sitting down and writing a letter drives me crazy let alone a book. Sometimes when I look at something beautiful like all that," he indicated the view, "or when I run across someone really brilliant like you are I feel low—honest to God I do—"

"Why?" said Evan.

"Because I'm such a damn fool of course. I couldn't write down what that looks like to me, not if you paid me a million dollars I couldn't. I couldn't paint it either, I couldn't even talk about it. What do I get out of life I ask you? Money, yes—I make a lot of dough and so what—Happiness, no—I'm one of the unhappiest sons of bitches in the whole world," he broke off.

"Cheer up," said Evan as cheerfully as he could. He was feeling depressed himself.

"It gets me down," murmured Don, pressing his forehead against the glass of the window. "It just gets me down."

Evan was pained and embarrassed to observe that he was crying. A concerted scream of laughter came from the living room. Evan peeped in. Everyone was grouped round Carola who, with a man's Homburg hat perched on her head, was doing an imitation of somebody. Evan glanced back at Don, who was still staring out into the night; his shoulders were heaving. Now was the moment to escape, everyone was far too occupied to notice whether he was there or not; if he could get into the hall without Louise seeing him, the rest was easy; he could get into his room, lock the door and go to bed. He crept along behind the buffet, avoiding Mr. Hockbridge, who was asleep on a chair, and reached the hall in safety. From behind the closed door of the library came sounds of strife, apparently Irene's fury at Dwight had in no way abated. Evan paused long enough to hear her scream angrily—"It was Luella's fault, was it—we'll see about that!"—then he darted down the passage, through Lester's room and the bathroom and reached his own room with a sigh of relief. He switched on the lights by the door and started back in horror. Stretched out on his bed was a woman in a heavy sleep. On closer examination he recognized the Countess Brancati. Her black dress was rumpled and her hair was spread over the pillow like pink hay.

A great rage shook Evan to the core. He seized her by the shoulder and pushed her backward and forward violently; she continued to sleep undisturbed. He knelt down on the floor by the bed and shouted "Wake up—please wake up" in her face to which she replied with a low moan. He shook her again and one of her earrings fell off; he picked it up and put it on the bed table and stood there looking at her, his whole body trembling with fury and frustration. He gave her one more despairing shove but she paid no attention. Then, with an expression of set determination, he marched back to the living room. On his way he met Bonwit emerging from the library. "My God," Bonwit said, "there's all hell breaking loose in there," and then, noticing Evan's face, "what's happened to you?"

"There's a woman on my bed," Evan almost shouted.

"I'll bet it's Mary Lou Brancati," said Bonwit. "She always passes out somewhere—come on—we'll get her out."

They went back together. The countess had turned over onto her face. Bonwit slapped her behind; she wriggled slightly and he did it again harder. Presently, after several more whacks, she turned over and muttered, "G'way and leave me alone—" Bonwit whereupon hoisted her up on to the side of the bed and shook her. She opened her eyes and looked at him malevolently. "Get the hell away from me," she said. "What d'you think you're doing!"

"Come on, baby," said Bonwit, "you're missing everything. There's a party going on."

"To hell with it," she replied. "G'way and leave me alone."

"Take her other arm," ordered Bonwit. Evan obeyed and they hauled her struggling and protesting into the bathroom. There Bonwit dabbed her face with a wet sponge; she gave a scream and tried to hit him. Finally they got her into the hall and deposited her in a chair. Bonwit slapped his hands together as though he had just felled a tree and said, "Now you're Okay, fellar."

At that moment the hall suddenly filled with people. Louise came out of the library with her arms around Irene who was sobbing. Dwight followed them miserably. Unfortunately Luella and Otis Meer came out of the living room at the same instant followed by Lester, Lady Kettering and the Grouper Wendelmanns. Irene, catching sight of Luella, wrested herself from Louise's arms. "So you're still here," she said harshly. "I'm surprised you have the nerve!"

Luella looked at her coolly. "You're tight, Irene," she said. "You'd better go home."

"You're a snake!" cried Irene, breathing heavily. "A double-faced, rotten snake!"

Lester tried to calm her. "Look here, honey," he said, "there's no cause in getting yourself all worked up."

Irene pushed him aside. "You shut up—you're as bad as she is—you're all of you jealous of Dwight and me and always have been—Luella's been trying to get him for years, and if you think I'm so dumb that I haven't seen what's been going on you're crazy."

"Really," murmured Lady Kettering. "This is too bloody—we'd better go—"

"Go and be damned to you!" said Irene.

Louise gave a cry of distress. Lady Kettering turned and tried to make a dignified exit into the living room, but was prevented by Ossie, Suki, the Hughes-Hitchcocks and Mrs. Hockbridge, who had crowded into the doorway to see what was happening.

Luella seized Irene by the arm in a grip of steel. "Behave yourself," she hissed. "What do you mean by making a disgusting scene like this about nothing?"

"Nothing!" Irene screamed and writhed in Luella's grasp. Otis Meer gave a crackle of shrill laughter. Dwight tried to coax Irene back into the library. Louise wept loudly and was comforted by Lester and Ossie. Lady Kettering struggled valiantly through the crowd to try to find her cloak. Carola, who had joined the group with Shirley and Leonie, announced in ringing tones that in her opinion the possession of an adequate singing voice was hardly sufficient excuse for behaving like a Broadway floozie. Lester turned on her and told her to shut up and not make everything worse, and in the indescribable pandemonium that ensued, Evan fled.

8

About an hour later, Evan, sitting up rigidly in his bed, began to relax. He had brushed his teeth, taken three aspirins, undressed, tried to lock the door but discovered there was no key, and read four chapters of *Sense and Sensibility* which he always traveled with as a gentle soporific. He had left no stone unturned in his efforts to drag his aching mind away from the horrors he had endured. He had turned out the light twice and attempted to sleep but to no avail. Incidents of the day, people's names, unrelated scraps of conversation crowded into his brain, making even the possibility of lying still out of the question let alone sleep. Sleep was eons away, he felt that it was well within the bounds of probability that he would never sleep again. The thought of the lecture he had to give that very night, it was now three A.M., tortured him. He felt incapable of uttering one coherent phrase and as for talking for an hour, his mind reeled at the very idea of it. The continual noise, the endless arrivals and departures, the impact of so many different atmospheres and personalities, the unleashing of vulgar passion he had witnessed to say nothing of the incredible amount of alcohol he had drunk, had lacerated his nerves beyond bearing. He was outraged, shamed, exhausted and bitterly angry.

Now at last he was beginning to feel calmer. The three aspirins he had taken had made his heart thump rather, his maximum dose as a rule being two, but it was apparently taking effect. He glanced at his watch, ten minutes past three, if he could manage to sleep until eleven he would have had nearly his eight hours and probably be able to get in an extra hour at his hotel before his lecture if he wasn't too nervous. "I'll give myself another ten minutes," he reflected, "and then turn out the light, by that time it ought to be all right."

He lay there still as a mouse, resolutely emptying his mind and concentrating on gentle, peaceful things, the waves of the sea, a vast four-poster bed in some remote English country house, the cool, soft lavender-scented sheets, the soughing of the wind outside in the elms— At this moment the door opened and Bonwit came in on tiptoe. He was in his pajamas and carrying a pillow and an eiderdown. He looked relieved when he saw that Evan wasn't asleep.

"I'm awfully sorry, fellar," he said, "but I've got to come and use your other bed—there's been all hell going on. Irene drove off in her car with Dwight, leaving Suki and Luella behind, the Brancatis went too, leaving Ossie and Otis, and we've only just found Don Lucas—he's in the living room on the sofa. Ossie and Otis are in with Lester, Luella's in with Louise and Suki's in my room. I've got to get up at seven to go into town but don't be afraid I'll disturb you—I've left my clothes in the bathroom so I can dress in there."

"Oh," said Evan hopelessly, the blackness of despair made further utterance impossible.

Bonwit clambered into bed and switched off his light. "I'm all in," he said. "Good night, fellar."

Evan switched off his light too, and lay staring into the darkness.

In a remarkably short space of time Bonwit began to snore. Evan groaned and tried to fold the pillow over his ears, but it was no good, the snores grew louder. They rose rhythmically to a certain pitch and then died away. Occasionally the rhythm would be broken by a grunt, then there would be silence for a moment, then they'd start again. Evan, after a half an hour of it, suddenly leapt up on an impulse of pure blinding rage, switched on the light and went over to Bonwit's bed and stood looking at him. Bonwit was lying on his back with his mouth wide open—the noise issuing from it was incredible. Evan, flinging all gentleness and consideration to the winds, seized him violently by the shoulders and turned him over. Bonwit gave a terrific snort, turned back again almost immediately and went on snoring louder than ever. Evan began to cry, tears coursed down his cheeks and fell onto his pajamas—panic assailed him—if this went on he would definitely go mad. He walked up and down the room fighting to prevent himself from losing control utterly and shrieking the house down. He went over to the window and looked out. The night was crystal clear, there wasn't a cloud in the sky. Suddenly he knew what he was going to do, the idea came to him in a flash. He was going away, that's what he was going to do. He was going to dress, telephone for a taxi and leave that horrible house for ever. It was idiotic not to have thought of it before. He would leave a note for Louise in the hall asking her to bring his suitcase into New York with her. He tore off his pajamas and began to dress. Bonwit stopped snoring and turned over. Evan switched off the light and stood still hardly daring to breathe. If Bonwit woke up and caught him trying to escape, he'd obviously try to prevent him—there would be arguments and persuasions and protests, probably ending in the whole house being roused.

Bonwit started to snore again and Evan, with a sigh of relief, finished dressing. Holding his shoes in his hand he crept down the passage, through the bathroom and into Lester's room. He could dimly make out two forms in one bed and one in the other. He banged against a chair on his way to the door and immediately lay down flat on the floor. Lester moved in his sleep but didn't wake; finally, on hands and knees, Evan crawled out into the other passage and into the hall. Once there, he put on his shoes and went cautiously in search of the telephone; just as he was about to go into the library he remembered that it was in the bar, he had heard Bonwit using it before lunch. He went into the living room. The curtains were not drawn and moonlight was flooding through the windows. Don was sleeping soundly on a sofa, he looked rather debauched but extraordinarily handsome. Poor Don. Evan shook his head at him sorrowfully and went over to the bar. There was a shutter down over it which was padlocked. This was a terrible blow. Evan thought for a moment of going back and waking Bonwit; but decided against it. If there was no taxi he'd walk and if he didn't know the way he'd find it, at all events he knew he would rather die in the snow than spend one more hour in that house. He scribbled a note to Louise in the library. "Dear Mrs. Steinhauser—" He debated for a moment whether or not to address her as Louise, she had certainly kissed him several times during the day and called him Darling frequently, also he knew her to be a kindly, well-intentioned woman, although at the moment he could cheerfully have strangled her. On the whole he felt that Mrs. Steinhauser better expressed the manner in which he was leaving her house. "Dear Mrs. Steinhauser—Finding myself unable to sleep I have decided to go back to New York. Please forgive this unconventional departure, but it is essential, if I am to lecture with any degree of success, that I relax for several hours beforehand. Please don't worry about me, I am sure I shall find my way to the station quite easily, but if you would be so kind as to have my suitcase packed and bring it in with you tomorrow, I should be more than grateful. With many thanks for your delightful hospitality I am, yours sincerely, Evan Lorrimer." He signed his name with a flourish. "She can stick that in her damned visitors' book," he said to himself. He left the note in a prominent position on a table in the hall, found his hat and coat in a cupboard and let himself quietly out of the front door. The cold air exhilarated him. It was odd, he reflected, how the excitement of escape had completely banished his nervous hysteria. He felt surprisingly well, all things considered. The snow shone in the moonlight and the country lay around him white and still. He noticed a glow in the sky behind a hill. That must be a village, he thought, and set off jauntily down the drive.

About an hour later, when he had walked several miles and his adventurous spirit had begun to wilt a trifle, he was picked up by a milk van. The driver was rugged and friendly and agreed to take him to the nearest station. They had some coffee together in an all-night lunchroom when they got there; the next train for New York wasn't due for three-quarters of an hour, and the driver talked freely about his home and domestic affairs with an accent that Evan found, at moments, extremely difficult to understand. Finally he drove away in his van, having allowed Evan to pay for the coffee, but refused to accept two dollars.

"Nuts to that," he said with a laugh. "I like you—you're not high-hat and kind of snooty like most Englishmen— So long, buddy."

Buddy, warmed by this tribute, went to the platform and waited for the train.

When he arrived in New York it was daylight. The night porter at his hotel greeted him in some surprise and handed him a pile of telephone messages and a letter. When he got to his room he opened the letter first. "Dear Mr. Lorrimer," he read, "Although we have never met, your books have given me so much pleasure that I am taking this opportunity of welcoming you to Chicago, where I understand you are going to talk to us next week on 'History and the Modern Novel.' My husband and I would be so pleased if you would come out to us for the weekend after your lecture. Our home is on the edge of the lake and we flatter ourselves it is the nearest approach to an English country house that you could find in the whole of the Middle West. It is peaceful and quiet, and no one would disturb you, you could just rest. If you have anyone with you we should, of course, be delighted to receive them, too. My husband joins me in the hope that you will honor us by accepting. Yours very sincerely, Irma Weinkopf." Evan undressed thoughtfully and got into bed.

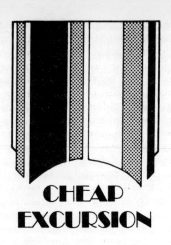

CHEAP
EXCURSION

Jimmy said, "Good night, Miss Reed," as she passed him in the passage. He did it ordinarily, no overtones or undertones, not the slightest indication of any secret knowledge between them, not even a glint in his eye, nothing beyond the correct subservience of an assistant stage manager to a star. She answered him vaguely, that well-known gracious smile, and went on to the stage door, her heart pounding violently as though someone had sprung at her out of the dark.

In the car, she sat very still with her hands folded in her lap, vainly hoping that this very stillness, this stern outward quietness might help to empty her mind. Presently she gave up and watched herself carefully taking a cigarette out of her case and lighting it. "I am Diana Reed. *The* Diana Reed, lighting a cigarette. I am Diana Reed driving home in my expensive car to my expensive flat—I am tired after my performance and as I have a matinee tomorrow it is sane and sensible for me to go straight home to bed after the show. I am having supper with Jimmy tomorrow night and probably Friday night, too—there are hundreds of other nights and there is no reason whatsoever for me to feel lonely and agonized and without peace. I am Diana Reed—I am celebrated, successful, sought after—my play is a hit—my notices were excellent—except for the *Sunday Times*. I am Diana Reed, famous, nearing forty and desperate. I am in love, not perhaps really in love like I was with Tony, nor even Pierre Chabron, but that was different, because it lasted such a little time and was foreign and mixed up with being abroad and everything, but I am in love all right and it's different again, it's always different and always difficult, and I wish to God I could be happy with it and give up to it, but there's too much to remember and too much to be careful of and too many people wanting to find out about it and gossip and smear it with their dirty fingers."

She let down the window and flicked her cigarette onto the pavement. It fell at the feet of a man in a mackintosh and a bowler hat, he looked up quickly and she drew herself back guiltily into the corner of the car. When she let herself into her flat and switched on the lights in the sitting room its smug tidy emptiness seemed to jeer at her. It was a charming room. The furniture was good, plain and luxuriously simple in line. There was the small Utrillo that Tony had given her so many years ago—it had been in her flat in Cavendish Street for ages, and she had even taken it on tour with her. That sharp sunny little street with the pinkish-white walls and neat row of plane trees making shadows across the road. The only other picture in the room was a Marie Laurencin of a woman in a sort of turban. It was quite small and framed in glass. That she had bought herself a couple of years ago when she was in Paris with Barbara and Nicky. Nicky said it looked like a very pale peach with currants in it.

She pitched her hat onto the sofa where it lay looking apologetic, almost cringing, and went over and opened the window. Outside it was very quiet, only dark rooftops and an occasional light here and there, but there was a glow in the sky over Oxford Street, and she could hear the noise of traffic far away muffled by the houses and squares in between. Just round the corner in George Street she heard a taxi stop, the slam of its door and the sharp ping as the driver shut off the motor. It might so easily be Jimmy, knowing that she was coming home alone, knowing how happy it would make her if he just came along for ten minutes to say good night. The taxi with a grind of its gears started up and drove away, she could hear it for quite a while until there was silence again. It might still be Jimmy, he wouldn't be so extravagant as to keep a taxi waiting—he might at this very moment be coming up in a lift. In a few seconds she would hear the lift doors opening and then the front-door bell. She listened, holding her breath. He might, of course, come up the stairs in order not to be seen by the lift man. Jimmy was nothing if not cautious. She waited, holding on to the windowsill tight to prevent herself from going to the front door. There was no sound, and presently her tension relaxed and, after rather a disdainful glance at herself in the glass over the mantelpiece, she went and opened the front door anyhow. The landing was deserted. When she came back into the room again she discovered, to her great irritation, that she was trembling.

She sat on a chair by the door, bolt upright, like somebody in a dentist's waiting room. It wouldn't have surprised her if a bright, professionally smiling nurse had suddenly appeared and announced that Doctor Martin was ready for her. Again she folded her hands in her lap. Someone had once told her that if you sat still as death with your hands relaxed, all the vitality ran out of the ends of your fingers and your nerves stopped being strained and tied up in knots. The Frigidaire in the kitchen suddenly gave a little click and started whirring. She stared at various things in the room, as though by concentrating, identifying herself with them she could become part of them and not feel so alone. The pickled wood Steinway with a pile of highly-colored American tunes on it; the low table in front of the fire with last week's *Sketch* and *Bystander*, and the week before last's *New Yorker*, symmetrically arranged with this morning's *Daily Telegraph* folded neatly on top; the Chinese horse on the mantelpiece, very aloof and graceful with its front hoof raised as though it were just about to stamp on something small and insignificant. Nicky had said it was "Ming" and Eileen had sworn it was "Sung" because she had once been to China on a cruise and became superior at the mention of anything remotely oriental.

There had been quite a scene about it culminating in Martha saying loudly that she'd settle for it being "Gong" or "Pong" if only everybody would bloody well shut up arguing and give her a drink.

Diana remembered how Jimmy had laughed, he was sitting on the floor next to Barbara. She looked at the empty space in front of the fireplace and saw him clearly, laughing, with his head thrown back and the firelight shining on his hair. That was during rehearsals, before anything had happened, before the opening night in Manchester and the fatal supper party at the Midland, when he had come over from his party at the other end of the French restaurant to tell her about the rehearsal for cuts the next afternoon. She remembered asking him to sit down and have a glass of champagne, and how politely he had accepted with a rather quizzical smile, almost an air of resignation. Then the long discussion about Duse and Bernhardt, and Jonathan getting excited and banging the table, and Jimmy sitting exactly opposite her where she could watch him out of the corner of her eye, listening intently to the conversation and twiddling the stem of his wine glass. They had all been dressed, of course. Jonathan and Mary had come up from London especially for the first night, also Violet and Dick and Maureen. Jimmy was wearing a gray flannel suit and a blue shirt and navy blue tie; occasionally the corners of his mouth twitched as though he were secretly amused, but didn't want to betray it. Then he had caught her looking at him, raised his eyebrows just for the fraction of a second and, with the most disarming friendliness, patted her hand. "You gave a brilliant performance tonight," he said. "I felt very proud to be there." That was the moment. That was the spark being struck. If she had had any sense she'd have run like a stag, but instead of running, instead of recognizing danger, there she had sat idiotically smiling, warmed and attracted. Not content with having had a successful first night and having given a good performance, not satisfied with the fact that her friends, her close intimate friends had trailed all the way from London to enjoy her triumph with her, she had had to reach out greedily for something more. Well, God knows she'd got it all right. Here it was, all the fun of the fair. The fruits of those few weeks of determined fascination. She remembered, with a slight shudder, how very much at her best she had been, how swiftly she had responded to her new audience, this nice-looking, physically attractive young man at least ten years younger than herself. How wittily she had joined in the general conversation. She remembered Jonathan laughing until he cried at the way she had described the dress rehearsal of *Lady from the East*, when the Japanese bridge had broken in the middle of her love scene. All the time, through all the laughter, through all the easy intimate jokes, she had had her eye on Jimmy, watching for his response, drawing him into the circle, appraising him, noting his slim wrists, the way he put his head on one side when he asked a question, his eyes, his thick eyelashes, his wide, square shoulders. She remembered saying "good night" to him with the others as they all went up in the lift together. Her suite was on the second floor, so she got out first. He was up on the top floor somewhere, sharing a room with Bob Harley, one of the small-part actors. She remembered, also, looking at herself in the glass in her bathroom and wondering, while she creamed her face, how attractive she was to him really, or how much of it was star glamour and position. Even then, so early in the business, she had begun to doubt. It was inevitable, of course, that doubt, particularly with someone younger than herself, more particularly still when that someone was assistant stage manager and general understudy. A few days after that, she had boldly asked him to supper in her suite. She remembered at the time being inwardly horrified at such flagrant indiscretion; however, no one had found out or even suspected. He accepted with alacrity, arrived a little late, having had a bath and changed his suit, and that was that.

Suddenly, the telephone bell rang. Diana jumped, and with a sigh of indescribable relief, went into her bedroom to answer it. Nobody but Jimmy knew that she was coming home early—nobody else would dream of finding her in at this time of night. She sat on the edge of the bed just in order to let it ring once more, just to give herself time to control the foolish happiness in her voice. Then she lifted the receiver and said "Hallo," in exactly the right tone of politeness only slightly touched with irritation. She heard Martha's voice at the other end, and the suddenness of the disappointment robbed her of all feeling for a moment. She sat there rigid and cold with a dead heart. "My God," Martha was saying, "you could knock me down with a crowbar, I couldn't be more surprised. I rang up Jonathan and Barbara and Nicky, and finally the Savoy Grill—this is only a forlorn hope—I never thought for a moment you'd be in." Diana muttered something about being tired and having a matinee tomorrow, her voice sounded false and toneless. Martha went on. "I don't want to be a bore, darling, but Helen and Jack have arrived from New York, and they're leaving on Saturday for Paris, and they've been trying all day to get seats for your show, and the nearest they could get was the fourteenth row, and I wondered if you could do anything about the house seats." With a great effort Diana said: "Of course, darling, I'll fix it with the box office tomorrow." "You're an angel—here are Helen and Jack, they want to say 'Hullo.'" There was a slight pause, then Helen's husky Southern voice: "Darling—"

Diana put her feet up and lay back on the bed, this was going to be a long business. She was in command of herself again, she had been a fool to imagine it was Jimmy, anyhow; he never telephoned unless she asked him to, that was one of the most maddening aspects of his good behavior. Good behavior to Jimmy was almost a religion. Excepting when they were alone together, he never for an instant betrayed by the flicker of an eyelash that they were anything more than casual acquaintances. There was no servility in his manner, no pandering to her stardom. On the contrary the brief words he had occasion to speak to her in public were, if anything, a trifle brusque, perfectly polite, of course, but definitely without warmth. Helen's voice went on. She and Jack had had a terrible trip on the *Queen Mary*, and Jack had been sick as a dog for three whole days. Presently Jack came to the telephone and took up the conversation where Helen had left off. Diana lay still, giving a confident, assured performance, laughing gaily, dismissing her present success with just enough disarming professional modesty to be becoming. "But, Jack dear, it's a marvelous part—nobody could go far wrong in a part like that. You wait until you see it—you'll see exactly what I mean. Not only that, but the cast's good too, Ronnie's superb. I think it's the best performance he's given since *The Lights Are Low,* and, of course, he's heaven to play with. He does a little bit of business with the breakfast tray at the beginning of the third act that's absolutely magical. I won't tell you what it is, because it would spoil it for you, but just watch out for it—No dear, I can't have supper tomorrow night—I've a date with some drearies that I've already put off twice—no, really I couldn't again—how about lunch on Friday? You'd better come here and bring old Martha, too—all right—it's lovely to hear your voice again. The seats will be in your name in the box office tomorrow night. Come backstage afterward, anyhow, even if you've hated it—good-bye!"

Diana put down the telephone and lit a cigarette, then she wrote on the pad by the bed: "Remember fix house seats, Jack and Helen." Next to the writing pad was a thermos jug of Ovaltine left for her by Dora. She looked at it irritably and then poured some out and sipped it.

Jimmy had probably gone straight home. He generally did. He wasn't a great one for going out, and didn't seem to have many friends except, of course, Elsie Lumley, who'd been in repertory with him, but that was all over now and she was safely married, or was she? Elsie Lumley, judging from what she knew of her, was the type that would be reluctant to let any old love die, married or not married. Elsie Lumley! Pretty, perhaps rather overvivacious, certainly talented. She'd be a star in a year or two if she behaved herself. The picture of Elsie and Jimmy together was unbearable—even though it all happened years ago—it *had* happened and had gone on for quite a long while, too. Elsie lying in his arms, pulling his head down to her mouth, running her fingers through his hair—Diana put down the cup of Ovaltine with a bang that spilt a lot of it into the saucer. She felt sick, as though something were dragging her heart down into her stomach. If Jimmy had gone straight home he'd be in his flat now, in bed probably, reading. There really wasn't any valid reason in the world why she shouldn't ring him up. If he didn't answer, he was out, and there was nothing else to do about it. If he was in, even if he had dropped off to sleep, he wouldn't really mind her just ringing up to say "Good night."

She put out her hand to dial his number, then withdrew it again. It would be awful if someone else was there and answered the telephone, not that it was very likely, he only had a bed-sitting room, but still he might have asked Bob Harley or Walter Grayson home for a drink. If Walter Grayson heard her voice on the telephone it would be all over the theater by tomorrow evening. He was one of those born theatrical gossips, amusing certainly, and quite a good actor, but definitely dangerous. She could, of course, disguise her voice. Just that twang of refined cockney that she had used in *The Short Year*. She put out her hand again, and again withdrew it. "I'll have another cigarette and by the time I've smoked it, I shall decide whether to ring him up or not." She hoisted herself up on the pillow and lit a cigarette, methodically and with pleasure. The ache had left her heart and she felt happier—unaccountably so, really; nothing had happened except the possibility of action, of lifting the receiver and dialing a number, of hearing his voice—rather sleepy, probably—saying: "Hallo, who is it?" She puffed at her cigarette luxuriously watching the smoke curl up into the air. It was blue when it spiraled up from the end of the cigarette and gray when she blew it out of her mouth. It might, of course, irritate him being rung up, he might think she was being indiscreet or tiresome or even trying to check up on him: trying to find out whether he'd gone straight home, and whether he was alone or not.

How horrible if she rang up and he wasn't alone: if she heard his voice say, just as he was lifting the receiver: "Don't move, darling, it's probably a wrong number," something ordinary like that, so simple and so ordinary, implying everything, giving the whole game away. After all, he was young and good-looking, and they had neither of them vowed any vows of fidelity. It really wouldn't be so surprising if he indulged in a little fun on the side every now and then. Conducting a secret liaison with the star of the theater in which you work must be a bit of a strain from time to time. A little undemanding, light, casual love with somebody else might be a relief.

Diana crushed out her cigarette angrily, her hands were shaking and she felt sick again. She swung her legs off the bed and, sitting on the edge of it, dialed his number viciously, as though she had found him out already; caught him red-handed. She listened to the ringing tone, it rang in twos—brrr-brrr—brrr-brrr. The telephone was next to his bed, that she knew, because once when she had dropped him home he had asked her in to see his hovel. It was a bed-sitting room on the ground floor in one of those small, old-fashioned streets that run down to the river from John Street, Adelphi. . . brr-brr—brr-brrr—she might have dialed the wrong number. She hung up and then redialed it, again the ringing tone, depressing and monotonous. He was out—he was out somewhere—but where could he possibly be? One more chance, she'd call the operator and ask her to give the number a special ring, just in case there had been a mistake.

The operator was most obliging, but after a few minutes her voice, detached and impersonal, announced that there was no reply from the number and that should she call again later? Diana said no, it didn't matter, she'd call in the morning. She replaced the receiver slowly, wearily, as though it were too heavy to hold any longer, then she buried her face in her hands.

Presently she got up again and began to walk up and down the room. The bed, rumpled where she had lain on it, but turned down, with her nightdress laid out, ready to get into, tortured her with the thought of the hours she would lie awake in it. Even medinal, if she were stupid enough to take a couple of tablets before a matinee, wouldn't be any use tonight. That was what was so wonderful about being in love, it made you so happy! She laughed bitterly aloud and then caught herself laughing bitterly aloud and, just for a second, really laughed. Just a grain of humor left after all. She stopped in front of a long glass and addressed herself in a whisper, but with clear, precise enunciation as though she were trying to explain something to an idiot child. "I don't care, " she said, "I don't care if it's cheap or humiliating or unwise or undignified or mad, I'm going to do it, so there. I'm going to do it now, and if I have to wait all night in the street I shall see him, do you understand? I shall see him before I go to sleep, I don't mind if it's only for a moment, I shall see him. If the play closes tomorrow night. If I'm the scandal of London. If the stars fall out of the sky. If the world comes to an end! I shall see him before I go to sleep tonight. If he's alone or with somebody else. If he's drunk, sober or doped, I intend to see him. If he is in and his lights are out I shall bang on the window until I wake him and if, when I wake him, he's in bed with man, woman or child, I shall at least know. Beyond arguments and excuses I shall *know*. I don't care how foolish and neurotic I may appear to him. I don't care how high my position is, or how much I trail my pride in the dust. What's position anyway, and what's pride? To hell with them. I'm in love and I'm desperately unhappy. I know there's no reason to be unhappy, no cause for jealousy and that I should be ashamed of myself at my age, or at any age, for being so uncontrolled and for allowing this God-damned passion or obsession or whatever it is to conquer me, but there it is. It can't be helped. No more fighting—no more efforts to behave beautifully. I'm going to see him—I'm going now—and if he is unkind or angry and turns away from me I shall lie down in the gutter and howl."

She picked up her hat from the sofa in the sitting room, turned out all the lights, glanced in her bag to see if she had her keys all right and enough money for a taxi, and went out onto the landing, shutting the door furtively behind her. She debated for a moment whether to ring for the lift or slip down the stairs, finally deciding on the latter as it would be better on the whole if the lift man didn't see her. He lived in the basement and there was little chance of him catching her unless by bad luck she happened to coincide with any of the other tenants coming in. She got out into the street unobserved and set off briskly in the direction of Orchard Street. It was a fine night, fortunately, but there had been rain earlier on and the roads were shining under the lights. She waited on the corner of Orchard Street and Portman Square for a taxi that came lolling toward her from the direction of Great Cumberland Place. She told the driver to stop just opposite the Little Theatre in John Street, Adelphi, and got in. The cab smelt musty and someone had been smoking a pipe in it. On the seat beside her something white caught her eye; she turned it over gingerly with her gloved hand, and discovered that it was a program of her own play, with a large photograph of herself on the cover. She looked at the photograph critically. The cab was rattling along Oxford Street now, and the light was bright enough. The photograph had been taken a year ago in a Molyneux sports dress and small hat. It was a three-quarter length and she was sitting on the edge of a sofa, her profile half turned away from the camera. She looked young in it, although the poise of the head was assured, perhaps a trifle too assured. She looked a little hard too, she thought, a little ruthless. She wondered if she was, really. If this journey she was making now, this unwise, neurotic excursion, merely boiled down to being an unregenerate determination to get what she wanted, when she wanted it, at no matter what price. She thought it over calmly, this business of being determined. After all, it was largely that, plus undoubted talent and personality, that got her where she was today. She wondered if she were popular in the theater. She knew the stagehands liked her, of course, they were easy; just remembering to say "thank you," when any of them held open a door for her or "good evening," when she passed them on the stage was enough—they were certainly easy because their manners were good, and so were hers; but the rest of the company—not Ronnie, naturally, he was in more or less the same position as herself; the others, little Cynthia French, for instance, the ingenue, did she hate her bitterly in secret? Did she envy her and wish her to fail? Was all that wide-eyed, faintly servile eagerness to please, merely masking an implacable ambition, a sweet, strong, female loathing? She thought not on the whole, Cynthia was far too timid a creature, unless, of course, she was a considerably finer actress off the stage than she was on. Walter Grayson, she knew, liked her all right. She'd known him for years, they'd been in several plays together. Lottie Carnegie was certainly waspish at moments, but only with that innate defensiveness of an elderly actress who hadn't quite achieved what she originally set out to achieve. There were several of them about, old-timers without any longer much hope left of becoming stars, but with enough successful work behind them to assure their getting good character parts. They all had their little mannerisms and peculiarities and private fortresses of pride. Lottie was all right really, in fact as far as she, Diana, was concerned she was all sweetness and light, but, of course, that might be because she hated Ronnie. Once, years ago apparently, he had been instrumental in having her turned down for a part for which he considered her unsuitable. The others liked her well enough, she thought, at least she hoped they did; it was horrid not to be liked; but she hadn't any illusions as to what would happen if she made a false step. This affair with Jimmy, for example. If that became known in the theater the whole of London would be buzzing with it. She winced at the thought. That would be horrible. Once more, by the light of a streetlamp at the bottom of the Haymarket, she looked at the photograph. She wondered if she had looked like that to the man with the pipe to whom the program had belonged; whether he had taken his wife with him or his mistress; whether they'd liked the play and cried dutifully in the last act, or been bored and disappointed and wished they'd gone to a musical comedy. How surprised they'd be if they knew that the next person to step into the taxi after they'd left it was Diana Reed, Diana Reed herself, the same woman they had so recently been applauding, as she bowed and smiled at them in that shimmering silver evening gown—that reminded her to tell Dora at the matinee tomorrow that the paillettes where her cloak fastened were getting tarnished and that she must either ring up the shop or see if Mrs. Blake could deal wih it in the wardrobe.

The taxi drew up with a jerk opposite to the Little Theatre. Diana got out and paid the driver. He said: "Good night, Miss," and drove away down the hill, leaving her on the edge of the curb feeling rather dazed, almost forgetting what she was there for. The urgency that had propelled her out of her flat and into that taxi seemed to have evaporated somewhere between Oxford Street and here. Perhaps it was the photograph on the program, the reminder of herself as others saw her, as she should be, poised and well-dressed with head held high, not in contempt, nothing supercilious about it, but secure and dignified, above the arena. Those people who had taken that taxi, who had been to the play—how shocked they'd be if they could see her now, not just standing alone in a dark street, that wouldn't of course shock them particularly, merely surprise them; but if they could know, by some horrid clairvoyance, why she was there. If, just for an instant, they could see into her mind. Diana Reed, that smooth, gracious creature whose stage loves and joys and sorrows they had so often enjoyed, furtively loitering about in the middle of the night in the hopes of spending a few minutes with a comparatively insignificant young man whom she liked going to bed with. Diana resolutely turned in the opposite direction from Jimmy's street and walked round by the side of the Tivoli into the Strand. Surely it was a little more than that? Surely she was being unnecessarily hard on herself. There was a sweetness about Jimmy, a quality, apart from his damned sex appeal. To begin with, he was well-bred, a gentleman. (What a weak, nauseating alibi, as though that could possibly matter one way or another and yet, of course, it did.) His very gentleness, his strict code of behavior. His fear, so much stronger even than hers, that anyone should discover their secret. Also he was intelligent, infinitely more knowledgeable and better read than she. All that surely made a difference, surely justified her behavior a little bit? She walked along the Strand toward Fleet Street, as though she were hurrying to keep an important appointment. There were still a lot of people about and on the other side of the street two drunken men were happily staggering along with their arms round each other's necks, singing "Ramona." Suddenly to her horror she saw Violet Cassel and Donald Ross approaching her, they had obviously been supping at the Savoy and decided to walk a little before taking a cab. With an instinctive gesture she jammed her hat down over her eyes and darted into Heppell's so quickly that she collided with a woman who was just coming out and nearly knocked her down. The woman said, "Christ, a fugitive from a chain gang?" and waving aside Diana's apologies, went unsteadily into the street. Diana, faced with the inquiring stare of the man behind the counter and slightly unhinged by her encounter in the doorway, and the fact that Donald and Violet were at that moment passing the shop, racked her brains for something to buy. Her eyes lighted on a bottle of emerald green liquid labeled "Ess Viotto for the hands." "I should like that," she said, pointing to it. The man, without looking at her again, wrapped it up and handed it to her. She paid for it and went out of the shop. Violet and Donald were crossing over further down. She walked slowly back the way she had come. An empty taxi cruising along close to the curb passed her and almost stopped. She hailed it, gave the driver her address, got in and sank thankfully back onto the seat. "A fugitive from a chain gang." She smiled and closed her eyes for a moment. "What an escape!" She felt utterly exhausted as if she had passed through a tremendous crisis, she was safe, safe as houses, safe from herself and humiliation and indignity. No more of such foolishness. She wondered whether or not she had replaced the stopper in the thermos. She hoped she had, because the prospect of sitting up, snug in bed, with a mind at peace and a cup of Ovaltine seemed heavenly. She opened her eyes as the taxi was turning into Lower Regent Street and looked out of the window. A man in a camel's-hair coat and a soft brown hat was waiting on the corner to cross the road. Jimmy! She leant forward hurriedly and tried to slide the glass window back in order to tell the driver to stop, but it wouldn't budge. She rapped on the glass violently. The driver looked round in surprise and drew into the curb. She was out on the pavement in a second, fumbling in her bag. "I've forgotten something," she said breathlessly. "Here"—she gave him a half a crown and turned and ran toward Jimmy. He had crossed over by now and was just turning into Cockspur Street. She had to wait a moment before crossing because two cars came by and then a bus. When she got round the corner she could still see him just passing the lower entrance to the Carlton. She put on a great spurt and caught up with him just as he was about to cross the Haymarket. He turned his head slightly just as she was about to clutch at his sleeve. He was a pleasant-looking young man with fair hair and a little moustache. Diana stopped dead in her tracks and watched him cross the road, a stream of traffic went by and he was lost to view. She stood there trying to get her breath and controlling an overpowering desire to burst into tears. She stamped her foot hard as though by so doing she could crush her agonizing, bitter disappointment into the ground.

A passing policeman looked at her suspiciously, so she moved miserably across the road and walked on toward Trafalgar Square, past the windows of the shipping agencies filled with smooth models of ocean liners. She stopped at one of them for a moment and rested her forehead against the cold glass, staring at a white steamer with two yellow funnels; its decks meticulously scrubbed and its paintwork shining in the light from the streetlamps. Then, pulling herself together, she set off firmly in the direction of the Adelphi. No use dithering about anymore. She had, in leaving the flat in the first place, obeyed an irresistible, but perfectly understandable impulse to see Jimmy. Since then, she had hesitated and vacillated and tormented herself into a state bordering on hysteria. No more of that, it was stupid, worse than stupid, this nerve-racking conflict between reason and emotion was insane. Reason had done its best and failed. No reason in the world could now woo her into going back to that empty flat without seeing Jimmy. If Fate hadn't dressed that idiotic young man with a moustache in Jimmy's camel's-hair coat and Jimmy's hat, all would have been well. If Fate had arbitrarily decided, as it apparently had, that she was to make a fool of herself, then make a fool of herself she would. Jimmy was probably fast asleep by now and would be furious at being awakened. She was, very possibly, by this lamentable, silly behavior, about to wreck something precious, something which, in future years, she might have been able to look back upon with a certain wistful nostalgia. Now of course, after she had observed Jimmy's irritation and thinly-veiled disgust, after he had kissed her and comforted her and packed her off home in a taxi, she would have to face one fact clearly and bravely and that fact would be that a love affair, just another love affair, was ended. Not a violent break or a quarrel or anything like that, just a gentle, painful decline, something to be glossed over and forgotten. By the time she had reached the top of Jimmy's street there were tears in her eyes.

She walked along the pavement on tiptoe. His windows were dark, she peered into them over the area railings. His curtains were not drawn, his room was empty. She walked over the road to where there was a streetlamp and looked at her wristwatch. Ten past two. She stood there leaning against a railing, not far from the lamp, for several minutes. There were no lights in any of the houses except one on the corner. On the top floor, a little square of yellow blind with a shadow occasionally moving behind it. On her left, beyond the end of the road which was a cul-de-sac, were the trees of the gardens along the embankment; they rustled slightly in the damp breeze. Now and then she heard the noise of a train rumbling hollowly over Charing Cross bridge, and occasionally the mournful hoot of a tug on the river. Where on earth could he be at this hour of the morning? He hated going out, or at least so he always said. He didn't drink much either. He wouldn't be sitting up with a lot of cronies just drinking. He was very responsible about his job too and in addition to a matinee tomorrow there was an understudy rehearsal at eleven—she knew that because she had happened to notice it on the board. He couldn't have gone home to his parents; they lived on the Isle of Wight. She sauntered slowly up to the corner of John Street and looked up and down it. No taxi in sight, nothing, only a cat stalking along by the railings. She stooped down and said "Puss, puss" to it but it ignored her and disappeared down some steps. Suddenly a taxi turned into the lower end of the street. Diana took to her heels and ran. Supposing it were Jimmy coming home with somebody— supposing he looked out and saw her standing on the pavement, watching him. Panic seized her. On the left, on the opposite side of the road from the house where he lived, was a dark archway. She dived into it and pressed herself flat against the wall. The taxi turned into the street and drew up. She peeped round the corner and saw a fat man and woman in evening dress get out of it and let themselves into one of the houses. When the taxi had backed and driven away she emerged from the archway. "I'll walk," she said to herself out loud. "I'll walk up and down this street twenty times and if he hasn't come by then I'll—I'll walk up and down it another twenty times." She started walking and laughing at herself at the same time, quite genuine laughter; she listened to it and it didn't sound in the least hysterical. I'm feeling better, she thought, none of it matters nearly as much as I think it does, I've been making mountains out of molehills. I'm enjoying this really, it's an adventure. There's something strange and exciting in being out alone in the city at dead of night, I must do it more often. She laughed again at the picture of herself solemnly setting out two or three times a week on solitary nocturnal jaunts. After about the fifteenth time she had turned and retraced her steps she met Jimmy face-to-face at the corner. He stopped in amazement and said, "My God—Diana—what on earth—"

She held out to him the parcel she'd been holding.

"I've brought you a present," she said with a little giggle. "It's Ess Viotto—for the hands!"

THE KINDNESS
OF
MRS. RADCLIFFE

Mrs. Radcliffe always awoke on the dot of half-past seven. It was a habit of years and from this regularity she derived a certain pride. It signified a disciplined mind in a disciplined body, and Mrs. Radcliffe was a great one for discipline. Life was a business that had to be handled with efficiency and dispatch otherwise where were you? She had a poor opinion of those, and alas there were all too many of them, who allowed themselves to be swayed this way and that by emotions and circumstances over which they had little or no control. To have little or no control over emotions and circumstances was, to Mrs. Radcliffe, anathema. Not only did she consider it was foolish to succumb to the manifold weaknesses inherent in our natures, and after all there are many of these in even the sternest of us, it was downright dangerous. Mrs. Radcliffe could quote several instances of people of her acquaintance, occasionally even relatives, who, owing either to self-indulgence, lack of sense of responsibility or, in some cases, willful stubbornness—such as Cousin Laura for example—had completely degenerated and failed. It must not be imagined that Mrs. Radcliffe, who heaven knows was a broad-minded and kindly woman, referred to failure merely in the worldly sense; many of those who from her point of view had "Failed" had, on basely materialistic counts, done exceedingly well for themselves. Failure was a hydra-headed monster. You could be shrewd and businesslike, marry well and become a senior partner in no time and still fail. You could bear children, bring them up firmly, embark them on promising careers, keep your figure, wear smart clothes and play bridge as well as Mrs. Poindexter and still fail. On the other hand you could be poor and of no account, an insignificant cog in the great wheel of life and succeed, succeed triumphantly, for surely success in the eyes of God is of more ultimate importance than the glittering transient satisfaction of success in the eyes of the world. This, to sum it up briefly, was Mrs. Radcliffe's philosophy and she was delighted with it. She felt herself to be on a footing with the Almighty which was, to say the least of it, cordial. She referred to Him frequently in her mind and even more frequently in her conversation, not, it must be understood, with the slightest trace of sanctimoniousness. Hers was far too healthy and sane a character for that, rather more in a spirit of reverend friendliness. Occasionally she even blasphemed mildly to the extent of saying "Good Lord" or "My God" in moments of light stress. This, she considered in her secret heart, to be rather amusingly racy provided she didn't allow it to become a habit.

On this particular morning in early April Mrs. Radcliffe awoke as usual and lay for a few moments in dreamy awareness of the comfort of her bed, the translucent greenish charm of her bedroom, and the fact that it was a sunny day. This was apparent from the bars of strong light shining through the venetian blind and making stripes on the corner of the dressing table and the chaise longue by the window. Presently she heard Mildred approaching with her early tea; a swift glance at the clock on the table by her bed informed her that Mildred was four and a half minutes late. She decided, however, not to mention it this time. Mildred's unpunctuality was, unfortunately, the least of her defects; in fact there were moments when Mrs. Radcliffe genuinely regretted her generous impulse in taking her from the orphanage when she might quite easily have found a girl from the Registry Office with a certain amount of previous training in domestic service. The training of Mildred presented many problems and showed every sign of being an uphill struggle. But still Mrs. Radcliffe in her capacity as one of the esteemed Vice-Presidents of the Orphanage Committee had felt it her bounden duty to set an example to some of the other members, who, although volubly free with suggestions for the future of their charges when the moment came to launch them onto the world, were singularly unresponsive when it came to the point of doing anything practical about it themselves. Mrs. Radcliffe often smiled whimsically as she recalled the various expressions on the faces of the committee when she had burst her bombshell. "I will take Mildred myself," she had said, quite simply, without undue emphasis on the magnanimity of her gesture, just like that, "I will take Mildred myself!" She remembered that Mrs. Weecock, who was overemotional and effusive, had risen impulsively and kissed her, and that Doctor Price had immediately proposed a vote of thanks which had been carried unanimously with the greatest enthusiasm.

Mildred, after several months of strenuous effort, had, as yet, only managed to scrape the surface of what was ultimately expected of her; however she was willing, sometimes almost too eager to please, all of which was natural enough, poor little thing; nobody could accuse Mrs. Radcliffe of being unable to recognize pathetic, overwhelming gratitude, however nervous.

At this moment the object of her reflections entered the room. She was an uncouth girl of eighteen. Her abundant sandy hair straggled widely away from her neat cap, giving it the appearance of a small white fort set in the middle of a desert. Her hands were large and pink and her feet, encased in cotton stockings and strap shoes, were larger still. Her face, however, apart from a few freckles, was pleasing. She had a generous mouth and well-set grayish-green eyes. She said "Good morning, 'um," in a breathy voice and, having deposited the tray temporarily on the chest of drawers, went over and pulled up the blind. She also closed the window, which during Mrs. Radcliffe's slumbers had been open a fraction at the top, rather too sharply, so that the panes rattled.

"Gently, Mildred, gently," said Mrs. Radcliffe as she hoisted herself up on her pillows preparatory to receiving the tea tray. Mildred, by drawing in her breath and clicking her tongue against her teeth several times, made a noise which, although intended to express bitter self-reproach, merely succeeded in being irritating. Mrs. Radcliffe winced and waited for her tray in silence. The tray was a complicated affair designed for the comfort of invalids. By pressing lightly with the hands, two pairs of wooden legs shot out from each side thereby forming a neat little bridge across the patient's knees. This was one of the banes of Mildred's life. If the eiderdown were rumpled or Mrs. Radcliffe had not arranged herself in a completely symmetrical position, the whole thing was liable to tip sideways causing everything on it to slide alarmingly and hover on the brink of disaster. This morning, aware that she had transgressed over the window shutting, Mildred was even more nervous than usual. Her large hands were trembling and she breathed heavily. She set the tray across Mrs. Radcliffe's legs with laborious care; so far so good, only a few drops slopped out of the milk jug. She straightened herself with a sigh of relief and in the moment of triumph God struck her down. The corner of her apron, unbeknownst to her, had been caught by the left legs of the tray and the straightening of her body jerked it free with just sufficient force to overbalance the teapot. It was one of those moments in life when Time ceases to exist, years of fear and agony are endured in the passing of a brief instant. Mildred watched, with dilating eyes, the fat blue teapot with the willow-pattern design on it wobble from side to side and then slowly, slowly, with the slowness of protracted death, fall off the tray, roll over twice on the smooth slope of the counterpane, shedding its lid on the way, and finally crash to the floor, emptying its contents with devilish exultance into Mrs. Radcliffe's ostrich feather bedroom slippers. In the deadly silence that ensued a train whistled in the cutting a mile away, causing Mildred to jump violently as though the last trump had sounded for her.

Mrs. Radcliffe, who as a rule could be relied upon to assume an attitude of splendid calm in any crisis, for once lost control and fairly let fly. Mildred stood before her wretchedly twisting her hands, dumb with misery, too frightened even to take in half of what was being said to her. Disjointed words flashed across her consciousness like those moving electric light signs which tell of immediate events but which, if your attention is not wholly concentrated on them, become a series of meaningless phrases. A few invectives like "Idiot," "Fool," "Clumsy" and "Stupid" seared her mind for a moment and then were gone with the rest, leaving her shivering in a void of hopelessness and shame.

Presently Mrs. Radcliffe regained control and, after a slight pause, spoke with icy precision: "Pick it up," she said, and then again: "PICK IT UP!" using each word as a sword. Mildred stooped and picked up the teapot and stood with it in her hands, only vaguely aware of its heat. "The tray," said Mrs. Radcliffe. "Take the tray." Mildred put the teapot down on the floor again and took the tray.

The next ten minutes were devoted, insofar as was possible, to restoring order to chaos. Mildred, galvanized suddenly into feverish activity, flew down to the kitchen, blurted out the disaster in a few stumbling words to Cook, flew upstairs again with a cloth, rubbed and scrubbed with hot water out of the silver-plated jug to erase the tea stains from the carpet amid a hail of frigidly patient directions from her mistress. Finally, when the best that could be done had been done, she blurted out, "I'm sure I'm very sorry, 'um, it was an accident," and made for the door. Mrs. Radcliffe halted her.

"Just a moment, Mildred."

Mildred waited, standing first on one foot then on the other. Mrs. Radcliffe's voice was cold and just, she was now in full command again and sailing to victory.

"To explain that it was an accident, Mildred," she said, "was unnecessary. I should hardly have imagined that you had done such a thing on purpose. But what I wish to point out to you is that the accident would never have occurred if you had not been both careless and slovenly. I have spoken to you, Heaven knows often enough, about your clumsiness, and if you don't try to improve I very much fear I shall have to give you your notice. This time, however, and it is the last time, I shall excuse you." Mildred's heart leapt with relief like a bird in her breast. "But," continued Mrs. Radcliffe, "in order that this shall be a lesson to you, in order that you shall think and be more careful in future, I intend to punish you." There was a slight pause. The small gilt clock on the mantelpiece gave a little whirr and struck eight. Mrs. Radcliffe waited portentously until it had finished. "I understand that today is your afternoon out?" The bird in Mildred's breast dropped like a stone to the earth and through the earth into deep caverns of despair. "Yes, 'um," she said huskily. "Well," went on the voice of doom, "you will stay in this afternoon and help with the silver. That is all, thank you." A tear coursed down the side of Mildred's nose. "Very good, 'um," she said in a voice so low as to be almost inaudible, and went out of the room.

The fact that every minute of every hour of every day of Mildred's week had been concentrated on the anticipatory bliss of that afternoon out was of course hidden from Mrs. Radcliffe. How could she possibly know that Fred, thrilling wonderful Fred, assistant to Mr. Lewis the chemist in the High Street, had arranged to meet Mildred at two-thirty outside Harvey Brown's and take her to see Spencer Tracy, Clark Gable and Myrna Loy in *Test Pilot*? How could she possibly know that Messrs. Tracy and Gable and Miss Loy would be up and away by next Thursday and their sacred screen occupied by an English historical picture featuring Sir Cedric Hardwicke? How also could she guess that as Fred would be out on his rounds all the morning there was no possible way of letting him know that Mildred would be unable to meet him and that, after waiting for a half an hour or so on the pavement outside Harvey Brown's, he would probably be so furious that he would never speak to her again?

Fortunately for Mrs. Radcliffe's peace of mind she was ignorant of all this and, in consequence, her sense of exhilaration at having handled a difficult and annoying domestic drama with her usual consummate calm and decision was in no way impaired.

2

Mr. Stanley Radcliffe stood five foot six inches and a half in his socks which, no matter with what fickleness the weather might change, were invariably of austere gray worsted. His hair, thin on the top but happily bushy at the sides, was of the same color as his socks. As a character he was amiable, temperate and industrious but, if criticize we must, a trifle lacking in spirit. This defect, however, could be understood, if not altogether excused, by the fact that he had been married to Mrs. Radcliffe for thirty-three years. It is a well-known sociological truism that two dominant personalities become ill-at-ease when compelled by force of circumstance to inhabit the same house for a long period of time. It is possible that Mr. Radcliffe wisely realized this early on in his married life and, being a man of peaceful and sensible disposition, relinquished the ever dubious joys of domestic authority to his wife. It must not be supposed, however, that outside his home he was anywhere near as weak as he was in it. On the contrary, in his of-fice—he was a partner in the firm of Eldridge, Eldridge and Black, Solicitors-at-Law—in his office he was often a veritable martinet. Times out of number Miss Hallett, his secretary, would emerge from taking the morning letters with pursed lips and a spread of scarlet stretching from her neck up to her ears that spoke volumes.

On the morning of the teapot tragedy he was feeling cheerful. It was a cheerful day. The birds were twittering in the garden. He had received a letter from Henry Boulder, a more or less private client, that is to say a client who combined the transaction of legal business with a pleasant personal relationship, inviting him to visit him that afternoon at his house near Bromley to discuss the details of a new building contract that Eldridge, Eldridge and Black were drawing up for him, and perhaps play a round of golf afterward. A game of golf to Stanley Radcliffe was as steel is to a magnet, or rather a magnet to steel. He loved golf deeply and truly with all the passion of his na-ture. He was also fond of Mrs. Boulder, not in any way lasciviously, Mr. Radcliffe's sex impulses had atrophied from neglect at least fif-teen years ago, but with a warm sense of comradeship. She was a gay, vivacious creature in the early forties, given to telling rather risqué stories, and she had a loud, infectious laugh. Life at the Boulders' home seemed to consist of one long joke. Henry Boulder laughed a lot too, and frequently said the most outrageous things, but with such an air of worldly geniality that no offense could pos-sibly be taken.

Mr. Radcliffe looked at his wife sipping her coffee and opening letters at the other side of the table. She had her glasses on and ap-peared to be in a tranquil mood. He wondered if the moment was at last ripe for him to suggest what he had been longing to suggest for weeks. Why not take the plunge? He cleared his throat. Mrs. Radcliffe looked up. "Such a nice letter from Mrs. Riddle," she said. "They've just come back from a cruise to the Holy Land."

A fleeting vision of Mrs. Riddle, a formidable woman of vicious piety, blustering through the Church of the Holy Sepulcher, flashed across Mr. Radcliffe's mind for a moment and was obliterated. Now or never.

"How nice, dear," he said. "I wanted to—"

"They bathed in the Dead Sea," went on Mrs. Radcliffe, glanc-ing at a closely written page of thin notepaper. "And it was so salt that they couldn't sink."

"I shouldn't have thought," said Mr. Radcliffe with a bold chuckle, "that they would have wished to."

Mrs. Radcliffe looked at him suspiciously and then smiled, but without mirth, and went on reading the letter. Humor was not her strong suit and flippancy definitely irritated her.

Mr. Radcliffe, realizing that he had made a tactical error, cleared his throat again. "Adela," he said, "I have just had a letter from Henry Boulder." This, he realized the moment the words were out of his mouth, was another tactical error implying as it did that a letter from Henry Boulder was on a par with a letter from Mrs. Riddle. Mrs. Radcliffe ignored him completely and went on reading. Then Mr. Radcliffe, in a determined effort to get what was in his mind out of it, committed the gravest blunder of all. He advanced recklessly into the open. "I thought of inviting the Boulders to dinner tonight," he said.

Mrs. Radcliffe slowly lowered her letter and stared at him. If he had suggested inviting two naked Zulus to dinner she could not have expressed more shocked surprise. "My dear Stanley!" she said in the exasperated tone one might use in addressing a particularly fractious invalid. "The Dukes are coming."

"I don't see that that would make any difference," he said suddenly.

Mrs. Radcliffe, scenting mutiny, decided to scotch it once and for all. She leant across the table and smiled. "I fully appreciate," she said, "that they are great friends of yours," the emphasis on the word "yours" implied just enough subtle contempt, "but they are certainly not great friends of mine, in fact I barely know them. Also, my dear, although I am sure they are very useful to you in business, they are hardly"—here she gave a little laugh—"hardly the sort of people I would invite to meet the Dukes!"

Mr. Radcliffe opened his mouth to speak, to speak sharply, to say with firmness and conviction that the Reverend Francis Duke, vicar or no vicar, was an overbearing, pretentious bore, and his wife a giggling fool, and that for good humor and pleasant company and making a dinner party a success Mr. and Mrs. Henry Boulder could knock spots off them any day of the week. All this and more was bubbling in his mind, clamoring to be said, but the habit of years was too strong for him. He met the unwinking stare of his wife's slightly protuberant blue eyes for a moment and then wavered, the game was up. "Very well, my dear," he said, and resumed his toast and marmalade. Mrs. Radcliffe relaxed and smiled indulgently, poor old Stanley! She, who was so used to triumph, could afford to be magnanimous. She leant across the table and patted his hand affectionately then, generously wiping the episode from her mind, she embarked on the fourth page of Mrs. Riddle's letter about the Holy Land.

Mr. Radcliffe, a half an hour later, sat in the corner of a third-class smoking compartment on the train to London puzzling out in his mind the most tactful way in which he could repay some of the Boulders' hospitality. He could, of course, invite them to dine at a restaurant and perhaps get seats for a play afterward, but even so he was terribly afraid that the absence of Adela and the fact that they had never been asked to the house might hurt their feelings. People were extremely touchy about things like that. The last time he had visited them Mrs. Boulder had dropped a few hints. Suddenly, with a rush of blood to his face, he remembered that that same evening, just after dinner, he had, in a moment of expansion, definitely invited them. He remembered his very words: "You must come and dine one night soon and we'll have some bridge—my wife is so anxious to get to know you better."

When the train arrived at Cannon Street he went straight to the telegraph office, walking slowly as if he were tired. He wrote out the telegram carefully. "Boulder, 'The Nook,' Bromley. Very disappointed unable accept your kind invitation for this afternoon regards Radcliffe."

3

Mrs. Radcliffe rose from her desk in the morning room with a sigh and patted her hair in front of a mirror on the wall. She had been absentmindedly disarranging it while writing that difficult letter to Cousin Laura. She looked at her reflection for a moment and then, smiling, shook her head sorrowfully at herself. "You must really break yourself of that bad habit," she said with mock firmness, and then looked hurriedly to see if Mildred had happened to come in without her noticing. It would be too ridiculous to be caught by a servant talking to oneself. All was well, however· Mildred had not come in. As a matter of fact Mildred was at that moment in her bedroom at the top of the house crying her eyes out.

That letter to Laura had certainly been difficult, but Mrs. Radcliffe felt a sense of great relief at having at last written it. It had been hanging over her for days. Laura was her Aunt Marion's daughter and they had been at school together. Laura's whole life, in Mrs. Radcliffe's opinion, had been untidy, inefficient and annoying. To begin with she had married a drunkard with no money who had finally deserted her and died in Rio de Janeiro. After that for several years and with two young children on her hands she had contrived to run a tea shop at Hove and carry on a scandalous affair with a married man at the same time. In the year 1912 she had married again, a handsome but vague young man also with no money to speak of, who had later been killed in the retreat from Mons. In the intervening years between the Armistice and 1930 she had fortunately been abroad running a pension in some dead-and-alive seaside town in Northern Italy. Meanwhile the children of her first marriage had grown up. The boy, Frank, had married and gone off to plant rubber in Burma and was seldom heard from, while the girl, Estelle, had also married and, with an inefficiency obviously inherited from her mother, had died in childbirth, having misjudged her time and been caught in labor on a Channel Island steamer in the middle of a storm. Laura, now a woman of over sixty, had been living ever since in a small house in Folkestone only just managing to pay the rent every quarter by taking in paying guests. Almost the most irritating thing about her was her unregenerate cheerfulness. Even in the begging letter Mrs. Radcliffe had received from her a few days back there had been an irrepressible note of flippancy. Mrs. Radcliffe picked it up from the desk and re-read it for the third time. "My dear Adela," she read, "I am in the soup this time and no mistake. Please forgive me for worrying you with my troubles, but I really don't know where to turn. Mr. Roland, one of my extra quality streamlined P.G.'s, upped and left me on Saturday without paying his month's board and lodging and I was counting on it to pay off the last instalment on my dining-room set. I owe eighteen pounds on it and unless I pay it by Friday they'll come and take every stick away and poor Mr. Clarence Sims and Mr. Brackett, my other two gents, will have to sit on the bare floor. I do feel dreadful asking you to lend me ten pounds temporarily. I can raise eight all right on mother's silver, but if you possibly can spare it do please help me as I am in a flat spin and worried to death. I promise to pay it back within the next three months. Your distracted but affectionate cousin, Laura." Mrs. Radcliffe replaced Laura's letter in its envelope and read once more her own firm and admirable answer to it.

> My dear Laura, your letter was a great surprise to me, not having heard from you for so long. Believe me, I sympathize with you more than I can say in all your worries. If you will remember I always have. (Underlined.) How very disgraceful of your lodger to leave without paying you. Wasn't it a little unwise to take in that sort of man in the first place? However, it's no use crying over spilt milk, is it? With regard to your request for ten pounds, I am afraid that is quite out of the question at the moment. As you know I have many calls upon my purse in these trying times especially now that the Orphanage, of which I am vice-president, is becoming so overcrowded that we find ourselves forced to build a new dormitory for the little ones to which we all, that is the committee and myself, have had to subscribe a great deal more than we can afford. You see we all

have our little troubles! However, as we are such old friends, let alone actual blood relations—I always think that sounds so unpleasant, don't you?—I cannot bear to think of you in such dire straits, so I am enclosing a check for three guineas. This is most emphatically not a loan as I cannot bear the thought of money transactions between friends. Please, dear Laura, accept it in the spirit in which it is offered. Stanley joins me in the warmest greetings. I remain, your affectionate cousin, Adela Radcliffe.

Mrs. Radcliffe sat down at the desk again and wrote out the check, then having placed it with the letter in an already addressed envelope, she licked it down and stuck a stamp on it with an authoritative thump of her fist. This done she sat back in her chair and relaxed for a moment. What a pleasant thing it is, she reflected, to be in the fortunate position of being able to help those who, owing to defects in character and general fecklessness, are so pitifully unable to help themselves. In this mood of justifiable satisfaction, and humming a little tune, she went down into the kitchen to interview the Cook.

4

Mrs. Brodie had cooked for Mrs. Radcliffe for nearly three years and had, on the whole, proved satisfactory. Mrs. Radcliffe's tastes were simple. She disapproved of high seasoning, rich sauces, and the complicated flubdubbery of the French school. She designated any dish that was not strictly in accordance with the wholesome English culinary tradition as "Messy," and nobody who knew Mrs. Radcliffe even casually could visualize her for a moment sitting down to anything messy. Mrs. Brodie filled the bill perfectly. True, there were times when she displayed a certain tendency to flightiness. There had been one or two slipups. The Malayan curry, for instance (Mrs. Brodie's brother was a sailor), and the dreadful time the Piggots came to dinner and had been offered soufflé en surprise, the cold middle part of which had so surprised Mrs. Piggot's wisdom tooth that she had had to lie down on Mrs. Radcliffe's bed and have her gum painted with oil of cloves. All that, however, was in the past, although an occasional reminder of it came in handy as a curb whenever Mrs. Brodie showed signs of rebellion.

This morning there was no spirit in Mrs. Brodie at all, she had her own private troubles, as indeed who has not, and today they had come to a head. In the first place her widowed sister had been whisked off to the hospital to be operated on for gallstones, thereby leaving no one to look after Mrs. Brodie's husband who had had two strokes in the last nine months and was due for another one at any moment. This had necessitated some quick thinking and the sending of a telegram first thing to a niece in Southampton, together with a money order for fare and expenses. Mrs. Brodie devoutly hoped that at this moment the niece was already in the train. In the meantime she had telephoned to Mrs. Marsh, her next-door neighbor, asking her to pop in from time to time during the day and see that Mr. Brodie was all right. She planned to slip over herself during the afternoon to see that the niece was safely installed, and call at the hospital for news of her sister. This obviously meant asking Mrs. Radcliffe's permission, as Mrs. Brodie's home was in Maidstone, twenty miles away by bus, and in order for her to get there and back dinner would have to be later than usual and a scratch meal at that. At Mrs. Radcliffe's first words her heart sank. "Good morning, Cook. I want a particularly nice dinner tonight. The Vicar and Mrs. Duke are coming, also Miss Layton and Mr. Baker. Have you any suggestions?" Mrs. Radcliffe spoke kindly, in the special smooth voice she reserved for the Lower Orders. The lower orders, she knew, appreciated differences in class as keenly as anybody, that was one of the fundamental virtues of the English social structure and the reason that no nonsensical experiments such as Bolshevism or Communism or anything like that could ever take root in the British Isles. Class was class and there was no getting away from it, you only had to look at the ineffectiveness of those little men who shouted from sugar boxes in Hyde Park to realize how secure England was from disintegration. Everybody knew that they were paid by the Russians anyhow.

Mrs. Brodie looked at her mistress's gentle, pale face and pleasant smile and, for one wild instant, contemplated telling her about her sister's gallstones and Mr. Brodie's imminent and probably final stroke and imploring her to cancel her dinner party for tonight. The impulse died as soon as it was born and she found herself trembling at her temerity in even having thought of such a thing.

"Very good, 'um," she said. "We might start with cream of tomato"—Mrs. Radcliffe nodded—"then fillets of plaice?" Mrs. Radcliffe pursed her lips thoughtfully and then shook her head. "Lemon sole," she said. Mrs. Brodie wrote "lemon sole" down on a slate; the slate pencil squeaked causing Mrs. Radcliffe to draw in her breath sharply and close her eyes. Mrs. Brodie went on—

"Rack of lamb, mint jelly, new potatoes, beans or peas?"

"Peas," said Mrs. Radcliffe laconically.

Here Mrs. Brodie, having gallantly consigned her personal sorrows to the back of her mind and feeling oppressed by the uncompromising ordinariness of the menu, ventured a daring suggestion—

"I read a lovely new receipt for a sweet in *Woman and Home* the other day," she said eagerly, doubtless feeling subconsciously that the thrill of a new experiment might drug her mind into forgetfulness of her troubles—"it's called 'Mousse Napoleon' and—"

Mrs. Radcliffe cut her short. "I would rather we took no risks tonight, Cook," she said firmly. "We will have Apple Charlotte and a baked custard for Mrs. Duke who, as you know, has only recently recovered from influenza"; then, detecting in Mrs. Brodie's eye a fleeting but unmistakable expression of defiance, she thought it advisable to show the whip, not use it, just show it. She laughed indulgently and with the suspicion of an edge in her voice said, "We don't want any repetition of that unfortunate experience we had with the soufflé for Mr. and Mrs. Piggot, do we?"

Mrs. Brodie lowered her head. "No, 'um," she murmured.

"Then that will be all," said Mrs. Radcliffe lightly. "I shall be out to lunch."

Mrs. Brodie watched the door close behind her and sat down at the kitchen table. She felt low, dispirited, as though the hand of God were against her. It wasn't only Alice's gallstones and Mr. Brodie and the nuisance of Eileen having to be sent for and boarded and fed. Those were the sort of things in life that had to be faced. It was less than that and yet somehow more. Suddenly her whole being was shaken by a blind, vindictive hatred for Mrs. Piggot. "Silly old bitch!" she said out loud. "Wisdom tooth indeed! I'd like to yank the whole lot out with the pliers!" In a moment her rage subsided and she felt ashamed. She sat there idly for a moment wondering whether or not it would do her good to give way and have a nice cry. She was a great believer in a nice cry from time to time when things got on her nerves, it sort of loosened you up; however, the fact that Mildred had been crying steadily for two hours dissuaded her. "It would never do for all of us to be mooching about the house with red eyes," she reflected. "Whatever would happen if someone came to the front door! A nice thing that would be!" The clock on the dresser struck half-past ten, at the same moment Mildred came into the kitchen, pink and swollen, but calm.

"Cheer up, Mildred," said Mrs. Brodie comfortingly. "There's just as good fish in the sea as ever come out of it. Let's make ourselves a nice hot cup of tea."

5

After her successful interview with Mrs. Brodie, Mrs. Radcliffe went upstairs to put on her hat. She debated in her mind whether she should catch the eleven o'clock train to London which would get her to Charing Cross at twelve-five, thus giving her a whole hour to fill in before she was due to lunch with Marjorie and Cecil, or wait for the twelve o'clock which would get her to Victoria at twelve-fifty. She could certainly utilize that extra hour in town by doing Swan and Edgar's before lunch instead of afterward, but on the other hand as she had arranged to spend the entire afternoon shopping with Marion anyhow, perhaps an hour in the morning as well might be too much of a good thing. Also, if she took the twelve o'clock she would have time to call in at the Orphanage on the way to the station and have a little chat with Matron. She made one of her characteristically quick decisions. The twelve o'clock.

Mrs. Radcliffe's little chats with Matron took place on an average of about once a fortnight. They were unofficial and the other members of the executive committee, who met on the first Tuesday of every month, were unaware that they took place at all. If they had they might conceivably have been a trifle annoyed, people were like that, reluctant to take a practical personal interest themselves over and above their official capacities and yet oddly resentful of anyone who did. This regrettable human weakness was clearly recognized by both Matron and Mrs. Radcliffe, and, without saying so in so many words, they had tacitly agreed upon a policy of discreet silence. As Matron boldly remarked one day, "What the eye doesn't see the heart doesn't grieve over." These clandestine meetings were very useful to Mrs. Radcliffe. The various tidbits of information and gossip concerning members of the staff, the oddities of the children, etc.—some of them not always pleasant—all combined to give her a knowledge of the inner workings of the institution that came in handy at meetings. Had it not been for Matron she would never have been able to unmask that most distressing business last year of Hermione Blake and Mr. Forrage, a hirsute young man who tended the garden and did any other odd manual jobs that were required of him. She remembered how, fortified by her private information, she had swayed the whole committee. Mr. Forrage, due to her eloquence, had been summarily dismissed, while Hermione Blake, a sullen girl obviously devoid of moral principles, had, after a long cross-examination and ultimate confession, been justly robbed of her status as a prefect and forbidden, on the threat of being sent to a Reformatory, to speak to anybody whatsoever for three months. This punishment had not worked out quite as effectively as had been hoped, for apparently, according to Matron, the girl, after moping and crying for a week or so, had decided to treat it as a sort of game and invented a series of extravagant gestures and signs that caused so much laughter in the dormitory that Matron had been forced to send her to sleep in one of the attics by herself.

A plump, spotty girl, Ivy Frost by name, ushered Mrs. Radcliffe into Matron's private sanctum. It was a small room congested with personal effects. There were a great number of photographs of Matron's friends and relatives; a varied selection of ornaments, notably a small china mandarin whose head wobbled if you trod on the loose board by the table on which he sat, and a procession of seven ivory elephants on the mantelpiece, graded in size, and being led by the largest one toward a forbidding photograph of Matron's mother sitting under a lamp.

"Well, Ivy," said Mrs. Radcliffe benevolently as she ensconced herself in a creaking cane armchair by the fireplace and loosened her furs, "and how are you?"

"Very well, thank you, mum."

"That's right." Mrs. Radcliffe put her head a little to one side and scrutinized her through half-closed eyes as though measuring the perspective in a watercolor with which she was not completely satisfied.

"Your spots seem to be worse than ever," she said.

Ivy blushed and looked down. Her spots were the curse of her existence. Nothing she did for them seemed to do any good. A whole pot of cuticura ointment in three weeks, to say nothing of hot compresses and boracic powder, had achieved no signs of improvement; on the contrary, two new ones had appeared within the last few day, one small, on her chin, and the other large, on the side of her nose. She had been teased about them a good deal by the other girls, Mabel Worsley in particular, who, on one occasion, had persuaded all her dormitory mates to shrink away from her shielding their faces with their hands for fear of contamination. This joke had lasted a long while and provided much merriment. Mrs. Radcliffe went on, kindly, but with a note of reproof: "You're at an age now when you should take an interest in your appearance. I expect you eat too many sweets and don't take enough exercise—isn't that so?"

"Yes, mum," muttered Ivy, her eyes still fixed on the carpet.

"Well there you are then," said Mrs. Radcliffe with finality.

Ivy shifted her feet unhappily. It was not true that she had been eating too many sweets. No sweet had crossed her lips for months. Nor was it true that she didn't take enough exercise. She took as much exercise as the other girls and, being a member of the hockey team, more than a great many of them. But she had learned from bitter experience that it was never any use denying anything to those in authority. Authority was always in the right and you were always in the wrong. Much better keep quiet and say as little as possible.

Mrs. Radcliffe, feeling that further discussion would be unproductive, spoke the longed-for words of dismissal:

"Run along now, child, and tell Matron I'm here."

Ivy darted to the door with alacrity and vanished through it, but not quickly enough to escape Mrs. Radcliffe's parting shot—"And the next time I come I expect to see a nice, clean, healthy skin!"

Ivy, safely in the passage with the door closed behind her, contorted her face into the most hideous grimace she could manage and then, with a deep sigh, went off in search of Matron.

The Matron was a small, faded woman of fifty. Her sight was poor, which necessitated her wearing glasses with very strong lenses. These gave her a sinister expression which sometimes had a scarifying effect on the smaller children. However, she was a kind enough creature on the whole, that is to say as kind as it is possible to be without imagination. This deficiency occasionally caused her to be crueler in the discharging of her duties than she really intended to be. A few of her charges liked her, the majority tolerated her, while only a very small number actually detested her.

She was in the middle of her weekly locker inspection when Ivy Frost burst in and told her that Mrs. Radcliffe had arrived, and notwithstanding the fact that she had just found a lipstick together with a packet of "papier poudré" in Beryl Carter's locker, cunningly concealed in the leg of a pair of combinations, and had already sent for Beryl in order to confront her with her guilt, she immediately decided that, shocking and urgent though the matter undoubtedly was, it would have to be dealt with later. Mrs. Radcliffe, not only in her capacity as vice-president, but by virtue of her social position in the town, was not the sort of person to be kept waiting for a moment. Also her visits were a great pleasure to Matron. It was, indeed, flattering to be on terms of almost conspiratorial intimacy with anyone so aristocratic and imposing. She hurried along the passages and down the stairs with the eagerness of a romantic girl on the way to meet her lover. By the time she arrived she was quite breathless. Mrs. Radcliffe shook hands cordially, but without rising, Matron pulled the chair away from her writing desk and sat down on it, quite close to her visitor as though to emphasize the confidential character of the interview.

"Well, well, well," she said, flushing with pleasure. "This *is* a nice surprise!"

"I am on my way up to town," said Mrs. Radcliffe, "to lunch with my daughter and her husband and do a little shopping, and I thought as I had a little time to spare, I would drop in and ask you if everything was running smoothly and satisfactorily."

Matron smiled deprecatingly and replied in a tone of bright resignation:

"As well as can be expected."

"You look a little tired, Matron. I hope you haven't been overdoing it?"

"Oh no, Mrs. Radcliffe." Matron shook her head. "Of course, there *is* a lot to be done and with such a small staff we all get a bit fagged sometimes, but still it's no use complaining, is it? After all, that's what we're here for."

119

Mrs. Radcliffe smiled understandingly and there was silence for a moment. These preliminaries had by now become almost a ritual, the actual phrasing might vary with different visits, but the essence remained the same. Mrs. Radcliffe was always on her way to somewhere else and just happened to drop in casually, and Matron was always overcome with flattered surprise. Mrs. Radcliffe unfailingly commented upon Matron's tiredness, and Matron invariably denied it with an air of gallant stoicism. This over, they wasted no time in getting down to brass tacks.

"How is Elsie Judd?" said Mrs. Radcliffe, lowering her voice and leaning forward in her chair, which gave an ominous crack as though anticipating the worst. The adolescent processes of Elsie Judd, an overdeveloped girl of fourteen, had been causing some anxiety.

"Better," replied Matron, also lowering her voice. "I thought it advisable to call in Doctor Willis. He examined her most thoroughly and told me afterward that if we kept her quiet and watched her carefully for a few months that it would all blow over."

Mrs. Radcliffe nodded approvingly. "Is the new gardener satisfactory?"

Matron gave a little shrug. "In a way he is," she said. "I mean, he keeps everything quite tidy, but he's very slow over odd jobs and, of course, he can't drive the Ford like Mr. Forrage could."

The truth of the matter was that Matron secretly regretted Mr. Forrage. She often reproached herself for having divulged the Hermione Blake business to Mrs. Radcliffe. There might not have been very much in it really, although everybody seemed to think there was, and if she had only kept her mouth shut, and perhaps spoken to Mr. Forrage privately, a great deal of fuss and trouble might have been avoided. The new man, viewed as a possible menace to the chastity of older girls, was, of course, as safe as houses! In addition to having a wall eye, he was seventy-three and suffered from rheumatism. This, together with his age, not unnaturally restricted the field of his activities somewhat. Running errands, chopping wood, and the various odd jobs of domestic plumbing and carpentry at which his predecessor had been so invaluable, were obviously out of the question. Apart from this, he was disagreeable, which Mr. Forrage had never been. Yes, Matron definitely regretted Mr. Forrage, and although nothing would have persuaded her to admit it to Mrs. Radcliffe, whose moral indignation had been the cause of his dismissal, she made an inward vow to be a little more wary of her disclosures in the future. However, no major upheaval could possibly result from her discussing with Mrs. Radcliffe the perfidy of Beryl Carter. On the contrary, Mrs. Radcliffe's advice, which was always sensible and the epitome of kindly justice, might prove very useful in helping her to deal with the situation.

"I am very worried," she said, lowering her voice still further, "about Beryl Carter!"

Mrs. Radcliffe rustled expectantly. "Beryl Carter? Isn't that the rather fast-looking girl we had trouble with at the theatricals?"

"It is," said Matron. "And she's been a nuisance ever since. I don't know what's to be done with her, really I don't. Only just now I found a lipstick and one of those 'papier poudré' things in her locker—wrapped up in her combinations," she added, as though that made the whole affair more shameful than ever. Mrs. Radcliffe assumed a judicial expression.

"How old is the girl?"

"Getting on for sixteen."

"Hum—" Mrs. Radcliffe thought for a moment. "What was her mother?"

Matron had her answer ready to this, clear and accurate. She had looked up Beryl's dossier in the files only the other day. "A prostitute," she said. "She died when Beryl was three. The child was looked after by a charwoman, some sort of relative I think until she was eight, then she was sent here."

"There's no doubt about it," said Mrs. Radcliffe sagely, "heredity accounts for a great deal. You'd better send for the girl and let me talk to her."

This was rather more than Matron had bargained for. A little wise advice was one thing, but cross-examination in her presence might conceivably undermine her own personal authority, and in defense of her personal authority Matron was prepared to fight like a tigress.

"I don't think that would be altogether advisable," she said, and observing Mrs. Radcliffe stiffen slightly, added hurriedly, "She's rather an unruly girl, I'm afraid, and she might be rude. I should hate there to be any unpleasantness."

"You needn't be afraid of that," said Mrs. Radcliffe in a voice that brooked no argument. "I flatter myself that I am capable of dealing with a child of fifteen, however unruly. Kindly send for her at once, Matron. We can decide what is to be done with her after I have talked to her."

It may have been the unexpected peremptoriness of Mrs. Radcliffe's tone, or it may have been that Matron, having passed a sleepless night owing to neuralgia, was inclined to be more irritable than usual that morning. It may have been the weather or it may even have been some obscure cosmic disturbance. Whatever it was; whatever the cause; what took place was shocking to a degree. Matron lost her temper. To do her justice, she felt it happening and made a tremendous effort to control it; but alas! to no purpose. She felt herself go scarlet and then white again. She was aware of a strange singing in her ears, of great forces at work, rumbling through the room, pushing her over the precipice. She looked Mrs. Radcliffe fair and square in the eye and said, "No!" Not even: "No, Mrs. Radcliffe." Not even: "I'm very sorry, Mrs. Radcliffe, but what you ask is quite impossible." Just a plain unequivocal: "No," spoken more loudly than she intended and without adornment. There ensued a silence so profound that even the infinitesimal creaking of Mrs. Radcliffe's stays as she breathed, could plainly be heard. So charged with tension was the atmosphere, that Matron felt numbed, robbed of all sensation, as though she had been electrocuted. She continued to stare at Mrs. Radcliffe's face, because there didn't seem to be anywhere else to look, also she couldn't have moved a muscle if you had paid her. She watched a small nerve in the region of Mrs. Radcliffe's right eyebrow twitch spasmodically and her expression of blank astonishment slowly give place to one of glacial anger. Still the silence persisted. From the world beyond those four walls, the ordinary, unheeding outside world, a few familiar sounds penetrated; the grinding gears of a car; a dog barking in the distance; a tram clanking around the corner of Cedar Avenue into the High Street; but Matron heard them vaguely, remotely, as though they belonged to another existence. She experienced the strange sensations of one who is coming to from an anesthetic. That unutterable fatigue. That reluctance to take up the threads of life again. That deadly, detached lassitude. At last Mrs. Radcliffe spoke. "I beg your pardon?" she said, with such terrifying emphasis on the "beg" that Matron jumped as though someone had fired off a revolver in her ear. Again, to her own amazement, anger seized her. How dare Mrs. Radcliffe speak to her in that tone as though she were a menial? What right had she to come here and demand to interview Beryl Carter, or anybody else for that matter? It was nothing more nor less than an unwarrantable liberty, that's what it was. "I'm very sorry, I'm sure," she said, "but I'm afraid I cannot allow you to interview any of the girls without the authority of the committee." This was shrewd of Matron, although not an entirely true statement of fact. Mrs. Radcliffe, as vice-president, was perfectly within her rights in asking to see any of the girls, and Matron knew it as well as she did, but Matron also knew, owing to Mrs. Radcliffe's expansiveness on one or two occasions, that the committee would be far from pleased if it discovered that she was in the habit of making surreptitious visits to the Orphanage behind its back. Mrs. Poindexter in particular who was also a vice-president and who, in addition, was well known to be on far from cordial terms with Mrs. Radcliffe, would undoubtedly take full advantage of such an excellent opportunity of attacking her in front of everyone. Mrs. Poindexter had a sharp tongue as Matron knew to her cost. If anyone could floor Mrs. Radcliffe she could. All this and more had already passed through Mrs. Radcliffe's mind and, angry as she was, she fully realized that an open quarrel with Matron would be impolitic to a degree. There were other ways, she reflected, of dealing with a woman of that type. Matron, after all, was not indispensable. She was efficient within her limits, but she was certainly getting on in years, the committee might well be persuaded in the course of the next few months to replace her with somebody younger and more in tune with modern ideas of hygiene. Obviously, poor thing, she had been denied the benefits of breeding and education over and above the regulation course of hospital training, but still an ignorant woman, in such a very responsible position, was perhaps just a trifle dangerous? She was convinced that the Hermione Blake affair could never have occurred had there been a younger, more authoritative Matron in charge. Observing the palpable vulnerability of her adversary as she sat there opposite her, strained and tense on the edge of her chair, her eyes staring through her spectacles immovably, as though they had been stuck into them from the back, she almost felt it in her heart to be sorry for her. In fact, she definitely was sorry for her; poor stupid woman, having the impertinence to say "No," to her in that shrill hysterical voice, the temerity of referring to the authority of the committee! Authority of the committee, indeed! Mrs. Radcliffe almost snorted, but restrained herself. She rose from her chair slowly and grandly, complete mistress of the situation, captain of her soul. "Matron," she said, and Matron, also rising, quivered at the sound of her voice as a small fish will quiver when transfixed by a spear. "I must admit I am very surprised, very surprised indeed." She spoke evenly and pleasantly without heat. "Not that you should consider it inadvisable to send for this girl when I asked you to, in that you are perfectly justified, after all, you are in charge here and I am sure we are all only too willing to accede you the fullest authority that your position entitles you to—but—" Here she paused for a moment and adjusted her silver fox—"that you should adopt an attitude that I'm afraid can only be described as downright rude is quite frankly beyond me—"

"Mrs. Radcliffe," began Matron cravenly. The grand manner had triumphed, all anger had evaporated, all passion spent, she felt abject and ashamed—Mrs. Radcliffe overruled her by holding up her hand and smiling, a smile in which there was worldly understanding with just a soupçon of grief—

"Please let me go on," she said gently. "The whole thing has been the most absurd misunderstanding. It was exceedingly tactless and foolish of me to suggest sending for Beryl Carter. I am sure you are perfectly capable of dealing with the matter as it should be dealt with. It was only that I allowed myself to be carried away by my very real interest in this Orphanage and all the young lives for which we

123

are responsible. I only wish sometimes that some of my fellow members of the committee felt as personally about it as I do, but doubtless they are too occupied with their own worries. But one thing I must say, Matron, before I leave, and I must go in a moment, otherwise I shall miss my train, and you really won't take offense at this will you?—you are a little touchy you know, sometimes—" She laughed lightly—Matron quivered again and braced herself. Mrs. Radcliffe went on. "It's this—I really hardly know how to put it—but for some time, and this I assure you has nothing to do with this morning whatever, for some time I have been rather concerned about you, in fact only the other day I mentioned it to Mrs. Weecock and Doctor Price at the end of the meeting. You see," here Mrs. Radcliffe paused again as though really at a loss to know how to handle a situation of such appalling delicacy, "you see, you really are a little old to be doing work which demands such an immense amount of physical energy. I am often amazed that you mange as well as you do—and I have noticed, especially just lately, that you have been looking very, very seedy—"

"I assure you, Mrs. Radcliffe—" began Matron again, but once more Mrs. Radcliffe silenced her—"We were wondering whether it wouldn't be a good idea for you to have a little change," she said. "Of course, I haven't mentioned this in full committee yet, I felt that I should like to discuss it with you first—what do you think?"

Here it was, retribution, the axe! Matron saw it there above her head suspended by a hair. A series of sickening pictures flashed across her mind—a letter from the committee containing her dismissal with, at best, a minute pension. The dismantling of her room, the packing of her things. The confused squalor of her married sister's house at Whitby, she wouldn't be able to afford to live anywhere else. All very well for Mrs. Radcliffe to talk about "a little change," she knew what that meant all right; the thin end of the wedge. She made a gallant effort to speak calmly, to prove by perfect poise that she was in the best of health and fit to manage a dozen orphanages for at least another twenty years, but her nerves, which for considerable time had been stretched beyond endurance, betrayed her. Her humiliation was complete. She burst into floods of tears. Mrs. Radcliffe regarded her pityingly for a moment and then put her arm round her. Matron, her glasses misted with tears and knocked half off her nose by Mrs. Radcliffe's bosom, was unable to see and could only hear and smell. She could hear Mrs. Radcliffe's heart beating and her even, comfortable breathing, and smell a sharp tang of eau-de-Cologne and the rather animal, fusty scent of her fur. Presently she withdrew herself and dabbed blindly at her eyes with her handkerchief. She heard, as though from a long way off, Mrs. Radcliffe's voice saying with a trace of impatience: "Come, come, Matron, there's nothing to cry about. The whole episode is forgiven and forgotten." Then she heard the shutting of the door and a brisk retreating step in the passage and realized that she was alone. Still sobbing, she sank down to her knees on the floor, groping for her glasses which had finally fallen off entirely. The small china mandarin nodded at her.

6

Mrs. Radcliffe walked to the station with a springy tread. It was a radiant morning. The air was balmy, the sun was shining and a procession of large white clouds was advancing across the sky. They looked beautiful, she thought, so majestic, so removed from the pettiness, the insignificant sorrows and joys of human existence. Mrs. Radcliffe often derived great pleasure from the changing sky. Times out of number she had sat at her window just gazing up into that vast infinity and allowing her thoughts to wander whither they would, occasionally chiding herself humorously for the extravagant fancies that took shape in her mind. How fortunate to be blessed with imagination, to possess that inestimable gift of being able to distinguish beauty in the ordinary. Many of her acquaintances, she knew for a fact, hardly glanced at the sky from one year's end to the other unless to see if it was going to rain. She remembered once saying to Cecil, Marjorie's husband, who after all was supposed to be a painter, when they were standing in the garden one summer evening before dinner, that sunset and sunrise were God's loveliest gifts to mortals if only they were not too blind to be able to appreciate them. Cecil had laughed, that irritating, cynical laugh of his, and replied that many thousands of people would appreciate them more if they were edible. She recalled how annoyed she had been, she could have bitten her tongue out for betraying a fragment of her own private self to someone who was obviously incapable of understanding it. On looking back, she realized that that was the first moment that she really knew that she disliked Cecil. Of course, she had never let Marjorie suspect it for an instant, and never would. What was done, was done, but still it was no use pretending. "Know thyself," was one of the cornerstones of her philosophy. Poor Marjorie. Poor willful, disillusioned Marjorie. That Marjorie was thoroughly disillusioned by now, Mrs. Radcliffe hadn't the faintest doubt. Nobody could be married for seven years to a man like Cecil with his so-called artistic temperament, his casualness about money, her money, and his complete inability to earn any for himself, without being disillusioned. Mrs. Radcliffe sighed as she turned into Station Road. What a tragedy!

Marjorie Radcliffe had met Cecil Garfield at a fancy-dress ball at the Albert Hall in 1930. She was up in town for a few days visiting a married school friend, Laura Courtney. There had been a buffet dinner before the ball, in Laura's house in St. John's Wood, and Marjorie, dressed as Cleopatra, a very effective costume that she had designed and made herself, was escorted to the Albert Hall by Roger Wood, a cousin of Laura's who was in the air force. Roger was not dressed as anything in particular. He was a hearty young man and balked at the idea of tidying himself up; the most he had conceded to the carnival spirit of the occasion was a false moustache and a dark blue cape lined with scarlet which he wore over his ordinary evening clothes. Marjorie had been rather bored with him and was much relieved when, upon arrival at the ball, they had been accosted in the foyer by a group of hilarious young people none of whom she knew, but all of whom seemed to know Roger. They were whirled off to the bar immediately to have a drink before even attempting to find Laura and the rest of their party. Among the group was Cecil Garfield, and Cecil was dressed as Mark Antony. This coincidence provided an excuse for a great deal of playful comment from everybody. It would be useless to deny that Cecil looked very attractive as Mark Antony. His physique, much of which was apparent, was magnificent. He had a quick wit and a charming smile and Marjorie danced several dances with him.

At about three in the morning everybody, Laura and her husband included, adjourned to Cecil's studio in Glebe Place to cook eggs and bacon. It was there that Marjorie first realized that he was an artist. Now the word "Artist," to Marjorie, held an imperishable glamour. She had long ago decided that a life such as her mother would have wished her to lead with a conventional husband, a cook and a baby, was out of the question. Marjorie wholeheartedly detested her suburban existence and, if the truth were known, was none too fond of her mother. Of this unnatural state of affairs, Mrs. Radcliffe was mercifully unaware, and if Mr. Radcliffe occasionally had an inkling of it, he was wise enough to keep his suspicions to himself. Marjorie's predilection for the artistic life had originally started when she was in her teens. Miss Lucas, her drawing mistress at school, had, perhaps unsuitably, lent her *The Life of Van Gogh*. Profoundly impressed by this, Marjorie had gone from bad to worse. *My Days with the French Romantics, The Beardsley Period, Isadora Duncan's Autobiography,* and *The Moon and Sixpence*, had followed each other in quick succession. By the time she was twenty, she had assimilated a view of life so diametrically opposed to her mother's, that existence at home became almost insupportable. She was an intelligent girl, however, wise beyond her years and practiced in deceit. A certain proficiency in this direction being essential with a mother like Mrs. Radcliffe, and with a secretiveness that could only be described as downright sly, she kept her own counsel.

When Marjorie first met Cecil she had just turned twenty-one. She was a tall girl with a pale, almost sallow skin, dark hair, and keen, well-set blue eyes. Her figure was good although, as Mrs. Radcliffe frequently remarked, her movements were inclined to be a little coltish; however, she would doubtless soon grow out of that. With common sense unusual in one so young, she had faced the fact that, though she longed for it above all things, she had no creative ability whatsoever. This does not mean that she had not explored every possibility. She had written poems and begun novels—she had taken a course of line drawing at the Slade School, this only after a series of endless arguments with her mother, who had finally given way on condition that she traveled back and forth to London in company with Phyllis Weecock who was taking a stenography course at the Polytechnic. She had sat at the piano for hours trying to string chords together into a tune but alas, with no success, as she invariably forgot the ones she had started with and was incapable of remembering any of it at all the next day. She had, of course, made a bid for the stage, but on this Mrs. Radcliffe had put her foot down firmly. Poor Marjorie. None of it was any good. Her musical ear was nonexistent, her drawing commonplace, and her writing devoid of the faintest originality. However, undaunted by all this, she flatly refused two offers of marriage, one from Kenneth Eldridge, the son of one of the partners in her father's firm, and, worse still, Norman Freemantle, whose aunt, Lady Walrond, was not only the widow of a baronet, but owned an enormous mansion near Dorking and was as rich as Croesus.

Mrs. Radcliffe had risen above Kenneth Eldridge, but the rejection of Norman Freemantle went through her like a knife.

Cecil and Marjorie had sat in a corner together that night after the ball and talked. A few days later they met by the Peter Pan statue in Kensington Gardens and talked a lot more. They talked of literature, music, religion and morals and agreed on all points. Of painting they talked more than anything. Cecil's gods were Cézanne, Van Gogh, Matisse and Manet. He considered Picasso an intrinsically fine painter, but misguided. Cecil, when he talked of painting, betrayed his heart. Marjorie watched him fascinated. She noted the way his body became tense, the swift, expressive movements of his hands, how, when he was describing some picture that meant much to him, he would screw up his eyes and look through her, beyond her, beyond the trees of the park and the red buses trundling along on the other side of the railings, beyond the autumn sunshine and the people and the houses, beyond the present into the future. It was himself he was staring at through those half-closed eyes, himself having painted a successful picture, several successful pictures. Not successful from other people's points of view, perhaps, but from his own.

127

It was when she first saw him like that, unself-conscious, almost arrogant, demanding so much of life and of himself and of anybody who had anything to do with him, that she knew she loved him. More than this, she knew that she could help him and comfort him and look after him. At last she had found someone in whom she could sublimate her passionate, unresolved yearning for creativeness. Five months later she had crept out of the house early on a bleak wet morning in February, traveled to London by the seven-forty-five train, met him under the clock at Victoria Station and married him at nine-thirty at a Registry Office in Fulham.

Needless to relate, this insane headstrong gesture left a wake of sorrow and suffering in the Radcliffe household only comparable to the darkest moments of Greek tragedy. However, after bitter letters had been exchanged and after over a year had passed, during which time Marjorie and Cecil had endured a penurious hand-to-mouth existence in a small flat in Yeoman's Row, a fortunate miscarriage of Marjorie's, if such an inefficient catastrophe could ever be called fortunate, and her subsequent illness, had at last effected a reunion. Mrs. Radcliffe had come to London. Still grieving, still shocked by filial ingratitude, still licking the wounds in her mother's heart, nevertheless she came. About a month later it was arranged that Mr. Radcliffe should resume the small allowance that he had given to his daughter before her disastrous marriage. This generosity undoubtedly owed something to a remark of Mrs. Poindexter's at a bridge party, when she was heard to say loudly to Mrs. Newcombe that the manners and cruelty of the Radcliffes in permitting their only child to live in abject poverty was nothing short of medieval.

All this had taken place six years ago. Since then the allowance had been raised, on the stubborn insistence of Mr. Radcliffe, to almost double. Consequently, the Garfields were enabled to live in comparative comfort in a small house behind Sloane Square with a studio at the back converted, at certain expense, from a conservatory.

The fact that Cecil only very rarely managed to sell a picture was a source of great irritation to Mrs. Radcliffe. Having at last, soothed by the passage of time, consented to bury the hatchet and accept her artistic son-in-law, it was extremely frustrating not to be able to refer to his work with any conviction. To say "My son-in-law is quite a well-known painter, you know," was one thing, but it was quite another to say, "My son-in-law is a painter," and upon being asked what kind of a painter, to be unable to explain. If only he would do portraits that had some resemblance to the sitter, or landscapes which gave some indication, however faint, of what they were supposed to be. It was all very fine to argue that a painter painted through his own eyes and nobody else's, and that what was green to one person might very possibly be bright pink to another. All that sort of talk smacked of affectation and highbrowism. What was good enough for Landseer and Alma Tadema was good enough for Mrs. Radcliffe, and, she would have thought, good enough for anybody who had their heads screwed on the right way.

With these reflections she settled herself into the corner seat of a first-class compartment and opened a copy of *Vogue* that she had bought at the bookstall. Just at the instant of the train's starting three people clambered into the carriage. Now it is an odd frailty in the human character that however benevolent and kindly you may be by nature, the influx of strangers into an empty compartment that you have already made your own by getting there first, is very annoying. Mrs. Radcliffe was no exception to this rule. She looked up testily and was shocked to observe that the interlopers, apart from the initial tiresomeness of their interloping, were quite obviously of the lower classes. Now one of the reasons that Mrs. Radcliffe, who was naturally thrifty, always paid without regret the extra money for a first-class ticket instead of a third, was in order to avoid contact with the lower classes. Not that she had anything against the lower classes, she hadn't. She defied anyone to be more democratic spirited, to have a warmer, more genuine sympathy and understanding for those who happened to be in less fortunate circumstances than herself. But when she bought a first-class ticket she demanded the first-class privileges that the ticket entitled her to. Therefore she was perfectly justified in regarding these three most unprepossessing-looking people, with marked disapproval. The man, who wore a cloth cap and a dirty handkerchief round his neck, was smoking a cigarette. The woman, probably his wife, was pasty and dressed in a shabby gray coat and skirt, a pink blouse, a mustard-colored beret and black button boots. The third interloper was a boy of about eleven. He had no hat, unbrushed hair, a sore on his lip and a long mackintosh with one of the pockets hanging out.

Mrs. Radcliffe gathered herself together. "I think you have made a mistake," she said. "This is a first-class carriage."

The man and woman looked guilty. The little boy didn't look anything at all, he just stared at her. The woman spoke in a husky, whining voice.

"The third class is full," she said. "If we 'adn't of 'opped in 'ere double-quick we'd 'ave missed the train."

"In that case," said Mrs. Radcliffe, "you will be able to get out at the next station and change."

"I don't see 'ow it's any of your business any'ow," muttered the man sullenly.

Mrs. Radcliffe ignored him and looked out of the window. There was silence for a moment which was broken by the little boy saying loudly, "'Oo does she think she is?"

The woman giggled.

"Never you mind," she said. "The Queen of Roumania as like as not!"

"Shut up!" said the man. There was another pause and then the woman spoke again. "I will say it's a treat to be able to take yer weight off yer feet for a minute," she murmured. "I'm worn out and that's a fact."

"Shut up grumbling," said the man.

"I wasn't grumbling," she replied with spirit. "Just talking to pass the time." The man shot a baleful glance at Mrs. Radcliffe. "Well, pass the time some other way," he said, "you might upset 'er lady-ship."

Mrs. Radcliffe peered out of the window as though she had suddenly recognized a horse that was grazing in a field.

"That would never do," said the woman with another giggle. "She might 'ave us sent to jail, I shouldn't wonder. Be quiet, Ernie, and stop fiddling with that mac, you'll 'ave the button off in a minute."

Presently the train drew into a station. Mrs. Radcliffe withdrew her gaze from the window and looked the man straight in the eye. He held his ground for a moment and then quailed. Nobody moved. The train stopped.

"I don't wish to have to complain to the guard," said Mrs. Radcliffe.

A thunderous look passed over the man's face, he spat out his cigarette violently so that it fell at Mrs. Radcliffe's feet, then he jumped up.

"Come on, Lil," he said. "Look lively." He opened the door and they all three clattered out onto the platform. He slammed the door and then pushed his face in at the window causing Mrs. Radcliffe to shrink back.

"I'll tell you what your sort need," he snarled. "And that's a nice swift kick up the What's-it!"

The woman giggled shrilly again and they were gone. Mrs. Radcliffe fanned herself with *Vogue*. What a very unpleasant experience.

7

When Mrs. Radcliffe arrived, Marjorie opened the door to her herself. They had a maid but she was in the kitchen preparing the lunch. Cecil was still working in the studio and so Marjorie and her mother sat in the drawing room to wait for him. The drawing room was on the ground floor and the dining room opened out of it. The house was small and rather dark and smelt of cooking. Marjorie had tried to mitigate it by burning some scent in a heated iron spoon, but she had done this a little too early, and by now the scent had mostly evaporated whereas the cooking had not. Mrs. Radcliffe glanced around the room with a scarcely perceptible sigh of regret. It was simply furnished and neat enough, and there was a profusion of flowers, but it was far far removed from the setting her maternal imagination had originally painted for her only daughter. Mrs. Radcliffe looked at her only daughter curled up in the corner of the sofa, so unlike her in every respect, with her dark cropped hair, her large horn-rimmed glasses and her serviceable oatmeal-colored frock over which she wore a flamboyant bolero jacket of bright scarlet, and marveled that from her loins should ever have sprung such a baffling disappointment. Marjorie at the same time was observing her mother with equal wonderment. It was always like this. They always met as strangers, and it usually took quite a while to establish a point of contact. Mrs. Radcliffe's visits were fortunately rare. Marjorie wholeheartedly dreaded them, and it is possible that her mother did too, but immutable forces insisted on them taking place. It is doubtful whether Marjorie would have shed a tear had she been told that she was never going to set eyes on her mother again. It is also doubtful whether Mrs. Radcliffe would have minded either. She would shed a tear certainly, many tears. She would be, for a time, inconsolable, but genuine grief, the desolate heart, would be lacking.

"How's father?" asked Marjorie.

"Very well indeed. He had one of his liver attacks last week but it didn't last too long. He made a great fuss about it, you know what father is."

Marjorie nodded understandingly, the ice thawed slightly in the warmth of their both knowing what father was. Marjorie jumped up from the sofa and went over to a table by the window.

"Let's have some sherry," she said. "Cecil will be here in a minute." She poured out two glasses and brought them over carefully. "I'm afraid I've filled them rather too full."

Mrs. Radcliffe took hers and held it away from her for the first sip in case a drop should fall on her knees.

"How is Cecil?"

"Bright as a button. He's been working like a dog for the last two weeks."

"Really?" The vision of Cecil working like a dog did not impress Mrs. Radcliffe. In the first place she didn't believe it. She didn't consider that painting away in that studio constituted work at all. It was just dabbing about. Cecil, as far as she could see, spent his whole life dabbing about. She naturally didn't say this to Marjorie. Marjorie was inclined to be overvehement in defense of her husband's activities.

"Has he managed to sell any more pictures lately?" she inquired. The "any more" was purely courtesy. As far as she could remember Cecil had only sold one picture in the last eighteen months and for that he had received only twenty pounds.

An expression of irritation passed over Marjorie's face, but she answered amiably enough. "He's planning to have an exhibition in June. Lady Bethel is lending him her house for it."

This caused Mrs. Radcliffe to sit up as Marjorie had intended that it should.

"Is that the Lady Bethel who organized that charity pageant just before Christmas?"

"Yes," said Marjorie. "She's a darling, there was a lovely picture of her in the *Tatler* last week: going to a Court ball," she added wickedly.

Mrs. Radcliffe was clearly puzzled. Lady Bethel was certainly an important figure. If she was willing to lend her house for an exhibition of Cecil's paintings it might mean—here her reflections were disturbed by Cecil himself coming into the room. He had washed and tidied himself for lunch, but for all that he looked ill-groomed. His hair was too long, he wore no tie and there were paint stains on his very old gray flannel trousers. He bent down and kissed Mrs. Radcliffe on the cheek and then poured himself out some sherry.

"How are you, Marm?" he said breezily. He always addressed her as "Marm" and there was a suggestion in his tone of mock reverence which never failed to annoy her. "You look shining and beautiful."

Mrs. Radcliffe deplored extravagance of phrase. She answered rather tartly, "Very well indeed, thank you, Cecil."

Cecil came over and leant against the mantelpiece, looking down at her. She was forced to admit to herself that he was handsome in a loose, slovenly sort of way, but she could never be reconciled to that hair, never, if she lived to be a thousand.

"I've been telling mother about Lady Bethel promising to lend her house for your exhibition," said Marjorie a trifle loudly.

Was it Mrs. Radcliffe's fancy or did Cecil give a slight start of surprise?

"Yes," he said with marked nonchalance. "It's sweet of the old girl, isn't it?"

Something in Mrs. Radcliffe revolted at Lady Bethel, *The* Lady Bethel, being referred to as an old girl, but she didn't betray it.

"It certainly is very nice of her," she said. "But she has a great reputation, hasn't she for giving a helping hand to struggling artists?"

Cecil, disconcertingly, burst out laughing. "Touché, Marm," he said. "Come along and let's have some lunch." He helped her out of her chair with elaborate solicitude and led the way into the dining room.

Lunch passed off without incident. The conversation, although it could not be said to sparkle, was at least more or less continuous. Cecil was in the best of spirits. He was extremely attentive to Mrs.

Radcliffe, always it is true with that slight overture of mockery, that subtle implication in his voice and his gestures that she was a great deal older than she was, and had to be humored at all costs. He insisted, with playful firmness, that she drink some Chianti which she didn't really want, as wine in the middle of the day was apt to make her headachy in the afternoon. He displayed the most flattering interest when she described her visit to the Orphanage and the tact and kindliness she had had to exert in dealing with Matron, and when she told of her unpleasant adventure in the train, he was shocked beyond measure and said that that sort of thing was outrageous and that something ought to be done about it. During this recital Mrs. Radcliffe observed that Marjorie was bending very low over her plate, and wondered whether her nearsightedness was getting worse. Although fully aware that her long experience and inherent social sense were responsible for the success of the lunch party, Mrs. Radcliffe was not too occupied to notice that the soup was tepid, the fillet of steak much too underdone and that there was garlic in the salad. All of this saddened her. It was indeed depressing to reflect that Marjorie, with the lifelong example of her mother's efficiency before her, was still unable to turn out a simple, well-cooked meal. However, with her usual good-humored philosophy she rose above it. It took all sorts to make a world and if, by some caprice of Fate, her own daughter had turned out to be one of the less competent sorts, so much the worse.

After lunch was over and they had had their coffee (lukewarm), in the drawing room, Mrs. Radcliffe expressed a desire to see Cecil's pictures. This request was made merely in the spirit of conventional politeness. She had no real wish to see his pictures, as she knew from experience that there was little or no chance of her admiring them. Cecil and Marjorie were also perfectly aware of this, but nevertheless, after a little humming and hawing Cecil led the way into the studio. Marjorie walked behind with a rather lagging tread. The untidiness of Cecil's studio always struck Mrs. Radcliffe with a fresh shock of distaste. It was inconceivable that anyone, however artistic, could live and breathe amid so much dirt and squalor. The table alone, which stood under the high window, was a sight to make the gorge rise. On it were ashtrays overflowing with days' old cigarette ends, two or three used and unwashed teacups, a bottle of gin, a noisome conglomeration of paint tubes of all shapes and sizes, many of them cracked and broken so that their contents was oozing out and all of them smeared with a brownish substance that looked like glue, a pile of books and magazines, countless pencils and crayons and pieces of charcoal and, most disgusting of all, a half-full glass of milk, round the rim of which a fly was walking delicately. The rest of the room was equally repulsive. There was a model throne draped with some dusty material, a gas-fire with a bowl of water in front of it, in which floated several more cigarette ends, two easels, several canvases stacked against the wall, a large divan covered in red case-ment cloth and banked with paint-stained cushions and a pedestal supporting a sculpture in bronze of a woman's breast. It was only by the greatest effort of self-control that Mrs. Radcliffe repressed a cry of horror.

The picture on which Cecil was working stood on the bigger of the two easels in the middle of the room. It represented a man, or what passed for a man, sitting in a crooked rocking chair without any clothes on. His legs, which were fortunately crossed, were enor-mously thick. Upon a slanting table at the right-hand side of the pic-ture was what appeared to be a guitar together with a vase of flowers, a bottle and a fish. The paint on the canvas looked as though it had been flung at it from the other side of the room. There was not a trace of what Mrs. Radcliffe had been brought up to recog-nize as "fine brush work." In fact there didn't appear to be any brush work at all. She regarded in silence for a moment and then shook her head. "It's no use," she said, trying to keep the irritation out of her voice. "I don't understand it."

"Never mind, Marm," said Cecil cheerfully. "It's not really fin-ished yet, anyhow."

"But what does it mean?"

"It's called 'Music,'" said Marjorie as though that explained ev-erything.

"I still don't understand what it *means*," said Mrs. Radcliffe.

Cecil exchanged a quick look with Marjorie, who shrugged her shoulders. This annoyed Mrs. Radcliffe. "I'm sure you think I'm very ignorant and old-fashioned," this time making no attempt to control her irritation, "but I don't approve of this modern futuristic art and I never shall. To my mind a picture should express beauty of some sort. Heaven knows, there is enough ugliness in the world without having to paint it—"

"But we don't think that picture is ugly, mother," said Marjorie with an edge on her voice. Cecil looked at her warningly. Mrs. Rad-cliffe sniffed.

"You may not think it's ugly and your highbrow friends may not think so either, but I do," she said.

"Our friends are not particularly highbrow, Marm," he said gently. "And as a matter of fact, nobody has seen this picture yet at all. You're the first, you should feel very honored," he added with a disarming smile. Unfortunately, however, the smile was not quite quick enough and failed to disarm. Mrs. Radcliffe was by now thor-oughly angry. The Chianti at lunch had upset her digestion as she had known it would and, having endured that inferior, badly cooked food and done her level best to be pleasant and entertaining into the bargain, to be stood in front of a daub like this and expected to admire it was really too much. In addition to this, both Cecil and Marjorie had a note of patronage in their voices which she found insufferable. All very fine for them to be patronizing when they were living entirely on her money, or rather Mr. Radcliffe's which was the same thing. All very fine for a strong, healthy young man of Cecil's age to fritter his time away painting these nonsensical pictures when he ought to be in some steady job shouldering his responsibilities and supporting his wife in the luxury to which she had been accustomed. All very fine to allude to Lady Bethel as an "old girl" and a "darling" in that casual intimate manner and boast that she was going to lend her house for an exhibition of Cecil's paintings. If Lady Bethel considered that that sort of nonsense was worthy of being exhibited she must be nothing short of an imbecile. In any case, she strongly doubted that Lady Bethel had promised any such thing. She recalled the swift look that had passed between Cecil and Marjorie before lunch, and the rather overdone nonchalance of Cecil's tone. The whole thing was nothing but a lie in order to impress her. The suspicion of this, which had lain dormant at the back of her mind throughout the whole of lunch, suddenly became a conviction. Of course that was what it was. A deliberate lie calculated to put her in the wrong, to make her feel that her criticisms of Cecil's painting in the past had been unjust, and to try to deceive her into the belief that he was appreciated and understood by people who really knew, whereas all the time he was nothing more nor less than the complete and utter failure he always had been and always would be. Mrs. Radcliffe decided to speak her mind.

"Cecil," she said in an ominous voice, "I have something to say to you that I have been wishing to say for some time past."

The smile faded from Cecil's face, and Marjorie walked across purposefully and slipped her arm through his.

"Fire away, Marm," he said with a certain bravado, but she saw him stiffen slightly.

"I want to suggest," went on Mrs. Radcliffe, "that you give up this absurd painting business once and for all and find some sort of job that will bring you in a steady income—"

"Give up his painting, mother, you must be mad!" said Marjorie angrily.

Cecil patted her arm. "Shut up, darling," he said.

Mrs. Radcliffe ignored the interruption and continued: "I have talked the matter over with my husband." This was untrue, but she felt that it solidified her position. "And we are both in complete agreement that it is nothing short of degrading that a young man of your age should be content to live indefinitely on his wife's money."

There was dead silence for a moment. Mrs. Radcliffe's face was flushed and the corners of Cecil's mouth twitched.

"I'm sure father said no such thing," said Marjorie.

"Kindly let me speak, Marjorie." Mrs. Radcliffe looked at her daughter coldly.

"I think, Marm," interposed Cecil, "that anything more you said might be redundant."

"Nevertheless," went on Mrs. Radcliffe, "I would like to say this—"

Marjorie broke away from Cecil and came close to her mother. Her face was white with anger. "You will not say another word," she said. "You will go away now out of this house and you will never set foot in it again!"

Mrs. Radcliffe fell back a step, genuinely horrified at the passionate fury in her daughter's face. "Marjorie!"

"I mean it," Marjorie was clenching and unclenching her hands. Cecil stepped forward and put his arm around her, but she shook him off.

"No, Cecil, this is between mother and me. She says that for a long time she's been wishing to say those cruel, insulting things to you. Well, I've been waiting a longer time to say a few things to her. I've been waiting all my life and now I'm going to—"

"Darling!" Cecil put his arm round her again and this time held her. He spoke gently, but with an unaccustomed note of sternness. "For God's sake don't. It won't do any good, really it won't, and you'll only regret it afterward. Whatever you said she'd never understand, never in a thousand years."

Marjorie looked up at his face and he gave a little smile, her lip trembled. "All right," she said in a low voice. "You needn't hang on to me, I won't do anything awful—"

He let her go and she went quickly over to the window and stood with her back turned looking out on to the narrow stretch of garden that separated their house from the house next door. For a moment, while he had been talking, something had pierced Mrs. Radcliffe. She was shocked, outraged, angry; all that her affronted pride demanded her to be, but in addition to this, for a brief instant, the flash of a second, she had been aware of a sharp, overwhelming sense of loneliness. It passed as swiftly as it had come and she was secure again, secure in righteous indignation, wounded as only a mother can be wounded by her daughter's base ingratitude. She closed her lips in a tight line and surveyed Cecil and Marjorie and the studio and everything in it with an expression of withering contempt. Cecil put his hand under her elbow and piloted her to the door. "I think it's time we put an end to this distressing scene," he said. "Come along, Marm, I'll see you to the front door."

They walked through the yard and in through the French windows of the dining room without a word. She collected her bag and fur from the sofa in the drawing room.

"Shall I telephone for a taxi?" he asked.

"Thank you no," she replied with frigid politeness. "I prefer to walk."

He held the front door open for her and she descended into the street. A child bowling an iron hoop nearly cannoned into her. She drew aside as an Empress might draw aside from some unmentionable offal in her path and, with a barely perceptible nod to Cecil, walked away.

When Cecil got back into the studio Marjorie was smoking a cigarette. She looked swiftly at him as he came in the door and noted, with a little tug at her heartstrings, that his face was white and drawn.

"Sorry, darling," she said as lightly as she could.

He looked at his unfinished picture for a moment and then flung himself on to the divan. "Well!" He spoke in a taut, strained voice. "That was highly instructive, I must say."

"Mother's a very stupid woman." Marjorie said perfectly evenly, there was no anger in her anymore. "She doesn't know anything about anything. The fact that we're happy together infuriates her."

"Are we!" said Cecil.

"Oh, Cecil!" Marjorie's eyes filled with tears and she turned away. "How can you be such a bloody fool!"

"There's a certain element of truth in what she says," went on Cecil, intent on masochism. "After all, I do live on your money, don't I?"

"And why in the name of God shouldn't you?" Marjorie flared. "What's money got to do with it? We love each other and trust each other, isn't that enough?"

"It would be nicer though," he said with fine sarcasm, "if *somebody* apart from you and Bobbie Schulter thought I was a good painter! It would be nicer, really a great deal nicer, if I could sell just one Goddamned picture occasionally."

"Oh, darling!" Marjorie came over and sat by him on the divan. "Please, please don't go on like that. It's absolutely idiotic and you know it as well as I do. It hurts me terribly when you lash out and say bitter, foolish things that I know in my heart that you don't really mean. Look at me—please look at me and snap out of it."

Cecil looked at her and made a gallant effort to smile. It wasn't entirely successful, but it was the best he could do. Marjorie flung both her arms round him and drew his head down onto her shoulder. She stroked his hair gently and he wouldn't have known she was crying if a tear hadn't happened to drop on to his neck.

8

Mrs. Radcliffe's blood was boiling and continued to boil through several quiet squares and streets until she turned into Brompton Road. Here she stopped for a moment and consulted her watch which hung from a little gold chain on her bosom. The watch said twenty minutes past two. Marion was meeting her in the piano department at Harrods at half-past, not that either she or Marion intended to buy a piano, but it was as good a place to meet as anywhere else and less crowded. It would never do for Marion to suspect that her blood was boiling, because she would inevitably ask why, and Mrs. Radcliffe would have either to tell her or invent a convincing lie, neither of which she felt inclined to do. She sauntered very slowly toward Harrods in order to give herself time to deal efficiently with her unruly emotions. It was no use pretending one way or the other, she reflected. Marjorie was no daughter of hers. This, of course, was rhetorical rather than accurate, her memories of the pain and indignity of Marjorie's arrival, even after thirty years, were still clear, but still the fact of disowning Marjorie in her mind, of denying her very existence in relation to herself, somehow reassured her. Mrs. Radcliffe searched in vain through the past to find one occasion on which Marjorie had proved to be anything but a disappointment. Even as a child she had been unresponsive and sometimes actually belligerent. She recalled, still with a blush of shame, the dreadful tea party when Marjorie, aged four, had spat a whole mouthful of Madeira cake at poor kind old Mrs. Woodwell, who had bent down to kiss her. She recalled how a few years later she had, quite unnecessarily, been sick over the edge of the dress circle during a matinée of *Peter Pan*. She remembered the countless times during adolescence that she had been rebellious, sly, untruthful and sulky. Heaven knew it had been explained to her often enough and with the utmost patience and kindness that an only daughter's primary duty was to be a comfort and support to her mother, and a fat lot of good it had done. Marjorie had never been even remotely a comfort to her mother. On the contrary she had been a constant source of grief and pain to her ever since she was born. Then, of course, the secretiveness and cruelty of running off and marrying Cecil without a word of warning, turning her back on her parents and her home and all the love and affection of years without a regret, without a shred of gratitude. No, Marjorie was certainly no daughter of hers. Much better to face the truth fair and square. The reconciliation a year after the marriage had been a great mistake, she realized that now; in any case, the miscarriage and illness and everything had probably been greatly exaggerated in order to play upon her sympathy and get the allowance renewed. There was no love in Marjorie, no gentleness, no affection. That was what was so heartbreaking. If she had been merely self-willed and obstinate. If she had done all she had done and yet betrayed at moments just a scrap of sweetness and understanding, an indication that there was just a little soft womanliness in her character somewhere, then Mrs. Radcliffe would have forgiven her and stood by her and done everything she could to mitigate the disastrous mess she had made of her life, but no, there was no love in Marjorie, not a speck of softness, she was as hard as nails. Better to cut the knot once and for all rather than compromise, rather than humiliate her spirit by making any further bids for a love and affection that, she knew now, had never existed and never could exist, and proceed in pride and loneliness to the grave. Mrs. Radcliffe stopped by a confectioner's at the corner of Ovington Street and wiped away a tear, then she blew her nose and proceeded in pride and loneliness to Harrods.

Marion was dutifully waiting in the cathedral quiet of the piano department. She was the type of woman who is always a little too early for everything, not from any pronounced sense of punctuality so much as an innate determination not to miss a moment. Life to Marion was a glorious adventure. Her zest for enjoyment even after fifty-seven years of strict virginity was unimpaired. She had a small income bequeathed by her father, who had been a colonel in the Indian Army, the top part of a house in Onslow Gardens, a collection of theater programs dating back to eighteen ninety-eight, and a parrot called Rajah, upon which she lavished a great deal of brusque affection. She smoked incessantly and belonged to a small ladies' club in Dover Street which was rather dull, but useful to pop into from time to time and write letters. Her friendship with Mrs. Radcliffe went back to their schooldays and was based on romance. Adela Radcliffe, Adela Wyecroft as she had been then, had captained the lacrosse team and had been revered and adored by most of the school and by Marion Kershaw most of all. She still possessed a snapshot of Adela taken when she was sixteen, standing against a background of fierce waves, wearing a small boater, a white dress with high, puffed sleeves and holding an anchor. It was a striking photograph and although the dust of ages lay over the tears that Marion had once shed over it, she cherished it with a certain merry nostalgia.

Adela's attitude to Marion had been then, and was still, one of affectionate tolerance, not entirely free from patronage. In her opinion, Marion was a good sort, but rather a fool and definitely unstable emotionally. She could have married quite well if she had only concentrated a little more. Mrs. Radcliffe could remember several occasions when a little common sense and proper management could have achieved the altar; that young Critchley boy for instance, he had been quite keen on her, and even Admiral Mortimer's son, although on the whole it was just as well she hadn't married him as he had had to be sent out of the Navy for something or other when he was twenty-four. But Marion was hopeless. She was always getting these wild enthusiasms for people and then dropping them like hot cakes. Look at that Sylvia Bale! A tiresome whining creature if ever there was one. Marion had gone on about how wonderful she was in the most ridiculous way and even went so far as to share a flat with her but not for long. Mrs. Radcliffe remembered how she had chuckled inwardly when Marion, trembling with rage, had recounted to her the beastly behavior of Sylvia Bale. Mrs. Radcliffe had refrained from saying "I told you so," she was not one to rub it in, but she certainly had known all along and warned her into the bargain.

Today, Marion was at her most exuberant. She was wearing a tailor-made, none too well cut, a white blouse with rather an arty-looking colored scarf tied in a knot in front and one of those newfangled hats perched much too far forward. She was smoking, needless to say. Mrs. Radcliffe was aware of the strong smell of tobacco as she kissed her. Marion, who had nearly finished her cigarette, couldn't find anywhere to crush it out and so before anything could be discussed at all they had to wander about among the Steinways in search of an ashtray. This was typical of Marion. Finally, of course, she had to stamp it out on the carpet and one of the assistants gave her a most disagreeable look.

Marion was full of conversation. She hadn't seen Adela for ages, but not for *ages!* and there was really so much to tell her that she couldn't think where to begin. Mrs. Radcliffe was really rather grateful for this volubility, for although by now she had regained complete command of herself and had contrived, at God alone knew what cost to her nerves, to present an outward mien as unruffled and tranquil as usual, the fact remained, she was still upset. However strong in character you may be, however bitterly you may have learned through sad experience to discipline yourself to withstand the cruel bludgeonings of Chance, you are after all but human. And Mrs. Radcliffe felt, in justice to herself, that in view of all she had recently gone through, to say nothing of the courage with which she had faced to the full the whole agonizing tragedy of the situation, she might be forgiven a little inward weakness, a little drooping of the spirit. There were not many others, she reflected, who were capable of cutting their only child out of their hearts at one blow and go out shopping with Marion as though nothing had happened.

Marion, unaware of the abyss of suffering so close to her, continued to chatter like a magpie. "You'd never believe it," she said. "But I did the most idiotic thing the other night. I'd been to the Old Vic with Deidre Waters, you remember Deidre Waters, she married Harry Waters and then he left her and now they're divorced and she's living with Nora Vines and they're doing those designs for textiles, some of them are damned good too, I can tell you. Well, Deidre arrived to call for me and kept the taxi waiting, fortunately, I was ready, but she rushed me out of the house so quickly that I forgot to take my latchkey out of my other bag. Well, my dear, of course I didn't think a thing about it, it never even crossed my mind, how I could have been such a fool I can't think and, of course, when I got home there I was! Can you imagine? Thank Heaven it wasn't raining but it was bitterly cold and I was in evening dress with only that Chinese coat between me and the elements." She laughed hilariously and went on. "Well, I really was in the most awful state, I couldn't think *what* to do. I knew it wouldn't be any use banging on Mrs. Bainbridge's window, she has the downstairs part you know, for even if I could have climbed across the area railings and reached it she'd never have heard, she's deaf as a post and sleeps at the back anyway. I was absolutely flummoxed. I looked up and down the street and there wasn't a soul in sight and then I walked to the corner to see if I could see a policeman. Of course I couldn't, you can never find one when you want one. I was in despair. I could have gone to the Club of course, but it would have meant waking up the night porter and I hadn't any night-things or anything and anyhow there probably wouldn't have been a room, it's awfully small you know. Then I thought of Deidre and Nora, but you can't swing a cat in their flat and the vision of spending the night on their sofa didn't appeal to me very much I can tell you."

She paused for breath as they turned into the scent department. "Well—just as I was about to just sit down on the pavement and cry I saw a man, quite a youngish-looking man in a silk hat! I rushed up to him and I must say he looked horrified, but *horrified;* I daren't imagine what he must have thought but I explained and he was absolutely charming. He walked back with me to the house and my dear, would you believe it? He noticed something that I hadn't noticed at all. Mrs. Bainbridge's window was open a little bit at the top! Well, what did he do but take off his coat and hat and put them on the top step and then climb over the railings and break into the house. I was terrified of course that old Mother Bainbridge would think it was a burglar and have a stroke or something but I couldn't help laughing. In a minute or two—I was shivering by this time as you can imagine—I saw the light go up in the hall and he opened the front door and let me in. Of course I asked him to come up and have a whiskey and soda but he refused; then I helped him on with his coat and hat and off he went! There now. Wasn't that fantastic? I mean the luck of him just coming along at that moment. I couldn't get over it honestly I couldn't. All the time I was undressing and going to bed I kept on saying to myself: 'Well, really!'" The recital might have continued even longer if Mrs. Radcliffe had not interrupted it by demanding of an assistant the price of a bottle of Elizabeth Arden vanishing cream. She had paid scant attention to what Marion had been saying, her thoughts being elsewhere. Even if Marion had known this it is doubtful whether she would have minded much. Talking, with

Marion, was an automatic process like breathing. She didn't talk to inform, or to entertain, or to be answered. She just talked.

They visited several departments and made several minor purchases, Mrs. Radcliffe leading the way, dignified and decisive, with Marion in full spate, yapping at her heels. When finally they emerged into the warm spring sunshine Mrs. Radcliffe was feeling distinctly better. The business of pricing things and buying things had occupied her mind and soothed her. Marion of course was still talking—"And when he walked up to the cage," she was saying, "Rajah put his head on one side and gave him a look and, my dear, if looks could kill that one would have! Needless to say I was *terrified!* You see he's always perfectly all right with women and of course he adores me but he hates *men.* Parrots are like that, you know, always much more affectionate with the opposite sex to what they are themselves; it is extraordinary, isn't it? I mean how sex instincts come out even in birds. Not of course that I ever look on Rajah as a bird, he's a person and a very definite person at that I can tell you. Well, my dear, poor Mr. Townsend said 'Poll, Pretty Poll,' or something and put his finger between the bars of the cage if you please. I gave a little scream. 'Oh, do be careful, Mr. Townsend,' I said. 'He takes a lot of knowing, he does really.' 'I'm used to parrots,' said Mr. Townsend, 'we had one at Epsom for years.' The Townsends live at Epsom you know, and my dear as he said it, before the words were out of his mouth Rajah bit his finger through to the bone! Now can you imagine?" Marion paused dramatically, this time evidently demanding some sort of response. Mrs. Radcliffe looked at her absently and with an effort wrenched her mind from wondering whether it would be better to do Swan and Edgar's now or leave it until another day.

"How dreadful," she said.

"I didn't know what to do—" Marion was off again having used Mrs. Radcliffe's perfunctory comment as a sort of springboard. Mrs. Radcliffe, still undecided, led the way up Knightsbridge toward Hyde Park Corner. Perhaps on the whole it would be wiser to leave Swan and Edgar's until next week. She felt she really couldn't face the exertion of getting into a crowded bus and going all that way. The most sensible thing to do would be to have a cup of tea somewhere. Just as they were crossing Sloane Street Marion broke off in the middle of a description of Mr. Townsend's obstinate refusal to allow her to telephone for a doctor. "Adela," she cried, "I'd nearly forgotten. I'd promised to go to Maud Fearnley's shop just for a minute, it's only a few doors down and she'd so love it if you came too. She's the one I told you about you know, whose husband was killed in that motor accident, not that she cared for him very much, but he left her without a penny and so she started this hat shop. I do think people are awfully plucky, don't you? I mean it takes a lot of grit to do a thing like that. Anyway she calls herself 'Yolande et Cie' and gets a lot of the newest models from Paris, at least, between you and me, I believe what she really does is to pop over there from time to time and just copy the models but for heaven's sake don't say I said so. She's a very old friend of mine and she really is having a terribly uphill struggle. Do come, she'd be so thrilled!"

Mrs. Radcliffe hesitated for a moment and then, swayed by the thought of the obvious pleasure she would be bestowing upon Yolande et Cie by visiting her shop and also by the reflection that if Yolande et Cie was having such an uphill struggle as all that she wasn't likely to be very expensive and it might be possible to find a smart new hat at a lower price than elsewhere, she consented benevolently and they turned down Sloane Street.

Maud Fearnley was a vague, faded woman in the early forties. Marion's enthusiastic allusion to pluck and spirit and her picture of her as a shrewd, capable businesswoman dashing back and forth between Paris and London, gallantly fighting step by step to conquer misfortune, was unhappily a trifle inaccurate. True she had been left penniless by the death of her husband and, bolstered up by the energy and financial support of a few strong-minded friends, she certainly had taken over the lease and "goodwill" of Yolande et Cie, but for all that Maud Fearnley was not the stuff of which conquerors are made. She was a drifter. She had drifted into marriage, drifted into widowhood, and now she had drifted into a milliner's shop in Sloane Street. On the one occasion when she had happened to drift over to Paris, the results, commercially speaking, had been so far from successful that her friends had implored her never to do it again.

She rose from a small desk when Mrs. Radcliffe and Marion entered the shop and advanced toward them with the incredulous smile of a lonely traveler who unexpectedly happens upon two old school friends in a jungle clearing. She embraced Marion gratefully and was introduced to Mrs. Radcliffe. Mrs. Radcliffe sized her up at a glance. Her quick eye noted the dejected beige dress, the blue knitted wool jacket slung round the shoulders with the sleeves hanging, the mouse-colored hair and the amiable, rather silly expression. The woman's a fool she decided immediately, probably another of Marion's ridiculous enthusiasms, likely as not they had both planned this casual visit to the shop in order to get her to spend some money. Mrs. Radcliffe, in common with a great many other women of her social position, cherished a firm belief that there existed a sort of tacit conspiracy among those not as comfortably situated as herself to get at her money. This was not meanness on her part, she knew herself to be generous to a fault, it was merely a resigned acceptance of the frailties of human nature. No one could accuse her of being disillusioned. She was an idealist first and last, but in her wide and varied experience of life she had been forced to admit that if you allowed people to suspect that you had an assured income it was often liable to bring out the worst in them. One of her complaints against Marion had always been that she never, if she could possibly help it, made the slightest gesture toward paying for anything. Not that she would have permitted her to for a moment, she was perfectly aware of her financial situation and anyhow to be paid for by Marion would have been somehow incongruous, as well imagine a bird of paradise being entertained by a woodpecker. No, it wasn't that she wished Marion to pay for a thing but if she just occasionally made the effort she would have respected her a good deal more. Now in this dim little shop, its whole atmosphere charged with genteel failure, Mrs. Radcliffe scented danger. Mrs. Fearnley's greeting of Marion had been a little too surprised, a tiny bit overdone. The whole thing had probably been arranged over the telephone that morning. To do Marion and Mrs. Fearnley justice it is only fair to say that Mrs. Radcliffe's suspicions on this occasion were unfounded. Mrs. Fearnley had been quite genuinely surprised to see them come into the shop; in fact, poor thing, she was always surprised if anyone came in, and one of her fundamental weaknesses as a saleswoman was her inability to control it. She betrayed too desperate an eagerness, too flagrant an anxiety to please her infrequent customers. She wooed them and fawned upon them to such an extent that they sometimes left the shop in extreme embarrassment without buying a thing. Today, confronted by the majesty of Mrs. Radcliffe, she could hardly contain herself. She gave a series of little gasps and cries of pleasure and one of pain when she happened to pinch her finger in the sliding glass door of one of the showcases. She showed Mrs. Radcliffe several hats, offering them to her with the despairing subservience of a beggar displaying the stump of an amputated arm and imploring charity. Marion kept up a running fire of comment on each model as it appeared—"There," she said, "isn't that sweet?"—"Ah, now that one I really *do* like." "Look, Adela, at the way that's turned up at the back! Isn't that the smartest thing you've ever seen?" Mrs. Radcliffe looked at them all but without enthusiasm. She even agreed to try two or three on after a lot of coaxing from both Mrs. Fearnley and Marion. They both fluttered about behind her as she stood in front of the glass, heading this way and that and regarding her ecstatically from all angles. Finally she discovered one that really wasn't so bad. It was perfectly plain, which was more than could be said for most of the others, made of black straw with just one greenish-blue quill in it. It really was quite stylish. Mrs. Radcliffe tried it on twice and then returned to it and tried it on once more. She revolved slowly before the mirror holding a hand glass and scrutinizing it from the back and from both sides. It certainly suited her, there was no doubt about that. The excitement of Mrs. Fearnley and Marion rose to fever pitch. At last she turned to Mrs. Fearnley.

"How much is it?" she asked.

Mrs. Fearnley was foolish enough to shoot a triumphant look at Marion.

"Four guineas," she said self-consciously.

"Four guineas!" Mrs. Radcliffe stared at her as though she had gone out of her mind. "Four guineas—for this!"

"It's my very latest model," said Mrs. Fearnley. "It came over from Paris only last week by airplane."

Mrs. Radcliffe took it off with a gesture that implied that it could circumnavigate the globe by airplane for all she cared and still not be worth four guineas.

"I'm afraid that's far beyond my poor resources!" she said with a cold smile.

"Oh, Adela!" wailed Marion. "It suits you down to the ground."

"I would be willing to make a slight reduction," ventured Mrs. Fearnley.

"I fear that it would have to be a great deal more than a *slight* reduction to satisfy me," said Mrs. Radcliffe with an acid note in her voice. She had not failed to note Mrs. Fearnley's exultant look at Marion before she had quoted the price and it had annoyed her profoundly. It was just as she suspected, nothing more nor less than a put-up job, she wouldn't be at all surprised if this Mrs. Fearnley hadn't agreed to pay Marion a commission. A nice state of affairs when you couldn't even trust your oldest friends. It really was too disheartening the way people behaved, always on the make; it was degrading. But they would find to their cost that it was not so easy to swindle her as they thought. She looked Mrs. Fearnley steadily in the eye. "To ask four guineas for that hat, Mrs. Fearnley," she said, "is nothing short of outrageous. You know as well as I do that it isn't worth a penny more than a guinea if that!"

Mrs. Fearnley, quailing before this onslaught, was about to speak when Marion forestalled her. Marion's face was quite pink and she look furious.

"Really, Adela," she said, "I don't think there's any necessity to talk to Mrs. Fearnley like that."

"I resent being swindled," said Mrs. Radcliffe picking up her own hat and putting it on carefully in front of the glass.

"Oh, Mrs. Radcliffe," Mrs. Fearnley burst out in horror, "how *can* you say such a thing. I'm sure I never—"

"Well, really," exclaimed Marion, "I never heard of such a thing, honestly I didn't, never in all my life. Adela, you should be ashamed of yourself, honestly you should. I mean—you can't behave like that, really you can't—"

Mrs. Radcliffe looked at her crushingly. "Don't talk to me like that, Marion," she said. "And don't imagine that I can't read you like an open book because I can. I know perfectly well why you're in such a state. I'm not quite such a fool as you and your friend seem to think I am. I should be interested to know how much commission you expected to receive if I had been stupid enough to pay four guineas for this, this monstrosity." There now, it was out, she had said it and a good job too. She looked coolly at Marion in the shocked silence that ensued and was gratified to observe that her eyes were filling with tears. Serve her right, that would teach her not to take advantage of a generous lifelong friendship.

Marion, making a tremendous effort not to cry, spoke with dignity. "If it was your intention to hurt me," she said, "you have succeeded beyond your wildest dreams. I am very sorry you said what you did, Adela, more sorry than I can say . . . "

"I must say," interposed Mrs. Fearnley, gaining a sort of bleak courage from Marion's obvious distress, "I have never been so insulted in all my life, never," she said bridling. "If it were not for the fact that you are a friend of dear Marion's, I should be forced to ask you to leave my shop."

"I have no wish to stay," said Mrs. Radcliffe with hauteur, "and I shall certainly never set foot in it again, nor, I assure you, will any of my friends." She glanced at Marion. "I mean naturally my real friends," she added. "Good afternoon."

Mrs. Fearnley and Marion watched the door swing shut behind her and her stately figure pace along by the window and disappear from view; then Marion gave up to the tears she had been so gallantly trying to restrain and sank down onto a small gilt chair with her face buried in her hands.

"Oh dear," she wept. "Oh dear, oh dear—how dreadful—how absolutely dreadful."

Mrs. Fearnley placed her arms around her for a moment and patted her sympathetically and then, with commendable tact, left her to have her cry out while she put the offending hat back into the showcase.

9

Those who knew Mrs. Radcliffe only slightly would have been surprised, whereas those who knew her well would have been downright amazed had they chanced to be strolling through Hyde Park between the hours of four o'clock and six o'clock and observed her sitting on a seat, not even a twopenny green chair, but a seat, alone! Their amazement would have been justifiable because with all her failings, and after all Mrs. Radcliffe was not perfect, she was no loiterer. One could imagine other people, Mrs. Weecock for instance or even, on occasion, the redoubtable Mrs. Poindexter, idling away an hour or so, but Mrs. Radcliffe, never. Hers was far too energetic and decisive a character for it to be conceivable that, in the admirable organization of her days, she should have an hour to spare. But there she was, sitting alone, leaning a trifle against the back of the seat, with her hands folded on her lap. She had taken off her glasses for a moment and on each side of the bridge of her nose there was a little pink line. Before her, in the mellow afternoon light, the unending pageant of London life passed by. Nurses with perambulators and straggling children; dim-looking gentlemen in bowler hats; a few soldiers arrogant in their uniforms; neatly dressed young women of uncertain profession; various representatives of the lower orders, their children making a great deal more noise than those of higher birth; occasionally somebody's paid companion walking along meekly with a dog, all parading before her weary eyes. In Knightsbridge the constant procession of taxis, private cars, lorries, bicycles and buses provided a soothing orchestration to the scene while every now and then a common London sparrow flew down from the trees and chirruped shrilly quite close to her.

Mrs. Radcliffe however was aware of all this only subconsciously, her conscious mind being occupied, to the exclusion of everything else, with the cruelty and ingratitude of human behavior. What a day! What a disillusioning day she had had, beset on all sides by ignorance, stupidity, defiance, deceit, rudeness and, in the case of Marion and Mrs. Fearnley, sheer treachery. Why, she wondered without anger—she was no longer angry—why should all this be visited on her? What had she done to deserve it? She put on her glasses and looked up at the sky, beyond which her indestructible faith envisaged a kindly God, in the vague hope that she might receive some miraculous sign, some indication of where she had erred to merit such harsh treatment. Perhaps, it was just within the bounds of possibility, she had unwittingly committed some trifling sin, some thoughtless act of omission which had brought down this avalanche of suffering upon her. She scanned the heavens humbly, supplicatingly, but no sign was forthcoming. True there was an airplane flying high over in the direction of Westminster Abbey, and for a moment the light of the sun caught it so that it shone like burnished silver before disappearing behind a cloud, but that could hardly be construed as a sort of reassuring wink from the Almighty. She lowered her eyes again. It was, she reflected without bitterness, inevitable that a woman of her temperament should feel things more keenly, with more poignance than ordinary people. It was one of the penalties of being highly strung. After all, that awareness of beauty, that unique sensitiveness to the finer things of life, had to be paid for. Everything had to be paid for. Your capacity for joy was inexorably balanced by your capacity for sorrow. Other people, such as Stanley for instance, just exIsted. Stanley really couldn't be said to live, really live, for a moment. Sometimes, she gave a wry smile, she almost envied him. No ups and downs for Stanley. No ecstasies, no despairs. Just an even, colorless monotony from the cradle to the grave. How extraordinary to be like that and, in some ways, how fortunate. Here she gave herself a little shake, she was becoming morbid. It was surely better to live life to the full and to pay the price, however high it might be, than to be a drone without punishment and without reward.

At this rather more comforting stage of her reflections her attention was diverted by a handsome, well-dressed woman in the middle forties and a distinguished gray-haired man in a silk hat and frock coat, who sat down on a seat almost immediately opposite her. They were unmistakably of high breeding, possibly even titled. They were talking with animation and every now and then, obviously in response to something amusing he had said, she gave a pleasant laugh. Mrs. Radcliffe looked at them with great interest. They had probably been to some grand social function, a reception perhaps or a wedding, although it was a little late for it to have been a wedding. The woman's face seemed familiar to her somehow, she racked her brains for a minute and then suddenly remembered, of course, it was Lady Elizabeth Vale, *The* Lady Elizabeth Vale, she was almost certain it was. Mrs. Radcliffe made no effort to repress a feeling of rising excitement. Lady Elizabeth Vale was one of the most famous women in London society, or in fact any society. An intimate friend of royalty and the wife of one of the most brilliant of the younger Cabinet Ministers, she was well known to combine impeccable breeding with considerable wealth. She was much photographed and she traveled extensively. Her moral reputation was as untarnished as could be expected with such a glare of limelight beating upon her. Her most ordinary activities received the closest attention in the gossip columns but so far no definite hint of scandal had stained her name. It was possible that even if it had Mrs. Radcliffe would have forgiven it. People of the social position of Lady Elizabeth Vale could demand from Mrs. Radcliffe, should they so wish, an inexhaustible meed of Tolerance and Christian Charity. As she sat there watching the couple out of the corner of her eye, she indulged in a few fleeting fancies. That capacity for reverie so soothing to the bruised ego was strongly developed in Mrs. Radcliffe. She often admonished herself with a lenient smile. "There you go," she'd say, "dreaming again!"

Today, possibly owing to the disillusionment she had suffered, her imagination was especially vivid. The real world was too pitiless, too sharply cruel. Was it not natural enough that she should seek refuge for a while in the rich gardens of her mind? She gave fantasy full rein. How pleasant it would be for instance if Fate, in the guise of some minor accident such as a child falling down and having to be picked up, should enable her to establish a friendship with Lady Elizabeth Vale. It would of course begin quite casually. "There dear, don't cry." "Poor little thing, I wonder where its mother is." Something quite simple and ordinary like that. Then, the child disposed of somehow or other, a little desultory conversation during which Lady Elizabeth would swiftly recognize what a charming, delightful creature Mrs. Radcliffe was and, with one of those graceful impulses that were so typical, invite her to tea! Mrs. Radcliffe saw herself clearly ensconced in a luxurious drawing room in Belgrave Square; discreet footmen hovering about with delicacies; the light from the fire gleaming on priceless old family silver; the conversation cozy and intimate—

"Dear Mrs. Radcliffe, I know you'll think it fearfully unconventional of me on the strength of such a short acquaintance, but I would so like it if you would call me Elizabeth, Lady Elizabeth sounds so stuffy somehow between friends and I'm sure we're going to be real friends, I felt it at once, the moment I saw you—" Here Mrs. Radcliffe paused for a moment in her flight to ponder the likelihood of it being "Elizabeth" or "Betty." "My dear Elizabeth." "My dear Betty." Betty won. "My dear Betty, of course I should be charmed, and you must call me Adela." Her mind jumped to a bridge party at Mrs. Poindexter's which she had accepted for next Wednesday. "I'm so sorry, I can't start another rubber, really I can't. I must fly home and dress, I'm dining with Betty Vale and going to the Opera—"

At this point her attention was dragged back to reality by the consciousness that a figure was standing close to her. She looked up and saw the most dreadful old woman. Mrs. Radcliffe positively jumped. The old woman was wearing a threadbare jacket, a skirt literally in rags, gaping boots and a man's old straw hat from under which straggled wisps of greasy white hair. Her face was gray and her eyes red-rimmed and watery. "Please lady," she murmured hoarsely, "spare us a copper, I 'aven't 'ad a bite to eat all day, honest I 'aven't." Mrs. Radcliffe's first instinct naturally was to tell her to go away at once. These beggars were everywhere nowadays, it was really disgraceful. She glanced round to see if there were a policeman in sight and in doing so observed Lady Elizabeth Vale looking full at her. Automatically, without thinking, like the reflex action of a motorist who suddenly swerves to avoid a dog that has run out into the road, she plunged her hand into her bag and gave the woman a half-a-crown. The woman looked at it incredulously and then burst into a wail of gratitude. "God bless yer, lady," she cried. "God bless yer kind 'eart"; she wandered away clutching the coin and still mumbling her blessings. Mrs. Radcliffe, with a smile of mingled pity and good-natured tolerance, looked across at Lady Elizabeth Vale for her reward. They would exchange a glance of mutual understanding, a glance expressing a subtle acknowledgment of what had passed, of the bonds of class and distinction that bound them together. That reciprocal glance would imply so much, administer such balm to Mrs. Radcliffe's battered spirit. Unfortunately, however, Lady Elizabeth didn't look at her again, she was immersed in conversation. After a little while she got up, her escort helped her to arrange her sable cape more comfortably round her shoulders and, still talking, they walked away. Mrs. Radcliffe only distinguished a few words as they passed her seat. The man, placing his hand protectively under Lady Elizabeth's elbow said, in an intimate tone of mock exasperation—"My *dear* Elizabeth—"

10

At a quarter to eleven that evening Mrs. Radcliffe went upstairs to bed. The dinner had been a success on the whole, marred only by the clumsiness of Mildred who had banged against Mrs. Duke's chair while proferring her the baked custard and caused the spoon, with a certain amount of custard in it, to fall onto her dress. Stanley had, as usual, not contributed very much, but the Vicar had been splendid, he had kept everyone highly amused with his imitation of Miss Lawrence trying not to sneeze while she was playing the organ at choir practice, and, after dinner, he had sung "Now Sleeps the Crimson Petal," by Roger Quilter, with great charm and feeling. Miss Layton of course had been rather silly, but then she always was, making sheep's eyes at Mr. Baker all the evening and laughing in that affected way, as though he'd ever look twice at a dried-up frump like her. That dress! Mrs. Radcliffe, as she was taking the pins out of her hair, paused for a moment to smile at the memory of Miss Layton's dress. It really was too absurd, a woman of her age, she must be fifty if she was a day, dolling herself up with all those frills and folderols. She'd have been much better advised to wear a plain black frock. Mrs. Radcliffe remembered having whispered this naughtily to Mr. Baker who had been on her left, and smiled again.

Presently Stanley came upstairs, she heard him go into his room on the other side of the landing. Stanley really was a very peculiar man. Fancy asking Miss Layton to play like that the moment the Vicar had sat down, indeed, before Mrs. Duke had even left the piano stool. How unobservant men were. Couldn't he have noticed that the one thing she had been trying to avoid was the possibility of Miss Layton playing. To begin with she had a very heavy touch and no style whatsoever, also she always insisted upon the piano being opened fully which was a great nuisance as it meant taking off the shawl, the vase and the photographs. In any case it was quite obvious that she only wanted to play at all in order to make an impression on Mr. Baker; however, she certainly hadn't succeeded. Mr. Baker had paid very little attention, even when she had embarked upon "The Gollywogs' Cake-Walk" by Debussy with all that banging in the bass, he had only nodded politely and raised his voice a trifle.

Presently Stanley came in to say "Good night." She came out of the bathroom and there he was, fiddling about with the things on her dressing table. Poor Stanley, he was undoubtedly beginning to show his age, she wished he'd learn to stand up a little straighter, stooping like that made him look much older than he really was. If only he had a little more grit, more strength of character. If only he were the sort of man upon whom she could lean occasionally when she felt weary and sick at heart, the sort of man who would put his arms round her and comfort her and bid her be of good cheer. But No; no use expecting any sympathy or demonstrativeness from Stanley. He was utterly wrapped up in himself and always had been. She had contemplated for a moment, while she was dressing for dinner, telling him about Marjorie's behavior, but she had quickly put the thought out of her mind. Stanley always stood up for Marjorie, he would be sure to have twisted the whole thing round into being her fault and then said something sarcastic. He had one of those blind, uncritical adorations for Marjorie that so many elderly fathers have for their only daughters. It was sometimes quite ridiculous the way he went on about her. He even liked Cecil, and said that in his opinion he was a damned intelligent, straightforward young fellow. Straightforward, if you please! Mrs. Radcliffe knew better.

Hearing his wife enter, Mr. Radcliffe stopped fiddling with the things on the dressing table and looked at her. She was in her nightdress and pink quilted silk dressing gown; on her feet were her ostrich feather bedroom slippers, looking a trifle draggled; on her large pale face was a layer of Elizabeth Arden cold cream which made it even paler. Her gray hair was tortured into several large curling pins.

"Stanley," she said. "What a fright you gave me." This was untrue. He hadn't given her a fright at all, she had known perfectly well he was there as she had heard him come in when she was in the bathroom, but still it was something to say.

"Sorry, dear," he replied. "I just came in to say 'good night.'"

Mrs. Radcliffe kissed him absently. "Good night, Stanley." This being said she turned away expecting him to have gone by the time she turned round again, but when she did he was still there, kicking at the edge of the rug with the toe of his shoe. He looked at her again, his forehead was wrinkled, he obviously had something on his mind.

"What's the matter, Stanley?" she asked, a little impatiently.

"I think you were a bit hard on poor Miss Layton tonight," he suddenly blurted out. "Talking to Mr. Baker like that all the time she was playing. She noticed, you know, and it upset her very much. I walked to the corner with her and she was nearly crying."

"Really, Stanley," said Mrs. Radcliffe with extreme exasperation, "you are too idiotic."

"Idiotic I may be," retorted her husband with unwonted spirit, "but you were unkind and that's worse!"

Mrs. Radcliffe opened her mouth to reply, to give full vent to the annoyance he had caused her, not only at this moment, but the whole evening long, but before she could utter a word he had gone out of the room and shut the door, almost slammed it, in her face. She stood quite still for an instant with her eyes closed and her hands tightly clenched at her sides. This was too much. At the end of a dreadful day like she'd had, for Stanley, her own husband, to fly at her and accuse her of being unkind. After a little she moved over to her bed quivering at the injustice of it all. She knelt down automatically to say her prayers, but it was quite a while before she was able to will herself into a suitable frame of mind. Suddenly, like a ray of light in the dark cavern of her unhappiness, the incident of the beggar woman in the park flashed into her memory, and with that all disquiet left her. It was like a miracle. When she had finished her prayers and got into bed she was smiling. Unkind indeed!

NATURE STUDY

The heartiness of Major Cartwright had grown beyond being an acquired attribute of mind and become organic. He exuded it chemically as a horse exudes horsiness; as a matter of fact he exuded a certain amount of horsiness as well. He was large and blond and his skin was brickish in color, the end of his fleshy nose shaded imperceptibly to mauve but not offensively, it blended in with the small purple veins round his eyes which were pale blue and amiable. His best point really was the even gleaming whiteness of his teeth, these he showed a good deal when he laughed, a loud, noninfectious, but frequent laugh.

The barman treated him with deference and he was popular on board owing to his genial efficiency at deck games. In the early morning and later afternoon he played Deck Tennis in saggy khaki shorts, below which he wore neatly rolled stockings and gym shoes and above a rather old blue silk polo shirt opened generously at the neck exposing a few curling fronds of dust-colored hair.

He was at his best in the smoking room after dinner, expanding into "outpost of Empire" reminiscence and calling for "stengahs," a bore really but somehow touching in his fidelity to type. It

153

wasn't until after Marseilles, where most of the cronies had disembarked to go home overland, that he turned his attention to me. We sat together in the little winter garden place aft of the promenade deck and had a drink before dinner. The lights of Marseilles were shimmering on the horizon and there was a feeling of emptiness in the ship as though the party were over and there were only a few stragglers left. The stragglers consisted of about a dozen planters and their families and three or four yellowish young men from the Shell company in Iraq, who had joined the ship at Port Said and were going home on leave.

He talked a lot but slowly and with great emphasis, principally, of course, about himself and his regiment. On the few occasions when he forsook the personal for the general it was merely to let fly a cliché such as "That's women all over," or "A man who has a light hand with a horse has a light hand with anything." I gently interposed "Except with pastry," but he didn't hear. He suggested that he should move over from his now deserted table in the saloon and join me at mine for the rest of the voyage. I was about to spring to my usual defense in such circumstances, which is that I always have to eat alone as I am concentrated on making mental notes for a book or play, but something in his eyes prevented me, they were almost pleading, so I said with as much sincerity as I could muster that nothing would please me more, and that was that.

Our tête-à-têtes for the next few days were, on the whole, not as bad as I feared—he was perfectly content to talk away without demanding too many answers. By the time we reached Gibraltar I knew a great deal about him. He had a wife, but the tropics didn't agree with her so she was at home living with her married sister just outside Newbury, a nice little place they had although the married sister's husband was a bit of a fool, a lawyer of some sort with apparently no initiative.

The major had no doubt that his wife would be damned glad to see him again. He was proposing to take a furnished flat in Town for part of his leave and do a few shows, after that Scotland and some shooting. A friend of his called, for some unexplained reason, "Old Bags," had quite a decent little shoot near a place the name of which the major had as much difficulty in pronouncing as I had in understanding.

I listened to this conversation attentively because I was anxious to discover what, if anything, he had learned from the strange places he had been to, the strange people he had met, the various and varied differences in climate, circumstances, motives and human life that he had encountered. There he sat, slouched back in a big armchair in the smoking room, his large legs stretched out in front of him and a brandy glass in his hand—talking—wandering here and there among his yesterdays without any particular aim and without, alas, the gift of expressing in the least what he really wanted to say and, worse still, without even the consciousness that he wasn't doing so. His limited vocabulary was shamefully overworked—most of his words did the duty of six, like a small orchestra of provincial musicians thinly attempting to play a complicated score by doubling and trebling up on their instruments. I wondered what he knew, actually knew of the facts of life, not complex psychological adjustments and abstractions, they were obviously beyond his ken and also unnecessary to his existence. But any truths, basic truths within his own circumscribed experience. Had he fathomed them or not? Was there any fundamental certainty of anything whatever in that untidy, meager, amiable mind? Were the badly-dressed phrases that he paraded so grandiloquently aware of their shabbiness, their pretentious gentility? Did they know themselves to be illgroomed and obscure, or were they upheld by their own conceit like dowdy British Matrons sniffing contemptuously at a Mannequin Parade?

I tried to visualize him in certain specified situations, crises, earthquakes or shipwrecks, or sudden native uprisings. He would behave well undoubtedly, but why? Could he ever possibly know why? The reason he stood aside to allow the women and children to go first; the exact motive that prompted him to rush out into the compound amid a hail of arrows, brandishing a Service revolver? The impulses that caused his actions, the instincts that pulled him hither and thither, had he any awareness of them, any curiosity about them at all? Was it possible that an adult man in the late forties with a pattern of strange journeys behind him, twenty years at least of potentially rich experience, could have lived through those hours and days and nights, through all those satisfactions, distastes, despondencies and exhilarations without even a trace of introspection or skepticism? Just a bland unthinking acceptance without one query? I looked at him wonderingly, he was describing a duck shoot in Albania at the moment, and decided that not only was it possible but very probable indeed.

After dinner on the night before we arrived at Plymouth he asked me into his cabin to see some of his snapshot albums. "They might interest you," he said in a deprecatory tone which was quite false, as I knew perfectly well that the thought that they might bore me to extinction would never cross his mind. "There's a damn good one of that sailfish I told you about," he went on. "And that little Siamese girl I ran across in K.L. after that Guest Night."

I sat on his bunk and was handed album after album in chronological order, fortunately I was also handed a whiskey and soda. They were all much the same; groups, picnic parties, bathing parties,

155

shoots, fishing parties, all neatly pasted in with names and initials written underneath. "Hong Kong, March 1927. Mrs. H. Cufly, Captain H., Miss Friedlands, Stella, Morgan, W. C." He always indicated his own presence in the group by his initials. I need hardly say that W. C. figured largely in all the albums. He had the traditional passion of his kind for the destruction of life, there was hardly a page that was not adorned with the grinning, morose head of some dismembered animal or fish.

Suddenly, amid all those groups of people I didn't know and was never likely to know, my eye lighted on a face that I recognized. A thin, rather sheeplike face with sparse hair brushed straight back and small eyes that looked as if it were only the narrow high-bridged nose that prevented them from rushing together and merging for ever.

"That," I said, "is Ellsworth Ponsonby."

The major's face lit up. "Do you know old Ponsonby?"

I replied that I had known him on and off for several years. The major seemed, quite agreeably, stricken by the coincidence.

"Fancy that now!" he said. "Fancy you knowing old Ponsonby." He sat down next to me on the bed and stared over my shoulder at the photograph as though by looking at it from the same angle he could find some explanation of the extraordinary coincidence of my knowing old Ponsonby. Old Ponsonby in the snapshot was sitting in the stern sheets of a small motorboat. Behind him was the rich, mountainous coastline of the Island of Java, on either side of him were two good-looking young men, one fair and one dark and both obviously bronzed by the sun. Ellsworth Ponsonby himself, even in those tropical surroundings, contrived to look as pale as usual. The word "old" as applied to him was merely affectionate. He was, I reflected, about forty-three. He was narrow-chested and wearing, in addition to his pince-nez, a striped fisherman's jersey which was several sizes too big for him. The young men were wearing, apparently, nothing at all. I asked who they were, to which the major replied that they were just a couple of pals of old Ponsonby's, quite decent chaps on the whole. They were making a tour of the Islands in Ponsonby's yacht, the noble proportions of which could just be discerned in the right-hand corner of the photograph.

"Never seen such a thing in my life," said the major. "Talk about every modern convenience, that yacht was a floating palace; marble bathrooms to every cabin, a grand piano, a cocktail bar, a French chef—those rich Americans certainly know how to do themselves well. I ran across him first in Batavia—I was taking a couple of months' sick leave—had a touch of Dengue, you know, and thought I'd pay a call on an old pal of mine, Topper Watson—wonder if you know him?—used to be in the Sixth—anyway, he'd been invalided out of the army and had this place in Java, plantation of some sort, quite good shooting and some decent horses, unfortunately married a Javanese girl—quite a nice little woman, but that sort of thing gives one the shudders a bit—not that it was any of my affair, after all a man's life's his own to do what he likes with, still it seemed a pity to see a chap like old Topper on the way to going native."

"Ellsworth," I said wearily. "Ellsworth Ponsonby."

"Oh yes, old Ponsonby." The major gave one of his strong laughs—"Ran up against him in the bar of the Hotel des Indes—got to yarning—you know how one does, and finally he asked me on board this damned yacht of his. By God, I hadn't eaten such a dinner for years, and the brandy he gave us afterward!" Here the major smacked his lips and blew a lumbering kiss into the air. "We sat on deck into the small hours talking."

I wondered if the major had really permitted Ponsonby to do any of the talking. Apparently he had for he heaved a sigh and said, "Damned sad life old Ponsonby's, he had a raw deal."

As that did not entirely fit in with what I knew of Ellsworth I asked in what way he had had such a sad life and such a raw deal.

"Wife left him," replied the major laconically, pursing up his large lips and ejecting a smoke ring with considerable force. "God, but women can be bitches sometimes! Did you ever know her?"

"Yes," I said. "I knew her."

"Ran off with his own chauffeur—can you imagine a decently bred woman doing such a thing? Old Ponsonby didn't say much but you could see it had broken him up completely—women like that ought to be bloody well horsewhipped. He showed me a photograph of her, pretty in rather a flash sort of way, you know, the modern type, flat-chested, no figure at all, not my idea of beauty, but each man to his own taste. After we'd looked at the photograph we went up on deck again—you could see old Ponsonby was in a state, he was trembling and hardly said a word for about ten minutes and then damn it if he didn't start blubbing! I must say I felt sorry for the poor devil, but there was nothing I could say so I poured him out some more brandy and after a bit he pulled himself together. That was when he told me about her running off with the chauffeur—after all he'd given her everything, you know—she was a nobody before she married him. He met her first in Rome—then he took her over to America to meet his people—Boston, I think it was. Then they had a house in London for a couple of seasons and another one in Paris, I believe. Then this awful thing happened." The major wiped his forehead with his handkerchief, it was getting rather stuffy in the cabin. "My God," he said pensively, "I don't know what I'd do if a woman did a thing like that to me—Poor old Ponsonby—" He broke off and was silent for a moment or two, then he turned to me. "But you knew her, didn't you?"

"Yes," I said. "I knew her."

2

Jennifer Hyde was nineteen when she first met Ellsworth Ponsonby in Alassio just after the War. She was staying at the Pension Floriana with her aunt and a couple of girl cousins. Ellsworth was at the Grand Hotel with his mother. Old Mrs. Ponsonby was remarkable more as a monument than a human being. Her white hair was so permanently waved and arranged that it looked like concrete. Her face was a mask of white powder and her eyes were cold and hard. Beneath her chin, which was beginning to sag, she wore a tight black velvet ribbon by day, and at night a dog collar of seed pearls and diamonds. She sat on the terrace of the hotel every morning from eleven until one, lunched, rather resentfully, at a window table in the dining room, retired to her bed regularly from two until four and then took a short drive through the surrounding country. She over-dressed for dinner and played bridge afterward, wearing an expression of thinly disguised exasperation whether she won or lost. Ells-worth sometimes ate with her, drove with her, and played bridge with her. Whenever he did, the look in her eyes softened a trifle and her face relaxed. She watched him greedily, every gesture that he made, when he was shuffling the cards, when he was taking a cigarette from his elaborate Cartier cigarette case and lighting it, whatever he did her eyes were on him sharp and terribly loving. When he was not with her he was usually with Father Robert. They would walk up and down the beach sometimes in the moonlight after dinner, their dark shadows bumping along behind them over the dry sand. Father Robert was plump with fine eyes, a thick, sensual mouth and wide soft hands which moved gently when he talked, not in any way to illus-trate what he was saying, but as though they were living a different, detached life of their own. Jennifer and her girl cousins used to al-lude to him as "The Black Beetle."

Ellsworth had been converted to the Catholic Faith when he was nineteen. Oddly enough his mother had put forward no objec-tions, in some strange intuitive way she probably felt that it would keep Ellsworth close to her, and in this she was right. He had always been emotional as a boy and this Catholic business seemed some-how to calm him, also it was an outlet that he could discuss with her without outraging any proprieties. She had hoped, in her secret heart, that once away from the strong guiding influence of Father Ryan in Boston, he might, amid the interests and excitements of travel, become a little less ardent; this hope, however, was doomed to disappointment, for on arrival in London they had been met by Fa-ther Hill; in Paris by Father Jules; in Lausanne by Father MacMichael; in Rome by Father Philipo; and here, in Alassio, by Father Robert. She had not really minded the other Fathers, in fact Father MacMichael had been quite amusing, but she quite unequivocally detested Father Robert. This was in no way apparent, as her Bostonian upbringing had taught her to control any but her more superficial feelings; however, the hate was there, lying in her heart, vital, alert, and waiting.

Ellsworth, even if he suspected it, showed no sign and continued to enjoy Father Robert's company as much as he could, which was a great deal.

Mrs. Ponsonby first noticed Jennifer in the lounge of the hotel, sitting with a young man in flannels and two nondescript girls. Jennifer looked far from nondescript. She radiated a clear, gay, animal vitality. She was wearing a neat white tennis dress and the ends of her dark hair were damp and curly from bathing. Mrs. Ponsonby watched her for a little, covertly, from behind a novel; quick movements, good teeth and skin, obviously a lady, she smiled a lot and talked eagerly in a pleasant, rather husky voice. When she got up to go on to the terrace with the two girls and the young man, still talking animatedly, Mrs. Ponsonby rose too and went up to her room.

From that moment onward Mrs. Ponsonby proceeded upon a course of stately espionage. Her sources of information were various. Mrs. Wortley, who was a friend of Jennifer's aunt; the English padre Mr. Selton; Giulio, the barman in the hotel, even the floor waiter was questioned discreetly as his wife was a laundress in the town and dealt with the washing from the Pension Floriana.

In a few days she had found out quite a lot. Jennifer was nineteen, the daughter of a doctor in Cornwall, her name was Hyde. She was evidently not well-off as she had traveled out from England second-class, but she apparently had some wealthy relatives in London, had been out for a season and been presented. Mrs. Wortley was quite enthusiastic about her. "A thoroughly nice girl," she said. "Modern in one way and yet old-fashioned at the same time, if you know what I mean. I do think, of course, that it's a pity she puts quite so much red on her lips, but after all I suppose that's the thing nowadays, and one is only young once. I remember myself when I was a girl my one idea was to be smart. I remember getting into the most dreadful hot water for turning one of my afternoon dresses into an evening frock by snipping off the sleeves and altering the front of the bodice—" Here Mrs. Wortley laughed indulgently, but Mrs. Ponsonby had lost interest.

A couple of evenings later on the terrace Mrs. Ponsonby dropped her book just as Jennifer was passing. Jennifer picked it up and returned it to her with a polite smile and, upon being pressed, agreed to sit down and have a glass of lemonade. She talked without shyness but also, Mrs. Ponsonby was pleased to observe, without too much self-possession. Before she left to join her friends who were standing about giggling slightly in the doorway, Mrs. Ponsonby had extracted a promise from her to come to lunch on the following day.

The lunch party was quite a success. At first Mrs. Ponsonby had been rather disconcerted to discover that Ellsworth had invited Father Robert, but it was not very long before she decided in her mind that it had been a good thing. To begin with the presence of Jennifer made Father Robert ill at ease. Mrs. Ponsonby watched with immense satisfaction the corners of his mouth nervously twitching. She also noted that he didn't talk as much as usual. Ellsworth, on the other hand, talked nineteen to the dozen; he was obviously, she observed happily, showing off. The general narrowness of Ellsworth was not so apparent in those days, he was only twenty-six and had a certain soft personal charm when he liked to exert it. On this occasion he was only too keen to exert it. He discussed books and plays wittily with Jennifer, and whenever she laughed at anything he said, he shot rather a smug look at Father Robert. Altogether everything was going very well and Mrs. Ponsonby's spirit purred with pleasure as she watched, with cold eyes, Father Robert's left hand irritably crumbling his bread.

About a week later, during which time Jennifer and Ellsworth had struck up a platonic friendship, Mrs. Ponsonby made her supreme gesture by dying suddenly in the lounge after dinner.

3

Jennifer Ponsonby was, to put it mildly, a reckless gambler, but her gaiety at the tables whether winning or losing was remarkable. She had a series of little superstitions, such as placing one card symmetrically on top of the other and giving the shoe two sharp peremptory little whacks before drawing—if she drew a nine she chuckled delightedly, if she made herself baccarat she chuckled equally delightedly. Her luck, on the whole, was good, but she won gracefully, shrugging her shoulders and giving a little deprecatory smile when anyone failed to win a banco against her.

It was the summer of 1933, and I had stopped off in Monte Carlo on my way home from Tunis. Everybody was there, of course, it was the height of the summer season. The Beach Hotel was full and I was staying at the Hôtel de Paris which, actually, I preferred. Jennifer was staying with old Lily Graziani on Cap Ferrat, but she escaped whenever she could and came over to Monte Carlo to dine and gamble. I played at the same table with her for an hour or two, and then when I had lost all that I intended to lose, I asked her to come and have a drink in the bar while the shoe was being made up.

We perched ourselves on high stools and ordered "Fine à l'eaus" and talked casually enough. She asked me where I'd been and whether or not I'd seen so-and-so. Presently a chasseur appeared and said that her table was starting again. She slipped down from her stool and said, almost defiantly, "You haven't asked after Ellsworth, but you'll be delighted to hear that he's very well indeed," then she gave a sharp little laugh, more high-pitched than usual, and disappeared into the baccarat room.

I felt a trifle embarrassed and also vaguely irritated. I hadn't mentioned Ellsworth on purpose. (A), because it might have been tactless as I hadn't the remotest idea whether they were still together or not; and (b), because I didn't care for him much anyhow, and never had. I ordered another drink and, when I had drunk it, strolled upstairs to watch the cabaret. There was an inferno of noise going on as I came in, the band was playing full out while two American Negroes were dancing a complicated routine in white evening suits and apparently enjoying it. I sat down at a corner table and watched the rest of the show. It was reasonably good. The usual paraphernalia of elaborately undressed beauties parading in and out. The usual low comedy acrobatic act. The usual mournful young woman crooning through the microphone. I glanced round the room occasionally. All the same faces were there. They had been here last year and the year before, and would be here next year and the year after. They changed round a bit, of course. Baby Leyland was with Georgie this year, and Bobbie had a new blonde. The Gruman-Lewis party looked tired and disgruntled, but then they always did. I felt oppressed and bored and far too hot. I watched Jennifer come in with Tiny Matlock. They were hailed by Freda and Gordon Blake and sat down at their table. It was one of the noisier tables. I think Alaistair, who was sitting at the end, must have been doing some of his dirtier imitations, because they were all laughing extravagantly, rather too loudly, I thought, considering the hundreds of times they must have heard them before.

Jennifer laughed with the rest, meanwhile refurbishing her makeup, holding the mirror from her vanity case at one angle in order to catch the light. Her movements were swift and nervous, she stabbed at her mouth with the lipstick and then, holding the glass at arm's length, looked at it through narrowed eyes and made a slight grimace. Suddenly, in that moment, I can't think why, I knew quite definitely that she was wretched. My memory ran back over the years that I had known her, never intimately, never beyond the easy casualness of Christian names, but always, I reflected, with pleasure. She had always been gay company, charming to dance with, fun to discover unexpectedly in a house party. I remembered the first time I had met her in London, it must have been 1920 or 1921, the pretty young wife of a rich American. That was a long time ago, nearly thirteen years, and those years had certainly changed her. I watched her across the room. She was talking now, obviously describing something, gesticulating a little with her right hand. There was a moment's lull in the general noise, and I caught for a second the sound of her husky laugh, quite a different timbre from that which she had given as she left the bar. "You haven't asked after Ellsworth, but you'll be delighted to hear that he's very well indeed."

I decided to walk back to my hotel, rather than take a taxi, the night was cool and quiet after the cigarette smoke and noise of the Casino. I had nearly reached the top of the first hill when I heard a car coming up behind me. It seemed to be coming a great deal too fast, so I stepped warily against the parapet to let it go by. It came whirling round the corner with a screech of brakes, a small open Fiat two-seater. It stopped noisily about a yard away from me and I saw that Jennifer was driving it. "I saw you leaving the Casino and chased you," she said rather breathlessly, "because I wanted to say I was sorry."

I stepped forward. "What on earth for?"

"If you didn't notice so much the better, but I've had a horrid feeling about it ever since I left you in the bar. I tossed my curls at you and spoke harshly, it's no use pretending I didn't because I did, I know I did."

"What nonsense!" I said.

"Get in, there's a darling, and I'll drive you wherever you want to go—where do you want to go? I've got to get to Cap Ferrat."

"Not as far as that anyhow, just the Hôtel de Paris."

I got in and sat down beside her. She let in the clutch and we drove on up into the town. The streets were deserted as it was getting on for three in the morning. Suddenly she stopped the car by the curb in front of a sports shop, the window was filled with tennis rackets, golf clubs and sweaters.

"I'm now going to do something unforgivable," she said in a strained voice. "I've been trying not to for hours, but it's no use." She sat back in the driving seat and looked at me. "I'm going to cry. I hate women who cry, but I can't help it, everything's absolutely bloody, and I know it's none of your business and that this is an imposition, but we've been friends on and off for years and—" Here she broke off and buried her face in her hands. I put my arm round her. "I don't think you'd better be too sympathetic," she muttered into my shoulder. "It'll probably make me worse." Then she started to sob, not hysterically, not even very noisily, but they were painful sobs as though she were fighting them too strongly—

"For God's sake let go!" I said sharply. "If you don't you'll probably burst!"

She gave me a little pat and relaxed a bit. Two or three cars passed, but she kept her head buried against my shoulder. I sat quite still and looked gloomily at the tennis rackets. I felt rather bewildered and quite definitely uncomfortable. Not that I wasn't touched, that out of all the people she knew she should surprisingly have selected me to break down with. My discomfort was caused by a strange feeling of oppression, a similar sensation to that which one experiences sometimes on entering a sad house, a house wherein unhappy, cruel things have taken place. I almost shuddered, but controlled it. Some intuition must have made her feel this, for she sat up and reached her hand behind her for her vanity case. "I am so dreadfully sorry," she said. I smiled as reassuringly as I could and lit a cigarette for her. She wiped her eyes, powdered her nose, took it and sat silently for a little—I noticed her lip tremble occasionally, but she didn't cry anymore. Suddenly she seemed to come to some sort of decision and leant forward and restarted the engine. "I'll drop you home now," she said in a stifled voice which struck me as infinitely pathetic, there was an almost childish gallantry in the way she said it, like a very small boy who has fallen down and broken his knee and is determined to be brave over it.

"You'll do nothing of the sort," I said quickly. "You'll drive me up onto the Middle Corniche and there we'll sit and smoke ourselves silly and watch the sun come up."

She protested: "Honestly, I'm all right now—I swear I am."

"Do what you're told," I said.

She gave the ghost of a smile and off we went.

We stopped just the other side of Eze, left the car parked close in to the side of the wood, having taken the cushions out of it, and arranged ourselves facing the view, with our backs against a low stone wall. Jennifer hardly spoke, and we sat there for quite a long while in silence. Far below us on the right, Cap Ferrat stretched out into the sea like a quiet sleeping animal. Occasionally a train, looking like an elaborate mechanical toy, emerged from a tunnel, ran along by the edge of the sea for a little way and then disappeared again, the lights from its carriage windows striping the trees and rocks and houses as it passed. The rumbling sound of it came to us late when it was no longer in sight. Every now and then, but not very often, a car whirred along the road behind us and we could see its headlights diminishing in the distance, carving the darkness into fantastic shapes and shadows as it went. The path of the moon glittered across the sea to the horizon and there were no ships passing.

"I suppose it would be too obvious if I said: 'Now then'?"

Jennifer sighed. "'Now then,' is a bit discouraging," she said. "Too arbitrary—couldn't we lead into it a little less abruptly?"

"How is Ellsworth?" I said airily. "Or rather, where is Ellsworth?"

"Very well indeed, and in Taormina."

"Why Taormina?"

She fidgeted a little. "He likes Taormina."

There was a long silence while we both looked at Ellsworth in Taormina. I can't vouch for Jennifer's view, but mine was clear. I saw him going down to bathe, wearing sandals, a discreetly colored jumper and flannel trousers with a faint stripe. I saw him at lunch in the cool monastic hotel dining room, talking earnestly with a couple of Catholic Fathers. I saw him in the evening, after dinner, sitting in a café with a few of the young locals round him, standing them drinks and speaking in precise, rather sibilant Italian with a strong Bostonian accent.

"He can't get sunburnt, you know," said Jennifer irrelevantly. "And he does try so hard. Isn't it sad?"

"Not even pink?"

"Only very occasionally, and that fades almost immediately."

"Freckles?"

"A few, but in the wrong places."

"How much does he mind?"

"Desperately, I think." Jennifer sighed again deeply. "It's become a sort of complex with him. He has quite a lot of complexes really. The Catholic Church, Italian Gothic, Walt Whitman and not overtipping. He's a beauty lover, I'm afraid."

"You should never have married a beauty lover."

She nodded. "Beauty lovers certainly are Hell."

"Why did you?"

"Why did I what?"

"Marry him."

"Hold on to your hats, boys, here we go!" She laughed faintly and said, "I think I'd better have another cigarette, I'm told it gives one social poise. I'm afraid my social poise has been rather overstrained during these last few years."

I gave her a cigarette. "Why not begin at the beginning?" I suggested. "You know it's all coming out eventually, you might just as well go the whole hog."

"I wonder where that expression originated?" she said. "It doesn't really make sense—you can't go a hog, whole or otherwise."

"Never mind about that."

"I don't really."

"Why did you marry him?"

"I was an innocent girl," she replied. "When I say innocent girl, I naturally mean a bloody fool. I was ignorant of even the most superficial facts of life. Circumstances conspired against me— doesn't that sound lovely?—but it's honestly true, they did. I was in Italy, staying with Aunt Dora in a pension, and Ellsworth and his mother were at the Grand Hotel. They had a suite, of course, and as far as the hotel was concerned they were the star turn on account of being American and very rich. The old girl took a fancy to me, why I shall never know, and asked me to lunch, and there was Ellsworth. He really was quite sweet in those days and funny; he said funny things and knew a lot and was nice to be with. There was a priest there, too, Father Robert, who I suspect had his eye on the Ponsonby fortune—some priests on behalf of their church have a strong commercial sense—anyhow, he took a hatred to me on sight which I rather enjoyed. Then came the moment when circumstances conspired against me. Old Mrs. Ponsonby upped and died of a heart attack in the lounge of the hotel just as we were all having our after-dinner coffee. It really was very horrid, and I was desperately sorry for poor Ellsworth. That was where the trouble started. Pity may be a Christian virtue, but it's dangerous to muck about with, and can play the devil with common sense. Well, to continue, as they say, from that moment onward, Ellsworth clung to me; you see, I had unwittingly and most unfortunately ousted Father Robert from his affections. He cried a good deal, which was natural enough, as he'd never been away from his mother all his life. I went with him to the funeral, which was pretty grim, and did my best to comfort him as well as I could. Then, the night after the funeral he suddenly appeared at our pension and said he wanted to talk to me. My Aunt Dora was in a fine flutter, being one of those nice-minded British matrons who can only see any rich young man as a prospective bed-mate for their younger unattached female relatives. I think she probably regretted that Ellsworth didn't want to talk to Grace or Vera, who were her own daughters—and God knows she couldn't have regretted it half as much as I did later—but still, I was an unmarried niece, and half a loaf is better than whatever it is, and so out I went into the sweet-scented Italian night with Ellsworth and her blessing. We walked for a long way, first of all through the town and then along the beach. Ellsworth didn't say much until we sat down with our backs to a wall, rather like we're sitting here, only without the view, just the sea lapping away and a lot of stars. Then he started. Oh dear!" Jennifer shifted herself into a more comfortable position. "He told me all about himself from the word go, not in any exhibitionistic way, but as though he just had to get it out of his system in spite of caution and decency and traditionally bred reticence—again like I'm doing now." She laughed rather sharply. "I wonder why people do it? I wonder if it's ever any use?"

"It's all right," I said, "when there are no strings attached. Don't get discouraged, it will do you a power of good."

"You're very sweet," she said. "I do hope I'm not going to cry again."

There was silence for a few moments and then she went on, speaking more quickly.

"I can't possibly tell you all he said, because it wouldn't be fair. I couldn't ever tell anybody, but the main thing was that he was frightened, frightened to death of himself. That was why he had become a Roman Catholic, that fear. He wasn't very articulate about it really, and he jumped from one thing to another so that on the whole I was pretty bewildered, but I did feel dreadfully touched and sad for him, and foolishly, wholeheartedly anxious to help him. He said, among other things, that he'd always been terrified of women until he met me and that the thought of marriage sort of revolted him. Of course, he hadn't had to worry about it much as long as his mother was alive, but now he was utterly lost, he couldn't face the loneliness of having no one. Father Robert had tried to persuade him to join the Church in some capacity or other, I don't exactly know what, but he fought shy of this, because he didn't feel that he had a genuine vocation or enough faith or something. He went on and on rambling here and there. One minute he'd be talking about Father Robert and how wonderful the Church was, because it knew everything about everyone, and could solve all problems if only one believed enough. Then he'd jump back, a long way back, into his childhood and talk about a friend he had at his prep school called Homer—aren't Americans awful giving their children names like that?—Homer was apparently very important, he kept on cropping up. You've no idea how strange it was sitting there on the sand with all that emotion and fright and unhappiness whirling round my head. I was only nineteen and didn't understand half of what he was talking about, but I do remember feeling pent-up and strained and rather wanting to scream. Presently he calmed down a bit and said something about how terrible it was to live in a world where no one understood you, and that Society was made for the normal, ordinary people, and there wasn't any place for the misfits. Then, then he asked me to marry him. To do him justice he was as honest as he could be. He said I was the only person he could trust and that we could travel and see the world and entertain and have fun. He didn't talk about the money side of it, but he implied a great deal. I knew perfectly well he was rich, anyhow—" She paused for a moment, and fumbled in her bag for her handkerchief. "But that wasn't why I married him, honestly it wasn't. Of course it had something to do with it, I suppose. You see, I'd been poor all my life, Father's practice wasn't up to much and the idea of having all the clothes and things that I wanted, and being able to travel, which I'd always longed to do, probably helped a bit, but it wasn't the whole reason or anything like it, I swear it wasn't. The real reason was much stranger and more complicated and difficult to explain. On looking back on it, I think I can see it clearly, but even now I'm not altogether sure. I was very emotional and romantic and really very nice inside when I was young, far nicer than I am now. There ought to be a law against bringing children up to have nice instincts and ideals, it makes some of the things that happen afterward so much more cruelly surprising than they need be. I can see, now, that I quite seriously married Ellsworth from a sense of duty—doing my good deed for the day. Girl Guides for ever. I knew perfectly well that I didn't love him, at least my brain knew it and told me so, but I didn't listen and allowed my emotions, my confused, adolescent, sentimental emotions, to drag me in the other direction. I remember forcing myself to imagine what it would be like, the actual sex part, I mean, and thinking, quite blithely, that it would be lovely and thrilling to lie in Ellsworth's arms and be a comfort to him and look after him and stand between him and his loneliness. Of course, my imagination over all this wasn't very clear, as my sex experience to date had consisted of little more than an unavowed and beautiful passion for Miss Hilton-Smith our games mistress at St. Mary's, Plymouth, and a few daring kisses from a young man at a hunt ball in Bodmin. Obviously, I hadn't the remotest idea what I was letting myself in for, so I said 'Yes,' and two days later, still in a haze of romantic and emotional confusion, we went off to Nice, without letting anyone suspect a thing, and were married in some sort of office by a man with a goiter."

Jennifer held out her hand for another cigarette. I lit one for her and, without saying a word, waited for her to go on.

"Then the trouble started." She gave a slight shudder. "I'm not going to tell you all the details, but it was all very frightening and horrid and humiliating, I think humiliating more than anything else. After a few weeks, during which time Father had appeared and Aunt Dora and a very pompous uncle of Ellsworth's, and there had been a series of scenes and discussions and a great deal of strain, Ellsworth and I went to Rome and stayed there for months. In due course I was received into the Church. I didn't have much feeling about that one way or another and Ellsworth was very insistent, so there it was. We were finally married properly with a great deal of music and rejoicing and a lot of American-born Italian Marchesas giving parties for us. As a matter of fact, old Lily Graziani was one of them, the nicest one, I'm staying with her now." She indicated Cap Ferrat with a vague gesture. "Then we went away, practically right round the world, starting with Boston and all Ellsworth's relations. Oh, dear!" she gave a little laugh. "That was very tricky, but some of them were all right. After that, we went to Honolulu and Japan and China, then to India and Egypt and back to England. That was when we first met, wasn't it, at the house in Great Cumberland Place? By that time, of course, I'd become a bit hardened. I was no longer romantic and innocent and nice. I'd learned a lot of things, I'd joined the Navy and seen the world. All those lovely places, all those chances for happiness, just out of reach, thrown away. Don't misunderstand me, it wasn't the sex business that was upsetting me, at least I don't think it was. I'd faced the failure of that ages before. Oh no, it was Ellsworth himself. I should have been perfectly happy, well, if not happy, at least content, if Ellsworth had played up and been kind and ordinary and a gay companion, but he didn't and he wasn't. I suppose people can't help being beastly, can they? It's something to do with glandular secretions and environment and things that happened to you when you were a child. I can only think that the most peculiar things certainly happened to Ellsworth when he was a child and his glandular secretions must have been something fierce. At any rate, I hadn't been with him long before I knew, beyond a shadow of doubt, that he was a thoroughly unpleasant character. Not in any way bad in the full sense of the word. Not violent or sadistic, or going off on dreadful drunks and coming back and beating me up. Nothing like that, nothing nearly so direct. He was far too refined and carefully cultured, you said it just now, a beauty lover, that's what he was, a hundred percent rip-snorting beauty lover. Oh dear, how can one reconcile being a beauty lover with being mean, prurient, sulky and pettishly tyrannical almost to a point of mania? The answer is that one can, because there are several sorts of beauty lovers. There are those who like kindness and good manners and wide seas and dignity, and others who like Bellini Madonnas and Giottos and mysticism and incense and being able to recognize, as publicly as possible, a genuine old this or old that. I don't believe it's enough—" Jennifer's voice rose a little. "I don't believe it's enough, all that preoccupation with the dead and done with, when there's living life all round you and sudden, lovely unexpected moments to be aware of. Sudden loving gestures from other people, without motives, nothing to do with being rich or poor or talented or cultured, just our old friend human nature at its best! That's the sort of beauty worth searching for; it may sound pompous, but I know what I mean. That's the sort of beauty lover that counts. I am right, aren't I? It's taken me so many miserable hours trying to puzzle things out." She stopped abruptly, almost breathless, and looked at me appealingly.

"Yes," I said, "I think you're right."

"The trouble with Ellsworth," she went on more calmly, "was that he had no love in his heart for any living soul except himself. Even his mother, who I suppose meant more to him than anyone else, faded quickly out of his memory. After the first few weeks he hardly ever referred to her, and if he did it was lightly, remotely, as though she had been someone of little importance whom he had once met and passed a summer with. If he had been honest with me or even honest with himself, it would have been all right, but he was neither. He dealt in lies, small, insignificant lies; this was at first, later the lies became bigger and more important. He made a lot of friends as we pursued our rather dreary social existence, some of them appeared to be genuinely fond of him, at any rate in the beginning; others quite blatantly fawned on him for what they could get out of him. I watched, rather anxiously sometimes, and occasionally tried to warn him. I still felt there was a chance, you know, not of reforming him, I wasn't as smug as that, but of reaching a plane of mutual companionship on which we could both live our own lives and discuss things, and have a certain amount of fun together without conflict and irritation and getting on each other's nerves. But it wasn't any use. He distrusted me, principally I think because I was a woman. There wasn't anything to be done. It was hopeless. Then, after we'd been married for several years, a situation occurred. It was in New York, we were staying at the Waldorf, and it was all very unpleasant and nearly developed into a front-page scandal. I'm a bit vague as to what actually happened myself, there were so many conflicting stories, but anyhow, Ellsworth was blackmailed, and I had to interview strange people and tell a lot of lies, and a lot of money was handed out and we sailed, very hurriedly, for Europe. After that, things were beastlier than ever. He was sulky and irritable and took to making sarcastic remarks at me in front of strangers. All the resentment of a weak nature, that had been badly frightened, came to the top. Finally, I could bear it no longer and asked him to divorce me. That was the only time I have ever seen him really furious. He went scarlet in the face with rage. He was a Catholic and I was a Catholic. That was that. There could be no question of such a thing. Then I lost my head, and told him what I really thought of him, and that I was perfectly sure that the Catholic business was not really the reason for his refusal at all. He was really worried about what people would say; terrified of being left without the nice social buttress of a wife who could preside at his table, arrive with him at pompous receptions and fashionable first nights and in fact, visually at least, cover his tracks. We had a blistering row, and I left the house, that was the house in Paris, you remember it, in the Avenue d'Iéna, and went to London to stay with Marjorie Bridges. He followed me in a week, and a series of dreary scenes took place. He actually cried during one of them, and said that he was really devoted to me deep down and that he would never again do anything to humiliate me in any way. I think he was honestly dreadfully frightened of me leaving him. Frightened of himself, I mean, that old fear that he had told me about, sitting on the beach, when he first asked me to marry him. I gave in in the end. There wasn't anything else to do really. And that's how we are now. He goes off on his own every now and then and does what he likes, but never for very long. He hasn't the courage for real adventure. Then we join up again, and open the house in Paris, and give parties, and do everything that everyone else does. Sometimes we go for a yachting cruise through the Greek Islands, or up the Dalmatian coast or round about here. Actually, I'm waiting now for him to come back, and I suppose we'll collect a dozen people that we don't care for, and who don't care for us, and off we shall go to Corsica or Mallorca or Tangier. It's a lovely life."

She sat silently for a moment, looking out over the sea, then she rose to her feet and began to kick a stone with the toe of her evening shoe. "That's about all," she said.

I got up, too, and we clambered over the wall and walked slowly over to the car.

"Not quite all," I said mildly, putting the cushions into the car. "You haven't yet told me why you were crying."

She got into the car and started fiddling with the engine. She spoke without looking at me. "I have never been unfaithful to Ellsworth," she said in a dry, flat voice. "I know I could have easily, but it always seemed to me that it might make the situation even more squalid than it is already. Anyhow, I have never found anyone among the people we meet whom I could love enough to make it worth it. Perhaps something will happen some day—I wouldn't like to die an old maid."

She started the car and drove me back to Monte Carlo. It was getting quite light and the whole landscape looked as though it had been newly washed. She dropped me at the Hôtel de Paris then, just as she was about to drive away, she leant over the side of the car and kissed me lightly on the cheek. She said: "Thank you, darling, I'll be grateful always to you for having been so really lovingly kind."

I watched the car until it had turned the corner and was out of sight.

4

"—But a chap's own chauffeur," the major was saying. "I mean that really is going too far—"

"Where are they now?" I interrupted. "She and the chauffeur—did he tell you?"

"Out in Canada, I believe, the man's a Canadian. They run a garage or a petrol station or something—funnily enough, she wouldn't take any of old Ponsonby's money, he offered it, of course, he's that sort of chap, you know 'quixotic,' is that the word?"

"Yes," I said, "that's the word."

The major collected the photograph albums and packed them in his suitcase, as he did so he hummed a tune rather breathily. My mind went back to that early, newly washed morning four years ago—driving down through the dawn to Monte Carlo. I remembered the emptiness in Jennifer's voice when she said: "Anyhow, I have never found anyone among the people we meet whom I could love enough to make it worth it—perhaps something will happen some day—I wouldn't like to die an old maid."

The major straightened himself. "What about a nightcap?" he said.

We went up on deck. The air was clear and cold, and there was hardly any wind. Far away on the port bow a lighthouse on the French coast flashed intermittently.

In the smoking room the major flung himself, with a certain breezy abandon, into a leather armchair which growled under the strain.

"Fancy you knowing old Ponsonby," he said. "The world certainly is a very small place. You know there's a lot of truth in those old chestnuts." I nodded absently and lit a cigarette. He snapped his fingers loudly to attract the steward's attention. "I shall never forget that night as long as I live, seeing that poor chap crying like a kid, absolutely broken up. It's a pretty bad show when a man's whole life is wrecked by some damned woman. What I can't get over—" he leant forward and lowered his voice; there was an expression of genuine, horrified bewilderment in his, by now, slightly bloodshot eyes—"is that she should have gone off with his own chauffeur!"

"I suspect," I said gently, "that was why he was crying."

"Steward! Two stengahs!" said the major.

A
RICHER
DUST

Sidney's letter arrived on May 12, 1941, and Joe brought it down to the pool. Lenore was at the bar mixing two tomato juice cocktails with an extra dash of Worcestershire sauce, as they both felt a bit liverish after Shirley's party and had made a mutual pact not to touch any hard liquor before sundown. Joe came shuffling down the white steps, and Morgan felt irritated even before he saw the letter—the scraping of Joe's shoes set his teeth on edge. He snatched the letter from Joe's hand, recognized the handwriting and felt more irritable than ever. Joe went off again up the steps, still shuffling his feet. Morgan dried his hands on the corner of the towel and opened the letter, and when Lenore came out with the cocktails he had read it and was gazing out over Beverly Hills to the sea with an expression of set exasperation.

Lenore noted the expression and placed the tomato juice gently beside him. Then she sat down herself on the edge of the diving board and rummaged in her bathing bag for her sunglasses. She was aware that she probably felt a bit better than he did because while mixing the tomato juice she had quite shamelessly cheated and given herself a shot of rye; her stomach felt smoother, and the sensation of nausea and dizziness which had been plaguing her all the morning had passed away. Morgan continued to gaze out into the blue distance in silence. Lenore contemplated for an instant making a little joke such as—"Cut—the scene stinks anyway!" or "Is there anything wrong with the sound?" but thought better of it and kept quiet.

She rubbed her sunglasses with her handkerchief and put them on. The world immediately became cooler and less harsh; the sky took on a pinky glow, and the light on the hills softened. Morgan's body looked even more tanned than it actually was—he never went very dark, just an even golden brown. It was certainly a fine body: long legs, strongly developed chest tapering to a perfect waistline, hardly any hips, and no bottom to speak of. She gave a little sigh and wistfully regretted that they had had a tumble that morning on waking; those "over-in-a-flash" hangover tumbles were never really satisfactory; it would have been much more sensible to have saved it for later; now, for instance, in the hot sun. Obeying an overwhelming impulse, she slid her hand along his thigh. Even as she did it she knew it was a mistake. He jumped violently, and said in a tone of bored petulance, "Lay off me for one minute, can't you?" Discouraged, she withdrew her hand, muttered, "Pardon me for living" and took a swig of tomato juice, which brought tears to her eyes, owing to the sharpness of the Worcestershire sauce. Morgan, his mood of retrospection shattered, gave a disagreeable grunt and went off into the change room to have a shower.

Lenore picked up the letter. The handwriting was neat and clear, and the address at the top was H.M.S. *Tagus*, c/o G.P.O., London. It started, "Dear Les." She smiled at this. He hated being called Les, and very few people in Hollywood knew that it was his name. She turned the page over and saw that it was signed, "Your affectionate brother, Sid." Then, still smiling, she read it through.

> Dear Les,
>
> I expect you'll be surprised to hear from me after so long, but I've been at sea now for several months. You'll see where I am by the postmark, and we're moving along in your direction in a few days' time, all being well. So expect me when you see me and hang out the holly and get the old calf fatted up because I shall probably get forty-eight hours' leave. Mum and Dad and Sheila were all well when last heard from. One of my mates wants to meet some film lovelies in the following order— Betty Grable, Loretta Young, Paulette Goddard and Marlene Dietrich. Failing these, he doesn't mind settling for Shirley Temple

at a pinch, as he likes them young. I just want to see you and a
nice big steak, done medium, with chips.

> *Your affectionate brother,*
> *Sid*

In the change room Morgan had a shower and dried himself
with grim efficiency, emptied some toilet water, tactfully labeled "For
Men Only," into the palms of his hands and rubbed it over his chest
and under his arms. The long mirror reflected his expression, which
was still set in exasperation; he stared at himself, for once almost
without enthusiasm, and lit a cigarette; his mouth felt tacky and
unpleasant, and the cigarette did nothing to improve it. "Dear Les"—
"Your affectionate brother, Sid." "Les and Sid." He shuddered, and
slowly pulled on a pair of dark red linen trousers and a sweater.

The awful thing was that "Your affectionate brother, Sid," was
true. Ever since they were tiny kids trudging home from school
across Southsea Common, Sid had been affectionate, much more so
than Sheila, really, although it was generally supposed to be sisters
who lavished adoration and hero worship on their elder brothers. Sheila, however, had never been the hero-worshiping type. Plain and practical, she had always, even when very young, refused to be impressed.
Sid, on the other hand, had been a pushover from the word go;
whatever Morgan, or rather "Les," said or did was perfection. There
were so many occasions that Morgan could remember when Sid had
taken the rap for him. During the roof-climbing phase, for instance,
when seventeen slates had been broken and gone crashing down into
Mrs. Herndon's back garden, Sid had taken all the blame for that and,
what was more, been punished for it. Then there was the ringing-
doorbells-and-running-away episode when Morgan, who had in-
stigated the whole affair, had managed to hop over somebody's
garden wall and lie panting in a shrubbery while Sid was captured and
led off to the police station. Sid, with admirable *Boy's-Own-Paper*
gallantry, had resolutely refused to divulge the name of his ac-
complice. The policeman had finally brought him home where, after a
big family scene during which Morgan remained ignobly silent, Sid
was whacked by Dad and sent to bed supperless.

There were many other like instances, through childhood and
adolescence and right on until they were grown men. Sid certainly
had the right to sign himself, "Your affectionate brother," and the
strange thing was that through all the years this steady, undemanding affection had merely served to annoy the recipient of it, sometimes almost intolerably. Perhaps deep down beneath the armored
shell of Morgan's self-esteem there were remnants of a conscience
which had not quite become atrophied. Perhaps, who knows, there
were moments every now and then when, in his secret private heart,

he was ashamed. Whether this was so or not, the presence or even the thought of Sid invariably made him ill at ease and irritable. Now Sid was going to appear in his life again. Six years had passed since they had seen each other; six eventful years for the world and even more eventful for Morgan, for in the course of them he had climbed from being a small-part English actor to one of the biggest stars in Hollywood.

2

In 1933 Leslie Booker, age twenty, was a floorwalker in the novelty department of Hadley's. This position was procured for him through the civic influence of his uncle Edward who, owing to certain connections on various boards and committees, knew Fred Cartwright, one of the directors of Hadley's. Uncle Edward privately thought no great shakes of his nephew, but, being strong in family conscience and devoted to his sister Nell, who was Leslie's mother, he decided to do what he could for the boy. His misgivings about Leslie were based more on intuition than actual knowledge of his character. This intuition told him that Leslie was idle, overgood-looking, excessively pleased with himself and flash, and that his younger brother Sid was worth twenty of him any day of the week; however, he was Nell's eldest and he couldn't ride about the countryside indefinitely on a secondhand motorcycle with a series of tartish young ladies in flannel slacks riding pillion behind him with their arms clasped tightly round his stomach. So something had to be done.

Mr. Cartwright was invited to the Queen's, given an excellent lunch, and, when sufficiently mellowed by hock and two double Martell Three Star brandies, was finally persuaded to give Leslie a three months' trial in the shop. The three months passed swiftly and proved little beyond the fact that Leslie was idle, over-good-looking, excessively pleased with himself and flash. However, he did more or less what was required of him, which was mostly to smile and look amiable and tactfully coax the customers to buy things that they did not really want, and so he was re-engaged for a further six months with a vague promise of a raise in salary if he did well.

It was during these six months' further probation that Adele Innes arrived in Portsmouth to play a week's tryout of a new farce which was due to open in the West End. Adele was a conscientious young actress with good legs and little talent. In the farce she played the heroine's best friend, who made a lot of pseudosophisticated wisecracks and was incapable of sitting down without crossing her legs ostentatiously and loosening her furs. On the Monday of tryout week, after a tiring dress rehearsal, she popped into Hadley's on her way home to the digs to buy a few roguish little first-night gifts for her friends in the company. Leslie Booker helped her assiduously to choose a china Pierrot scent burner, two green elephant bookends, a cunning replica of an apple made of china which could be used, Leslie assured her, either as a paperweight or a doorstop and a small scarlet leather bookshelf containing four minute dictionaires which were illegible owing to the smallness of print.

Having made these purchases, she lingered a little chatting nonchalantly with him. She was a democratic girl quite uninhibited by any sense of class distinction, so uninhibited, indeed, that she deliberately allowed her hand to rest against his while he was totting up the bill. During the ensuing week they had morning coffee twice at the Cadena, went to Gosport and back three times on the ferry in between the matinee and evening performances on the Wednesday, which was early closing day; and went to bed together once in her digs between the matinee and evening performances on the Saturday which, although not early closing day, was perfectly convenient as the shop shut at six and she did not have be in the theater again until eight.

A few weeks later, after some impassioned correspondence, Leslie abandoned Hadley's novelty department forever and arrived in London with seventeen pounds ten shillings, nine pounds of which were savings and the rest borrowed from brother Sid. According to prearranged plan he went directly to Adele's flat just off the Fulham Road, which she shared with a girl friend who was at present away on tour. Thus comfortably established with bed and board and convivial company, he managed, through Adele's influence, to get into the chorus of the current revue at the Caravel Theatre which, as he was without theatrical experience and could neither sing nor dance, said a great deal for Adele's influence.

By 1934 the revue at the Caravel had closed, and he was sharing the flat of a husky-voiced singer called Diana Grant in St. John's Wood. Diana was large, possessive, generous, exceedingly bad-tempered, and had a rooted objection to going to bed before 5 A.M. and rising before noon. Leslie's brief but tempestuous association with her depleted his natural vitality to such a degree that when he was offered, through a friend of a friend of hers, a general understudy and small-part job in a repertory company in Dundee, he accepted it from sheer self-preservation.

By 1936 he had played several insignificant parts in several insignificant productions both in the provinces and in London and was playing a young dope fiend in a thriller called *Blood on the Stairs*. In this piece he had one of those surefire scenes in Act Three in which he had to break down under relentless cross-examination and confess to a murder. The breakdown entailed all the routine gurglings and throat-clutchings which never fail to impress the dramatic critics, and so consequently he received glowing tributes from the *Daily Mirror,* the *Daily Express,* and the *Star,* an honorable mention in the *Daily Telegraph,* and an admonition against the overacting in *Time and Tide* which he immediately ascribed to personal jealousy and wrote a dignified letter of protest to the editor.

Blood on the Stairs was a fatuous, badly written little melodrama which, having received enthusiastic notices, closed after a run of seven and a half weeks, but, as far as Leslie Booker was concerned, it achieved some purpose, for during its brief run he was sent for and interviewed at the Savoy Hotel by a visiting American manager who was on the lookout for a clean English type to play a young dope fiend in a murder mystery play he was to present in New York in the fall. The visiting American manager's name was Sol Katsenberg and he prided himself, inaccurately, upon his unique flair for discovering new talent. He was noisy and friendly and gave Leslie two double whiskeys and sodas which he described as highballs and which contained too much ice, too much whiskey and too little soda. He also gave him a graphic description of the superefficiency of the American theater as opposed to the English. He said "Christ Almighty" a great many times but without religious implication, and by the end of the interview Leslie, slightly dizzy, had signed a contract for three hundred dollars a week and had agreed to change his name, for, as Sol explained, Leslie Booker sounded too Christ Almighty dull. The name agreed upon after a great deal of discussion was Morgan Kent, a name that, had they but known it, was destined to flash over all the movie screens of the world.

The Sol Katsenberg production of *Blood Will Tell* opened in Long Branch on September 17, 1936, and closed, after three changes of cast and two changes of author, on October 29 in Pittsburgh. The name Morgan Kent rang no urgent tocsin in the stony hearts of the American out-of-town critics, which was odd, because in the last act of the play he had a scene in which crazed with dope, he had to break down under relentless cross-examination and confess to a murder. He gurgled and clutched his throat with even more abandon than he had exhibited in *Blood on the Stairs,* but to no avail. Nobody cared, not even *Variety,* which merely listed him among the minor players and spelled his name Kant instead of Kent.

Reeling under this blow to his pride, Leslie, or rather Morgan, was driven to sharing a small apartment on West Thirty-first Street, New York City, with Myra Masters, a statuesque, red-haired ex-showgirl who had played a vampire in the deceased *Blood Will Tell.* Myra was a cheerful, openhearted girl with what is known as "contacts." These contacts were mostly square-looking businessmen from Detroit and points Middle West who cherished tender memories of her in George White's *Scandals* and Earl Carroll's *Vanities.* One of them, fortunately for Morgan, was in advertising, and, before Christmas had cast its pall of goodwill over Manhattan, magazine readers were being daily tantalized by photographs of Morgan Kent (nameless) discussing with another young man (also nameless) the merits of "Snugfit" men's underwear. Both young men were depicted practically nude in the change room of a country club where presumably they had been swimming or playing polo or doing something equally virile, but whereas one was wearing what appeared to be rather baggy old-fashioned underpants, the other, Morgan, was pointing proudly to his groin which was adorned with none other than the new "Snugfit." The dialogue beneath the photograph, although uninspired, proved its point. 1st Y.M.: "Gee, Buddy, don't you find that those loose little old pants you're wearing spoil your game?" 2d Y.M.: "Well, Chuck, as a matter of fact they do." 1st Y.M. (triumphantly): "Well, you old son of a gun, why not follow my example and try SNUGFIT!"

The result of this well-paid but unromantic publicity was as inevitable as the March of Time. Morgan was traced through Myra Masters, sent for and interviewed brusquely by a film agent in an ornate office in Rockefeller Plaza. The film agent, Al Tierney, had astute eyes jockeying for position over a long, ponderous nose, a gentle, rather high voice and a sapphire-and-platinum ring. He explained to Morgan that his fortune was in his face and figure and that, if he would sign a contract authorizing him, Al Tierney, to deal exclusively with his affairs, within the year he would be on the up-and-up and saving thousands of dollars a week.

In due course Morgan bade farewell to Myra, and set out for Hollywood.

3

The first months in Hollywood were conventionally difficult. Morgan virtually starved, waited in queues outside casting offices; wandered up and down the boulevards homesick and weary; lived on inadequate sandwiches in snack bars; made innumerable tests; acquired a few casual friends on the same plane of frustration and failure as himself, and lived in celibate squalor in a psuedo-Mexican apartment house in a side street off Wilshire Boulevard in which he had one room with shower and could, when desperate and his financial circumstances permitted, have a blue-plate dinner in a teeming restaurant on the ground floor for seventy-five cents, service included.

Al Tierney, his exclusive agent, remained exclusively in New York; occasionally his Hollywood representative, Wally Newman, granted Morgan an interview in course of which he outlined in glowing colors the lucky breaks and golden opportunities which were waiting just round the corner; in addition to these optimistic flights of fancy he contrived now and then to get Morgan a few days' crowd work which was of more practical value although less heartening. In these dreary months Morgan deteriorated in looks owing to malnutrition but gained perceptibly in moral stature, it being a well-known fact that, just as travel broadens the mind, so a little near-starvation frequently broadens the spirit.

Leslie Booker, alias Morgan Kent, the assured, charming, flash, young salesman from Southsea; the complacent, attractive, promising young actor from London, had suddenly time, far too much time, to reflect; to look at himself, into himself and around himself; to discover bitterly that a handsome face, wide shoulders and small hips were not enough in this much-publicized land of opportunity. Day after day he waited about in casting offices with dozens of handsome young men with as wide if not wider shoulders and as small if not smaller hips. Women, who hitherto had been his solace both physically and financially in times of stress, in Hollywood were either too tough, too blasé or too preoccupied with their own ambitions to devote their time and energy to a young film extra, by now only comparatively good-looking.

Morgan was forced to face the unpalatable truth that masculine good looks in the outer fringes of the movie industry were as monotonously prevalent as the eternal sunshine, the painted mountains and the cellophane-wrapped sandwiches. Had this dismal state of affairs continued much longer; had his self-esteem received just a few more kicks in the teeth; had his shrinking ego shuddered under just a few more bludgeonings of Fate, who knows what might have happened? He might conceivably have given up the struggle, begged, borrowed, earned or stolen enough money to get himself back to New York or London and started again playing small parts and learning to become a good actor. He might have given up all idea of either stage or screen and worked his way home on a freighter or even as a steward on a liner, in which capacity he would have done very well. There are a thousand things he might have done had not Fate suddenly relented and whisked him from penury and frustration into such flamboyant notoriety that he was dazzled, bewildered and lost forever.

It all came about, as usual, through hazard, chance, an accident, somebody else's misfortune. The somebody else was a young man called Freddie Branch, and the accident occurred on number seven stage on the M-G-M lot when they were in course of shooting a big ballroom scene which purported to be taking place in one of the stately homes of England. The set was impressive. There was a Tudor staircase at the top of which stood the stand-in for the hostess wearing satin and a tiara and elbow-length gloves. At the foot of the stairs stretched the vast ballroom flanked by footmen in powdered wigs; there were also heraldic shields, suits of armor, Gothic windows and two immense Norman fireplaces, one on each side, in which gargantuan logs were waiting to flicker realistically. The floor, rather erratically, was made of composition black marble and upon it were grouped hundreds of extras cunningly disguised as members of the effete British aristocracy.

The accident, which was negligible, happened to poor Freddie Branch after he had been standing quite still clasping his hostess's hand for three hours and four minutes. The whistles blew for a rehearsal, bejeweled ladies and eccentrically be-uniformed and be-tailed gentlemen stiffened to attention, and proceeded, as previously rehearsed, to revolve like automatons. Freddie Branch retreated to the foot of the stairs and proceeded, as previously rehearsed, to walk up it again. Upon gaining the top step, he suddenly felt an overwhelming desire to be sick, grabbed frenziedly at his collar, murmured "Jesus" audibly and fainted dead away. Morgan, whose proud task it was to follow him, jumped nimbly aside, and watched his inert body roll and sprawl to the bottom of the stairs. There was an immediate uproar; more whistles blew, the unconscious Freddie was carried off the set and Morgan was detailed to take over his business.

That was Fate's gesture to Morgan Kent—the striking down of the wretched Freddie Branch, who had barely had time to come to from his faint before Morgan was ascending those shining stairs in his place. He continued to ascend them at intervals for the rest of the morning. Miss Carola Blake, the star, finally emerged from her dressing room and took over from her stand-in, and the scene was taken. It was taken at two o'clock, at two-twenty, at two forty-five, at three-ten, at three-forty, at four-fifteen and, owing to a hitch in the sound, at eight, eight-thirty and nine onward during the following morning.

By the following evening Miss Carola Blake had shaken Morgan's hand—plus rehearsals—forty-seven times and become aware in the process that he had fine eyelashes, an excellent physique, although a little on the thin side, and a deep and attractive speaking voice. (As she had spent the thirty years of her life in Illinois and California, her ear was naturally oblivious to any subtle cockney intonations and, to do Morgan justice, these were becoming increasingly rare.) When the ballroom scene had been packed away in the can, Morgan together with the other extras was paid off. Only a few days later, however, he received a peremptory call to report at the casting office where to his surprise he was greeted with a welcoming smile from the outer secretary, archfriendliness by the inner secretary and downright effusiveness by the casting director himself. It appeared, after some casual conversation and the offer and refusal of a cigar, that the sharp-eyed observers on the set had noted his charm, poise and talent and that he was to be tested for a scene in a speedboat. Miss Carola Blake, the casting director added with an oblique look, had actually consented to do the test with him herself. Later, on the same day, Morgan wearing abbreviated swimming trunks, spent three and a half hours with Miss Carola Blake, also scantily clad, sitting in the built-up bows of a speedboat with, behind them, a back projection screen upon which were monotonously depicted the swirling waters of the Caribbean.

Five weeks later he moved unostentatiously into Carola Blake's elaborate house in Beverly Hills.

A little later still they were married.

4

By the autumn of 1938, while the English prime minister was shuttling back and forth between England and Germany, two things of considerable importance had happened to Morgan Kent. The first was his sensational success in a picture called *Loving Rover*, in which he played an eighteenth-century pirate who, after many nautical and amorous vicissitudes, finally evaded death by a hairbreadth and found true love in the arms of a beautiful New England girl with a pronounced Middle Western accent. The second was his divorce from Carola Blake on the grounds of mental cruelty. The publicity of the latter almost surpassed that of the former, with the result that his fan mail reached unheard-of proportions, and he signed a new seven-year starring contract, the terms of which were published inaccurately in every newspaper in the United States.

Throughout 1939 and the beginning of 1940 he made no less than seven successful pictures, one of which was quite good. He bought a delightful house in the hills of Hollywood which commanded a spectacular view of the town, especially at night when the myriad lights blazed from Sunset Boulevard to the sea. Here he enjoyed a carefree bachelor existence with, in order of their appearance and disappearance, Jane Fleming, Beejie Lemaire, Dandy Lovat, Glory Benson and Brenda Covelin.

In the spring of 1940, at the time of the evacuation of the British Expeditionary Force from the beaches of Dunkirk, he had just completed a grim but exciting war picture entitled *Altitude*, in which he portrayed to perfection a taciturn but gallant fighter pilot whose ultimate death for the sake of his fiancée and his best friend created on the screen a dramatic climax hitherto unparalleled in the art of filmmaking. While making *Altitude* he met for the first time Lenore Fingal, who was cast as his fiancée. Their meeting was described by all observers as an absolute and concrete example of love at first sight, and before the picture was half finished they had flown together over the border into Mexico on Saturday, been married on Sunday and flown back again in time for work on Monday. A little later he gave up his bachelor establishment, and they moved into a larger and more convenient house in Beverly Hills.

5

Lenore Fingal, at the time of her marriage to Morgan Kent, was twenty-five years old. She was small and dark, with a good figure, an attractive husky voice and very lovely gray-blue eyes. These eyes were undoubtedly her best feature, but they were deceptive. There was an appealing expression in them, a tender naïveté, a trusting, friendly generosity which, although effective in "close-ups," actually was at variance with her character. Lenore was neither tender, naïve, trusting nor particularly generous. The exigencies of her life in the treacherous shallows of the motion picture industry had not allowed her much time for the development of these qualities. She was hard, calculating and, although occasionally sentimental, never emotional. In course of her journey from the slums of Los Angeles to the heights of Beverly Hills she had, once or twice, permitted herself the luxury of a love affair; that is to say, she had consciously directed her will into an emotional channel in order, presumably, to discover what it was all about, but, as her heart had never been involved seriously, she had discovered very little. She had played a few stormy scenes, shed a few tears and emerged unscathed and tougher than ever.

It is doubtful that she even imagined herself in love with Morgan. He was physically attractive to her and, in the dazzling light of his rise to stardom, an excellent matrimonial proposition. Now, in the spring of 1941, they had been married for a year, a professionally successful year for them both. He had made three pictures and was in the process of making a fourth. She had made two apart from him and one with him in which she had portrayed a gallant British Red Cross nurse who rescued her lover (Morgan) from the beaches of Dunkirk by rowing out from Dover in a dinghy. The picture when shown in New York and London had had a disappointing reception from the critics and so it had been decided, for the time being anyway, that it would be wiser to cast Lenore and Morgan separately, and wiser still to keep Lenore away from the perils of English pronunciation and allow her to exhibit her undoubted talent securely enclosed in her own idiom. Domestically their first year of marriage also had been fairly successful. They had quarreled a good deal, naturally enough, and had once come to blows, but the blows given and received had not been violent, and the original cause of the row swiftly lost forever in a haze of alcohol.

The arrival of the letter from brother Sid, coming as it did on the morning of a hangover, had both irritated and depressed Morgan considerably, and the arrival of brother Sid himself a few days later irritated and depressed him still more.

They were all sitting round the pool drinking old-fashioneds before going over to dinner at Beejie's: Morgan, Lenore, Coral Leroy, Sammy Feisner, Charlie Bragg and Doll Hartley. Sammy was just reaching the point of a long story about a scene between Hester Norbury and Louis B. Mayer when there was a loud "Hallo, there!" from the upper terrace, and Sid came bounding down the steps, followed by another sailor who was red-haired and covered with freckles. Sammy stopped abruptly on the verge of his story's denouement; Morgan rose from a canvas chair, leaving on it the dark imprint of his damp swimming trunks, and, with a valiant smile masking his annoyance, advanced to meet his brother.

Sid in appearance, temperament and character was everything Morgan was not. Whereas Morgan was tall, lithe and dark, Sid was short, square and fair. Whereas Morgan's temperament was naturally solemn, Sid's was ebullient and permanently cheerful. Sid was trusting, kind and uninhibited; Morgan was suspicious, egocentric and, since his early Hollywood struggles, frequently a prey to misgivings. Sid had none. It would never have occurred to him that he was not immediately welcome wherever he went. He flung his arms affectionately round Morgan and banged him heartily on the back.

"My God, Les," he said, "I've been looking forward to this for months!"

The word "Les" went through Morgan's heart like a poisoned spear, and he shuddered. Lenore, who also had got up to greet the new arrivals, noticed it and giggled. Morgan, with an excellent display of brotherly affection, introduced Sid to everyone. Sid introduced his friend, Pete Kirkwall, who shyly shook hands all round; Charlie Bragg got up to mix fresh drinks; there was a lot of shifting of chairs, and finally Sid found himself ensconced between Morgan and Lenore on a striped swing seat which creaked plaintively whenever any of them moved.

Morgan realized with a sinking heart that Sid and his friend would not only have to be offered the best guest room, but would have to be taken with the others to dinner at Beejie's. They would also without doubt expect a personally conducted tour of the studios the next day and a glamorous lunch in the cafeteria. It was not that he was ashamed of Sid. There was nothing to be ashamed of in a reasonably nice-looking sailor brother, but there was, as there always is in such circumstances, a wide gulf to be bridged. None of his friends, either at the studio or at Beejie's, would have much in common with Sid and Pete. In envisaging the social strain involved, the effort he would have to make not to shudder when called "Les," nor to flush at Sid's over-British naval repartee, and, above all, not to betray to anybody the fact that he devoutly wished that his brother had never been born, almost overwhelmed him. He knew that Lenore was watching, waiting for a chance to sneer, to get in a crack at him. He also knew that she would extract from Sid as much information as possible about his early years and fling it in his face the next time an opportunity offered.

Sid, on the other hand, sublimely unaware of the conflict raging in his brother's heart, was perfectly happy and at ease. He kept a weather eye open to see that Pete was doing all right, and was relieved to see that he was thawing out a bit and exchanging Player's cigarettes for Lucky Strikes with a blond woman whose breasts seemed about to burst exuberantly from a tightly stretched bandanna handkerchief. Sid had already taken a fancy to Lenore, whom he considered to be on the skinny side but friendly and attractive. Charlie Bragg handed him an old-fashioned, and called him "Pal"; Les—good old Les—asked him how long his leave was and said that of course he and Pete must stay in the house and that he'd take them round some studios the next day. Everything, in fact, had turned out as well, if not better, than he had hoped. After a few more drinks and a swim in the pool, during which he churned up and down doing rather a clumsy "crawl" and treating the water as though it were a personal enemy, he squeezed himself back into his "tiddley" suit which, being his best, was molded tightly to his stocky figure, and, with bell-bottomed trousers flapping and vitality unimpaired, he climbed into a blue Packard with Lenore, Sammy Feisner and Coral Leroy. Pete was with Morgan and the others in a beige Chrysler convertible.

Beejie's house was in another canyon, and this entailed a sharp and tortuous descent from Morgan's house with a sharper and more tortuous ascent on the other side of the valley. Sid, who was sitting next to Lenore in the front seat, was both fascinated and alarmed at the firm assurance with which her small brown hands gripped the wheel. During the drive she gave him a few hints as to what he was to expect from the evening.

"It isn't that Beejie isn't all right," she explained. "Beejie's as right as rain, but don't go outside with her after she's had more than three drinks."

"If you take my advice," interposed Coral from the backseat, "you won't go outside with her at all, drink or no drink. She's the biggest ripsnorting nympho between here and Palm Springs!"

"Maybe the sailor would like to have a few passes made at him," said Sammy, "after all, he's only got forty-eight hours."

"He's my brother-in-law"—here Lenore swerved sharply round a curve—"my baby brother-in-law, and so help me God I'm going to protect him from evil if it kills me!"

Sid laughed loudly at this, and was rewarded by an affectionate pat on the thigh. He gathered in course of the drive that his imminent hostess had been married four times; had made a smash hit some years before in a picture called *Honey-Face*, but had never really had a success since; that her present husband was a surgeon whose specialty was the quasi-miraculous removal of gallbladders, and that in 1939 she had had a brief but tempestuous affair with Morgan. This neither shocked nor surprised him. He had always viewed Les's sexual promiscuities with tolerant good humor not entirely devoid of admiration. Good old Les had always been a quick worker even way back in the old days in Southsea. He recounted with brotherly pride an episode in Morgan's adolescence which concerned a chemist's daughter called Dodo Platt and her official fiancé who was in the wool business. As a story it was not extravagantly amusing, but Coral, Sammy and Lenore laughed satisfactorily, and Lenore made a mental note of Dodo Platt. Encouraged by this and the general atmosphere of warm conviviality, Sid obliged with a few more lighthearted anecdotes about Morgan's early youth, all of which were rapturously received. At last, with a screaming of brakes, the car swirled through a pink plaster archway and drew up before what looked like a Spanish sanatorium.

The phrase "Hollywood party" has become synonymous in the public mind with drink, debauch, frequent violence and occasional murder. This is both unjust and inaccurate, but the reason for it is not far to see, and it lies, obviously enough, in the publicity value of the hosts, or the guests, or both. The movie colony lives, breathes and functions in a blaze of publicity. Many members of it make a point of leading quiet lives and evading the limelight as much as possible. In the old days, when the various social strata were more clearly defined, it was easier for certain groups of the upper hierarchy to move about unobtrusively among themselves, to give little dinners and to visit each other's houses without the world at large being informed of it. But during the last few years this has become increasingly difficult owing to the misguided encouragement of a new form of social parasite, the gossip columnist. This curious phenomenon has insinuated itself into the lifestream not only of Hollywood but of the whole of America, and what began as a minor form of local, social and professional scandalmongering has now developed into a major espionage system the power of which, aided and abetted by the radio, has reached fabulous porportions.

It would not be incorrect to say that today the minds of millions of citizens of the United States are affected by it. A column of inconsequential gossip is written daily by Mr. So-and-So or Miss

185

Such-and-Such. This column, in addition to being printed in the news-paper for which it is written is syndicated throughout the country. Mr. So-and-So and Miss Such-and-Such also—as a rule—have a week-ly, or sometimes daily, half hour on the radio, during which they re-capitulate what they have already written and give pointers as to what they are going to write. The effect of this widespread assault upon the credulity of an entire nation must inevitably be confusing. It would not be so were the information given checked and counter-checked and based on solid truth, but unfortunately it seldom is; con-sequently anybody who has the faintest claim to celebrity is likely to have his character, motives and private and public actions cheer-fully misrepresented to an entire continent.

This is not done, except on rare occasions, with any particu-larly malicious intent, but merely to gratify one of the least admira-ble qualities of human nature: vulgar curiosity. The accuracy of what is written, stated, listened to and believed is immaterial. The monster must be fed, and the professionally employed feeder of it is highly paid and acquires a position of power in the land which would be ri-diculous were it not so ominous. In Hollywood, where this epidemic first began to sap the nation's mental vitality, no large and very few small social gatherings can take place without one or several poten-tial spies being present. An exchange of views between two directors; a light argument between two leading ladies; a sharp word, spoken perhaps only jokingly, by a young husband to his young wife, by the next day will have been misquoted, distorted, magnified, read and believed by several million people. This reprehensible state of affairs concerns our story vitally because at Beejie Lemaire's party, in the regretted absence of Miss Louella Parsons and Miss Hedda Hopper, there was present an up-and-coming young lady journalist called Ruthie Binner who ran a column in a comparatively obscure but lo-cally read magazine: *Hollywood Highlights*. The column was headed "Nest Eggs" and consisted of a series of staccato misstatements purporting to have been whispered to Ruthie by a little bird. The in-ventive capacities of Ruthie's little bird could have found no parallel in the annals of ornithology.

To describe Beejie's party as "informal" would be an under-statement. It began hilariously with one of her ex-husbands, Peppo Ragale, falling down three steps in the bar with a plate of cheese appetizers and breaking his ankle. Her present husband, Grant Law-rence, who, apart from his deft manipulation of gallbladders, could also set bones and apply compresses, dealt with the matter with gay efficiency, and the party went on from there. Morgan drank steadily throughout the evening, and became more and more depressed. Le-nore drank too, but not to excess; she was anxious not to miss any-thing that was going on. Sid and Pete were received enthusiastically by Beejie and everyone present. Soon after the buffet dinner Pete retired into the garden with Doll Hartley and was not retrieved until it was time to go home.

Sid enjoyed every moment. He had seven old-fashioneds before dinner and a number of Scotch highballs after dinner. He answered questions about the war, the British Navy, "Dear old London" and, volubly, about his brother. He had an unproductive but enjoyable interlude with Beejie on a chintz-covered divan in what she laughingly described as "the library." He helped Beejie's husband to scramble eggs in the kitchen at 2 A.M. At 2:20 A.M. he was beckoned alluringly to a seat at the edge of the swimming pool by a vivacious dark girl who said her name was Ruthie. He found her outspoken, amusing and sincerely concerned about the progress of the war. He was also touched and charmed by her evident devotion to "Les" and his career. They talked cozily for a long while, and finally returned to the house to find Lenore rounding up her party to go home.

On the following morning Morgan, who was not working, stayed in bed, and turned Sid and Pete over to Lenore, who took them onto several of the M-G-M stages and showed them Joan Crawford, Jeanette MacDonald and Myrna Loy in the distance and Mickey Rooney, Spencer Tracy, Judy Garland and Nelson Eddy close to. They lunched in the cafeteria and consumed vast glasses of milk and cartwheel slices of tomato on acres of hygienic lettuce. They were then shown some convulsive rough cuts of incomplete movies in a projection room where they sprawled in gargantuan armchairs flanked by ashtrays and cuspidors so that they could sleep and smoke and spit whenever they so desired.

In the evening, after a merry cocktail gathering down by the pool, they were taken by Morgan and Lenore to a much grander dinner party than Beejie's. This was given by Arch Bowdler, one of the most prominent Hollywood executives, in a resplendent house that had been furnished with the utmost care. Attired as they were in the usual "square rig" of British ordinary seamen, they caused a mild sensation except among the English actors present who of course recognized it immediately. After a suitable sojourn in a cocktail bar laboriously decorated to represent an open-air café in the Place Pigalle, they were ushered into a long, pale-green room where they were placed at little tables for dinner.

Sid found himself opposite a dim English actor who asked him a few lachrymose questions about New Malden, where apparently he had been born, and then lapsed into a gloomy silence, and between two ladies of outstanding glamour. One was Mae Leitzig, who had been whisked by the host from under the iron heel of the Nazis in Vienna and was about to star in a picture about Charlotte Corday, and the other, Zenda Hicks, a tough little blonde, who had recently won an award for the best minor performance of February 1941. She explained to Sid during the meal that it was just "one of those crazy things" and that no one had been more surprised than she was.

On the whole he got along better with her than with Mae Leitzig, who was rather somber and seemed to be worried about something. Zenda obviously was not worried about anything. She told him all about her first marriage and divorce and also about her present husband, who was Mexican and terribly jealous. She told him the entire story of the picture she was working in at the moment, and gave her free and unprejudiced opinion of her director who had a knowledge of life and humanity in general which was nothing short of "dreamy." He also, it appeared, thought very highly of her own talents and was in the habit of sitting up to all hours in the morning with her asking her advice about his unhappy marriage, discussing world affairs and occasionally breaking into uncomfortable sobs at the sheer hopelessness of everything. These nocturnal but strictly platonic interludes had been the cause of many bitter quarrels between her and Juano, but, as Juano was apparently nothing but a big baby anyway, everyone was as friendly as could be and there was no harm done.

She was just about to describe her early life in Omaha, Nebraska, when there was a sharp call for silence, and the host rose to his feet. He was a round man with very small hands and black hair. He made a long speech bidding everyone welcome to his house and board, and then, to Sid's slight embarrassment, launched forth into an impassioned eulogy of England and the British war effort. He sat down at last amid loud applause, having called upon Robert Bailey, one of the leading British actors present, to respond. Robert Bailey spoke well and slowly with an underlying throb of patriotism in his voice. He paused once or twice to find a word, and it was obvious to all that he was making a brave effort to restrain his emotion. He was followed by an English character actress of high repute who waved her arms a good deal and talked about the women of England and how staunchly they had behaved during the blitzes. She concluded by reading a letter from her married sister in St. John's Wood upon which, it appeared, bombs had been raining incessantly for months. By this time Sid was getting restless, bored and a little sleepy. He roused himself, however, when Morgan was called upon to speak.

Morgan rose shyly to his feet and stood in silence for a moment, twisting the stem of his champagne glass. His speech was mercifully brief, but in every word of it there pulsated a love of his native land which was intensely moving. Sid was genuinely surprised, having had no idea that "Les" thought of the Old Country in those terms. He was still more surprised and utterly shattered when "Les" finished by asking everyone to join him in drinking the health of "My sailor brother and the British Navy."

There were resounding cheers at this, and everyone rose solemnly and clinked glasses. Sid, sweating with embarrassment, was forced to stand up and make a brief response. He cleared his throat, wishing devoutly that he was safely in his ship and at the other side of the world, and said: "On behalf of my friend and I—thanks a lot for making us so welcome here tonight and for giving us such a good time! When we tell our shipmates about all the wonderful people we've seen they'll be green with envy and that's no lie." Here he paused for a moment and cleared his throat again. "As you are all aware"—realizing that he was speaking rather loudly, he lowered his voice—"as you are all aware, the Navy is known as 'The Silent Service,' so you will not expect from an ordinary seaman such as I myself am anything highfalutin in the way of a speech, speechmaking not being much in my line as you might say. But I would like to say, on behalf of the Old Country which I proudly belong to and the fleet in which I serve—thanks a lot for all the kind things that have been said here tonight and, as far as the war goes, down with old Hitler and Musso, and God save the King."

He sat down abruptly amid tumultuous applause; someone shouted, "Good old England!" and an Irish actress who had been playing bit parts for thirteen years burst into loud sobs.

After this everyone was shepherded into an enormous blue room, the walls of which were lined with sets of the classics bound in different colors. Here trays of highballs were handed round, a movie screen rose noiselessly from the floor and the party settled down to a preview of Clyde Oliver in *The Eagle Has Wings*. The screen titles, which were printed in glittering white against a background of moving planes and clouds, proclaimed that the story was a simple human document concerning a New York playboy who found his true self in the crucible of war, and that the producer was Arch Bowdler; the associate producers, Josh Spiegal and Chuck Mosenthal; the director, Bud Capelli; and the cameraman, Vernon Chang. The titles further stated that the story was by Norma and Perce Fennimore, adapted from the novel by Cynthia Stein; that the screenplay was by Max Macgowan and Eloise Hunt, with additional dialogue by Olaf Hansen and Benny Zeist; and that the music had been specially composed by Gregor Borowitz, with orchestrations and vocal arrangements by Otto von Stollmeyer. Then came a long list of lesser people who had operated the sound, supervised the makeup, designed the hairstyles, organized the publicity and supplied extra effects. As an afterthought it was explained that the whole thing was a "Bowdler-L.N.G.-Peerless Production."

It took one hour and fifty-five minutes for the hero to find his true self in the crucible of war, because before doing so he was constrained to find a great many other things as well. These included a tough friend with a hairy chest who cried on the least provocation; a

drunken Canadian sergeant pilot with a heart of gold who crashed in
flames halfway through the picture; a lovable but brusque British
peeress who lived in a Tudor tearoom on the Yorkshire moors, and
last, but unfortunately not least, an adorable American girl of great
courage and vivacity who was continually hiding herself in the
cockpits of Eagle Squadron bombers. Finally, after a moving scene in
a hospital run by some over-made-up nuns, all misunderstandings
were straightened out, and the picture ended with the hero and heroine walking up a steep hill to the deafening accompaniment of a celestial choir.

When the lights went up, several members of the party were
discovered to be in tears. Pete was fast asleep with his head resting
on the bare breast of his dinner partner; Morgan and Lenore were
bickering in a corner and Sid was utterly exhausted and wished to
go home.

The next day, Sunday, was passed peacefully. A few people
came over for drinks before lunch and stayed until three. After lunch
everyone slept, either in the house or by the pool, and at seven
o'clock, fortified by some old-fashioneds and peanut-butter appetizers, Sid and Pete were dispatched to their ship in Morgan's car.
When they had gone, Morgan and Lenore continued the squabble they
had begun the night before, and went on with it intermittently for the
rest of the evening. The gist of it was, of course, Sid. Actually Lenore
had found him rather boring, but she spoke of him with enthusiastic
admiration in order to irritate Morgan. In this she succeeded easily. He
rose to the bait every time. Finally, toward the end of dinner, he got up
from the table violently and retired to the pool, where he remained for
an hour by himself, leaving Lenore in lonely triumph with the straw-
berry shortcake.

The visit of the two sailors had undoubtedly been a great success. Neither of them had behaved badly nor said anything shaming.
Of the two, Sid had been the more popular because of his natural ease,
lack of shyness and vitality, but they both had made a good impression on everyone they had met and they had been pressed on all sides
to return for further hospitality should their ship ever again be in the
vicinity.

Morgan was not much given to introspection, nor was he particularly adept at analyzing his own feelings. In his early years,
when his ego was more easily satisfied and assuaged by sexual pro-
miscuity and his ambition was goading him to succeed, he had had little time to sift, weigh and evaluate his motives. Perhaps if he had, the
impact of his sudden fame might have steadied him instead of confusing him. As it was, he was in a muddle, and somewhere, deep in his
subconscious, he knew it. He was aware, dimly, that he had changed;
that his reactions were less gay, less volatile, than they used to be;

that his capacity for enjoyment seemed to have dwindled and that with the increasing burden of his stardom he was considerably less happy than he had been before. He was also aware, not dimly but very clearly, that he was much to be envied. He was young, successful, immensely publicized and sought-after. Big executives argued and fought for the loan of his services; his financial position was assured, and his contract with C.R.P.I. (Cinesond Radiant Pictures, Incorporated) was watertight, with automatic raises of salary for the next four years. True, he was sick of Lenore, but she was still physically satisfactory and, when not determined to be bitchy, fairly good company.

The arrival of Sid had disturbed him by bringing into his mind something that for years he had been striving to shut out; memory of the past, concern for his family, perhaps—who knows?—even a little concern for his country. During the last years he had written home occasionally; dutifully remembered his mother's and Sheila's birthdays, and had sent them presents at Christmas. Sid he had ignored. Sid had always been a thorn in his flesh. He knew that there was no reason for this. Sid was devoted to him; was loyal, affectionate and true whereas he, Morgan, was none of these things and was not even sure that he wanted to be. Sid was the trouble, all right. Sid was the weight of his conscience. Ordinary Seaman Sidney Booker, brother of Morgan Kent—sailor brother of Morgan Kent. What the hell had Sid wanted to join the Navy for in the first place, and, having joined it, why the hell couldn't he have stayed with the Home Fleet and not come dashing romantically out to the Pacific in a destroyer?

Sitting gloomily by the pool while Lenore amused herself up in the house with the radio, Morgan was compelled to face one fact honestly and without compromise, and that was that he wished his good-humored, loyal, affectionate sailor brother dead and at the bottom of the sea. He crushed down this unedifying reflection as soon it seared across his mind, but it remained there dormant until the next morning, when it re-emerged with even greater force.

Lenore wandered into his bedroom wearing peach-colored pajamas. She had a glint in her eye and *Hollywood Highlights*, which was published with dreadful regularity every Monday, in her hand.

"Well, 'Les,'" she said cheerfully, "our Ruthie's little bird certainly worked overtime at Beejie's the other night. Just cast those dway big violet eyes over this."

She threw the magazine lighty onto his chest and lit a cigarette. Morgan, with a dry mouth and a sinking heart, read Ruthie's column, flung the magazine to the floor, stamped into the bathroom and slammed the door. Lenore languidly picked it up and read it again with a quizzical smile.

"A very cute little bird talked to Ruthie the other evening—the cutest little bird you've ever seen, with curly fair hair, blue eyes and bell-bottomed pants—now don't try to guess, girls, because you never will. It was our Morgan Kent's sailor brother, and was our Morg's face red when S.B. called him 'Les.' Because, girls, 'Les' is what his name really is. Les Booker from Southsea, England. There have been a lot of bombs falling on Southsea lately, so it's nice to think that at least one of the Booker boys is out trying to stop them."

6

In the December following Sid's visit to Hollywood, the Japanese, to the astonishment of a great many people, dropped a number of bombs on Pearl Harbor, an American naval base on the island of Oahu. The reverberations of those bombs echoed across the Western world, and that lesser world, bounded by Los Angeles in the East and Santa Monica in the West, was shaken to its foundations. Enemy invasion was expected hourly; vital and momentous decisions were made; the course of many a contract was drastically changed, and several important projects abandoned. One of these was a Technicolor musical with a Japanese setting entitled provisionally, *Get Yourself a Geisha,* which was to have been a starring vehicle for Linda Lakai, a new Hungarian soprano with tiny eyes and an enormous range. A quarter of the picture had already been shot and so its sudden abandonment caused acute financial anxiety, until fortunately one of the scriptwriters conceived the brilliant idea of altering the locale from Japan to China, a gallant country with which everyone was in sympathy. This change was immediately put into effect and, with only minor alterations to the costumes, the picture ultimately emerged as *Pekin Parade* starring Laurine Murphy.

There were, of course, other equally momentous but more personal upheavals in the movie colony, among them the sudden discovery, by careful X ray, of an ulcer in Morgan Kent's duodenum. This unforeseen disaster, although not directly attributable to oriental treachery, must certainly have been aggravated by it and it entailed immediate and radical changes in Morgan's professional and private life as well as in his diet. His alcohol consumption was grimly rationed to two Scotch highballs a day and no old-fashioneds at all. He was obliged to withdraw from a "period" picture he had only just begun called *Hail Hannibal* and retire sadly to a rented bungalow in Palm Springs for a prolonged rest.

Here Lenore visited him occasionally for weekends, bringing with her the gossip of the town and a few friends to cheer his loneliness. The gossip of the town at that time was rich in surmise and agitation. Nationwide conscription was inevitable; Robert Bailey had flown to Canada to enlist, but had been invalided out after three

weeks' training on account of an undescended testicle, an embarrassment which hitherto had been unsuspected by his friends. Ross
Cheeseman, Sonny Blake and Jimmy Clunes were on the verge of
being drafted, and Joan Ziegler, obsessed by the fear of Japanese invasion, had had a nervous collapse, left poor Charlie and fled to her
mother's home in Iowa with the three children. Dear old Paul Newcombe had been absolutely splendid and was organizing vast
projects for British War Relief, and Lulu Frazer had volunteered to
make a tour of personal appearances for the Red Cross and had designed for herself two uniforms, one for day work and one for night
work, and both in sharkskin. There were many other tidbits of news
to relieve the tedium of Morgan's enforced seclusion, but happily,
after three months, Doc Mowbray—who was a personal friend as well
as a physician and had originally diagnosed the ulcer and arranged
the X ray—announced that the patient had so much improved in his
general condition that, provided he took things easily and remained
true to his diet, he could come back and start work on a new picture.

The next year was a successful one for Morgan. He happened
to be given two good scripts one after the other and both pictures
were completed within seven months. In November he was loaned to
the "Arch Bowdler–L.N.G. Studios" to play the much-coveted role of
Jumbo in *Jumbo R.A.F.*, a story based on the sensationally successful novel of the same name and which, as everyone in the industry
had already prophesied, would certainly be the Picture of the Year
and had as good as won the critics' award before the first reel was in
the can. This, being an "Epic" production, took a long while to make
and it was not until June 1943 that it was finished, sneak-previewed
and finally given its world première at Grauman's Chinese Theatre.

Of all the premières given in that great theater since war had
cast its shadow over American life, none had approached within a
thousand miles of the brilliance and distinction of this one. To begin
with, the picture had been discussed and publicized over a long period. There had also been trouble with the Hays office over certain
scenes which were considered to be too realistic and outspoken, notably one in which a tough but good-hearted squadron leader said to
the hero: "By God, Jumbo, in spite of your crazy flying, you're a lovable bastard!" This phrase had, of course, been viewed with slight
skepticism at the preliminary script conferences, but, as it was the
climax of one of the most memorable scenes in the original book, it
had been left in in the hope that it would get by. The Hays office, however, its ears protectively attuned to the fragile sensibilities of the
American moviegoing public, was inexorable, and the line had to be
changed to "By gosh, Jumbo, in spite of your crazy flying, you're a
fine kid." This, together with some other similar assaults upon national decency, necessitated retakes which put several weeks' extra

time into the production schedule. Also, as the whole Hays episode had been widely discussed in the press, public anticipation had been worked up to fever pitch.

The première itself was attended by everyone who was of note in the motion picture industry and by a great many who were not. Special cordons of police were employed to beat back the eager crowds; arc lamps bathed the occasion in shrill blue light; the immaculately shod feet of certain stars were pressed into wet cement and the imprints duly autographed, and every celebrity upon arrival was led to a microphone in the lobby where, amid the whirring and clicking of cameras, he or she gave his or her message of goodwill to an expectant radio public of several millions.

The auditorium of the theater had been draped with R.A.F. flags, and on the stage was grouped the Los Angeles Civic Choir in its entirety, appropriately dressed in R.A.F. uniforms. When finally the audience was seated and the choir had rendered "Oh, for the Wings of a Dove!" and "There'll Always Be an England," a British Ministry of Information "Documentary" was shown which, although a little slow in tempo, proved conclusively that London really had been bombed. This was followed by an inaudible speech from the British Consul and a Donald Duck cartoon. Then at last—at long last—came the picture itself which, on the whole, was very good. There were, of course, a few minor anachronisms here and there: a Brittany fishergirl who spoke French with a pronounced Hessian accent; a scene in a blossom-laden English orchard in June at the end of which the hero's humble mother, wearing a tea gown, presented her son's fiancée with a large bunch of chrysanthemums; and an amusing, but unconvincing, episode between the hero and a cockney greengrocer who, late at night in the spring of 1942, happened to be wheeling a barrow down Piccadilly piled with Sunkist oranges. Apart from these insignificant errors, which only a carping mind would have noted, the story moved along to its climax with gathering emotional strength and commendable speed. Some of the air-battle sequences were magnificent, and the escape of the hero from a Nazi prison camp was breathtaking. Morgan Kent as Jumbo gave unquestionably the finest performance in his career. He played his love scenes with sincerity and beautifully restrained passion, and his portrayal of grim determination, mixed with terror when he was forced to bail out of a blazing plane, brought forth a spontaneous burst of applause. When it was all over, there was prolonged cheering from the audience, and Morgan was almost torn to pieces by the crowd outside who unhappily had not been able to see the picture at all.

There was a party afterward at the Arc de Triomphe nightclub, which had been taken over for the occasion by Arch Bowdler, and it was not until 3:30 A.M. that Morgan and Lenore, tired but exalted, let themselves into their house and found, propped up on the bar, a telegram. Lenore opened it while Morgan was fixing a "nightcap." She said "My God!" under her breath, and handed it to him. He read it, and slowly put the bottle of bourbon he was holding back on the shelf. It said: "Sid reported missing presumably killed. Mother terribly upset. Please cable. Love, Sheila."

7

In the months following, Morgan, on the advice of the studio publicity department, went out very little and wore a black band. People were wonderfully kind and sympathetic, and he received many letters of condolence. Arch Bowdler indeed was so profoundly moved when he heard the news that he suggested organizing a memorial service for Morgan's sailor brother in the Sweetlawn Baptist Temple on Sunset Boulevard. Upon reflection, however, the idea was abandoned and instead he gave a small dinner for twenty-eight people in Morgan's honor, at which Sid's memory was toasted reverently before the party adjourned to the Blue Room to see the new L.N.G. musical, starring Glenda Crane and Bozo Browning.

Morgan, who had cabled his mother immediately upon receiving the telegram and flogged himself into writing a long letter of commiseration, accepted the attitude of his friends and acquaintances with dignity and restraint, and it was evident to all that he was bearing his loss with the utmost fortitude. Another effect of his bereavement was the strange lessening of friction in his home life. Lenore, softened perhaps by the passing wings of the Angel of Death, became kinder in her everyday manner, drank a little less and made fewer sarcastic wisecracks. Life went on much as usual except that in the autumn of 1943 both Morgan and Lenore, together with a group of other stars, went on a flying tour through the United States and Canada in order to make personal appeals for a great War Bond drive. This was publicly a great success and privately not without its rewards. They had a special plane to take them from place to place; they were entertained lavishly and photographed and interviewed ad nauseum; they had to sign thousands of autograph books, which was dreadfully tiring of course, but they took it in their stride upheld by the reflection that they were working for a magnificent cause and doing something really worthwhile.

Morgan actually enjoyed the Canadian part of the tour a little less. His well-rehearsed and beautifully delivered patriotic appeal was received politely, but without quite the same vibrant acclaim that it had been in the States. In fact, on one occasion, in an enormous cinema in Toronto, someone at the back shouted something apparently uncomplimentary. No one ever found out exactly what it was, but the tension of the moment was snapped, and he found it difficult to re-capture the audience's attention. The War Bond tour came to an end in Washington, where they were all entertained at the White House and photographed still more, inside and outside and in the garden. Later on they were photographed again: outside the Capitol and out-side the headquarters of the F.B.I.; and posed reverentially in front of the Lincoln Memorial. *Life* magazine published a six-page photo-graphic survey of the whole expedition and *Time* devoted an entire page to a eulogistic article under the heading, "Stars Calling."

8

In November 1943 Morgan celebrated his thirtieth birthday by giving a party. This had to take place on a Saturday night because he was in the middle of a French Resistance picture called *Hidden Flames* and had to get up at six o'clock every morning excepting Sundays. The party was a great success up to a certain point. A large number of people came, most of them bearing gifts; there was an entertaining quarrel between Hester Roach and Lois Levine, two exquisitely pro-portioned young starlets who had unfortunately both fallen in love with the same agent; Tonio Lopez brought his guitar and sang Mexi-can folk songs for an hour and a half by the pool; the buffet supper was delicious; Gloria Marlow choked over a fishbone in the kedgeree and had to be taken to the bathroom to be sick; everyone drank and enjoyed themselves immensely.

Morgan himself was at the top of his form and, in addition to being a perfect host and seeing that all his guests were looked after, contrived to have a brief but satisfactory affair with Opal Myers in the bathhouse. He emerged with admirable suavity from this epi-sode, leaving Opal to reappear a little later. Tonio was still singing his songs; the moon was shining and, although it was cold by the pool, there were enough mink coats to go around and everyone seemed to be happy. From the house above, where Lenore was dispensing drinks in the bar, came a cheerful buzz of chatter and laughter. Mor-gan picked his way through the group of muffled figures lying about on the canvas furniture, their cigarettes glowing like red fireflies in the moonlight, and went up the steps. He was aware of contentment. Life was good and God was in His heaven.

It was at this moment, this instant of rare and perfect fulfill-ment, that Destiny elected to kick him violently in the stomach. There was a honking of a klaxon in the drive and, coinciding with Morgan's arrival on the porch, a taxi drew up. Morgan, still serene, still swathed in physical satisfaction and mental ease, went forward hospitably to welcome the latecomers. There was, however, only one latecomer. The taxi stopped with a screech of brakes, there was a hearty roar of "Les" from inside it and Sid leapt out of it, bounded up the porch steps and clasped Morgan in his arms. It was a moment of extraordinary poignancy. Lenore, hearing the noise, came out of the bar with several others and gave a loud shriek. The distant murmur of Tonio's baritone down by the pool came to an abrupt stop; there was a babble of voices; Sid was hugged and kissed and slapped on the back and swept into the bar.

With him was swept into bitter oblivion Morgan's peace of mind. His sudden, transient awareness of joy of living turned brown at the edges, curled up and died. The moon went behind a cloud; the wind from the Pacific Palisades blew chill and his heart writhed with dreadful, unacknowledged dismay. From then on the party, for him, became a nightmare. The gay, excited clamor of his guests rasped his nerves; the very recent memory of Opal Myers's surrender lay stalely on his senses, and Lenore's fatuous, incredulous, welcoming screams irritated him to such an extent that he longed to bash her perfectly capped teeth down her throat.

To do him justice, however, his outward behavior was beyond reproach. He installed Sid in a comfortable chair, plied him with drink and food and gave over the whole evening to him without stint and without betrayal. It must frankly be admitted that Sid accepted it wholeheartedly. Wearing creased khaki slacks and a stained tropical tunic, he was looking ill and emaciated, but his good spirits were in no way impaired. Before the party was over he had told the story of his escape four times, each time leavening its drama with impeccable British understatement. It was a thrilling, almost incredible, story and was received by the assembled company with gasps and groans of excitement. To begin with, his ship had been sunk off the coast of Borneo in the summer of 1942. He had clung to a raft in shark-infested waters for eleven hours before being picked up by an armed Japanese trawler. He had escaped from a pestilential prison camp in Malaya with two comrades, both American, in July 1943. One of them was a big, husky fellow from Texas and the other a Jewish boy from Brooklyn who possessed qualities of courage and endurance which were nothing short of fantastic. The three of them, after terrible vicissitudes, managed to get to Ceylon in an open boat. From there, after weeks in hospital, they were sent in a transport plane to Honolulu via Australia, New Zealand, New Caledonia and Fiji. In Honolulu they parted company. Tex and Lew, the Brooklyn boy, remained in Schofield barracks awaiting leave while Sid, through the goodwill of an American Naval Intelligence officer, was given space in a bomber which was flying to San Francisco. In San Francisco he reported to the British Consul, who had notified the naval attaché in Washington, who in turn notified the Admiralty in London. After three days, during which he had lived in a small hotel on money supplied by the Consul, who had been extremely decent to him, the order came through from London that he was to take a week's leave and report to H.M.S. *Taragon* which was refitting in Norfolk, Virginia. He had cabled his mother and Sheila, but purposely had not let Morgan know that he was alive and safe because he wanted it to be a surprise. Well, here he was, and it was certainly a surprise. He was finally led to bed, happily drunk, and the party broke up.

The next three days, the duration of Sid's dramatic visit, were a perpetual embarrassment to Morgan. Of course he told himself repeatedly how delighted he was that Sid, instead of being missing and presumed killed, was alive and kicking and exuberantly cheerful, but the strain was considerable.

The Sunday following upon Sid's dramatic arrival was hectic beyond all bearing. The house was besieged by reporters and cameramen. Sid was photographed interminably: inside the house, outside the house, by the pool, on the porch, with Morgan, without Morgan, with Lenore, without Lenore, with Fred, the colored butler, and alone, in the shower. The telephone rang incessantly; sheaves of telegrams arrived; Arch Bowdler called personally and insisted on giving a dinner for Sid that very night. It was enormous, noisy and successful. Everybody, as usual, made speeches and for once no movie was shown, the emergence of Morgan's sailor brother from the jaws of death being a far greater attraction than any preview.

On the Monday, Ruthie's column in *Hollywood Highlights* was one long scream of hero worship. All the other papers also were plastered with photographs of Sid, articles on Sid, anecdotes about Sid and interviews with Sid. Louella Parsons flung her arms round him in the Brown Derby and burst into tears, and Hedda Hopper, looking extremely chic, appeared at a cocktail party wearing a new toque made entirely of palm fronds and white ensigns. To do Sid justice, all this embarrassed him almost as much as it embarrassed Morgan, but for different reasons. Morgan's reactions, entangled as they were with family conscience, subconscious jealousy and an agitated inferiority complex, were difficult to define accurately. Sid's were quite simple. He was glad to be alive; delighted to see "Old Les" again; pleased up to a point with all the fuss that was being made of him, but aware in his heart that it was perhaps a bit overdone, and above all else impatient to get home—via Norfolk, Virginia—as soon as possible.

Fortunately, on the second day of his visit, Gareth Gibbons, a new and handsome L.N.G. "heartthrob," was arrested for driving a car while under the influence of alcohol and attempting to rape a sixteen-year-old waitress in a milk bar on Brentwood Heights. This happily deflected the full blaze of publicity away from Sid, and his departure on the Wednesday was achieved, much to his relief, almost without comment.

The repercussions of his visit, however, were apparent for a long while. Morgan's behavior had been exemplary throughout, and most people had taken his carefully adjusted acceptance of Sid's reflected glory at its face value. Hollywood, however, is a strange place. It is filled with charming and talented people who work hard and do much to alleviate the miseries and troubles of the world. It is climatically amiable and steady; scenically it has much to offer; beautiful mountains surround it, efficient, clear-cut architecture adorns it, and blue skies, as a rule, smile down upon it. In spite of these advantages and a great many more besides, there is, as in all highly sensitive communities, an inevitable streak of cruelty and personal envy lying just below the radiant surface. There are, the fact must be frankly admitted, a few hard-boiled, oversophisticated, unkind characters abroad whose pleasure it is to strike down the successful, undermine the contented and distort, whenever possible, the pure motives of human behavior. These minds, it must also be frankly admitted, are frequently employed by the newspapers, for is it not from the newspapers that we first receive intimations that all is not well with our friends?

In Morgan's case it was Ruthie's little bird that first started the trouble. The ungenerous innuendo made by that feathered scavenger two years before had been quickly forgotten, but now, reinforced by Sid's second and far more spectacular arrival in the colony, it chirped again and again with increasingly malicious effect. Presently, in the columns of larger, more revered periodicals than *Hollywood Highlights*, unpleasant paragraphs about Morgan began to appear. Several of his magnanimous gestures toward the war effort were deprecated and questioned. His successful War Bond tour of the preceding year was alleged to have been mere publicity hunting; his duodenal ulcer, which had been troubling him acutely since Sid's visit, was mocked at and above all the fact that he had largeheartedly given his entire salary for *High Adventure* to the British War Relief was smeared with the suggestion that, as this picture was one over his schedule for the year, he evaded a great deal of super-tax by doing so.

All this, of course, was unmannerly and reprehensible, but, alas, in public life it is often necessary to take the rough with the smooth, and occasionally with the rough. This Morgan was temperamentally incapable of doing. His spirits were not particularly resilient, and his morale crumbled easily. As the insidious attacks upon his integrity increased and spread, he became more and more nervy, irritable and morose. Lenore, to her eternal credit, stood by him loyally. On one occasion she even went so far as to slap Mona Melody's face in the Beachcomber when that lady unequivocally stated that Morgan's moving-picture career was shot to hell.

But in spite of his wife's steadfastness and the devotion of his friends, things went from bad to worse. *High Adventure* opened simultaneously in New York, Chicago and Hollywood, and was unanimously voted by the critics to be the worst picture to come out of Hollywood since the war. Morgan's personal notices were insulting and occasionally downright vituperative. He was torn to pieces with all the gleeful savagery that only well-established, perenially successful stars can ever inspire. Al Tierney, his agent, flew especially to the Coast from New York, and grave consultations ensued between him, the studio publicity department, Lenore and Morgan himself. It was finally decided that he must publicly renounce his next two contracted pictures and go immediately on a tour of the war areas under the aegis of U.S.O.

Morgan protested against this decision at first, on the reasonable grounds that, being unable either to sing or dance, there was little that he could contribute to the entertainment of troops. He ultimately gave in, however, on the assurance that his role would be that of Master of Ceremonies and that all that would be required of him would be to talk nonchalantly into a microphone, tell a few funny stories and introduce the more musical artists supporting him.

In March 1944 the party set forth across the Atlantic in a transport plane. They all wore khaki uniforms with U.S.O. "flashes" on their shoulders, and had a farewell party given for them at the Stork Club in New York on the eve of their departure.

The tour was strenuous but triumphant. They played Gibraltar, Oran, Algiers, Tunis, Tripoli, Malta and Cairo. Then, after a few days' rest, they went on to Sicily, Naples and Rome. The show, being speedy, efficient and abundantly noisy, was received enthusiastically almost everywhere. Morgan had been paralyzed with nerves at the first few performances, but he gradually became more relaxed and began to enjoy himself. He discovered that the less effort he made, the more the troops liked him. He had been supplied with a few good stories before leaving and these he interspersed with impromptu comments of his own, some of which brought forth gratifying roars of laughter. The company consisted of Zaza Carryl, a slumbrous "blues" singer, who moaned lugubriously into the microphone and was invariably cheered to the echo; Ella Rosing, a very small starlet with a piercing coloratura, who went on first and sang, "Je Suis Titania" and "The Bells of St. Mary's"; Gus Gruber, who did card tricks interlarded with rather suggestive patter, and finished up by playing a ukulele and singing and dancing at the same time; and Okie Wood and Buzzie Beckman, a vaudeville act who had the star position at the end of the program and monotonously tore the place up. Lenore had been left behind in Beverly Hills, and Morgan, after a few halfhearted approaches to Ella Rosing, who was not really his type, finally settled on

Zaza Carryl as the partner of his private pleasures. She was an amiable, uncomplicated creature, and they got on very well.

Upon arrival in Rome toward the end of May, orders came through that when their week there was over they were to proceed to England. This caused a lot of discussion in the troupe, and a great many jokes were made about food rationing, doodlebugs and rocket bombs. Morgan, naturally enough, was tremendously excited at the thought of returning to his homeland after so many years' absence and in such circumstances. He realized without cynicism but with sheer common sense that, from the publicity angle alone, it would be an excellent thing to do.

Imagine, therefore, his bitter disappointment when three days before they were due to leave, he collapsed in agony halfway through a performance they were giving at an air base in the Campagna. He was hurried immediately into hospital, examined by several doctors and X-rayed. Nothing definite appeared in the X ray, but as his pains, although sporadic, were intense and he was also in a bad state of nervous exhaustion, it was deemed wiser to fly him directly back to the States rather than let him risk continuing the tour.

His plane was met at Los Angeles by Lenore, Arch Bowdler, the deputy head of the studio publicity department, Doc Mowbray and an ambulance in which he was whisked off to a clinic, where he stayed for three weeks undergoing various tests and gradually regaining his strength. The publicity accruing from his misfortune was, on the whole, innocuous. Even Ruthie's little bird, although a trifle skeptical, was forced to admit that Morgan's tour of the battle areas had been an unqualified success and that he had done a fine job and been popular with the "boys."

9

In the autumn of 1945 Morgan's dream of returning home to England at last came true. During the defeat of the Nazis in Europe and the dropping of the atomic bomb on Hiroshima he had made two immensely successful pictures. His position now was more unassailable than it had ever been even in the year of his first meteoric rise to stardom.

Only one thing marred the joy and gratification of his spectacular "comeback" into public favor, and that was Lenore's unexpected and crude announcement that she was sick to death of him, was passionately in love with Tonio Lopez and wished for a divorce as soon as it conveniently could be arranged. There were some violent scenes and much bitter mutual recrimination during which the names of Opal Myers and Zaza Carryl were hurled at his head with certain justification. Finally, with the assistance of two lawyers and the studio publicity department and a lot of bickering, it was arranged that Lenore should divorce him on grounds of mental cruelty and acute incompatibility of temperament. Soon after this Lenore unostentatiously left the house and retired, for discretion's sake, to her married sister's home in Salt Lake City. Morgan meanwhile, oppressed by a sense of matrimonial failure, was dispatched, in a blaze of publicity, to attend a Royal Command performance of his latest picture *The Boy from the Hills* at the Empire Theatre, Leicester Square, London.

His reception in England surpassed not only his own but the studio publicity department's wildest dreams. From the moment he stepped ashore from the *Queen Elizabeth* at Southampton he was mobbed by wildly cheering crowds. Sid, wearing inconspicuous civilian clothes, met him at the dock. His mother and Sheila remained at home on the advice of the English representative of the studio publicity department, who had organized for Morgan a triumphant return to Southsea on the coming Saturday and wished the long-awaited reunion of mother and son to be handled in the proper manner at the proper time.

At Waterloo Station Morgan was nearly trampled underfoot by his English fans, and the expectant crowd outside Claridge's was so vast that special mounted police had to be deployed to keep it in order and deflect the traffic. The première at the Empire the next evening was, to Morgan, the accolade of his whole career. He received an ovation upon entering the theater; was presented, with others, to the King and the Queen, and cheered with heartwarming enthusiasm at the end when he stepped onto the stage to make his personal appearance.

His return to his home town of Southsea on the Saturday was even more tumultuous, and, although not graced by the presence of Royalty, almost equally moving. The streets were hung with banners and flags; his mother and Sheila and the mayor greeted him on the steps of the Town Hall, and it was not until after a reception at the Queen's Hotel, at which he was called upon to make one speech for the newsreels and another for the B.B.C., that he was allowed to relax in the bosom of his family. Even then the street remained thronged with adolescent enthusiasts for quite a while.

His first impression on entering the familar sitting room was that it was much smaller than he remembered it to be. Sheila, married now and with two children, was as brusque and downright as ever. His mother had aged a good deal, but her eyes were glistening with excitement and she was inclined to be tearful. After tea conversation flagged a bit. All family news had been exhausted. Father's death and funeral in 1943 had been described in detail, also Sheila's wedding, the birth of both her children and Sid's intended marriage to a Miss Doris Solway in a few months' time. Strangely enough, the devastation of the town in the early years of the war was hardly mentioned. Even the fact that Hadley's, where Morgan had once worked as a floorwalker, was now nothing but a mound of grass-covered rubble, was only once lightly commented upon by Sheila. Morgan found himself glancing furtively at his watch and hoping that the studio car would soon arrive to drive him back to London.

It is sad to reflect how many family reunions are spoiled by anticlimax. The excitement and anticipation have been so strong; the moment so often and so gloriously pre-envisaged that the human heart seems unable to sustain the joy of actuality. Morgan's homecoming was naturally poignant and touching and happy. Not only this, but it was publicly spectacular into the bargain. And yet, inevitably, when the first greetings were over, the occasion wilted and became soggy; little nervous jokes were made and there were unexplained silences.

Presently the car arrived and Morgan got up to go. He kissed Sheila, wrung Sheila's husband's hand and banged Sid on the back. There was suddenly a renewed burst of conversation, as though everything was perfectly normal. Morgan's mother, after a swift, appealing glance at Sheila, went out with him into the hall. He took her in his arms and was aware of a genuine surge of emotion. She felt frail and old and somehow pathetic. She stood away from him and gave her hair a little pat.

"Come back soon, Les." she said, and then with a tremor in her voice, "We didn't know anything about the ulcer, dear. It must have been dreadful."

Morgan squeezed her arm affectionately. "That's all over now, Mum, don't worry."

"It isn't that"—she seemed to be speaking with an effort—"but if anyone mentions your tubercular lung—do remember that we had to say something!"

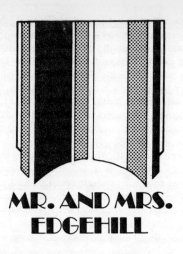

MR. AND MRS.
EDGEHILL

Mrs. Edgehill had walked along to the "Split" and sat down with her back against Roper's Folly. Roper's Folly was the remains of a wooden lookout house which Mr. Roper, since deceased, had begun to build many years ago and had discarded. It was a pleasant place to sit, and she came there often in the evenings when she had washed up the tea things. It was silly of poor Mr. Roper ever to have thought of building a house on that particular spot; for one thing, it was too exposed and lay right in the path of the trade winds. Also, if he had ever completed it, it would have necessitated making a path all the way from the landing stage. There would have been no peace in the house either, stuck right out there on the edge of the surf, and in really bad weather it might quite conceivably have been washed away—indeed, bits of it already had been. Last March year, when the cyclone had passed quite close to the island, waves had broken clean over it.

Mrs. Edgehill sat there idly with her hands in her lap. She could, of course, have brought her knitting or a book, but it was nicer just to do nothing at all. On her right the vivid water swirled through the "Split" into the lagoon; when it had escaped the foam and turbulence of the surf, it flowed swiftly and smoothly and looked solid like blue-green glass. Directly in front of her was nothing but sea and sky. The sky, as usual at this time of year, was pale and without a cloud; the line of the horizon was sharp, and the enormous rollers advanced monotonously, as though they had been strictly disciplined, to break on the outer rocks of the reef. Occasionally in the troubled water she would see the sinister dorsal fin of a shark slip by, or a school of porpoises flinging themselves through the waves just before they broke. She had a soft corner in her heart for the porpoises; they were so gay and abandoned, and seemed to enjoy life. At her feet, among the shells and seaweed and myriad pieces of broken coral, hermit crabs scuttled about; some of them were enormous and had almost outgrown their borrowed shells. She always longed to catch one in the act of changing into a larger shell, but she had never been lucky.

Her back was to the island—it was not really an island in the proper sense of the word, merely a coral reef some hundred yards wide enclosing a large lagoon—but when the sun went down she would, of course, turn round. This was a ritual. Eustace pulled the flag down at sunset, and he liked her to stand up wherever she happened to be just for those few solemn moments. She loved him for insisting on this, even if there was no one to see; even when they had been alone on the island for months, she had always stood rigidly and watched the flag slowly fluttering down the mast and Eustace in his faded khaki shorts hauling away at the ropes.

There was still half an hour or so to go before sunset, so she could afford to relax and let her thoughts wander. She was rather given to doing this; Eustace had said, years and years and years ago when they were first married, that her mind was like a ragbag. She remembered having been vaguely hurt by this at the time, but later she had had to admit that there was a certain justification for what he said. Her mind was rather like a ragbag—she viewed it quite literally as being a hotchpotch of odds and ends and bits of colored stuff and thimbles and needles and whatnot—but the trouble was that she could never get it really tidied up, and by nature she was a tidy woman.

Here, of course, sitting by herself looking at the sea, it didn't matter how casually her mind behaved; it could jump backward and forward through time and space as much as it liked. She could even talk out loud to herself if she wanted to; there was nobody to hear her except the hermit crabs. Sometimes she tried to string together piece by piece the last twenty years, all the adventures and excitements and joys and despairs, but she nearly always got sidetracked; some particular memory would hold the stage for too long and, in reliving it, the story would become unstuck and muddled. It was quite a story, too, when you came to think of it, if you could write it for a magazine and put it down clearly, without having to worry about spelling or keep on stopping to think of the right words.

Up until she had first met Eustace, of course, there hadn't

been any story at all; that is, nothing out of the ordinary. Just a girl with a mother and father and three sisters and one brother living in a country town. She closed her eyes for a moment against the bright, alien sea, and walked along Hythe High Street; she turned to the left just after passing the Red Lion, and walked across the bridge over the dike, past Mrs. Vernon's, and along for a bit until she got on to the Front. The tide was out, but only just out, because the sands still looked wet. Away to the right were the Romney Marshes and the sea wall with the Martello towers sticking up against the evening sky. There was Eustace coming toward her, arm in arm with that awful Elsie Mallet; there was her Fate walking into her life with a slight sailor's roll and his cap too much on the back of his head and a tuft of towlike hair jutting out over his forehead. She had often, in later years, felt slight conscience pangs about Elsie Mallet. After all, he was her second cousin and had come down from Chatham on week-end leave.

Mrs. Edgehill opened her eyes again, and permitted herself a complacent smile. Poor Elsie! No need to pity her really; they hadn't been actually engaged, but still. . . . That had been the beginning—the very beginning—twenty-five years ago.

She turned her head, and looked back toward the hotel and the landing stage. Eustace was still fiddling with the canoe. He looked very small and thin in the distance, like a sunburned little boy. She did wish he could put on a little more weight, but still he was the thin type, and although he was over fifty he would always look young for his age.

Her mind ran lightly back to the honeymoon at Blackpool. That was 1919—she never liked thinking about it very much because she hadn't enjoyed it. It wasn't Eustace's fault—it wasn't anybody's fault really—but she hadn't known it was going to be quite like that. Later on she had to admit that she'd been a bit silly over the whole thing, but Blackpool of all places, so common and noisy and all those thousands of people and that awful bedroom in the Marine Hotel and the picture of the soldier saying good-bye to the dead horse. Waking up to that every morning was no picnic. It almost made her cry to think of it. And being sick on the scenic railway, and Eustace getting drunk on the Saturday night, and then having that dreadful quarrel on the pier. . . . Then came London, and the flat in Acacia Mansions, and Eustace leaving the Navy and getting the job at Bartlett's. Whoever it was that said the first year of married life is the most difficult was dead right and no mistake.

It was funny to look back on bitterness and utter misery and not mind about it anymore. Perhaps if it had not been for the operation, and the baby dying and her being so ill for all those months, nothing would ever have come right. Eustace might have gone on at

Bartlett's; they might have had other children, and gone on living in that flat and quarreling and not understanding about each other or anything. Eustace might have left her eventually—run off with somebody else (her heart contracted painfully at the very thought of it)—none of the rest might ever have happened, none of the adventures and troubles, none of the true love (she sighed and then smiled)—she wouldn't change places, not with anyone in the world, she wouldn't go back five minutes, but she wouldn't change! She looked back again. Eustace had at last left the canoe and was walking back to the house. He saw her and waved his hand. She watched him go in by the back door, followed faithfully by Sandy; Sandy probably thought that there was a bit of fish going.

The sun was getting lower and the sea color was changing; a spider crab suddenly popped out of a hole in the sand and went dancing down to the water's edge on its high, spindly legs as though it were being blown by the wind. Mrs. Edgehill settled herself comfortably again. There was no hurry.

2

Cowrie Island is a small coral ring in the Southwest Pacific. Officially it is designated as belonging to the outer Samolan Group, but this is merely for the purpose of identification as it is entirely isolated. Actually it is nearer to Fiji than to Samolo, but it comes under the jurisdiction of the Samolan governor. It was first charted in the year 1786 by the redoubtable Captain Evangelus Cobb, who was driven by a gale onto its reefs. Fortunately the damage to his ship was comparatively slight, for there was no water on the island and had he been forced to stay there he and his crew would have died of thirst. As it was, however, he was stranded for only a few days and was able to report with lyric enthusiasm in his logbook that it was "..... a reef of personable size o'er which fluttered small white birds of exquisite beauty . . . so tame were these gentle, fragile creatures that they were willing, nay, eager to accept biscuit crumbs from the naked hand."

In the nineteenth century, when the Samolan group was taken over by the British, Cowrie Island was, rather casually, included in the deal. Since then it had remained uninhabited until the early nineteen twenties, when the then governor of Samolo, Sir Vivian Cragshore, with extraordinary foresight for a colonial governor, had realized its possible potentialities as a future seaplane base.

With commendable promptitude, and in the face of considerable opposition from the Colonial Office, he had equipped an expedition consisting of ten people, three Samolans, four half-castes (all of whom had passed with honors through an engineering course at

Pendarla University) and three Englishmen, or rather two Englishmen and a Scotsman named Ian Strachan.

Ian Strachan was in charge of the party, and they swiftly and efficiently set to work to build rain tanks, several huts—most of which were demolished by the weather in later years—and a flagstaff which, although it blew down every now and then, survives to this day. After a few months of extremely primitive living the expedition departed, leaving only Strachan and the hardy Samolans. These exiles were supplied with necessities by a ship which called twice a year. Strachan lived there in solitude with the exception of the Samolans, who fished incessantly, until 1935, when he died of blood poisoning, having had his heel torn off by a barracuda while swimming in the lagoon.

At this time the Trans-National Airways were already casting covetous eyes on the island with a view to using it as a convenient overnight stop for their intended Trans-Pacific Clipper service. Representations were made from Washington to the British Government for either a lease or sale of the island. Meanwhile Sir Humphrey Logan, who had succeeded Sir Vivian Cragshore in Samolo, dispatched Eustace Edgehill, who had been trying for two years, not very successfully, to run a pineapple plantation on the seacoast near Naruchi, and bade him build a house and install himself as British Resident, pending the results of the Anglo-American discussions.

In May 1936 Eustace Edgehill arrived at Cowrie Island. He brought with him adequate but not extravagant supplies and six Samolan boys of excellent physique but dubious reputation, dubious that is to say from the standpoint of the Church of England Mission School in Naruchi. They were beach boys, and beach boys, in the view of the God-fearing, were definitely lesser breeds without the law. They had spent most of their extreme youth and adolescence diving for pennies for the edification of visiting tourists. For the further edification of the tourists they were known to be obliging in many other ways. They were cheerful, amoral, and they could all play the "akula" (a local form of ukulele) with impeccable rhythm. They could also sing charmingly, although some of their native hybrid songs were not entirely guiltless of sensual implication. They were expert fishermen and were tough, willing and without malice.

It was for these latter qualifications that Eustace Edgehill chose them to accompany him. There was a certain amount of fuss in church circles in Naruchi—in fact, a question was asked in the House of Assembly in Pendarla—but Eustace, who took a bleak view of missionaries and was none too enthusiastic about the Church of England anyhow, finally got his way and, amid scenes of local jubilation, they set sail.

For Eustace the whole thing was a tremendous adventure. In

the first place the title "British Resident" filled him with pride; secondly, the thought of going off into the unknown, starting as it were from scratch, building himself a house, and installing himself as monarch of all he surveyed, fluttered his heart with excitement and gratification. All his life he had been like that, not only willing but eager to cast away the substance for the shadow. Not that the pineapple plantation could in truth be called substance. It had been unsatisfactory and unremunerative from the word go, and for him, with his irrepressible spirit of adventure, far too sedentary.

For his wife, Dorrie, this new challenge to Fate was full of menace. After all, they were neither of them as young as they used to be and he, like poor Mr. Strachan, might be bitten by a barracuda or get sunstroke all by himself on an exposed coral reef. She had not enjoyed the pineapple experiment any more than he had, but at least, with all its disappointments and difficulties, they had been together. Now he was leaving her behind, by order of the governor, until the house was built and he could send for her. He swore that it would only be a question of a few months at the outside, but she remained skeptical, heavyhearted and full of dark forebodings. When he had finally sailed she went dismally back to the house, looked with distaste at the crop of undersized pineapples and had a good cry.

3

The arrival at Cowrie Island was, on the whole, discouraging. There was a heavy sea running, a seventy-mile-an-hour gale and driving rain. Three days of this had to be endured before they could come close enough in to land a boat and negotiate the "Split." After several hazardous journeys, during one of which the boats nearly capsized, they finally managed to get themselves and their supplies ashore. Eustace, wearing a pair of shorts, gum boots, a raincoat and a topee, looked around him and sighed.

The sight that met his eyes was not entirely up to what his imagination had pictured. The driving rain did little to enhance the cheerfulness of the scene. The island was about twenty-eight miles in circumference and, where he stood by the rickety landing stage, about three to four hundred yards wide; beyond the "Split" on the right, and also about a quarter of a mile away on the left, it narrowed until at certain places there was less than a hundred yards between the pounding surf and the lagoon. There were no trees or shrubs of any sort, except one large, rather sullen-looking bush that looked like a vast green hedgehog.

The huts that the Strachan expedition had built were still standing, but were in a bad state of disintegration. Over by the "Split" stood a strange stone edifice which had obviously never been finished at all. This had been started in a moment of enthusiasm by Mr. Roper, who had been Ian Strachan's second in command. The captain of the ship was standing with Eustace on the landing stage. He waved his hand contemptuously in the direction of Mr. Roper's unfulfilled dream. "Bloody silly," he said; "any fool would have known better than to try to build a house right on the point like that." Eustace smiled desolately and agreed with him.

The largest of the Strachan huts still had enough roof over half of it to keep out the rain, and so, pending further explorations, Eustace directed the boys to dump the supplies and themselves in there until the weather abated a little. The captain, who was obviously concerned about getting his boat through the "Split" and back to the ship, wrung Eustace's hand with ill-disguised sympathy, slapped him a thought too heartily on the back and departed with many shouted promises to see him again in about three months' time.

Eustace walked over to the sea side of the reef and watched the boat battling through the surf. When it had safely navigated it and was rapidly becoming a small black speck in the distance, he turned and walked back to the hut. The boys were still staggering up from the landing stage with packing cases. Ippaga, the eldest of them, was sucking at a sodden cigarette and shouting orders. He smiled broadly at Eustace, exposing two rows of perfect teeth, and shrugged his shoulders as much as to say, "Well—here we are—it's bloody awful, but all we can do is to make the best of it." Eustace smiled back at him, and suddenly felt more cheerful.

A few hours later, a little before sundown, a miracle happened. The rain stopped abruptly, the skies cleared and the whole island was bathed in soft, luminous yellow light; the lagoon was transformed from a waste of choppy gray waves into a sheet of vivid emerald and blue with multicolored coral heads pushing up above the surface of the water. The boys, who had been profitably employed in rigging up a tarpaulin over the unroofed part of the principal hut, gave loud whoops of joy and, tearing off whatever odd garments they happened to have, ran down to the landing stage, from which they dived, clean as arrows, and with hardly any splash at all.

Eustace watched them indulgently and, lighting a cigarette, sat down on one of the rotting wooden rails of the verandah. While he was sitting there a very small, delicate white bird circled twice round the hut, and then, quite unafraid, settled on his hand. The sky suddenly became a pageant; the vanished storm had left wisps of cloud that took fire from the last rays of the sun; every color imaginable flamed across the heavens. Eustace nodded his head contentedly. "Dorrie will like this," he said to himself.

4

Doris Edgehill was a woman of fortitude. She was also what has been described in a popular song as a "One-Man Girl." She had met and fallen in love with Eustace in 1917, and, in spite of the disappointments, difficulties and, in her case, actual tragedies of early married life, she had remained in love with him and would continue to love him until the end of her days. It is indeed fortunate for the sanctity of marriage vows that women of her type still exist. Not that she ever gave much thought to sanctity of any sort. Once Eustace had whisked her away from her home and family and the ambiguous religious ministrations of the local vicar, she was perfectly content to accept his views on God and man and the universe without argument and without question. She seldom troubled her mind with conjectures on the life hereafter, being far too occupied with the continued effort of adapting herself to the occasionally alarming circumstances of life as it was.

Eustace's incorrigible adventurousness and sudden inexplicable enthusiasms led her convulsively, but on the whole happily, through the years. It is true that she sometimes reflected on the strange unorthodoxy of her married life as compared with the romantic visions of it that she had cherished originally. These visions, of course, had been the natural outcome of her home environment, which was nothing if not conventional: a hardworking husband, a house or flat, several children and a tranquil old age. This perhaps was what she had hoped for, but it was so long ago that she could not really accurately remember. At all events it certainly could not have panned out more differently.

If, during those far-off early days, any prophetic instinct had so much as hinted at the shape of the years to come, she would have been aghast. Here she was, rising forty-five, with graying hair and a skin toughened by tropic suns and varied weathers, sitting, grass-widowed, on a failing pineapple plantation on one of the remoter British Colonial possessions. It really was laughable. If it weren't for being worried about Eustace and separated from him by hundreds of miles of ocean, she could have laughed with more wholehearted enjoyment. Even as it was, she could not help seeing the funny side.

This perverse but undaunted sense of humor had come to her aid in far worse situations than the one in which she now found herself. There was the time when they had first come out to the South Seas and landed themselves in Suva with that dreadful copra business. Then there was the collapsible airplane which Eustace had sent out in crates from England with a view to revolutionizing the inter-island communications. That had been the worst really, on account of it being so dangerous—let alone all their savings being invested in the damn thing.

She could never remember without a shudder the black day when Eustace and Joe Mortimer and the native boys had at last managed to put the machine together and were preparing for the trial flight. Joe Mortimer had been in the Royal Flying Corps in the last war, and so he was the pilot. Eustace, poor old Eustace, apart from being the promoter of the whole enterprise, was the observer. She could see it now, that long stretch of sandy beach with the airplane, surrounded by giggling natives and Eustace in a cap and goggles that made him look like a beetle. Then the propeller being "revved" up; going round faster and faster, then a lot of shouting, and the natives scattering in all directions, and the machine, slowly but with gathering speed, starting off along the beach.

It was all over in less than five minutes, but it had seemed to her like five years. On it went, growing smaller and smaller in the distance until it almost reached the bluff of coco palms jutting out into the sea; then it took off—she remembered distinctly giving a loud scream—and flew out over the lagoon cumbersomely and jerkily as though it were being pulled by a string. Then, horror of horrors, wallop it went into the sea, just the other side of the reef, where there was heavy surf. She stood transfixed with misery and waited. All her life it seemed that she waited, watching the plane like a large wounded bird bobbing about in the waves. A big roller took it as lightly as though it were a paper boat, and, turning it upside down, dashed it against the reef.

It was then that she started to shout loudly. Kumani, the fisherman, had the canoe ready, and was just pushing it off when she, sobbing and breathless, jumped into it. Eustace and Joe were both on the reef when they got there. Joe looked all right, but Eustace was lying twisted up and deathly still. When they finally managed to get him into the canoe he had regained consciousness and was groaning. He had three broken ribs, a fractured thigh and a lump on his head the size of a cricket ball, and that was that. Joe's nose was bleeding pretty badly, but apart from that he was unhurt. The airplane, having been repeatedly dashed against the rocks, finally disappeared from view. With it disappeared their joint savings of several years.

After that there were no other adventures for quite a long time. Eustace was in the hospital at Suva for eleven months, and in a plaster cast for six of them. During this time Dorrie had managed to get a job as teacher in the mission school. She taught only the very smallest native children and hated every minute of it, but it sufficed to keep a roof over her head. A little later on, just before Eustace was well enough to leave the hospital, Providence, which always favors the reckless, obligingly arranged for Uncle Ernest to die in Cumberland, and Uncle Ernest, whom she hadn't clapped eyes on since she was fourteen, by some oversight had left her five hundred pounds in his will. On receipt of the solicitors' letter from London explaining this incredible bit of good fortune, she had gone immediately to Eustace in the hospital, and they had made plans for the future.

There had been a lot of argument and, on her part, some tears, but Eustace was quite determined. They had had enough of Fiji. They must go away somewhere quite different, and make a fresh start. Dorrie fought this gallantly, but without much conviction. She never had much conviction when Eustace was really set on something, and finally they decided that the moment he was well enough they would set sail for the Samolan Islands. Eustace was wildly enthusiastic about this because a man who had been in the next bed to him when he first came into the hospital had been Samolan born and swore that it was a veritable paradise and full of the most fantastic opportunities for anyone who had the faintest grit and initiative. Dorrie ultimately gave up the struggle, and so to Samolo they went.

That was all ten years ago. Samolo had not turned out to be quite the heaven on earth that Eustace's bedmate had depicted, but on the whole, up until the pineapples, they had not done so badly. During the years Eustace had been respectively a barman in a new luxury hotel in Pendarla which failed; a warder in the prison, which unenviable job he relinquished voluntarily because he said it depressed his spirit; an assistant office manager in the Royal Hawaiian and Samolan Shipping Company, which lasted over three years and might have gone on indefinitely if Eustace had not had a blood row with one of the directors; and finally came the pineapple scheme, which she was now concerned with liquidating as soon as possible.

Eustace's appointment as Resident on Cowrie Island had come as a staggering surprise to them both. Dorrie privately considered it to be a wild eccentricity on the part of the governor, who had met Eustace at a Rotary luncheon and taken a fancy to him. Her innate loyalty to Eustace prevented her from ever implying, either by word or deed, that in her humble opinion he was not of the stuff of which successful Residents are made—Residents, that is to say, according to the conventional conception of what a Resident, a representative of His Majesty's Government, should really be.

Eustace was small and undistinguished physically by either height or girth; his attitude toward religion was undoubtedly tinged with mockery; he was utterly lacking in pomposity; he had a slight but quite unmistakable cockney accent. True, his loyalty to his country and its traditions was strong and at moments downright truculent; he had an undisguised passion for four-letter words and bawdy songs, and very little tolerance of any kind. Still, if the governor thought he was suitable for the job, she would obviously be the last person to say anything against it.

Once the immediate depression of his departure was over, she set to work diligently to get rid of the pineapple plantation as soon as possible. She actually had some good luck over this, and finally managed to dispose of three-quarters of the land to a new real estate company which wished to turn the East Naruchi beach into a bathing resort. The other quarter, which was to the west and slightly elevated above sea level, she held on to, reflecting logically that land was land whichever way you looked at it and that if the Naruchi beach scheme ever amounted to anything it would probably treble its value in a few years' time. Having achieved all this, she stored all their furniture and personal belongings against the happy day when the house on Cowrie Island should be ready for her, and rented a small furnished flat in Pendarla.

Pendarla was the main town on the island and the seat of government. It was situated on the north coast, and boasted a wide and lovely harbor. A range of mountains swept straight up from the sea and, over the foothills, sprawled the town itself. Dorrie's flat was in a new building at the far end of the Mallaliea road. This meant that she was within an easy tram ride from the center of the town, with the additional advantage of being more or less in the country. Her flat was on the seventh story, one floor from the top, and she had a small balcony which commanded a view over the harbor to the right and to the left over Mano point to the open sea. She spent many hours sitting there with her sewing and gazing, a trifle forlornly, out over the curling breakers to where she imagined Cowrie Island lay. As a matter of fact, it really lay about three hundred miles directly behind her, but maps and distances and geography had never been her strong point, and it didn't really matter anyway.

After she had been there a few weeks she was astonished, and considerably shattered, to receive an invitation to lunch at Government House. It had not yet occurred to her that as the wife of the new Resident of Cowrie Island she would automatically be received into the higher Samolan social circles. This unexpected contingency upset her very much. She knew herself to be completely lacking in social graces; she had no gloves, and only one passable afternoon dress which she knew to be several years out of date. She was also oppressed with the fear that either by talking too much, or too little, or losing her head and doing something stupid, she might let Eustace down.

It was therefore in a state of miserable panic that she finally drove up in a taxi and turned into the impressive drive of Government House. An immense Samolan in a white tunic and a scarlet fez opened the door of the cab, and she was received by a cherubic young naval officer with an unmistakable twinkle in his eyes. He led her through a large hall and along a shady patio into the drawing room. She was painfully aware that her shoes were squeaking loudly on the parquet. There was a small group of people clustered round a sort of trolley table, on which were decanters and jugs and glasses. She was too nervous to notice who anybody was.

Lady Logan came forward to meet her, followed by Sir Humphrey. Lady Logan was tall, immeasurably distinguished, with rather untidy white hair and an easy, friendly smile. Sir Humphrey was large and shaggy and exuded an air of benign frowziness; his white silk tropic suit hung on his enormous frame with the utmost casualness. He placed a vast hand under her elbow, and piloted her toward the other guests. There was a smartly dressed, drained-looking woman, Lady Something-or-Other, who was on a visit from England and staying in the house; an admiral with gentle blue eyes and aggressive eyebrows; a captain of marines, very handsome with curly hair, a curly mouth and a most curly moustache. Vivienne and Sylvia, the two Logan daughters, came forward and greeted her warmly. She, of course, knew them by sight, but had never spoken to them before. They were pretty, fresh-looking girls in cool linen frocks. Last of all she was introduced to a Professor Carmichael who, the governor explained, was making a tour of the islands at the head of an entomological mission. Dorrie had not the faintest idea what that meant, but she nodded knowingly as she shook his withered little hand. The naval A.D.C. offered her the choice of either a dry Martini, sherry or tomato juice. She chose the dry Martini and then wished she'd plumped for the tomato juice. Lady Logan motioned her to a place beside her on the sofa and asked her if she had had any news of Eustace, and whether or not she was looking forward to her exile on Cowrie Island. Dorrie replied in a prim, constricted voice that she was certainly looking forward to going to the Island, but that she was afraid that it would be a long time before she got there.

Lady Whatever-It-Was chimed in and said that the whole thing sounded too entrancing for words and that she envied her with every fiber of her being.

Vivienne, the elder Logan girl, said, "Really, Aunt Cynthia, you know perfectly well you'd hate it."

Lady Logan laughed. "I'm afraid it wouldn't be quite your affair, darling," she said. "You've always been a great one for your comforts, and on Cowrie Island there is apparently nothing but coral, coral and more coral."

"But I adore coral," protested Lady Cynthia, handing her empty cocktail glass to the A.D.C. "I don't mean those dismal little pink necklaces that German governesses wear—they're absolutely bloody, of course—but coral qua coral is sheer heaven!"

Dorrie, who had jumped slightly at the surprising use of the word "bloody" in such high circles, was trying to decide in her mind whether Lady Cynthia really was idiotic or merely, for some obscure reason, pretending to be, when luncheon was announced and they all went into the dining room. Lady Cynthia sat on the governor's left and Dorrie on his right. As the meal progressed, Dorrie began to lose a little of her shyness. Lady Cynthia continued to talk and behave like somebody out of a back number of the *Tatler*, but Dorrie had to admit to herself that she was now and then quite amusing and apparently without guile. H. E. talked incessantly on a variety of topics. The two girls chattered gaily in high, shrill, very English voices, and flirted mildly with the captain of marines. Lady Logan, at the other end of the table, grappled gallantly with the professor, who was obviously rather heavy in the hand. The admiral uttered a short bark at intervals.

When lunch was over, they all sat out on the patio and had coffee. The afternoon sun blazed down on the smooth, perfectly kept lawn, but under cover, in the shade of the pink plaster arches, it was pleasantly cool. Dorrie relaxed and allowed the gentle, effortless atmosphere to smooth away her agitation. It was stupid, she reflected, to be shy of people and get into a state. After all, as long as you were yourself and didn't pretend or try to show off, nothing much could happen to you. Lady Cynthia, who had been upstairs to powder her nose, came back and sat down next to her on a swing seat; she rocked it languidly backward and forward with her foot, and offered Dorrie a cigarette. "I must say," she said pensively, "I really do think you're bloody brave."

"Why?" said Dorrie in surprise.

"Well"—Lady Cynthia held up her hand and scrutinized her nails with some distaste—"going off into the blue like that and settling down on a little dump and not clapping eyes on anybody from one year's end to another."

"It won't be so bad as all that," said Dorrie. She suddenly felt confident and almost superior. Perhaps she really was a good deal more dashing than she had ever thought she was. "After all, I shall be with my husband." This sounded rather flat, and she immediately wished that she hadn't said it. Lady Cynthia gave a little laugh, and then suddenly her face looked sad and much older.

"What's he like?" she said.

Dorrie stiffened as though to ward off an attack, and then, realizing that there was really no offensive intent in Lady Cynthia's question but merely a frank curiosity, she relaxed and gave a little laugh. "He's not much to look at really," she said, "that is, he isn't what you'd call exactly handsome. But still it's a nice face, if you know what I mean, and he's full of go and always keen on getting things done."

"What sort of things?" said Lady Cynthia inexorably.

"All sorts. . . ." There was pride in Dorrie's voice. "He can turn his hand to anything. The trouble is"—she paused—"he sometimes gets a bit carried away."

"I shouldn't imagine that he'd have many opportunities of getting carried away on Cowrie Island."

"Well, you never know," said Dorrie simply. "He's building a house at the moment, and I must say I wish I was there to keep an eye on it."

"How long have you been married?"

"Twenty-eight years next August."

"Good God!" Lady Cynthia looked genuinely astonished. "And you still love him all that much?"

Dorrie tightened up again, and Lady Cynthia, immediately realizing it, suddenly patted her hand and smiled—a charming smile, which completely banished the habitual look of weary boredom from her face. "Please forgive me," she said gently. "You mustn't think I'm being bloody. I'm always far too inquisitive about people, particularly if I happen to take a fancy to them."

The unmistakable sincerity of Lady Cynthia's tone flabbergasted Dorrie. The idea of being taken a fancy to by anyone so ineffably poised and remote from her own way of life as Lady Cynthia seemed quite fantastic. How surprised Eustace would be when she told him about it! "How did you know I loved him so much?" she asked.

"It's pretty obvious really." Lady Cynthia smiled again, but this time a trifle wryly. "I envy you. I've run through three husbands in far less time than twenty-eight years. Perhaps I'm not as lucky as you, or as sensible—or even as nice," she added.

This was plainly Dorrie's cue, and she took it unstintingly. "I'm quite sure you couldn't be nicer," she said boldly, and then was glad she had done so, because Lady Cynthia looked so obviously pleased.

"It's always pleasant, isn't it," she said, "to meet new friends? I shall be here for another two weeks—do ring me up and we might have lunch and gossip or go to a movie or something."

Dorrie, quite overcome, murmured that she'd certainly love to. Then Lady Logan made a slight but perceptible movement indicating that it really was time that the party broke up. There was a brief flurry of general conversation. The naval A.D.C. said that he was driving into the town and would give Dorrie a lift, and, after the various good-byes had been accomplished, she followed him out through the vast, echoing hall into the hot sunshine.

5

On Christmas Eve 1936 Eustace sat down on an upturned canoe a few hundred yards away from the landing stage and lit a pipe. In order to do this he had to crouch down and bend himself almost double because there was quite a strong southwester blowing. Having lit it successfully, he sighed luxuriously, wriggled his right sandal to shake a pebble out of it and looked with pride on his achievements of the last seven months.

First and foremost there was the house. It stood about twenty yards back from the narrow beach. The last coat of bright blue paint was still drying on the doors and window frames. It was, to him, a beautiful house. It was his; he had built it, and he loved it with all his heart. It consisted of two large rooms separated by a partition that reached not quite up to the roof, so that whatever cool breeze there might be could blow through it. The kitchen, scullery and larder were built out on one side. This, although unsymmetrical from the more aesthetic architectural point of view, was undeniably convenient, as it ensured that the smell of cooking would invade the main rooms only when the wind was blowing from the north, which it very seldom did.

The lower part of the house up to the level of the windowsills was constructed of thick coral rocks, hewn roughly but efficiently by the boys. Above this was ordinary teak clapboarding stained brown and varnished in order the better to withstand the elements. The roof was pink corrugated tin and fitted snugly. He had been held up for weeks waiting for that damned roofing to arrive in the supply ship. However, there it was complete in every detail except for the crazy paving path which he intended to start work on on Boxing Day. At the moment, of course, there was no furniture beyond a camp bed, a couple of wooden tables and chairs and a Frigidaire. This worked on an oil burner and was surprisingly successful.

Dorrie was due to arrive any time within the next week with the rest of their belongings. His heart fairly jumped in his chest when he thought of showing it all to her. To the left of the house, slightly nearer to the lagoon, was the radio station (nearly complete as far as equipment went) and the flagstaff, with the Union Jack fluttering bravely in the evening sunshine. Two of the disintegrating Strachan huts had been pulled down and the materials used for bolstering up the remaining three. In one of these the boys lived in haphazard chaos, ruled authoritatively by Ippaga. The other two were used for stores. The landing stage had been reinforced and repainted, and net paths had been made so that it was possible to walk in comfort from hut to hut without crunching along through loose coral.

At the moment, work being over for the day, the boys were

whooping and splashing down by the landing stage. Eustace looked at them affectionately. They were good boys and had worked well and were to have tomorrow off entirely in addition to an extra ration of beer and cigarettes. They were also, he reflected dispassionately, extremely beautiful. He watched Ayialo, who had won the native swimming championship three years running at Naruchi, do a double-back somersault into the lagoon.

Still puffing at his pipe, he sauntered down to the landing stage to join them. The water at the end of the landing stage was about twenty feet deep and crystal clear. Shoals of vividly colored coral fish glittered just below the surface like precious stones. He slipped off his shorts and dived in. The water was still a bit too warm for his liking. It would cool off a bit after the sun had gone down. He swam out a couple of hundred yards to a coral head; his swimming was of the sedentary, Margate breast-stroke variety. Three of the boys accompanied him, streaking through the water like seals, their arms and legs acting apparently independently of each other but with perfect rhythm and grace; their heads seemed to be almost continually submerged as though they were able to breathe as comfortably below the surface as above it. Eustace rather envied them this easy familiarity with an element that he had always regarded with slight suspicion. They had often attempted to teach him how to "crawl" and do other aquatic contortions, but it was never any good. He invariably choked and spluttered and got too much water up his nose, and finally decided that he was too old a dog to learn such exhausting and complicated tricks.

He clambered up on to the coral head, wriggled his bottom into a comparatively comfortable position and sat looking back at the shore. Ayialo and Ippaga sprang out of the water and sat down next to him. He glanced at their sleek, glistening bodies and wondered, rather perplexedly, whether or not he ought to insist on them wearing bathing trunks when Dorrie arrived. Not that Dorrie would give a hoot, of course, but perhaps from the point of view of Christian decency. . . . He suddenly laughed out loud. Ippaga looked at him questioningly. Eustace, whose Samolan was still, after several years, far from fluent, felt that the effort of explaining what he was laughing at would be too complicated, and so he waved his hand vaguely and said, "Mo Imana," which meant, "I am very happy." Ippaga nodded understandingly and, looking toward the house, clapped his hands violently as though to applaud their combined handiwork. Then he and Ayialo, almost in one combined movement, shot into the sea.

Eustace watched them swimming strongly down and down through the clear water, their bodies becoming increasingly paler in the blue depths; their breath control was really fantastic, and it seemed to be several minutes before their heads bobbed up above the surface again. They decided to race each other to the shore. Ippaga gave a loud cry, and off they went at an astonishing rate. Eustace sighed a trifle enviously and remembered, when he was their age, the nightmare swimming lessons he had had to endure in St. Michael's baths; the damp, dank smell; the hairy-chested, implacable swimming instructor shouting at him from the side, and the clammy nastiness of the water wings rubbing against his shoulders. This was certainly a far cry from Sydenham all right!

A few days after Christmas, Eustace was awakened from his afternoon snooze by a great commotion outside. He jumped up from the camp bed and looked out of the window. Ippaga was jumping up and down in a frenzy of excitement, and all the other boys were yelling and pointing out to sea.

His heart gave a leap, and he dashed out, hurriedly doing up the top two buttons of his shorts which he always undid before relaxing after lunch in order to give his stomach freedom to expand and help the digestion. It had often been a false alarm before, but this time it was not. There was the ship, a smudge on the horizon with a thin wisp of black smoke curling up from its funnel into the pale sky. He stood stock-still for a moment or two, and suddenly was aware that his eyes were stinging with tears. He ran back into the house again, began to find a clean shirt, then sat down on the bed and started to laugh. There was an hour at least to go before the ship came in close enough to send off a boat, and here he was carrying on as though the house were on fire! He had ample time to have a salt-water shower and a shave and get the cups out for tea. He laughed again, this time with less hysteria and more wholehearted glee, and went out to the hut where the shower was. He caught himself doing a little dance step as he went; then he stopped because he did not want to betray too much emotion in front of the boys.

An hour and a half later he was standing in clean white shorts and shirt and stockings and shoes on the edge of the "Split" by Roper's Folly, watching the ship's boat slowly, maddeningly slowly, making its way toward the surf. He had been there for three-quarters of an hour. Horrible macabre thoughts rushed through his mind. The boat might capsize; Dorrie would be flung into the sea among the sharks—there were always hundreds of them just out there beyond where the waves broke—he would see her disappearing and be powerless to do anything—perhaps he would even hear her scream—her last dying despairing shriek. . . . He began to jump up and down in an agony of agitation. The boat came nearer and nearer. Just before it reached the surf he saw Dorrie.

She was sitting in the stern and she waved a white handkerchief. He waved back frantically and shouted, but she could not possibly have heard because of the wind and the sea. The boat got through the surf without any trouble at all, and slid into the smooth water of the "Split." Suddenly there she was, just a couple of yards away from him, looking very cool and calm in a pink cotton dress and a white sun helmet. He called out "Welcome, darling" in a strangled voice, quite unaware that the tears were streaming down his cheeks. He started to run, breathlessly, to the landing stage.

Late that evening they were sitting in deck chairs side by side just outside the house. The moon was up and made a glittering path of light across the lagoon. The furniture had been dumped, some of it in the house and the rest down by the landing stage; the captain and the first officer had gone back to the ship. The boys had all gone to bed for the night. Dorrie and Eustace had each a whiskey and soda and a cigarette, but they had to keep putting one or other of them down in order to hold hands. Dorrie had told him all about the pineapple plantation sale and Lady Cynthia and Government House and the various incidents and discomforts of her journey. Eustace had told her all about the building of the house and the setbacks and the four days' gale in November and the giant stingray that had got right into the lagoon through the "Split." Lots of other bits and pieces of news would come to light later; there was infinite time, all the time in the world. At the moment there seemed to be nothing more to say. There they were, together again; the stars were blazing down on them; they could hear the gentle lap of the small wavelets of the lagoon against the supports of the landing stage and the steady, soothing roar of the surf behind them.

Eustace flipped his cigarette away, placed his whiskey glass carefully down on a bit of rock and, kneeling by the side of Dorrie's deck chair, put his arms tightly round her and buried his face in her breast.

"Careful!" she said automatically, putting down her glass too.

"Do you like it?" he asked huskily, "the house, I mean, and the island and the whole place?"

Dorrie smiled in the darkness and stroked his hair. "I will say this for it," she said, "it's one up on Blackpool."

6

By the end of the year 1937 Washington and London had finally come to an arrangement about Cowrie Island. For months and months negotiations had been under way. Thousands of civil servants in thousands of offices had typed memoranda and filed and unfiled letters, telegrams, reports, ciphers and suggestions in duplicate, triplicate and often quadruplicate. There had been meetings, conferences and discussions; official, semiofficial and private. Clerks and secretaries and shorthand-typists and stenographers had gone wearily home evening after evening on buses in England and trolley cars in Washington, sick and tired and bored with the very name of Cowrie Island.

Finally, at long last, the deicsion was arrived at that America and Britain should share the island fifty-fifty. It was, in fact, to be known henceforward as a Condominion. In many high official quarters it was confidently asserted that this arrangement would have a beneficial and lasting effect on Anglo-American relations. The President of the United States was jubilant; the President of Trans-National Airways positively ecstatic, and the Colonial Minister in London relieved, resigned and, on the whole, indifferent. A few Middle Western senators asked some irrelevant questions; one of them, a slightly obtuse gentleman who had been inaccurately briefed on the situation, made a rambling speech in Des Moines, Iowa, filled with withering references to "Perfidious Albion" while Sir Humphrey Logan, His Majesty's representative in Samolo, who had been opposed to the whole business from the start, bowed his head to the inevitable.

The only people who knew nothing about the transaction whatever were the British Resident and his wife on the island itself. For them the months slipped by in peace and contentment. The crazy paving was laid down and completed. Ippaga and Ayialo were chased by a nine-foot shark in the very middle of the lagoon, but managed to clamber to safety on a coral head. (The shark was later caught by the combined efforts of all the boys together and a chunk of bleeding raw meat from the Resident's Frigidaire.)

Dorrie found a wounded love tern, one of the island's little white birds, and nursed it devotedly back to health and strength, after which it refused to leave her, and Eustace built a little dovecote for it behind the house. Sandy, the little ginger cat which had been presented to the Edgehills by the captain of the supply ship, in defiance of all apparent biological laws, suddenly produced a litter of five kittens in the middle of Roper's Folly. This, to all intents and purposes, immaculate conception, caused a profound sensation on the island.

As far as Dorrie was concerned it was the happiest year she had ever spent in her life. She learnt to float on her back without moving at all, an accomplishment that she had always envied in others. She went off with Eustace on excursions to the far side of the lagoon in a little boat which the boys had built and for which Eustace had rigged up a sail. She became a passionate collector of shells, and sometimes one or other of the boys would dive down deep enough to procure for her some lettuce coral which, when bleached by the sun, made the loveliest house decorations imaginable.

Every morning at dawn and every evening at sunset Eustace performed, with correct solemnity, the ritual of the Flag. For this all the boys, in brightly colored sarongs, the only moments of the day or night in which they wore anything, stood respectfully to attention. Dorrie stood to attention too, and, once in a while, permitted herself the luxury of a nostalgic tear or two. Thoughts of Home dropped into her mind. The soft wet green of the Romney Marshes; the brightly colored traffic in Piccadilly on a spring morning; the crowded pavements of Oxford Street; the bargain basement at Selfridge's and the Changing of the Guard.

She occasionally received letters from Home, from her sisters and her brother and one or two faithful friends. She devoured these eagerly enough, but they never moved her so much as watching Eustace hauling away at that little flag. She had been away for many years and she realized that, if she did go back, everyone she had ever known would be changed beyond all recognition. Only the aspects of England that were unchangeable would be familiar still. This thought saddened her a little sometimes, but not for long. She had Eustace and the house and the sun and the sea and the sky, and her world was at peace

7

In March 1941 Lady Cynthia Marchmont was sitting in the American-bound trans-Pacific clipper reading a rather highly colored romantic novel about the American Civil War. Her mind, however, was only partially concentrated on what she was reading. She was dressed in the uniform of the Mechanized Transport Corps. It was a smart uniform, and it suited her. She took a small compact containing powder, lipstick and mirror out of her pocket, and scrutinized her face with detached interest. She decided that she looked a bit tired and that the lines were deepening under her eyes and around her mouth.

This, oddly enough, depressed her far less than it might have done a few years ago. There was every reason for her to be looking tired, as she had just completed a lecture tour of Australia and New Zealand, and the whole business had been fairly exhausting. She was perfectly aware that she was a not particularly experienced or inspired public speaker, but the lecture tour, on the whole, had been a success. Her subject had been the women of Britain in wartime and the efficiency of their contribution to the war effort. She herself since September 1939 had been working unremittingly. In the beginning she had plunged immediately into the organization of canteens and rest rooms for the troops. Later, being an excellent driver, she had enlisted in the M.T.C. as an ordinary private and had worked her way up to her present rank of commandant. She was conscious, sometimes almost shamefacedly so, that for the first time for many years she was no longer bored. It was strange to reflect that all the distractions and small happinesses she had so assiduously sought during the twenties and the thirties were no longer attractive or even valid. On the surface, they had been gay, those years—monotonously gay. Looking back, her mind refreshed and renovated by so much violent change, she was astonished to realize that her memories even lacked poignancy. There they lay, strewn behind her, all the love affairs and parties and yachting trips and summers in the south of France and the Lido; all the trivial strains and stresses and febrile emotions that had woven the pattern of her life and the lives of her friends.

She remembered a phrase that she had read years ago in a book of historical memoirs, a phrase spoken by a dying French actress of the eighteenth century who had achieved triumph and fame and been reduced to penury. *"Ah les beaux jours, les beaux jours, j'étais si malheureuse!"* She smiled to herself and wondered how miserable she had really been? Certainly a great deal more than she had realized at the time. Not the obvious, genuine unhappinesses, like Clare dying in that frowzy little hospital in Paris, and Henry being killed in the motor smash, and poor Philip getting muddled up with that bloody woman and finally commiting suicide—those tragedies and sufferings had been real, and would have been real in any circumstances, whatever sort of life she had led—but the general tone of all those years, the perpetual, unrecognized, hectic boredom. She had lived through so much of all that, pretending to herself and to everyone else that she was enjoying it. She smiled again, and then sighed and put her compact back into her pocket. It really had been too idiotic.

She looked out of the window of the plane. They were flying at about eight thousand feet, and the evening sky was clear except for a bank of fantastic cloud formations far away on the horizon. She glanced at her wristwatch. According to schedule they should have arrived at Cowrie Island an hour ago, but there had been a head wind nearly all day since they had left Noumea in the gray hours of the morning. The light faded from the sky, and the empty, outside world disappeared. About an hour and half later there was a slight commotion in the forward end of the plane, and the steward came bustling through with a tray of cocktails in little cardboard cups.

"It's all right," he said, "we've sighted the Island." There was a ring of restrained excitement in his voice, and Lady Cynthia wondered idly whether or not the pilot and observer had perhaps been getting a little agitated. She looked out of the window and there—far,

far below them in the darkness—was a little cluster of twinkling lights. One of them seemed to be moving and was changing alternately, red and green and white. That would be the pilot launch.

Lady Cynthia began to collect her things, and the lighted notice flashed on: "Please fasten your belts." The clipper, sweeping lower and lower over the lagoon, finally with an almost imperceptible bump touched down on the water; spray obscured the windows; the passengers unfastened their belts and began to move about, collecting their books and overnight bags. The engines stopped; there was a confused noise of shouting outside, and, after a considerable time, the giant machine was towed gently alongside the landing stage. The pilot went out first; then two of the officers. Lady Cynthia waited, sitting quite still in her seat. She always hated hurrying for no particular reason, and she much preferred the other passengers to disembark before her. When they had all gone she rose, a little wearily, and stepped onto the landing stage.

The hot night air seemed to strike her in the face. She walked along the wooden pier, brightly illuminated by two enormous arc lamps, and up a short rock path to the hotel. It was all on one story and on entering the main lounge she was immediately impressed by the incongruity of so much expensive luxuriousness flourishing on a small coral reef in the middle of the Pacific Ocean. She registered at the reception desk and the manageress, Mrs. Handley, a smartly dressed little American woman, insisted on showing her to her room herself. The room was pleasantly furnished with its own private shower and toilet. Mrs. Handley was both amiable and voluble and said that dinner would be ready in about half an hour, and would Lady Marchmont, when she had washed and freshened up, care to come along to her private suite and meet her husband, Robb, and have a cocktail? Lady Cynthia accepted gracefully, although inwardly she would much rather have been left alone, and Mrs. Handley departed saying that she would send one of the boys for her in ten minutes.

The Handleys were an oddly assorted couple. It would be impossible, reflected Lady Cynthia, to imagine two people more thoroughly opposite from each other in every respect. Mrs. Handley—Irma—had shrewd, sharp eyes and was impeccably soignée; her simple linen frock was perfectly cut and pressed, and her hair looked as if it had been done by an expert Fifth Avenue hairdresser that very afternoon. Robb, her husband, was entirely casual both in appearance and manner. He was nice-looking and had a certain loose-limbed charm. His eyes were a trifle too pale and his fair hair was untidy.

Captain Elliot, the pilot of the clipper, a large, friendly, beefy man, was also present together with the airport manager, a tall, austere young man whose surname Lady Cynthia did not catch but who was referred to by everybody as "Brod."

Robb Handley mixed an excellent dry Martini with the efficiency of an expert. Lady Cynthia was very grateful for it. She felt tired, and the drumming of the plane was still in her ears. Conversation was general and consisted mainly of "shop." The new hospital for the ground staff was nearly finished; the westbound clipper had been held up in Honolulu and would be a couple of days late at least; there was a cyclone about a hundred miles off, which would probably mean that the supply ship would be late too, which was irritating because they were beginning to run out of cereals and cigarettes.

Lady Cynthia allowed the talk to flow around her and, sipping her cocktail, idly took in the details of the room. It was pleasantly done, in excellent taste. There were no flowers except for one vase of zinnias on a side table. The whole atmosphere was typical of a well-run hotel or country club anywhere in the United States. The windows were shuttered; the air-conditioning plant made an occasional clicking sound, and, apart from the distant noise of the surf pounding on the reef, it was impossible to imagine that you were anywhere but in the midst of civilization.

Suddenly a name in the conversation galvanized her into attention—"Edgehill"—it struck a forgotten chord in her mind. Brod was talking.

"That guy makes me tired. He's always beefing about something or other."

Mrs. Handley laughed.

"Well"—there was a slightly amused drawl in her voice—"he hasn't got much else to do, has he?"

"But it isn't as if we didn't do all we could to be cooperative." Brod turned earnestly to Captain Elliot. "We never have a film showing without inviting them to it—Robb and Irma are constantly sending them over supplies whenever they run short. . . ."

"I like her," said Irma. "I think she's just darling, but I must admit he gives me a bit of a headache now and then."

"Who are the Edgehills?" interjected Lady Cynthia.

Robb refilled her cocktail glass. "He's the British Resident, ma'am."

Lady Cynthia, flinching slightly at suddenly being addressed as royalty, remembered in a flash—Mrs. Edgehill! The nice little woman at Government House, Pendarla, when she was staying with Humphrey and Eloise. "Is she here now?" she asked.

"All of two hundred yards away," said Robb. "In the Residency." Everybody laughed at this, obviously a standard joke. Lady Cynthia felt definitely irritated. She rose and said with a sweet smile: "They're very old friends of mine. I must call on them at once."

At this there was a general outcry. Mrs. Handley protested that dinner would be ready in a few minutes—wouldn't it be better to go over afterward? Lady Cynthia was inflexible. "I had no idea they were still here," she said. "I really must go. I really don't want any dinner. I ate far too much in the plane." She smiled at the captain. "The food was delicious. I wonder if anyone would be kind enough to show me the way to"—she paused—"to the Residency?"

Robb escorted her out of the side door of the hotel. It was a very dark night, and he had brought a large electric torch with him. Hermit crabs scuttled away from the coral path as the beam of light struck them. The air was soft and a little cooler; a wind had sprung up and the noise of the surf was like thunder. In a minute or two they arrived at Edgehill's house; there was a glow of lamplight showing through the window. Robb shouted "Huroo" loudly, and then knocked on the front door. After a moment a man opened. Lady Cynthia could not see what he looked like, as he was silhouetted against the light inside.

"Here's a friend to see you," said Robb with great breeziness. Eustace peered into the darkness. "Oh, who is it?" he asked rather dimly.

Lady Cynthia, remembering that five minutes ago she had asserted that they were her oldest friends, rested her hand lightly on Robb's arm and whispered, "I want it to be a surprise—thank you so much for showing me the way." She gave him a little push, but, obtusely, he would not move. "What about you getting back?" he asked.

"I can get back perfectly all right," she said firmly.

"Okay, ma'am," he said and, to her immense relief, called out, "Good night, Mr. Edgehill," and went off into the night.

Eustace Edgehill was still standing at the door. Behind him appeared Mrs. Edgehill. Lady Cynthia really felt a little foolish; she had obeyed a sudden impulse, and now it looked as if it might all be a great failure. After all, Mrs. Edgehill had met her only once and probably wouldn't know who she was from Adam. She spoke quickly and was surprised to note that there was definitely a note of nervousness in her voice.

"I'm Lady Cynthia Marchmont," she said. "I had the pleasure of meeting your wife at Government House in Pendarla years ago. I'm just here for the night and am leaving again in the clipper at crack of dawn. I do hope I'm not disturbing you by coming so late, but I should hate to leave without seeing her again."

Mrs. Edgehill gave a little cry.

"Well!" she gasped, "isn't that extraordinary! Just fancy you remembering me."

She gave Eustace a little shove. "Get out of the way, dear."

She seized both Lady Cynthia's hands in hers. "Please come

in—this is the nicest surprise I've ever had in my life." She drew her inside. "This is my husband." Her voice sounded breathless. "You never met him, did you, but I remember we talked about him."

Eustace shook hands. He was a wizened little man, deeply tanned by the sun, and wearing nothing but shorts and sandshoes. Lady Cynthia noticed that, in spite of the fact that his hair was thinning a little, he retained a slightly boyish air, as though he had never quite grown up. He shut the door carefully and led her politely to a rickety-looking but comfortable chair.

"If only I'd known," cried Mrs. Edgehill, "I'd have put on a dress instead of receiving you in old shorts and a blouse like this."

As a matter of fact, she did look rather peculiar. Her shorts had obviously originally belonged to her husband, and her blouse was of startlingly flowered printed silk. It would have been an excellent design for chintz chair covers but was a trifle overpowering as it was.

"Get out the whiskey, Eustace," she said, and then, a thought striking her, "Have you had dinner?"

Lady Cynthia's eye quickly took in the cups and plates and dishes on the table. It was obvious that they had just finished. She nodded. "Yes," she said, "I dined the moment I got off the plane, but I should love a soft drink of some sort."

"You must have some Johnnie Walker, you really must," said Mrs. Edgehill. "This is an occasion!" Lady Cynthia was touched to see that her whole face was quivering with pleasure. She called out to her husband, who had disappeared into what was probably the kitchen, "The soda's in the Frigidaire." She produced a packet of Gold Flake cigarettes. "I'm afraid these are all we have to offer you until the next supply ship comes, unless you'd rather have an American one. Eustace can pop over to the hotel in a minute."

Lady Cynthia shook her head. "I much prefer these."

Mrs. Edgehill lit her cigarette, then lit one for herself and drew up a chair. "I wish I'd known, really I do. I'd have had the house tidy for you. It does look like a pigsty, doesn't it?"

At this moment Eustace came back bearing a bottle of whiskey, two bottles of soda and an opener. Lady Cynthia looked round the room. It certainly was the strangest mix-up she had ever seen. There was an old sofa with a faded chintz cover; rather a good Spanish-looking sideboard; a gramophone, one of the old-fashioned kind with a livid green horn; two or three deck chairs; a portable radio, and a table covered with shells of different shapes and colors and some gleaming white, graceful branches of bleached coral. On the stained wooden walls there were two or three dim watercolors; a whole row of six perfectly charming old prints of London; and in the place of honor, on the wall of the partition facing the stove, a framed photograph of the King and Queen. The frame, obviously homemade, was of varnished wood and the photograph was quite dreadful. It had apparently been cut out of one of the illustrated papers, and some kind of disaster had happened to it. Mrs. Edgehill caught her looking at it and smiled sadly.

"Isn't that awful?" she asked. "We had a terrible storm about six months ago, and the rain came in and trickled all down the inside of the frame and ruined it. It makes me feel ashamed every time I look at it, but we can't take it down because it's the only one we have."

"Surely," said Lady Cynthia, "as official British Resident you should have an official portrait of the King and Queen."

"We've asked for one over and over again," said Eustace, prizing open one of the bottles of soda, "But there's a new governor in Samolo now, and nobody's ever paid any attention."

"As a matter of fact, we really do feel it a bit," said Mrs. Edgehill, with an overbright little smile. "You see, we are the only two British people here, and it's been a little difficult to keep our end up since the Americans came."

8

It was long after midnight when Lady Cynthia finally tore herself away. Eustace accompanied her back to the hotel, took her in through the side door and showed her the way to her room. When she said good night to him he gripped her hand and held it for quite a while.

"It was awfully nice of you to drop in," he said, his voice sounding rather hoarse. "It'll set Dorrie up no end. She has so often talked about you. She always wanted to ring you up, you know, when you asked her to that time at Government House, but she never dared. You've no idea how much this evening has meant to her, really you haven't."

He let go her hand, and then added shyly, "You won't forget about that photograph, will you? It isn't really for us, ourselves— we're little people and we don't matter very much—But I would like these Americans to know that we had it. You see, they don't quite understand how difficult it is sometimes for us to be the only British people here, with the war going on and everything and being such a long way away from home. . . ." He broke off abruptly, and, with a muttered "Good night," turned and walked away along the passage.

Lady Cynthia went into her room and, closing the door quietly behind her, sat down at her dressing table and observed, without surprise, that her eyes were filled with tears.

"I'm getting old," she reflected, "old, and possibly rather

maudlin, but all the same I'm learning a good deal more than I ever learned before."

She undressed slowly and lay on the bed without switching out the light, knowing that sleep was miles away from her. She glanced at her traveling clock: ten past one. She was to be called at three-thirty, because they were taking off just before dawn. It really wasn't any use attempting to sleep—she could sleep all day tomorrow in the plane anyway. She lit a cigarette and let her mind wander back over the evening.

She was not at all sure why it was that she had felt so highly strung and emotional all the time; perhaps because she hadn't had any dinner, or maybe it was that she was overtired and had had two strongish whiskey and sodas on top of the Handleys' dry Martinis. There was nothing in the least sad about the Edgehills. They were obviously a devoted couple and serenely happy in each other's company from morning till night; whatever troubles had assailed them in their lives, they had had each other, and had been able to share them.

Perhaps this was what had given her that slight ache in her heart: the spectacle of two people who were secure in the knowledge that, whatever might happen to them, providing it was not death or separation, they could never be lonely!

Lady Cynthia sighed lightly and tried unsuccessfully to remember any one period of her life when she had felt that sense of security. There was Henry, of course, but then he had died too soon, before either of them had had time to get through the first painful ecstasies and miseries of being married and in love. There had certainly been no security there—not even a semblance of tranquillity ever. She tried to imagine what would have happened if he had lived, and their possessive, demanding passion for each other had simmered down with the passing of the years. What would have been left? Gentle domesticity, quiet acquiescence—understanding—tolerance?

She suddenly laughed aloud, and stubbed her cigarette out in the ashtray on the table by the bed. What nonsense! They would never have had the remotest chance of it; all the cards would have been stacked against them; too much money and leisure and far too many shrill, predatory friends. The period had been against them too; those overgay, strained nineteen twenties.

Still, the Edgehills had lived through that period also—but that was different. They belonged to another world. They had had the inestimable advantage of having to work in order to live; every bit of pleasure or happiness they ever had they had earned, striven for, and fully appreciated when they got it. That was where the difference lay, and it was a basic difference. She and Henry had had everything—everything but the essentials; an abundance of treacherous gifts poured into their laps. The Edgehills had had nothing, nothing but the essentials. Their security and gentleness and love for each other; their tranquil acceptance of life as it was; their immutable, inner convictions about themselves and each other, had not been showered on them in colored wrappings like so many wedding presents. Those things were never showered on anyone. But they were the lucky ones, luckier even than they knew.

She fixed the pillow behind her head, and stared up at the ceiling. There was a small lizard in the corner using all its wiles to catch a fly. It stalked it very, very slowly, and then, suddenly, out shot its long tongue, there was no more fly, and the lizard relaxed. Lady Cynthia relaxed too. What an extraordinary evening! After the first half hour, when they had had a drink and the inital shyness had evaporated, the whole atmosphere had changed, become intimate. Eustace Edgehill, who had hurriedly put on a clean shirt in her honor, had taken it off again, and lay back in his deck chair. Dorrie—Lady Cynthia smiled—Dorrie had put a large conch shell at her feet for cigarette ends, and turned on the news on the portable radio. There they had sat, three English people, listening to an American voice, rich in dramatic overtones, describing a heavy air raid on London. Lady Cynthia remembered watching the expression on the Edgehills' faces, or rather the lack of expression. They had sat quite still, staring straight in front of them. At one moment Dorrie had frowned, and then closed her eyes wearily. After a while Eustace had got up and turned the radio off.

"No sense in sitting here and upsetting ourselves," he said, and poured himself out another drink.

Presently they had begun to talk about "Home" and ask questions. Did Lady Cynthia know Hythe, and had it been knocked about much? Was London really as badly hit as the radio said it was? Eustace had a married sister living in Clapham who wrote to him occasionally. They had not heard from her lately, but she never said much about the blitzes in her letters—perhaps they hadn't had it very badly in Clapham?

Lady Cynthia told them all she could think of about London. She described the first dreary, anticlimactic months of the war, and then the tension when it really started; the miraculous, agonizing days when the men came pouring back from Dunkirk. She had been at Dover, running a canteen on the station. Dorrie and Eustace drank in every word with passionate eagerness; Dorrie's right hand was tapping ceaselessly on the edge of her chair, and her eyes were glistening. She said that one of her cousins had been through Dunkirk, but that she hadn't seen him since he was a little boy and didn't even know what he looked like now. Then they had sat silent for a little while; the refrigerator made a whirring sound every now and then, and the noise of the sea seemed to get louder and louder. Later on in the evening they had told her about their lives on the island from the very beginning when Eustace had come out with the boys and built the house.

They spoke eagerly, interrupting each other and passing the story back and forth. It had been a bit of a shock when the Americans had first arrived, but they had got used to it after a bit, although, of course, it wasn't half so quiet and peaceful as it had been before. They had had official instructions to do their level best to cooperate with them in every way possible. The Handleys were quite nice in their way. They had arrived just before the hotel was finished. They had been nothing if not friendly and civil from the word go really, but, of course, you couldn't get away from the fact that, being Americans, they weren't in the war and didn't really understand. All they really seemed to be interested in was Trans-National Airways.

Then Broderick Sarnton, the new airport manager, had arrived. He was all right really, but the one who had been there before had been much nicer. Inevitably there had had to be several changes. The Americans had imported a whole lot of Chamorro boys from Guam, and there had been quarrels between them and the Samolans until finally, after a lot of rows and arguments, Eustace had had to give in and send the Samolans home—except Ippaga, who helped in the radio office.

The Americans really weren't so bad. They were awfully kind about sending over cartons of Lucky Strikes and Camels, but unfortunately they didn't like Lucky Strikes or Camels very much. They also asked them regularly every week to see the newest films, which were brought by the clippers, but they accepted only once in a while because they really didn't care to put themselves too much under obligation, and they had no way of returning the hospitality.

There had been a rather unhappy incident. Lady St. Merrion, the wife of the new Governor General of Samolo, had arrived one night in the American-bound clipper. There had been bad flying weather and the plane was unable to take off the next morning as usual. Dorrie, naturally expecting that Lady St. Merrion would come to call, as Eustace was the official British Resident, had worn her one and only afternoon frock all day long for three days, and Eustace had put on a shirt and tie and white flannel trousers, but she had never come. They had watched her every morning strolling by toward the "Split" with the captain of the clipper and one or two of the other passengers. They used to fish for barracuda off the point by Roper's Folly. By the time Dorrie had finished retailing this unfortunate exposé of aristocratic bad manners, her face was quite red. "You see," she said to Lady Cynthia, "it didn't matter about us really, but it was the flag. She never once even looked up at the flag."

9

In October 1940 there was a crisis on Cowrie Island. The crisis had no international complications and was brought about entirely by the weather. For three whole weeks a gale had been blowing. No clipper had arrived, either from Honolulu or Noumea, and the supply ship was over a month late. There were no cigarettes left on the island and very little food. The food situation, of course was not really serious, because fish could always be obtained easily from the farther side of the lagoon. It was impossible to fish in the open sea, because the waves were tumultuous, and to attempt to get a boat out through the "Split" was obviously out of the question. The lagoon fish, however, were reasonably edible although small and a trifle monotonous. Everyone's nerves became rather frayed. Brod had a row with the Handleys. Some of the mechanics fell out with each other, with the result that one of them had his head split open with a bottle and had to be put in hospital.

The hotel passed its days in echoing emptiness and acquired a greater air of incongruity than ever. Robb Handley, who had a secret store of bourbon whiskey, elected to get wildly drunk one night with the assistant airport manager, and they both swam out to one of the farther coral heads in the lagoon. Having reached it, they collapsed in complete exhaustion and had to stay there until the following morning, when they were rescued by the launch and brought back to the landing stage, stark naked and shivering violently.

The Edgehills, as usual, kept to themselves. Eustace continued to perform the ritual of the flag every morning and evening. He was fully aware that this might appear foolish to the Americans, if not somewhat irritating. On three occasions the flagstaff blew down, but he got it up again all right, assisted by Dorrie and Ippaga. They, too, were completely out of cigarettes, but Eustace had some pipe tobacco, and so they shared a pipe amicably each evening. Dorrie almost grew to enjoy it.

At last, on a dreadful day, when the rain was driving across the reef almost horizontally like staves of music, the supply ship was sighted. Everyone on the island was immediately galvanized into frenzied activity. Brod rather lost his head and, against the advice of Eustace, the assistant airport manager and several others, insisted on sending the barge out through the "Split." Eustace and Dorrie, crouching in the lee of the rock walls of Roper's Folly, watched the barge anxiously as it edged out into the surf. Miraculously, it managed to get through, or rather over, the gigantic rollers, and headed for the ship. In about two hours it returned, laden with packing cases.

This time disaster overtook it. It had just reached the entrance to the "Split" when an extra-large wave knocked it round broadside onto the reef. There was a panic-stricken shout from the seven men on board, then an agonizing pause, until another wave capsized it completely. Dorrie gave a scream and sprang to her feet. Eustace left her side and started to run over the coral to the edge of the surf. She called after him to come back. There was nothing that he could possibly do beyond just stand there in the driving wind and rain, and watch the barge being battered to matchwood. Fortunately, the men managed to get themselves ashore. They were badly cut and bruised, and three of them had to go to hospital. The worst aspect of the whole business was that all the packing cases contained food supplies and cigarettes.

Four days later the weather abated sufficiently to enable the ship to send in a boat. It made three journeys during the day and managed to land the remaining supplies, among them a mail bag for the Edgehills. It was a very small mail bag, containing two letters from Eustace's married sister; a long, rambling letter from Ena Harris, a friend of Dorrie's in Pendarla; and an impressive-looking flat parcel. They opened the parcel last. Inside it was a typewritten letter and two thick pieces of cardboard, sandwiching between them a signed photograph of Their Majesties, the King and Queen. The letter was from a lady-in-waiting and started: "Dear Mr. Edgehill: The Queen has commanded me to send you the enclosed photograph of Their Majesties. Her Majesty was most interested to hear from Lady Cynthia Marchmont . . ." Dorrie said, "Oh dear!" in a choking voice and, sinking down on the bed, burst into tears.

10

In the spring of 1942 the American authorities decided to evacuate Cowrie Island. The process took several weeks. Two destroyers appeared escorting a large freighter. The clipper service had been canceled ever since the month following Pearl Harbor. The Handleys had gone, and the hotel had been closed for some months. The Edgehills, having received no instructions of any sort, were slightly at a loss and, as the weeks passed and the island grew more and more denuded, they realized that they would have to make a decision. The captain of one of the American destroyers had called politely on arrival and offered them passage on his ship, bound for Honolulu, which offer they had felt bound to refuse pending instructions from Samolo.

Now the evacuation was nearly completed, no instructions had come, and they were faced with having to decide whether to accept passage in the American ship and pack all their belongings on to the freighter, or to stay where they were and await events. The young American captain, who was both helpful and sympathetic, strongly advised them to come with him. He explained that, since the Japanese had declared war, all radio communications in the Pacific had gone haywire, and that once they arrived in Honolulu the British consul there would advise them what to do.

Eustace, who felt that the dignity of his position demanded advice from rather higher authority than a mere consul, was torn with indecision. Finally, after an anguished discussion with Dorrie, which lasted nearly all night, he decided to go, and they started to pack. The Americans were leaving on the following evening, and the captain was to call in the morning for their final decision. They had started to pack at about 4:30 A.M. listlessly and miserably. Any thought of sleep was out of the question. Just after dawn Dorrie went into the kitchen to cook some eggs and bacon. They were both worn out with arguing and were utterly depressed, and she thought that a little sustenance might cheer them up a bit. While she was putting the kettle on for the tea, she happened to glance out of the window. The kitchen window was at the back and looked out over the reef to the open sea. There was the freighter in the same place it had been for the last few weeks. A little to the right and to the left of it lay the destroyers, but—she blinked her eyes and stared—there was a third ship, smaller than the American destroyers, but unmistakably warlike. She gave a loud cry.

Eustace came running into the kitchen. She pointed with a quivering finger.

"Look at the flag," she said breathlessly. "Look at the flag!"

From the third ship fluttered the White Ensign. Eustace gave a whoop of joy and flung his arms round her; the coffeepot went flying off the stove and broke on the floor. Still with his arm tightly round her, he rushed her out of the side door, and they started to run toward the edge of the reef. Eustace was shouting, which was very foolish, as the ship was at least a mile off shore.

Just before sundown that evening they were sitting together in the stern of a boat being rowed out through the "Split." The boat's crew were sunburned British sailors. Dorrie was clasping her handbag and a large, flat package very carefully done up in sacking and string. She glanced at poor old Roper's Folly as they passed, and felt a sudden catch in her throat. There were the hermit crabs and the little mound with the colored shells on it where the love bird was buried. There was the house, their house that Eustace had built so lovingly; the lowering sun glinted on the windows, making it look as though it were on fire. She almost wished that it was. It was hateful going away like this and leaving the house empty and alone. The Union Jack still fluttered from the flagstaff; she wondered sadly how long it would stay there.

Eustace, after a sidelong look at her face, leant close to her

235

and put his hand on hers. "Never mind, old girl," he said softly. "It was lovely while it lasted." She returned the pressure of his hand, and tried to smile, but it was not a great success, so she turned her face toward the open sea and did not look at the island any more.

H.M.S. *Rapid.*
May 1944

STOP ME IF YOU'VE HEARD IT

Please God," she whispered to herself. "Don't let it be the one about the Englishman and the Scotsman and the American in the railway carriage, nor the one about the old lady and the parrot, nor the one about the couple arriving at the seaside hotel on their honeymoon night! I'll settle for any of the others, but please, please merciful God, not one of those three—I can't bear it. If it's one of those three, particularly the Englishman and the Scotsman and the American in the railway carriage, I shall go mad—I shall do something awful—I'll shriek—I'll make a hideous scene—I'll bash his head in with a bottle—"

Her husband, sitting opposite to her at the table, cleared his throat. Her whole body became rigid at the sound. With a great effort she took a cigarette out of a little blue enamel pot in front of her and lit it. Some of the general conversation at the table died away into polite attentiveness. She was aware, wretchedly aware, of the quick, resigned glance that Louis Bennet exchanged with Susan Lake. She looked at her host, Carroll Davis, leaning forward politely, his good-looking face blank. Carroll was kind; Carroll understood; his manners were dictated by his heart—he wouldn't hurt Budge's feelings for the world; he would listen appreciatively and laugh at the right moments, saving his loudest, most convincing laugh for the point at the end, and Budge would never know, never remotely suspect for an instant, that he hadn't been amused.

The others would laugh too, of course, but there would be an undertone of malice—their alert, cruel minds would be silently communicating with one another. "Poor Budge," they would be saying, "the kiss of death on every party—he never knows when to stop. In the old days he used to be funny on the stage, but now he's even lost that. Why does Carroll ask him? Obviously, for Marty's sake—she *must* know how awful he is. She *must* realize, deep down, that she's married to the most monumental cracking bore. Why doesn't she leave him? Why doesn't she at least come to parties without him? She knows we're all old friends—she knows we love her. Why the hell doesn't she leave that aggressive, overeager little megalomaniac at home?"

Marty drew deeply at her cigarette. Jane and Shirley and Bobby Peek were still talking and laughing at the other end of the table. They had not noticed—yet. They were still unaware of doom. Budge shot them a quick, resentful look and cleared his throat again. They glanced up, and the light went out of their faces. Shirley stabbed out her cigarette, put her head back and closed her eyes. Marty felt an insane desire to lean forward and slap her face violently. "Listen, you languid, supercilious bitch, Budge Ripley's going to tell a story. Sit up and listen, and mind your manners! He was telling stories—amusing people—millions of people—making them laugh until they cried, making them forget their troubles—making them happy—before you were born. All right, all right—he may be a bore now—he may have lost his touch, but mind your manners—lean forward, look interested, whatever you feel—bitch—spoiled, supercilious bitch."

"Stop me if you've heard it." Budge's voice grated in the silence. He caught her eye, and, painting an encouraging smile on her face, she leaned forward. No more than a split second could have passed before he began, but in that split second the years of her life with him rolled out before her—jerkily and confused in memory, like a panorama she had been taken to see at Earl's Court when she was a child.

She had been getting on quite well twenty years ago when she had first met him—chorus and understudy and small parts here and there. She had never been pretty, but there was something about her that people liked, a comic quality of personality. Carroll had always asked her to his grandest parties regardless of the fact that she was really small fry in the theater compared with his other guests. She had had wit always, a realistic, unaffected cockney humor, quick as a whip but without malice. It was at one of Carroll's parties, in this same house, that Budge had first noticed her. It was in this same house three years later, after she had slept with him hundreds of times, that he had told her that his divorce was through and that they could get married. Seventeen years ago that was. They had moved into Number 18—she had been so proud, so grateful, and he had been so sweet. No more stage work for her, no more prancing on and off for finales and opening choruses. She ran the house fairly well, went to all Budge's first nights in a box or stalls; stood with him afterward in the dressing room while people came rushing in to say how marvelous he was. "Funnier than ever." "I laughed till I was sick." "Nobody like you, Budge, the comic genius of the age—your inventiveness—your pathos too—only really great comedians have that particular quality, that subtle balance between grave and gay—"

They gave parties at Number 18—gay and amusing, lasting sometimes until dawn. Several years of happiness passed—several years of excitement and success and occasional holidays in the South of France. Then, insidiously, the rot began to set in—very gradually at first, so gradually, indeed, that it was a long time before she even suspected it. A strange rot, composed of circumstances, small, psychological maladjustments, mutual irritations, sudden outbursts of temper; the subtle cause of it all still obscure, still buried deep.

It was about then that he began to be unfaithful to her—nothing serious—just an occasional roll in the hay with someone who took his fancy. Marty found out about this almost immediately, and it hurt her immeasurably. She reasoned with herself, of course; she exerted every ounce of common sense and self-control, and succeeded bleakly insofar that she said nothing and did nothing, but from then on everything was different. There was no security anymore, and no peace of mind. It was not that she cared so desperately about him popping into bed every now and then with someone else—only a fool, married happily for years to a famous star, would make a fuss about that. It was something deeper, something that bewildered and gnawed at her, something more important that she knew to exist but somehow could not identify.

It was later—quite a long while later—that the truth suddenly became clear to her, that the answer to this riddle, which had tortured her for so long, suddenly flashed into her consciousness with all the blatant clarity of a neon light—a neon light sign flashing on and off with hideous monotony one vulgar, piteous word, jealousy. Budge was jealous of her. He was jealous of her wit, her gaiety, her friends. She could have slept with other men as much as she liked, and he would have forgiven her; she could have drunk herself into a coma every night, and he would have been loving and concerned and understanding; but because she was herself, because people of all kinds found her good company, because she could, without effort, embroider an ordinary anecdote with genuine humor and infectious gaiety and be loved and welcomed for it—this he could never forgive; for this, she realized in that blinding flash of revelation, he would hate her until the day he died.

"Stop me if you've heard it!" That idiotic, insincere phrase—that false, unconvincing opening gambit—as though people ever had the courage to stop anyone however many times they'd heard it! Human beings could be brave—incredibly brave about many things. They could fly in jet-propelled planes; fling themselves from the sky in parachutes; hurl themselves fully clothed into turbulent seas to rescue drowning children; crawl on their mortal stomachs through bullet-spattered mud and take pins out of unexploded bombs or shells or whatever they were, but no one, no one in the whole twisting, agonized world was brave enough to say loudly and clearly, "Yes, I have heard it. It is dull and unfunny; it bores the liver and lights out of me. I have heard it over and over again, and if I have to hear it once more in any of the years that lie between me and the grave, I'll plunge a fork into your silly throat—I'll pull out your clacking tongue with my nails."

Marty suddenly caught sight of her hands. One was resting on the table; the other was holding her cigarette; both were trembling. She looked miserably round the table. They were all listening with exaggerated courtesy. Shirley was looking down, her long scarlet-tipped fingers scratching about among the bread crumbs by her plate, making them into little patterns, a circle with one larger one in the middle, then a triangle. Budge's voice grated on. The Englishman, the Scotsman and the American, "I say you know," "Och aye," "Gee." Marty stared across the years at his face. There it was, aged a little, but not much changed since she had loved it so; the same kindly, rather protuberant blue eyes, the fleshy nose, the straw-colored hair, the wide comedian's mouth. His head was bent forward eagerly. He was talking a trifle too quickly because somewhere writhing deep within him was a suspicion that his audience was not wholly with him, he hadn't quite got them. He finished the Scotsman's bit. Bobby Peek laughed, and Marty could have flung her arms round his neck and hugged him for it.

Budge's eyes shone with pleasure—"Gee, Buddy!" There was quite a loud laugh at the end of the story.

Carroll's kindness triumphed over his wisdom. "That was wonderful, Budge," he said. "Nobody can tell a story like you!"

Marty's heart died in her. She made a swift, instinctive movement to get up from the table. Budge looked at her, and his eyes hardened. She sat still as death, chained to her chair. He cleared his throat again.

"Marty half getting up like that reminded me of a good one," he said. "Do you know the one about the shy lady at the dinner party who wanted to go to the telephone?"

There was a polite murmur round the table. Shirley took her compact out of her bag and scrutinized her face in the little mirror. Louis Bennet coughed and exchanged another meaning glance with Susan. Budge pushed back his chair, recrossed his legs and started. . . .

Marty stared down into her lap. There was some gold embroidery on her dress and it seemed to be expanding and changing into curious shapes because her eyes were filled with tears.

A hundred years later they were driving home. It was very late and the streets were almost empty. Budge was bunched up in his corner, sulky and silent. Marty stared at the back of Gordon's neck. Gordon drove well, but he was inclined to take risks. As a rule she was nervous and made him go slowly, but tonight she didn't care; she wouldn't have minded if he had driven at sixty miles an hour, careering along Oxford Street, crashing all the lights.

They arrived at Number 18 still in silence. Budge said good night to Gordon, and they went into the house. Rose had left the drink tray on the dining-room table and a plate of curly-looking sandwiches.

Budge poured himself out a whiskey and soda. "I'm going on up," he said. "I'm tired."

Suddenly something seemed to crack inside Marty's head and she started to laugh. There was an ugly note in the laugh which she recognized, but she had neither the strength nor the will to do anything about it.

"You must be," she said. "Oh, my God, you certainly must be!"

Budge stopped at the door and turned and looked at her.

"And what exactly do you mean by that?" he asked.

"Don't you know?" she said, and her voice sounded shrill and hysterical. "Don't you really know? Haven't you got the faintest idea?"

Budge's already red face flushed, and he advanced two steps toward her. "What's the matter with you?"

Marty backed away from him, still laughing miserably.

"This is a good one," she said. "Stop me if you've heard it. Stop me if you've heard it or not, because if you don't you'll never forgive me and I shall never forgive myself."

Budge frowned. "Are you drunk?"

Marty shook her head dumbly. She felt the tears starting and tried to wipe them away with the back of her hand. Budge came closer to her and looked carefully into her face. There was no more anger in his eyes, only bewilderment. She tried to look away, to escape from that puzzled, anxious face. She backed farther and, feeling the edge of a chair under her knees, sank down into it.

"What's the matter?" Budge persisted. "You're not ill or anything, are you? Is it anything to do with me? What have I done?"

He put his hand on her arm. She felt the warmth of it through her sleeve. Suddenly her hysteria evaporated. She felt utterly exhausted, but no longer wild, no longer shrill and nerve-strained and cruel. She put her hand up, and pressed his more firmly onto her arm. Then she gave a little giggle, not a very convincing one really, but good enough.

"You may well ask what you've done," she said. "You may well ask if it's anything to do with you—"

Her voice broke, and, bringing her face against his stomach, she started crying thoroughly and satisfyingly.

Budge remained silent, but his other hand smoothed her hair away from her forehead. After a moment or two she controlled herself a bit and pushed him gently away.

"You've given me a miserable evening," she said huskily. "You never took your eyes off Shirley Dale from the beginning of supper to the end. You then behave like a sulky little boy all the way home in the car, and, to round the whole thing off, you help yourself to a drink without even asking if I want one and tell me you're tired! You're an inconsiderate, lecherous little pig and I can't imagine why I ever let you lead me to the Registry Office."

She rose to her feet and put her arms round him tightly. She felt his body relax.

He gave a complacent chuckle. "Of all the bloody fools," he said. The warmth was back in his voice, the crisis had passed and the truth was stamped down again deep into the ground.

He led her over to the table and mixed her a drink. "Shirley Dale, indeed—you must be out of your mind!"

She stood there with one arm still around him, sipping her drink. Nothing more was said until he had switched off the lights and they had gone upstairs. They talked ordinarily while they undressed; the familiarity of the bedroom seemed overeager to put their hearts at ease.

Later on, after he had attacked his teeth in the bathroom with his customary violence, sprinkled himself with Floris 127 and put on his pajamas, he came over and sat on the edge of her bed.

She smiled and reached out and patted his hand. Then gently, almost timidly, as though she were not quite sure of her ground, she pulled him toward her. "I've got something to tell you," she said. "Stop me if you've heard it."

ASHES
OF
ROSES

Leonora glanced idly through the pile of fan letters on her dressing table. She had got in for the matinee earlier than usual, and Alice had not arrived yet, otherwise the letters would already have been opened and neatly arranged for her.

Suddenly, among the genteelly colored envelopes she came upon one that was white and quite plain. It looked businesslike, but was not typed. She turned it over in her hands and read an embossed address in an oval on the flap: "Hogarth and Currie—Solicitors."

She looked at the writing again. It seemed vaguely familiar; the envelope was very tightly stuck down, so she slit it open with her nail file.

> My dear Leonora,
>
> I expect you will be surprised to hear from me after so many years. Perhaps you will have forgotten my very existence. In case you have, I will remind you of Lorelei in 1924 and Hyde Park on a May afternoon. Those days seem very far away. I have spent most of the intervening years in Malaya, but came home in 1939 just after War broke out. Having been

*refused for the Army, I have been up here ever since working
for the above firm. I have been married twice since the old days
when we knew each other. Time does march on, doesn't it?
Judging by your photographs in the papers you have hardly
changed at all! I am coming to the play tonight and wondered
if you would be free to have supper with me afterward at the
Caledonian. It would be so nice to see you again and talk over
old times. If by any lucky chance you are free, could you leave
a message for me with the stage-door man? I do hope you will
be able to.*

*Yours sincerely,
Felix Mesurier*

Leonora slowly put the letter down and closed her eyes. She
then opened them again, and looked at herself in the glass with interest to see if the shock had done anything to her face; it hadn't.
There she was, looking exactly the same as she always looked when
she was about to make up. The butter muslin was tied round her
head as usual to prevent the powder getting into her hair; nothing
erratic had happened to her features. She passed her hand wearily
across her forehead—the gesture she always used in the last act in
the "Good-bye" scene with Henry. She looked lovely as she did it,
lovely and hopeless and resigned. Then she shook her head and
smiled wanly, and suddenly, with neither loveliness, wanness nor resignation, she clapped her hand over her mouth and burst out laughing. Felix Meseurier!—Felix! After nearly twenty years! It wasn't possible. She picked up the letter and reread it: "Judging by your
photographs in the papers you have hardly changed at all!" Like hell
she hadn't!

She leaned forward and scrutinized her face in the mirror.
"Hardly" was the operative word. She remembered herself distinctly,
too distinctly, in *Lorelei* in 1924. That was the year she'd had the
Foulsham and Banfield photographs taken at considerable personal
expense, and had finally persuaded the "Guv'nor" to allow a frame
containing four of the best poses to be hung in the theater foyer. She
could see them clearly even now. One was a large head with the eyes
looking upward with a rather startled expression, as if someone
were going to throw something at her from a great height. In two of
the others she was posed in an unrelaxed manner on a sort of music
stool with spindly legs, and in the fourth she was looking archly
round a screen with her hair down.

She had been nineteen when those photograhs were taken.
Now, looking at herself in the glass in the star dressing room of the
King's Theatre, Edinburgh, it was 1944 and she was forty. The face
peering with such roguish assurance round that screen in Foulsham

and Banfield's studio had been unlined and chubby; the face now looking back at her from the mirror was neither. It was a lovely face, certainly, actually lovelier perhaps than it had been twenty years ago, but youth had vanished from it for ever.

Alice came fussing in full of apologies: she had waited in a queue for twenty minutes for the tram and then, just as she reached the step, the conductress had shouted "Full up," and given her a push into the bargain. Leonora began to make up. Helen, the assistant stage manageress, knocked on the door and said, "Half an hour please, Miss Jarvis." Alice bustled about the room getting her first-act dress ready and running the tap into the basin so that the water would be warm and ready to wash in. Felix Meseurier!

Leonora expertly massaged the Max Factor foundation into her skin and sighed; Lorelei—Hyde Park on a May afternoon! A little while later, when the first act had been called and she was getting into her dress, she said with a casualness that was only a fraction overdone, "Alice, dear, leave a message at the stage door for a Mr. Meseurier— you'd better spell it out because that old man's awfully stupid. MESEURIER—say that I shall be delighted to have supper with him tonight, and will he come round after the show and pick me up."

2

One of the greatest attractions of Lorelei at the Walgrave Theatre was undoubtedly the sextet which came in the middle of the third act. The girls who sang it were Maureen Clayton, Josie Gay, Phyllis Greville, Leonora Jarvis, Etta Malvern and Violet Primrose. They all dressed together in Number 14 dressing room on the third floor. They were a carefully picked little bunch of houris, and all their twelve legs were impeccable although their voices were less uniformly perfect. Maureen, Etta and Phyllis carried the vocal ardor of the number, while Josie, Leonora and Violet opened and shut their pretty mouths and emitted occasional thin, but not entirely unpleasant, sounds. All six of them, however, had the charm of youth and the assurance of comparative inexperience. Maureen, aged twenty-six, was the eldest and had actually played two leads on tour. Josie Gay, twenty-five, was actually the veteran because she had been on the stage since she was nine. Etta, a pretty creature utterly devoid of ambition, was the same age as Leonora. In fact, they both celebrated their twentieth birthdays in the same week, and there was a write-up about it in the Daily Mirror with a photograph of them both cutting a large cake with candles on it and a few of the principals standing around wearing strained, good-humored smiles. Phyllis and Violet were the babies, being nineteen and eighteen respectively.

In the show the girls had comparatively little to do apart from the sextet. They had a concerted entrance in the first act, when they all came chattering and laughing down a ship's gangway and, for a few minutes, provided a demure background for Martha Dorcas's first number. She was the leading comedienne and they were all supposed to be her daughters. After this they were not on again until the finale of the second act when, together with the entire company, they had to stand about while Judy Clandon, the leading lady, sang a loud and reproachful aria to Clyde Markham, the leading man, at the end of which she flung a glass of champagne into his face and collapsed, sobbing violently, into the arms of Martha Dorcas. In the third act there were the sextet and the finale of the whole show. None of the girls had any lines to speak, except Maureen, who played a brief "feed" scene with Budge Ripley, the comedian, in the opening of Act Three and in addition understudied Judy Clandon.

Number 14, therefore, was the real hub of their theater lives. Here they argued, quarreled, giggled, manicured their nails, tried new ways of doing their hair, made underclothes, gave tea parties on matinee days to other members of the company (nobody outside the theater was allowed backstage during performances) and discussed sex in general and their own love affairs in particular. The dressing room was presided over and kept in reasonable order by Mrs. Leftwich, "Leffie," their dresser. "Leffie" was overworked, harassed, sharp-tongued and beloved by them all. She had been in the profession herself years ago and, at one time, had played quite good parts on tour. However, she had sacrificed her career at the age of twenty-nine and married an electrician in Bradford who had taken to the bottle. After some years of acute conjugal incompatibility he had been knocked down by a tram just outside the Kennington Oval tube station, and had died in St. Thomas's Hospital, leaving Leffie with the relief of his departure offset by the burden of having to bring up two children. Both of these were now adult. The son, Bob, had gone to Canada and married and settled down; the daughter, Nora, had also married, but far from settling down had run off with someone else only a month after the wedding. It was the general opinion of Number 14 that Nora had gone thoroughly to the bad because, however pressed, Leffie would seldom speak of her.

Number 14 came to life every evening at about seven-thirty and on Wednesdays and Saturdays at one-thirty. Leffie always arrived on the dot, took the key off the hook in the stage-door box and trudged up the three flights. She invariably unlocked the door and went in with a faint sinking of the heart just in case everything wasn't all right. There was really no reason why it should not be, as she herself was the last to leave at night having tidied up meticulously and placed neat chintz covers over each of the six dressing places, but this daily apprehensiveness was accounted for by the fact that, years ago when she had been dressing May Garson at the Vaudeville, she had come in one night as usual to find that the room had been ransacked and all May Garson's clothes pinched, including her fur coat which, like a fool, she'd left hanging up in the cupboard. That had been a "do" and no mistake—policemen and cross-questionings and one thing and another. The nightmare of it still lingered in her mind.

One evening toward the end of April 1924, when the show had been on for three months and had settled into an established success, Leffie was just about to take the key off the hook as usual when Frank, the doorman, jerked his head in the direction of a figure standing in the rather cramped space between the outer and inner doors. "Someone wants to speak to you." He gave a lewd wink and wiggled his tongue up and down in his cheek. "I think he's after one of your young specials!"

Leffie went up to the stranger. He was a good-looking, well-dressed young man with a soft black hat pulled down over his eyes, which he raised politely. "Are you Miss Jarvis's dresser?"

Leffie nodded. "That's right," she said.

The young man smiled, a charming smile exposing very white teeth. "I wonder if you would be very kind and give her this note when she comes in?" He handed her an envelope and two half crowns which she took rather dubiously.

"Do you know Miss Jarvis?"

He smiled again. "Unfortunately not—that is, not personally. I've seen her several times in the show."

"I see." Leffie put her head a little on one side and looked at him appraisingly.

"I know I could have left it in the rack in the ordinary way," he went on, "but I thought I'd rather give it to you and be sure she'd get it all right. My intentions," he added, "are quite honorable."

Leffie nodded laconically. "All right," she said, "I'll see she gets it."

The young man raised his hat again. "Thank you so much—I'm very grateful."

He went out into the alley. Leffie turned the note over in her hands, put the five shillings into her pocket and went thoughtfully upstairs. While she was whisking the covers off the dressing places and setting the various wrappers over the backs of the chairs all ready to be slipped on the moment their owners arrived, she hummed breathily a little tune to herself, but, behind the tune, somewhere in the back of her mind, she was aware of a certain perplexity, a faint pang of questioning conscience. It was not taking the note and the five shillings exactly: there was nothing either wrong or unusual in that, but there was something all the same, something that made her feel uneasy. He was a nice-looking young man all right and his clothes were good—she looked at the note which she had propped up against Leonora's powder box—quite gentlemanly writing.

Suddenly she sat down, still staring at the note, and rubbed her chin pensively. Concentrated thought processes were difficult for Leffie; she lived her life almost entirely by instinct. What really was gnawing at her conscience was a sense of responsibility. Not that there was any logical reason for this. It was not part of her duties to guard the moral behavior of her charges; all she was paid for was to dress them, keep them in order as much as possible and see to it they went down when they were called and did not miss any entrances; still, she was an elderly woman and they were young, and she wouldn't like any harm to come to a hair of their heads.

A romanticist would, of course, be lyrically moved at the thought of those six young creatures, so full of life and potentialities all starting their careers together with the glamorous possibilities of stardom or wealthy marriages beckoning them on into the future. A cynic would merely have seen Number 14 dressing room as a forcing house for egoism, artificiality and female predatoriness.

Mrs. Leftwich was neither a romanticist nor a cynic; she was a realist. To her, Maureen, Josie, Phyllis, Leonora, Etta and Violet were six girls whose job it was to make successes of their lives or their careers, or both if possible. She had grown fond of them and they of her; each of them tipped her regularly every Saturday night—always the same sum, which had obviously been agreed on among themselves in secret conclave. They sometimes borrowed money from her which was invariably paid back at the end of the week. They always shared whatever they had with her in the way of food or drink, and, above all, they trusted her and frequently asked her advice.

Occasionally the advice was extremely difficult to give. There was, for instance, that dreadful Saturday not long after the show opened when Phyllis had lingered on in the dressing room until all the others had gone and then burst into floods of hysterical tears and confessed that she was over two months gone and that something would have to be done about it or she would kill herself. That was a teaser and no mistake. Leffie had sent her home in a taxi, having promised to meet her next day outside the Piccadilly Hotel at two-thirty, and that same night had gone traipsing round to the Palace Theatre to see old Mrs. Greerson, who knew a woman who knew a doctor somewhere near Olympia.

The next afternoon they had met as arranged, and had gone off to Addison Road. Leffie would never forget that little jaunt to her dying day. The doctor was an oily-looking man with spurts of iron-gray hair growing out of his ears. Leffie had had to wait for two hours in a sort of front parlor with nothing to look at but a back number of *Woman and Home* without a cover and a large picture over the mantelpiece of a dog with a rabbit in its mouth. Fortunately it had all gone off all right, and she had taken Phyllis away in a taxi and deposited her at her cousin's, well briefed with a trumped-up story of having fainted at the pictures.

It must here be noted that the ethics of stage life differ considerably from those of other, more conventional worlds. Leffie, it is true, had been extremely shocked by this incident, but not on account of its moral aspects. Having been born and bred in the theater she had no inherent reverence for virginity. In her experience it was an overrated commodity at the best of times and far too much fuss was made about it at that. What shocked her over this particular episode was not that Phyllis had had an affair with a gentleman unnamed, but that she should have been silly and inefficient enough to let herself get into trouble through it and thereby jeopardize her professional career. In Leffie's opinion, a strapping girl of nineteen ought to have more sense. The silliest part of it all, of course, was to let it drag on until she was well into her third month. However, all was well that ended well.

What was worrying her now, about the young man and the note and the two half crowns, she was unable to explain to herself. Perhaps it was something to do with his teeth or his voice—a gentle, dangerous voice. At all events, she shrugged her shoulders, Leonora was a bright, ambitious girl and well capable of looking after herself.

3

Felix Meseurier stood in the foyer of the Walgrave Theatre casually smoking a cigarette and occasionally glancing at his wristwatch to give any of the attendants who might be observing him the impression that he was waiting for someone. From his particular point of vantage just to the left of the box office he commanded an excellent view of a large frame on the opposite wall containing four portrait studies of Leonora Jarvis. If being in love means a physical attraction of the first magnitude then Felix Meseurier was in love. He could hardly look at the photographs without trembling.

There he stood, slim and handsome in his dinner jacket, listening to the orchestra tuning up for the overture, and staring across the heads of the people passing by him. Every now and then he would look away, but his eyes always returned avidly to that pert, lovely little face and those long, exciting legs. He was rather a saturnine-looking young man, a fact of which he was perfectly aware and which secretly pleased him. His father had been French and had died years ago. His mother, a determined and thoroughly efficient woman, ran a small chemist's shop in Uxbridge. Her one weakness in life had been, and still was, Felix. He on his side was fond of her and reasonably filial, in that he visited her dutifully once a week.

He was a selfish creature, but not more so than many other young men of his generation. Having been called up in 1916, he had been invalided out of the Army in 1917 with incipient t.b. This had necessitated his spending a year at a sanatorium near Woking, from which he emerged completely cured a few weeks after the Armistice was signed. His sojourn in the Army had been undistinguished to the point of bathos, a dismal little record of influenzas, bad colds and finally pleurisy, the results of which obtained for him his ultimate discharge. With one part of his mind he regretted this. He liked to visualize himself as romantically valiant, as indeed who does not? His sense of realism, however, caused him to admit to himself in secret that he was relieved beyond words that he had never got nearer to the war than a bleak camp in Derbyshire.

In 1919, through his mother's resolute determination, he got a job as a clerk in a shipping office in the City, and now, after four years, he had laboriously climbed to being a sort of secretary-cum-assistant to the manager of the branch. This dazzling eminence had been achieved less by hard work than by a romantic attachment to the manager's daughter, a plain but fiercely emotional girl two years his senior. It was an understood thing that ultimately when, in the words of the girl's father, he had "proved himself," they were to be married.

This whole situation might have been intolerable were it not for the fact that the manager, Herbert Renshaw, his wife and Sheila lived at Sevenoaks, just mercifully far enough away to make constant propinquity difficult. Felix lived on his salary, with occasional assistance from his mother, in a bed-sitting room in Ebury Street. Every now and then he went to Sevenoaks—as dutifully as, but even less enthusiastically than, he went to Uxbridge. Sometimes, fortunately not very often, Sheila Renshaw came to London for the day. This involved much playacting and nerve strain. First of all, there would be the halting, boyish request to Mr. Renshaw for an afternoon off; then lunch and a matinee, followed by the inevitable embarrassing taxi drive, hand in hand, to Victoria. Sometimes Mrs. Renshaw would come up too and meet them archly for tea; this at least ameliorated the horror of the latter part of the afternoon. It was perfectly apparent that Sheila loved him intensely. She was a stocky girl with nice eyes and no neck to speak of. Felix alternated between tolerating her and actively loathing her. He had not yet really faced up to the ultimate showdown, but knew that sooner or later he would have to. In the meantime life jogged along pleasantly and he had enough leisure to enjoy himself as much as he could.

The fact must be faced that Felix's principal preoccupation was sex. Sex in any reasonable form whatever. This may or may not have been something to do with his t.b. tendencies, but, whatever the cause, it was his preeminent interest and it had been for almost as long as he could remember. There was never a day in his life that he had not been ready and willing to respond to physical contact. So engrossed was he with the manifold physical pleasures that his body could provide that he had never given a desultory thought to other safety valves, such as reading, debate, music or drink. What was most curious of all was the fact that he had never once experienced the emotion of being in love. He was highly predatory, but completely unpossessive; sensual and passionate, but incapable of jealousy. To go to bed with another fellow creature who attracted him seemed to him the most natural thing in the world, and it was astonishing how far this amiable conviction carried him. But to feel himself in any way bound to them or in their debt would never have occurred to him. With all this it must not be imagined that he lacked subtlety when in pursuit of what he wanted; far from it, he was capable of infinite patience and also, alas, of infinite charm.

This, then, was the affable young wolf who was standing in the foyer of the Walgrave Theatre gazing romantically at photographs of an attractive young woman of twenty.

4

Leonora Jarvis had been on the stage for four years. Her father and mother had died when she was a baby, and she had no memory of them; her earliest recollections were of Aunt May and Uncle Hubert and the house in Sandgate, a light, clean, chilly house overlooking the sea. At the age of eight she had been sent to a small day school nearby and, two years later, to a larger school in Folkestone in which she was a weekly boarder and could come home for weekends every Saturday afternoon by catching a bus outside Timothy White's.

Aunt May and Uncle Hubert were kind but undemonstrative, and, although her early years may have lacked the warmth of parental affection, they in no way lacked creature comforts. The house, during the summer months, accommodated boarders of aggressive gentility. Leonora naturally preferred the off-seasons, when there was no one left but old Mr. Radlett, who was a permanent, because then she was permitted to move from the poky little room on the top floor at the back which she inhabited when the house was full, and to spread herself in the second-floor front. Here she could kneel on clear winter nights, with the window wide open and an eiderdown wrapped around her, and look out over the dark sea. Sometimes, when it was very clear, she could see the rhythmic flash of the Gris Nez lighthouse below the horizon but reflected in the sky. Here, with the smell of the sea, the sound of the waves pounding the shingle and the sharp wind blowing the curtains out into the room, she could make plans for the future.

She was not a particularly romantic child, but she had always been determined, and since the second January of the War, when she had been taken by a school friend and family to a pantomime at the Pleasure Garden Theatre, she had formed one steadfast resolution, and that was to be an actress. It took her three years to achieve even the beginnings of this ambition, but through Uncle Hubert dying, and Aunt May giving up the house and moving into a flat in Maida Vale, and various other helpful circumstances, achieve it she did.

In the year 1919, after a series of impassioned scenes with Aunt May and Miss Bridgeman, the rather fierce companion whom Aunt May had taken to live with her, Leonora was sent to Madame Alvani's Acting and Dancing Academy in Baker Street. In 1920—aged sixteen—she played an animated water lily in a Christmas production at the Villiers Theatre. For this she was paid three pounds a week, from which Madame Alvani deducted ten percent commission. Her next engagement was on tour with an ancient but select farce. In this she played a small part and understudied the ingenue lead. Her salary was again three pounds a week, but this time she did not have to pay commission, as she had got the job through Kay Larkin, an associate water lily a year older than herself who knew the ropes and had taken her straight to the management. Aunt May's and Miss Bridgeman's fears for her chastity were allayed by the fact that she was sharing rooms with Kay and, what was better still, Kay's mother. Had either of the good ladies ever clapped eyes on Kay's mother they might have been less tranquil. However, no moral harm came to Leonora during the engagement, and even if it had they would certainly have been the last to hear about it.

By the end of November 1923, when Oscar Morley (the Guv'nor) had engaged her for the sextet in the forthcoming production of *Lorelei*, she had achieved quite a lot of experience, if little fame. She had toured, been in the chorus of two West End revues, done a whole season of repertory in Nottingham and played a bright, gay prostitute with a heart of gold in an ambitious problem play at the Everyman in Hampstead which never came to the West End. Through all these routine vicissitudes she had managed to remain, through circumstance and a certain natural fastidiousness, a virgin.

She had imagined herself to be in love on two occasions, once with the leading man in Nottingham, who was at least fifteen years older than she and heavily and happily married, and then with a young man who had been invalided out of the Navy and had appeared in her life when she was in the chorus of the *1922 Revue* at the Parthenon. This had been quite serious and lasted all through the summer. He had taken her out to supper at Rule's and occasionally the Savoy Grill. He had driven her on warm, languorous Sunday evenings in a small, spluttering two-seater to Maidenhead, where they had danced at Murray's and driven home through the dawn, stopping at the side of the road at frequent intervals to exchange ardent, but innocuous, embraces. He was a nice, good-looking boy, shy, and with impeccable manners.

On one of these romantic jaunts he had stammeringly proposed marriage, but Leonora, who by that time had been introduced to his mother and sister at tea at the Carlton, knew with every instinct in her that no good would come of it and that, if she accepted him, she would somehow be betraying him as well as herself. So she refused him firmly but with a sad heart, and a few weeks later he came tragically to say good-bye to her. His mother and sister had decided to go out to visit his other sister, who was married and lived in New Zealand. He was to go with them on account of his health and being able to live an outdoor life and one thing and another. It all sounded rather garbled, but Leonora thought she detected the underlying truth, which was that he really did love her more than was good for him, and his family, reasonably enough, were intent on getting him out of harm's way.

They had a farewell supper at Rule's, sitting in an alcove staring miserably at each other over sausages and bacon and gins and tonics. The two-seater was outside, and they drove down to Richmond and back although it was a raw October night. He dropped her off outside the flat at Fulham Road that she was sharing with Hester Lancaster. They stood sadly on the pavement hand in hand, looking abstractedly at a streetlamp swinging on the other side of the road. Then he suddenly kissed her almost violently, and said in a choked voice, "I shall never forget you and some part of me will always love you." With this he had jumped into the car and driven away. Leonora, blinded with tears, had fumbled for her latchkey, let herself in and flung herself sobbing onto Hester's bed, where finally, soothed by wise, sympathetic advice and hot Ovaltine, she fell into a deep sleep.

For quite a while after that she had been heavyhearted, but gradually, assisted by Hester and her own natural resilience, she forgot lost love in the everyday excitements of living. Hester was a laconic, drily humorous woman in her late twenties. They had met, shared digs and become close friends during the tour of *Lady from Spain*. Hester's talent for acting was meager; as far as a successful theatrical career was concerned, she was doomed to disappointment and she knew it, but she had a swift, cultured mind, and was a wise and restraining influence on Leonora. For over two years since the death of Aunt May they had been sharing the flat in Fulham Road.

Leonora came gaily into the dressing room with Josie. Phyllis,

Violet and Etta were already making up, but Maureen was late as usual. Leffie took her hat, bag and coat from her and hung them on a peg.

"There's a billy doo for you, dear," she said laconically. "I propped it up against the tin."

Leonora glanced at it casually as she slipped out of her dress. "It's probably from the Prince of Wales," she said. "Badgering me to go to one of those dreary evenings at Buckingham Palace."

"It might be from Alfie Stein," said Josie, "badgering you for his ten percent."

"Not me," Leonora sat down and pulled her wrapper round her. "I've never had an agent in my life since Miriam Moss got me a tour that only lasted for three split weeks." She opened the letter and read it through. Leffie, watching her in the glass, saw her frown for a moment, smile and then pass her hand rather abstractedly across her forehead.

"Well—come on, dear—don't keep us in suspense!" Josie banged on the dressing table with the back of her brush.

Leonora folded the letter carefully and put it back in the envelope and sighed. "Sorry to disappoint you all," she said, slapping some grease on her face. "It's only from my cousin Edward. He's eighteen, lives in Birmingham and has spots, and he's coming to the Saturday matinee." She turned to Leffie. "Leffie, darling, put that in my bag for me, will you, or I shall forget to answer it." Leffie, unsmiling, took it from her, put it in Leonora's handbag and snapped it to quite hard. Leonora gave her a swift look in the glass and went on with her makeup.

5

Felix stood in the alley outside the stage door. There was a group of girls near him, clutching autograph books and talking in whispers; occasionally one of them giggled. Felix, with elaborate nonchalance, took out his cigarette case and lit a cigarette. His whole body was taut and tremulous with suppressed excitement. He had watched the show from the front row of the dress circle on the side: it was the seventh time he had seen it, but he had never before been so near. During the second verse of the sextet Leonora had been actually only a few yards away from him. He had never taken his eyes off her for an instant; noting avidly every turn of her head; the little flounce she gave to her dress as she danced upstage; a secret smile she exchanged with one of the other girls when they were standing in a row right on the footlights for the last refrain; the demure, provocative swing of her hips as she went off, last but one, and the lissome grace of her curtsy when they all ran on to take the call. When the encore was over and they had finally gone, he had discovered that his hands, gripping the edge of the circle, were moist with excitement and had left a damp mark on the plush.

One by one and in groups, various members of the company emerged from the stage door. Budge Ripley, the comedian, came out in a hurry and went, almost at a run, up the steps at the end of the alley, where a taxi was waiting for him. The autograph collectors argued among themselves as to whether it really had been he or not. One of the show girls came out in a chinchilla coat, a spray of gardenias fastened to the lapel with a jeweled clip. A uniformed chauffeur was waiting for her. He raised his cap respectfully and helped her carefully up the steps toward the car as though she were infinitely fragile and might break.

Felix waited on. He recognized Maureen Clayton and Etta Malvern walking by him engrossed in animated conversation. He nearly accosted them to ask if Lenora was on her way down, but thought better of it and lit another cigarette. Judy Clandon came out followed by an elderly man in tails and a silk hat. The group of girls closed round her, and she signed their books and said good-bye to them with a great display of unaffected charm. When she had gone they moved off. Felix was left alone, except for a man in a mackintosh standing a little farther down. He was smoking a pipe and reading an evening paper in the light of the hanging lamp over the upper circle exit. At last Leonora came out. His heart seemed to jump into his throat; she was alone. Raising his hat, he stepped forward.

"Miss Jarvis." His voice sounded as though it belonged to someone else.

She stopped and smiled. "Are you Mr. Mes—Meseurier?" She had a little trouble with the name.

"Yes." He put out his hand which she accepted without embarrassment. "I hope you didn't mind me writing that letter. I couldn't help it."

She let her hand lie in his for a moment and then gently withdrew it. "I thought it was a very nice letter."

Suddenly Felix's overstrung, nervous shyness vanished. Everything was going to be all right. He grinned with a mixture of boyish humility and slight roguishness. "Is there any hope of your doing what I asked? Coming to have supper with me?"

Leonora shook her head. "I'm afraid not," she said. "I have to get straight home."

"Oh!" His voice was heavy with disappointment. They moved off together up the alley steps and into the street.

"You see," said Leonora, "I share a flat with a friend of mine, and if I go out without letting her know she gets rather worried."

"Couldn't you telephone her? We needn't be late."

255

Leonora shook her head. "Not tonight—honestly, I'd rather not tonight."

"Where is your flat? Is it far?"

"It's in the Fulham Road—I get the tube from Leicester Square."

"Would you mind if I came with you?"

Leonora shot him a look out of the corner of her eye as they turned into Garrick Street.

"Wouldn't it be taking you out of your way?"

Felix smiled—rather a nice smile, she thought. "I wish you lived at Hendon!"

He slipped his hand under her elbow to guide her across the road and kept it there when they reached the other side. She gave him another sidelong glance; his face was serious and, she had to admit, extremely attractive, and he wore his soft dark hat with an air. She began to wonder if, after all, she hadn't been a little hasty in refusing to have supper with him; there really wouldn't be any harm in it, and she was perfectly capable of looking after herself. The prospect of going straight home was rather dreary. Of course what she had said about Hester being worried about her wasn't strictly true. Hester probably wouldn't be home herself for an hour or more; she was playing a small part in a straight play at the Shaftesbury, it did not ring down until half-past eleven, and Hester always took her time anyway. She felt his hand tighten under her arm as they crossed St. Martin's Lane. He must have sensed that her obduracy was cracking a little, for he returned to the attack gently and very persuasively.

"I wouldn't like you to think that I made a habit of waiting outside stage doors and badgering girls to have supper with me." There was a tone of urgent sincerity in his voice. "As a matter of fact, this is the first time in my life that I've ever done it, and at that it's taken me weeks to summon up enough courage—as you see." He slowed down perceptibly—the Leicester Square station was distressingly near.

"You see, I really meant what I said in the letter. It would mean so very much to me to get to know you a little. Don't you think you could possibly change your mind—about supper, I mean? I'll drive you straight home in a taxi afterward, so you really wouldn't be so very much later than if you went in the tube."

They came to a standstill in the entrance of the station. Leonora disengaged her arm from him and looked up at the clock. It was only twenty-five minutes to twelve. There were a lot of people about, and there was a long queue at the ticket window. The hot, familiar smell of the station assailed her nostrils unpleasantly. It would be far nicer to go home in a taxi, and if they weren't more than an hour over supper she could be in bed by one o'clock at the latest.

Felix watched her, and again was aware of an inward trembling: her fawn-colored coat was tight-fitting and most tantalizingly outlined the curves of her young body; she was wearing a perky red cloche hat from under which a wisp of chestnut hair escaped in a jaunty little curl; her eyes were gray green, heavily lashed and set wide apart; her nose, which was short and retroussé, while it may have impaired the beauty of her face from the strictly classical point of view, undoubtedly enhanced its vitality and charm; her mouth was enchanting, full-lipped and with a dimple in each corner, and as Felix looked at it with longing it suddenly opened in a radiant smile and she said, "Oh, all right!"

They had supper in a small restaurant in Soho. The atmosphere was oppressively Italian and there was a pervasive smell of garlic and cigar smoke, but the food was good, the chianti passable and the red-shaded lamp on the table seemed to isolate them from the rest of the room and to enclose them in a glowing, shadowed, intimate world of their own. Felix ordered hors d'oeuvres, ravioli with powdered Parmesan cheese to sprinkle over it, and zabaglione in little shallow cups. He suggested liqueurs with the coffee, but she refused, finally compromising by having a crème de menthe frappé. Felix had brandy and bought himself a cigar.

By this time all restraint and shyness had fled. Felix, with a masterly sensitivity that many an older roué would have envied, refrained from any suggestion of lovemaking. He talked gaily and naturally without a trace of flirtatiousness. His acute hunting instinct warned him to establish firmly a friendly basis before attempting anything further.

Leonora, although not entirely deceived, thoroughly enjoyed herself. Her instincts also were fairly acute, and she had been about with ardent young men enough to be able to size up the situation without undue confusion. She found him attractive and nice-looking; she liked the way his eyes went up at the corners and the wave of his glossy dark hair. His eyes were brown and perhaps just a little too close together; he had a deep voice and his smile was infectious and charming; his teeth were perfect, even and gleaming white—no toothpaste firm could wish for a better advertisement. His greatest attraction, however, was his hands, muscular and slim with long, tapering fingers; his wrists, she had to admit, were rather hairy, but still you couldn't have everything.

They were almost the last to leave the restaurant. He took her coat from the cloakroom woman and helped her on with it himself. The patron wished them an expansive good night. Leonora noticed with satisfaction that Felix had tipped generously. When they got outside, the street was deserted and shone under the lights as though it had been raining. Their footsteps echoed in the silence as they walked down toward Shaftesbury Avenue. Felix hailed a taxi just outside the Queen's Theatre, and Leonora told the driver the address. When they had driven about halfway down Piccadilly Felix gently took her hand and held it. He said rather huskily, "You don't mind, do you?" She said, "Of course not," and inwardly commenting, "Here we go," she braced herself for the inevitable kiss. This, however, was not forthcoming. He seemed quite content to sit there silently holding her hand; every now and then he gave it a little friendly squeeze, but that was all.

When the cab drew up outside her front door, Felix jumped out immediately and held her arm carefully as she stepped down onto the curb. They stood there looking at each other for a moment. Leonora was aware of a faint but unmistakable disappointment that he had not kissed her.

"You were a darling," he said, allowing a note of passionate intensity to creep into his voice, "to come to supper after all. You've no idea how much it meant to me!"

Leonora gave a slight giggle. She felt suddenly unaccountably nervous. "Don't be silly," she said, aware that her voice sounded rather breathless. "I had a lovely time."

She began fumbling in her bag for her latchkey; she found it and looked up at him. In the light from the streetlamp she observed a little pulse beating in his temple. She held out her hand. "Good night, and thanks a lot."

He shook hands with her silently, and she turned and went up a little path to the front door. When she had, rather agitatedly, fitted the key into the lock, she turned back and waved. He was still standing there staring after her. Her wave seemed to snap him out of his trance, for he waved back, called, "Good night," quite ordinarily, gave an address to the driver and jumped into the cab. As she closed the door behind her she heard it drive away. She walked upstairs feeling a bit deflated. He hadn't kissed her; he hadn't even asked to see her again.

6

There is much to recommend Hyde Park on a sunny Sunday afternoon, particularly in spring when the grass is newly green and there is a feeling of lightness in the air. Subconsciously affected by this, the most prosaic citizens frequently give way to a certain abandon. Fathers of families take off their coats and waistcoats and lie on their backs chewing bits of grass and gazing up at the sky; their wives sit near them, keeping an eye on the children and allowing the sun to burn semicircular areas of pink onto their necks. Younger people lie unashamedly very close, sometimes asleep, sometimes lazily awake, murmuring laconically to each other, sucking sweets, smoking cigarettes, relaxed and content, soothed into a sensual lassitude by the promise in the air and the gentle weather. As a general rule decorum is observed, although occasionally passion flames suddenly between them and they lie with arms and legs entwined, oblivious of passersby, lost in brief ecstasy. Police constables regulate these transient excesses with admirable discretion; nothing is allowed to get out of control, the decencies are upheld, the birds sing, and the cries of children, the barking of dogs and the far-off strains of a military band, together with the gentle, incessant rumble of traffic in the distance, provide a muted orchestration to this unremarkable, but at the same time unique, London pastoral.

On a Sunday afternoon in May 1924 Leonora and Felix, having lunched at the Rendezvous and strolled down Piccadilly into the Park, lay in the shade of a tree near the Round Pond. At least Leonora was in the shade because she was afraid of getting freckles. Felix, intent on acquiring a tan, had taken off his shirt and was stripped to the waist in the sun. This was their third meeting since the evening two weeks ago when they had had supper at the Italian restaurant and he had driven her home in a taxi. He had called for her unexpectedly one Wednesday after the matinee and taken her to tea at the Thistle tearooms at the top of the Haymarket. The day after that he had sent a large bunch of flowers to her at the theater with a card on which was written, "The words are old and ever new—forgive my heart for loving you." This was a quotation from Judy Clandon's number in Act Three of *Lorelei,* and under it were the initials F. M. The following Monday night after the show he had called for her in the pouring rain and they had supper together again, this time impressively at the Savoy Grill. This time, also, he had kissed her on the way home in the taxi, but not until they were past Brompton Oratory and the drive was nearly over; the kiss, however, well-timed and admirably executed, had lasted with mounting intensity until the taxi drew up before her front door.

Today from the moment they had met outside the Piccadilly Circus tube station until now there had been no indication, either in his voice or in his manner, that he had ever kissed her at all or had the faintest intention of kissing her again. Throughout lunch he had been gay and talkative. Never once had his hand closed over hers; never once had she detected in his cheerful brown eyes that look of sudden longing, of suppressed desire. He had actually made fun of a couple sitting in the far corner of the restaurant because they looked so obliviously, so overwhelmingly, in love.

Leonora's first reaction to this technique was one of acute irritation. This was presently superseded by a strange unhappiness, a desolation of the heart, an inexplicable desire to burst into tears. She rallied, however, with commendable poise and chattered and laughed as gaily as he. This successful effort at self-control had not only carried her triumphantly through lunch and down Shaftesbury Avenue and the whole length of Piccadilly, but had strung her nerves high. She had worked herself into a mood of tingling, brittle defiance. She'd show him all right, the next time he started any of his nonsense, that that kiss—the tremulous memory of which she hastily put out of her mind—had meant as little to her as it obviously had to him.

Now, sitting under the tree with the warm spring sunshine all around her, this mood suddenly and unaccountably evaporated, leaving her shivering and vulnerable. Felix was lying a yard or so away from her. His naked chest and arms shone in the strong light. She felt a violent urge to fling herself onto him, to feel his mouth under hers, and the warmth of his body pressed against her. Appalled by this sudden wave of passion which swept over her and receded, leaving her trembling and exhausted, she leant her head back against the tree trunk and closed her eyes.

Felix, whose telepathic instincts seldom failed him, turned his head sharply and looked at her; swiftly and almost in one movement his arms were around her and his lips pressed into the hollow of her neck. She gave a little cry. He kissed her mouth lingeringly, and then, when her whole being seemed to be fused in an agony of surrender, he rolled away from her and lay face downward on the grass, still as death, with his face turned away from her.

A little while later, his hand, familiar and comforting under her arm, guided her gently across Knightsbridge into the deserted Sabbath peace of Lowndes Square. She walked automatically in step with him; neither of them spoke, but the feeling between them was tense. Somewhere below her surface consciousness a conflict was raging: this was silly, cheap, immodest, dangerous—she would regret it until the end of her life. Walking through the empty, echoing London squares in the clear afternoon sunlight with her lover, a comparative stranger; being led inexorably to the glamour and squalor and ecstasy and defeat of a bed-sitting room in Ebury Street. An empty taxi hoping for a fare drew up close to them as they crossed Eaton Square. She longed for the courage to shake off Felix's arm and jump into it. It ground its gears and drove off. They walked on in silence along Elizabeth Street and turned the corner.

Felix's bed-sitting room was on the third floor at the back of a tall, narrow house. The window looked out over a small yard, a grimy brick wall and the backs of the houses in Chester Square. The landlady lived in the basement, and they had crept in and up the stairs unheard and unobserved. Leonora noticed a bottle of bright green hairwash on the dressing table and a photograph of a squat dark girl in an embossed leather frame. The bed, pretending to be a divan, had neither head nor foot and was pushed against the wall. There were some colored Liberty cushions on it, arranged three-cornerwise and looking self-conscious; on the mantelpiece there were a few books leaning against a china dog, a tin of Gold Flake cigarettes, a large photograph of three young men in bathing trunks and a pair of dumbbells. Leonora stood quite still in the middle of the room, staring uncertainly at the three young men and imagining vaguely that the one in the middle of the group was Felix himself; a beam of sunlight cut sharply through the net curtains, and in the distance there was the noise of a train shunting. Felix turned the key in the door, and then came over to her. He stood looking at her for a moment with a strange, furtive little smile, and then, with a sort of gentle violence, he pulled her to him and as his mouth opened on hers she felt his left hand slip into the bosom of her dress.

7

On a Saturday evening a few weeks later Leonora came into the theater with Josie Gay. They were late and breathless, having run all the way from Josie's family flat in Covent Garden, the "half" had already been called, and if Len Baxter, the stage manager, saw them they would be ticked off. The stage-door man handed Leonora a letter from the rack as she and Josie rushed through the folding doors, and she took it without looking at it. Leffie glanced at them disapprovingly as they burst into the dressing room.

Leonora flung the letter face downward on her dressing table while she tore her clothes off and got into her wrapper. She felt gay and without a care in the world. Tomorrow was Sunday and she was meeting Felix as usual; she had had a lovely time having dinner with Josie and the Prout family. Josie's father, Syd Prout, the well-known comedian, had died some years ago, leaving his wife with three daughters to bring up. Dawn (Dawn Lawrence), the eldest, had made quite a name for herself playing cockney character parts. Josie came next and was doing reasonably well; she was a hard-boiled, thoroughly experienced little "pro" and looked a great deal younger than twenty-five with her chubby face and fluffy blond hair.

The family's pride was Shirley, the youngest—the famous Shirley Dale, who already at twenty-four was an established star. Leonora had met her for the first time this evening and had been duly thrilled and impressed. Shirley had arrived unexpectedly and tempestuously just as they were sitting down to dinner. Her clothes were perfect and her manner entirely natural and unaffected, the aura of stardom, although unmistakable, seemed in no way to have interfered with her alert, utterly theatrical sense of humor, a quality which most emphatically distinguished the whole family.

Mrs. Prout (at one time Rosie Claire) was obviously adored by the three girls. They laughed at her and teased her and told hilarious stories of her absentmindedness, her occassional predilection for having a "couple over the odds," her swiftness of repartee and her frequent, but always unsuccessful, attempts to become what they described as "county." None of them ever called her "Mother" or even "Mum." She was always "Rosie" or sometimes "Our Rosie." There was certainly a warmth, a coziness, an intrinsic, down-to-earth reality about the Prout family.

Leonora had been taken to their ramshackle, untidy house in Covent Garden several times, and each time she had come away happy and stimulated and with a little envy in her heart, a regret that she had not had the luck to be born of a comedienne and a principal boy and to be brought up with the fun and jokes and glamour of the theater as her natural background.

It was not until she had put on the foundation of her makeup and was about to start on her eyelashes that she remembered the letter. She wiped her fingers on her face towel, picked up the letter and turned it over in her hands. With a slight sinking of the heart she recognized Felix's handwriting; perhaps he was putting her off for tomorrow, perhaps he was ill, or had to go and see his mother at Uxbridge or something.

She opened it quickly and read it. Then she sat quite still feeling sick, as though someone had hit her hard in the solar plexus. The chattering voices of the other girls seemed to recede into the remote distance. Like a sound from another world she dimly heard the callboy's voice in the passage shouting, "Quarter of an hour, please." With an immense effort she read the letter through again.

> *Dearest Lee,*
>
> *I hate writing you this letter, but I've got to do it—there is no other way out. I know you'll think me an awful cad for never having told you that I was engaged to be married, but somehow I couldn't screw up the courage—I felt that it would spoil everything if you knew. I am utterly heartbroken and miserable—my fiancée's father has found out about you and me. I don't know how, but he tackled me with it and there's been the most awful row. He has forced me to promise never to see you again and he is sending me away to Holland for three months on the firm's business. By the time you receive this I shall already have left. Please try to forgive me. I daren't break my word to him because he is my boss and my whole job depends*

on it. I feel so dreadfully unhappy—I can't write any more. Good-bye.

Felix

Leonora folded the letter and put it carefully back into the envelope and automatically began to do her eyelashes. Nobody must see that she was upset; nobody must notice anything wrong. She caught Leffie's eye in the mirror, and forced herself to smile at her. Her hand was shaking, and it caused her to smudge some eye black on her cheek. She said, "Blast!" loudly, and heard, to her surprise and relief, that her voice sounded quite ordinary. She managed to get through the performance without betraying herself. Only once, during the sextet, she nearly broke down. It was in the second chorus when she had her little solo bit to sing, and just as she stepped forward out of the line a burning, agonizing memory of Felix sprang at her from the darkness of the auditorium. Last Sunday afternoon—could it really only be last Sunday?—they had been lying together on the divan and he had suddenly jumped up and, wrapping a towel round his middle, minced across the roon in an imitation of her singing these very words. She had laughed immoderately and he had silenced her by sliding on top of her and kissing her repeatedly. . . .

Now, with the other five girls humming *bouches fermées* behind her, she suddenly felt her throat contract. She gave a painful little gulp, and forced the rhymed couplet out the wrong way round. As they were dancing off at the end of the number Josie hissed out of the corner of her mouth, "Drunk again, dear!" Leonora giggled as naturally as she could, "I suddenly got the chokes!"

When the show was over, she took longer than usual to get her makeup off. She was feeling exhausted and wretched, and the strain of keeping up the pretense that nothing out of the way had happened to her was beginning to wear her down. When she had finally got her outdoor clothes on, all the others had gone and she was fumbling in her bag to find Leffie's Saturday night tip when her fingers encountered the shameful, heartbreaking letter. She had put it carefully in her bag before going down for the first act. Again a wave of sickness engulfed her. She caught Leffie's eye looking at her curiously, her legs seemed to give way under her and she sank down abruptly on a chair. In a moment Leffie's arms were round her.

"What's the matter, dear? You've been looking peaky all the evening."

Leonora tried gallantly to mutter that she was all right, but the sympathy in Leffie's voice and the hopelessness and misery in her heart were too much for her. She buried her face against Leffie's shoulder and broke into violent, shaking sobs. Leffie, with the tact born of long experience, said nothing at all for quite a long while, merely holding her close and occasionally giving her a gentle, affectionate little pat. Presently, when the violence of her weeping had spent itself, Leffie went over to the cupboard over the washing basin and, taking out a medicine bottle with brandy in it, poured some into a glass and held it to Leonora's lips.

"Here, love," she said, "take a sip of this, and I'll light you a nice cigarette."

Leonora obeyed weakly. The brandy made her gasp a little. Leffie lit a cigarette and handed it to her, then sat down purposefully opposite her with her gnarled hands on her knees and said firmly, "Now then—what's wrong? You'd better tell me and be quick about it, for if it's what I think it is, there's no sense in fiddling about and wasting time!"

Leonora made a great effort. "I don't think," she gulped, "I don't think it *is* what you think it is, Leffie—it's just that—that—" Her eyes filled with tears again, and she broke off.

"Is it that young man with the smarmy voice and the funny name?"

Leonora nodded.

"I knew it." Leffie clicked her tongue against her teeth. "Has he got you into trouble?"

Leonora shook her head wearily. "No, not exactly—that is—not that sort of trouble." Somewhere at the back of her misery she was aware of a flicker of amusement at Leffie's insistence on the obstetrical aspect of the situation.

"What *has* 'e done then?" went on Leffie inexorably, "led you up the garden path and then buggered off and left you?"

"That's right, Leffie." This time Leonora really did manage a wan smile. "That's exactly what he's done." She reached for her bag, opened it, took out the letter and handed it to Leffie.

"Here—you'd better read it."

Leffie took it, fixed her glasses on her nose and read it slowly through. Leonora watched her without emotion. She felt drained of all feeling and immeasurably tired. Leffie finished the letter and put it back in its envelope. "Well," she said. "That's a nice thing, I *must* say! I knew that young gentleman was no good the first time 'e come here with that note for you and give me five bob." She looked at Leonora sharply over her glasses.

"Have you been the 'ole 'og with him?"

Leonora nodded.

"Was it the first time you ever 'ad with anybody?"

"Yes."

"Well then," said Leffie with finality, "the first thing you've got to do is to forget all about him—he's a bad lot if ever I saw one—and the second thing is to keep a careful eye on yourself for the next few weeks—let's see now." Leffie wrinkled her brow with the effort of calculation. "You're not due again until the first week of July, are you?"

Leonora frowned slightly, Leffie's aggressive realism was a trifle distasteful. "It's nothing to do with that, Leffie," she said with a slight edge on her voice. "That's not what's worrying me, really it isn't—"

Leffie's face softened suddenly. "I know, dear," she said. "You mustn't take any notice of me—I always look at the practical side of things first—I always 'ave done all my life, that is ever since I was old enough to learn a bit of horse sense and that's going back a bit, I give you my word." She leant forward and patted Leonora's hand. "Now, look 'ere, dear—"

Leonora looked at her pale, kindly eyes and was surprised to see that there were tears in them.

"I know what's upsetting you all right—don't you make any mistake about that—you've let yourself fall in love with him, and you thought that he was in love with you, and now you suddenly find that all he was after was just one thing and that one thing you were fathead enough to let 'im have! Well—that's that, isn't it? What's done's done and you can't get away from it, but it isn't right to work yourself into a state and cry your 'eart out for a slimy young rotter who takes advantage of you and leaves you flat without as much as a by-your-leave, is it, now? He's not worth one minute of your time if you only knew it. Mind you, I'm not saying he isn't good-looking and nicely spoken and all that sort of thing. They always are, that type, but look at you now. You're young and pretty and getting on fine, with your whole life before you. Why should you worry just because some la-di-da young bastard 'asn't got the decency to treat you right! Why, if he had any sense he'd be jumping for joy at having the luck to take you out to tea, let alone have an affair with you. Let him go, dear, and a bloody good riddance to him at that. Don't cry anymore, and don't get upstage with me for speaking what's in my mind. You're the lucky one if you only knew it, and a day will come—and not so far off either—when you'll laugh your 'ead off to think what a state you got yourself into over someone who wasn't fit to black your boots!" Leffie, exhausted by this peroration, rose to her feet. "If you'll wait two shakes of a duck's arse, I'll tidy up and walk with you to the tube."

Leonora got up too and straightened her hat in front of the glass; then she turned, her underlip trembling a little, and flung her arms round Leffie's angular, undernourished little body. "Thank you, Leffie," she said with a catch in her voice; "thank you a lot."

8

Leonora Jarvis was certainly a big draw in Edinburgh. As a matter of fact, she was a big draw all over the country. Since 1940 she had, in common with most of the other West End stars, played in the provinces more consistently than ever before in her life. Mr. Gilmour, the house manager, stood by the box office at the end of the performance and watched the crowds passing through the foyer and on through the exit doors into the blackout. They all looked cheerful and animated, as though they had had a good time.

Leonora had made, as usual, a charming little curtain speech. Gilmour had stopped on the way down from his office to listen to it. Despite all his years of managerial experience, it always amused and pleased him to observe the technical grace and courtesy with which established stars handled their applause. Leonora Jarvis was actually one of his favorites. She had played the theater countless times and never been in any trouble, always polite and charming to the staff, always controlled and assured and untemperamental even when things went wrong. He remembered the first time she had appeared there a long while ago, 1927 or 1928. She had played the second part in a Clarence Wellman comedy supporting Charles Lucas and poor old Jane Lorrimer. It had been the first week of the play's provincial tryout before going to the West End, and on the opening night, after a disastrous dress rehearsal on the Sunday, Leonora had unquestionably walked away with the show. He remembered going round to her dressing room to congratulate her—she had dressed upstairs in those days, not in the star room on the stage level where she was now—he remembered how flushed and happy and excited she had been, and how proudly she had introduced him to her husband, a good-looking young naval lieutenant. Mr. Gilmour sighed sentimentally; that completely happy marriage had been broken by Fate in 1933, when the husband had been killed in an air crash while on his way to rejoin his ship at Malta. The papers had been full of praise of Leonora's behavior, all the usual journalistic tripe about her playing with a broken heart and never missing a performance; being an old ex-actor himself, he realized only too well how fortunate she had been in a crisis like that to have a performance to give. There's nothing like having responsibility and a job to get you through trouble.

Tonight, watching her make her curtain speech, he had suddenly felt a surge of emotion. Nothing particularly personal, just professional emotion; the theater was the thing all right, a good artiste in a good play, gracefully acknowledging the enthusiasm of a packed house—you could never achieve a thrill like that in all the ornate super-cinemas in the world! He nodded cheerfully to the doorman, and, stubbing his cigar out in a brass ashtray affixed to the wall outside one of the entrances to the stalls, he pushed the door open, walked down along the side of the empty auditorium and went through the pass door onto the stage.

A little while later, when he was seated in Leonora's dressing room having his usual chat with her while she put the finishing touches to her street makeup, there was a knock on the door. Alice, Leonora's maid, disappeared discreetly into the passage for a moment and then came back. "It's that Mr.—that gentleman who you was expecting," she said. Mr. Gilmour saw a quick smile flit across Leonora's face. "Tell him to give me just two minutes," she said. Gilmour immediately rose to his feet. "I must be pushing off," he said. "Everything all right—no complaints?"

"A million complaints." Leonora patted his mottled red face affectionately. "Those damned girls with their coffee trays rattling all through the beginning of the second act—one of these nights I shall jump over the orchestra pit and bash their heads in!"

"All right, all right." He held up his hand pacifically. "It won't happen tomorrow night, I promise."

"Does that go for tea as well? Tomorrow's a matinee day!"

"Tea trays out before the curtain—cross my heart," said Mr. Gilmour. "Good night, my dear."

"Good night, Gillie." Leonora kissed her hand to him as he went out of the door. She stood still for a moment in the middle of the room, surveying herself in the long glass. Her tailor-made was good, new silk stockings wonderful! God bless darling Bobbie Craig for coming back from Bermuda via Lisbon. Her mink coat, of course, was the crowning glory. Yes, she certainly looked well enough. "It's all right, Alice," she said with the faintest suspicion of a tremor in her voice. "You can ask Mr. Meseurier to come in now."

Alice disappeared into the passage again and, after a moment or two, flung open the door. Leonora heard her say, "This way, sir."

Into the room walked briskly, if a trifle nervously, the first lover of her life, and at the sight of him her heart stopped dead in her breast and the charming welcoming smile was frozen onto her face.

"Leonora!" He took her hand. "This is wonderful—wonderful—I can hardly believe it's really you!"

She felt her hand warmly enveloped in his and watched with awful fascination as with forced, self-conscious gallantry he bent down to kiss it. His head was practically bald except for a few strands of hair which were plastered across his scalp with infinite care like strips of damp patent leather. He straightened himself and gazed into her eyes with a whimsical expression tinged with stale amorousness, a macabre travesty of the way she remembered him looking at her in the past. His figure, the once lithe and graceful body, had assumed with the years the shape of a pear-drop, sloping from the shoulders and swelling into a paunch; his sagging skin was a yellowish-gray and his eyes, the whites of which were slightly bleared, seemed to have crept closer to the bridge of his nose as though they were scared and anxious to get as near to one another as possible. He was wearing a debonair pin-striped brown suit which was a little tight for him, and on the third finger of his left hand was a large ruby ring. He had laid his bowler hat and mackintosh on the couch when he came in.

With a supreme effort Leonora pulled herself together. "Why, Felix!" The words seemed to stick in her throat. "What a lovely surprise! After all these years!" She was horribly aware of the falseness in her voice, but he was blandly unconscious of it.

"You were splendid in the play tonight." He gave a little nod as though to emphasize his approval of her performance. "What I said in my letter proved to be quite true. You've hardly changed at all."

"Neither have you—I should have known you anywhere." Mortified, she noted his serene acceptance of the glib, conventional lie. Suddenly feeling that she could not bear to look at him for another moment, she hurriedly turned and snatched up a cigarette box from the dressing table. "Let's sit down quietly and have a cigarette," she said, "before we go to supper. Alice, ask the taximan to be a dear and wait for five minutes, will you? Then you can go."

"All right, Miss Jarvis." Alice took her hat and coat from the peg behind the door. "Good night, miss—good night, sir." She went out and closed the door behind her. Leonora and Felix were alone. With a quick, almost subservient gesture, he whipped a lighter from his pocket and lit her cigarette and then his own. She murmured, "Thank you," motioned him into the armchair and inhaled the smoke deeply into her lungs. "If only," she thought wildly, "this one particular Player's Mild might by magic contain some strong anesthetic that would send me off into complete unconsciousness!" She sat down at the dressing table and, giving a nervous little dab at her hair, tried frantically to think of something to say, but the leaden silence crushed her down and numbed her brian. After an eternity he broke it by leaning forward and saying, with pregnant meaning, "Well?"

She forced herself to turn and look at him. "Well, what?" She gave a gay little laugh.

"Have you forgiven me?"

Aware of the strain in the atmosphere but happily misunderstanding the cause, he allowed a distinctly roguish look to come into his eyes and grinned, a slow, knowing, resolutely seductive grin. That grin was the final horror, for, in place of the gleaming white teeth that in the past had so tremendously enhanced his charm, he was now exhibiting, with the utmost complacency, a double set of shining dentures surmounted by gums of gutta percha.

Leonora stared at them hypnotized. Then the dreadful thing happened: her control snapped, and she started to laugh. His grin persisted for a little, but gradually faded. She saw his expression change from arch coquetry to bitter, tight-lipped rage. He stood up. She tried incoherently to cover her mounting hysteria by murmuring something about the sudden shock and the excitement of seeing him again, but it was no use. She was gone, sunk, lost irretrievably. The tears rolled down her cheeks; she felt her face becoming suffused and scarlet; some mascara ran into her eyes, and the sharp, stinging pain of it, far from pulling her together, merely sent her off into further agonizing paroxysms. She scrabbled wildly in her bag for her handkerchief and, having found it, dabbed ineffectually at her streaming eyes. She was aware also that she was making awful explosive noises, groans and gasps and grunts, her whole body was shaking uncontrollably, and finally, beyond shame and far beyond all hope of restraint, she stretched her arms out on the dressing table and, burying her face in them, lay there in utter abandon, sobbing helplessly, with her shoulders heaving.

When, after a considerable time, spent and exhausted, she raised her head, the room was empty.

THIS
TIME
TOMORROW

Louise came out of the Airways Terminal into the spring sunlight and walked briskly along Buckingham Palace Road in the direction of Victoria Station. It was only a quarter of twelve, and Sheila was not expecting her until one o'clock, so there was lots of time. Realizing that she was almost running, she slowed down and, waiting at the corner of Ebury Bridge for the traffic lights to change, crossed over to the other side. It would be sublimely idiotic to be knocked down by a bus now, at this particular moment of her life, after all that money had been expended and the man with the pince-nez had been so nice and reassuring.

Everything was in order; her passport, with a half-dozen extra photographs, her vaccination certificate, her ticket, and a wad of B.O.A.C. brochures which explained in incomprehensible detail the flying hours and arrivals and departures of a myriad aircraft which now, at this very instant while her high heels were clicking along on the secure, comforting pavement, were hurtling above the clouds of the world, taking off and landing, rocketing and bumping through electric storms, droning interminably along at immense altitudes over mountains and deserts and far-off seas, gliding down through velvety tropical darkness onto illuminated strips of asphalt, rising up through fogs and rains and snows into Arctic dawns and scarifying infinity. It was absurd nowadays to be agitated at the thought of traveling by air. Everybody did it; it was no longer spectacular or dashing or even romantic; ordinary people, people like herself, without any claims to heroism or gallantry, without even the impetus of urgency, clambered in and out of airplanes without a qualm. Even poor Eileen, who had been so terrified of the blitzes that she had buried herself gloomily in Chiddingfold for the duration of the War, had flown to South Africa and back with her dreadful sister-in-law and never turned a hair!

The man with the pince-nez really had been extremely considerate; he may have noticed that her hand was trembling when she wrote out the check, he may even have heard her heart pounding, but if so he had certainly given no sign; his attitude had been calm, businesslike and benignly unaware of the very possibility of anxiety. He had told her with gentle firmness that she must be at the terminal not one minute later than seven-fifteen, that on arrival at the airport her baggage would be weighed in, and that if there were any excess she would be permitted to pay for it by check at the last minute. He had explained, patiently but unsuccessfully, the confusing differences in time that she would encounter in course of the journey and, when she had finally gathered up all the papers he had given her, he wished her "Happy landings" and turned the soothing balm of his personality to a mad-looking woman in a red beret who had been standing just behind Louise for quite a while and breathing stertorously.

This time tomorrow, she reflected as she turned into Eccleston Street, I shall be up very high indeed above the sea and the clouds and sitting in a pressurized cabin. Her heart missed a beat and, feeling that she might suddenly be sick or fall down, she stopped in front of an antique shop and pressed her forehead against the cool glass of the window. A woman inside, presumably the owner, wearing a mauve overall and a string of amber beads, looked at her suspiciously. Louise fixed her gaze intently on a pair of dusty red leather bellows and frowned as though she were trying to decide whether they were genuine or fake; then with an almost imperceptible smile of contempt she shrugged her shoulders and walked on.

"I must pull myself together," she said to herself. "I can't go staggering about the streets leaning against shop windows and making a craven, cracking fool of myself."

She glanced at her watch, and, seeing that it was only five to twelve, she sighed irritably. Still more than an hour to go and only Cadogan Place to get to at the end of it, which was not more than a

271

few minutes' walk. If only Sheila lived at Hampstead she could have got into a bus and sat down. She felt more than anything in the world a passionate longing to sit down. There were unfortunately no seats in Ebury Street, and it was improbable that there would be any in Eaton Square.

She strolled along aimlessly in the direction of Sloane Square, where at least there was a restaurant where she could have a cup of coffee. Ebury Street was at last showing signs of rejuvenation after the drab deprivations of the War. There were still gaps between some of the houses and remains of rubble overgrown with grass and weeds, but a few front doors had been newly painted and there was a general feeling of spring-cleaning in the air; a piece of newspaper blew out of the gutter and across the road, and a small boy on roller skates charged at her with his head down and she had to step onto one of the doorsteps to avoid him cannoning into her. If, of course, he had cannoned into her and knocked her down she might have broken her leg and been taken to hospital.

She closed her eyes for a moment, and stopped dead in her tracks at the blissful thought of lying in a clean, cool, hospital bed, pain or no pain, relieved of awful fears, resigned and at peace. She wrote out in her mind the telegram to Henry: "Darling, have had to cancel flight owing slight accident—nothing serious—don't worry—writing—love love love."

She wondered, as she walked on again after her temporary sojourn in St. George's Hospital, how and where, if such a telegram were sent, Henry would receive it. She visualized him clearly on a dim, green-shaded verandah, sipping a long, cool drink through a straw and wearing tropical shorts; not the baggy British-Raj kind that flapped around the knees and sometimes even below them, but the neat, abbreviated variety like those her cousin Derek had worn when he came back on leave from Cairo during the War. Henry would open the telegram casually, probably making a gay little joke over his shoulder to his friends as he did so. Then he would read the words, "Cancel flight—slight accident—nothing serious," and stand quite still for a moment, stunned with disappointment, while his left hand mechanically crumbled the telegram envelope into a ball.

Perhaps, on the other hand, he would not be stunned with disappointment at all, but merely exasperated at the thought of all his plans and arrangements being upset, and would stamp off with his cronies to the club, where he would get drunk and curse the day that he had been stupid enough to tie himself up to a neurotic ass.

"That's what I am," she told herself miserably as she turned into South Eaton Place, "nothing more nor less than a neurotic ass!" She said the words "neurotic ass" out loud in the hope that hearing them scathingly enunciated might shame her into a calmer attitude of mind and lay by the heels the foolish panic that had been tormenting her ever since Henry's letter had arrived ten days ago. A woman pushing a perambulator shot her a sharp, apprehensive glance as she passed, and quickened her pace.

In a restaurant just off Sloane Square she ordered a cup of coffee, fished for her cigarette case in her bag, lit a cigarette, inhaled deeply and looked around her, pressing the familiarity, the ordinariness of the crowded café against her mind's eye, endeavoring by staring at it so closely, so clinically, to relegate its hordes of complacent shopping ladies, its clamorous children and anemic waitresses to a limbo of commonplace, unadventurous servitude from which she, by means of the colored papers in her bag, was about to escape forever.

Seen thus from the viewpoint of her imminent emancipation from all that they were and all that they represented, the very safety and security of their lives provided her with a bulwark against her fear, and fortified her courage. A woman at the next table was wiping a smear of jam from her child's face. It was a fat child and its nose was running. A little farther off two elderly ladies were squabbling politely with each other as to which of them should pay the bill. A highly made-up waitress flounced up to Louise's table and banged down a cup of coffee on it so sharply that some of it slopped over into the saucer. She gave a slight grunt of perfunctory apology, and went away again.

"This time tomorrow—" Louise drew a deep breath and with a concentrated effort of her will stared firmly and unwinkingly at "this time tomorrow." There it was, so near in the future, waiting for her inexorably. It was no use trying to evade it or frighten it away or beat it out of her consciousness. It would not give up and go home, like one of those lazy sharks she had read about which scurry off in dismay when a local pearl fisher slaps the water with the flat of his hand. It would stay there smugly and inevitably until, after God knows how many more eons of terror-stricken imaginings, she would finally reach and pass it.

"Most of the time," the man with pince-nez had said, "you will be flying at approximately eighteen thousand feet." He had said this pleasantly and informatively, without a suspicion of dramatic implication just as he might have said, "You will pass a pillar-box on the right, after which you turn sharp left and you will find the shop you require standing on the corner." She wondered if the whole business was as normal and commonplace to him as he made it sound; if the routine monotony, day after day, of consigning his fellow creatures to excessive altitudes had atrophied his imagination; or if, perhaps when he was a young man himself, he had flown so much and so far that the perils of the air held no surprises and no fears for him,

273

and now, in sedentary middle age, he could look back on electric storms, forced landings, blazing port engines and alien airfields blanketed in impenetrable fog, with nothing more than pleasurable nostalgia.

She stirred the beige, unappetizing coffee, and stubbed out her cigarette. It really was too ridiculous that a woman of her age, thirty-two in May, five years married and in full posession of her faculties, should work herself into a state bordering on nervous collapse at the prospect of traveling in an airplane for the first time. It was degrading enough in any case to have to admit that it was the first time. Everyone she knew flew as a matter of course. It just so happened that, for one reason or another, she never had; and, during the last few years owing to gruesome accounts of crashes in the newspapers—and poor Ellen and Charlie being burnt to death on their honeymoon when their plane overshot the runway at Marseilles and nose-dived into a hangar—she had become more and more firmly resolved that she never would.

Now, of course, there was no help for it. Henry was in Jamaica and she was England. Henry wanted her, and she wanted him. Her timorous resolution had to go by the board; the die was cast, and there was no turning back. Except, of course, for engine trouble. She repeated in her mind the sinister phrase, "engine trouble." It was so ambiguous, so noncommittal. It might mean so little, no more than an hour's delay, a temporary inconvenience set to rights with brisk efficiency by a few mechanics in blue dungarees with screwdrivers. On the other hand, it might mean a great deal—the difference between life and death! One little nut or screw or bolt working itself loose balefully and secretly, unobserved by the pilot, undreamed of by the passengers, and then, suddenly—probably at eighteen thousand feet—engine trouble!

She sipped her coffee and shivered. There were, of course, alternatives to flying to Jamaica. There were occasional cruise ships sailing from New York or from New Orleans; there were also fruit boats that sailed from Tilbury direct and took fourteen days, but these were very difficult to get on to because of limited space and limitless priorities, and traveling by them almost inevitably would entail sharing a small cabin with two, three or possibly four strangers. The thought of two long weeks of seasickness on the gray Atlantic, mewed up in a confined space with dubious members of her own sex, made Louise shudder again. Flaming death, although not exactly preferable, would at least be quicker and more final. In any event, further surmise and havering was out of the question. Her ticket was bought and paid for, her light fiber suitcase was packed and ready, except for her toilet things which would be put in at the last minute, and she was leaving tomorrow morning at crack of dawn and no nonsense.

2

"I envy you," said Sheila vivaciously. "I envy you with all my heart and soul. Just imagine." She turned to Alice Layton, who was seven months gone and poking indecisively at her salad. "This time tomorrow, while I'm sitting gloomily under the dryer looking at *Picture Post* and you're lunching with your in-laws, and poor Mona's flogging along the Great West Road in the Austin, Louise will be in midair!"

"At eighteen thousand feet," said Louise mechanically.

"It's almost unbelievable," Sheila rattled on, "when you think that practically in our lifetime, or at any rate only a minute or two before, those what-you-may-call-'em brothers were flying for the first time in a thing that looked like a kite made of string and three-ply, and now here's Louise calmly hopping off across the Atlantic as if it were the most ordinary thing in the world!"

"Rather her than me," said Mona with feeling. "I loathe flying; I'm either sick as a dog, bored stiff or terrified out of my wits."

"Have you flown much?" Louise's determined effort to speak calmly made her voice sound supercilious.

"Constantly," said Mona. "Robert adores it. Every holiday we've had since we've been married has been ruined for me by air travel—including our honeymoon."

The thought of poor Ellen and Charlie rushed immediately back into Louise's mind and was resolutely dismissed.

"The thing I hate about it," Sheila went on, "is the hideous uncertainty. I don't mean crashes or coming down in the sea or anything dramatic like that. I mean the waiting about at airports and not being able to take off because of the weather, and people keeping on coming to see you off and you never going. It took Laura Warren five days to get away from New York last winter which really, what with the money restrictions and a whole week of farewell parties, was a bit too much!"

"I'd rather go by sea and have done with it," said Alice. "At least you know you're going to get there."

"During the War that was the last thing you knew." Sheila signaled to the sullen parlormaid to take away the plates. "I came back in a convoy from Gibraltar in 1942 just before Simon was born, and it was absolute hell, nothing but emergency drills and life-belt inspections and everybody being strained and brave and making dreadful little jokes. I never took the damn safety jacket off night or day until we reached the mouth of the Mersey."

"After all, that was wartime," said Alice plaintively. "It isn't quite the same thing, is it?"

"There have been shipwrecks in peacetime, you know, dear. Look at the *Titanic* and the *Empress of Whatever-it-was* that sank like a stone in the St. Lawrence River."

"That was before my day," said Alice firmly.

Sheila laughed. "It was before mine too, but it did happen, didn't it? I mean, whatever way of traveling you choose you've always got to take some sort of risk, haven't you?"

"At least, in a shipwreck or a railway accident or a car smash you have a chance," said Mona. "But a plane crash is so horribly final."

"Not necessarily," Sheila spoke with authority. "The thing to do at the first sign of trouble is to rush to that little lavatory at the back."

"I do that automatically," said Mona.

"But seriously," Sheila went on, "I was reading about it in Nevil Shute's book. You just wedge yourself in, and when the front of the plane hits the ground, there you are up in the air and as right as rain!"

"What happens if the back of the plane hits the ground first?"

"I don't think it can." Sheila frowned thoughtfully. "Somebody told me why once, but I've forgotten."

"It's being burnt to death that I shouldn't like." Alice helped herself to crème caramel.

"How curious," said Louise tartly. "Most of us love it."

"I think we'd better change the subject." Sheila patted Louise's hand. "After all, it isn't very tactful, is it, to go on nattering about flying accidents and horrors when Louise is on the verge of taking to the air for the first time?"

"The first time?" said Mona. "Do you mean to say that you've never flown before?"

"I used to swing very high as a girl," Louise replied lightly, and everybody laughed.

3

Louise's great-aunt Esther lived in Connaught Square in a thin dark house crammed with Victorian and Edwardian knickknacks. She was small and ivory-colored and rising ninety; her faculties were unimpaired, except for her hearing, which defect she sought to ameliorate by a series of patented appliances which invariably were "miracles" at first and "disgraceful swindles" when the initial enthusiasm had worn off. Her energy was boundless and her affection for Louise conscientious rather than effusive. Being her only living relative, she felt in duty bound to admonish, criticize and disapprove whenever she considered it necessary—and she usually seemed to consider it necessary for one reason or another whenever she saw her.

Louise, having rung the bell and discreetly rat-tat-ed the brass knocker, braced herself against the inevitable. The door was opened as usual by Clara, a gray woman of sixty, who had tended Aunt Esther despotically for nineteen years. She showed Louise into the drawing room on the first floor, announcing her name loudly and clearly, but in a tone of resigned disapprobation, as though she suspected her of some sinister purpose.

Aunt Esther was sitting by the fire with an exquisite cashmere shawl round her shoulders, reading the latest volume of Sir Osbert Sitwell's memoirs. "The thing about this man," she said putting the book down as Louise kissed her, "is that he's a gentleman."

"He also writes well." Louise sat down in a chair facing her.

"That's what I meant," said Aunt Esther, pushing forward a cigarette box. "You can smoke if you want to. I know you can't sit still for a minute without puffing away like a chimney, so I told Clara to have all the paraphernalia ready for you. There's an ashtray just by you."

"Thank you, darling," said Louise gratefully. "You're sure it won't make you cough or anything?"

"I seldom cough," replied Aunt Esther, "unless I happen to have a cold or bronchial asthma, and at the moment I have neither."

"You're hearing very well," said Louise ingratiatingly.

"Telex," replied Aunt Esther. "I put in a new battery because I knew you were coming, so there's no need to shout."

"I wasn't shouting."

"I didn't say you were, I merely warned you that it wasn't necessary. It makes a horrible buzzing in my ears and I can't distinguish a word. Eva Collington came to see me last week and made such a din that I had to tell her to go."

"How is she?" inquired Louise.

"In the depths as usual." Aunt Esther complacently adjusted the shawl round her shoulders. "She's years younger than I am, but you'd think she was ninety the way she carries on; had to be helped up the stairs, if you please. You should have seen Clara's face—it was killing!"

"But she did have an accident of some sort, didn't she? I remember you telling me about it last time I was here."

"Accident!" Aunt Esther snorted contemptuously. "She twisted her ankle getting out of a taxi in Pelham Crescent last December and we've never heard the last of it. Such a hullabaloo—you'd think she'd broken every bone in her body."

There was silence for a moment broken only by the ticking of the clock on the mantelpiece and the distant yapping of a dog on the other side of the square; the atmosphere of the room was close and oppressive. The furniture, the silver photograph frames, the accumulated bric-a-brac of years; snuffboxes, miniatures, paperweights, porcelain cups and saucers and plates—all seemed to be immured in a subaqueous vacuum of old age. Life, eighty-eight vigorous years of it, had been reduced to this stuffy quiescence. Louise looked at her aunt curiously and repressed a wild impulse to ask her suddenly how it felt to be so immeasurably old, with everything over and done with and nothing to look forward to but further gentle decay; to face her point-blank with the imminence of death and see how she reacted; to find out, once and for all, if the fear of it was still alive in her or if the weight of her years had crushed it out of existence, leaving her with nothing more than a vague, unspeculative resignation.

At this moment Clara came in with the tea things, which she placed on a low table beside Aunt Esther's chair. "I brought it up earlier than usual," she said loudly, "because I thought Mrs. Goodrich would be wanting to rush away."

"Don't yell like that, Clara," said Aunt Esther. "You know perfectly well I've got a fresh battery in."

"You can never be sure they'll work, however fresh they are." Clara straightened herself. "It's always hit or miss with those things, as we know to our cost. One day we're up in the clouds, and the next we're down in the dumps. There's no telling what's going to happen." She turned to Louise. "Talking about being up in the clouds, I hear you're going off in an airplane tomorrow!"

"Yes," said Louise with a bright smile. "I've got my ticket in my bag and everything's packed and ready. I'm looking forward to it very much," she added defiantly.

"Well, there's no accounting for tastes," said Clara, "but you wouldn't get me to set foot in one of those contraptions, not if you were to offer me a thousand pounds down."

"That contingency is unlikely to arise," snapped Aunt Esther.

"It's flirting with death, if you ask me," Clara went on, "fairly begging for it. Look at Mrs. Morpeth and those two lovely little girls— the eldest couldn't have been more than five—setting off as gay as you please to join their daddy in Egypt—"

"Never mind about Mrs. Morpeth and her little girls now, Clara; that will be all for the moment." She turned to Louise. "Perhaps you'd like to pour out, dear? My hands are rather shaky."

"Mine are none too steady," said Louise.

"If God had intended us to fly he'd have given us wings, wouldn't he?" said Clara with finality, and went out of the room.

"Clara's been getting more and more aggressive lately." Aunt Esther sighed. "She bites my head off at the least thing. Just give me the tea, dear, I prefer to put in my own milk and sugar. I'm afraid I shall have to talk to her seriously."

Louise handed her her cup of tea and pushed the milk jug and sugar basin gently toward her. "Poor Clara," she said with a smile, "I don't suppose she meant to be discouraging."

"I wasn't thinking of that," said Aunt Esther. "I was thinking of the way she pounced at me about my new battery—really quite insufferable. She's becoming too big for her boots, that's what's the matter with her. Give that class an inch and they take an ell."

"After all she has been with you for nearly twenty years!"

Aunt Esther was not to be placated. "That's what she trades on. She thinks just because I'm chained to this house most of the time and more or less dependent on her that she can do and say whatever she likes. She was downright rude to poor Oliver Elliot when he came to luncheon the other day, just because he asked for some scraps for that dog of his that he always insists on dragging everywhere with him. He got quite hysterical when she'd gone out of the room. You know what an old woman he is."

"I haven't seen him for ages," said Louise.

"You haven't missed much." Aunt Esther gave an evil little chuckle. "He's sillier than ever and talks about nothing but his gallbladder. I expect it will carry him off one of these days." She paused and looked at Louise critically. "Is that hat supposed to be the latest thing?"

Louise laughed. "Not particularly, it's just a hat. As a matter of fact, I've had it for some time. Don't you like it?"

"Not very much," said Aunt Esther. "It makes your face look too big."

"I'm afraid that's my face's fault more than the hat's."

"Harriet Macclefield's girl came to see me the other day wearing one of the most idiotic hats I've ever seen. It looked as if it were going to fly off her head. She's managed to get herself engaged at last, you know."

"No," said Louise, "I didn't know."

"Something in the Foreign Office, I think she said he was. She showed me his photograph and I must say he looked half dotty. He can't be quite all there to want to marry her. She's grown into such a great fat lump, you'd never recognize her."

"I don't suppose I should even if she hadn't," said Louise. "I've never seen her in my life."

"Nonsense," said Aunt Esther impatiently. "She was one of your bridesmaids."

"I didn't have any bridesmaids. Henry and I were married in a Registry Office."

"I remember now—it was Maureen's wedding I was thinking of.

I knew she'd been somebody's bridesmaid." Aunt Esther paused. "How is he?" she asked abruptly.

"Henry? Very well, I believe. I shall know for certain the day after tomorrow. It's incredible, isn't it"—she went on with a rush—"to think one can get all the way to Jamaica—five thousand miles—in so little time."

"I thought he was in Bermuda," said Aunt Esther, "but after all I suppose it's much the same thing."

"No, darling," Louise spoke firmly, "it's quite quite different. Jamaica is much more tropical."

"A woman I met in that hotel at Bournemouth had lived in Bermuda for years," said Aunt Esther. "She swore by it."

"I'm sure that Bermuda is charming," said Louise, a slight note of exasperation creeping into her voice, "but Henry happens to be in Jamaica, which is why I'm going there."

"Well, I must say I don't envy you," said Aunt Esther. "Henry or no Henry. All that rattling and banging and discomfort. I suppose they strap you in, don't they?"

"Only when the plane's taking off or landing, I believe."

"If you ask me, the whole world is going mad! All this scrambling about here, there and everywhere at breakneck speed. I can't see the point of it. No wonder everybody has nervous breakdowns."

Louise, feeling that it would be useless to contest this statement, merely nodded reluctantly, as though she were really in complete agreement but was not prepared to commit herself.

"When I was a girl," Aunt Esther went on, "the actual traveling to places was just as much fun as getting to them. I shall never forget, when I was very young, going all the way to Sicily with your great-aunt Mary and the whole family. My dear, the excitement of that journey you can't imagine! We laughed and laughed and laughed! I shall remember it to my dying day."

"I may laugh hysterically all the way to Jamaica."

"You'll laugh on the wrong side of your face if the airplane falls into the sea," said Aunt Esther grimly.

"There's always the remote chance that it won't fall into the sea." Louise underlined the word "remote" with deliberate sarcasm. "After all, the percentage of air crashes is relatively small, all things considered. Everybody flies nowadays. Look at Princess Elizabeth! I saw a newsreel of her getting into a plane at Malta only the other day."

"More fool her!" said Aunt Esther.

"That," said Louise reprovingly, "is *lèse-majesté*."

Aunt Esther pushed a plate of scones toward her. "You'd better have some of these. Clara made them especially for you."

"How sweet of her!" Louise took one.

"You ought to feel very flattered. She doesn't put herself out as a rule. I don't know what's been the matter with her lately. She's forever grumbling and getting lazier and lazier. I'm sick and tired of her. To hear the way she carries on sometimes you'd think I was a slave driver. But that's typical of the lower classes. They get overbearing and spoilt before you can say Jack Robinson, and now of course with this unspeakable Government they're getting worse and worse."

"There *have* been cases of the upper classes being overbearing and spoilt."

Aunt Esther ignored the interruption and went on. "Actually, apart from getting me up in the morning, giving me my meals and getting me to bed at night, she has nothing to do but sit in the kitchen and twiddle her thumbs."

Louise made no reply to this petulant outburst; such barefaced, obtuse ingratitude, if genuine, was quite shocking and beyond comment. If, in the face of Clara's long years of unremitting servitude, Aunt Esther could so glibly dispose of her as a human being; so arbitrarily relegate her to the status of a well-paid automaton, an automaton that might understandably by now be wearing out a little, growing rusty, creaking at the joints; if she could deceive herself into the sincere belief that the task of tending efficiently a querulous, self-centered octogenarian morning, noon and night, year in, year out, was such a sinecure that it allowed time to spare for thumb twiddling—then, Louise reflected, she was a wicked, graceless old megalomaniac and the sooner the grave closed over her the better.

But of course it wasn't genuine. The words, however arrogant and bitter they sounded, had no depth and no validity, not even any particular impetus beyond a surface irritation, a sudden urge to show off, a determination to prove that, in spite of her great age and increasing infirmities, she was not yet done for, not yet subject to any dominance other than her own will.

"Well," cried Louise conciliatingly, "however tiresome Clara may be, her scones are certainly a dream!"

"Fiddle!" cried Aunt Esther unexpectedly, hitting herself sharply on the chest. "The battery's gone dead." Clucking her tongue with irritation, she proceeded to haul from the bosom of her dress a small biscuit-colored box which she opened expertly, disclosing two little batteries. She scrutinized them angrily for a moment and then, with surprising energy, rose and pressed the bell by the fireplace. "I suppose this will give Clara another opportunity to gloat over me," she said, and, observing that Louise was about to say something, made a quick, impatient gesture with her hand to silence her and sat down again. "It's no use trying to say anything, so you might just as well sit still until Clara comes. I've got another set upstairs."

Louise obediently sat back in her chair and lit a cigarette. Her recent resentment of Aunt Esther's crotchety arrogance evaporated, and she felt a sudden uprush of sentimental pity, an impulse to fling her arms protectively around those sharp bony shoulders. There was something infinitely pathetic in the spectacle of that gallant, disagreeable old woman sitting there in the dusk of her long life; her mind still alert, her indestructible will to fight, to get her own way, to dominate, still alive and kicking, but trapped into irascible dependence by the treachery of her body.

Louise looked at her wonderingly, trying to envisage Aunt Esther's drained, parchment-colored skin with the bloom of adolescence on it; the hollow cheeks filled out and glowing with youth; the little withered mouth full-lipped and stretched wide in convulsive laughter all the way to Sicily. Perhaps, after all, the prospect of sudden death, however violent and frightening, was less to be dreaded than this slow, implacable disintegration.

"What are you staring at?" asked Aunt Esther sharply. "Is my hair coming down?"

"I was admiring your shawl," Louise replied hurriedly. "It looks so pretty and soft."

Aunt Esther looked at her bleakly and leant forward.

"Your shawl"—Louise leant forward too and enunciated the words carefully—"your shawl looks so pretty and soft."

"Oh!" grunted Aunt Esther, "is that all!" She fingered the shawl disdainfully. "Hubert's wife sent it to me from Scotland at Christmas. I should think it would be more useful to her than me, shut up all the year round in that drafty barrack miles away from anywhere."

Louise, remembering that Hubert's wife was Lady Macleven, one of Aunt Esther's grander nieces, smiled and nodded appreciatively.

"I stayed there once," went on Aunt Esther reminiscently, "but never again!"

"It's a very lovely old house, though, isn't it?"

"What?"

Louise repeated the question more loudly.

"Hideous," said Aunt Esther. "Filled with antlers and stuffed pike."

At this moment Clara came in carrying two little batteries which she gave to Aunt Esther. "Here," she said. "I expect these are what you wanted, aren't they?"

Aunt Esther took them from her with a muttered, "Thank you," and proceeded to fit them into the little box.

"How on earth did you know?" asked Louise.

"I could tell by the ring," said Clara laconically. "When she jabs at the bell like that it nearly always means battery trouble."

Aunt Esther closed the box and lowered it carefully into her bosom. She then struck herself briskly again and said, "That's better."

Louise rose to her feet. "I really must go now, darling, I've got a million things to do and I have to be up at six in the morning."

"I'm always up at six in the morning," said Aunt Esther, "winter or summer."

Clara sniffed. "Awake maybe, but up, never."

Aunt Esther ignored her and looked at Louise critically. "You're as thin as a scarecrow. I suppose you've been reducing or some such nonsense!"

"No, I haven't," Louise replied. "I just don't eat fattening things."

"If I'd been as skinny as that when I was your age they would have thought I was going into a decline and sent for the doctor."

"You needn't worry about me." Louise bent down to kiss her. "I'm as strong as a horse."

"Thank you for coming to see me." Aunt Esther returned Louise's kiss by pecking the air. "I fully realize that it can't be very exciting talking to a deaf old woman like me."

"You know perfectly well I love coming to see you."

"Fiddlesticks!" said Aunt Esther with a gleam in her eye. "If you loved it all that much you'd come more often." She gave a little cackle at her own wickedness. "Anyhow, send me a postcard from Bermuda if you have time."

"I will," said Louise, feeling unequal to further argument.

"I remember the woman's name now."

"Which woman?"

"The one at Bournemouth who told me all about it," said Aunt Esther testily. "Mrs. Cutler-Harrison. She was rather common, poor thing, but quite amiable. If you should run into her tell her you've seen me. She might introduce you to some of her friends. She seemed to know everyone on the island."

"She'll have to bring them all down to the airport at one in the morning. The plane only stops there for an hour."

Aunt Esther either did not notice the flippancy of Louise's tone or decided to rise above it. "Good-bye, then," she said, making a gesture of dismissal with her clawlike hand. "I don't suppose I shall be here when you come back. One more winter like this will finish me off, I should imagine. And a good job too!" she added briskly.

Louise, suddenly stricken with compassion and restraining an impulse to burst into tears, kissed the old lady again swiftly and unexpectedly and fled from the room.

4

"Now, then"—Mrs. Peverance peeled off her gray suede gloves and placed them on the arm of the sofa beside her—"what exactly is your husband going to do in Jamaica?"

Louise shot an appealing look at Boy Sullivan, who was leaning against the mantelpiece sipping a dry Martini. Myra, Mrs. Peverance's daughter, a pasty girl of sixteen, was sitting in an armchair clutching a glass of orangeade and staring into space.

"Well," said Louise with a forced smile, determined not to allow Mrs. Peverance's didactic manner to fluster her, "it's all rather complicated really. You see, Henry—that's him, my husband—had a little money left him last year and, as he's never felt particularly fit in this climate after being a prisoner of war in Malaya for three years, he decided, with two friends of his, one of whom knows Jamaica well, to buy some property there with a view to building a hotel."

"Good heavens!" Mrs. Peverance could not have looked more startled if Louise had announced that Henry and his friends were planning to erect a chain of brothels. "Where?"

"On the north shore, I believe."

"The north shore!" Mrs. Peverance stared at her incredulously.

"Yes. Somewhere near a place called Port Maria."

"I know it well. It's where the hurricane struck in 1944."

"Well, let's hope that the next one will strike somewhere quite different," said Louise. "Hurricanes are fairly unpredictable, aren't they? I mean, you can't rely on them hitting exactly the same place every time."

"You can't rely on them at all," put in Boy Sullivan flippantly.

"A hurricane is no joke, I can assure you," said Mrs. Peverance. "When we were in Barbados, before my husband was transferred to his present position, our entire garage was blown into the sea."

"It was only a temporary one," said Myra.

"Apparently a little more temporary than you bargained for!"

Louise, gathering from Mrs. Peverance's expression that she was definitely not amused, changed the subject hastily. "I'm terribly excited by the whole idea, as you can well imagine, never having seen a tropical island in my life. It all sounds to me so romantic and *Boy's-Own-Paper*ish. Is it true that you can send little native boys shinnying up palm trees to get delicious green coconuts?"

"Quite true," admitted Mrs. Peverance grudgingly. "But I fear you won't find them so very delicious."

"Mother, how can you!" protested Myra. "They're lovely!" She turned to Louise. "You cut off their tops with a machete and fill them up with ice and put in gin too if you like. We did it last January when I was staying with the Croker-Wallaces, and old Mrs. Croker-Wallace was simply furious when she found out, about the gin, I mean—she's very straitlaced."

"There's a family you must meet," said Mrs. Peverance. "They own an enormous banana plantation near Port Antonio. She used to be a Crutchley, you know!"

Louise managed to look suitably astonished. "No, really?"

"Her father, old Sir Kenneth Crutchley, was one of the most famous figures on the island in the old days. They say he used to ride fifty and sixty miles a day without turning a hair. Then, of course, the slump came and he had to get rid of all his horses."

"I wonder that there were any left to get rid of," said Louise.

Mrs. Peverance looked at her dimly, and continued, "He was a very remarkable man and he did a tremendous lot for the natives. They absolutely worshipped him. It was quite a common sight, I believe, to see vast crowds of them following him wherever he went."

"How nice!" Louise, aware that her reply was inadequate, endeavored to enhance it with a knowing smile.

"He died in 1923," went on Mrs. Peverance, "and his widow survived him by only two years. Her eldest daughter married Adrian Croker-Wallace shortly afterward and they had five children, all girls, unfortunately, but full of fun. They're Myra's greatest friends, aren't they, dear?"

"Vivienne isn't bad," said Myra, "but I can't stand the other four."

"Nonsense." Her mother quelled any further signs of mutiny with a glance. "At all events"—she turned once more to Louise—"Adrian Croker-Wallace's mother, that's the one Myra was talking about just now, is one of the most fascinating characters in Jamaica, over eighty and bursting with energy. She became a Roman Catholic a few years ago and always says exactly what comes into her mind, but you mustn't let her intimidate you. Just stand up to her and answer her back, and she'll be your friend for life!"

"I'll do my best," said Louise, repressing a shudder.

"She's an old beast!" said Myra sullenly. "And she spits when she talks. I hate her."

"You are not to say things like that, Myra," said Mrs. Peverance sharply. "I won't have it!" She turned to Louise and, leaning forward a little, spoke with the steely authority of a detective trying to coax vital information from a recalcitrant criminal. "Who is this friend of your husband's who knows Jamaica so well?"

"His name is Edgar Jarvis," said Louise. "He's apparently lived there on and off most of his life."

Mrs. Peverance relaxed and gave a pitying little laugh. "Poor old Edgar! I might have guessed it. He's always getting himself involved in some harebrained scheme or other, but still," she added charitably, "he's as straight as a die and most amusing—we're all devoted to him."

"I'm glad," said Louise.

"His grandfather, old Sir Pelham Jarvis, was one of the richest men in the island. He owned thousands of acres all over the place—sugar, bananas, coconuts—and then, of course, everything went."

"Why?"

"He died in 1911, but it had all begun to disintegrate long before that. Stephen Jarvis, Edgar's father, inherited everything, but, of course, he was absolutely hopeless, one of those weak, head-in-the-clouds sort of men, quite irresponsible, no business sense, full of crackpot ideas and an appalling gambler into the bargain. You can well imagine that, what with various slumps and one thing and another, there was soon nothing left but a ramshackle old house up in the hills behind St. Ann's Bay with no light and no water. That's where poor Edgar lives now."

"It's got a marvelous view," interpolated Myra.

"You can't live on a view," said her mother severely. "But there he sticks, year in, year out with that wife of his and all those children—do you know her?" she asked Louise abruptly.

Louise shook her head. "I don't know either of them."

"She's a common little thing but quite pretty if you care for those kind of looks."

"What kind of looks are they?" Louise felt herself becoming increasingly irritated by Mrs. Peverance's illusions of grandeur.

"Flashy!" replied Mrs. Peverance. "She touches up her hair and uses too much makeup, but you will probably quite like her once you get over her accent. She's Australian, I think, or South African, I can never remember which." She smiled superciliously.

"There's a considerable difference," put in Boy Sullivan from the mantelpiece.

Mrs. Peverance ignored this and, fixing Louise with a penetrating look, said in businesslike tones, "But this hotel project of your husband's—I presume that he has gone into the whole matter very carefully?"

"Naturally he has," Louise replied with dignity. "He's been planning it and discussing it for ages, and the whole proposition has been worked out to the last detail on a solid financial basis."

"I'm sure I'm very glad to hear it." Mrs. Peverance spoke with such palpable disbelief that Louise longed to slap her face. Conscious, however, that such a gesture might be a little too drastic, but determined to endure no further patronage at the expense of Henry and his plans, she rose to her feet.

"Do let me get you a fresh Martini. That one must be quite scalding by now." Swiftly taking Mrs. Peverance's glass from her hand, she went over to the drink table, noting, as she measured the gin and vermouth into the shaker, that she was trembling. This was all Boy's fault. She glanced at him out of the corner of her eye: he was still leaning nonchalantly against the mantelpiece and blowing smoke rings, serenely oblivious to any tension in the atmosphere and apparently still convinced that by bringing Mrs. Peverance to the flat he had done Louise a signal service.

"She'll be frightfully useful to you out there," he had said over the telephone. "She's tremendously important socially, and knows everybody, and she'll be able to advise you and keep you from getting in with the wrong people. She'll also be able to put you wise about domestic problems and servants and what clothes to wear and generally prevent you from making a silly twit of yourself."

Louise looked at Mrs. Peverance's hat, which was skittish and unbecoming, and at her dress which was devoid of line and badly cut, and shook the cocktail shaker with considerable violence, at the same time running over in her mind a few of the things that she would have to say to Boy afterward. It really was too much.

She had had a nerve-racking day. What with her recurrent jitters about flying; the tedious hen lunch at Alice's; then having to say good-bye to Aunt Esther, probably for the last time, and getting herself so upset by the heartbreaking poignancy of old age and change and decay that she had left the house in Connaught Square feeling miserable and utterly depleted. So much so indeed that, instead of going to see Freda and her new baby, which she had fully intended to do and which at least would have been cheerful, she had had to come straight home, take a hot bath and three aspirins and lie down! And now, on top of everything else, to have to be polite to this insufferable woman and her idiotic daughter, on her last day in London, possibly her last day on earth! She gave the shaker an extra shake of such force that the top came off and a stream of dry Martini shot up her sleeve.

"Goddamn it!" she said, regardless of Myra's tender years. "It's always doing that!"

"You were bashing it about a bit, you know," said Boy, advancing with a handkerchief which Louise accepted with a baleful look.

"Here," she said, handing him the shaker, "give Mrs. Peverance her drink while I dry myself."

Mrs. Peverance, protesting shrilly, allowed her glass to be filled to the brim. "I really oughtn't to," she cried. "It's dreadfully strong."

Louise, having dabbed at her bedraggled sleeve and wiped her wrist, gave the handkerchief back to Boy, permitted him to pour her out another cocktail and sat down again.

Mrs. Peverance bared her irregular teeth in an affable smile. "You'll like Jamaica," she said authoritatively, as though she had been weighing up all the pros and cons with meticulous care and had arrived at an irrevocable decision, "but from the social point of view you must be prepared to make allowances."

"I always do," replied Louise.

"We're a small community. Everybody knows everybody else and on the whole we manage to have quite a lot of fun in our way, but, of course, as in all small places, there are certain little cliques that it's as well to steer clear of."

"I quite understand," said Louise with deceptive meekness.

"Then there's the color question." Mrs. Peverance assumed an air of worldly tolerance. "That's very complicated and has to be handled with the utmost tact. I mean to say you have to accept conditions as they are and not be too surprised when, for instance, you suddenly notice that the gentleman next to you at dinner is, well—on the dark side!" She gave a metallic laugh, apparently convulsed at the thought of Louise's dismay upon finding herself in such a bizarre situation. "Some of them are very intelligent, quite brilliant, in fact; you'd be astounded at their scientific knowledge."

"I'm always astounded at anyone's scientific knowledge," said Louise.

"Take Dr. Mellish now." Mrs. Peverance turned to her daughter for support, but was greeted with a stony stare. "He's a real Jamaican born and bred and quite definitely colored, but my dear"—she paused dramatically—"to hear him talk about all the technical aspects of the atom bomb—well it's perfectly fascinating!"

"It must be," said Louise, making a private resolve to avoid Dr. Mellish like the plague.

"Then there are the De Laras," continued Mrs. Peverance. "They're an enormous family. You're bound to run into some of them, particularly on the north shore."

Louise, confronted suddenly with a vivid mental picture of a palm-fringed coral beach littered with De Laras, giggled. Mrs. Peverance, however, paid no attention and continued. "Where are you going to stay when you arrive?" she inquired, dismissing for the moment the De Laras and the social intricacies of the color question.

"My husband has rented a small house near a place called Ora—something."

"Oracabessa." Mrs. Peverance nodded. "I expect they've charged him the earth. They ask the most fantastic prices along that coast, particularly if they think you're green and don't know your way about."

"I think Edgar Jarvis arranged it."

"Poor old Edgar would be fleeced quicker than anyone. He has no money sense at all. He's just one of those people who drift through life, you know, thriftless and improvident, never a thought for the morrow. I only hope that this hotel scheme of your husband's will come to something for his sake."

"I hope so too," murmured Louise.

Mrs. Peverance sighed. "I always think it's so tragic to see a man like poor old Edgar; well-born, carefully educated, starting off with so many advantages and yet somehow quite incapable of carrying anything through—do you know what I mean?" She looked at Louise with a pained expression in her eyes, as though she were at a loss to explain, to anyone so obviously imperceptive, such a unique psychological phenomenon. "It's as if something vital, something essential, had been left out of him entirely, as if a wicked fairy had appeared at his christening and cursed him with total lack of ambition, lack of will to succeed!"

Louise's patience snapped; she felt suddenly overwhelmed by a surge of irrational loyalty to the wretched Edgar Jarvis whom she had never even clapped eyes on, and exasperated beyond endurance by the pretentious smugness of Mrs. Peverance.

"I like people like that," she said.

Boy Sullivan, detecting the change in her tone, gave her a quick look, and frowned warningly, but ignoring both the look and the frown, she continued in a bright, edgy voice: "I find them agreeable and friendly and easy to get along with, whereas I must confess that people crammed with implacable ambition and bursting with the will to succeed bore me to extinction. They're so unrestful, so perpetually on the *qui vive*, so terrified that they might be missing something, so vulgar! You can hear their unsatisfied egos rattling a mile off!"

Mrs. Peverance, contriving to look both bewildered and shocked at the same time, opened her mouth to speak, but Louise mowed her down.

"As for this Edgar Jarvis, I'm perfectly certain that I shall adore him. He sounds just my cup of tea. Henry, of course, is already devoted to him, but then he's known him for some time. You should just read his letters! Nothing but 'Edgar says this' and 'Edgar says that'—just like a schoolboy getting a crush on the head prefect!" She laughed indulgently. "But that's typical of Henry. I don't mean about the prefect exactly, although nowadays one never quite knows, does one? I mean, the whole world is becoming more and more uninhibited every day—but he's always getting violent enthusiasms for people. I can't wait for you to meet him. You'll get along like a house on fire! He's a really genuine bohemian, you know—not exactly eccentric, but quite definitely unpredictable. You never have the faintest idea what he is going to do from one minute to the next. And as for colored people, he has an absolute mania for them, so you need have no fears for us on that score. Our house is certain to be chock-full of them from morning till night! That Negro poet there was such a fuss about—I can't recall his name for the moment, but you must know whom I mean—the one who was an ardent communist and then suddenly gave up the whole thing and became a Seventh Day Adventist or something peculiar and wrote all those lovely, turgid things about the Deep South—well, he was one of Henry's closest friends before the War. They used to go to workers' meetings together and have a whale of a time."

Mrs. Peverance, with commendable poise, smiled emptily and proceeded to put on her gloves. "I'm afraid he will have to modify his views a little if he wishes to be a success in Jamaica," she said, "particularly if he is contemplating building a hotel."

"But the hotel is going to be exclusively for Negroes," cried Louise. "Didn't I tell you? Henry has been studying living conditions over there very carefully, and he is convinced that a really comfortable hotel, run on a communal basis, of course, will go far toward solving a most pressing and urgent problem. It's going to have a swimming pool!" she added recklessly.

"Come, Myra," said Mrs. Peverance. "It's dreadfully late and we shall have to hurry if we are to change and be at the theater by seven-thirty."

"How extraordinary to think that the next time we meet it will be in Jamaica!" said Louise blandly. "When do you expect to be back?"

"At the end of next month." Mrs. Peverance looked Louise full in the eye; her expression was forbidding. "I have to take Myra to Switzerland, and then spend a few days in Paris." She rose and shook hands coldly with Boy Sullivan. "Good-bye, Major Sullivan. It was so nice seeing you again."

"Are you flying out?" asked Louise.

"I never fly," said Mrs. Peverance.

"Mother's airsick," put in Myra with sudden animation. "She's sick from the moment she gets into the plane until the moment she gets out of it. When we flew to Nassau last year she had to be carried off in a stretcher."

"That will do, Myra," said Mrs. Peverance. She offered Louise a limp hand. "Good-bye, Mrs. Goodrich."

"Good-bye." Louise shook it warmly. "It was so kind of you to come, and I shall remember all you've told me."

"I expect you will find your own friends in the island," said Mrs. Peverance in a tone that left no doubt of her personal determination not to be one of them. "People always do, don't they? At all events, I wish you a pleasant journey."

"Thank you," said Louise.

"As you and your husband will be so far away on the north

coast and as I scarcely ever leave Kingston, I don't suppose we shall find many opportunities of meeting." Mrs. Peverance's anxiety to scotch once and for all even the faintest possibility of any further intimacy was almost painful in its intensity. "However, we must hope for the best, mustn't we?"

With a smile of ineffable remoteness she took Myra firmly by the arm and swept out of the room. Boy Sullivan followed politely in order to see them into the lift, and Louise was left alone. She wandered about the room for a moment, seething with irritation and restraining an impulse to fly at Boy when he came back and beat him with her fists. When he did come back, however, she was sitting on the sofa lighting a cigarette with a shaking hand.

"Well!" he said cheerfully. "You certainly bitched that little enterprise."

"What did you expect?" asked Louise with dangerous calm. "I've always been allergic to excessive patronage. That woman's a pretentious ass, and you know it."

"My intentions were pure. I hardly knew her myself. I merely ran into her at Angie's the other day and, discovering that she was a social big shot in Jamaica, I genuinely thought it might be useful to you to meet her."

"If she's a social big shot I'll settle for the riffraff."

"How was I to know you'd take a black hatred to each other on sight?"

"By just taking one clear look at her," said Louise crossly. "You couldn't seriously imagine that either Henry or I would be likely to form a lasting friendship with that desiccated old *mem-sahib*."

"At any rate," replied Boy equably, "you definitely couldn't now, even if you wanted to."

"Was I abominably rude?"

"Yes. You certainly were."

"Oh, dear!" Louise felt a pang of conscience.

"Not that it matters all that much." He laughed. "Poor old Henry!"

"Why poor old Henry?"

"I suspect that Mrs. Peverance is a keen letter writer—that type of woman usually is—and as you made it abundantly clear to her that your husband was an eccentric bohemian, a communistic negrophile with homosexual tendencies—"

"Don't!" cried Louise, burying her face in her hands and rocking to and fro. "It's too awful! I knew I was going too far, but I couldn't stop myself."

"He will probably be blackballed immediately from the local tennis club and cut stone dead from one end of the island to the other."

"Give me your handkerchief again," said Louise, laughing help-lessly. "Mine's in my bag, and my bag's in the bedroom, and I wish I were dead!"

"As far as Jamaican society goes, you already are," replied Boy, giving it to her. "Perhaps it would be a good idea if Henry changed his plans and built a hotel in Trinidad!"

5

The taxi was at the door and Mrs. Meaker had taken her luggage down in the lift. Louise went into the sitting room for one last valedictory look around; her eyes were prickly from lack of sleep, for she had been awake most of the night, and in spite of two cups of strong coffee she still felt half anesthetized, as if only part of her brain was functioning and that part liable to pack up at any moment leaving her stranded, without volition, in a mindless trance. She wondered drearily whether, if this should occur, Mrs. Meaker would have the presence of mind to lead her to the air terminal and deposit her in the bus, or whether she would lose her head, telephone the nearest hospital and have her carried off, mouthing vacuously, in an ambulance. The sitting room looked, in her exhausted imagination, a little unfriendly, almost as if it resented being stared at so early in the morning or perhaps had already accepted the idea of her deser-tion and was placidly adjusting itself to receive the Warrilows.

The Warrilows! Louise gave a sudden cry, and, galvanized into action, dashed to the writing desk to scribble a note to Grace Warrilow about the tap in the spare-room lavatory which had been dribbling for the last week and needed a new washer. Having ex-plained that she had meant to have it fixed days ago but had forgot-ten and that the name and address of the plumber were to be found in the small blue house-telephone book in the top right-hand drawer, she sealed up the note in an envelope, wrote "Grace" on it in block capitals and propped it against the clock on the mantelpiece. The clock announced that it was ten minutes past seven, and her heart jumped in her breast as though someone had crept up behind her and suddenly shrieked in her ear.

She turned to look at the room again, desolate and near to tears. She and Henry had lived in this flat ever since their honey-moon five years ago, except for the three months in Ireland in 1947 when they had let Annabelle have it. The Warrilows had taken it for a year with options; they were old friends and fairly quiet in their habits, so there was little likelihood of them giving wild parties and emptying Pernod into the piano and burning holes in everything. She patted the sofa cushions despairingly, as though they were dumb, devoted pets who would miss her when she had gone and howl all night.

At this moment Mrs. Meaker appeared in the doorway. "All ready," she said morosely. "You'd better be getting a move on."

"Good-bye, Mrs. Meaker. You will clean up, won't you, and see that everything's nice and tidy?"

"Trust me." Mrs. Meaker nodded. "Remember me to Mr. Goodrich, and I hope you get there all right I'm sure. The weather doesn't look good."

"We shall fly above the weather," said Louise with forced brightness. "It's a Constellation plane, you know, and they go very high indeed."

"Good heavens!" Mrs. Meaker looked incredulous. "It makes me dizzy to even think of it!"

"Well—good-bye again." Louise shook hands with her. A parting gift of three pounds in an envelope had been presented and accepted in the kitchen earlier, and there did not seem much more to say. "I've left a note for Mrs. Warrilow on the mantelpiece explaining about the tap. You might telephone Mr. What's-his-name later in the morning, but if you can't get hold of him I've told her that his name and address are in my blue book."

"All right," said Mrs. Meaker. "Happy landings!"

Louise collected her handbag and book from the hall table and went out to the lift.

6

"Please fasten your safety belts." The stewardess smiled as she said it, hoping to rob the sinister command of any urgent implication. She was a tall, thin girl with reddish hair and a very slight cast in her left eye; her manner was mercilessly affable and her voice was so constricted with refinement that Louise was surprised that she was able to get any words out at all. She helped, or rather assisted, Louise with her belt, and retired to the back of the plane, where she disappeared behind a curtain.

A moment or two later the steward, a short, tubby man with twinkling eyes and a cheerful smile, appeared through a door in the front of the plane and, taking up a stance in the center of the aisle between the two rows of double seats, made a routine speech to the passengers. In this he explained that life-saving apparatuses, in case of sudden immersion, were to be found beneath the chairs; that there were two emergency exits marked clearly in red on each side of the fuselage; that the plane was about to take off, would fly at an average altitude of eighteen thousand feet and would arrive in Lisbon in approximately four hours' time. He added that once they were airborne smoking would be permitted, but that smokers were requested to confine themselves to cigarettes and not light pipes. He concluded by wishing everyone a pleasant flight, and disappeared in the direction of the stewardess.

The airplane, which had been vibrating for some time while each of its four engines was switched on in turn, now proceeded to lumber slowly along the tarmac. Louise shut her eyes so as not to have to look at the actual takeoff, and then opened them again immediately so as not to miss it. It was the takeoff, she remembered with numb resignation, that was always considered to be the most perilous moment; it was during the takeoff, or just after, that engines were most likely to "cut out," plunging the plane nose-first into the ground, where it would at once explode and burst into fierce flames. She fingered her safety belt anxiously and wondered just how quickly she could release herself and bash her way out of one of the emergency exits if, after the first impact, she was still capable of moving at all.

The plane, having reached the farthermost end of the runway, turned around bumpily and stopped. There was a moment's pause, a loud moaning sound like a prolonged burglar alarm and then a sudden, reverberating roar as all four engines went into action together and the plane began to move forward faster and faster. She gripped the arms of her chair and stared, hypnotized, at the ground slipping away in streaks of gray and gunmetal beneath the vast silver wing. After a few moments of rapidly increasing momentum there was a sudden lessening of sound and vibration, and she saw the earth drop down. . . . The stewardess touched her on the shoulder and she jumped violently.

"Can I tempt yeow to a little chewing gum or barley sugar?"

Louise shook her head dumbly, and she passed on to the next passenger. The moaning recommenced and Louise watched the flaps along the edges of the wing sliding slowly out of sight. Trees, fields, houses and telegraph poles were by now reduced to miniature, and cars crawling along the highways looked like small shining insects. A few wisps of cloud appeared, increasing gradually, until the English countryside, the solid, comforting land upon which she had lived and breathed and walked for thirty-two years, was hidden from her sight. . . . The stewardess once more made her jump by hissing sibilantly in her ear, "You can unfasten your belt neow—alleow me." With expert hands she loosened her belt, smiled compassionately and moved away. Louise leant her head back and envisaged bitterly the calm, inevitable heroism of the stewardess in the event of a crisis. She would be efficient, reassuring and refined to the last. "Please alleow me to assist you to bleow up your rubber dinghy!" "Can I tempt you to a tayny shot of morphine?" She would, beyond a shadow of doubt, be singing "Roll Out the Barrel" in a birdlike soprano as the plane slid finally and for ever beneath the cold gray waves.

Presently, in spite of herself, Louise felt her nerves beginning to relax; the noise of the engines was now steady and soothing, and there was no sensation of movement whatsoever. It was impossible to believe that she was being whirled through the sky at several hundred miles an hour. She glanced across the aisle at a red-faced man in a Palm Beach suit methodically taking off his tie preparatory to going to sleep; when he had put his tie in the pocket of his coat and also taken off his shoes, he gave a practiced jerk to the green knob at the side of his seat and, shooting himself backward into a recumbent position, closed his eyes.

Louise decided enviously that he was an experienced air traveler and without fear. Not for him the night of horror that she had endured; the continual waking up and lighting cigarettes with a shaking hand; the periodic stumblings into the bathroom for glasses of water. Not for him the graphic mental pictures of sudden crashes, searing flames, people trapped and suffocating, trampling on each other, shrieking and fighting to escape from a blazing inferno! On the contrary, he had probably clambered into bed with some accommodating lady friend and finally slept like a top, without a pang, without a qualm, without even a momentary stab of dread that possibly this time, this particular flight, this particular plane, might just be the one destined to hit the mountainside, to crash into the sea, to encounter that fatal, unexpected electric storm and disintegrate in midair, flinging him twisting and turning grotesquely through infinities of space until the ultimate, sickening thud shattered the life out of him.

At this moment the stewardess appeared suddenly with a pillow. "Can I assist you with your chair?" she inquired. "We shall not be serving a meal just yet, and I thought that perhaps you might like to lie back."

"Thank you," murmured Louise.

The stewardess twisted the knob until Louise was comfortably extended; then, placing the pillow solicitously behind her head, she smiled again, that same smile of indulgent compassion, and minced away. A few seconds later the steady hum of the engines seemed to change its tone, to become muffled and far-away, then there was no sound at all, no anxiety, no piercing fears, no airplane, no life, no death; nothing but profound and dreamless sleep.

At London Airport Louise had been too dazed and wretched to pay much attention to her fellow passengers. They had all shuffled out together into the windy gray morning, and once in the plane they had been hidden from her by the high backs of the seats. She remembered vaguely noticing a small yellow baby being carried by its equally yellow parents in an oblong box with handles. They had looked so utterly depressed that she had averted her eyes and banished from her mind the immediate vision of baby, box and parents hurtling down through the clouds from a great height. At Lisbon Airport, feeling calmer and clearer after her sleep and the dainty meal that the stewardess had brought her on a tray, and also deeply thankful for the ground under her feet, Louise was more inclined to look about her, to work up a little interest in her surroundings. After all the first takeoff and landing had been accomplished without mishap, and there were only eight more to go including the ultimate arrival in Jamaica!

Herded with the others into a dark, fly-infested restaurant, she observed a vacant table in a corner and sat down at it. A harassed waiter rushed up to her, banged a cup of coffee and a stale rusk onto the table and rushed away again, and she was left alone. The yellow baby in the box was at the other side of the room; its parents leaned over it from time to time, pursing their mouths and making clucking noises in an effort to wring from it some sign of animation, but it remained comatose with its eyes shut.

At the table next to hers was the man in the Palm Beach suit with a large, thick-set Negro wearing a creased gray alpaca coat and trousers, a beige shirt and a green-and-orange tie. The Negro was talking in a light, singsong voice with a strong Welsh intonation which made it difficult for her to hear what he was saying. Perhaps, like Dr. Mellish, he was expounding with scientific brilliance the technical intricacies of the atom bomb. Whatever he was talking about, the man in the Palm Beach suit was obviously exceedingly bored by it, because he kept fidgeting and looking around the restaurant like a prisoner scanning the walls of his cell in the desperate hope that there might be some slab of stone that moved aside disclosing a secret exit, or that the bars of the window might have been filed through and could be whipped out with a flick of the wrist.

At a farther table there was a tiny, freckled nun sitting with a heavy-bosomed girl of about sixteen; the girl, whose skin was waxy and moist, looked uncomfortably hot. Sharing the table with them was a swarthy young couple who sat quite still, holding hands and staring straight before them. Probably they were just married and this was the beginning of their honeymoon. Poor Ellen and Charlie came into Louise's mind again. They had been so ecstatic, so very much in love, starting their lives together so gaily! Then that ghastly, tearing crash. . . . She pulled herself together and took a large gulp of coffee, which was so hot that it burnt her throat and brought tears to her eyes; then, after lighting a cigarette, she looked firmly at the couple again. At least they could not be described as either ecstatic or gay. They were just sitting there, silent and unsmiling, apparently in a trance. They both appeared to be so utterly lacking in vitality that they probably wouldn't notice whether the plane crashed or not. There was another group, farther away still, over by the yellow baby, composed of three men and one lush-looking woman, all gesticulating a great deal and talking at the top of their lungs in Spanish or Portuguese.

Presently, irritated by the buzzing flies and the fusty atmosphere of the restaurant, Louise got up from her table and wandered out. There was nothing to do and nowhere to go. She contemplated for a moment going to the lavatory, but remembering that she was on Latin territory, thought better of it and decided to wait until she got back on the plane. She strolled up and down for a little while and stared idly at a curio shop filled with straw hats and cheap jewelry, and a bookstall that had little to offer beyond foreign movie magazines, some ancient copies of the *Illustrated London News* and a few Penguin thrillers. Finally she found a wooden bench in the customs hall upon which she settled herself and watched the agitated crowds rushing back and forth under the contemptuous eyes of various officials; the porters yelling and staggering in and out with luggage of all shapes and sizes; the frantic travelers struggling to cram mountains of soiled clothes back into fiber suitcases which had been pitilessly ransacked.

The noise was deafening. Everybody was talking at once. The Latin races, she decided with insular detachment, obviously regarded travel as an emotional experience of the greatest intensity. Shrill cries rent the air. Families, either arriving or departing, embraced each other violently, laughed, wept and waved their arms about with the utmost abandon. She watched with interest the entrance, through the swing doors, of a tall, distinguished man in a dark suit and an Eden hat. It was clear that he was someone of importance because the customs officials greeted him with obsequious smiles and marked his expensive suitcases swiftly and delicately, as though the very thought of opening them in search of contraband would be sacrilege. This having been accomplished in record time, he thanked them courteously and, still maintaining his air of suave, diplomatic dignity, turned toward a group of people who had been waiting at the other side of the barrier.

In a flash his studied composure fell from him and he became transformed into a screaming maniac. Three ladies in black flung themselves into his arms one after the other, emitting groans and shrieks of excitement; two young men with pockmarked faces and straw hats kissed him repeatedly and a very small boy in a sailor suit was hoisted, gibbering, onto his shoulder. The reunion was brought to a climax by the elder of the three ladies in black giving a wailing cry and bursting into floods of tears, upon which the erstwhile suave diplomat seized her in his arms and, raining kisses on her face with such fervor that he knocked her hat on one side, led her, followed by the others screaming in unison, through the swing doors and out of sight. Louise's reflections on this curiously uninhibited display of family feeling were shattered by a raucous voice from the loudspeaker ordering the passengers of Flight 445 back to the plane.

Ten minutes later the sun-stained houses and churches and twisting streets of Lisbon lay far below her, like a map flung down onto a rumpled green carpet. She unfastened her safety seat belt hurriedly in order to circumvent the stewardess, who was approaching her with a solicitous gleam in her eye, and breathed a sigh of relief. Takeoff number two over and done with! She looked out of the window; the flaps had creaked out of sight again and the wing, like a sheet of molten silver, was so dazzling that she had to turn her eyes away and draw the curtain.

She picked up the novel that Boy Sullivan had brought her yesterday as a parting present and looked at it without enthusiasm. It was called *The Seeker and the Found* and was written by a young American journalist, Elwyn Brace Courtland, who, the blurb informed her, had served with conspicuous gallantry as a fighter pilot in the War and now lived with his wife and two children on a barge in Salem, Massachusetts. A photograph of him adorned the back flap showing him looking rather anxiously at a sheep dog. It was a strange face, with wide-apart eyes and high cheekbones; his hair, which was cut in a fringe, made him look artificial, like a Dutch doll. The blurb went on to say that *The Seeker and the Found* was unquestionably the most courageous, forceful and outspoken contribution to American literature that the postwar generation had yet produced, and that the reader would be moved, repelled, fascinated and enthralled by it from the first page to the last. Louise opened it at random and read:

> *Marise lay back wantonly on the rug Buck had spread for her on the sand. Her naked flesh, honeyed by the shrill sunlight, challenged his senses until his groin ached and his mouth became harsh and dry and drained of spittle like that time when he won the race at school and Mom and Pop were there and old Doc and Zelma too with her wild colt's legs and flying hair. In the blue shadows of Marise's armpits where she had shaved, beads of sweat glistened like jewels; like the silvery tinsel snow Mom used to sprinkle on the Christmas tree; like tiny sharp-pointed spears of light stabbing ruthlessly into the heart of his desire. He leant over her and cupped her eager, up-tilted breasts in his lean brown hand. "Christ, kid," he muttered hoarsely. . . .*

Louise closed the book firmly and put it down on the seat beside her. It was high time, she reflected, that Boy Sullivan took a course in psychology. First Mrs. Peverance and then this! I must send it to Aunt Esther, she thought with a giggle, just as an antidote to Sir Osbert. The man in the Palm Beach suit, apparently taking her giggle as an invitation to a little chat, got up from his seat and leant over her, steadying himself by resting his arm on the chair immediately in front. "Well," he said cheerfully, "so far so good!"

Louise, not wishing to appear disagreeable, smiled vaguely and nodded.

"I must say I didn't expect such a smooth flight when I saw that baby being yanked on board this morning," he went on. "They're always bad luck in an airplane, you know."

"No." Louise's smile faded. "I didn't know."

"Babies and nuns." He looked cautiously over his shoulder and lowered his voice. "Fortunately we've only got one nun this time. When you get a couple of 'em together it's disaster! You're not a Catholic by any chance?" he added anxiously.

Louise shook her head reassuringly and he looked relieved.

"Not that I'm all that superstitious myself, but when you notice the same sort of thing happening again and again in the same sort of circumstances you can't help but put two and two together, can you?"

"No—I suppose you can't."

"I remember once, just after the War it was, I was flying from Montreal down to New York with a friend of mine. We'd had a few drinks in the bar and we were both feeling, well—a little gay, as you might say—and just as we were about to board the plane he suddenly gripped my arm. 'Harry,' he said, and I could hear the panic in his voice, 'do you see what I see?' I looked to where he was pointing with a shaking hand and there they were, two of 'em climbing in just in front of us!"

"Babies or nuns?" Louise inquired with rising hysteria.

"Nuns!" he said dramatically. "And in the middle of the night too!"

"I don't think there's any hard-and-fast rule about them traveling only by day," said Louise.

"Well, I'm here to tell you that the sight of 'em sobered us up double quick pronto and we stopped dead in our tracks. 'I'm not going,' said Mac—my friend's name was Maclure—'I wouldn't get into that plane now, not if you gave me the Koh-i-noor diamond!'"

"That's supposed to be fairly unlucky too!" murmured Louise, but the man in the Palm Beach suit was not to be deflected by any flippant irrelevancies.

"'Don't be a fool,' I said, 'we can't go back now. I've got a conference at nine-thirty in the morning and you've got to get the midday plane to Baltimore.' 'I don't care,' said Mac, and I could tell by his tone that he meant it. 'You can go if you like, but I'm staying here!'—and he started to walk back into the airport. I ran after him and grabbed his arm, but he shook me off. I was in a fine state, I can tell you, not knowing whether to stay with him or leave him behind and get onto the plane myself. But it was he who made up my mind for me, as a matter of fact. He suddenly gripped both my hands and looked me straight in the eye—I can see his face now—'Don't go, Harry boy,' he said, and I could feel him trembling. 'If you do I shall never see you again—I feel it in my bones—I know it!' Well, that decided me. 'Come back and have another drink,' I said, and that was that." He paused, and Louise, realizing that the denouement was yet to come, thought it best to get it over quickly.

"What happened to the plane?" she asked.

"Crashed just after takeoff," he said. "We saw it happen from the window of the bar—the most terrible sight I've ever seen. It exploded as it hit the ground, and in a split second it was a sheet of flame. Nobody could get near it, and not a single soul survived! Burnt to a crisp every man jack of 'em!" He paused and smacked his lips thoughtfully. "That's the narrowest squeak I've ever had in my life, and no fooling! You can see what I mean about two nuns being unlucky, though, can't you?"

"Yes," replied Louise dimly. "I certainly can."

Four hours later the plane flew in low over a coast of somber black rocks and landed delicately at Santa Maria in the Azores, so delicately indeed that there was scarcely any bump at all when the heavy wheels touched down on the runway. Louise unfastened her belt with a sigh of relief. One more lap accomplished; quite an agreeable lap, all things considered, apart from the man in the Palm Beach suit, and he at least, upon observing her close her eyes, either in appreciative horror or sheer boredom at the climax of his story, had had the grace to move away. She had dozed a little and read a little. In addition to *The Seeker and the Found* she had wisely packed *Persuasion* and *The Oxford Book of Victorian Verse* into her overnight bag at the last minute. The stewardess had served another dainty meal; the yellow baby, in a sudden access of vitality, had had a screaming fit, which proved at any rate that it was alive. Nothing had happened in the heavens; no dangerous weather, no unforeseen meteoric disturbances; the plane had droned along monotonously over an endless prairie of white clouds which occasionally thinned and parted for a moment showing the flat blue of the sea far below. She had been stabbed by no sharp alarms, no sickening terrors, and the dead weight of fear that lay permanently at the back of her mind had remained obligingly dormant.

The pervasive melancholy of *The Oxford Book of Victorian Verse*—its recurrent preoccupation with the quiet grave, its nostalgic sentiment, its emphasis on gentle death, its almost smug avoidance of violence and of shrill agony—had been very soothing: soothing and at the same time tantalizing! Viewed from a pressurized metal tube hurtling through space at an altitude of eighteen thousand feet, the nineteenth century seemed remote and most enviably secure.

How little they had to fear, those Victorians, compared with us today! Of course, occasionally there were routine disasters like the Tay Bridge blowing down with a train on it, and the sinking of the *Princess Alice*, and that awful fire in the Charity Bazaar, but that, after all, was in Paris and so didn't quite count. True, many more people died of appendicitis than they did nowadays, and there were no anesthetics, not in the early part of the reign anyway, but taken by and large they had had an easy time of it. They had had leisure to think and plan and get their minds into a peaceful state of acceptance. The idea of death had so much more dignity and grace. Lovesick girls went into "declines" and had a little calf's-foot jelly and expired; poets coughed their lives away in sanatoriums and died peacefully, murmuring lovely things to their loved ones. There was hardly any banging and burning and being blown to bits and torn by jagged steel.

After the man in the Palm Beach suit had gone away to embark on an arch conversation with the stewardess, she had turned to Walter Savage Landor and read:

> *Death stands above me, whispering low*
> *I know not what into my ear;*
> *Of this strange language all I know*
> *Is there is not a word of fear.*

Then Christina Rossetti: "When I am dead, my dearest, sing no sad songs for me"—and the charming bit about not seeing the shadows and not feeling the rain; and then dear Algernon Charles:

> *So long as I endure, no longer, and laugh not again, neither*
> *weep*
> *For there is no God stronger than death; and death is a sleep.*

There now! she reflected. What could be more comforting than that?

The airport at Santa Maria was smaller than the one at Lisbon and a little cleaner. Once again the passengers were herded into a restaurant, but Louise, perceiving the gray sandwiches, the dirty tablecloths and the flies, rebelled and went to the bar where she discovered that she could buy a whiskey and soda with English money. While she was sitting there sipping it, the pilot of the plane and another officer came up and ordered, she was grateful to observe, two glasses of lemonade. She glanced at the pilot's hands, which were

301

well-shaped and brown and looked efficient; his eyes were very blue and he had a pleasant voice; he smiled politely at her and then went on chatting to his companion, apparently in no way overwhelmed by the terrifying magnitude of his responsibility.

Some words of Tennyson's that she had read only an hour ago flashed into her mind and she repressed a giggle:

> For tho' from out our bourne of Time and Place
> > The flood may bear me far,
> I hope to meet my Pilot face to face
> > When I have crossed the bar.

In due course they were all ordered back to the plane and, obediently disposing of their cigarettes, they climbed on board and strapped themselves in. The steward reappeared and gave an abbreviated rendering of his original speech for the benefit of two new passengers who were blue-black and looked furtively about them as though they were expecting some blatant display of racial discrimination. The stewardess, with painstaking gentility, gave them chewing gum, wool for their ears and two pillows; she also strapped them in and, with a smile of ineffable condescension, left them.

Louise, warmed by the whiskey and soda, watched the takeoff with splendid calm. The plane slid off the ground and out over the black rocks and churning sea, rising smoothly and gradually until presently the clouds intervened again, blotting out the diminishing land. The sky was lemon and orange in the evening light, and far above, where it deepened into blue, she saw a star. She glanced at her watch, which she had kept at London time; it said six-thirty. She tried fruitlessly for a little to work out in her mind if two hours had already been lost or gained; then, remembering that someone had said something about daylight saving either operating or not operating in Portugal, she gave up the whole idea and decided to eat, go to sleep and wake up when the stewardess told her to. This, at all events, was the longest lap of the whole journey—nine to ten hours! She shuddered and hurriedly opened *The Oxford Book of Victorian Verse* at random:

> Let me be gathered to the quiet west
> The sundown pleasant and serene,
> Death.

Nine and a half hours later Louise was awakened from an uneasy sleep by the stewardess hissing in her ear, "We shall be landing in Bermuda in twenty minutes' time." She untwisted her cramped limbs, having been lying half on the seat next to her which had fortunately been unoccupied for the whole journey and half on her own. She had a crick in her neck and the right cheek of her behind was entirely numb. There was a dim blue light in the plane, and the man in the Palm Beach suit was snoring with his mouth wide open; the upper plate of his false teeth had slipped down, which gave the impression that he was grinning obscenely at some private bawdiness.

Louise, seizing the moment to stagger to the lavatory before anyone else was wakeful enough to get there, plunged her face in cold water and brushed her teeth. She scrutinized herself in the mirror, and arrived at the conclusion that air travel, although comparatively clean, was definitely not becoming. Her face was quivering violently, not from fear this time but from the vibration of the plane; it looked wan and tired, and her hair was terrible. She did the best she could with it and, after dabbing herself with some eau de cologne and putting on some lipstick, she went back to her seat again feeling a little better.

Her watch said five-thirty and she peered out of the window, expecting to see at least the vague beginnings of sunrise, but it was still pitch dark and there weren't even any stars. The yellow baby, lolling in its mother's arms, passed her, looking far from well. Louise was profoundly thankful that she had managed to get to the lavatory ahead of it. Suddenly the stewardess switched all the lights on, and the man in the Palm Beach suit woke in the middle of a loud snore and stared angrily and incredulously at Louise, as though she were an unwelcome stranger who had forced her way into his bedroom. After a moment he realized where he was, snapped his teeth back, gave a sickly smile and heaved himself off to the lavatory.

The stewardess reappeared and walked up and down from seat to seat collecting pillows and rugs, while the steward, with a sort of flit gun, appeared through the door in the front and proceeded to spray the air with sickly smelling disinfectant. Presently the "Fasten your belts—No smoking" sign flashed on, and Louise felt her ears clicking as the plane began to descend. She looked out the window and saw some scattered lights in the darkness below; some of them were reflected in water and she could distinguish shadowy shapes of land and low white houses. The engine nearest to her, which had frightened her dreadfully in the night by suddenly emitting jets of flame, coughed out a few sparks; there was a gentle crunching bump, and she loosened her hands, which had been gripping the arms of the chair in a vise, and relaxed.

The waiting room in the Bermuda airport, where coffee and sandwiches were served, was a marked contrast to the drab restaurants of Lisbon and Santa Maria. Here there were no harassed waiters, no grubby tablecloths and no flies. There were, however, to her great astonishment, two women and a man in evening dress. The man was fairly drunk, and a red carnation had died in the buttonhole of his white dinner jacket. It was not until she heard the younger of the two women, who was wearing a very décolleté pink dress, urging the young man to let the plane go on without him and come back to the party, that she realized that whereas, as far as she was concerned this was the beginning of a new day, as far as they were concerned it was still last night. She looked at her watch, which said five-fifty-five and then up at the clock over the door, which said one-fifteen, and her heart sank. The night had already seemed to be interminable, and now she was faced with the prospect of several more hours of it.

The girl in the pink dress was obviously in a state of considerable agitation; her voice was deep and hoarse and very American and she was arguing heatedly.

"I think you're mean," she said, "just as mean as a little old skunk. You know Lenore won't give a goddamn if you get there tomorrow or the day after. As a matter of fact, she won't give a goddamn if you don't get there at all."

"Now, don't talk that way, honey—"

"It's true and you know it. Isn't it true, Gloria?" She turned to the older woman, who had bright blue hair and was sitting on the arm of a chair doing up her face.

"Isn't what true?"

"About Lenore not caring whether Elsworth gets there or not."

"Listen, dear." The woman with blue hair had a strong Middle Western accent and stared at herself critically in the mirror of her compact with her head on one side. "You've been harping on that same tired theme ever since before we got in the car to go to Marion's, and I'm here to tell you that you're driving me crackers. Why the hell can't you lay off Lenore for two minutes and shut up?"

"Lenore's a bitch, and you know it."

"All right, all right—so Lenore's a bitch. Let's leave it at that."

"I hate her!"

"All right, that's fine. You hate her. But she does happen to be Elsworth's wife and she is expecting him home on this plane tomorrow. Whether she cares or not is his problem, not yours. For heaven's sake stop bellyaching about it and let's get the hell out of here and go back to the party."

"It won't be the same without Elsworth."

"Oh yes, it will. Except that Marion will be a little more stinking than she was when we left, and so will everybody else, everybody but us! That's what's burning me up, just loitering about here in this glamorized toilet and not getting anyplace. Come on—let's go."

"Go on, honey—do like Gloria says!" The young man put his arm tentatively round her shoulders, but she wriggled away.

"Leave me alone!"

"Now, don't get mad, sweetheart. You know I'd stay if I could, but we did agree to let everything ride for a bit, didn't we? Won't you kiss me good-bye now and go back to Marion's like Gloria said?"

"I'm sick of Gloria!" said the girl, at bay. "And I'm sick of you too—so there!"

"You know you don't mean that, honey—"

"I do too mean it!"

"Oh for God's sake!" said Gloria.

"And what's more—I don't ever want to see you again. I'm through!"

"Here, dear"—Gloria pacifically offered her a packet of cigarettes—"try one of these—they're toasted."

The girl pushed Gloria's arm away, violently knocking the packet of cigarettes onto the floor. Elsworth bent down unsteadily to pick it up.

"And if your plane falls into sea—it's okay by me!"

"Don't talk like that—it's unlucky," said Gloria sharply.

The girl, suddenly abandoning all belligerence, burst into tears and flung herself into the young man's arms.

"I didn't mean it!" she sobbed. "But don't go—not on this plane—please, please don't. Catch the next one, if you like, but not this one! I had a presentiment coming along in the car—I swear I did—"

Louise, feeling suddenly sick, got up and moved away out of earshot. Back in the plane she steeled herself to face three and a half hours more of dreadful night. She decided against trying to go to sleep again, realizing that the attempt would be doomed to failure anyway, as she had had two cups of black coffee and her nerves were strung to such a pitch of acute wakefulness that she felt she would twang like a guitar if anyone touched her.

A different steward appeared and gave his own version of the routine speech. There was also a different stewardess, brisk and dumpy, altogether a tougher proposition than her predecessor. She bustled up and down distributing chewing gum and cotton wool, with the hard, detached efficiency of an overworked matron in a crowded hospital ward.

The young American, having finally shaken himself free from the girl in pink, had taken off his coat and tie, settled down in his seat and was staring glumly at a copy of *Esquire.*

Shortly after the takeoff the stewardess switched out the lights and the interior of the plane became blue again. Louise discovered a button which when she pressed it shed a small beam of white light from the ceiling onto her lap. She opened *Persuasion*, hoping that Miss Austen's impeccable gentility would soothe her nerves and waft her away from the dangerous sky into a less agitating world wherein young ladies and gentlemen drove about in curricles and went to assemblies and viewed life, not in terms of speed and swift achievement and vulgar publicity, but sedately; sometimes with sly humor, sometimes even with exasperation but always, always with dignity and discretion.

But it was no use. Her mind, like a tired gramophone needle, skidded across the gentle attitudes and verbal arabesques, and refused to hold. She read one sentence over three times without gaining any impression from it whatever: "From situation, Mrs. Clay was, in Lady Russell's estimate, a very unequal, and in her character she believed a very dangerous companion—and a removal, that would leave Mrs. Clay behind and bring a choice of more suitable intimates within Miss Elliot's reach, was therefore an object of first-rate importance."

With a sigh she closed the book and leant her head against the back of the chair. Only a few more hours and this journey, this insecure, nerve-racking and continually anxious journey, would be over. She would be on land again; solid, comforting land. Earthquakes might shake and rend it, tropical storms might flood it and hurricanes devastate it, but it would remain land upon which she could walk and sit and lie without the scarifying knowledge that immediately beneath her was a void, a vast infinity of space, with nothing between her and utter oblivion but a few wisps of insubstantial cloud. There would also be Henry—dear, darling Henry! She was suddenly overwhelmed by such a passionate longing for him that her eyes filled with tears. She would lie, safe and at peace, in his arms, perhaps under a mosquito net, perhaps not—she was not sure about the mosquito situation, but at any rate she would be relaxed and happy, and this exhausting, idiotic nightmare would be past and done with and she would never leave him again in any vehicle of any sort or allow him to leave her either. She rested her forehead against the window and stared out into the dark. The engine nearest to her continued to glow in a sinister way and occasionally shot out jets of blue flame. She remembered the beastly girl in pink and her hysterical, drunken babbling about a presentiment, and down went her heart again and she sat back, rigid with fear and claustrophobia, and wanting to scream.

Dawn was breaking as the plane circled over the turquoise lagoons and white beaches of Nassau. It must have been raining an hour or so before, because Louise noticed oily puddles on the tarmac as she stepped out of the plane and walked down the gangway. She had not slept; she had not read; she had just sat quite still for over three hours trying as much as possible to make her mind a blank, to think of nothing, to indulge in no imaginative flights, pleasant or otherwise. She had partially succeeded, but the effort had left her worn out and lethargic.

She walked over to a sort of bungalow restaurant the verandah of which was being swept indolently by two colored maids. There was a tropical warmth in the air, even at that early hour; she sniffed it gratefully after the curious ozonic smell of the plane and, selecting a table by a window, ordered orange juice, coffee and eggs and bacon, in the hope that solid food might mitigate the pervasive tiredness that seemed to have settled into her joints and bones and made even the powdering of her nose a major endeavor.

The rest of the passengers, looking sleepy and disgruntled, were dotted about at the other tables. The yellow baby and its parents arrived last; the mother's eyes were puffy from lack of sleep and a bit of the father's wiry black hair was sticking out at the back like a handle. The freckled nun and the fat girl were silently devouring cornflakes and milk. The blue-black couple and the Jamaican Negro, having apparently bridged successfully the subtle shade of color that differentiated them, were strolling up and down outside and talking animatedly, occasionally baring their brilliant teeth in wide laughter. The man in the Palm Beach suit had left the plane in Bermuda, and the young man in the white dinner jacket had been met by a small, hatchet-faced young woman in green slacks, presumably Lenore, and whisked away in a shiny station wagon. There were some other people sitting about whom she failed to identify; they had got on at Bermuda and been placed up in the front of the plane beyond her vision. She ate her eggs and bacon listlessly, drank some coffee and lit a cigarette. Her watch said ten minutes to ten, but the restaurant clock blandly contradicted it by pointing to five minutes to six.

At six-fifteen (by the restaurant clock) the plane took off again. The last lap! Only one more landing, only one more strapping on of the safety belt, only one more cold sweat of fear as the ground rose nearer and nearer. Louise twisted the knob of her seat and tilted it back a little, not too far, as she did not wish to sleep, but just at a comfortable angle at which she could lie peacefully with her eyes closed and count the minutes.

Presently she opened her eyes and was surprised to see that the plane was no longer flying steadily along through a clear sky, but seemed to be climbing almost vertically through dense banks of cloud. She tried vainly to rise, but was unable to lever herself up from her chair; she wrenched violently at the knob but it wouldn't budge.

At this moment the pilot appeared through the door in the front, encased in a life jacket and smiling charmingly. "We are now flying at an altitude of approximately eighty-five thousand feet," he said in a hoarse, rather drunken voice that sounded curiously familiar. "But owing to serious engine trouble I fear that it will be necessary for you to fasten your safety belts and have some chewing gum."

He advanced toward Louise and she saw to her dismay that he was no longer smiling, but crying bitterly. "I had a presentiment that this would happen," he muttered, "I swear I did. The first moment I saw those nuns I knew that we hadn't got a chance of survival, and it's all my own fault for not traveling to Sicily with Mrs. Morpeth and those two lovely little girls—"

He leaned close to her face and she saw that his front teeth had slipped over his underlip and that he was quivering with dreadful terror. She strained away from him and turned to the window; as she did so, the engine nearest to her was suddenly enveloped in a sheet of flame and, as sick with horror she watched it, it detached itself from the plane entirely and went spinning away upward into the sky like a vast Catherine wheel. She gave a strangled shriek and began to pummel the pilot's chest with her fists, but it sank in like soft rubber as she touched it, and he seized her arms and began shaking her.

"If the plane falls into the sea," he screamed malignantly, "it will be okay by me—okay by me!" There was a sharp jolt and she fell forward.

"Wake up, please," said the voice of the stewardess, edgy with controlled impatience. "We shall be landing at Kingston in ten minutes' time." Seeing that Louise was at last awake, she stopped shaking her, and with a tight-lipped smile moved away.

Louise, feeling as though she had been dragged up by her hair from the furthermost pit of hell, started to laugh weakly. She glanced out of the window and saw below her a range of corrugated green mountains; in the distance their color changed to deep blue, and they looked as though they had been cut out of some opaque material and gummed rather untidily onto a paler blue background. There were deep, shadowed valleys with the gleam of water in the bottom of them; little roads, twisting up and down through groves of feathery bamboo, and scattered clusters of straw-colored houses clinging to the summits of the lower hills. Ten minutes' time! She dashed hurriedly to the lavatory, but had to wait while one of the Bermuda passengers, a tall, horsy woman in a shantung suit, finished her ablutions at the basin and put on her rings. When at last she had gone, Louise washed hastily, wrestled with her face and hair, upset about half of her bottle of eau de cologne up her sleeve and returned, trembling with excitement, to her seat.

The plane was sweeping lower and lower over the wide bay of Kingston. She looked down at a spit of land stretching out into the sea, with behind it an immense wall of purple-gray mountains. She fastened her belt; her ears clicked. "Please God!" she prayed silently, "not now! Don't let it crash now. Don't let it overshoot the runway; don't let it nosedive into the sea; don't let it explode and burst into flames! I want so very much to see Henry again—just once! I know we were married in a Registry Office and not in a church, and so from Your point of view we probably aren't married at all, but I do love him—more than anyone or anything in the world—and love is important. You've said so often Yourself—!"

The plane touched down lightly with an almost imperceptible bounce; the airport, with some white-clad figures standing outside it, flashed by the window and, for the last time, she unfastened her safety belt.

A little while later she was standing in a small yellowish room with a thermometer in her mouth, gazing raptly at Henry through some wire netting. A nurse with magnolia skin and enormous dark eyes whipped the thermometer from her mouth, and Louise rushed forward. Henry poked a brown finger through the netting, and she clung to it tightly, trying hard not to cry.

"Well, cookie," he said, "did you have a good trip? Were you scared?"

"Of course not," she replied. "I adored every minute of it!"

STAR QUALITY

She'll do it," said J. C. Roebuck. "To begin with she hasn't had an original script since *Dear Yesterday*. Also, she hasn't got a man at the moment and she's in serious trouble over her taxes. Oh yes, she'll do it all right, and if you feel, Ray, that you can stand the wear and tear, it's okay with me, but never say I didn't warn you!"

Ray Malcolm laughed. "I'm sure I can deal with her." He leaned forward and took a cigarette out of a massive silver box. There was about him an intensity, a wiry vitality, that made his recent meteoric rise to fame as a director clearly understandable. His movements were alert and his speech decisive; his personality embodied all the requisite qualities—drive, force and authority.

Bryan Snow, who had been sitting silently for some time on the edge of the sofa trying valiantly to appear calm while the fate of his play was being discussed, watched him with wholehearted admiration. "I'm sure I can deal with her." There was something so firm, so charmingly confident, in the way it was said. Bryan was convinced that this dynamic, fascinating young man of the theater would find no difficulty whatsoever in dealing with a cage full of ravening lionesses, let along one allegedly temperamental leading lady.

Ray Malcolm turned on him the full force of his concentrated charm.

"You want her, don't you, Bryan? You feel that she really would be right for the play?"

"Yes," said Bryan, "I do."

"Well, then, that's settled. Will you handle it, J.C., or do you think I'd better go along and see her first?"

J. C. Roebuck scribbled something on his telephone pad and smiled. There was a certain benign resignation in the smile.

"I'll handle it," he said. "I'll call up Clemson, her agent. He'll be very relieved. I don't think you'd better have anything to do with it until it's all signed and sealed: you'll have quite enough of her later on."

"She's read the script?"

"Probably. She's had it for two weeks."

"What about Gerald Wentworth? Does she get on with him all right?"

J.C. smiled. "As well as she gets on with any leading man; a little better, if anything. She had a swing round with him when they were in *Wise Man's Folly* a few years ago; since then they've appeared together fairly painlessly several times. I suspect that he hates her guts, but he's far too easygoing to allow her to ruffle him."

"You do too, don't you?" Ray fired the question sharply, almost challengingly.

"What?"

"Hate her guts."

"Not at all." J.C. spoke blandly. "On the contrary, I'm very fond of her. I admit I did say on one occasion that I'd never allow her to appear in a theater of mine again. That was after she'd given poor Ella Craven a nervous breakdown and driven Scott Gurney into a nursing home."

"Scott Gurney." Ray snorted contemptuously. "Scott Gurney couldn't direct a church social."

"But since then," J.C. went on, "we've kissed and made friends."

"She's looking wonderful," volunteered Bryan. "I saw her in the Savoy Grill the other night."

"She always looks wonderful," said J.C. "And, what is more, she knows she looks wonderful."

"I've spoken to her only once in my life," said Bryan. "I thought she had tremendous charm."

"She's always had tremendous charm," said J.C., "and she knows that too."

311

Ray Malcolm quizzically raised one eyebrow a trifle higher than the other. "You'd fall dead with surprise, wouldn't you, if we got through this whole production without a single row—without a single argument?"

J.C. laughed outright. "I certainly would," he said, "but before I fell dead I should have the presence of mind to give you a check for a thousand pounds."

"Is that a bet?"

"Most definitely not. But it's a promise."

"You're a witness to that Bryan," Ray said gaily, as he rose and put on his overcoat. Then, with an abrupt change of expression, he said very seriously: "I know, J.C., that you think I'm overconfident when I say so surely that I can deal with her, but, believe me, I have a very good reason for saying it, and the reason is that underneath all her fiddle-faddle and nonsense I know her to be a bloody good actress. Her talent is true and clear, in addition to which she has the quality that this play needs. I know a dozen women who could play it technically as well, if not better, but none of them could bring to it that peculiar magic that she has, that extraordinary capacity for investing whatever she touches with her own truth."

"Yes," said J.C., a thought absently. "She can do that well enough, but she sometimes does it at the expense of the play."

"She hasn't been properly directed for years. Not since old Jimmy died, really."

"All right, all right." J.C. began to show signs of impatience. "I've said my say. I agree with you that she's a fine actress. I agree with you that she has a quality of magic that is completely and entirely her own. I agree with you that in the right part in the right play she can be one of the biggest draws in the country. I also agree with you that she has never been properly directed since Jimmy died, but where I don't agree with you is in your supposition that she ever *can* be properly directed. If anybody can do it, you can; I have a profound respect for your knowledge and your determination. But apart from her talent and her magic and her truth, there is one thing that you don't know about and that I do."

"What is it?"

J.C. sighed and got up from his swivel chair. "She is the least intelligent, most conceited and most tiresome bitch that I have ever encountered in all my long experience of the theater."

2

Lorraine Barrie's house was in a mews near Knightsbridge. It was easy to identify from quite a long way off because it was painted pale pink and had blue shutters and a blue front door. It also had window boxes glowing with scarlet geraniums, and obviously could belong to no one but a famous actress or a scene designer. Bryan hesitated before ringing the bell. He felt distinctly nervous and needed a moment or two to gather himself together. He was irritated with himself for feeling nervous, although he realized that it was natural enough that he should. This was an important occasion, this first official meeting with the star who was, he hoped, prepared to lavish her talent, charm and technique on a play by an unknown playwright.

It was not actually his first play; there had been *The Unconquered*, which had been produced the year before in a small artistic theater in Bayswater where it had run for a week, but unfortunately, in spite of excellent press notices and a competent performance by an all-male cast, failed to achieve a West End production. This had been a bitter disappointment at the time, but the fact of it having been produced at all had spurred him on. This new play, *Sorrow in Sunlight*, was therefore his first real bid for commercial success.

The Unconquered had been raw and autobiographical, with patches of good writing in it, but apparently little popular appeal. Nobody, it seemed, wanted to know about life in a prisoner of war camp. The War was over, and the sooner it was forgotten the better. The intricate psychological problems, both tragic and comic, of a group of men mewed up for years in a drafty barrack in a remote German village were not considered by theatrical managements to have entertainment value. True, certain critics had said that the play had strength and realism and moments of sheer nobility, but the fact had to be faced that strength and realism and sheer nobility were not enough. Other ingredients were needed, most particularly love interest—or at least sex conflict. One eminent manager who had been sufficiently interested in the play to invite Bryan to lunch at Scott's had suggested the introduction into the prison camp of a female parachutist who, apart from being brave and tough, could have immense glamour which in itself would create an emotional situation acceptable to the larger theatergoing public. He had also implied that if Bryan were willing to go away to Cornwall or somewhere quiet and rewrite the whole play on those lines there would be a very good chance of popping it into the Jupiter Theatre when *Sweet Ladies* closed. Bryan, diplomatically concealing his irritation, had agreed to think about it, and returned fuming to his flat in Ebury Street.

Sorrow in Sunlight was different in every way from *The Unconquered*. It was what might have been described in earlier years as a "drawing room" drama. That is to say, its protagonists were educated people with money who lived their lives in comfortable surroundings. The play was primarily the study of a neurotic woman whose subconscious jealousy of her husband's heroism in the war caused her to run off to the South of France with a worthless but attractive man

313

younger than herself. The main theme of the play was her gradual disillusionment, not only with the young man, who inevitably let her down, but with herself. In the last scene of all she left a superficially gay lunch party and committed suicide by crashing a speedboat into a lighthouse at fifty miles an hour. It was, on the whole, a well-written play; the dialogue was natural without being scintillating, and the characterization of the husband was particularly clear. The heroine, though neurotic and at moments tiresome, commanded enough sympathy to justify her rather arbitrary behavior, and, if played by an actress of outstanding personality, had every chance of charming the audience into believing in her and the validity of her suffering.

Ray Malcolm had been right when he said that Lorraine Barrie had the exact quality that the play needed; he was also right when he said that, leaving aside the temperamental excesses that had tarnished her reputation among theatrical people, she was a bloody good actress. She was. She had been a bloody good actress right from the beginning. Her instinct for timing, her natural grace of movement, her gift for expressing, without apparent effort, the subtle nuances either of comedy or tragedy, had all been part of her stock-in-trade since she had stepped onto the stage of the Theatre Royal, Sunderland, at the age of nine and piped, with the utmost emotional authority, "Oh, Hubert, spare mine eyes!" Throughout her dazzling career in the theater these rare and unaccountable gifts, this almost incredible facility for expression, had seldom failed her. She had, with the years, acquired by experience certain technical tricks and mannerisms, none of which had impaired the purity of her talent. Occasionally perhaps they may have obscured it, but never for long; it always popped up again, the peculiar magic that Ray had described, endowing a turgid, unreal play with truth; decorating a clumsy, inept comedy with such enchanting personal arabesques that the author on reading his press notices would be gratified to discover that he was the wittiest playwright since Congreve.

It was a little unfair of J. C. Roebuck to say that she was unintelligent; unfair and inaccurate, for she had a native intelligence where her own desires were concerned that was quite remarkable. He was also a little off true when he said she was conceited. Lorraine Barrie's ingrained convictions about herself far transcended mere conceit. Her profound, magnificent egocentricity was far removed from such paltry bathos. A mountain peak lit by the first light of dawn is superior to a slag heap in size and shape and design, but it is not conceited. Niagara Falls are unquestionably more impressive than the artificial cascade in Battersea Park, but they are singularly devoid of personal vanity. It would never have occurred to Lorraine to compare herself either favorably or unfavorably with Bernhardt,

Duse or Réjane. She was Lorraine Barrie, and that was enough; it was more than enough—it was unequivocally and eternally right.

When Bryan finally summoned up courage to ring the bell, there was an immediate outburst of ferocious barking, the sound of smothered imprecations, further barking and footsteps in the passage. Then, to his surprise, the door was flung open by Lorraine Barrie herself. She was wearing gray linen slacks, a lime-colored sports shirt and enormous dark glasses, and she had in her hand a blue-covered typescript.

"Look," she cried triumphantly, waving it in his face, "you've come at exactly the right moment. I was just reading your wonderful play for the seventh time!"

Before he had time to make a suitable reply, a snarling Aberdeen terrier rushed at him from between her legs and sank its teeth into the cuff of his trousers. Lorraine gave it a sharp blow with the script, whereupon it yelped and retired into the hall.

"It's only excitement," she said. "Bothwell always goes on like that when anyone comes to the house for the first time, don't you, my angel?"

Bothwell, who had taken up a menacing attitude at the foot of the small staircase, growled. Lorraine shooed him up the stairs.

"Come on up," she went on. "My maid's out for the afternoon, so we're all alone and can talk in peace. Tea's all ready except for just popping the water into the pot. You can leave your coat here or bring it upstairs, whichever you like."

Bryan took his overcoat off and laid it on a chair and followed her up into a charmingly furnished sitting room on the first floor. There was a fire crackling in the grate, in front of which was a low table with tea things spread invitingly upon it. Above the fireplace was a large painting of Lorraine herself in a wide gray wooden frame flecked with gilt. In it she was portrayed in her dressing room staring at herself fixedly in a mirror; behind her hovered a bulky woman with sandy hair.

Lorraine laughed gaily when she saw Bryan looking at it.

"It's a Charles Donovan," she said. "He did it three years ago. Personally I loathe it, although it's supposed to be one of the best things he ever did. That's Nellie, my dresser, who's been with me ever since I was at the Haymarket before the War—it's really far better of her than it is of me. Look at the way he's done the hair just on the verge of coming down, and the painting of the hands and that heavenly safety pin! It's terrifying, isn't it? I need hardly tell you that she despises it—she says it makes her look like a lavatory attendant, and I've never had the heart to tell the poor sweet that's exactly what she does look like. Here, darling, have a biscuit and shut your trap." Her

315

last remark was addressed to Bothwell, who was still eyeing Bryan malignantly and snarling. She threw him a chocolate biscuit, and he disappeared with it behind the sofa.

"Now just sit down and relax"—she gave Bryan a gentle push toward a low armchair by the fire—"while I go and make the tea. There are cigarettes in that hideous silver box; it was presented to me on the last night of *Dear Yesterday* by the whole company and they'd all subscribed their little pennies and put their signatures on it and it really was heartrending and took me so completely by surprise that I literally hadn't a word to say; I just stood there stammering like a fool with the tears cascading down my face. If Bothwell makes a beast of himself, just give him another chocolate biscuit and he'll adore you."

She went swiftly out of the room, shutting the door behind her. Bryan obediently sat down and helped himself to a cigarette. Bothwell came out from behind the sofa, sat down by the tea table and stared at him. Bryan said "Good dog" automatically, and stared back. Then he looked up at the picture again wondering why, if Lorraine hated it as much as she said, she had hung it in such a prominent position. It was unquestionably a good painting; it had strength and sureness, but it was not attractive. The face staring into the mirror with such intensity had an unreal, masklike quality; the modeling of the features was perfect, the texture of the skin shone in the bright light shed by the two symmetrical dressing-table lamps. It was not a beautiful face in the classical sense; the nose was too formless and the mouth too big. The eyes were widely spaced and the high cheekbones, which the artist had slightly overemphasized, gave an impression of Asiatic exoticism which was somehow out of key. It was perhaps this that accounted for the general artificiality of the whole picture. It was clever, arresting and highly decorative both in execution and design, but there was no life in it.

His reflections were interrupted by Bothwell giving a conciliatory whine and rearing himself, with some effort, into a sitting position on his short back legs. Bryan leaned forward obligingly and gave him a chocolate biscuit, which he received with a satisfied grunt and withdrew once more behind the sofa. A moment later Lorraine reappeared carrying a teapot and a hot-water jug on a small tray.

"It's China tea," she said. "If you prefer Indian, there's masses in the kitchen and you can have a little pot all to yourself." Bryan rose to his feet and relieved her of the tray and was about to reply that he was devoted to China tea when she cut him short by saying abruptly, "You know you're quite different from what I thought you'd be. I can't imagine why, but I expected someone much older and drier—in fact, I can tell you now that I was really quite nervous. I've always had a dreadful inferiority complex about authors. To me there's something incredible about people being able to sit down and write plays and books. It's torture to me to have to write so much as a postcard. I'm just physically incapable of stringing three words together on paper. I suppose it's never having been to school properly and having to earn my living ever since I was tiny. I'm completely uneducated, you know; I used to drive poor Doodie Rawlings quite frantic when he was directing me in *The Cup That Clears*. He was an Oxford don, you know, with a passion for the theater and, of course, madly intellectual, and he was astounded that anyone in the world could know as little as I did. He was a darling, of course, but frightfully twisted up emotionally, and if I hadn't a sort of instinctive feeling for what he wanted we should never have got beyond the first week of rehearsal.

"I remember quite early on going to Clemmie—that's my agent—in absolute despair. 'It's no use,' I said. 'I can't do it.' It isn't that I don't want to be directed. I do. I want it more than anyone else in the world; I want to be told every gesture, every intonation, but this man, poor angel, doesn't *know* the theater! He may adore it; he may write brilliant essays on the Restoration playwrights or Shakespeare and God knows who, but he doesn't really *know*—I mean, one can tell in a flash, can't one?

"I remember at the very first reading of the play, when we were all sitting round a table, he kept on getting up and walking about and *explaining* our parts to us. It really was disaster. Finally, of course, Clemmie calmed me down, and back I went with my heart literally in my boots and went straight up to Doodie in front of the whole company and had it out with him. 'It's no good,' I said, 'expecting me to give what I have to give before I've got the book out of my hand. God knows I'm willing to rehearse until I drop at any time of the day or night, but you must let me work it out in my own way to begin with. Later on, when I'm sure of my words and not trying to think of a million things at once and worrying about my fittings into the bargain, you can do what you like with me. You can tear me to pieces, turn me inside out, but not yet—not yet—not yet!'"

On the last "not yet" she struck the tea table sharply with her left hand, which caused the sugar tongs to shoot out of the bowl and clatter into the fender. Bryan stooped down to retrieve them, and Bothwell charged out from behind the sofa, barking loudly.

"There I go," said Lorraine with a gay, unaffected laugh, "overacting again." She handed Bryan a cup of tea. "I don't know whether you like sugar or milk or neither, so just help yourself. I made those little scones myself specially for you, so you must eat them all up to the last crumb. I adore cooking, but I never dare go into the kitchen when my maid's in the house, so I send her off to the movies every so often and have a real field day. Can you cook?"

"Only scrambled eggs," said Bryan modestly.

"There's nothing in the world," said Lorraine simply, "more divine than scrambled eggs." She turned to Bothwell, who was once more wobbling uneasily on his hindquarters. "You're Mother's sweetheart angel pie and the cleverest dog that ever drew breath, but this is definitely and finally the last chocolate biscuit you're going to have today." She threw him a biscuit, which he caught in midair. "And if you go on whining and begging and making a revolting greedy pig of yourself, Mother will lock you in the bathroom." She turned back to Bryan. "He simply hates the bathroom," she said, "because the smell of the bath essence makes him sneeze. Where was I?"

"We were talking about scrambled eggs really," replied Bryan. "But, just before that, you were telling me about Doodie Rawlings."

"Poor Doodie." Lorraine sighed and nibbled a sandwich pensively. "He went back to Oxford after the play opened, and I haven't clapped my eyes on him from that day to this. Tell me about this new man that J.C. says is going to direct our play, Ray Something-or-other. I missed the thing he did at Hammersmith, and wild horses wouldn't drag me to Stratford, particularly with poor Etta Marling flogging her way through all those long parts, so I've never really seen any of his work at all."

"I think he's brilliant," said Bryan firmly, aware of a sudden uprush of loyalty to Ray Malcolm. "He has a terrific personality and great charm."

Lorraine assumed an expression of grave interest.

"But does he really know about the theater?" she asked, "or is he one of those artsy-craftsy boys who pop out of the Services bursting with theories and keep on doing *The Cherry Orchard*?"

"He's not a bit artsy-craftsy." Bryan decided that the moment demanded a little diplomatic flattery. "He was holding forth about you for ages the other day in J.C.'s office. He said that your talent was clear and true and that you had a particular magic of your own that no other living actress possessed."

"Did J.C. agree with him, or say I was a bitch?"

Bryan, taken aback by the suddenness of the question, stammered for a moment and then said "Both" before he could stop himself. To his relief Lorraine only laughed and offered him another scone.

"J.C. adores me really," she said tranquilly. "He's always telling people I'm a bitch because I won't stand for any of his nonsense. As a matter of fact, in many ways he's quite right. I can be dreadful when I'm driven to it, and he certainly drove me to it when, not content with forcing me to do that dreadful play of Caldwell Rogers', he wished Scott Gurney on to me as a director. Have you ever seen Scott Gurney?"

Bryan shook his head.

"Well." Lorraine gathered herself together. "To begin with, he isn't a director at all. He's a glorified stage manager. He hasn't the faintest idea of timing or grouping or tempo. He used to leave me and the wretched company wandering about the stage and tying our-selves into knots while he sat in the stalls and dictated letters to a stenographer. Finally I couldn't stand it any longer, so I went to Clemmie and said, 'Either he goes, or I do.' Then there was a terrific hullabaloo and I refused to rehearse, and J.C. came and pleaded, and Scott Gurney came and apologized and sent me flowers, and for the sake of the company I agreed to go on with the damn thing, a deci-sion I have never for one instant ceased to regret. It was a moldy script from the word go, and with that red-faced, drunken little butcher in charge of it it hadn't a chance.

"Then J.C., who really ought to have known better, came burst-ing into a rehearsal without so much as a by-your-leave—it was one of those nightmare days when we were working on the set for the first time—and fired Maureen Raleigh on the spot and put in Ella Craven! Without consulting me or even discussing it with me! You can imagine how I felt—there we were, four days off production in complete chaos. I'm not saying that poor Maureen was very good in the part, in fact, she ought never to have been engaged for it in the first place, but what I am saying is that, compared to Ella Craven, she was Rachel and Ellen Terry rolled into one."

Here Lorraine paused to pour herself some more tea. Bryan, who was feeling a trifle dizzy, stumped out his cigarette and shifted his position in the chair. Lorraine waved the teapot inquiringly at him, and he shook his head. "What happened then?" he asked, feel-ing that some sort of comment was expected.

"What happened!" Lorraine put down the teapot with a crash. "What happened was that Miss Craven came flouncing on on the opening night without ever having learnt it properly, threw the whole play out of balance and played the end of the second act like a Lyceum melodrama. All I could do was just stand about and pray for the cur-tain to come down. Afterward, of course, I bearded J.C. in his office and really told him what I thought of him. Then, to cap everything, the critics, who are always incapable of telling the difference between a good part and a good actress, gave her rave notices. I don't think I have ever been so really deeply angry in my life. After all, it wasn't myself I was thinking of—it was the play. That's where I'm such a fool, but I can't help it. I always put the play first. From the moment that woman came on the stage we were sunk; you could feel the whole thing disintegrating. It was heartbreaking. I've never quite forgiven

J.C. for that, although we are outwardly as friendly as we always were. His behavior to me over the whole production killed something in me; do you know what I mean? It isn't that one wants to go nursing grievances. One wants to make up and be friends—and forget. But there are some things one just can't forget. He rang me up, you know, about this Ray Whatever-his-name is. . . ."

"Malcolm," said Bryan.

"He said that in his opinion he was the most exciting new talent that had appeared in the English theater for years."

"He's quite right," said Bryan, "I'm sure he is."

"Anyhow," said Lorraine resignedly, "the die is cast now. It's too late to go back. I've signed the contract."

"I really do want to tell you," said Bryan with sincerity, "how proud and thrilled I am. It will make the whole difference to my play, the fact that you're playing it. I can hardly believe in my good luck."

"Wait and see." Lorraine, who was obviously pleased, smiled indulgently. "I may ruin it for you."

"You'll make it for me," went on Bryan enthusiastically. "You'll be magnificent."

Lorraine leaned forward and looked at him intently for a moment, and when she spoke the whole timbre of her voice changed, and with it her whole personality seemed to change too. Her inconsequential manner dropped away, and it was as though the light in the room had been lowered.

"I want you to promise me something here and now," she said, taking off her dark glasses and fixing him with her lovely gray eyes. "I want you to promise me that from this moment onward you will always be absolutely and completely honest with me. I have a strange feeling that we are really friends even though we first met only half an hour ago. I have the advantage over you, of course, because whereas you have never known me before, I have known you. I have learnt to know you and become fond of you through your lovely, lovely play. . . ."

Bryan made a slight movement to speak, but she silenced him with a gesture.

"Don't say anything for a moment, my dear. Let me finish. I have never been good at saying flattering things or paying extravagant compliments, particularly to anyone whom I respect; on the contrary, it's generally my idiotic honesty that gets me into trouble and makes people hate me. I just cannot and will not lie, and I want to tell you frankly now, at this first step of our adventure together, that this agonizing, twisted, moving play of yours is one of the most beautiful things I have ever read, and I can only swear solemnly that I will do my best to be worthy of it."

She flashed him a brave smile of ineffable sweetness, and he

320

was startled to see her eyes were filled with tears. With a quick, businesslike gesture she drew a green chiffon handkerchief from her waist belt, blew her nose delicately into it and put her dark glasses on again. Bryan, in an agony of embarrassment mixed with gratification, racked his brains to find something simple and appropriate to say, but his mind was blank and so, smiling rather fatuously, he offered her a cigarette, which she refused with a weary shake of the head. He took one himself and lit it, and the silence continued. The clock on the mantelpiece struck five very quickly, as though it were in a hurry, and outside in the mews there was a noise of a car starting up, which elicited an ominous growl from Bothwell. Lorraine, with a change of mood as sudden as a slap in the face, said, "Goddamn it, I forgot to telephone Clemmie! Forgive me a moment, will you?" and, reaching over to the telephone which was on a small table at the end of the sofa, proceeded to dial a number.

Bryan, thankful that the quivering emotional tension had at last been dissipated, relaxed and sat back in his chair. Lorraine at the telephone said in an authoritative tone, "Mr. Clemson, please. This is Miss Barrie." Then, placing her hand over the receiver, she hissed at Bryan, "Be an angel and shut the window, will you? That's the hell of living in a mews; one can't hear oneself think." Bryan, ignoring hostile noises from Bothwell, got up, closed the window and sat down again.

"Clemmie, dear," said Lorraine into the telephone, "I would have called you before, but Bryan Snow is here and I got so carried away talking about the script that I completely forgot what the time was. Yes, darling, of course I do. I do think you might have warned me that he was young and attractive and had a divine sense of humor. . . ." Here she smiled roguishly across at Bryan and threw him a kiss. "I expected someone middle-aged and starchy and difficult, and was fully prepared to tear myself to shreds in order to break down his reserves and make him approve of me. I even made some of my special scones. . . . Yes, of course, he does." She smiled again at Bryan. "You do approve of me, don't you?" Bryan nodded enthusiastically, and she turned to the telephone again. "What news from J.C.'s office? Have they got anyone for Stella yet? What about Marion Blake? In heaven's name, why not? Well, really. . ." She bit her lip angrily, and when she spoke again there was an edge to her voice. "I've never heard such nonsense in my life. She's one of the best actresses we've got. Oh, it was Mr. Ray Malcolm who turned her down, was it? I see. Who does he suggest? What! Carole Wylde! He must be out of his mind. Hold on a minute." She put her hand over the receiver and turned to Bryan. "Your Mr. Thingamejig wants Carole Wylde for Stella."

"Yes," said Bryan uncomfortably, "I know he does."

"Have you ever seen Carole Wylde?"

"Only once, in *Leave Me My Heart*. I thought she was quite good."

"You can't possibly go by that. It was a foolproof part anyway. She couldn't play Stella in a thousand years. She's far too young to begin with, and with that maddening voice she'd drive people out of the theater."

"Oh," murmured Bryan inadequately.

Lorraine returned to the telephone. "Listen, Clemmie, you can tell Mr. Ray Malcolm from me that he'll have to think again. I couldn't possibly play that important scene in the last act with Carole Wylde; she's utterly and completely wrong for it. Yes, dear, I know the critics like her and I also know she won the R.A.D.A. medal, but if she plays Stella it will be over my dead body. The part cries out for Marion Blake. I don't know whether he likes her or not, and anyway I have yet to be convinced that he really knows anything about the theater at all. Yes, all right. Of course, and the sooner the better. The first reading is in two weeks' time, and I must certainly meet him before that. As a matter of fact, I ought to have met him at the very outset, and you can tell J.C. from me that I consider it was very high-handed of him to engage a director that I've never even clapped eyes on in my life. Very well. I'll leave it to you to arrange it within the next two days. Yes, dear. Call me in the morning, I shall be in until lunchtime."

Lorraine hung up the telephone and held out her hand. "I'll have a cigarette now," she said. "Just to calm me down, because really that has put me into the most terrible rage." Bryan handed her a cigarette and lit it for her. She inhaled deeply and gave a bitter little laugh. "It's incredible. Quite incredible!"

"I don't think Ray is all that set on Carole Wylde," he said tentatively. "I'm quite sure that if you talk it over with him he'll see exactly what you mean."

"He ought to know without me telling him that Carole Wylde in that part would throw the whole play out of balance. That's what's worrying me really. I'm in despair. I honestly am."

"Please don't be," said Bryan soothingly. "I am sure it will all be all right."

"All this is quite typical of J.C.," went on Lorraine. "To start with, he's not a true man of the theater at all. He's a real estate agent. I swore that I'd never work for him again and I wish to God I'd never weakened, and if it hadn't been that I fell in love with your play the very first minute I read it, I wouldn't have. He's as obstinate as a mule, and I wouldn't trust him an inch. He's always getting idiotic crazes for 'exciting new talent' as he calls them. Do you remember Yvonne Laurie?"

"No," said Bryan, "I don't think I do."

"Neither does anyone else," said Lorraine. "She was one of J.C.'s finds, one of his 'exciting new talents.' He dragged the poor thing out of the provinces, where she was perfectly happy pottering about in small repertory companies, and gave her the lead in that French play that Edgar Price translated into basic Surbiton. You should have seen her got up as a symbolic prostitute from Marseilles. Exciting new talent indeed! She was so exciting that the play ran three whole nights."

"What happened to her?"

"The Old Vic, of course," said Lorraine witheringly.

"There was once talk of you doing a season with the Old Vic, wasn't there?" asked Bryan unwisely.

Lorraine shuddered.

"There certainly was," she said. "They've been badgering me for years, but I'd rather die. I'm too old and too tired." She sighed and gazed into the fire. "I expect I'm old-fashioned too," she went on. "I've been at the game too long. I learnt the hard way. Now everything's different. Amateurs have taken possession of the theater. Some of them are quite talented, I'm willing to admit, but their talent never really develops; everything is made too easy for them. Take this Mr. Ray Malcolm that you're all so mad about. How long has he been in the theater?"

"I don't know," said Bryan. "I think he ran a small repertory before the War. Then, of course, he was in the Army for five years."

"I've nothing against that," said Lorraine decisively. "Nothing against it at all. He may be a genius for all I know. But this play you've written doesn't need genius. It has that already in the writing. What it does need is a real down-to-earth professional to direct it, a man who has all the technical tricks at his fingertips. God preserve us all from enthusiastic intellectuals like poor Doodie who have theories about acting and talk about rhythm and color. As I said before, I need direction more than any actress living. I'm an absolute fool at rehearsals and so slow that I drive myself mad and everybody else too. In this play of yours I don't have to have the character explained to me. I don't have to be told what she feels and why she does this or that or the other. I knew all that from reading it the first time. I have always, ever since I was tiny, had that particular gift of understanding a part immediately. I have often, in fact, electrified authors by quite obviously knowing a great deal more about the inside workings of their characters than they do themselves. But what I do need all the time is guidance; to be told how to do it. Now, in your honest opinion, do you think Mr. Malcolm can do this?"

"I really don't know," said Bryan, who was becoming a trifle irritated at Ray Malcolm continually being alluded to as his own personal property. "I have never seen anything that he has directed. In fact, I met him for the first time only about ten days ago."

"Then we're both more or less in the same boat!" cried Lorraine triumphantly. "We can be allies against a common foe!"

"I don't see why he should necessarily be regarded as an enemy," said Bryan.

Lorraine laughed charmingly. "That was only a joke," she said. "Actually I can't wait to meet him. And when I do I shall probably be completely bowled over by his charm, obey him slavishly and follow him about like a lap dog!"

Bryan took the plunge that he had been contemplating in his mind for the last ten minutes. "Will you come and dine with me tomorrow night or the night after, and I'll ask Ray, and you can get to know each other sort of officially?"

"I should simply adore to," said Lorraine. "But I can't either tomorrow or Thursday. What about Friday?"

Bryan, who had arranged to go away for the weekend on Friday afternoon, hesitated for the fraction of a second and then, realizing how important it was to his play that Ray Malcolm and Lorraine Barrie should meet in the most amicable circumstances possible, rose to his feet and said, "Friday will be perfect providing that I can get hold of him. May I telephone you in the morning?"

"Done," said Lorraine, holding out her hand boyishly. "I shall leave it all to you. Would you like a cocktail before you go?"

"No, thanks." Bryan shook his head. "I'm late as it is." He paused. "I can't tell you how excited I am. And how grateful too."

Lorraine snatched up the script from the sofa and held it up solemnly. "This is our talisman," she cried. "The token of our lovely new friendship."

The enchanting quality of her voice when she said these words was still echoing in Bryan's ears as he walked up the mews in search of a taxi.

3

Bryan, in a state of irritable nervousness, arrived at the Vert Galant a full half-hour early. He had been to a film at the Empire which he had had to leave before the end. He had chosen the Vert Galant after careful consideration. It was quieter than the Savoy Grill, less vibrantly theatrical than the Ivy and not quite so crowded as the Caprice. Upon arrival he verified the corner table he had reserved by telephone two days before, and sat down to wait in the bar. Having ordered himself a dry Martini, he lit a cigarette and contemplated, with rising agitation, the ordeal before him.

Ray Malcolm had shown signs of petulance when he had called

him up to invite him. First he said he couldn't possibly manage it as he was going to an opening night with Martha Field and couldn't ditch her. Then he said that supper parties in public restaurants were always dangerous for first meetings on account of there being too many distractions and too much noise, and that he would rather his initial encounter with Lorraine Barrie took place in some peaceful office somewhere, preferably in the morning, when they could meet on a professional rather than a social basis, get down to brass tacks and discuss the play seriously.

Finally, after a good deal of coaxing and argument, he had given in, agreed to shake himself free from Martha Field and promised to be at the Vert Galant not one minute later than ten-thirty. Lorraine, on the other hand, had put no difficulties in the way. She had agreed enthusiastically to the Vert Galant on the grounds that it had always been for her the luckiest restaurant in London, even going so far as to ascribe to Bryan a certain clairvoyant tact in choosing it. She might, she had added, be the tiniest bit late, and so they had better start eating at once and she would have whatever they were having when she arrived.

In due course Ray appeared in an immaculate dinner jacket, flashed Bryan an affectionate smile and ordered himself a double whiskey and soda.

"It was all right about poor Martha," he said. "She was going to a managerial party at the Savoy, so it was all quite painless. What's happened to our glamorous star?"

"She said she might be a little late and that we were to start without her."

"Nonsense," said Ray. "We will sit here and sozzle ourselves into a nice coma so that when she does arrive we shall be past caring. Tell me about your baptismal tea with her. You weren't very communicative on the telephone. Did you fall madly in love with her? Did she fascinate you within an inch of your life, or did you find her tiresome, affected and utterly repellent?"

"She was much nicer than I thought she'd be," replied Bryan with care.

"Oh, God!" said Ray. "Simple, dreamy and unspoiled by her great success, I suppose?"

"Yes." Bryan gave a conspiratorial giggle. "But you're going to have your work cut out if you want Carole Wylde to play Stella. She hates her. She wants Marion Blake."

"All dynamic leading ladies like having Marion Blake in the cast," said Ray equably. "She is dull, competent and offers no competition. Also, she's far too old for Stella."

"Lorraine Barrie thinks that Carole Wylde is too young."

"We'll cross that old-world bridge when we come to it," said

325

Ray. "No one is actually engaged yet anyway. I am feeling benign to-night. I have seen quite a good play, reasonably well acted. I am about, I trust, to eat a very good dinner, God's in His Heaven, and all's right with the world. Let's have another drink!"

The next three-quarters of an hour passed happily for Bryan. The nervousness that had beset him earlier in the evening evaporated and he became aware of a warm glow not entirely engendered by alcohol, although he had two more double Martinis and Ray two more double whiskeys and sodas. The warmth, the sense of ease and well-being, were caused principally by the knowledge of growing intimacy. There was a sweet friendliness in the air, an aura of mutual discovery, which, whether Ray was equally aware of it or not, gave a special enchantment to the occasion. One of the most glittering facets of Ray's personality was his capacity for concentrating the full force of his intelligence and vitality upon the person he was talking to. He questioned Bryan penetratingly, sometimes quizzically, but always kindly about his hopes and ambitions, his war experiences and his life in the prison camp; he commiserated with him on the commercial failure of *The Unconquered,* implying with flattering sincerity that it had been far above the heads of the present-day public. He even remembered and described certain emotional scenes in the play, holding them up to the light and scrutinizing them and then handing them back to Bryan embellished and made more important by his expert analysis of them. His hands were slim and flexible, and he used them graphically to illustrate his comments. Bryan, who had never really enjoyed being on the stage during his brief prewar apprentice-ship in repertory, found himself longing to be an actor again, if only for the chance of being directed by Ray Malcolm. For one moment he actually toyed with the idea of suggesting himself for the small part of Maurice in the second act of *Sorrow in Sunlight,* but discarded it on the reflection that not only would it be a waste of time, but that he was entirely the wrong type for it.

Ray, at the beginning of his third whiskey and soda, began to outline wittily and vividly his own early experience in the theater. He recounted incidents and disappointments and jokes against himself so lightly and so gaily that Bryan was entranced. How enviable, how truly remarkable, to be able so cheerfully to rise above heart-break and despair and turn every defeat into victory by sheer force of character and sense of humor. Ray was in the middle of describing the first rehearsals of the first big success he had ever had and Bryan, enthralled, was hanging on to every word, when Lorraine Barrie arrived wearing a mink coat over a black evening dress and a spray of white gardenias.

"Never," she announced dramatically, "until the grave closes over me will I go to a first night again. The strain is too much. I am utterly worn out!"

Ray and Bryan sprang to their feet, helped her off with her mink coat and installed her between them on the banquette. Bryan stumblingly attempted introductions, but it was quite unnecessary. Lorraine seized both Ray's hands in hers, looked deeply into his eyes and said, "At last I meet the one man I've really wanted to meet for years!"

For the next hour and a half Bryan was a comparatively silent spectator of two remarkable performances. Perhaps if he had had a little less to drink he might have been more cynically appreciative of the subtleties and overtones of the acting, more genuinely amused at this superficially suave but fundamentally ruthless conflict between two violent egos, each one inexorably resolved to charm, conquer and dominate the other. Even as it was, he was fascinated most of the time, although he found his mind wandering occasionally. Both Lorraine and Ray talked incessantly; the rather expensive dinner that Bryan had ordered with such care was served and devoured automatically and without comment. He reflected with a slight tinge of bitterness, as he watched smoked salmon, crème vichyssoise, filet mignon and pineapple salad vanish down their gullets, that he might just as well have ordered shepherd's pie and stewed prunes for all the attention they were paying to it. Also at the back of his mind he was aware from time to time of a little stab of sadness, of undefined disappointment. In other less hectic circumstances he might have recognized this for what it was—nothing more nor less than jealousy; not profound, not the tearing agony of outraged love, but a dim, dreary sense of disillusion.

Ray, before the arrival of Lorraine, had been so true and clear and understanding. There had been a sincerity underlying his words and a certain tenderness in his voice even when he was joking and laughing at himself. There was no tenderness in his voice now. It was brittle and sharp and supremely conscious of its effects. Lorraine was radiant. Her conversation, devoted to the theater in general and herself in particular, was gay, ironic and devoid of the slightest trace of the imperious grandeur usually attributable to a great star. On the contrary, she was occasionally overrealistic; stripping even from her acknowledged successes the trappings of glamour, and showing them up mercilessly in their true light as just jobs of work well done. Admittedly, most of the poignant little anecdotes she recounted ended with the balance of credit heavily weighted on the side of her own extraordinary perception and strength of character, but the possible monotony of gallant virtue invariably being its own reward was largely mitigated by her lightness of touch and calculated flashes of humor. Whether or not Ray was as enchanted by her as he appeared to be, Bryan was unable to decide. Even later, when they had dropped Lorraine at the corner of her mews and were sitting in Ray's flat having a final drink, he was not sure. Ray's comments on the

327

evening were amiable but sardonic; his mood of amused cynicism seemed genuine enough, but it might well be assumed in order to deceive either Bryan or himself.

Bryan ultimately left him, and walked home to Ebury Street in a haze of indecision. The evening had undoubtedly been of value; he had brought his director and his leading lady, the two most important protagonists of his brain child, successfully together. The future of his play lay in their hands. By rights, he reflected, he should be feeling elated and triumphant; this, after all, was the chance he had dreamed of—a West End production under the best possible auspices: "J. C. Roebuck presents Lorraine Barrie in *Sorrow in Sunlight* by Bryan Snow. Directed by Ray Malcolm." But as he let himself in with his latchkey and walked up the dark stairs to his bed-sitting room he was aware of no elation at all—nothing but utter weariness and a slight headache.

4

The first reading of *Sorrow in Sunlight* took place on the stage of the Caravel Theatre at ten-thirty in the morning. Bryan arrived at ten twenty-five and was immediately conscious of the atmosphere of subdued tension that usually characterizes such occasions. Various members of the cast were standing about chatting in low tones; one man, whom he was unable to identify, was sitting on an upturned rostrum reading the *Daily Telegraph*. The current attraction at the Caravel was a whimsical comedy in verse called *The Last Troubadour*, which, having hovered for some months between success and failure, was now within two weeks of closing. The action of this play took place in the banqueting hall of a medieval castle, a setting designed by Robin Birkett which had received enthusiastic notices from the press but had failed to compensate for the roguish dullness of the play. It was a built set and therefore immovable, and any company wishing to use the theater for rehearsals on non-matinee days were forced to rehearse in it or not at all.

The safety curtain was down, and in front of it was a table around which were placed a dozen chairs in a semicircle. At a smaller table sat a harassed young man with unruly hair, dark green corduroy trousers and horn-rimmed glasses. On the table in front of him was a pile of typewritten "parts" bound in dull pink paper which he was sorting feverishly. A working light hung from the flies, betraying with its harsh effulgence the pseudo-Gothic glories of poor Robin Birkett's decor. A large armchair upholstered in faded chintz, obviously a tribute to Lorraine Barrie's position as a star, was placed prominently in front of a huge open fireplace in which a papiermâché ox was wobbling uneasily on a spit.

Bryan's arrival coincided with that of Gerald Wentworth, a florid, handsome man of about forty-five. The harassed young man at the prompt table sprang up and greeted him respectfully, and a lady with a curious green bird in her hat gave a little squeal and flung her arms round his neck. No one paid any attention to Bryan, so he sat down on a vacant chair, lit a cigarette and read with frowning concentration a bill from the Electrical Supply Company which he happened to find in his pocket.

Presently Ray Malcolm strode onto the stage, and immediately the atmosphere became so intensified that Bryan would not have been surprised if the stage manager had handed everyone oxygen masks. Ray was followed purposefully by a short, thick-set young man in a camel's-hair coat whom he introduced to Bryan as his assistant, Tony Orford.

"My dear," said Tony Orford, as they shook hands, "Ray has talked about you so much that I've been positively counting the moments. This must be a great day for you; are you in a terrible tizz?"

Bryan, disliking him on sight, shook his head with what he hoped was bland assurance, and before he had time to explain that, far from being in a "tizz," he was as cool as a cucumber, they were interrupted by another shrill squeal, and the lady with the green bird in her hat kissed Tony Orford effusively and then turned to Bryan.

"I saw you sitting there and I wasn't sure," she said, "but now I know, and if nobody is going to introduce us I shall introduce myself. My name is Marion Blake, and I've read your play, and to my mind it's got everything—but everything. I don't believe I've been so excited over a script since I first read *Love Child*, and God knows I was right about that—"

"*Love Child*," interposed Tony, "was my *un*favorite play of all time."

"Be that as it may," cried Marion Blake, "it ran two solid years, and we never dropped, even during the election!" She turned to Bryan. "Isn't he horrid? He's always like that. So damping!"

Further revelations of Tony's character were cut short by Ray rapping a pencil on the table and announcing in a voice only faintly tinged with irritation that they would start without Miss Barrie as she was not in the first scene anyhow. There was a general movement toward the chairs; the stage manager distributed the parts; Ray motioned to Bryan to come and sit next to him at the table. Bryan, with a thrill of pride, sat down. There was a brief argument between Gerald Wentworth and Ray as to whether he should read from his script or from the "part." In course of this Ray hurriedly introduced him to Bryan, who rose to his feet and sat down again. Finally it was decided that Wentworth should read from the script. He took a chair exactly facing the table and put on his glasses. A hush descended, Ray cleared his throat and proceeded to read a preliminary description of the set. He read swiftly and concisely; the authority in his voice was unmistakable. From outside in the street came the muted noises of traffic; the company sat expectantly, waiting for their moments to begin. The unidentified man sitting on the upturned rostrum continued to read the *Daily Telegraph*. Suddenly there was the sound of barking in the passage leading to the stage; the swing door with "Silence" painted on it in large white letters burst open, and Bothwell appeared on a leash dragging Lorraine Barrie after him. She was simply dressed in a neat blue tailor-made suit and a black hat; a fur cape hung from her shoulders, and she was hugging to herself three parcels, a big scarlet handbag, a rolled umbrella and the script.

"This," she cried gaily as she approached the table, "is quite definitely the worst entrance I've ever made. I know I'm late and I'm bitterly, bitterly ashamed. Please, please will you all forgive me?"

She looked appealingly at Ray and then smiled at the company. Gerald Wentworth rose, kissed her solemnly and sat down again. Marion Blake, emitting shrill noises, hugged her emotionally as though she had just been rescued from a foundering liner; Bothwell snarled and yapped until Lorraine struck him with her umbrella.

"Listen, angel pie," she said grimly. "Mother only brought you to rehearsal because she was sorry for you being left all alone and you have been making a maddening beast of yourself ever since we left the house. Here, Harry!"—she beckoned to the stage manager—"take him to the property room and tie him up to something really heavy." She glanced round the set. "With any luck you might find a script of this play!" There was an obsequious titter from the company. She handed Bothwell's lead to Harry, who reluctantly took it and dragged Bothwell off the stage. Lorraine deposited her parcels on the table in front of Ray and smiled radiantly at him.

"You'll have to forgive me for all this. You really will," she said. "Because I *know* my first act! Not quite all of it, but I can do up to Stella's exit without the book!"

"It's all right," said Ray pleasantly. "We were only just starting the first scene."

Lorraine leaned across the table and patted Bryan's hand. "Good morning, dear author," she said affectionately, "this is all wildly exciting, isn't it?" Bryan gave a nervous smile of agreement. Lorraine gathered up her parcels and sat down on a small hard chair at the side.

"The armchair is for you," said Ray courteously. "Harry routed it out from somewhere or other specially."

Lorraine shook her head firmly.

"I couldn't, darling, I really couldn't. Once I sank into that I should go into a deep, deep sleep. Laura must have it." She beckoned to Laura Witby, a tired-looking character actress who was playing the maid. "Take this chair, Laura dear. I absolutely insist."

Laura Witby looked anxiously at Ray and mumbled something about being perfectly comfortable where she was. However, her timid protests were overruled by Lorraine who, after embracing her affectionately and knocking her hat over her eye, led her firmly to the armchair and forced her down into it. Lorraine, thus having established at the outset that she was brimming with democratic goodfellowship, returned to her wooden chair, deposited her umbrella and bag on the floor beside her and opened her script. The reading of the play began. In course of it Ray made occasional comments, corrected an intonation here and there and scribbled notes on a pad that lay on the table in front of him. Bryan, smoking incessantly, watched the pile of cigarette ends growing in a tin ashtray and tried vainly to resist a mounting feeling of disappointment.

Lorraine, far from proving her boast that she knew the first act up to Stella's exit, kept her eyes glued to the script and read stumblingly, without expression; at moments her voice was so low that Bryan could not hear what she was saying. Gerald Wentworth lost his place several times and muttered, "Sorry, that's me." Marion Blake read swiftly and brightly, so brightly indeed that Ray winced several times quite openly.

At the end of the reading Ray gave a little talk to the company. What he said was highly technical and was concerned mainly with the tempo at which certain scenes should be played. He concentrated his attention for a moment or two on Marion Blake, explaining firmly that, although her reading had been clear and competent, she had obviously not quite grasped the psychological significance of Stella's character. Lorraine at one point made an attempt to interrupt, but he quelled her with a courteous smile, and she tapped her lips chidingly with her right forefinger and relapsed into silence, passing off this minor defeat by rummaging in her bag for her compact.

Bryan, Lorraine, Ray and Tony Orford lunched together at the Ivy. Marion Blake was sitting alone at a table nearby and blew them kisses repeatedly. At two-thirty they were back in the theatre. There was no longer a semicircle of chairs, for Harry, the stage manager, had arranged them in various formations according to the ground plan of the first act. Bothwell, who had behaved surprisingly well during the reading and barked only twice at lunch, was again consigned to the property room. The first rehearsal began.

To a layman, unless he happens to be abnormally interested in the theater, the preliminary rehearsals of a new play are dull in the extreme. Most of the proceedings are conducted in undertones; the actors wander about, reading from parts and making occasional vague gestures to indicate that they are closing a door or opening a window. Each time a new movement is set for them by the director they stop dead and borrow pencils from each other with which they scribble hieroglyphics on their scripts. There is a staleness in the air, an atmosphere of insecurity, slowness and frustration. To the actors themselves, of course, none of this applies. For them it is a period of great nervous activity. Not only are they concentrated on trying to remember the words in relation to the movements, but their minds are seething with secret plans and projects for effective little bits of "business" they intend to do when they get their books out of their hands. Many of them are also beset with nightmare worries about billing, clothes, dressing rooms and ultimate press notices. In addition, they are all, as a general rule, a prey to agonizing nerves. This malaise takes various forms, and years of experience are likely to increase rather than assuage it. In some it expresses itself by over-emphasis; a sharp, bright, too quick-on-the-trigger efficiency; in others by a hesitant, constricted self-consciousness. It is one of the primary duties of a good director to recognize these temperamental and psychological symptoms early and make reasonable allowances for them.

Bryan sat with Tony Orford at the side of the stage and watched intently. Ray did nothing beyond indicating an occasional movement and saying from time to time such phrases as, "Go back to your entrance," or, "Try it again from where you move down to the window." He sat hunched up in a chair against the safety curtain with his overcoat slung from his shoulders and his hat tilted over his eyes. Tony Orford hissed comments into Bryan's ear every now and then, but Bryan discouraged him by leaning forward still more intently. He had disliked Tony on sight, and up to date had found no cause to revise his opinion. Admittedly, he had been a help at lunch, having talked a lot in rather a bitchy strain and lightened the distracted gloom which usually prevails after a first reading. Ray had introduced him as his assistant, but Bryan was still confused as to the exact scope of his activities. It could not possibly be of any great assistance to Ray that Orford should sit at the side of the stage, whispering irrelevant and occasionally scurrilous gossip into the author's left ear.

Lorraine walked through the rehearsal with lamblike docility. On the few occasions that Ray made a suggestion to her she merely nodded thoughtfully, scribbled something in her script and went back a few lines in order to set what he had said securely in her memory.

At five o'clock the rehearsal came to an end, and the company dispersed. Bothwell was retrieved from the property room and flew onto the stage, barking wildly. When his first emotional transports had calmed down a little, Lorraine produced a biscuit from her bag which she made him sit up and beg for. Presently Ray, without even a look in the direction of Bryan and Tony, went off with Lorraine and Bothwell, and the door marked "Silence" closed behind them.

"I thought as much," said Tony laconically. "He's going to start work on her."

"How do you mean?" asked Bryan.

Tony began to struggle into his coat, Bryan helping him find the sleeve.

"He will drive her back to her house, dog and all," said Tony. "Once there, happily ensconced with a whiskey and soda and in a general atmosphere of peace and goodwill, he will proceed to tear the liver and lights out of her."

Bryan was genuinely startled. "But why? Do you think he didn't like the way she read? After all, it was only a first run-through."

"Come and have a drink," said Tony. "And I'll tell you the facts of life with Father. To begin with," he went on, as they walked up the stairs and out of the stage door, "he will explain to her sweetly but firmly that her whole approach to the character is wrong. He will then list accurately every mannerism and trick she has ever used, and tell her to throw all she has ever learned into the alley. When he has successfully asserted his dominance over her and reduced her either to maudlin tears or screaming hysterics, he will inform her with almost clairvoyant intensity that she is a great, great actress with more talent in that well-known little finger than Duse had in her whole frail body. After which he will kiss her affectionately and bugger off. The results," he added, "will be discernible on a clear day at the beginning of the second week of rehearsals."

5

The first week of rehearsals passed without incident. Lorraine continued to be docile, and accepted Ray's direction with businesslike submissiveness. The young man whom Bryan had failed to identify at the first reading continued to sit on the rostrum with the *Daily Telegraph*, discarding it only every now and then when called upon to make his one brief appearance as the chauffeur at the beginning of Act Three. Bryan was fascinated by his almost insolent lack of interest in the proceedings. Marion Blake continued to play her part with stubborn archness and, to Bryan's surprise, Ray allowed her to do so without protest.

On the Thursday afternoon Ray was absent, and Tony Orford

took a word rehearsal. Once more the chairs were arranged in a semi-circle and the cast, in an atmosphere of controlled irritation, were forced to go through the entire first act three times without their books. Bryan, with grudging admiration, had to admit that Tony conducted the whole business with patience and firmness. Gerald Wentworth wasted a good deal of time and energy by striking himself violently on the forehead every time he forgot a line and insisting that he had known it backward the night before, and Laura Witby created a diversion by having a nosebleed, upon which the stage manager produced a key, which he dropped discreetly down her back, and led her to the property room, where she lay on the floor. Apart from this, the afternoon was dull in the extreme.

That evening Bryan dined by himself at an oyster bar in Gerrard Street and went to a movie at the Plaza. He was feeling low in spirit, and the movie, a historical romance in blinding Technicolor, did little to alleviate his gloom. It was raining when he came out, and he had to wait in the covered entrance to the cinema for over ten minutes while the commissionaire darted backward and forward between the road and the curb blowing a whistle for a taxi. Finally one appeared, and Bryan, having given the commissionaire half a crown because he hadn't anything smaller, huddled himself into the corner of the cab and tried, as it rattled through the sodden streets, to analyze the feeling of deflated melancholy which had been gradually mounting during the last few days and now threatened to overwhelm him entirely. By rights, he reflected angrily, he should be supremely happy. His career as a playwright had taken a pronounced upward curve. Everything was going well, rehearsals were smooth and orderly, there had been, to date, no turbulent moments, no nerve-shattering scenes, none of those sudden preproduction crises which he had been led to believe were fairly inevitable in the putting on of a new play. True, there were still two and a half weeks to go before the actual opening; there was still time and to spare for the battles and tears and anguish, but, even so, this sense of vague disappointment, almost of boredom, was surely unusual. There must be, lurking in the back of his consciousness, some cause for it, some acknowledged reason why, instead of eagerness, pride and pleasurable anticipation, there was nothing in his heart but listlessness and an undefined sense of unhappiness.

Having paid the taxi and let himself into his bed-sitting room, he undressed quickly, mixed himself a strong gin and tonic and got into bed. While he sipped his drink he surveyed the room thoughtfully and decided that, whether *Sorrow in Sunlight* was a success or not, he would at least get enough money out of it to be able to afford a flat. The bed-sitting room was all right as bed-sitting rooms go, but it was small and dingy and congested with his personal possessions, none of which seemed to take kindly to it. His framed reproduction of "The Bridge at Arles" by Van Gogh looked out of place against the flowered wallpaper. His writing desk was piled untidily with books and papers and was dominated by two large leather frames containing photographs of his mother and sister respectively. His mother was sitting on a garden seat wearing a pained expression and holding a Cairn terrier, which had moved while the picture was being taken and consequently looked like a muff. His sister Margaret, a pretty girl of twenty-five, was posed on a staircase in her wedding dress. Her expression was noncommittal.

On the mantelpiece, together with two empty glass vases and a clock which remained monotonously at eleven-twenty, was an enlarged snapshot, framed in passe partout, of a good-looking young man holding a large fish in his right hand and pointing to it triumphantly with his left. This was Bryan's closest friend, Stuart Raikes, who had gone to Barbados after the War to grow bananas and wrote rather dull letters every month or so. Bryan missed him very much. The rest of the room was impersonal as such rooms usually are. Two of the rings were missing from the blue curtains, which made them sag unattractively, and the window rattled.

Having finished his drink and smoked two cigarettes, Bryan was about to switch out the light when the telephone rang downstairs. He lifted the receiver of the extension by his bed in the forlorn hope that the call might be for him and was startled to hear Ray Malcolm's voice. In the split second before he replied, his imagination envisaged a lightning series of disasters. Lorraine Barrie had been run over on her way home from rehearsal; J. C. Roebuck had decided that the play was no good after all and had canceled the production; Ray himself had been offered a monumental movie contract and was flying to Hollywood the next day. He murmured "Hello" in a strangled voice which sounded as though he had been crying.

"Thank God," said Ray fervently. "I was afraid that you would be out gallivanting with your fine friends, and I want to talk to you. Are you alone?

"Quite alone," replied Bryan, wondering blankly who Ray imagined was sharing his bed with him.

"It's the end of the play," said Ray. "Lorraine isn't happy about it, and I must say I'm not either." Bryan's heart sank even lower than it was already.

"What's the matter with it?" he asked, trying to keep his voice free from agitation.

"Well," said Ray, "to begin with it's too like *The Green Hat.* I never realized it until Lorraine pointed it out to me."

"I've never read *The Green Hat*," said Bryan defensively.

"It doesn't matter whether you've read it or not," said Ray with

335

genial firmness. "Your suffering heroine decides to 'end it all' in a big way by flinging herself into a speedboat and ramming a lighthouse at fifty miles an hour. Iris March, the suffering heroine of *The Green Hat*, decided to 'end it all' in a big way too, only she chose a Hispano and an oak tree which she called, with whimsical sophistication, Harrods. At least you haven't called your lighthouse, 'Pontings.'" Bryan heard Ray chuckling to himself at this little sally, and said with undisguised irritation, "I don't quite see what I can do about it. It's a little late to start making major alterations now. She's got to commit suicide somehow, hasn't she? It's the climax of the whole play!"

"Of course she has," said Ray gently. "For heaven's sake, don't get upset about it. I've got a lot of ideas which I can't possibly go into on the telephone. All I want you to do is to think about it quietly before I say anything more, then I should like you to come down to the country with me tomorrow afternoon after rehearsal, and we'll have a peaceful weekend hashing it all over. It's only an hour and a half's drive, and we'll have all the time in the world. How's that?"

Bryan, aware of a sudden quite irrational lifting of his spirits, said, "That will be fine. I'd love it."

"Good," said Ray. "Small suitcase, no dinner clothes, just ourselves. Until tomorrow—good night, sweet prince."

Bryan heard the click as Ray hung up the receiver.

Ray Malcolm's cottage was in Kent, halfway between Maidstone and Ashford. The bedrooms had sloping ceilings, exposed oak beams and small, low windows. There was a minute bathroom with a lavatory adjoining it, distempered in shrimp pink, which commanded a superb view of the weald of Kent and, as an added attraction for the contemplative guest, contained a series of eighteenth-century playbills framed in bright green. Downstairs two small rooms had been knocked into one to make a dining room, and outside, a few yards away, was the living room which had once been a stable. This was enormous, with a wide open fireplace built in at the end of it. The whitewashed walls were alive with theatrical implications: highly colored engravings of dead-and-gone actors picked out with tinsel; large Victorian prints of crowded opera houses and a whole series of Robin Birkett's original designs for *'Tis Pity She's a Whore*, the production of which a few years earlier had established Ray in the modern theater.

Ray and Bryan arrived at about seven-thirty and were received, to Bryan's surprise and dismay, by Tony Orford, who had come down by train during the afternoon. He was wearing a Canadian lumberjack's shirt, maroon trousers and sandals.

"Mrs. Hartley," he said as he greeted them, "is in a terrible tizz on account of the joint not having come for tomorrow's lunch. She also went off into a Mrs. Siddons tirade about Colonel Spencer's red setter."

"What's it done now?" asked Ray irritably.

"Killed three chickens," replied Tony. "It is now sitting under a tree in Colonel Spencer's garden with one of the corpses tied round its neck, the idea being that twenty-four hours' worth of decomposing fowl will teach it that Crime Does Not Pay. My personal guess is that the higher it gets the more the dog will adore it. Like Stilton."

Later, after Bryan had been taken to his room and shown where to wash, they all three sat round the fire in the living room drinking whiskeys and sodas and waiting for dinner to be announced. The daylight faded, and the windows became blue in the dusk. Tony and Ray got into an argument about a review in *The New Statesman* of a recent play, Tony maintaining that the critic was a Bloomsbury highbrow whose knowledge of the theater began and ended with *Murder in the Cathedral*, and Ray insisting that, whether the play in question was good, bad or indifferent, the critic had a perfect right to state his opinion of it.

Bryan lay back in his armchair and closed his eyes; the country air, the pungent smell of wood smoke in the room and the warming effect of the whiskey, were beginning to make him drowsy. His initial annoyance on discovering that Tony was in the house gave place to a feeling of benign resignation. After all, he wasn't bad and had certainly gone out of his way to be friendly ever since they had met at the first reading; he was quite attractive, too, if you were prepared to bridge the bewildering gulf between his appearance and his conversation.

Bryan regarded him critically through half-closed eyes: the bright checked lumber jacket enhanced his general stockiness, making him look as though he had just climbed off a tractor and sluiced himself down under a pump in the yard; his curly hair, which was rather too long, glinted in the firelight. It was his voice that was the trouble, Bryan decided; it was too light and high-pitched, and his choice of phrase and manner of speaking were too startlingly at variance with his looks. His sense of humor was quick and destructive and essentially of the theater. He described, with affectionate, contemptuous gusto, the carryings-on of famous stars and elderly character actresses. He seemed to have little interest in the younger ones. He was now recounting gleefully some fresh details of a famous feud between Dame Laura Cavendish and Miss Lavinia Kirk, who had apparently loathed each other since they had appeared together with the late Sir Herbert Tree in the palmy days of His Majesty's; his voice and his laugh pierced Bryan's sleepiness like a stiletto.

"Darling Laura arrived late, of course, and there was Lavinia literally on the Queen's lap, my dear, nattering away as if they had

337

known each other for years! Laura gave one look, turned bright green and would have dropped dead if she hadn't remembered she had a matinee the next day. Then with a supreme effort she pulled herself together and became ze life and death of ze party, but it wasn't until after the Royalties had left that she really pounced. She churned up to Lavinia like an old Thames steamboat with her paddles thrashing the water into a frenzy. 'Lavvy, dear'"—here Tony imitated Dame Laura's voice—"'How lovely for you to have had the Queen to yourself for such a long time. I thought she looked dreadfully tired, didn't you?'" Tony's rendering of this, with an emphasis on the words, "Lovely," "long" and "dreadfully," was so cruelly accurate that Ray laughed immoderately and was about to help himself to another whiskey and soda when Mrs. Hartley, a fat woman with a scarlet face, flung open the door and announced breathlessly that dinner was served.

After dinner they returned to the living room, and Bryan steeled himself against the dreaded discussion of his play which he felt was now imminent. He had lain awake most of the night after Ray's telephone call, vainly endeavoring to figure out an effective way for his heroine to dispose of herself. She could not jump under the Blue Train, because of Anna Karenina; nor could she shoot herself offstage, because of Paula Tanqueray; an overdose of sleeping tablets would be too slow and would necessitate reconstructing the whole last act and inserting a time lapse of several hours. A sudden heart attack of course was always possible, if a trifle farfetched, and there would have to be a lot of rewriting of the earlier part of the play to explain her cardiac condition. There were no ramparts from which she could fling herself, like Floria Tosca, and no Samurai sword on which to impale herself like Madame Butterfly. Tuberculosis was obviously out of the question, quite apart from it being reminiscent of La Dame aux Camellias and La Bohème because, modern therapy being what it is, the whole last act would have to be transferred to a sanatorium in Switzerland. Bryan, in the still silence of the night, had worked himself into a furious rage against Lorraine Barrie. She had obviously argued Ray into agreeing with her. It was also obvious that the whole situation had been brought about merely for her to assert her idiotic ego. He had fallen asleep just before dawn and awakened at ten o'clock, calmer but devoid of any constructive ideas whatsoever. Ray had said that he had some ideas of his own, and so the only wise course was to wait and see what they were, and then, without stubbornness or prejudice, try to do the best he could with them.

Ray settled himself comfortably on the sofa and regarded Bryan benevolently.

"Now then," he said. "Coats off. Shoulders to the wheel. Cards on the table."

"Wigs on the green," murmured Tony with a giggle.

"Shut up," said Ray. "This is business, and we've got to concentrate."

A long while later Bryan, utterly dazed and with a blinding headache, undressed in a trance and fell into bed. He had drunk six whiskeys and sodas, smoked countless cigarettes and listened to his play being twisted, changed and entirely reconstructed no less than three times, each version being completely different from the others. Ray's demonic vitality was inexhaustible, and Bryan had received the full brunt of it for five hours, Tony having long since retired to bed.

Now, with throbbing head and jittery nerves, he lay staring at a patch of moonlight on the ceiling, regretting bitterly that he had ever thought of writing a play in the first place, and trying to sort out in his mind at least some of the drastic alterations that Ray had suggested. Finally, he gave it up as hopeless. A church clock struck three somewhere in the distance. His brain was too tired and confused to be capable of coherent thought. After stumbling along the dark passage to the bathroom for a glass of water, he swallowed three aspirins, clambered back into bed and went miserably to sleep.

The next morning at eleven o'clock Tony came into his room with a breakfast tray, which he deposited on the bedside table. He was wearing a peacock-blue and scarlet sarong, and the upper part of his body was naked. Bryan, who had been dozing uneasily, was startled into full wakefulness.

"It's all right, dear," said Tony cheerfully, "it's only me and not Dorothy Lamour as you thought. My sister sends me these things from Malaya. They're wonderful to sleep in, and you can kick your legs about all night long if you feel like it without them riding up and strangling you. How did you sleep?"

Bryan hoisted himself up on his pillow and blinked. "I don't quite know yet," he said huskily.

"I brought you some breakfast myself because I thought that the sight of Mrs. Hartley in the cold light of remorseless dawn might be too much for you."

"Thanks very much," said Bryan. "I think I'd better brush my teeth."

"But *do*," said Tony. "I'll wait here and nurse you back to health and strength."

Bryan groped for his slippers with his bare feet and stumbled off to the bathroom. When he came back, Tony was sitting on the end of the bed smoking a cigarette.

"If this cigarette sends you off into a frenzy of vomiting I'll put it out," he said obligingly. "You'd better get back into bed, and I'll put the tray on your knees."

"Thanks very much," said Bryan. "I've got a slight hangover." He kicked off his slippers and got back into bed obediently.

339

"I rather thought you might have," said Tony. "I gave one look at the Maestro stretched out like a fish on a slab, and put two and two brightly together. He's just coming to now. I suppose you sat up till all hours?"

"Yes," said Bryan with a wan smile. "I'm afraid we did."

'I knew he was working up for one of his big virtuoso performances." Tony arranged the tray on Bryan's knees, and proceeded to pour out the tea. "And so I went to bed. I suppose he rewrote your entire script for you, played out every scene and tore himself to shreds?"

"I was the one who was torn to shreds," said Bryan bitterly.

"You poor dear!" Tony looked at him with genuine anxiety. "He didn't really upset you, did he?"

Bryan, valiantly resisting an impulse to burst into tears of self-pity, mumbled, almost inaudibly, "I'm afraid he did rather!"

"Drink some tea," said Tony with practical sympathy. "Have a stab at that sensational brown egg and relax. Meanwhile Mother will give you a little kindly advice based on long experience."

Bryan sipped some tea and, with an effort, attacked the brown egg with a spoon. Tony lit another cigarette, retired to the end of the bed again, hunched up his knees and looked at Bryan thoughtfully.

"To begin with," he said, "there is no need for you to be upset at all. You've written a very good play, and J. C. Roebuck wouldn't have considered doing it for a moment unless he thought it had an excellent chance of success. What you've got to get into your poor fuddled head is that Ray, although he has genius as a director, is a frustrated actor. He would also give his eyeteeth to write one page of creative dialogue, but he can't—and, what's more, he knows he can't because writing is a gift. Either you have it, or you haven't!

"What happened to you last night has happened to every author of every play Ray's ever done. He gets carried away by his own virtuosity; his imagination, which is fantastic, works overtime, and, before you know where you are, you have fifteen plots instead of one, an entirely new set of characters and the whole thing looks like a dog's dinner." Tony paused and patted Bryan's foot affectionately.

"I don't want you to think I'm being disloyal to Ray," he went on gently. "I adore him and admire him more than anybody in the world, but I've been with him too long not to know his little failings, and his principal one is that his own violent energy makes it impossible to let well alone. You may have had a bloody evening last night, but I can assure you that he didn't. He enjoyed every minute of it! He got rid of a lot of superfluous vitality and gave himself the whale of a time. Lorraine Barrie got at him about the end of the play, and that gave him a springboard. Now he's got it all out of his system, and he'll be mild as a kitten until next time. What is important, of course, is whether the end of the play is right as it is or whether it should be altered. What do you think yourself? Really and honestly?"

"I don't know," said Bryan. "I'm in a muddle."

"Would you forgive me," asked Tony, "if I made one small, insignificant suggestion?"

"Of course I would." Bryan smiled gratefully. "You're being very kind and very sympathetic."

"Don't kill Eleanor off at all," said Tony. "Make the scene where she discovers Aubrey and Stella together much stronger. Let the audience think for a little while that she really is in such despair that she is going to do herself in. Then let her pull herself together, and, at the end, after the cocktail scene, get all the others onto the patio for lunch, and let the curtain fall on her telephoning to Robert, quite quietly with a smile on her lips and tears rolling down her face. Lorraine can do that sort of 'Smiling, the boy fell dead' performance better than anyone alive. It's not so melodramatic as the way you've written it, but I think it's more real."

There was silence for a moment, while Bryan's mind sniffed warily at Tony's suggestion. There was certainly a good deal of sense in it, although it would necessitate rewriting nearly the whole of the last act.

He sipped his tea, and was aware of a lightening of his spirits. Spring sunlight flooded the room, and from outside in the garden came the clicking purr of a lawn mower. The high-powered tension of the night before receded farther and farther away, and he found that now, in the fresh light of morning, he could view the whole situation in clearer perspective.

He looked at Tony who, with concentrated determination, was trying vainly to make smoke rings, and the last shreds of his initial prejudice against him vanished. He remembered, with shame, how at the first reading he had sneered to himself when Ray had said, "This is my assistant, Tony Orford." He saw now with sudden clarity how valuable Tony's assistance must be.

Tony abruptly stopped blowing smoke rings and jumped off the bed.

"Think it all over quietly," he said, "and don't allow yourself to be barracked. It's your play and nobody else's. Have you finished with the tray?"

"Yes," said Bryan, "and I can't tell you how grateful I am. I'm going to have a shot at rewriting the last act on your lines, only I really would like to go over it all with you in detail before I start it, if you can spare the time."

"All the time in the world," said Tony, balancing the tray on the upturned palm of his right hand like a waiter. "We'll creep away somewhere after lunch, while Ray goes off into his afternoon coma, and if you take my advice you won't say a word about it until you've got it down or at least clear in your mind."

He went out of the room, closing the door after him.

341

The rest of the day passed without incident. Ray appeared just before lunch in a turtleneck sweater and a tweed jacket, carrying the Sunday papers bunched up under one arm and a number of play scripts under the other. He plumped the whole lot down on a deck chair, screamed for Tony and they all three walked down a lane to the village and had gins and vermouths in the "local." Ray exchanged neighborhood gossip with the lady behind the bar, played a game of darts with three laborers, who, Bryan suspected, infinitely would have preferred to play by themselves, laughed overloudly when his darts missed the board entirely and generally gave a rather unconvincing performance of a country squire. Tony sipped his drink and observed the proceedings with a quizzical eye.

On the way back to the house Ray squeezed Bryan's arm affectionately and said he was the most receptive and attractive author he had ever worked with. Apart from this there was no allusion made to the night before. At lunch he recounted anecdotes of the theater with consummate brilliance. To anyone uninterested in the drama, some of the incidents he retailed might have appeared to be a trifle drawn-out, a little overelaborated, but, as his audience consisted solely of Bryan and Tony, the atmosphere was unclouded by criticism. At moments Bryan felt a little sorry for Mrs. Hartley, who frequently was forced to wait for a considerable time before proffering a dish of vegetables while Ray was leading slowly but wittily to a histrionic climax. On one occasion indeed he made an unexpected gesture with his left hand which nearly sent a sauceboat full of gravy flying across the room, but Mrs. Hartley, with a swiftness obviously born of long training, whisked it out of the way in the nick of time.

Tony's phrase "frustrated actor" recurred to Bryan's mind once or twice, but he crushed it down loyally and gave himself up wholeheartedly to enjoying the vivid play of Ray's words and the extraordinary fascination of his personality.

After lunch Ray retired upstairs with the scripts and the papers, and Tony and Bryan went for a walk. They climbed over a stile at the end of the garden and walked up a muddy path through a small wood, emerging finally on a grass plateau which commanded a sweeping view. Here, with the gentle Kentish countryside at their feet, they sat down with their backs against a tree trunk and reconstructed methodically the last act of *Sorrow in Sunlight*. Tony talked concisely and professionally, and Bryan, making notes on a piece of paper, was astonished to find how easily everything seemed to fall into place. Now, in the light of Tony's kindly but ironic intelligence, the original ending of the play appeared to be almost childishly melodramatic. The only thing that perplexed Bryan was the fact that neither he himself, Lorraine, Ray nor J. C. Roebuck had noticed it in the first place.

At last, when the sun was low across the hills, Tony got up. "It's teatime," he said, "and the Maestro will be in a tizz and think we have run away together to start a new life. Also," he added, "if we stay here any longer we shall catch the Universal Complaint, if we haven't got it already."

Bryan got up, stuffed the notes into his pocket and they walked arm in arm down through the wood to the house. He felt happy and relaxed and burning with ambition to start rewriting at once. Tony warned him against too much sudden enthusiasm.

"Let it simmer for a bit," he said as they clambered over the stile. "Type out all your notes before you start, and see that there aren't any sticky passages."

They found Ray lying on a sofa in the living room. "The tea," he said laconically, "is jet black and very cold indeed."

"In that case," said Tony, pressing the bell by the fireplace, "we will have some fresh."

Bryan, immediately aware of tension in the atmosphere, began to explain loyally that it was entirely his fault that they were late. Tony cut him short. "Run upstairs like a good obedient author," he said, "and wash those pudgy little hands."

Bryan, reflecting that it ill became the most dynamic director in the English theater to be as crotchety as an aged spinster because someone was late for tea, said, "All right," cheerfully and went upstairs. When he came down again a few minutes later Ray, who had risen from the sofa and was standing in front of the fire, came forward smilingly and flung his arms round him.

"Tony's just told me about the new ending for the play," he said enthusiastically, "and I'm genuinely thrilled with it. And if Lorraine isn't as delighted as I am, I shall thrash her within about two inches of her artificial life! How long do you think it will take you to write it?"

Bryan felt a sharp stab of panic. "I don't know," he said. "Probably not more than a few days once I get started."

"You shall start tomorrow," Ray said decisively. "And, what's more, you shall stay here in peace and quiet until it's done. Tony and I have arranged it all. I'll concentrate this whole week on the first and second acts so that they're word perfect and out of the way. Mrs. Hartley will wait on you hand and foot. Tony will drive up with me tonight, and come down again tomorrow afternoon to keep you company."

"What about my typewriter?" asked Bryan, aware of a vague resentment of this arbitrary rearranging of his life.

"I'll bring it down tomorrow," said Tony, handing him a cup of tea, "or you can use mine—it works like a dream, except for the Y, which is a little bent."

"I think I'd rather have my own," said Bryan a little doubtfully.

343

Ray laughed gaily. "Nothing could be easier," he said. "You can give Tony a brisk little note to your landlady, spend the whole of tomorrow lying in the sun, relaxing your mind and contemplating your navel. Tony will arrive, typewriter and all, on the five-fifteen, and you can start bashing away first thing on Tuesday morning. How's that?"

"Fine," said Bryan, not quite certain in his mind whether it was fine or not. "It's awfully nice of you to suggest it."

"Nonsense," said Ray. "The house is here. Mrs. Hartley is here. She does nothing but eat like a horse from the beginning of the week to the end. You can stay on in the room you're in now, or move into mine, whichever you like. Perhaps mine would be better, because the telephone is by the bed and you can call me whenever you want to."

"Stay in your own room," said Tony. "That telephone cuts both ways. He can call you too, and what's more he will if he suddenly feels the 'fluence' coming on—you won't get a wink of sleep."

"You see," said Ray, flinging out his arms in a gesture of suffering resignation, "how this sardonic little son of a bitch tries to undermine me at every turn!"

Bryan intercepted a wink from Tony, and smiled. "I do," he said.

6

Bryan, after Ray and Tony had driven away in the car, returned to the living room, poured himself a drink and sat down before the fire. The room, bereft of Ray and Tony's physical presence, felt stale and uncooperative and the silence was oppressive. A log crashed in the open fireplace and made him jump so violently that he spilled some of his whiskey onto the brocaded arm of the sofa. He was dabbing it furtively with his handkerchief when Mrs. Hartley came in to ask him at what time he wanted to be called in the morning. He said that he would like tea and toast at nine o'clock, upon which she said good night politely and went out, shutting the door behind her. The silence closed in on him once more, and he got up irritably and wandered about, regretting wholeheartedly his own weakness in giving way to Ray's no doubt well-meant suggestion that he should stay and work in the peace of the country. At the moment he felt an active distaste for the peace of the country and a nostalgic longing for the less peaceful but more familiar atmosphere of Ebury Street. The personality of the house, even when empty, was obtrusive, and, far from giving him a feeling of quiet relaxation, made him nervous and self-conscious. He took an early volume of the *Play Pictorial* from the shelves and returned with it to the sofa.

At all costs, he decided, he would think no more about the dreaded rewriting of the last act until he had had a good night's sleep, and if, as he suspected, it turned out that he could not do it satisfactorily, even with Tony's help, they would just have to get on with it as it was or not do it at all.

Slightly comforted by his own fatalistic defiance, he sipped his drink and turned the pages of the *Play Pictorial* and found they did little to dissipate his feeling of general futility about the theater and everything connected with it. Being a very early volume it contained photographs of actors and actresses long since dead, playing scenes in plays long since forgotten, sometimes by authors of whom he had never even heard.

His attention was caught by the picture of a radiant young woman, full-bosomed and plump, lying in a hammock and smiling seductively at a slim young man in flannels and a straw hat. The letterpress beneath gave only the names of the characters they were playing, but Bryan, with a slight shudder, identified them, for he had seen them fairly recently. The slim young man was now a very old character actor who appeared from time to time in small supporting roles on the screen. The radiant young woman of thirty-five years ago was acting currently in a mediocre farce in which she played a fat comedy charwoman. He had seen her the week before last and thought she overacted appallingly. He wondered bleakly whether or not, in her heyday, she had insisted on last acts being rewritten for her, and also if she had been able to coerce vital young producers into doing what she wanted them to do against their better judgment, and whether or not she had had an Aberdeen terrier. Realizing that the taboo subject was forcing its way ruthlessly into his mind, he slammed the book shut, turned out the lights and went up to bed.

The next day it rained incessantly. He spent most of the morning elaborating the rough notes he had made with Tony the day before. In the afternoon he found a raincoat in a cupboard under the stairs and went for a walk. Tony arrived on the five-fifteen train, bringing with him Bryan's typewriter as promised. He also brought with him the news that Lorraine was absolutely enchanted with the suggested changes for the last act and sent him her fondest love and a pot of caviar from Fortnum's. Bryan, warmed by this gesture, was about to telephone her immediately in a glow of gratitude, but Tony stopped him.

"Write her a note tomorrow," he said. "Don't give way to too much schoolboy enthusiasm. After all, it's you who are doing her the favor, you know, not the other way round, and it's only a very small pot anyhow!"

The next three days were arduous. Bryan was called each morning at seven-thirty and worked alone at his typewriter until one. The afternoons were devoted to reading and discussing what he had written. Actually, after the first plunge, the newly constructed last act took shape more swiftly and more easily than he would have believed possible. Tony contented himself with a few minor criticisms and suggestions, and by five o'clock on the Thursday afternoon the job was done. After an early dinner that night they caught the eight-thirty to London and took a taxi straight from Charing Cross Station to Ray's flat. Bryan was in a mood of exaltation. An urgent and difficult task had been accomplished, and he felt unutterably relieved and very pleased with himself. Tony, vicariously sharing his satisfaction, was in high spirits.

"It's good," he said with conviction as the taxi turned out of the station yard into the Strand. "I know it's good, and I'm pretty certain that Ray will think so too. The last bit at the telephone is beautifully done, and if Lorraine Barrie doesn't like it I have a very neat suggestion as to what she can do with it." Tony opened the door of Ray's flat with a latchkey, and Ray met them in the hall.

"Lorraine's here," he whispered. "I thought if Bryan was going to read it, it would be better to get it all over at one fell swoop."

"I see," said Tony, and Bryan was surprised at the tone of his voice. It was sharp and almost angry. When they went into the sitting room, Lorraine was standing in front of the mirror over the fireplace tidying her hair. She turned with a little cry of welcome, and seized Bryan's hands.

"I'm so excited!" she said. "When Ray telephoned me and said you'd finished it and were actually on the way up to London I felt as though a great leaden weight had been lifted from my mind." She turned to Tony. "Are you pleased with it? Is it really good?"

Tony turned away with a noncommittal smile. "Bryan's worked like a slave," he said.

Lorraine slipped her arm through Bryan's and led him over to the drink table. "You poor darling," she said. "Was it hell, torment and despair? I always think that to have to go back and redo something you've already done must be one of the most ghastly things in the world. You don't hate me, do you? I mean, for feeling the way I did? I just knew, when I was trying to learn it, that it wasn't right somehow. I tried and tried, but something was in the way. I could not get the words into my head, and then suddenly I realized what it was. . . . I mean, I felt absolutely that somehow or other she wouldn't do just that. I don't know why or how, but it didn't ring true to me. *She* didn't ring true. It was— How can I put it? *Contrived!* That's the word! *Contrived!* How you must have cursed the day I was born!" She laughed wistfully. "Now you must have a drink quickly and read what you've done. I can't wait another minute."

Bryan looked appealingly to Tony, but he was talking in an undertone to Ray at the other side of the room. He felt suddenly panic-stricken. Lorraine mixed him a strong whiskey and soda and shouted gaily to Ray and Tony.

"What are you two whispering about in that sinister way? This is the most thrilling moment! I can hardly bear it. I adore being read to anyway, whatever it is. For God's sake let's all sit down!"

7

Two weeks later Bryan drove through the empty Sunday streets to Euston Station. As he got out of the taxi and waited while a porter collected his two suitcases, Marion Blake, wearing tweeds and an unsuitable hat, waved vivaciously to him and disappeared into the station. His heart sank. Her smile was so assured, her wave of the hand so carefree and cheerful—obviously she was sublimely unaware that she was to receive her fortnight's notice after the opening performance on Monday night. No premonition of disaster marred her bright insouciance; she clearly had no suspicion that she had been the focal point of a nerve-shattering battle which had raged for three days and nights.

The trouble had started during the first run-through in the set on Wednesday, but Tony had foretold it many days before. "Mark my words," he had said, "the infant Reinhardt will not stand for that vintage coquetry much longer. He never wanted her in the first place, but Lorraine insisted on having her. Just you wait and see—one more coy gurgle, one more frisky exit through those French windows, and ze storm she will break and ze land she will be laid waste, and there will be a great wailing and gnashing of teeth."

His forecast had proved to be dismally accurate. After the rehearsal on that fateful day, Ray had called a conference in the bar behind the dress circle of the theater. The conference consisted of Bryan, Tony and J. C. Roebuck, who had been summoned by telephone from his office. It started quietly enough by Ray announcing firmly that he had no intention of allowing the play to open in London with Marion Blake playing Stella.

"It isn't that she's a bad actress," he said, with restrained fury. "I can forgive a bad actress, and occasionally coax her into being a good one. But this poor, overpaid repertory hack is worse than a bad actress; she's thoroughly and appallingly competent. There is no cheap technical trick that she doesn't know and use with cunning unscrupulousness. No prayers, no exhortations, no carefully phrased explanations will budge her inner conviction that she knows how to do it, and what is so macabre is that she's right. She does know how to do it, but she knows how to do it *wrong*—she has always known how to do it wrong! In this particular part she is sweet, tolerant, understanding and lethal. She's a bloody murderess—she kills the character and the play stone dead with the first line she speaks."

"I am not questioning your judgment for a moment," interposed

J.C. gently. "In fact, I agree with you, but I must, for all our sakes', deliver one word of warning."

Ray turned on him. "I know what your warning is going to be—Lorraine loves her. Lorraine must have her in the theater to wait on her hand and foot, to toady to her, to be a foil to her"—his voice rose—"of course Lorraine loves her. Any star would love Marion Blake; she's the megalomaniac's dream. She offers no competition. Her clothes are catastrophic, she's a monumental bum-crawler and makes tea at matinees, but all that, J.C., is not enough for me! All I ask is a decent, hardworking actress who can take direction and give the proper value to the play, and the woods are full of them. One glance through *Spotlight* and I could get you a dozen who could play this part perfectly. Here I am landed with this fifth-rate, clacking soubrette just because Lorraine likes her."

"The fact remains," said J.C. imperturbably, "that if you fire her there will be all hell to pay, and God help anyone you engage in her place."

"I want Carole Wylde!" shouted Ray, "and, what's more, I intend to have her."

"That," said J.C., "will put the lid on it."

J. C. Roebuck, as usual, was perfectly right. It did.

On the following day Ray sent for Carole Wylde, gave her the part of Stella and told her to learn it and stand by for a telephone call from Manchester during the week. This secret interview had taken place in J.C.'s office, after morning rehearsal. Unfortunately, however, just as Ray and Carole Wylde were coming down in the lift they met Lorraine face to face on her way to discuss some clause in her contract with J.C. Lorraine, realizing in a flash that conspiracy was in the air, had bowed icily to Carole Wylde, dug her fingers urgently into Ray's arm, and swept him into the lift again and back into J.C.'s office, leaving Carole Wylde alone in the lobby apprehensively clutching the script and wondering if Lorraine's acknowledged dislike of her would prove strong enough to do her out of the job. Up in the office the storm broke, and had raged and rumbled intermittently ever since. There had been tears, accusations, refusals to appear—all the routine posturings of an outraged leading lady whose dictatorship has been challenged and whose personal wishes have been ignored and thwarted.

Tony, sitting next to Bryan in a first-class compartment in the train to Manchester, gave his view of the existing situation with a certain gleeful cynicism. "The whole thing," he said, with a giggle, "is primarily biological. It began way back in the beginning of the world when the Almighty, for reasons best known to Himself, arranged that ladies should be differently constructed physically from gentlemen. All temperamental scenes made by all temperamental female stars since the theater was first invented have been based on that inescapable fact. It isn't, of course, their fault entirely. It is drummed into their fluffy little heads from infancy, through adolescence and on into adult life that they posses something unique and infinitely precious, something that every man they meet desires more than anything else. The dawning realization that, in the theatrical profession at least, this comforting conviction is not always true, flings them into paroxysms of fury and frustration. They hate the men who do want them and the men who don't, and they hate each other profoundly and mercilessly. Actresses, entirely on account of this mystically overrated aperture, are fussed over and spoilt out of all proportion to their actual status in the theater. They receive cartloads of flowers on opening night, whereas the poor leading man, or the author, or the director, considers himself lucky if some fan gives him one carnation wrapped in cellophane. Male actors, poor sods, are never temperamental to the same extent as their female counterparts. They cannot afford to be. They can be morose, nervous, wretched, miscast and sometimes tearful, but that is as far as it goes. They must not stamp or shriek or tear their clothes off and jump on them, or refuse to appear because they are denied their own way over some trifle—oh, dear, no! They must press on gallantly, standing aside for the leading lady, presenting her graciously to the audience; they must dress in a less comfortable dressing room, give up cheerfully many privileges their talent may have earned them, all to feed the already overweening vanity of some gifted, hysterical, domineering harridan whose every thought and feeling is motivated by sex-consciousness, treachery and illusion."

"You make it fairly obvious that you don't care for women," said Bryan, rather tartly.

"Don't be silly, dear," replied Tony. "I adore women, but not in what is known as 'that way.' Some of my greatest friends are women, and they're a damn sight more loyal and sweet to me than they are to each other. Above all, I love great big diamond-studded glamour stars; they fascinate me; I love watching them and foreseeing how they will react. I love all their little tricks and carryings-on; their unscrupulousness, their inflexible determination, their courage, their magnificent dishonesty with themselves and everyone else. I love and pity their eternal gullibility and their tragic, silly loneliness.

"Take our little treasure, Lorraine Barrie. There you have a perfect, glittering example of bona fide ripsnorting megalomania. She could only exist in the theater or the film studios. No other career, not even that of a brilliantly successful courtesan, could ever provide enough food for her ravening ego. Her basic power lies in her talent, her superb natural gift for acting. I don't suppose she has ever acted really badly in her life. I don't believe she could if she tried. That is her reality; the only reality she herself or anyone who knows her can be sure of. That is the foundation upon which the whole structure of her charm and personality rests, and, believe you me, it's rock solid. Apart from it, she has nothing that thousands of other women don't possess in richer measure. Her figure and looks are little more than attractively adequate. She is virtually illiterate; her conversation is adroit and empty, and, although she has immense reserves of cunning and shrewdness, she is not particularly intelligent. Whatever genuine emotional equipment she originally started with has long since withered and atrophied in the consuming flame of her vanity. Her whole life is passed in a sort of hermetically sealed projection room watching her own 'rushes.' She loves nobody, and nobody loves her. Occasionally they think they do for a little; occasionally she may think she does, but there's no truth in it. To meet, she can be alluring, charming, very grand, utterly simple, kind, cruel, a good sort or a fiend—it all depends on what performance she is putting on for herself at the moment. What really goes on, what is really happening deep down inside, no one will ever know—least of all herself.

"Then, my boy, you pay your money at the box office and go in and watch her on a matinee day with a dull audience, in a bad play with the fortnight's notice up on the board, and the house half full, and suddenly you are aware that you are in the presence of something very great indeed—something abstract that is beyond definition and beyond praise. Quality—star quality, plus. It is there as strongly in comedy as in tragedy, magical and unmistakable, and the hair will rise on your addled little head, chills will swirl up and down your spine and you will solemnly bless the day that you were born.

"All this, of course, only applies if you happen to love the theater, and I suspect that you might learn to if you stick around a bit." Tony paused. "And it's no use," he added, "accusing me in that prim, disapproving voice of not liking women, because it just doesn't make sense. Nobody can love the theater without liking women. They are the most fascinating, unpredictable and exciting part of it." He rose to his feet. "Let's go and have some railway lunch."

In the restaurant car Lorraine was sitting at a small table for two with her maid, Nora. She bowed coldly to Bryan as he passed and flashed Tony a look of unmistakable loathing. They moved on up the car and found two vacant places at a table with Gerald Wentworth and Marion Blake. Bryan, in an agony of embarrassment, squeezed Tony's arm protestingly, but it was too late. Marion welcomed them effusively, and they were forced to sit down. She was in high spirits and talked incessantly. A spate of theatrical reminiscences gushed from her, anecdotes of her early years in touring companies, play titles, actors' names, trivial little scandals, vivacious descriptions of bad "digs" and dead-and-gone landladies. Gerald Wentworth occasionally attempted a modest contribution of his own, but was inexorably mown down.

Bryan and Tony ploughed through the watery tomato soup, gray fish, overcooked mutton and nauseating sweet in anxious silence, dreading any reference to the imminent dress rehearsal and opening night. Fortunately Marion was so carried away by her volubility as a raconteuse that *Sorrow in Sunlight* was never mentioned at all until they had drunk some strangely metallic coffee and the usual squabble about the bill had been settled. Then she announced in a hissing whisper that she had a terrible feeling that poor darling Lorraine was either not well or very worried about something.

Tony quickly rose to his feet, mumbled something about Lorraine probably suffering from preproduction nerves, grabbed Bryan by the elbow and piloted him back to their compartment. Once back in it with the sliding door closed, he flung himself down on the seat and groaned.

"That," he murmured with his eyes closed, "was sheer, undiluted hell. The poor beast hasn't got a clue. She's as merry as a cartload of grigs, whatever they may be. The blow will fall on Monday night, if not before, and she will be caught completely unawares. The gutters will run with blood, and it will be terrible. Terrible!" He opened his eyes and smiled wanly. "Before that dreadful little meal I felt sorrow for her; pity and compassion were twanging at my old heartstrings, but now—oh, baby!—now, after that death-dealing monologue, that vomit-making welter of stale memories, that soul-destroying archness, that hideous, protracted torture of boredom, I'm glad she's going to get the sack. See? Glad, glad, glad! And, what is more, I hope she suffers and remains out of work and in dire poverty for seventeen and a half years." He flung himself full-length on the seat and groaned again. Bryan threw the *New Statesman* at him, and the train rattled on.

They arrived at London Road, Manchester, at four twenty-five. Ray was waiting on the platform with some press reporters and photographers. He was holding, rather self-consciously, a large bunch of red roses. He stepped forward as Lorraine descended from the train and presented the roses to her while the cameras clicked. She received them with a frigid bow, handed them immediately to her maid and swept off up the platform without saying a word. For a moment Ray looked nonplussed, and a gleam of livid anger shone in his eye. Then he recovered himself, chatted and laughed with the reporters, introduced Bryan to them and posed casually arm in arm with him while the cameras clicked and the light bulbs flashed. In the car he dropped his gay insouciance and swore articulately all the way to the Midland Hotel. A little while later, in his suite, he and Bryan and Tony had tea and discussed the situation at some length.

Ray was obviously nervy and apprehensive and quite incapable of sitting down for two minutes at a time. He strode up and down the room with a cup of tea in one hand and a bridge roll, with watercress hanging out of it, in the other.

"This is going to be murder," he said savagely. "She's going to make our lives a misery, bitch the dress rehearsal and have the whole company in a state of jitters."

"Don't let her," said Tony. "You're stronger than she is. Take the offensive. She hasn't got a leg to stand on, really. You have a perfect right to engage or fire anyone you like."

"Of course I have," snapped Ray. "I know that as well as you do. She knows it too. She's not going to compromise herself and commit herself by having a public row with me over Marion Blake. She's far too shrewd for that. She'll think up something else."

"What will she do?" inquired Bryan rashly. Ray turned on him so violently that the teacup shot from its saucer and crashed into the fireplace.

"Listen, my poor, innocent dreamer, the time has come for you to stop gurgling idiotic questions at me like Alice in Wonderland and face the facts of life. A woman of Lorraine's temperament and position with a run-of-the-play contract can inflict torture on her director, her fellow actors, the management and the play that would make Torquemada sob with envy. Not possessing the gift of clairvoyance, being pitifully unversed in the arts of sorcery, black magic, spirit rapping, table turning, thought reading, telepathy and crystal gazing, and having inadvertently mislaid my ouija board, I am unable to tell you *what* she will do or *how* and *when* she will do it. All I can tell you is that you had better hold on to your hat, throw away your cigarette, tighten your safety belt and prepare for a crash landing!"

"It's no use flying at poor Bryan," said Tony. "He didn't engage Marion Blake. You did, and if you hadn't been so besotted over Lorraine Barrie and allowed her to get round you, you would have thrown Blake out on her ear after the first reading. You can rant and roar as much as you like about not having the gift of clairvoyance, but it seems to me that as far as this situation is concerned you haven't even used common sense."

"Christ!" demanded Ray. "Whose side are you on?"

"Have some more tea and calm down." Tony smiled equably. "You can have my cup, as yours is in the fireplace."

Ray groaned with rage and sank onto the sofa, burying his head in his hands.

"I don't want any bloody tea."

"Come, come, dear," said Tony, taking up the teapot. "You're getting a big boy now."

Bryan got up from his chair by the fireplace. "I think I'll go and have a bath and change before the dress rehearsal," he said. "I shall have time, shan't I, Tony?"

"As things are going now," replied Tony, handing Ray his cup of tea, "I should think you'd have ample time for a mastoid operation and a permanent wave."

8

The dress rehearsal, which was timed to begin at seven-thirty, actually began at ten forty-five. The reason for the delay was a message from Lorraine Barrie, telephoned through to the theater at six-thirty, when most of the cast were already dressed and made up. The message stated that Miss Barrie was dreadfully sorry, but she was in bed with incipient laryngitis, that a doctor was in attendance and had forbidden her to speak at all for three hours and even after that only in a whisper. She would, however, make a supreme effort and be ready to go on at ten o'clock, if Mr. Malcolm would be kind enough to excuse her from either dressing or making up.

On receipt of this, Ray gritted his teeth, dismissed the company, with the exception of the understudies, and decided to concentrate on the relighting of certain scenes. Tony and Bryan sat in the back row of the stalls and watched. Bryan was genuinely worried at first about the laryngitis, but Tony soothed him.

"Keep calm, my poor duck," he said. "If Lorraine Barrie has laryngitis, I have curvature of the spine. I'd be willing to bet a thousand pounds to sixpence that she is at this moment sitting up in bed having a delicious little something on a tray. She is perfectly aware that from eleven o'clock onward the stage staff work on double time. She will be ready to start just before that breathless moment; she will perform veree, veree slowly for the first hour or so; then she will suddenly fling away her truss and give a full-throated magnificent performance of the second and third acts. The company will be overwhelmed by her 'old trouper' gallantry, applaud her to the echo, and she will faint just before the final curtain and have to be carried to her dressing room. All this will come true—it is written in the sand."

In due course Lorraine arrived at the theater and walked on to the stage at ten minutes past ten. Ray had finished his lighting and was sitting silently in the third row, smoking. Lorraine, clutching her mink coat round her, looked deathly pale and ineffably weary. "I am very sorry, Ray," she said in a hoarse whisper, "but I don't think I can go through with it."

Ray got up and walked down to the orchestra rail.

"Why not?" he asked briefly.

"You know perfectly well why not." Her voice increased a little in volume. "I presume that you got my message?"

"Yes," said Ray, "I got your message."

"Well, then . . . "

"I think you'd better come to my dressing room," she said, still in a hoarse whisper, but with a note of anger underlying it. "I want to talk to you."

"What about?" Ray's voice rang out in the empty theater with the sharpness of a pistol shot.

Lorraine jumped perceptibly at his tone and took a step back. She opened her mouth to speak, thought better of it, bit her lip and opened her eyes wide instead. They filled with tears. "Nothing can be gained by continuing this unpleasant little scene," she said with dignity. "You'll find me in my dressing room if you want me." She turned to go, but Ray's voice stopped her.

"I don't want to find you in your dressing room," he said. "I want to find you on the stage in exactly half an hour from now, dressed and made up for Act One. Is that clear?"

"Quite clear," said Lorraine. "Thank you for your courtesy."

She walked swiftly off the stage. Ray clapped his hands loudly. "Harry," he shouted. "Call the half an hour!"

Without looking at Bryan and Tony, he marched up the aisle in the direction of one of the exit doors. Tony was up like a flash.

"Stay where you are," he hissed urgently to Bryan. "That was a brief but famous victory. From now on he's going to need help."

Bryan gloomily lit a cigarette and watched them both disappear into the lobby.

At ten forty-five the curtain rose on Act One. A handful of people had appeared in the auditorium. The resident house manager and his wife and a large girl in a pink beret, presumably their daughter; the four walking understudies, who spent their time before the curtain rose eating sandwiches from a paper bag; Madame Nadia, a Russian Jewess who had made Lorraine's dresses, with her two assistants, and the actor who played the chauffeur in Act Three who was made up and was concentrating on the *Sunday Times* crossword.

Tony's prediction that Lorraine would play the first act slowly proved to be painfully accurate. Not only did she play it slowly, but almost entirely inaudibly; in fact, it would be an exaggeration to say that she played it at all. She merely walked about like an automaton and made no effort whatsoever. This naturally paralyzed the action and reduced the rest of the cast to a uniform flatness, with the notable exception of Marion Blake, whose professional vivacity was nothing short of terrifying.

When the curtain fell, it rose again immediately, and the cast stood about in various attitudes of despondency, waiting for Ray to make his way from the dress circle and give them their notes. Lorraine waited patiently with the others. Ray strode on to the stage, gave them their notes briskly and told them to get ready for the second act. He neither spoke to Lorraine nor even looked at her. She went off with the others, and he, after a short consultation with the stage manager, returned to his seat in the dress circle. Tony popped his head over the rail and beckoned Bryan to come up and join them. Bryan stumbled up the dark staircase, feeling utterly miserable and playing with a half-formulated decision to go back to the hotel, pack his bag and catch the midnight train back to London.

To his surprise, he found that Ray and Tony were quite cheerful and drinking neat whiskey from a large silver flask. They offered him a swig, which he accepted eagerly.

"So far so good," said Ray complacently.

"Good!" Bryan looked at him in astonishment. "I thought it was awful."

"From your point of view, of course it was awful," said Ray, patting his knee reassuringly. "But as far as mechanics go it was perfectly satisfactory, and that's all I'm worried about tonight. If we can get through the whole play once without any waits or hitches, we're all right for tomorrow."

"But what about Lorraine?"

"That remains to be seen," replied Ray. "She won't walk through as she's doing tonight with an audience, you know."

Bryan shook his head glumly. "I don't think she'll open at all," he said.

At that moment the stage manager appeared at the side of the circle and groped his way along the front row toward them. The expression on his face was grim.

"Mr. Malcolm."

Ray turned swiftly. "What's the matter, Harry?"

"Miss Barrie wants to speak to you in her dressing room."

"Here we go," said Tony. "Up the barricades."

"Shut up, Tony," said Ray sharply. He thought for a moment. "Tell Miss Barrie that I will come to her dressing room at the end of rehearsal."

"Miss Barrie wants to see you now. Otherwise, she says, she won't go on for the second act."

"I see," said Ray. "An ultimatum."

"She's in a bit of a state, sir," said Harry. "Trembling like a leaf."

Tony took a swig at the flask. "I'll bet the hell she is."

"I think, sir," said Harry tentatively, "you'd better go and see her and get it over with. It's a waste of time going on as we are—the whole company's upset, and nobody knows where they're at!"

"Harry's right," said Tony. "The time has come for a showdown. Grasp the nettle danger, and have a bash."

"I'll be Goddamned if I'll be dictated to," said Ray through clenched teeth.

Tony sighed. "That comes under the heading of naughty pride, and this is no moment for personal considerations. We've got to open tomorrow night. So far you've been in the right, but, if you refuse to see her when she asks you to, you'll be putting yourself in the wrong."

"All right," said Ray decisively. "We'll all three go. Come on, Bryan."

"Include me out," said Tony. "She hates me like poison anyway. I'll stay here with my thoughts. The thoughts of Youth are long, long thoughts, and there's still a little liquor left in the flask."

"Is it really necessary for me to come?" asked Bryan apprehensively.

"Certainly," said Ray. "You're the author. It's perfectly in order for you to be there. After all, the fate of your opus is hanging in the balance. Also, I like a witness on these occasions. Come on!" He grabbed Bryan by the arm and started off with him along the front row.

"Good luck, girls," shouted Tony after them. "The honor of St. Monica's is at stake."

Ray knocked on Lorraine's dressing-room door. After a slight pause, Nellie, her dresser, opened it and ushered them in. Lorraine was sitting at the dressing table staring at herself in the glass. She was wearing a man's dressing gown of dark blue foulard with white polka dots. Bryan immediately remembered the painting over the mantelpiece in her house when he had gone to tea with her and met her for the first time. She turned and indicated the chaise longue with a weary gesture. They sat down on it in silence.

"Wait outside, Nellie dear," she said huskily. Nellie went out, heavy with doom, and closed the door after her. Lorraine offered them a cigarette box with remote politeness. "I'm afraid I haven't got a light."

"I have," said Ray. She took one herself and Ray produced a small gold lighter and lit her cigarette and his own. Bryan noticed that his hand was trembling.

"Now then." Lorraine spoke as though the effort were draining her to the dregs. "I asked you to come to see me because I just can't go on like this any longer. I can't work under these conditions. This atmosphere of mistrust and suspicion and hatred is breaking me completely. I want you to be as honest with me as I intend to be with you. Let's put our cards on the table and try—for the sake of the company and Bryan's play—to find a way out."

"Willingly," said Ray. "How is your laryngitis?" There was no cynicism in his tone, no trace of irony; he merely asked the question, plainly and simply.

Lorraine looked at him long enough for her eyes to brim over with tears. Then she turned her head away.

"I haven't got laryngitis," she said. "I only said I had because I had to think of something to explain why I couldn't rehearse. What I am suffering from is far worse and far more dangerous than laryngitis. I don't think you quite understand, Ray, what the effort of creating a new part means to someone like me. After all, you are still—from the point of view of professional experience—fairly young in the theater. With me it's different. It has been the be-all and end-all of my life ever since I was a small child. I need help and encouragement and understanding every step of the way. I can't concentrate, I can't—how shall I put it?—come to life unless I am happy and relaxed and know that my director is on my side, rooting for me, willing me to succeed. God knows it isn't hard work I mind; I welcome it, I adore it, I'll work until I drop. The play comes first—that is my creed. It always has been, and I have never deviated from it for one instant. But this situation is new to me, something I have never experienced before—this deadly remoteness, this strange, twisted cruelty. Don't think I'm blaming you entirely, Ray. I know you were in the War, and war can do terrible things to people's minds. But I'm appealing to you now from my heart; this is a cry for help because I'm lost, utterly lost, and I don't know where to turn. . . ." Her voice broke, she gave up all pretense of controlling her tears and, burying her head in her hands, she sobbed helplessly.

Ray rose to his feet, stubbed out his cigarette in an ashtray, and put his arm round her shoulder.

"Snap out of it," he said. "There's a good girl!"

Lorraine pushed his arm away, firmly and without petulance. "I don't want to be babied," she said in a muffled voice. "You still don't understand. You merely think that I'm making a scene."

"Well, you are really, aren't you?" said Ray with an attempt at lightness.

Lorraine dabbed at her streaming eyes with a face towel and turned on him. "You're a very clever man, Ray," she said bitterly. "Very clever and very talented, but you have no heart, my dear. And you'll achieve nothing real and lasting in the theater without it."

"Are you accusing me of lack of consideration to you as a director?"

Bryan detected an undertone of exasperation in Ray's voice.

Lorraine smiled wanly and shook her head.

"Not as a director," she said. "I have found working with you extremely interesting. You have great talent and a brilliant mind, but . . ." She gave a little frown as though the words she needed were eluding her. "You'll probably think I'm affected and tiresome when I say that I want more than brilliance and talent. More, and yet less at the same time. I know I'm expressing myself badly and that you are probably laughing at me inside, but I must say what I feel, however incoherent and foolish it sounds; I must say honestly what is in my heart, even though you and your Tony What's-his-name do discuss me and mock at me behind my back."

Ray made an attempt to protest, but she lifted her hand and silenced him.

"Please let me go on. I don't want this to be a quarrel or even an argument, I merely want to state my case. I'll be only too pleased to listen to whatever you have to say afterward."

Ray heaved a sigh of resignation. "Very well," he said, "state away."

Bryan, acutely embarrassed, bit his underlip. That "state away" was a mistake. Lorraine, however, gave no indication that she had noticed it.

"My case is this," she said simply. "I am lonely and frightened and completely bewildered. I don't know what I have done! Before rehearsals and during the first two weeks we were close, you and I. We were growing day by day to like each other and respect each other more. Then suddenly, without warning, everything changed. I put out my hand trustingly as a comrade for your help and support when the path was difficult, and you were no longer there—you had withdrawn. I'd watch you and Tony—and Bryan too"—she paused for an instant, and looked at Bryan reproachfully—"come into the theater, and go out of the theater, I sometimes heard you laughing together in the stalls—I know how tremendously amusing Tony can be—but I was never included in the jokes. I am sure I was the butt of many of them. I was shut out, left stumbling along in the dark alone. I tried to reason with myself, to tell myself that it was imagination and silliness, but it wasn't, and I knew it wasn't. My instincts never lie to me, and I am too honest with myself not to face the truth at all times, however unpleasant it may be. Why did you suddenly change toward me, Ray? Was it my fault? What did I do? What did I say? It couldn't have been because I was slow and sometimes stupid at rehearsals—even you are theatrically experienced enough to know about that. Was I uncooperative? Did I offend you in any way? If I did, I swear it was unintentional—for God's sake, tell me and let's make an end of it."

Tears sprang to her eyes again, but she dashed them away with the back of her hand. She rose to her feet.

"Don't you understand?"—her voice took on a stronger, deeper note—"are you both so blind and lacking in perception that you don't realize one thing, and that is that I *love this play!* I have lived with it for weeks, for months really, ever since I first read it. It has been part of me night and day, waking and sleeping, and now, because of something strange, something sinister that is beyond my comprehension, I have lost my way to it, I can't do it—I can't—I can't—I can't!"

Sobbing, she sank down again on the stool in front of her dressing table and once more buried her face in her hands. Ray shot Bryan a quizzical look and shrugged his shoulders. Bryan, feeling that somebody must do something, got up and went to her.

"Don't cry like that, Lorraine," he begged. "Please don't cry. You're wonderful in the part—far, far more wonderful than I ever hoped anyone could ever be. Please don't be upset."

Lorraine seized his hand and pressed her wet face against it.

"Thank you, Bryan," she said brokenly. "Thank you, at least for understanding a little."

Bryan looked at Ray in the mirror. He was taking another cigarette from his case and lighting it.

"Is that all?" Bryan's blood congealed at the coldness of Ray's voice. He felt a tremor go through Lorraine. She lifted her head and looked Ray in the eye.

"Yes," she said. "That's all."

"Are you sure that you've been quite honest in this—this 'case' you've presented?"

Lorraine met his gaze unwaveringly. "Absolutely honest," she sighed. "But I realize already, only too clearly, that you haven't believed me."

"Dead right," said Ray, briskly. "Not a bloody word."

"I see." Lorraine rose with dignity. "Then there is nothing more to be said."

"On the contrary." Ray got up and went toward her. She quailed a little and sat down again. "There is a great deal more to be said."

"For God's sake, Ray," cried Bryan, "let's not go on about any of it any more. Let's finish the rehearsal."

"Shut up!" said Ray with some ferocity. He turned again to Lorraine. "You graciously said a little while ago that you would be only too pleased to listen to whatever I had to say afterward. In that, as in everything else you have said, you were inaccurate. You will not be at all pleased to listen to what I have to say, and it's this. Never in all

359

my limited experience of the theater have I seen such an inept, soggy and insincere performance as that you have just given in this dressing room. Every gesture and every intonation was ham and false as hell. And, if I may say so, your improvised script was lousy. You are *not* lonely or lost or bewildered. You are *not* honest with yourself or with anybody else. You never have been, and you never will be! You don't give a good Goddamn whether I've changed toward you or not. All you're upset about is that you have been thwarted, denied your own way over a comparative triviality, and that is more than your overblown ego can stand. You sent for me to see you because, having deliberately wrecked the rehearsal, sent a phony message about mythical laryngitis, mumbled through the first act, thereby throwing the whole company for six and utterly destroying Bryan's play which you assert you love so much—having achieved all this unnecessary tension and chaos, your well-trained professional instincts probably warned you that you were going too far. So you sent for me in order to declare a temporary truce. You longed for a nice satisfying scene ending up with all of us in tears and me soothing you and comforting you and telling you you were the most glorious, God-given genius the theater has ever known. Then we should have billed and cooed our way through the rest of the rehearsal—which incidentally is just as important for you as for the rest of the cast. Once firmly established on a sickening kiss-and-be-friends basis, you would immediately have set to work again insidiously and unscrupulously to win back the point that you lost at the outset, and that point is that Marion Blake should continue playing Stella, for which she is too old and entirely unsuited. You've wanted her in the cast from the first for one reason only, because she is a good foil to you and is shrewd enough to allow herself to be your offstage toady and bottle washer!"

"How dare you!" Lorraine's voice was shrill. She was shaking with fury. "How dare you speak to me like that! Get out of my room." She rose impressively, but Ray pushed her down again onto the stool; she made an attempt to strike his hand away, but missed. He towered over her threateningly, and Bryan noticed a vein throbbing in his forehead.

"Keep quiet!" he shouted violently. "I haven't finished."

"Get out! Get out! Get out!" Lorraine screamed, and in a frenzy of rage jumped up and smacked his face so hard that he staggered back and fell onto the chaise longue. Bryan made a movement to intervene, but she pushed him back and advanced until she was standing over Ray with blazing eyes.

"I'll teach you to insult me in my own dressing room, you tawdry, fifth-rate amateur"—she spat the words venomously into his face—"the most brilliant, dynamic new director my foot! Do you think I haven't met your sort before, camping in and out of the theater with your giggling boy friends! Who the hell gave you the right to throw your weight about and attempt to tell experienced actors what to do and what not to do? Get out of this room before I have you thrown out! Go and peddle your insipid artsy-craftsy theories to some cheap summer repertory theater where they'll be properly appreciated. Go and do *Uncle Vanya* in drapes at New Brighton! Go and breathe new life into Shakespeare at the Cotswold Festival of Dramatic Art, but get out of my sight!"

At this moment a diversion was caused by the door opening violently to admit Marion Blake, who bounced into the room, attired in an Alice-blue satin wrapper with some cheesecloth swathed round her head and carrying a tortoiseshell hairbrush. With a piercing cry she flung herself between Ray and Lorraine. "Don't, don't, don't," she wailed dramatically. "The whole theater can hear you, and I love you both!" She flung her arms round Lorraine, who pushed her away. Ray, seething with rage, rose to his feet.

"That, Marion," he said icily, "is entirely irrelevant. You are fired anyway!" He strode out of the room, slamming the door after him.

An hour or so later Bryan walked along the gray, wet, cobbled street to the hotel. Immediately following the scene in the dressing room Ray had dismissed the rehearsal and disappeared with Tony. Bryan, having extricated himself from the hysteria raging in Lorraine's room, had been buttonholed and questioned by various members of the company. Gerald Wentworth had given him two large gins in a toothglass, and he now felt dizzy in the head and utterly wretched. He walked, aching with nerve strain and weariness, through the deserted lobby of the Midland, got into the lift, exchanged mechanical "good nights" with the liftman, who had one arm and smelt of shag, staggered along the long, dreary corridor, let himself into his room and fell onto the bed in tears.

9

At nine o'clock the next morning Bryan was awakened by the usual saturnalia of breakfast trolleys bumping and rattling along the corridor. For a brief moment he lay staring at the ceiling and trying sleepily to account for the leaden feeling of depression that was weighing on his spirit. He had been dreaming deeply, and his mind was confused. Then, with sudden clarity, memory of the night before came back to him, and with a groan he staggered into the bathroom, sponged his face with cold water and brushed his teeth. He went back into the bedroom and drew aside the curtains; the day was gray and a steady rain was falling. He watched, abstractedly, an elderly man in a mackintosh running through the puddles after a tram, but the tram quickened its speed and the man had to give up and return to the pavement.

Bryan returned to bed. This was the day, the great day he had been living for, the first important steppingstone of his career. Tonight people from all over this gray city and the suburbs beyond would be getting into trams and buses and private cars to come to the theater to see Lorraine Barrie in *Sorrow in Sunlight* by Bryan Snow. What they would actually see would probably be a notice pinned into the box office stating that, owing to the sudden indisposition of Miss Lorraine Barrie, there would be no performance. A day or two later the papers would announce that the play had been indefinitely postponed. The story would eventually get out that there had been quarrels and scenes and disunity, but by that time nobody would care—nobody beyond the actual people concerned. Bryan, with tears of self-pity pricking his eyelids, reached for the telephone and ordered, in a hollow voice devoid of emotion, China tea for one and rolls and marmalade.

An hour or so later, when he was lying in the bath, trying in his mind to compose explanatory letters to his mother and sister, Tony came in cheerfully and sat down on the lavatory seat.

"Your door was not locked, dear," he said, "which only goes to prove that you are an incurable optimist and open your arms wide to life. It also shows a refreshing ignorance of L.M.S. hotels. Why, you poor, foolish, heedless creature, *anything* might happen to you with all these lusty cotton manufacturers pounding up and down the corridors. I really don't know whether to slap you or kiss you."

"Please don't do either at the moment," said Bryan, sponging his head violently. "I'm feeling bloody miserable."

"I know." Tony lit a cigarette and flipped the match into the bath. "Lorraine won't appear; the play won't open; we shall all go back to London defeated and humiliated. All is lost. There is no hope anywhere. . . . Isn't that what your poor, storm-tossed mind is telling you?"

"Yes, it is," said Bryan gloomily. "And it's probably right at that."

"Balls," said Tony. "I am your fairy godmother and all I have to do is wave my wand, which up to now I have been unable to locate owing to the cold weather, and all will be well."

"What are you talking about?"

"I won't keep you on those well-known tenterhooks any longer." Tony grinned benignly. "J. C. Roebuck has arrived. He came up on the midnight. He and Ray have been having breakfast together, and they are now closeted with La Belle."

"Do you really think there's any chance of her appearing? After last night?"

"Elemental, my darling little Watson." Tony sprang up and kissed him on the forehead. "There never has been the slightest question of her not appearing. I could have told you that last night."

"Well, it's a pity you didn't," said Bryan, getting out of the bath and reaching for the towel.

"I couldn't. Really I couldn't." There was genuine contrition in Tony's voice. "I had a terrible time with the Maestro, and it lasted for hours. Then, when I'd finally got him to bed and stoked him up with Seconal, it was too late."

"What makes you so sure, anyway?"

"No actress of her position and reputation could afford not to appear just because she'd had a row with her director. It would be breach of contract to start with. Also, that sort of thing just doesn't happen. If she had stuck to her illness story she might have worked it, but she'd have to have produced a doctor's certificate. Believe me, she's never had any intention of not appearing. All she wanted was to establish a nice cozy atmosphere of chaos, make everyone uncertain and wretched, get her own way over Marion Blake and then bounce onto the stage as though nothing had happened."

"If that's true," said Bryan, stamping into the bedroom, "she's a tiresome bitch, and deserves a bloody good hiding."

"For God's sake, pull yourself together, old man," said Tony. "You can't talk like that about a woman."

"All right," said Bryan, throwing a shoetree at him. "You win!"

At five past seven that evening Ray, Tony and Bryan took their places in the box nearest the stage; a small passage at the back of it led to the pass door. The theater orchestra was playing brassily a selection from *Glamorous Night*. The large auditorium was already nearly full. The day had passed without incident beyond the fact that J. C. Roebuck had insisted upon Lorraine and Ray declaring a formal armistice. In the afternoon, after an uneasy lunch in the restaurant, Ray had retired to bed and Tony had taken Bryan firmly to the pictures, in order, he said, to calm his nerves. They saw a newsreel, which showed several dead bodies being taken from a train wreck; some violent army maneuvers in the United States exploiting a new flame thrower; a famous boxer being carried from the ring streaming with blood, and an admiral's wife launching a new destroyer in the pouring rain. Then came an admonitory "short" issued by the Ministry of Health which portrayed, in revolting detail, the inevitability of food poisoning. After this there was a trailer of the next week's attraction which, peppered with alliterative adjectives, showed a man being shot in the stomach, a mother weeping over the body of her dead baby and a plane crashing into a stormy sea. After this came an exquisitely acted but rather tedious picture about a psychiatrist who committed suicide. Tony had slipped his arm through Bryan's as they stepped out of the cinema into the drizzle.

"Nothing," he said, "can hurt us now."

They had just had time to get back to the hotel, change and have a sandwich and a drink in Ray's suite and here they were. Bryan shot a quick glance at Ray, who was absently turning the pages of the program. He seemed perfectly calm and, if anything, a little bored. He had made no reference whatever to last night's scene in the dressing room, either during lunch or while they were having drinks before the show. In fact, he had not mentioned Lorraine Barrie or the play at all. Bryan wondered anxiously what he was really thinking, whether he was expecting success or failure, whether he minded one way or the other. Tony was peering over the edge of the box at the audience.

"You will be interested to know," he said to Bryan, "that Mrs. J. C. Roebuck has elected to wear silver lamé with a large red rose tucked into that fascinating hollow between her bosoms. The whole idea was a grave mistake!"

At this moment the overture came to an end and the house lights went down. Ray patted Bryan's knee kindly.

"Here we go," he said.

After a few minutes, when Lorraine had made her entrance, been duly applauded and embarked on her first scene with Gerald Wentworth, Bryan's nervousness began to ebb away. She was obviously in complete control and playing with consummate charm and authority. She looked younger and more attractive than he had ever seen her look before; every gesture, every movement she made, was exquisitely graceful and exquisitely right. For the quarter of an hour that the first scene lasted Bryan was spellbound, and when she made her exit and the whole audience applauded he closed his eyes with a feeling of infinite relief. Tony pressed a cigarette into his hand.

"Don't go to sleep yet, dear," he said. "It gets better later on."

Marion Blake made her first vivacious entrance through the French windows, and Ray groaned audibly. At the end of the first act the applause was good. The three of them went quickly to the office, where the house manager, an amiable little man with a scarlet face, was waiting for them.

"So far, so good," he said effusively. "Now, what shall it be? Scotch, gin, sherry or tea?"

"All four," said Tony.

The manager laughed delightedly. "Mr. Roebuck is coming up in the next interval," he said proudly. "We're old friends, you know. We were together at the Royal years and years ago before it was a cinema, long before your day, Mr. Malcolm. But old J.C.! What a man! He hasn't changed a bit!"

He poured the drinks and handed them round. Bryan sat on the edge of the desk and felt himself getting nervous again. He wished he was back in the box. At last the second-act bell went. The house manager, still talking volubly, ushered them out.

During the second act there was less tension in the box. Ray relaxed and whispered comments to Tony, who made notes on a pad with a pencil with a small electric bulb on the end of it. Bryan sat in the corner of the box nearest to the stage and concentrated on the performance. There were no technical hitches, except at one point during a scene between Marion Blake and Lorraine when the light brackets over the fireplace began to flicker in and out distractingly. Ray writhed with irritation and murmured, "Sweet God!"

Tony giggled and said in a hoarse whisper, "Don't worry, it's only the head electrician giving Marion Blake her notice in Morse!"

At the end of the act Bryan, feeling unequal to facing further conviviality in the manager's office, went backstage and sat for a while in Gerald Wentworth's dressing room. Gerald Wentworth had taken off his coat and was sitting at his dressing table having a cup of tea.

"They seem to be liking it," he said, "but, of course, they're missing all the finer points. That bit, for instance, when I'm waiting for the telephone to ring and playing with the paper knife went for nothing! In London, you'll see—they'll eat it up!"

"You're giving a wonderful performance," said Bryan gratefully. "So sure and so steady."

"That's my best act," Gerald Wentworth sighed. "The whole part goes to pieces in the last act. Not that it's your fault," he added hurriedly. "I know that Lorraine and Ray bullied you into rewriting the end of the play, but if you want my candid opinion, it was better as it was. Of course I see Lorraine's point. If we'd played the original version she'd have been offstage committing suicide for the last ten minutes of the play. As it is, she finishes on the stage by herself with the telephone. I'm not saying, mind you, that she doesn't do it beautifully. Nobody can smile through her tears better than she can. After all, she made her first great success in *Sheila Goes Away* doing precisely the same scene—not as well written, of course, but the same idea—and she's done it in different ways ever since. Did you ever see her in *Winter Wind* at the Strand?"

"No," said Bryan. "I'm afraid I didn't."

"More or less the same situation all over again, except that there was no telephone on account of it being Victorian. But there she was, crinoline and all, giving up her lover and going back to her husband with a gay smile and a breaking heart. You've never read such notices. Old Agate—God rest his soul!—compared her with that French actress that there was such a hullabaloo about."

"Bernhardt?" suggested Bryan hopefully.

"No, dear boy, not Bernhardt." Gerald gave an indulgent smile. "One of the other ones."

"She's giving a magnificent performance tonight, at any rate," said Bryan.

"Slow in the first act." Gerald scrutinized his teeth in the mirror. "But she always takes time to build. I've played with her enough to know all her little tricks."

The assistant stage manager rapped politely on the door and said, "Beginners Act Three, Mr. Wentworth."

"Only one more river to cross," said Gerald mechanically, as Bryan left him.

As he passed Lorraine's dressing-room door it opened and she came out. Bryan's heart fluttered with terror at meeting her face to face after his unwilling participation in last night's drama, but she smiled serenely at him and, linking her arm with his, walked with him onto the stage.

"How are you enjoying your baptism of fire?" she said.

"Very much indeed," Bryan stammered. "You're absolutely superb. The audience adores you."

"Lot of cods' heads," she said contemptuously. "We ought to have opened in Edinburgh!"

When the curtain fell on the last act there was an outburst of cheering from the upper parts of the house. Bryan, whose fingers had been tensely clutching the plush edge of the box, relaxed his grip and sat back. His throat was constricted, and there were tears in his eyes. Ray and Tony were both applauding with wholehearted sincerity. The curtain went up and down again, disclosing various members of the company bowing to the audience and to each other.

When Lorraine walked on alone for her star call, the applause and cheers were thunderous. The curtain fell and rose again on the whole company standing in a row with Lorraine in the center. Ray had definitely decided that neither he nor Bryan was to take a call and so, after a number of curtains, Lorraine, with a warning look at the stage manager, stepped forward and held up her hands graciously for silence. The noise died away. She made a brief and charming speech beginning with the tactful statement that Manchester audiences were well known to be the most receptive and intelligent in England. She acknowledged gratefully the splendid performance of her old and valued friend, Gerald Wentworth. Applause. "That gay and versatile comedienne, Marion Blake." Tumultuous applause.

("That," hissed Tony, "was unwise from every point of view.")

Then she made a charming reference to Bryan, and said how proud she was to be appearing in a first play by such a promising young author. Bryan flushed and felt a little dizzy. She finally said, with touching simplicity, that neither she herself nor any of the cast could have achieved anything without the sensitive guidance of the most brilliant young director in the theater today—Mr. Ray Malcolm.

She shot a swift glance up at the box and finished up by thanking the audience once more and wishing them good night.

The house lights came up, the orchestra played "God Save the King," during which Bryan stood rigidly to attention and stared at a lady wearing maroon satin in the opposite box.

"Come on," said Ray. "We'd better get it over with."

"I shall come too," said Tony, with a giggle. "I dote on family reunions."

They went through the pass door and onto the stage. Lorraine was standing in the center of a group of people who were congratulating her effusively. Ray broke through their ranks and, taking Lorraine in his arms, kissed her. There was a little murmur of indulgent appreciation from the onlookers. Lorraine stepped back from Ray's embrace then, taking both his hands in hers, she looked wistfully in his face.

"Were you pleased?" she said. "Was I a good girl?"

"You were beyond praise," said Ray, with complete sincerity. "You gave the most lyrical, moving performance I have ever seen."

"Thank you." Her eyes filled with tears. "Thank you, Ray, for everything." She brushed away her tears with her hand and gave a gallant little laugh. "And when I say 'everything' I mean 'everything.' You've taught me so much, so much, my dear."

"This," said Tony, sotto voce to Bryan, "is where we came in."

PRETTY
POLLY

The ship was due to dock at 8:00 A.M., but long before that the sprawling city of Singapore had emerged from the morning haze. At first it had looked muddled and gray and rather sinister because the sky was overcast, but as the ship chugged its way cautiously through the myriad craft of all shapes and sizes riding at anchor on the flat silky water of the harbor, the clouds suddenly disappeared and sharp morning sunlight brought the waterfront to life. There were several massive buildings; architecturally municipal, gleaming white against flowering trees; there were also one or two skyscrapers whose serried ranks of windows blazed momentarily in dazzling squares of reflected light. Polly Barlow, who had been leaning on the rail of the boat deck since six-thirty, adjusted her aunt's mother-of-pearl opera glasses and scanned the crowded harbor. They weren't very good opera glasses but better than nothing and they did bring one or two things into focus such as a brown Malay woman in a scarlet sarong feeding a baby on the afterdeck of a Chinese junk, and a stark naked Negro on the foc'sle of a freighter cheerfully emptying pails of water over himself; he looked as if he were singing but she could hear no sound. Polly glanced at her wristwatch and, with a reluctant sigh, left the boat deck and went down to her aunt's cabin. Mrs. Innes-Hook was sitting up in bed with a breakfast tray across her knees. She was wearing, as usual, a pink quilted bed jacket because the cabin was air-conditioned and she was not one to take risks. Curlers gleamed malignly from her acid yellow hair and her pasty face shone with cold cream. Her small, pale eyes glared at Polly irascibly.

"Where in heaven's name have you been? I sent the stewardess down to your cabin an hour ago."

"I've been on the boat deck. I woke early because there was an awful lot of noise going on and I felt too excited to go to sleep again, so I dressed and came along to see if you were all right and you were fast asleep so I took your opera glasses off the table to look at the harbor through—I hope you don't mind . . ." Polly's voice, trailed off and she dropped her eyes before her aunt's cold, contemptuous stare.

"I do not mind about the damned opera glasses." Mrs. Innes-Hook spoke with measured calm. "But I do most certainly mind you disappearing to God knows where without so much as letting me know."

"I'm sorry Aunt Eva."

"Have you done your packing yet?"

"Yes. Just one small case—enough for two nights, as you told me."

"Well you can now take this bloody tray off my stomach and start on mine." Mrs. Innes-Hook reached over to the bed table for a cigarette. Polly lit it for her and took the tray. Her aunt inhaled a mouthful of smoke and coughed violently. She coughed with the abandon of one who is completely insensitive to the feelings of other people, which was not surprising because she was, as a rule, completely insensitive to the feelings of other people. The exceptions to this rule were the rare occasions when for some reason or other she wished to ingratiate herself with someone whom she considered superior to herself either in rank or fortune; Polly, her niece, most emphatically belonged in neither of these categories. Polly, in fact, existed in her eyes only as a meek and faintly anemic slave, useful principally as a focal point for her frequent outbursts of temper. She was also her "good deed in a naughty world," for had it not been for her saintly kindness and generosity in bringing her as her personal companion on this world cruise, the poor thing would still be a salesgirl in Derry and Tom's and beating her silly brains out learning stenography three times a week at night school. In her self-congratulatory moments, which were fairly frequent, Mrs. Innes-Hook was given to chiding herself for being so irrepressibly good-natured. Here she was, in the greatness of her fond heart, giving this dull, undemonstrative girl the chance of a lifetime, a trip round the world in the most comfortable circumstances imaginable. She had not, it must be admitted, seen Polly's vibrating inside cabin which she shared with Lady Babcock's maid, a sullen, squat little Belgian woman who snored like a rhinoceros in the intervals of being resonantly seasick. Even if Mrs. Innes-Hook had condescended to visit Polly's cabin she would doubtless have considered it perfectly adequate. It could do no harm to a girl of Polly's age and circumstances to have to rough it once in a while: she was certainly in no position in life to demand luxury.

In all justice to Polly she never complained. She did what she was told to do quietly and efficiently: she fetched and carried, washed out stockings and underclothes in the basin in Mrs. Innes-Hook's bathroom, galloped back and forth to the ship's library to bring her aunt the books she imagined she read and, on the whole, being fortunately a good sailor, she managed to get through a great many more menial tasks per day than Lady Babcock's maid.

Mrs. Innes-Hook's mind, not being geared to unflattering introspection, refused to admit that Polly's utter calmness even in the face of the most vituperative unbraiding could be deliberately irritating. Time and time again, when Mrs. Innes-Hook, exasperated by some outrageous sling or arrow combined with the monotony of shipboard's daily routines, indulged herself in a comforting bout of uninhibited bad temper, her niece would stand quietly looking at her through her double-lens glasses and wait until the tirade faded into anticlimax through sheer lack of response. Then she would say meekly, "I'm sorry Aunt Eva." And although a perceptive observer might detect in the slight twitch of her lips the tiniest hint of an ironic smile, it was too fleeting and evanescent to be pounced on as a sign of incipient rebellion. It was also too subtle for Mrs. Innes-Hook, who was far from being a perceptive observer, to notice at all.

Polly pulled a small blue suitcase from under the bed and propped it up on the sofa which lined the opposite wall of the cabin. Mrs. Innes-Hook, puffing away at her cigarette, regarded her balefully from her pillows.

"I don't see what use opera glasses could be to you anyhow," she said. "You're as blind as a bat."

"Only near to," replied Polly. "I can see faraway things all right."

"In that case it's a waste of time to use my opera glasses. The whole point of opera glasses is to bring faraway things nearer." Mrs. Innes-Hook permitted herself a grunt of triumph.

"When I focus them they work beautifully." Polly proceeded to lay some underclothes in the bottom of the suitcase. "I saw a naked black man washing himself," she added. "He was on a ship with a blue funnel at the back, and there was a junk with brown sails and a woman feeding a baby at the breast."

Mrs. Innes-Hook gave a snort of disgust. "Please remember that I've only just finished my breakfast."

"I expect the baby has too by now." Polly gave a little giggle. Mrs. Innes-Hook shot her a withering look, put one fat, blue-veined leg followed by the other out of the bed, groped about with her toes for her mules, which were trimmed with draggled Alice-blue marabou, and walked majestically into the bathroom. Her creased pink chiffon nightgown had molded itself unbecomingly in between her large buttocks. Polly peered at her myopically as she passed and, when the bathroom door had slammed, giggled again.

Some time later, Mrs. Innes-Hook, bathed, made up and squeezed into a mauve cotton frock that was at least two sizes too small for her, sat on the bed displaying all the signs of mounting fury. She had twice put her hat on and taken it off again. She had sent Polly three times to the purser's office and to the head of the gangway to see whether her brother-in-law, Bob Hook, had arrived or not. It had all been arranged by letter and cable that he should meet them and motor them out to his rubber plantation about fifty miles outside Singapore.

Obviously he should have bounded on board to welcome his loving sister-in-law the very moment the ship docked, but the ship had docked over three hours ago and he still hadn't appeared. Polly came back into the cabin after one more fruitless journey to the head of the gangway. She was wearing a flowered print "Horrocks" dress that had belonged to a friend of hers at the Polytechnic and contrived, in spite of all her enforced running about, to look quite cool and almost pretty. She never looked entirely pretty because her skin was too sallow and her hair too mousy, also those double-lens glasses were enough to put anyone off. Polly's nearsightedness was a cross she had learned to bear with outward equanimity at least. Ever since she could remember she had been tormented about it, first by her brothers and sisters and later by her school friends who had often, in ecstasies of sadistic merriment, hidden her glasses at moments when she most needed them. To begin with this joke had the desired effect, which was to send her off into a wild fury, but after a while experience taught her that it was more effective to display no emotion whatever and just wait icily until they were returned. Her aunt's frequent references to her being blind as a bat left her unmoved. As a matter of fact most of her aunt's vituperative gibes at her expense left her unmoved. She had, early on, sized up her aunt's character accurately and had arrived with neither surprise nor dismay at the final conclusion that she was a disagreeable, common-minded, snobbish, conceited, ill-mannered old woman with nothing to recommend her whatsoever beyond a certain ghastly vitality and a lot of money. She realized that any display on her part of resentment or hurt feelings would merely be an invitation to further unkindness so she wisely exercised an iron control of her temper and managed to maintain an outward demeanor of almost intolerable docility.

At the moment, successfully hiding her inward amusement at Mrs. Innes-Hook's discomfiture, she sat down a trifle breathlessly.

"There's still no sign of him," she said. "The man at the gangway said that perhaps he hadn't got a pass to come on board and that he might be waiting at the entrance to the dock."

"Nonsense," said Mrs. Innes-Hook. "He wouldn't be so idiotic as not to get a pass. He's had ample warning. I cabled him from Colombo the exact time the ship was arriving." She stubbed her cigarette out irritably. "And even if for some reason or other he couldn't come he would certainly have sent somebody to explain. There's obviously been a muddle."

"Shall I go out to the entrance gate and see?"

"We'll both go." Mrs. Innes-Hook got up from the bed and put on her hat again. "If I have to stay one moment longer in this cabin with all that damned noise going on outside, I shall go mad. Come along."

Polly glanced at herself in the looking glass before following her aunt out of the cabin and made her usual little grimace at her own reflection. It didn't matter how much trouble she took with her face and her hair, the miserable glasses always ruined the whole effect. Her eyes looked back at her contemptuously from the mirror, magnified like two large gray oysters. She put out her tongue at them, and slammed the cabin door behind her.

The heat at the entrance to the dock was considerable. The sun blazed down on the milling crowd of passengers, rickshaw boys, porters and gesticulating taxi drivers. A red-faced man in the uniform of Thomas Cook & Sons was shepherding a group of about fifteen people into a small green bus. Polly observed that a little rivulet of sweat was running down by the side of his nose. An elderly rickshaw boy rushed up to Mrs. Innes-Hook and shouted some unintelligible words at her while he pointed invitingly to his rickshaw, which was painted red and looked dirty. Mrs. Innes-Hook, with an imperial gesture, waved him away. At this moment a young Indian, immaculately dressed in black trousers, a white shirt and a black tie, came up to them and bowed, doffing his straw hat at the same time with exaggerated elegance.

"You will be the Mistress Eenishook?" He smiled, displaying two rows of dazzling white teeth, one of which had a gold filling that glittered bravely in the violent light. Mrs. Innes-Hook nodded and took a step back as though she feared that he might suddenly embrace her.

"My name is Amazahudin. I have here a car to take you to the

Raffles Hotel." He smiled again. "It is most fortunate that I at last find you. Your honorable brother-in-law Tuan Hook tried to describe your person to me over the telephone but the line was unsatisfactory and I have been searching in desperation."

"My brother-in-law sent you to meet me?"

"Oh my goodness yes. He called me with the utmost urgency at a very early hour to make reservations for you at the hotel."

"Why didn't he come himself? Is he ill?"

"Yes—he indeed is ill. He has written to you a letter by post yesterday which will be awaiting you. He has a most high fever and is incommoded from coming to you. It is all a very unhappy coincidence that this illness should strike him down at the moment of your eagerly awaited arrival. He has said that if his temperature should fall a trifle he will drive in to see you tomorrow but it is fifty miles of jungle road and he is most doubtful that he will be strong enough. You will come please now with me? I have made all necessary arrangements and I am high qualified guide. This is my card." He handed Mrs. Innes-Hook a card which he extracted from a crocodile-leather wallet. "You will see upon it my address and telephone number so that if there is anything you may require during your stay I am at your most honorable service day and night."

Mrs. Innes-Hook, having given an ungracious snort of assent, motioned to Polly and they followed him to an ancient Cadillac which was standing by the curb on the opposite side of the road. The Malay driver was engaged in an argument with three half-naked Chinese boys when, having dodged through the traffic, they finally arrived at the car. Amazahudin shouted something at him and he sprang forward to open the door. When Polly and her aunt were installed on the backseat Amazahudin hopped up into the seat next to the driver, leaned over the back of it and smiled engagingly. The three half-naked Chinese boys jeered as the car moved away. Amazahudin, his face suddenly suffused with rage, shook his fist at them and shrieked some incomprehensible abuse, then, all passion spent, he smiled again and, producing a rather battered silver cigarette case, asked them if they would care to smoke. Mrs. Innes-Hook accepted one and he lit it for her, almost falling over the back of the seat in doing so. Polly, peering slyly at Amazahudin's face through her glasses, was suddenly struck by the clear beauty of it. His eyes were set wide apart and were of a melting brown, fringed with long black lashes. His nose was delicate and his mouth full and sensual; the texture of his skin looked ivory smooth and she was aware of a sudden longing to stroke his face. Mrs. Innes-Hook, fortunately unconscious of what was passing through her niece's mind, was firing questions at him. Why hadn't her brother-in-law sent a telegram to the ship?—Why hadn't he, Amazahudin, come on board instead of keeping her waiting about for three hours?—What was the exact disease from which her brother-in-law was suffering and was there or was there not an efficient doctor in attendance? Amazahudin withstood this barrage with beguiling serenity. He explained that he had been unable to come on board because there hadn't been time to procure a pass from the shipping office and that had he gone there first in order to get one he might in all probability have missed meeting them altogether. He had no idea what specific fever Tuan Hook was suffering from but he suspected that it was malaria and if so the only sensible thing was to remain in bed until it had run its course. As to whether or not there was an efficient doctor available he was unable to say as he was not personally familiar with the particular district in which the Tuan's plantation was situated. In any case, he assured Mrs. Innes-Hook, there would doubtless be a full explanation in the Tuan's letter which would be waiting for her at the Raffles Hotel. He added that if she were satisfied with the reservations that he had made for her that he would personally arrange for her luggage to be brought off the ship and delivered to her within an hour. In the face of so much common sense so charmingly and humbly expressed, Mrs. Innes-Hook's ill humor evaporated somewhat and she resigned herself to the inevitable. While all this was going on Polly, inwardly delighted at the whole situation, looked out of the window at the colored streets, the sudden, sedate stretches of grass in front of the more imposing buildings, the unexpected clumps of ragged banana leaves and palm trees and, with a lift of the heart, the fully blossoming frangipani trees, delicate pink or dazzling white. Presently the car turned sharply left into a small drive and drew up under the portico of the Raffles Hotel. Amazahudin was out like a flash and holding the door open for them before the hotel porter had a chance to come down the steps. He ushered them tenderly into the cool dark lobby. The punkahs in the ceiling made a whirring sound. Three American ladies were clustered round a glass showcase in which were some dubious antiques dominated by a large Buddha made of rose quartz. "I wouldn't have it in the house if you paid me a thousand dollars," said one of them vehemently. "Look what happened to poor Janey and Ed! Nothing but disaster ever since they came back from that world cruise on the *Caronia* and brought that gold Buddha with them. First of all Ed's hepatitis, then Janey's miscarriage, and then the dog being run over right opposite the front porch. They bring bad luck to some people just like opals these Buddhas do and it's no use trying to tell me they don't. No thank *you!*"

Polly laughed as they followed Amazahudin to the reception desk. Mrs. Innes-Hook shot her a sharp look.

"What are you laughing at?"

"Poor Ed and Janey," Polly replied.

"Who on earth are Ed and Janey?"

"I don't know," said Polly truthfully. "But they were terribly un-lucky."

Fortunately at this moment Mrs. Innes-Hook's attention was distracted by a slim Eurasian behind the reception desk who handed her a letter. Amazahudin, having asked for it, stood by at the alert. He watched her face anxiously while she opened and read it. When she had done so she folded it and put it back in its envelope.

"Well—that's that," she said tersely, her fat lips set in a grim line of displeasure. "I suppose we shall have to stay here whether we like it or not." She turned to Amazahudin. "You'd better tell them to show us these rooms we've heard such a lot about." The Eurasian behind the desk bowed and handed two keys to a bellboy who looked like a small brown monkey. He led the way to the lift. They followed him, Amazahudin smilingly bringing up the rear.

2

Material fortune had unaccountably smiled on Eva Shanks ever since the year of grace 1928 when she had been engaged as a dance hostess by the management of the Metropole Hotel Folkestone. Up until that date her life had been fairly rugged. She had obscurely adorned the stage during her teens, appearing sporadically in the chorus of various touring revues. She had been seduced, married and divorced before the age of twenty-four and had inadvertently given birth to an undersized baby in Rugby in 1923. The baby, lacking its mother's stamina, had not outlasted that particular tour and had been buried, rather hurriedly, on a matinee day in Stoke-on-Trent. Eva's career as a hotel dance hostess, although unsensational from the terpsichorean point of view, proved to be highly successful in other ways. She was a big-busted, blond young woman in her early twenties and her sexual allure, although far from subtle, was strong. Concealed by vitality, youth and a surface geniality, her inherent meagerness of soul was not, at that time, easily discernible. In due course a Lancashire cotton manufacturer called Alfred Innes fell in love with her, married her and, with a tact and consideration rare in most hardheaded North-countrymen, died of a heart attack three and a half years later, leaving her a considerable fortune and a Victorian Gothic mansion on the outskirts of Manchester. This she immediately sold at a handsome profit and moved to an expensive flat in South Kensington. Amply provided for for life, she spent the years immediately preceding World War Two traveling to and from the South of France and other fashionable resorts, playing bridge exhaustively and making a number of superficial friends and an even greater number of abiding enemies. It was after the war, in the summer of 1946, that she encountered Edgar Hook, Polly's uncle, at a party at the Dorchester Hotel. Edgar Hook was weak, amiable, good-looking and by birth what was in those far-off days described as a gentleman. This was an entirely new experience for Eva, and, attracted by his looks and urged on by a curious inborn snobbery, she married him, tortured him and finally murdered him. Not by means of any sharp implement or lethal drug, but by the slow wearing away of his weak and vulnerable spirit. He contracted a bad cold in 1955 which turned to pneumonia and, having neither the wish nor the will to endure any longer the nagging misery of his life with Eva, he turned his face gratefully to the wall and died. Curiously enough Eva missed him more than she could have believed possible. It cannot truthfully be said that she ever loved him, but he was a presence in her life, a permanent scapegoat, a continual and convenient target in her sadistic ill temper, and a constantly gratifying and existent proof of her financial superiority. She held the purse strings. He was idle and lazy and fair game for her petty meanness. When he was gone she felt frustrated and, although she would be the last to admit it, lonely.

It was during a bad bout of this inadmissible weakness that she conceived the idea of embarking on a world cruise and taking her niece with her as companion. Mrs. Barlow, Polly's mother, an easily flustered widow, had been harassed by one thing and another since the day she was born. In her early years she had been flurried and teased unmercifully by an obstreperous horde of brothers and sisters. Throughout her married life her own brood of four boys and three girls had very soon cottoned on to the fact that she was one of life's victims; an easy crier, prone to hysterics and a woolly-minded muddler. Her husband, Henry Barlow, was handsome, courteous and blatantly unfaithful to her until he drove his Austin Seven into a lorry on the Maidstone bypass and was killed instantly. Her growing family patiently endured her excessive mourning until they were old enough to go out into the world and fend for themselves. Three of them were by now married and they all subscribed to her upkeep. Polly, the youngest, was the last to leave the untidy nest near Malden. When the letter from her wealthy but heartily disliked sister-in-law arrived suggesting that Polly should accompany her round the world, Mrs. Barlow was immediately flung into a frenzy of agitation. It was obviously a wonderful opportunity for the girl in one way; she would undoubtedly gain invaluable experience traveling in such circumstances and would be freed, at least temporarily, from the bondage of being a salesgirl. On the other hand there might be terrible hazards involved. Mrs. Barlow was only very slightly acquainted with her sister-in-law. They had only met a few times on which occasions Mrs. Innes-Hook had ridden over her like a juggernaut. No member of the Hook family had a good word to say for her and since the death of poor Edgar few of them had even spoken to her. Mrs. Barlow after frantic discussions with her friend Mrs. Ruddle, who was a practicing medium, and the Reverend Elwyn Evans, the local vicar, finally decided that the only way out of the dilemma was to let Polly decide for herself. After all she was rising twenty-three and a sober-minded, sensible girl. Polly, on being told of the project, agreed with alacrity. In her view the disadvantages of Mrs. Innes-Hook's notorious temperament would be more than offset by the excitements of the voyage itself plus her escape from the clamorous customers of Derry and Tom's. A tea party was therefore organized in the lounge of the Hyde Park Hotel consisting of her mother, Mrs. Innes-Hook and herself, and everything was satisfactorily arranged. In course of this tea party Polly remained comparatively silent while her mother trembled on the verge of tears and Mrs. Innes-Hook, in one of her better moods, indulged in a lot of raucous laughter, told three unsavory and not very funny stories and abused the waiter. Polly, demurely picking at a coffee éclair, noted, through her double-lens glasses, several significant facts. One was that Mrs. Innes-Hook was a heavy eater and, judging by the small veins on the side of her nose, a fairly heavy drinker as well. Another was that she lapped up praise as a thirsty dromedary laps up water. Polly, having admired her hat and a rather vulgar diamond bracelet, and laughed with becoming appreciativeness at the unfunny stories, knew, from the complacent glint of approval in her aunt's pale eye, exactly what course it would be expedient to pursue. Mrs. Barlow's summing up of her daughter's character as being sober-minded and sensible was only partially accurate. Polly was sensible all right but her sober-mindedness was deceptive. Her glasses of course and her general air of mousiness contributed to the illusion that she was a dull, rather uninteresting girl. Actually she was observant, acutely sensitive to the humorous values in any given situation and, after a lifetime passed in the flickering shadow of her mother's congenital indecisiveness, a tough and determined realist.

A few hours later Polly was lying down in a thin, high room which opened onto a small balcony and overlooked the hotel garden. She had unpacked her overnight bag and her aunt's overnight bag. She had endured, from her aunt, a long garrulous tirade against the unkind circumstance which had forced her to alter all her carefully formulated plans. Not only was she obliged to stay in a hotel which she had no intention of doing, but she realized only too well that she would have to pay for the rooms instead of spending two days free of charge on her brother-in-law's rubber plantation. The fact of having to pay out good money was actually the aspect of the whole business that upset her most. Mrs. Innes-Hook, like so many rich women, was mean. She could easily have afforded the most luxurious suite in the whole hotel, and had there been anybody near to impress, might even have done so in order to emphasize her own importance. But alas there was nobody to impress but Polly and Amazahudin.

Polly stared blindly up at the ceiling and meditated happily on the incredible good fortune that had seen fit to strike Uncle Bob down with malaria. If it hadn't she would at this very moment be bumping along a jungle road with her aunt toward the unalluring prospect of two nights and a day in an isolated bungalow on a rubber plantation. At the back of her mind she was suspicious of her uncle's sudden malaise. From what she could remember of him he was a rather sardonic man with a bland sense of humor and the amiable, self-centered assurance of a determined bachelor who is accustomed to living alone in out-of-the-way places and would be unlikely to have any nostalgic urge to welcome a sister-in-law he hardly knew. She had seized the opportunity to read his letter while she was unpacking and her aunt was in the bathroom. It was polite but uneffusive and the regret it expressed at not being able to entertain them had not rung entirely true. If, as she suspected, the whole thing was a put-up job, she felt a wicked longing to write him a bread and butter letter thanking him for not having them to stay. She put on her glasses and glanced at her watch. Aunt Eva would probably sleep for another hour at least. She had knocked back three large gin slings before lunch and an enormous plate of prawn curry at lunch and was likely to be fairly comatose for quite a while longer. Polly took off her glasses again and wondered if she dared take the risk of going out and having a ride in a rickshaw. At this moment the telephone by her bed rang loudly. She groped for the receiver and put it to her ear. "Come quickly—come quickly—" her aunt's voice sounded panic-stricken. "I'm ill—come at once." There was a click at the other end of the line as her aunt hung up. Polly leapt off the bed, grabbed her glasses, slipped into her dress and shoes as fast as she could and rushed along the wide, dim passage of her aunt's room. Fortunately the door was not locked. She pushed it open and went in. Mrs. Innes-Hook, wearing a mauve taffeta dressing gown, was half lying on the floor with her head leaning against the bed. Her skin was a grayish color and her forehead and cheeks were shining with sweat. She grunted something incomprehensible and tried to haul herself higher against the bed. Polly, gazing at her in horror, noticed that her lower lip was trembling and that she looked as though she were about to cry. She crouched down on her knees and helped her into a sitting posture. Mrs. Innes-Hook leant her head back against the coverlet and, breathing stertorously, closed her eyes. "It's my right arm," she muttered thickly. "It hurts—I can hardly move it."

Polly got up quickly and went over to the bed table on which there was a chromium thermos jug of iced water; she poured some into a tumbler and, returning to where her aunt was lying, knelt down and tried to force some between her blue lips. Mrs. Innes-Hook, bad-tempered even in extremis, pushed it aside with a violent gesture of her left hand, thereby upsetting most of the water into her lap, then, with a raucous sound that was half a choke and half a sob, she toppled over sideways and lay, unconscious but still breathing noisily, on the floor. Her dressing gown had burst open exposing her vast, mottled breasts, the marks left by her recently discarded corsets and a wide brown appendicitis scar. Polly, leaving her as she was, ran to the telephone and dialed the operator. "Please send for a doctor immediately," she said. There was a tremor in her voice but it was calm. "This is room seventy-two. My aunt, Mrs. Innes-Hook, has been taken seriously ill." She hung up the receiver and picked up the tumbler, which was lying on the floor; beside it was her aunt's diamond and sapphire ring. This she also picked up and put thoughtfully into her pocket. With an effort she managed to drag Mrs. Innes-Hook into a sitting position. There was no hope of getting her onto the bed so she wedged her against it with pillows and cushions from the sofa. With an exclamation of distaste she rearranged the mauve taffeta dressing gown, prized off the rest of her aunt's rings, with the exception of a gold wedding ring which seemed to be embedded in the thick flesh, and, with some difficulty, finally succeeded in unclasping the heavy ruby and diamond bracelet. This, with the rings and the other one she had picked up earlier, she wrapped carefully in her handkerchief and put into her handbag, which she had left in her aunt's room after lunch. She then lit a cigarette but crushed it out in the ashtray after a few puffs because it occurred to her that it might look a little too nonchalant to be discovered smoking when the doctor arrived. She saw no harm however in taking a reassuring gulp of brandy from her aunt's flask, which was in the top drawer of the dressing table.

After a few minutes there was a gentle tap on the door. Polly opened it and was surprised to see Amazahudin. He had discarded his black trousers, white shirt and black tie and was wearing sandals, beige slacks and an open-necked blue silk shirt. He bowed unsmilingly.

"You have trouble?" He looked past her into the room. "I was happening to be by the desk below and heard that the doctor was to be required. May I in the meanwhile be of any small assistance?"

Polly looked at him and observed, perhaps irrelevantly, the silky black hairs on his forearms and how the blue of the shirt enhanced the color of his skin.

"You are very kind," she said. "I certainly do have trouble. My aunt has been taken ill. I think it must be a heart attack." She stood aside and motioned him into the room. They stood together in silence for a moment looking at Mrs. Innes-Hook, who, although bolstered by the pillows and cushions, had slipped a trifle to one side. She was breathing more easily but her face looked moist and gray and her eyes were closed.

"Oh my goodness me," said Amazahudin in a subdued voice. "This is indeed a most pitiful occasion."

"Will the doctor come soon?"

"I have ascertained before coming here to the room that he is on his way," said Amazahudin. "He is in office not far from the hotel. Please honor me by accepting while we await him my most grievous sympathy."

"Thank you." Polly bit her lip thoughtfully. "I really don't quite know what to do. I suppose I should telephone my uncle."

"Goodness yes." Amazahudin gave a small but encouraging smile. "I will personally call him but perhaps when the doctor has already examined the poor lady."

"Yes. I suppose it would be better to wait." Polly sighed and wandered over to the window. She looked out absently at the traffic streaming back and forth along the high road and at the gray-blue sea beyond on which the ships lay still as though embalmed in light. Amazahudin came and stood beside her.

"You are most brave Miss Polly," he said. "In evil circumstances such as these it is wholly remarkable to be brave."

"Thank you." Polly looked at him. His face was composed and his expression decorously grave, but she thought she detected a faint gleam of a smile in his eye.

At this moment there was a knock on the door. Amazahudin ran to open it and ushered in the hotel manager followed by the doctor.

Dr. Renshaw, a portly Englishman in his early fifties, dismissed the manager's suggestion that they lift Mrs. Innes-Hook onto the bed with an authoritative wave of his hand and knelt down beside her on the floor. The manager, Amazahudin and Polly retired to the other end of the room while he proceeded to examine her. Nobody spoke. Polly took off her glasses and polished them with her handkerchief. She felt curiously detached and almost light-headed as though all that was happening was happening to somebody else and not to herself at all. She put her glasses on again and watched the doctor rise to his feet and go to the telephone. Amazahudin took a packet of cigarettes out of his pocket and then, thinking better of it, was about to put it back again, when Polly put out her hand.

"Please," she smiled apologetically, "I think I would like one if you don't mind."

Amazahudin handed her the packet, she took a cigarette from it which he lit with a small Ronson lighter, then he lit one for himself. Polly sat down on the arm of a chair and, feeling the silence was becoming intolerable, said "Thank you" rather more loudly than she had intended to. The doctor put down the telephone and came over to her.

"I have ordered an ambulance," he said. "It should be here in a few minutes. Usually in cases like this it is wiser not to move the patient, but I think in this instance it would be advisable to take the risk." He consulted a piece of paper he held in his hand. "You are Miss Barlow?"

"Yes." Polly answered a trifle tremulously. "I am Mrs. Innes-Hook's niece. I am traveling with her."

The doctor looked at her appraisingly. "Perhaps you would like to drive to the hospital with me in my car," he said. "When we have got your aunt safely into the ambulance."

"Thank you. You're very kind . . ." Polly hesitated. "Is it—is it really very serious?"

"Yes," he said, "I'm afraid it is. Your aunt has suffered a severe stroke. I am risking moving her to the hospital because I think it is better for her to be where she can be properly looked after. Perhaps you would tell me where I can wash my hands?"

"In there." Polly pointed to the bathroom. The doctor looked at her sharply as though trying to assess the measure of her self-control, then he gave her a reassuring little pat on the shoulder. "I assure you that everything possible that can be done will be done, but I think you should be prepared for—for—" he was about to say "the worst" but changed it to "any eventuality." Then with a brusque nod he went into the bathroom and shut the door. Polly crushed out her cigarette in an ashtray on the table by her side and got up from the chair. Aware that both the manager and Amazahudin were staring at her, she forced a smile.

"I think I'd better go along to my room and pack my overnight bag," she said. "It will only take a few minutes." She picked up her handbag, Amazahudin sprang to open the door for her. "I am most grateful to you for all your kindness and consideration," she said, almost primly. "Perhaps you would be kind enough to telephone me later at the hospital?"

Amazahudin bowed and watched her walk away along the corridor.

3

"Goddamn bloody hell!" Robert Hook banged down the telephone receiver and stamped, naked, onto the verandah. Miss Lorelei Chang, who was sitting in a rattan swing chair painting her nails, looked up languidly. She was wearing an open, gold Chinese jacket over a scarlet silk sarong and her shining black hair was dragged up in a knot on the top of her head and secured by a small ivory comb.

"What's the matter now? Is the old bitch coming after all?"

"No," said Robert Hook, flinging himself down on the swing seat beside her. "The old bitch is *not* coming after all. The old bitch has upped and died!"

"Look out," said Lorelei, "you'll upset my nail varnish." She put the bottle down on a little bamboo table out of harm's way. "How do you mean she upped and died?"

"Just that. She arrived this morning with her bloody niece, stuffed herself with curry at the Raffles, and had a heart attack. Amaz just telephoned. She died about a half an hour ago in the hospital."

"Can you beat that?" Lorelei's fluent English had recently been idiomatically enriched by the visit to Singapore of an American air-craft carrier.

"They're burying her in the English cemetery tomorrow after-noon at four o'clock. I'll have to drive in tonight."

"You can't." Lorelei gave a final dab at the little fingernail of her left hand with a brush of vermilion varnish. "You've got malaria. You've also got me." She ran her right hand skittishly up and down his thigh, keeping her left in the air so that the varnish would dry.

"I'll have to," he said gloomily. "I'll really have to, there's no way out of it. I can't leave that poor wretched girl to cope with every-thing all by herself."

"Bobee." Lorelei leant seductively against him. "We planned these few days ages ago. I'll have to go back to work on Monday, which only leaves tomorrow and Sunday. Can't you say your ma-laria's much worse and ring up and send some flowers or some-thing?"

"We'll drive in after dinner." Bob slipped his hand inside her loose jacket and pulled her over onto him. She wriggled expertly out of his grasp.

"I had not planned on a fifty-mile *drive* after dinner," she said sulkily. "I had planned something quite different."

"We'll drive in *after* something quite different." He made a grab for her but she evaded him.

"The morning will do just as well. You can call Amaz and tell him to look after the girl and that we'll be in in time for lunch. Bobee—please . . ." She slipped behind the swing seat and twined her arms round his neck, he leaned his head back and she kissed him on the mouth.

"All right—all right—have it your own way."

4

Polly left the hospital at six-fifteen and stepped out into the sticky, humid evening. The sun was about to set and there was a smell in the air compounded of spices, petrol fumes, charcoal fires, cooking and the heady scent of frangipani blossom. The low, evening light catching the banana leaves and evergreen shrubs near the hospital entrance made them shine as though they had been varnished.

From the shadows of the portico Amazahudin appeared and bowed. He was formally dressed, as he had been in the morning; in addition to black trousers, white shirt and black tie, he was wearing a black coat. He looked at Polly's set expression and a slight frown puckered his smooth forehead.

"I have been awaiting here," he said, "to hear of the news of Mistress Eenishook. I am trusting that it is good."

"I'm afraid it isn't." Polly spoke in a flat voice devoid of emotion. "My aunt died a half an hour ago. She is to be buried tomorrow afternoon at four o'clock."

"Aie—Aie! That is indeed evil tidings." He clasped his hands and gazed up at the sky as though reproaching some celestial divinity for whisking Mrs. Innes-Hook so abruptly into nirvana. "I have the car here," he added practically. "I was thinking that perhaps it would be required."

"The doctor offered to drive me back to the hotel," said Polly. "But I told him I would rather go back alone. It's all very difficult. I don't quite know what to do."

"You will come with me," Amazahudin said firmly, and, taking her bag, led her to the Cadillac, which was parked by the curb in the shade of an immense tree covered with flame-colored blossoms. Before getting into the car Polly glanced up at it.

"That is a flamboyant tree." There was a slight note of apology in Amazahudin's voice as though he found the vividness of the color tactless in such a mournful situation. "Some people allude to it as 'Flame in the Forest,'" he added, "but I believe that that is not botanically correct." He hopped lightly into the car and sat next to her. As the car started Polly looked back at the flamboyant.

"I should like an evening dress of that color," she said.

When they arrived at the hotel Amazahudin collected the keys from the desk and accompanied her up in the lift and to her door. He opened it for her and stood back hesitantly.

"Please come in for a moment," said Polly. "I think I should like a cigarette. We might even order a drink," she added recklessly.

Amazahudin permitted himself a smile, still faintly tinged with mourning, and followed her into the room.

They sat side by side on the bed because, apart from one unyielding-looking chair in front of the dressing table, there was nowhere else to sit. Amazahudin telephoned to room service and ordered a large gin and tonic for Polly and a Coca-Cola for himself. They sat in silence for a while staring at a mediocre watercolor of a Chinese junk in a lacquered bamboo frame.

"That is a junk," said Amazahudin.

"I know." Polly nodded. "I saw a lot of them in the harbor this morning."

"It is often the custom for many many families to live on them all their lives. The conditions of this living are not the most sanitary. We also have much river living in India," he went on. "It is not very sanitary there either."

"No," said Polly absently. "I don't suppose it would be."

After a further silence there was a knock at the door and a Malay boy in a blue sarong and a red uniform coat came in with the gin and tonic and the Coca-Cola. Polly signed the chit he handed her and he bowed and went out, closing the door behind him. Polly lifted her glass.

"Here's luck," she said.

"I wish you, too, the most good luck now and forever and a day," said Amazahudin.

Polly, aware of a rather intense expression in his eyes, smiled remotely, and looked away.

"Thank you Mr. Amazahudin. You have been so very kind. I don't know how I can ever repay you."

"If you would be pleased to call me Amaz I would be richly honored."

"Very well—Amaz."

Amaz swiftly took her hand and kissed it, then got up from the bed and put his half-finished glass of Coca-Cola down on the corner of the dressing table.

"I have been most lacking in sensibleness," he said contritely. "I have taken the vulgar advantage of your most sweet politeness. It must be that you wish now to be alone to think your sad thoughts without the presence of a stranger. Please may I have the honor of returning to you at a later hour because my only wish is to be of service on this most tragic occasion."

"Yes," replied Polly, also getting up and standing facing him. "It would be better if I could be alone for a little. I have a great many things to think about. If you'd come back in an hour"—she glanced at her watch—"say at eight-fifteen?"

"It will be my most great pleasure," said Amaz.

"I intend to move to my aunt's room. It is larger and the view is more interesting. It also has a bath."

Amaz gave her a penetrating look, clasped his hands briefly in front of his face and with a little bow went out of the room.

When he had gone, Polly, with her gin and tonic still in her hand, sat on the chair opposite the looking glass on the dressing table and stared at herself reflectively. Her face was pale and her skin lifeless; her nose was shiny and her nondescript hair looked damp and badly needed a wash and set; it could also, she decided, do with a great deal of expert attention in other ways. A rather more definite color would be an improvement anyhow. She put her head on one side, frowning a little. On the whole, she thought, it should be lightened rather than darkened. She reached into her bag for her compact and her hand encountered the handkerchief in which she had wrapped Mrs. Innes-Hook's rings and bracelet. She took it out, laid the jewelry on the table and made a little pattern of it, with the bracelet curled in the middle with the rings ranged round it. She then peered more closely at the bracelet. It was heavily encrusted with rubies and diamonds in a platinum setting. She lifted it up and weighed it in her hand, then she tried on the rings one by one; there were five in all, but they were all too big for her. She put them down with a sigh, and, reaching into the bag again for her compact, took it out, opened it, powdered her nose and put on some lipstick. Then she put everything back into the bag, collected her overnight suitcase and went along to her aunt's room. The curtains had been drawn and the bed turned down. On the table by the side of it was Mrs Innes-Hook's cigarette case and lighter, which Polly had forgotten to pack with the other things before going to the hospital. The cigarette case was intricately patterned with a sort of trelliswork of sapphires and diamonds on a gold base. The lighter matched it. Polly picked up both objects and popped them into her bag with the rest of the jewelry, making a slight clucking sound with her tongue against her teeth at her original carelessness in leaving them lying about. She then went over to the dressing table on which was standing Mrs. Innes-Hook's makeup box. She tried to open this but discovered that it was locked. She fumbled in her bag for the keyring, which she had collected from her aunt's handbag in the hospital bedroom, found it and opened the box. It contained the usual paraphernalia of bottles, Kleenex tissues, pots of face cream and various other articles of makeup. On one side there was a bulge in the blue silk pocket in the lining. Polly felt inside it and produced a thick wad of five-pound notes. She counted these and discovered that they amounted to three hundred pounds. In the opposite pocket she found a dark-blue leather book of traveler's cheques. The contents of this amounted to 428 pounds. Polly counted them through again to make quite sure, then put them back. The bank notes, however, she put into her bag. Then, pulling back the curtains and drawing up an armchair to the window, she lit a cigarette and sat down quietly to contemplate the flashing lights of the passing traffic and her own immediate prospects.

5

Punctually at eight-fifteen there came a discreet tap on the door. Polly, who had had a bath and changed into the one of her two evening frocks that happened to be black, ran lightly across the room and opened it. Amaz, still in the austere attire in which he had accompanied her from the hospital, bowed as usual, and, with a tentative smile, offered her a small bunch of white gardenias.

"I have been hoping that you would honor me by accepting this small token of my heartfelt sympathy and esteem," he said.

"Thank you—they're lovely." She sniffed them. "Please come in."

Amaz regarded her anxiously for a moment. "I have been worried in my mind," he said when she had closed the door and motioned him to a chair, "if it would be insensible on my part to invite you, in these morose circumstances, to take a small dinner with me?"

"It wouldn't be in the least insensible," said Polly. "It would be lovely."

Amaz exposed his gleaming teeth in a gratified smile. "That is most thrilling," he said. "Would you—" he went on, "in the present deep sadness of your heart be interested in Chinese food, Japanese food or Indian food? Here, in this famous crossroad of the world, everything is obtainable."

"Whatever you suggest." Polly offered him a cigarette from Mrs. Innes-Hook's case, which she had filled before taking her bath.

"The choice is for you, Miss Polly," he said, taking one.

"Indian food generally means curry doesn't it?" said Polly, taking a cigarette herself and lighting them both with Mrs. Innes-Hook's lighter. "And we had a lot of that at lunch. I once went to a Chinese restaurant in the Brompton Road." She made a little grimace. "It wasn't very nice, but of course I am sure it would be very different here. I think it would be fun to try Japanese for a change."

Amaz clapped his hands delightedly. "That I hoped is what you would select. There is a small place here that I know called Aki Soo's that is most discreet and peaceful. We will have a sukiyaki dinner and rice wine and take off our shoes and enjoy ourselves. You will not object to sitting low on the floor?" he added anxiously.

"Not at all. I often sit low on the floor at home in the flat I share with a friend. It is a very small flat and there is only a sofa and one armchair so when people come it gets rather crowded." She paused. "I think that before we go I should telephone to my uncle. I know I should have throught of it before, but everything seems to have been happening so quickly."

Amaz leaned forward and smiled reassuringly. "I myself have already spoken with Tuan Hook," he said. "He has expressed most profound regret at your most tragic situation and loss and will be here to greet you at twelve o'clock tomorrow."

"How is his malaria?" inquired Polly.

"It is better," replied Amaz cautiously. "But not well enough to permit him to arrive tonight, which he would have most earnestly desired."

"What is he like, my uncle? I haven't seen him since I was about fifteen."

"He is a splendid fellow." Amaz's eyes gleamed with enthusiasm. "Most genial and go-as-you-please. When he comes into Singapore for the races or for business occasions I drive him here there and everywhere because the parking of his own car renders him irritable. Sometimes we have had evenings together of unforgettable merriment."

"Does he live all alone on his rubber plantation?"

Amaz shrugged his shoulders. "Sometimes he is alone but he is a man of roving spirits and many friends who are most devoted."

"Is he alone now?"

Amaz shrugged again and looked away in slight embarrassment. "I think . . ." he said after a moment's pause, "that he may possibly be entertaining for the weekend some casual acquaintance. He is wiry and strong and, for his years, most young." He caught her eye guilelessly.

"I see," said Polly. "Let's go and have dinner."

"I have discarded the big car," said Amaz, resting his hand lightly under her elbow as they walked along the corridor, "because it is for professional service only and the presence of the driver makes too much formality. You will not object if I drive you myself. It is a small MG which was given to me by an English friend three years ago before he sailed for home. It is I fear an open job so I have thought fit to bring a small scarf for your hair."

"That's very considerate of you," said Polly, "but I'm afraid it doesn't really matter about my hair. I have a comb in my bag anyhow."

Aki Soo's was a small, low building lying back from a wide, main road. The path leading to the entrance was fringed on one side by a hibiscus hedge and on the other by a row of dustbins. There was a red and gold Japanese lantern hanging above the door. They were received by a giggling Japanese girl in a gray kimono, and, after removing their shoes and easing their feet into leather slippers, were shown into a small, square room the walls and floor of which appeared to be made of yellow straw. There was a low, shiny black table in the middle and a number of little cushions. They sat cross-legged on the cushions and Amaz clapped his hands. After a moment a mature and over-made-up Japanese lady slid open a panel of the screen wall and sidled into the room hissing slightly and bearing a lacquer tray on which was a bottle of sake and two glasses. She put the tray down on the table, genuflected, still hissing, and crouched on her haunches. Having poured out a glass of the rice wine for each of them, she muttered something unintelligible and went off into a gale of high-pitched laughter. She was wearing an embroidered pink and blue kimono and Polly observed that no line or wrinkle disfigured the enameled mask of her face. Amaz tapped the table reprovingly and proceeded to issue a series of brisk orders in what sounded to Polly to be faultless Japanese. Whether it was faultless or not the lady obviously understood him for she immediately assumed a more sober and attentive expression, nodded a few times, hissed again twice and, with a constrained curtsy to both of them, insinuated herself out of the room, sliding the screen to behind her.

"She was once a geisha in Osaka," explained Amaz. "Then she made the friendship of a Dutch sugar planter who had much money and took her to live with him in Batavia in Java. It was after he was killed in the war that she arrived here and formulated this establishment."

"I envy you being able to speak Japanese so well." Polly smiled at him admiringly.

"For one year and a half I have had a Japanese friend who is a most big shot in the confectionary business. He visits Singapore many times a year and brings me biscuits for cocktails made of seaweed."

"What a lot of useful friends you have." Polly sipped her sake, which, to her surprise, was hot and tasted faintly of turpentine.

"You like?" Amaz raised his eyebrows inquiringly.

"Very much indeed." She held out her glass to be refilled. "But I didn't expect it to be hot."

"That is good," said Amaz, pouring it out. "It will be warming to your sorrowful heart."

"I think," said Polly gently, "that we had better get things straight about my sorrowful heart." She took another gulp of wine and put the glass down on the table. "It would be deceitful of me to pretend a sadness that I do not feel. The fact that my aunt died this afternoon was a shock I admit—I mean somebody dying suddenly is bound to be a bit agitating isn't it? But as a matter of fact I have only known her for just over a month and I didn't care for her very much."

"She was a grand lady of high breeding, however, was she not?"

"No," said Polly. "She was a common, disagreeable old pig."

"Ai—Ai—Ai!" cried Amaz, clasping his hands together. "That will be explaining what the Tuan Hook say to me over the telephone."

"What did the Tuan Hook say to you over the telephone?"

"He say, 'Keep the old bitch away from me at all costs!'"

"I thought as much," said Polly. "Good for Uncle Bob!" She raised her glass and gave a little giggle.

Amaz leaned across the table and pressed her hand; there was no hint of amorousness in the gesture, it was more like tacit acknowledgment of an unspoken pact. "I am still of the strong opinion," he said, "that you are a most brave and sensible young lady."

"I don't know about being brave and sensible," said Polly, "but I do believe in facing facts. And the principal fact that I have to face at the moment is what on earth am I going to do?" She looked at Amaz searchingly, as though she was trying to decide how far he was to be trusted. After all, she had only set eyes on him for the first time that very morning, a handsome, affable young Indian with long eyelashes and the slightly dubious recommendation of being a professional guide. And yet there was something, something more than surface charm and physical attraction that drew her to him. He had been kind and attentive and considerate ever since he had met her and Mrs. Innes-Hook at the dock and conducted them to the hotel. This, of course, was perfectly in line with his professional duties. But his attitude to her during and since the sudden, macabre drama of her aunt's illness and death had far exceeded professional duty. The doctor had been kind; the nurses at the hospital had been kind; the manager and the assistant manager at the Raffles Hotel had been kind, but their kindness had been, however well meant, more remote and automatic than the practical friendliness Amaz had given her ever since he had stepped into her aunt's bedroom in his bright blue shirt, beige trousers and sandals. She looked at him now, watching her as intently as she was watching him. His slim brown hands were placed, palms downward, on the dark table. His eyes met hers politely and unwaveringly, but there was, in their depths, an expression she was not quite able to fathom. It might be wariness, pity, that strange, unavowed contempt of the East for the West, or even physical desire. Having no great opinion of her own attractions and being conscious, as always, of her aggressive spectacles, she dimissed the last hypothesis as being the least likely. Feeling deflated and suddenly sad, she looked down.

"Why are you looking at me like that?" she said.

"I think because you were looking at me like that." There was a slight pause, and then he leaned forward and with a deft gesture removed her glasses and laid them on the table. "You have most pretty eyes," he said.

"Have I?" There was a slight tremor in her voice. She looked toward him but could only see the blurred image of his face.

"You should be wearing the contact lenses," he said practically. "A friend of mine here in Victoria Road makes them most brilliantly. He is a Chinese who studied the art of oculism in San Francisco. We will visit him the first thing in the morning. He will for you make a special price. They will perhaps be not comfortable at first but the habit will soon form. I have as well another Chinese friend," he went on, "who is an expert specialist in the business of ladies' hairdressing and facial making-up. He, too, will make you a special price and is well known by many movie stars. You will come with me to these people?"

"Yes," said Polly meekly. "I might also get a black dress for the funeral while I'm at it."

At this moment there was the sound of scuffling, the screen panel was slid back and the Japanese lady reappeared accompanied by two others, bearing a number of dishes which they set down on the table. From then on the complicated ritual of a sukiyaki dinner occupied Polly's mind to the exclusion of anything else. First of all she was presented with a bowl in which floated a raw egg, and a small oblong dish on which reposed a minute piece of ham, some brown stuff that reminded her of grapenuts, but which turned out on later inspection to be ground salt beef; one slice of pickled cucumber and a startled-looking shrimp. Amaz patiently taught her how to hold and use her chopsticks, first of all beating up the egg with them until it was a uniform yellow mess, then, most precariously, dipping the food into it and conveying it to her mouth. Some more sake was brought and she began to get the giggles. While she was struggling with the intricacies of the hors d'oeuvres, the three Japanese ladies, cackling like geese, heated a large iron pan with a spirit lamp and proceeded to fill it with flat slices of raw beef, sliced onions, bamboo-shoots, some unidentifiable green vegetable and a lot of mauvish sticky stuff which looked like the glue used for sticking photographs into albums. Onto all this was poured sugar water from a china kettle and reddish soya sauce from another china kettle. Polly, game to the last, plunged her chopsticks into the steaming pan and managed, unsteadily, to extract a large slice of gray meat, which she managed to get as far as her mouth when it dropped with a splash into her bowl of egg, spattering her neck and the upper part of her dress. The three Japanese ladies were immediately convulsed with laughter and fluttered round her like birds, dabbing at her with little napkins made of colored paper. Her next shot was more successful and by the end of the meal she had become quite adept. The taste of the food, much to her surprise, was subtle, vaguely sweet and quite delicious. When they both had managed to eat about half the contents of the pan they sat back exhausted and lit cigarettes. The three ladies then clattered to their feet, whisked all the dishes away and vanished sibilantly behind the screen. They sat in silence for a few moments. Polly leaned back against the wall because her legs were getting cramped. The occasional sharp honk of a klaxon sounded from the main road, and, far off in the distance, a radio was playing "My Funny Valentine." The sake had gone to Polly's head a little and she felt pleasantly relaxed and the tiniest bit dizzy. She took off her glasses, carefully wiped some egg off the left lens and put them back on again. Amaz, also leaning back against the wall, had his eyes closed. His exquisitely molded face in repose looked smooth and young and somehow defenseless; high up on the side of his angular cheekbone was a small, dark mole and there was a faint line of shadow on his upper lip. He opened his eyes and caught Polly peering at him. His lips parted in a lazy smile.

"You are looking at me again," he said, "as though you were wishing to find some special thoughts in my mind."

"You're quite right," said Polly seriously, "and the special thought I was wishing to find was—was . . ." she hesitated, "why have you put yourself out to be so specially kind to me?"

"Must there be a reason?"

"Yes I think there must and I really and truly want to know what it is because—well I mean—we only met for the first time this morning—" She broke off, feeling suddenly that she might be going to cry.

"What reason would you wish me to say?" he asked. "There might be many small reasons which, when they are added together, become one very big reason. It is most difficult to tell in one swift moment at the end of a long day when so much strange has happened. In the beginning this morning you looked at me most happily and I thought to myself Ha Ha here is a quiet young lady of deep humorousness with whom I could be gay and jolly if her big auntie was not near. That is why I came back to the hotel dressed in my clothes for the beach. I waited by the desk hoping that you might come down alone for perhaps a little private walk to see maybe the shops or ride in a rickshaw. It was then I heard the doctor being demanded most urgently and so I came up to find what was cooking and assist."

"You did assist," said Polly tremulously. "Just by being there. I was feeling horribly scared inside although I tried not to show it. You made me feel that I had a friend, someone to turn to. And then later when I came out of the hospital and found you there waiting—well I can never tell you how touched and relieved I was." She broke off abruptly, and, with a paper napkin, dabbed at a tear which was trickling down her cheek. Amaz rose quickly to his feet, jumped across the table, sat down beside her on the floor and put his arms tenderly round her. With great delicacy he removed her glasses and pulled her head gently onto his shoulder.

"You will wish to cry for a little," he said. "It is a good thing to ease the nerves."

"I do not wish to cry," said Polly in a muffled voice. "I hate crying."

"There—there," he said soothingly. "Rockabye baby on the tree top."

At this Polly made a stifled sound and began to laugh. Amaz, unmoved, proceeded to rock her backward and forward, rhythmically humming a wordless little tune as he did so. At this moment the proprietress slid back the screen and came in bearing two bowls of yellow fruit. She looked at them both impassively, placed the fruit on the table and went out again.

"Please stop," muttered Polly, fighting to control herself. "I shall be sick if you go on doing that. The room's going round quite enough as it is." She wriggled free from him and groped on the table for another paper napkin. He sat back on his haunches and looked at her with a quizzical smile on his face.

"My goodness!" he said. "You are a most sweet young lady."

"I'm afraid I'm not. But you certainly are a most, most sweet young man." She leaned forward and kissed him on the cheek. He looked at her for a moment intently, his brow puckered with a slight frown, then he rose slowly and pulling her up gently from the floor, pressed his mouth onto hers. She twined her arms tightly round his slim body to bring him even closer to her. They stood there silently in the little straw-colored room until the long kiss ended. She bent down to feel for her glasses, but he was too quick for her.

"Not yet," he said, picking them up and holding them out of her reach. "I would wish please to kiss your pretty eyes before you once more hide them."

She stood quite still while he solemnly kissed both her eyes. Then she turned away.

"Perhaps you have now found the special thought in my mind for which before you were seeking," he said.

"Yes," said Polly unsteadily. "I really believe I have."

A half an hour later, driving along a wide, tree-fringed boulevard, Amaz slowed down and turned the car into a narrow, rutted lane which led through a grove of coco palms to the sea. There was no moon but the sky was brilliant with stars. He switched off the engine and the headlights and, taking her by the hand, led her along a strip of beach to where there was a ruined gun emplacement half hidden by oleander trees. Here they sat down side by side, leaning back against the cool stone wall, and looked out across the dark lagoon. The sea was motionless and a little way from the shore the lights of a small fishing boat sent orange spears across the still water. Amaz produced a packet of cigarettes, lit two with one match and flicked the match, still burning, into the sea, where it expired with a little fizz. There was no sound but the trilling of cicadas in the trees and the occasional convulsive "guk guk" of a gecko lizard. Amaz reached for Polly's hand and held it gently and without passion. They smoked their cigarettes in silence for a while, then, still without speaking, he detached Polly's cigarette from the fingers of her left hand and threw it away, flicking his own after it onto the wet sand. With infinite tenderness he turned her face toward him, kissed her lingeringly and, slipping her hand under his shirt, pressed it against his chest. She felt his heart thudding against her fingers as he suddenly heaved his body onto her, his mouth pressing her head back onto the sand. The stars, through her maddening glasses, twisted into wild arabesques of dazzling light; with a clumsy gesture she managed to get them off and when, for a moment, she opened her eyes again, the sky was nothing but a blur of gold.

6

Mr. Archibald Critch, the purser of the S.S. *Arcalla*, was a heavily built, red-faced man in his middle forties. He had awakened with a racking hangover having been on the town the night before with the chief steward and two Eurasian girls they had happened to pick up in the New World pleasure gardens. They had visited several bars, eaten, hazily, a confused Chinese dinner and finished up, sexually incompetent but defiantly cheerful, in a small flat belonging to one of the Eurasians. Now, at 7:30 A.M., he was seated gloomily in his office on A Deck staring, with loathing, at the pile of papers on his desk. He had had a cup of tea, two Alka-Seltzers, and nearly a dessert-spoonful of bicarbonate of soda, but there was still a stabbing pain above his right eye and his head felt as if it had been stuffed with hot cotton wool.

Archie Critch, in normal circumstances, was a genial, well-disposed character. He performed his duties, on the whole, to his own and everyone else's satisfaction. He had tact and authority and just the correct amount of smiling obsequiousness when dealing with the more wealthy and important passengers. His jovial bonhomie at ship's galas, bingo tournaments and fancy-dress dinners earned him a well-deserved popularity on board and if this popularity bloomed with a trifle less effulgence in the Economy and Tourist classes and among the lesser members of the ship's personnel, who could blame him? He had his hands full enough in all conscience with the First Class lot.

He was in the act of scrutinizing, rather glassily, a list of the passengers due to embark on the morrow when his attention was distracted by a sharp rap on the counter. He looked up and was surprised to see a young woman in a pink cotton frock regarding him coolly through heavily-lensed glasses.

"Good morning, Mr. Critch," she said. "I do hope I'm not disturbing you. I know it's very early but I need your help."

For a moment he failed to recognize her and then, with a supreme effort of will, managed to identify her as the mousy little niece–companion who was always trailing about after Mrs. Innes-Hook, who inhabited B42.

"Miss Barlow!" The name came back to him in a flash of trained inspiration. "Up with the lark I see." He forced a merry little laugh and was rewarded with an extra stab of pain in his temple. "I hope your esteemed aunt is enjoying her stay in Singapore?"

"I'm afraid she isn't exactly," said Polly. "She's being buried at four o'clock this afternoon."

For a moment Mr. Critch was thrown completely off balance. His jaw dropped and he stared at her incredulously, "Good God!" he said, "you don't mean it!"

"She died of a heart attack yesterday evening. I understand they have to bury people rather quickly out here because of the climate."

"Yes, I believe that is so." He pressed his hand against his forehead. "What a terrible thing!" he said inadequately.

"Yes, isn't it?" Polly agreed. "I am afraid I shall need your advice and help about quite a lot of things."

"I am entirely at your service," Mr. Critch mumbled, breathing heavily.

"In the first place," continued Polly in a businesslike tone, "I shall have to pack her belongings and take them ashore. I naturally do not feel that I can continue the cruise in the present circumstances. I suppose I can get a refund on my own ticket as I shall not be using it anymore, and perhaps a transfer for my aunt's ticket for a later sailing."

"Certainly, Miss Barlow, I will arrange for our office here in Singapore to be notified. All you will have to do regarding the refund and the transfer is to check with them. Here is a card with the address and telephone number. Any taxi driver will take you to it."

"Thank you," said Polly, "I have a car."

"I trust that you will be returning home in one of our ships?" Mr. Critch, against his will, felt himself becoming a trifle flustered in the face of Polly's decisive coolness. "I will give you a list of our sailings for you to peruse at your leisure."

"I haven't quite made up my mind yet. I may fly back to England in a few days time."

"Please—" said Mr. Critch, rallying his forces, "please accept my most profound sympathy in this most unhappy situation."

"Thank you—you are very kind." Polly vouchsafed him a fleeting smile. "Now then—" she went on, returning briskly to the matter in hand. "I believe my aunt deposited her private papers and a jewel case in your strong box on the day we came on board at Southampton?"

"That is so." He looked at her warily.

"I would like to have them. Here is my aunt's keyring. Perhaps you can identify the key yourself?"

"I fear that it would be quite irregular for me to deliver them to you without written authority—" began Mr. Critch, but Polly gently interrupted him.

"I quite understand that," she said. "But the only written authority you could possibly have would have to be my aunt's signature and she is unfortunately in no position to give it."

Mr. Critch, nonplussed by this palpable logic, scratched his aching head unhappily. "I hope you will appreciate my position," he said, "but before I hand over to you Mrs. Innes-Hook's valuables and papers I must, I fear, have a little more concrete proof that all you say is true—please understand that I am only too eager to cooperate in any way I can but—" He shrugged his shoulders and looked at her uneasily.

"Of course I appreciate your position," replied Polly with a slight hint of impatience in her voice, "which is why I brought this . . ." She opened her handbag and produced a piece of paper, which she handed to him. "It is my aunt's death certificate. Dr. E. R. Renshaw signed it at five forty-five yesterday evening at the Singapore General Hospital. His address and telephone, as you will see, are on the top right-hand corner. You may verify it if you wish while I am packing my aunt's things. In the meantime please may I have the key of her cabin. I will collect the jewel case and the papers later."

Mr. Critch silently took a key from a pigeonhole and handed it to her. She took it, nodded graciously and disappeared down the stairs. He watched her go and once more passed his hand wearily across his forehead. "Well I'll be buggered!" he murmured to himself and, with a shaking hand, lit a cigarette.

About an hour later Polly drove away from the dock in the Cadillac. Amaz was sitting demurely in front next to the driver. Beside Polly on the seat was Mrs. Innes-Hook's crocodile jewel case and a bundle of papers in an envelope tied with pink tape. In the boot at the back, in addition to Polly's own rather drab little valise, were three Revelation suitcases and a large cardboard box containing a pink and mauve embroidered sari which Mrs. Innes-Hook, in a sudden burst of reckless extravagance, had paid a lot of money for in Colombo. Polly had tried it on in the cabin.

The packing had been accomplished entirely successfully. Miss Garry, the stewardess, had popped in and out once or twice in a flurry of inarticulate commiseration and accepted a gift of ten pounds after many protestations. Polly had also tipped Joe, the steward, who had been helpful to her during the voyage and had once given her a friendly little nip on the bottom as she was going along the passage laden with a bundle of her aunt's laundry.

As the car purred along through the early morning sunlight, Polly reflected, not without satisfaction, that her late aunt's inherent meanness with regard to money had, for once, proved exceedingly fortunate. Mrs. Innes-Hook had obviously been one of those women who, like certain French peasants, cherish a superstitious distrust of safes and banks. She belonged to the cash-in-the-stocking school. Proof of this lay snugly in Polly's handbag in two separate bundles of 350 pounds each. She had discovered one bundle rammed in the toe of a shoe and the other, wrapped in cellophane, in the bottom of an overstuffed sponge bag.

She intended to wait until after the funeral to examine the papers and open the jewel case. She suspected that there would probably be an itemized list of the jewelry among the papers and possibly some informative insurance policies. She realized that she required time to check these matters and she had a busy morning ahead of her.

At nine o'clock Amaz had made an appointment for her with the Chinese oculist.

At nine-thirty a Mr. Ambrose Wah Hai had agreed to lay aside two hours of his most valuable time in order to wash, set, wave, tint, spray and entirely reorganize her hair. He would also, Amaz assured her, be only too delighted to give her some vital hints on makeup. Still another crony of Amaz's, a lady called Mrs. Ackbar Singh, who was the proprietress of Yvonne et Cie in the Victoria Road, had agreed to send round to the Raffles Hotel two or three simple black frocks on approval. Polly had decided to leave the question of a suitable black hat until after her hair had been done; after all, as a last resort, she could always put on a black veil. In addition to all these arrangements, Amaz, carried away by his own unbounded enthusiasm in the cause of Polly's metamorphosis, had telephoned Tuan Robert Hook at a very early hour to request him not to be at the hotel until one o'clock as Polly would be too occupied to receive him at noon as planned. Apparently this telephone call had been received a trifle querulously.

At seven minutes to nine, having locked up the valuables in one of her aunt's suitcases, Polly set off, accompanied by Amaz, to buy the contact lenses and receive her first lesson as to how to use them. This proved to be a rather complicated and painful business, but after she had been shown how to put them in and take them out several times she began to get the hang of it. Mr. Wing Foo, the oculist, took infinite trouble and advised her to wear them for only two hours a day to begin with, moving on to four hours and eight hours a day as time went on and she became used to them. He also warned her that they would almost certainly itch violently at first and that she was on no account to rub her eyes but try to endure it with fortitude. She bought two pairs to be on the safe side. They were packed daintily in plastic boxes and lay side by side on some sort of mauve, spongy material looking like minute blobs of water.

The two hours she spent in Mr. Ambrose Wah Hai's Beauty Parlour were interesting but exhausting. Mr. Wah Hai himself was a bundle of dynamic energy. Assisted by two sullen-looking girls attired in cheongsams, he danced round her like some sort of oriental dervish. His English was perfect, but he spoke it with a strong American accent, having spent three years studying his trade in San Francisco and Los Angeles. He also hissed with even more wholehearted abandon than the three Japanese ladies who had served the sukiyaki dinner the night before.

"My dear!" he cried to Amaz, standing back and gazing at Polly with half-closed eyes, "have you ever *seen* such a fuzz? It looks exactly like something's nest!" He gave a high-pitched giggle and darted at Polly with a comb as though he were going to scalp her with it. "Don't worry honey-chile," he went on, noticing a look of dismay on her face, "it's just my way of talking. I'm as kooky as a sand crab! Aren't I, dear?" He glanced archly over his shoulder at Amaz, who was sitting in a cane chair against the wall, observing operations with a watchful eye.

Amaz nodded indulgently. "Ambrose is a most screaming character," he explained. The two hours seemed an eternity to Polly although she was fascinated by the unending flow of irrelevant conversation that cascaded from Ambrose's lips. Having removed her glasses, she was unable to see what was happening very clearly, so she gave herself up to the situation and hoped for the best. Amaz occasionally got up and went out, returning a minute or two later with a cup of thin, scented Chinese tea for her. He also lit cigarettes for her whenever she made a sign. Sometimes he touched her bare arm with his hand, and her heart melted.

Just after twelve o'clock Polly got back to the hotel and went up to the room. Amaz followed her discreetly a few moments later and, the moment he had closed the door behind him, they flew into a passionate embrace.

"Be careful darling," said Polly breathlessly wriggling out of his grasp, "remember my makeup!" Laughing, she took him by the hand and walked over to the looking glass on the dressing table. They stood there, side by side, staring at the rather tartish reflection staring back at them. Mr. Ambrose Wah Hai had certainly made a thorough job of it. Polly's now ash blond hair had been blown up into a sort of bouffant hive which made her head look enormous and her face tiny. Her eyes were elaborately shaded and painted and her scarlet lips gaped at her in clownish astonishment. She took off her glasses, put them on and then took them off again. "Oh dear!" she moaned, "that won't do at all. I look raving mad!" She stood back and rummaged in her handbag. "We'll have one try with the contact lenses," she said, "and then we really will have to do something about it. I can't possibly even go into the grillroom like this, let alone a funeral."

After a certain amount of concentrated effort from them both they managed to get the lenses into her eyes correctly. She gave a little blink and a sigh of pain.

"They feel like bits of broken glass," she said. "I shall never get used to them, I know I shan't."

"Do not allow your eyes to blink," said Amaz firmly. "Look now clearly and most tranquilly into the mirror." He led her back to the dressing table from which she had retreated in panic. She gazed at herself and was forced to admit, agony or no agony, that the lenses did work.

"They do make little shooting lights on the right and the left every now and then," she said. "But the man did say that that would pass off didn't he?"

Amaz put his arm round her shoulder and patted her soothingly. "You are beautiful!" he said. "I am in agreement that the hair is much too high up and the makeup on the face most strong. But you are beautiful—as from the first I was knowing that you would be."

"Oh, Amaz!" She turned her face to him. "Do you think they will wash out if I cry?"

7

For Robert Hook, the long drive into town from his plantation had been dusty and uncomfortable and rendered even more intolerable than it need have been by Lorelei Chang's determination to be disagreeable. She left him in no doubt of her resentment at being dragged back into the stuffiness of the city on a Saturday morning, when she didn't actually have to be back until late on Sunday evening. She was tearful, vituperative and sarcastic by turns, and by the time they had arrived at the vast white apartment building in which she occupied a minute flat, she had grumbled herself into a sullen silence. When the car drew alongside the curb she jumped out almost before it came to a stop, slammed the door viciously and clattered across the pavement without even looking back at him. He watched her bottom wobbling eloquently in its blue cheongsam and, with a great effort, controlled an impulse to jump out after her and slap it hard before it disappeared inside the entrance hall. Women, he reflected irritably, were a bloody nuisance. Particularly the pampered little sexpots who happened to be good in the hay. Bob Hook, in his middle forties, was still physically attractive and knew it. He had no illusions about his relationship with Lorelei Chang. She went to bed with him because she wanted to and he went to bed with her because he wanted to. There was no emotion involved and hardly any basis even for companionship. She amused him occasionally when she happened to be in a gay mood, but at the moment he could willingly have throttled her. She was one of the most highly paid models in Singapore, in addition to which she was amply provided for by a wealthy Chinese silk merchant who happened at the moment to be in Hong Kong. Beautiful and sexually alluring she undoubtedly was, but she was also a damned sight too pleased with herself and a spoilt little brat. He glanced at his wristwatch and, noting that it was only 12:15, let in the clutch and drove at a slow pace along the wide sun-baked boulevard in the direction of the Adelphi Hotel. He felt he needed a wash and a soothing drink before the ordeal of facing a probably tear-stained and hysterical niece who, he vaguely remembered, wore fearsome spectacles. In the air-conditioned bar of the Adelphi he ordered himself a gin sling and a packet of cigarettes and retired to the lavatory, where he removed his coat, tie and shirt, which was sticking uncomfortably to his skin. When he had sluiced himself with cold water the Chinese attendant rubbed him down with a towel and then proceeded to massage his chest delicately with talcum powder. The sensation was relaxing and faintly lascivious. He regarded his torso thoughtfully in the mirror and found the spectacle not unpleasing. He flexed his muscles lazily and, taking a deep breath, expanded his chest. The Chinese boy smiled at him hopefully and fluttered his fingers lightly over his stomach. Bob laughed, gave him a gentle cuff on the side of the head and tipped him a dollar; then he put on his damp shirt again, with a slight shudder, and returned to the bar. A half an hour later, feeling refreshed but still exasperated, he parked his car in the drive of the Raffles Hotel and walked up the steps into the lobby. Although not air-conditioned, it was agreeably cool and dim. He was on his way to the reception desk when a pretty young woman in a black frock who was sitting at one of the tables put down what looked suspiciously like a dry Martini, and rose to intercept him.

"Uncle Bob!—It is you, isn't it?"

"Polly!" He looked at her in some astonishment, hesitated for the fraction of a second and then kissed her on the cheek. "You certainly have changed since I saw you last."

"I know," replied Polly. "It's all happened rather suddenly." She smiled and motioned him to the other chair at her table. "Please sit down and have a drink while I finish mine. I don't generally drink in the middle of the day but I felt that this was rather a special occasion what with you coming and the funeral and everything. Also I've had rather a busy morning." She clapped her hands to summon the waiter. "What would you like?"

"Is that a dry Martini?"

"Yes."

"All right. I'll have the same."

A young Malay in a jacket and sarong came up to the table.

"A dry Martini please." Polly sat back with a little sigh and, taking a cigarette case from her bag, offered him one which he accepted mechanically. The cigarette case was heavy, gold encrusted with diamonds and sapphires. She noticed him staring at it.

"It was Aunt Eva's," she said. "It has a lighter to match." She fumbled in her bag again, produced the lighter, snapped it open and lit his cigarette. "Aren't they pretty?"

"Very pretty. A bit ornate perhaps."

"Poor Aunt Eva loved ornate things. Wait until you see the rest of her jewelry."

"The rest of her jewelry?"

"Yes. I collected it this morning from the purser. It's all upstairs locked in a suitcase. There are some papers as well. I thought we might look over them together after lunch. I'm not very good at legal documents."

Bob's seething astonishment at her complete self-possession suddenly exploded. "Well I'll be damned!"

She raised her eyebrows. "What's the matter?"

"You seem to be taking the whole business very calmly. I expected you to be in a terrible state, weeping hysterically and having to be comforted."

"I'm not the hysterical type."

"No," said Bob a trifle grimly. "I see you're not."

"Would you rather I was? Have I shocked you?"

"No." He suddenly laughed. "You haven't exactly shocked me, at least, if you have, the shock is entirely pleasant, in fact it's a great relief."

"I'm so glad." She rested her hand on his for a moment. "It was most awfully sweet of you to come. I do appreciate it. How's your malaria?"

He looked at her sharply, but her face was without irony. "Much better. It comes and goes you know," he added not very convincingly.

"Yes," said Polly. "I expect it does. Here's your Martini." She signed the chit and tipped the waiter, who bowed and retired to the bar. She raised her glass and clinked it gently against his—"Here goes!" she said.

"Here goes!" He looked at her curiously. "Surely you used to wear glasses?"

"Yes. They're upstairs. I've got contact lenses in. They itch a bit, but the man Amaz took me to explained that that would happen and that I would get used to them in time."

"Amaz?"

"Yes. He's been really wonderful to me. He took me to a hair-dresser, too, who's a friend of his. My hair was a musty brown when I woke up this morning and look at it now!"

"It looks charming."

"It didn't at first. The silly man made it into a sort of beehive, but we managed to get it back to a more suitable shape."

"We?"

"Amaz and I. He's been a tower of strength ever since he met Aunt Eva and me at the dock yesterday. He took me to a Japanese restaurant last night and taught me how to use chopsticks."

"You really are a most peculiar girl."

"Surely there's nothing so very peculiar about using chop-sticks in a Japanese restaurant? It's what you're supposed to do isn't it?"

"I wasn't referring to the chopsticks."

"Oh!" She looked at him searchingly. "You mean I oughtn't to have had dinner with Amaz?"

"Not—not exactly—" Bob found himself floundering a little under her level gaze. "It's only—only—" He broke off and took a hur-ried gulp of his Martini.

"Only what?"

"Well—Amaz is after all a professional guide and a Eurasian, half Indian and half Chinese and—"

"He adores you," Polly interposed. "He told me that you were very genial and go-as-you-please and that you and he had spent eve-nings together of unforgettable merriment."

"Did he indeed?"

"He also said you were strong and wiry and most young for your age."

"Now look here Polly"—Bob made an effort to speak severely—"Amaz is admittedly an attractive and efficient young man, but I can-not feel that he is an entirely suitable companion for a young girl of your age who is visiting the Orient for the first time in—we must face it—the most distressing circumstances."

"That's just it," said Polly. "If it hadn't been for the distressing circumstances I should never have got to know him. If it hadn't been for him I really don't know what I should have done. When Aunt Eva had the stroke and was lying on the floor it was Amaz who sud-denly appeared and coped with everything. It was he who was wait-ing for me with a car outside the hospital yesterday evening just after she died. It was he who telephoned you and explained the situ-ation—"

"It was also he who took you to the hairdresser and made you get the contact lenses?"

"Certainly it was, and this black dress for the funeral and a rather horrid little hat which is upstairs because I couldn't bear to put it on until the last possible moment. You can't expect me not to be fond of Amaz. He was the only one I had to turn to. After all you were miles away on your rubber plantation racked with malaria weren't you?" She paused and regarded him with the suspicion of a smile. "I do hope it isn't catching."

"Why do you say that?"

"I was thinking of Miss Lorelei Chang."

"What do you know about Lorelei Chang?"

Polly giggled. "I wormed it out of Amaz this morning. Is her name really Lorelei?"

"I'll wring that little bastard's neck."

"Don't be cross, Uncle Bob. I never thought you had malaria anyway. I read that letter you wrote to Aunt Eva and I didn't believe a word of it."

"I think," said Bob weakly, "we'd better go and have lunch."

"Good." Polly rose to her feet. "Don't let's order curry though. Aunt Eva had two whacks at it yesterday and I'm superstitious about it."

They walked into the grillroom in silence.

After lunch, fortified by two further dry Martinis, a carafe of vin rosé and two Grand Marniers in the hotel lounge, Polly and her uncle retired to the late Mrs. Innes-Hook's bedroom and settled themselves comfortably on either side of a small rosewood table on which Polly had placed the jewel case and papers she had extracted from the reluctant purser of the S.S. *Arcadia*. Polly looked at her watch.

"Amaz will be here at quarter of four with the Cadillac, so we've got nearly an hour. You can leave your car where it is in the drive and we can pick it up afterward."

"I don't know what poor old Nell would say, I really don't."

"Don't let's worry about mother for a moment. She's miles away and probably at a seance."

"A seance?"

"Yes. She's got a new friend who's a medium, rather dusty-looking, her name's Alma Ruddle. They constantly get in touch with departed loved ones on what they call 'the other side.' They're probably gossiping away with Aunt Eva at this very minute."

"There's a certain callousness in your approach to this whole situation that I cannot but deplore," said Bob, lighting a cigarette.

"Yes," agreed Polly. "It is bad, isn't it?"

"Have you cabled to your mother?"

"Not yet. I thought we'd wait until after the funeral and send one together. Or perhaps it would be better if you sent one on your own, explaining that I am naturally very upset and will write as soon as I feel up to it."

"Admirable," said Bob. "You think of everything. When are you going home?"

"I haven't decided yet. It seems silly to rush things. After all I've never been to the Far East before so I might just as well see as much of it as I can now that I have the opportunity." She paused. "I'm going to take my contact lenses out now," she said, "because they're driving me mad. You won't mind my glasses for a little will you?"

"Not at all. Go right ahead."

Polly went over to the dressing table and took a little box out of the drawer, then, with a slight groan, she poked about in her eyes with her finger until she had extracted the lenses. With a sigh of relief she placed them carefully on the mauve cushion in the box, put on her glasses and came back to the table.

"I *know* I shall get used to them in time because the old man swore I would, but I'm afraid it's going to be a long haul."

"Come on," said Bob practically. "To our muttons. We must concentrate." He winked at her conspiratorially, whereupon she jumped up, came round the table and kissed him on the cheek.

"You are a dear, Uncle Bob. I had no idea you'd be quite so gay and understanding. I suppose it's something to do with being the black sheep of the family. Black sheep are always more fun than the white ones."

"I didn't know I *was* the black sheep of the family."

Polly laughed and returned to her chair. "Of course you are. Think of Uncle Stanley and Uncle Fred and poor Aunt Sylvia, all married and respectable and as dull as ditchwater. You're mysterious and a bachelor and leading a secret, sinful life in the exotic East. If that doesn't make you a black sheep I should like to know what does."

"Why should you assume that my life is sinful?"

"*I* don't think so at all, but they would. Can you imagine what Aunt Sylvia would say if she knew about Miss Lorelei Chang?"

"Damn Miss Lorelei Chang," said Bob. "She's a tiresome little bitch and I'm sick to death of her."

"That's what I mean," said Polly. "Off with the old love and on with the new. No moral stamina."

"I had no idea that Derry and Tom's was such a hotbed of sophistication!" He looked at her keenly. "Do you consider yourself to be typical of the younger generation?"

"Inside, yes." Polly thought for a moment. "But not outside— that is, until now."

"Were you a virgin when you left England?"

"Why do you ask that?"

"Because I'd like to know."

"Technically, yes, principally because nobody found me very attractive. I did have an almost-but-not-quite carry-on with a friend of the girl I'm sharing a flat with. But it was late at night and he'd had a lot to drink and I think he was, if anything, more scared than I was. Anyhow it never really came to anything."

"And since you left England?"

Polly gave a quick frown and turned her head away. "Uncle Bob—please—"

"We've been entirely frank with each other all through lunch. We talked away as if we were old friends. Why shouldn't we now?"

"It's Amaz you're thinking of isn't it?" she said after a pause.

"Yes, it is Amaz that I am thinking of."

"All right." Polly sighed. "Have it your own way."

"I'd like to make it clear that I'm not taking up a moral attitude. Moral attitudes are not exactly my strong suit. But I would like to warn you to be a little careful."

"Careful? You mean careful about—about getting into trouble?"

"Actually I didn't mean careful about your body, I meant careful about your heart."

Polly removed her glasses, took a handkerchief out of her bag and dabbed her eyes with it.

"I'm not crying," she said in a muffled voice. "Not really crying I mean, but I might, if we go on with this conversation." She steadied herself with an effort. "Amaz made love to me last night," she said flatly. "I suppose it had all been built up to by what had happened during the day. I know I didn't truly mind about Aunt Eva dying because I didn't care for her, but it was all rather a shock and Amaz was there all the time standing by and helping me. Then of course there was the Japanese dinner and the chopsticks and everything and—" she faltered. "Nobody had ever really wanted me like that before, so I—I just gave up and let it happen. I can't honestly say whether I'm in love with him or not because I just don't know. All I do know is that I shall be grateful to him to the end of my days." She paused. "Now I really am going to cry which is just as well really because it will make my eyes nice and red for the funeral." She buried her head in her hands and wept without restraint. Bob patted her hand consolingly across the table and sat back to give her time to recover herself.

"Well," he said, "now we know where we are." He got up, walked over to the dressing table and brought over a box of pink Kleenex, which he put down beside her.

"Have a good cry if you feel like it, but don't keep it up for too long. We have a lot to discuss and we don't want to waste time."

Polly looked up at him, gave one more convulsive sob followed by a fleeting smile and blew her nose firmly.

"I'm not a crier as a rule," she said. "I'm in rather an emotional state I expect, subconsciously. After all it's not to be wondered at is it?"

"No." Bob lit a cigarette and handed it to her. "It's certainly not to be wondered at. But the sooner you snap out of it the better."

Polly blew her nose again and polished her glasses with a fresh piece of Kleenex.

"Why do you disapprove of Amaz?"

"I don't disapprove of Amaz. As a matter of fact I'm very fond of him. He's an oversexed little rabbit. He's quick, bright and efficient and he's been useful to me on many occasions."

"Useful?" she asked sharply. "In what way—useful?"

"Lots of ways. Among other things he has a remarkable talent for organization. Actually it was through me that he got his present job. I introduced him to Keith Machin, who is the chairman of the Tourist Board."

"You've known him a long time? Amaz I mean, not the man on the Tourist Board."

"I've known them both for a long time." Bob smiled blandly.

"When did you first meet him?"

"Several years ago, in a rather dubious bar. In those days he was even more attractive than he is now. Indians age very quickly you know."

"He's only half Indian," said Polly defensively. "The other half's Chinese and they don't age at all. What was he doing in the—dubious bar?"

"He was a sort of gigolo."

"Gigolo?"

"Yes. That's a polite way of saying that he was willing to sleep with anyone whom he thought could be useful to him. I'm not trying to shock you," he added gently. "Oriental moral values are very different from those of West Kensington."

"You should come home on leave more often Uncle Bob. You'd be surprised."

Bob laughed. "I see you are not convinced."

"Convinced of what?"

"That Amaz, owing to his mixed blood, his mixed relationships and the rather ramshackle pattern of his life up to date, may not turn out to be entirely satisfactory as a lover, on a long-term basis at any rate."

"I have no complaints so far," said Polly calmly, taking a compact out of her bag and powdering her nose.

"Good God!" cried Bob explosively. "You're talking like a blasé woman of forty instead of a girl of twenty-three."

"It's not only Indians who age quickly." Polly regarded herself thoughtfully in the mirror of her compact. "I've aged a lot during the last twenty-four hours. In any case," she added, "I have no intention that my relationship with Amaz should be on a long-term basis. As a matter of fact I have arranged to sail for Hong Kong on Monday. I went to the shipping office this morning after I'd had my hair done. The ship is called the *Alcona* and I have an outside cabin on A Deck."

"Be that as it may. I am your uncle, your mother's brother, and I cannot, without at least registering a protest, allow you to pop into bed with every Eurasian you meet."

"I am your niece, your sister's daughter, and it certainly doesn't matter to me how many Eurasians you pop into bed with."

"Surely that's a little different?"

Polly smiled radiantly and, leaning across the table, placed both her hands on his.

"Dear, dear, Uncle Bob," she said. "You're being a terrible hypocrite and you know it. You don't really care whether I have an affair with Amaz or whether I don't. It's only a sort of conscience hangover that's making you suddenly pompous. You have a feeling that because you're my uncle you ought to be responsible for me, but you know perfectly well that this really isn't true. There is no earthly reason for you to be responsible for me beyond standing by me at this particular crisis and seeing me through the funeral, and you're doing that all right so your conscience should be quite, quite clear. If you had been a conventional respectable white-sheep uncle instead of a cozy, immoral black-sheep one, I should never have talked to you as I have done. I would never have let you even guess about Amaz and I would never have let you catch me having a dry Martini. It was only by reading your letter to Aunt Eva and listening to Amaz talk about you that I got in advance a slight inkling of what sort of man you were. . . . You and I have a great deal in common. We neither of us have very strong family ties. I've really been living abroad in London just as much as you have been here. I see Jack and Ted and Ronnie and Mavis and Joan occasionally on birthdays and Christmases, and I sometimes go to lunch with poor mother in Malden on Sundays, but apart from that I've led my own life and done my own thinking. The difference is of course that you've always been the black sheep and attractive whereas I've been the ugly duckling and unattractive. However, thanks to Aunt Eva dying and Amaz suggesting the contact lenses and the hairdo and one thing and another, things seem to be leveling out. I loathed being at Derry and Tom's and I only came away with Aunt Eva so as to escape and see a bit of the world. I knew she was a mean, vulgar-minded old horror before we started, so her treatment of me on the ship was no surprise. I was well prepared for it and it didn't upset me in the least. As a matter of fact, I rather enjoyed her tantrums, particularly when she made a beast of herself in front of other people. I always had a strange feeling at the back of my mind that something was going to happen, and that whatever it was it would prove somehow to be fortunate for me. Naturally I didn't expect her to have a heart attack and die, but when she did, I felt instinctively that this was it, the happening, the opportunity I had been waiting for. It was unpleasant of course, and rather frightening, but I couldn't feel sorry. I tried once or twice to work up a little decent compassion but I couldn't manage it. All I could remember were her little meannesses, her rudeness to the stewards, the cruel jokes she was always making about me being short-sighted, her smarmy obsequiousness to the captain and her harsh, ugly voice—" Polly broke off and frowned.

"My God!" said Bob. "You did hate her didn't you?"

"No." Polly shook her head vigorously. "I didn't even hate her. I despised her and dismissed her."

"You are what might be described as a cool customer aren't you?" Bob chuckled.

"I'm a realist," said Polly. "I lived with mother too long to be anything else."

"Poor old Nell. I wonder if she has any idea of what sort of an ugly duckling she hatched out?"

"Of course not. She doesn't know what I'm like any more than she knows what you're like, and you're her favorite brother, next to Uncle Edgar, who Aunt Eva ate up. She doesn't know anything about any of us really. She's invented a sort of private woman's-magazine world of her own, full of spirit rappings, superstitions and sudden unneccessary little frights. She's never seen anything as it really is since the day she was born. She's vague, kind, woolly-minded, sentimental and a perfect ass. You know that as well as I do."

"I don't know what the younger generation is coming to, upon my soul I don't."

"Well you and she at least have that in common." Polly laughed.

"I'll tell you one thing," said Bob. "If I were not a case-hardened, amoral, dyed-in-the-wool black sheep, you'd terrify the bloody life out of me."

"Dear Uncle Bob." Polly blew him a kiss. "I'm beginning to love you very much indeed."

"Would you like to have dinner with me tonight, after this ghastly business is over?"

"I've already promised to have dinner with Amaz."

"Bring him too. We'll all dine together."

"That would be conniving."

"I don't object to a little shady connivance once in a while."

"That"—said Polly—"is what I hoped you would say. Now let's open the jewel case and see what can be salvaged. There's an itemized list of all the stuff that's insured among those papers. I had a quick look at them before lunch. But Aunt Eva did some quite extensive shopping in Colombo. She belonged to the 'diamonds are a girl's best friend' school of thought. Here's the key. You open it while I get the insurance list, and we'll check."

"To be a realist is one thing," said Bob, fumbling with the lock. "To be a potential criminal is another."

"Dear Uncle Bob," said Polly absently as she wrestled with the pink tape with which the papers were tied, "what nonsense you do talk."

8

The interment of the late Mrs. Innes-Hook was conducted with almost military efficiency. The hospital chaplain, a Mr. Bleaker, mumbled through a brief service which took place in a small gray chapel which smelt of onions because there was an open-air Chinese restaurant a little way down the road and the wind happened to be blowing from the west.

The mourners consisted of Polly, her uncle, Mrs. Renshaw, the doctor's wife and, to Polly's surprise, Miss Elaine Gudgeon, the cruise hostess from the *Arcalia*. Miss Gudgeon was a tinted blonde in her early forties with a professionally vivacious manner and slightly protruding teeth. When Polly got out of the car she sprang at her with a shrill yelp and enfolded her in her arms.

"I had to come," she said, "I just couldn't bear to think of you facing this terrible ordeal all alone."

Polly gently disengaged herself from Miss Gudgeon's embrace and rewarded her with a wan smile. "How very very kind of you." She turned toward Bob. "This is my uncle, Mr. Robert Hook."

Miss Gudgeon wrung Bob's hand fervently. "What a dreadful, dreadful tragedy! And so sudden!" She looked at him with almost canine eagerness. Polly felt that if he had thrown a stone she would have retrieved it immediately.

Bob bowed gravely. "In the midst of life we are in death," he said.

Polly turned away hurriedly. The last memory she had of Miss Gudgeon was at the captain's gala fancy-dress dinner when she had been wearing a tired blue satin pierette's costume and a dunce's cap made of sequins. The transition from that to her present somber black was too startling a contrast to be faced with equanimity.

After the service, the coffin, on a sort of trolley, was trundled briskly out into the late afternoon sunlight and deposited, with reverent dispatch, in the grave. While this was going on Mrs. Renshaw, a dumpy little woman like a small gray pigeon, squeezed Polly's hand.

When the last rites had been concluded, Mr. Bleaker accompanied Polly and Bob back to the car where Amaz was waiting, wearing a black sombrero and a suitably morose expression. Mrs. Renshaw and Miss Elaine Gudgeon followed behind. They all stood about for a few minutes in embarrassed silence. Bob, noticing that Polly's head was averted and that she was savagely biting her underlip, took charge of the situation with impressive authority. He shook hands first with Mr. Bleaker, then with Mrs. Renshaw, and Miss Gudgeon.

"On behalf of my niece," he said, "who, as you know, has been under a tremendous strain during the last twenty-four hours, I would like to thank you for your immense kindness and consideration on this most distressing occasion. My late sister-in-law was a woman of strong character and remarkable vitality. For us, her relatives here, and for her sorrowing loved ones at home, it is indeed a desolate thought that she should have been struck down in such sudden and tragic circumstances, however"—he added after a pregnant pause— "the ways of God are incalculable and it is not for us to question them. Thank you again very, very much."

At the end of this delicate oration Miss Gudgeon, obviously moved, gave a subdued whine. Polly, her head still averted, shook hands solemnly all round and got into the car. Bob raised his hat with sad dignity and got in after her. Amaz bounded into the front seat next to the Malay driver, who had been watching the proceedings with conventional oriental impassivity. Obeying a peremptory whack on the shoulder from Bob, he let in the clutch and the car moved slowly away.

Polly glanced back through the rear window. The trio of darkly clad figures diminished in the distance until they looked like three little black dolls that someone had placed haphazardly under a scarlet tree.

9

Upon returning to the Raffles Hotel, Polly pulled down the blinds, drew the curtains and, having undressed and taken out her lenses, put on a dressing gown and lay on the bed. . . . The air-conditioning plant made a subdued roaring noise occasionally punctuated by muted traffic noises from the street outside. Uncle Bob and Amaz were to pick her up at eight-thirty and it was now only ten to six, so she had ample time to relax. She stared up at the ceiling on which something suddenly moved. Being unable to see clearly enough to identify it, she frowned and closed her eyes. It might be an ordinary lizard, a scorpion or a tarantula. After a moment's reflection she decided that scorpions, as a general rule, did not frequent ceilings but were more likely to creep out from under the bed and secrete themselves in your bedroom slippers. To be on the safe side she leaned over, picked up her bedroom slippers, shook them carefully and placed them on the counterpane. If it were a tarantula, however, it might quite possibly elect to drop onto her face and bite her, whereupon in a matter of minutes she would swell up and die in agony. On the whole, she thought with a slight giggle, it would serve her right for being wily, scheming and unscrupulous. She stared up at the ceiling again, but this time nothing either ambulant or static marred its surface. It was white and smooth and void of menace. A clock, far away in the distance, struck six. She closed her eyes and drifted into sleep. While she slept she saw herself, dressed neatly as a ship's stewardess, wheeling a perambulator along a tree-lined suburban road. In the perambulator were two tiny, chocolate-colored babies dressed in batik sarongs and heavily bedecked with ornate jewelry. Beside her walked Amaz, stark naked, singing "Rockabye Baby on the Tree Top." She realized with a shudder of dismay that they were approaching her mother's house. At this moment Uncle Bob suddenly drove up at great speed in an open MG. When he stepped out of it and saluted smartly she saw that he was in the uniform of a London policeman and wearing large emerald earrings. With a debonair smile he detached them from his ears and presented them to her with a low bow. "These," he said, in the singsong voice the Reverend Mr. Bleaker had employed while reading the funeral service, "are not on the insurance list and should fetch anything from fifteen to sixteen thousand pounds, Amen." Whereupon Amaz darted forward and snatched them from her hand. "What a tragic occasion," he said, "and so *sudden!*" With that he proceeded to fit the earrings carefully into his eyes. "They are bound to itch a bit at first," he said, "but that will wear off in time." Then, as though pulled by an invisible string, both the babies shot into the air and fluttered round and round in circles emitting shrill cries. To her horror Polly suddenly realized that they were not babies at all but large black spiders. She tried to run away but her feet sank deeper and deeper into the asphalt pavement. She woke in panic, frantically groped for the light by the bed and switched it on. She lay still for a minute or two while the memory of the dream receded from her mind, then she looked at Aunt Eva's traveling clock. Twenty minutes past seven. She jumped off the bed and ran into the bathroom. When she emerged from the refreshingly tepid bath, she draped herself in a towel, went back into the bedroom and fitted in her contact lenses. They slipped in quite easily and almost painlessly. She sat down at the dressing table and went to work with the cosmetics she had brought away from Mr. Ambrose Wah Hai's beauty salon. After about a quarter of an hour's cautious endeavor she leant back and regarded the results critically. The face that looked back at her was so startlingly different from the one she had woken up with that morning that she found herself peering forward to see if it really was true and not some sort of optical illusion. Her skin looked clear and smooth; the shading on her eyes was just right; her face was naturally pale and she experimented for a moment with a little dry rouge, then, deciding that pallor looked more effective with her ash blond hair, she wiped it off again with a Kleenex tissue. She had eliminated Mr. Wah Hai's elaborate bouffant balloon and brushed her hair straight back into a little bun, which gave her a demure, rather Victorian look. When she was satisfied with her face she went to the wardrobe and took out the dresses Mrs. Ackbar Singh (Yvonne et Cie) had brought her on approval that morning. They were all three black of course, Amaz having explained to Mrs. Singh that the occasion was one of mourning. The one Polly had worn at the funeral lay over the back of a chair. It had not really fitted very comfortably and was not particularly well cut. She looked at the other two. One was high-necked and bunchy and she discarded it on sight. The other was a sleeveless black chiffon completely spoiled by a gold lamé belt. Polly detached the belt and, having slipped the dress on, looked at herself in the wardrobe mirror. It fitted her surprisingly well. She moved about and pirouetted twice to see how it flowed. It was perhaps a shade too long but, on the whole, not bad at all. She unlocked the suitcase in which Uncle Bob had packed those pieces of her aunt's jewelry which had not been marked on the insurance list and could therefore be appropriated with the minimum danger of discovery. The rest had been put back in the jewel case which, with the papers, was to be dispatched, via Uncle Bob's bank manager, to Aunt Eva's London lawyers. The non-itemized articles, however, as treasure trove, were certainly not to be sneezed at. Apart from a number of pretty, but comparatively valueless trinkets, there was the cigarette case with the lighter to match; three clips, one, plain diamond, one, diamond and ruby, and one, gold, in the shape of a bird with sapphire eyes and a sapphire tail; two diamond rings, one set in platinum; a diamond and pearl bracelet and, best of all, an exquisite diamond and emerald necklace with earrings of single emeralds which could also be used as clips if required. This, the gold bird, and the two diamond rings, Mrs. Innes-Hook had bought in Colombo and paid for with traveler's cheques. This, Polly remembered distinctly, because her aunt, who couldn't abide being watched while conducting any financial transaction, had ordered her to wait outside the shop in the blazing sun for nearly half an hour while she countersigned two entire folders. Uncle Bob had assessed the necklace and earrings alone at approximately fifteen hundred pounds. He had also given her a letter of introduction to a diamond merchant he knew in Hong Kong who, he assured her, would dispose of them for her without question and for a most modest commission. Polly poked about among the trinkets of lesser value and finally selected a string of cultured pearls with an amethyst clasp. (The real pearls, which she had rather shudderingly removed from her deceased aunt's neck in the hospital, were, alas, on the insurance list and therefore locked in the case destined for London together with the sapphire and diamond bracelet and all five of the rings that Polly had wrapped in her handkerchief when Mrs. Innes-Hook had first been taken ill.) She also selected a quite pretty aquamarine and pearl bracelet and a pearl and enamel clip. She toyed for a moment with the idea of wearing the bird but decided that this might be going too far. Having put on the necklace, the bracelet and the clip and studying the effect in the glass, she saluted herself with a businesslike nod of approval. There was no doubt whatever that the metamorphosis was a triumphant success. A simply dressed, discreetly made up and most attractive young woman looked back at her from the mirror and winked.

"Well," she said out loud, "all you need now is a crystal coach with six white horses and you're home and dry."

She shut and locked the suitcase, popped the key into her handbag and her glasses in case the contact lenses should become insupportable during the evening and walked down the corridor to the lift. When the door slid open a tall man in a white tropical suit sprang out and nearly bumped into her. The lift boy motioned him back. "This is the fifth floor," he said. The man stepped back into the lift and smiled at Polly apologetically. "Sorry, ma'am," he said. "I guess I nearly knocked you out for the count!"

Polly bowed graciously and lowered her eyes, but not before she had observed that he was one of the handsomest men she had ever seen. He was about six-foot-two; his shoulders were wide and his hips slim; his fair hair was crew-cut and his deeply tanned skin emphasized the clear blue of his eyes. She noticed that the hair on his brown wrists had been bleached almost white by the sun. He exuded animal health and vitality and might have been any age between thirty-five and forty-five. When they reached the main floor he stood aside to allow her to walk out. Aware that his eyes were appraising her, she walked, a little more languidly than usual, to a table under one of the punkahs after looking around casually to see if Uncle Bob or Amaz had arrived. She sat down with the unhurried poise that a movie star would have envied, took Aunt Eva's cigarette case and lighter from her bag, lit herself a cigarette and beckoned to a waiter who was hovering nearby. Having ordered a gin sling, she leaned back in her chair and gazed, perhaps a trifle arrogantly, round the lounge. She noticed that the tall American was standing by the reception desk staring at her intently. Out of the corner of her eye she saw him motion to the reception clerk and lean over the desk to talk to him. A moment later, after one more glance in her direction, he sauntered off toward the entrance lobby. Suddenly, with an almost childlike gesture, she put her hand to her mouth as if to prevent herself from bursting out laughing. "I can't believe it!" she said exultantly to herself. "I just can't believe it. I don't suppose that ever in my life will I feel as happy as this again. I've certainly never felt it before—never—never—never!" Three burlesque outpost-of-the-Empire Englishmen strolled from the bar past her table on their way out to the street. One of them, wearing overlong white shorts and an open shirt, turned and glanced at her. His immense, incongruous moustache looked as if it had been painted onto his pink, anxious young face. He muttered something to his more soberly dressed companions and they, too, looked back at her. She met their gaze with bland indifference, and then looked past them at the lacquer-red wall on which swam different varieties of brightly colored tropical fish. The waiter placed her gin sling on the table before her with a small white chit. She signed the chit, sipped the gin sling through two straws and watched Amaz threading his way through the tables toward her. He looked smooth and neat and a little harassed.

"I am most rudely late," he said. "It is quite abominable and mischievous to keep a young lady waiting, but it has not been all my fault." He sat down opposite her. "You will forgive me?"

"Of course." Polly looked at the clock over the reception desk, which registered twenty minutes to nine. "You're only ten minutes late anyhow," she said dreamily. "I can see the clock quite clearly. Isn't that wonderful?"

"It was the fault of Tuan Bob really. He is in the Adelphi Hotel waiting for Miss Lorelei Chang. He was ready to come a half an hour ago but just as we were to leave she telephoned and they first talked most furiously to one another and then he said 'All right—all right—all right—come on over but be here in five minutes.' And so there we waited and waited until I said I must first think of you so here I am."

"Have a gin sling," said Polly. "They're delicious."

"I will not drink until I know you are not angry."

"I'm not in the least angry." She reached for his hand across the table. His fingers clutched hers and, with the physical contact, she suddenly saw him again, not as intruder into her dream but as an essential part of it. She recalled with an urgent thrill of desire the feel and texture of his naked body lying with her under the stars. Her hand trembled in his and she felt her heart thumping. He, watching her face, gave a sigh of relief.

"I thought most sadly that I had lost you," he said huskily.

"Oh Amaz!" She bit her lip and looked down with a sudden sharp pang of remorse. What he had suspected had been, for a moment, true. Her newfound joy in her appearance, the handsome American in the lift, the sudden awareness that for the first time in her life she was being looked at and admired by strangers had plunged her into a complacent reverie from which Amaz, who had been so largely responsible for her abrupt translation from ugly duckling into self-satisfied swan, had been excluded. Thoroughly ashamed, she lifted her eyes and smiled at him gratefully and tenderly.

"I desire you most strongly, Miss Polly." He gripped her hand more tightly to prevent her from withdrawing it. "But when I saw you as I came in, I did not for one moment know that it was you. I was look-ing for the young, smiling mouth, the brown hair and the pretty soft eyes looking at me through the glasses. You have become most proudly beautiful now, but for me you were beautiful then."

"Would you like me to put the glasses on again?" she said contritely. "I really wouldn't mind. These damned things are begin-ning to hurt a bit."

"Not yet. Wait until late. It will be more right for Miss Lorelei Chang to see you as you are now."

"Is she really coming with us?"

"Tuan Bob said that a party of four was more easy to enjoy than a party of three because in a party of three there must always be one left outside."

Polly sighed. "I expect he's right. But I rather dread Miss Lorelei Chang."

"Don't worry," said Amaz reassuringly. "She is of no great ac-count except for making love with the gentlemen. She has most hot pants for Tuan Bob, who for ladies has still the enormously desirable body. The weight to him is of the largest importance and he makes daily rowing exercises in a boat that is fastened to the floor."

"Oh Amaz!" Polly burst out laughing.

"Is it my English that is at fault?"

"No, no—not at fault. Just—just sort of different. I wouldn't change it for the world." She got up. "I suppose we'd better be going?"

"I am to drive you in my car to the far-off restaurant. Tuan Bob will bring Miss Chang in his. This was my most cunning idea because I could be more with you alone."

"How far off is this far-off restaurant?"

"About twenty miles. It is out in the direction of Changi. Very new and modern and excellent with a garden in which are colored lights hung in the trees."

"I shall need a scarf for my hair."

"I have brought one in the car."

"Dear Amaz. You think of everything."

10

Mr. Hoo Yin, the designer, proprietor and owner of the Jacaranda Club, had every reason to congratulate himself. From the night of its open-ing only a few months previously, it had been an unqualified success. It was far enough but not too far from the stuffy clamor of the town and was ideally situated between the main road and the sea in a grove of coconut palms and wild almond trees. The sea being muddy and unalluring on that particular part of the coast, he had built an impressive kidney-shaped swimming pool complete with underwater lighting, a semicircular cocktail bar and a number of changing rooms elaborately equipped with showers and divans, in case guests might wish to lie down for a little after swimming. Having traveled extensively in the United States, he had decided to eschew all oriental atmosphere which, in Singapore, he considered to be redundant anyway, and go all out for the American style of luxury entertainment. This meant that, among other advantages of Western culture, the inside cocktail bar and restaurant were almost pitch dark, so that it was impossible to read the vast, gold-embossed menus without the assistance of the waiters, all of whom were provided with electric torches, and equally impossible to see what you were eating when the dishes you ordered were finally put before you. The stereo phonocized voices of popular American recording stars moaned disconsolately from somewhere in the dark ceiling overhead and scarcely any dish arrived at the table unaccompanied by lettuce.

Business during the week was usually rather slack, but this was happily compensated for by the crush on Saturday and Sunday nights when the crème-de-la-crème of Singapore society arrived from the city in droves. A feature of these weekly gala evenings was a barbecued steak dinner served by the pool, during and after which the clientele danced to the music of an erratic little jazz orchestra consisting of a Chinese saxophonist, a Malay double bass player, a Negro drummer and a pale Australian pianist who found it necessary, every so often, to push back with a skittish gesture the shrill yellow hair that tumbled over his eyes. Now and then a minute Eurasian girl in a sheath dress of mauve sequins emerged from behind the bar and slunk to the microphone through which she crooned harshly whatever tune the band happened to be playing at the moment.

Polly and Amaz had been sitting at the bar by the pool for almost half an hour before Bob and Lorelei Chang finally appeared. Uncle Bob, Polly quickly observed, was in none too good a temper. Lorelei Chang, on the other hand, appeared to be merry as a grig. There was no denying that she was very attractive indeed. She was wearing a tight-fitting cheongsam of vivid emerald green silk, her shining black hair was piled high and from her ears hung two little gold pagodas which tinkled faintly whenever she moved her head. She greeted Polly enthusiastically, realizing in a split second that, although she was prettier than she had expected, she was so different in type from herself that no competition need be anticipated. She shook hands coolly with Amaz as though by acknowledging him at all she was doing him much honor. He accepted the honor with a dazzling smile and eyes of dark hatred. Bob ordered drinks all round, lit a cigarette and lapsed into gloomy silence. Lorelei gave him a sharp little nudge with her elbow.

"For Christ's sake snap out of it, honey. You're not still at the funeral you know." Then, realizing that what she had said might be considered tactless, she turned to Polly. "I'm sorry, dear. After all it was your aunt that was buried wasn't it?"

"Yes," replied Polly. "But please don't apologize."

"I'm always talking out of turn," went on Lorelei vivaciously. "I say the most terrible things. Bobee says it's because I speak without thinking."

"You might try thinking without speaking for a change," said Bob.

"If you go on acting like a grouchy old bear, mother will spank!" Lorelei flashed Polly a gay, conspiratorial smile. "You'll really have to help me get him out of this mood. He's been like this ever since we left the plantation this morning."

"You seem to forget that you abused me without drawing breath during the entire drive."

"That's only sex antagonism, lamby-pie. Didn't you know?" She turned to Polly again. "I'm crazy about him," she said. "And what's more he's crazy about me although he acts sometimes as if I were something the cat brought in. Some men just don't know when they're well off."

Polly, fascinated by the violent contrast between Lorelei's exotic appearance and her strong American vocabulary, laughed obligingly and offered her a cigarette. Lorelei's eyes glinted at the sight of Mrs. Innes-Hook's cigarette case.

"Jesus!" she said. "That's a knockout! Are those stones real?"

"I hope so," said Polly devoutly.

At this moment the waiter appeared with the drinks. When they had been consumed and a second round ordered, Bob's gloom evaporated somewhat and the atmosphere lightened. This had been achieved almost entirely by an exhibition of feminine allure and grimly determined cajolery on Lorelei's part which Polly found wholly admirable. What she found far from admirable was her continued condescension to Amaz. He had spoken seldom, but whenever he had volunteered a casual remark Lorelei's face had hardened and she had waited, with marked disdain, for him to finish. Amaz, on his side, was trembling with suppressed rage and although he succeeded in controlling it fairly well Polly was uneasily aware that an explosion might occur at any moment. Occasionally she felt for his hand under the table and squeezed it consolingly. Bob and Lorelei continued to bicker back and forth, but the genuine anger that had been seething just below the surface at first, gradually evaporated and when Polly, who had retired to the ladies' room to replace her intolerably itching contact lenses with her familiar, comfortable glasses, came back to the table, they were almost cooing at each other. Bob consulted the menu and ordered the dinner without removing his arm from round Lorelei's waist. Lorelei looked at Polly and winked one of her almond eyes triumphantly.

After dinner when Polly was dancing with Amaz she asked him why Lorelei had so gone out of her way to be uncivil to him.

"She is an evil, no-good little bitch," he said. "And tough as old shoes."

"Surely not as bad as all that?"

"Most bad! Most bad!" he hissed vehemently. "She is a whore and it is of no advantage to Tuan Bob's upright nobility to sleep with a whore."

"I believe you're jealous."

"Jealous!" He stopped dancing abruptly. "Why do you say that?"

"It was just an idea," said Polly. "Do le's go on dancing, everyone's bumping into us."

"No." Amaz was quivering. "I do not care to dance further. I am most enraged."

"Don't be. It's waste of energy."

"For you to say such an idea is hurtful to my pride." He took her arm and led her back to the table. They had it to themselves because Bob and Lorelei were dancing.

"You really mustn't be so touchy, Amaz. You've been in a state all the evening."

"She will get round him and lie in his arms and make him deeply unhappy."

"On the contrary," said Polly. "I have a feeling that he'll enjoy it very much."

"He is no longer so merry and genial since he has known her. To me, and to everyone, he has changed."

"Snap out of it, honey," said Polly in a passable imitation of Lorelei's accent. "Stop acting like a grouchy old bear or mother will spank!"

"You are so sweet, Miss Polly. So humorous and sweet." He pressed her hand across the table in a sudden access of remorse. "I am being mischievous and of no social value. You will forgive me if I go to the toilet?"

"Lavatory," said Polly. "Toilet sounds common."

"Ai, Ai, Ai! I am never in the right!" He jumped up violently, almost knocking his chair over, and rushed away. Polly, left alone, shrugged her shoulders and scrutinized her face calmly in the mirror of her compact. Even the glasses didn't look so bad with the new hairdo and the makeup. At this moment, aware that someone was standing by the table, she looked up and saw the handsome American she had met in the lift.

"Good evening," he said. "We met in the elevator at the Raffles. Remember?"

"Yes. I remember." Polly took off her glasses and smiled up at his face, which had become a brown blur.

"Would you care to dance?"

She hesitated for a fraction of a second. "Yes," she said. "I'd love to."

"I guess I'd better introduce myself," he said, placing his hand under her elbow and propelling her gently toward the dance floor. "My name is Rick. Rick Barlow."

"How very odd!" said Polly. "My name is Barlow too. Polly Barlow."

"I guess I must have known we had something in common."

They began to dance. He danced effortlessly and well. So, fortunately, did Polly. Dancing had always been one of her assets. Even in her mousiest days in London when she had occasionally gone out for an evening with Eileen Mace, escorted by a couple of Eileen's boy friends, whichever boy friend had been allotted to Polly invariably forgot his initial disappointment at being stuck with the "dull one" when he got the "dull one" onto the dance floor. Mr. Rick Barlow, obviously equally impressed, held her a little more closely and gave a little grunt of satisfaction.

"I hadn't any *ahdee*," he said, "that English girls could dance like you."

"We're a strange race." Polly smiled blindly up into his face. "Full of surprises."

The dance came to an end and they stood in the middle of the floor applauding until the next one began. It happened to be a slow rhumba. The diminutive lady in mauve reappeared and screeched through the microphone in uneasy Spanish.

"People shouldn't sing in foreign languages unless they know what they're singing about."

"I sing very few songs in foreign languages," said Polly. "I once learned a lullaby in Gaelic when I was a child, but I've fogotton it now."

"You've got quite a sense of humor haven't you?"

"Yes," Polly sighed. "But I try to keep it under control. It's apt to put people off."

"You've had a tough couple of days what with one thing and another haven't you?"

"How did you know?"

"I asked the clerk at the hotel who you were. He told me about your aunt's passing away. I reckon it takes a hell of a lot of guts to do what you're doing."

"I'm not doing anything particularly, except dancing with you."

"I mean—to come out like this and act as if nothing had happened."

"If my aunt hadn't died I shouldn't have been able to come out at all."

"Were you very close?"

"Terribly close," said Polly. "Right up to the end."

"Poor kid." He gave her arm an affectionate little squeeze.

"She had a very ugly voice."

He looked puzzled. "What a queer thing to say."

"As I said before," said Polly, "the English are a strange race."

They danced in silence for a minute. When next he spoke she detected a note of urgency in his voice.

"Shall I see you again?"

"I expect so. I seem to spend quite a lot of time in that lift."

"I've only got tomorrow. I'm sailing on Monday morning. Are you busy all day?"

"I'm afraid I am. I have to be with my uncle. He came all the way from his plantation in the country to be with me during this," she paused, "this difficult time. He's been wonderfully kind and helped me to sort out my poor aunt's personal possessions and deal with all the legal documents and cables and things."

"Who's that Chinese cookie he's with?"

"That's the daughter of one of his overseers. I understand she's a model or something. She's had rather a tragic life I believe."

"She doesn't look very tragic."

"The Chinese are a strange race too," said Polly. "Impassive you know. Where are you sailing to on Monday?"

"Hong Kong. I've got business to do there. I'm in oil."

"Like a sardine." Polly gave a slight giggle. "What ship are you sailing on?"

"The *Alcona*. Too much flying makes me jittery. A few days on shipboard gives me time to relax."

"What a coincidence!" said Polly. "I'm sailing on the *Alcona* too."

"Gee that's wonderful! Have you ever been to Hong Kong before?"

"I've never been anywhere before really, except Weston-super-Mare. I'm seeing the world for the first time."

"You must let me show you around."

"Wouldn't that take rather a long while?"

"You slay me!" Rick Barlow laughed. "The way you say things, kind of deadpan."

The dance came to an end and the couples began to drift off the floor. "I'd like to meet this uncle of yours."

"By all means." Polly took his proffered arm. "You'll like him. He's a sweet old thing."

When they arrived at the table, Bob, Amaz and Lorelei were sitting in silence. The atmosphere had obviously become cloudy again. Bob and Amaz rose to their feet. Lorelei sat back in blank amazement, with her mouth slightly open.

"This is Mr. Rick Barlow," said Polly. "We sort of picked each other up. My uncle—Miss Chang—Mr. Amazahudin."

Rick shook hands all round.

"Sit down and have a drink?" said Bob hospitably.

"No thanks. I'm with a party." Rick indicated a table at the far end of the pool at which were seated a group of elderly Americans. "Your niece is a swell dancer," he said to Bob. Then he turned to Polly and bowed. "Thanks a lot. You've made my evening. The lot I'm with are not exactly dull but kind of executive. I'll phone you sometime in the morning."

"That," said Polly, "would be a very nice ahdee."

Rick laughed, nodded casually to everyone and walked away. Bob and Amaz sat down again. Polly sipped a glass of water and put on her spectacles.

"Jesus!" said Lorelei, breaking the silence. "You sure do work fast."

"The race is to the swift." Polly reached for her compact and powdered her nose.

"Where did you meet him?" inquired Bob.

"In the lift at the Raffles when I was on my way down to meet you and Amaz."

"How deep is the ocean how high is the sky!" said Lorelei none too amiably. "I suppose you know who he is?"

"Apart from his name being Barlow the same as mine and that he seems very nice, I don't know anything about him."

"He's just a bloody millionaire, dear, that's all. He has so many oil wells in Texas that he can't see straight."

"Congratulations, Polly." Bob signaled to the waiter to bring the bill. "You've obviously made quite a killing."

"This way of talking is most nasty," said Amaz with some vehemence. "It is not right that Miss Polly should be spoken of as a loose lady."

"God Almighty!" said Lorelei. "Listen to Billy Graham!"

Amaz turned to her. "You will not sneer at me for any longer," he said, quivering. "You have had with me the most nose-in-the-air, kiss-me-arse grandness the whole evening. You must remember that I know you for many a day, before you were the great splendid model, before you were Tuan Bob's mistress, before even you were fancy girl of old Kai Ling Foo, whose belly is so fat that he cannot stand up to make the water."

"Now see here you no-good little chi-chi—"

Amaz, his voice rising, mowed her down. "I know you when you were working in the Yum Yum Bar on Bugis Street and sleeping with every Tom, Dick and Harry for a drink of beer and a cheese sandwich—"

"If you go on like that much more Amaz," Bob interposed calmly, "Little Princess Lotus Blossom here will bash you over the head with a bottle."

"I suppose you think it's funny," cried Lorelei furiously. "To sit back and let this swishy little half-breed insult me!"

"You will not speak such words to me—" Amaz was about to rise but Bob pushed him down again and held on to his arm.

"Shut *up!*" he said firmly. "You've said quite enough. Now cool off and behave yourself." He turned to Lorelei. "And you can behave yourself, too, for the matter of that. Up to a point what Amaz said was perfectly true. You've been patronizing the hell out of him ever since we got here. I don't exactly know why you should suddenly acquire these delusions of social superiority, but I should like to remind you that Amaz happens to be an old friend of mine."

"Everyone in Singapore knows that," said Lorelei viciously.

"Any more cracks like that and I'll smack your bloody little bottom, so be quiet."

At this moment the waiter arrived with the bill. A smoldering silence reigned while Bob paid it. When the waiter had gone away he leant across the table to Polly.

"I apologize for this little scene my dear," he said. "I am sure that you have had quite enough drama for one day. I had planned that we should all go on to Bugis Street, but taking into consideration the slight strain in the atmosphere I think it would be better if I took Lorelei home and left you with Amaz. I have a feeling he needs cheering up. He hasn't had a very pleasant evening." He rose. "Come on, duchess," he said to Lorelei. "You can grumble all the way back to the car."

Lorelei got up and shot him a withering look. "You are a self-satisfied son-of-a-bitch and I will not speak again."

"Oh yes, you will. Come on." He took her by the arm but she wriggled petulantly out of his grasp.

"Good night, Polly," she said with a forced smile. "It's been swell meeting you."

"I shall come round to the hotel in the morning," said Bob. "There are some letters to be done and those cables to be sent. I'm staying over to see you to the ship on Monday morning." He slapped Amaz lightly on the back and looked at Polly with a twinkle in his eye. "Enjoy yourselves, children," he said with avuncular heartiness. "Don't do anything I wouldn't do."

"Thank you, Uncle Bob," replied Polly demurely. "We won't."

Bob and Lorelei walked away. Polly in silence, watched them go and then turned to Amaz. "Shall we dance?"

He shook his head dumbly and she was distressed to see that his eyes were brimming with tears. She reached for his hand and held it tightly.

"Oh, Amaz, don't be upset—please don't be upset. None of it matters, really it doesn't."

"Why have you not told me the news that you are sailing away on Monday morning?" A tear escaped from his eye and he brushed it away with his hand. "This is a most cruel and unkind surprise."

"I wanted to wait to tell you when we were alone."

"I must have indeed been most wicked to bring such heavy punishment on my head."

"Please, Amaz, dear dear Amaz, it's nothing to do with being wicked and bringing punishments on your head. I have to sail for Hong Kong on Monday. There isn't another ship until next week. You knew I could only stay for a little."

"I shall never see you again and you will forget that we ever have met each other."

"I shall never forget you. And I shall never stop being grateful to you until the end of my days. You really must believe that because it's true."

"I have been vulgar and unmannered," he said in a choked voice, looking down miserably. "I have this night made ugliness between us for the first time. I would like at this very moment to cut out my evil tongue."

"Please don't. It would ruin your lovely English."

"It is cruel to laugh at me when I am so unhappy and have so crudely played the fool."

"Your English is one of the things that I love most about you."

He looked up at her. "There are other things that you love about me?"

"Yes," said Polly gently. "A great many."

Amaz bent down and kissed her lingeringly in the palm of her hand. "You are most dear and sweet, Miss Polly, and for even a little piece of your heart I am tenderly grateful."

Polly, aware that the people at the next table were looking at them rather curiously, gently withdrew her hand and got up. "Let's go," she said. "What is this whatever-it-is street that Uncle Bob was talking about?"

"Bugis Street is no place for a young lady of fine breeding."

"My breeding hasn't been all that fine. And believe it or not, under this noble, aristocratic exterior, I am as tough as old shoes."

"You mustn't say such things even as a little joke, because they are not true."

"'What is truth?' said Jesting Pilate," murmured Polly as they walked toward the car park.

"I knew a pilot once." Amaz took her arm. "He had a most large moustache and worked for the B.O.A.C."

"It wasn't that sort of pilot who said 'What is truth?'" Polly explained dreamily. "It was the one who washed his hands."

"Here is the car," said Amaz. "And the scarf for your pretty hair."

11

Amaz, having parked the car in a dimly lit street of shuttered shops and unlighted houses, guided Polly delicately among the refuse lying in the gutter and hugged her arm protectively to his side. They crossed, with necessary caution, a wide main street along which sped lorries and cars at lethal speed, and arrived on a broad square of pavement which narrowed into a densely crowded causeway no more than a few yards across.

On one side of the causeway stretched a series of small bars from which blared a ceaseless din of amplified gramophone records both oriental and European. In front of these bars, set on the pavement, were a number of tables with grubby white tablecloths. On the opposite side were a few more café-bars and a row of brilliantly lit fruit and vegetable stalls, their contents glowing like gargantuan multicolored jewels under the tall, shadowed houses and the dark sky. Amaz, still holding on to Polly, conducted an urgent whispered conversation with the Chinese proprietor of one of the bars, who was immensely fat and had a glass right eye which stared with a fixed expression of wild surmise in the opposite direction from his left. The result of the conversation was that an extra table was produced and set between a party of English sailors on one side and a Chinese family on the other who were gobbling rice out of small green bowls. Polly, who had put back her contact lenses in the car, surveyed the curious pageant passing before her with fascinated interest. Every nationality in the world seemed to be represented in the endless procession of tightly packed humanity shuffling slowly along. Indians, Malays, Chinese, Javanese, Arabs, British, Dutch, Americans and, darting in and out, stopping at crowded tables, squeaking, giggling and soliciting, were the ubiquitous whores none of whom were young or even remotely attractive. The majority were squat, bow-legged Chinese or Eurasians, squeezed into cheap European dresses, with desperately eager smiles and cold, greedy eyes set in the thick paint on their faces like little black stones in colored clay. Even more predominant than the whores were the beggars. Beggars of every age, ranging from small limpid-eyed Indian girls of eight or nine with straight hair like shiny black seaweed, to ancient, incredibly wrinkled crones in dusty rags who stretched out twisted claws and moaned with professional piteousness. Then there were the insistent pedlars wandering from table to table bearing trays of watches, cigarette lighters, colored beads, cheap tin souvenirs of Singapore, ashtrays, lacquer boxes and mechanical toys. Above all, however, supreme in importance and for whom most of the fantastic spectacle was organized, were the men of the sea; the visiting gods from distant worlds. Sailors, marines, merchantmen of every nationality and from every variety of ship that sails the wide oceans; all set for adventure of some kind, sexual, alcoholic or merely pugnacious. And every one of them, and this was of paramount interest to the inhabitants of Bugis Street on a Saturday night, newly paid.

The proprietor with the glass eye brought two glasses of whiskey and ice to the table and a large bottle of soda water. When he had gone, Amaz, with an expression of resigned disapproval, poured out some soda water. Polly nudged his elbow gaily.

"Cheer up, dear Amaz," she said. "All this may be a bore for you because you're used to it, but you must remember that I'm seeing it all for the first time. It's what we refer to in England as the Glamorous East." She looked round happily. "It's certainly one up on the Burlington Arcade."

"This is a most evil place."

"Of course it is. That's the whole point of it isn't it?"

"It is most uncorrect that a refined young English lady should be seated among such riffle-raffle."

"You can't call English sailors riffle-raffle." Polly glanced at the next table. "They're the salt of the earth."

"I do not understand what that means."

"Neither do I actually. But it's something to do with them being the backbone of the nation and the Silent Service and True Blue and all that sort of thing."

"Sometimes, Miss Polly," said Amaz reproachfully, "the words you speak make no meaning to me at all."

"Lack of communication is a terrible thing," said Polly. "Lots of the plays they do at the Royal Court Theatre are about people who talk away for hours and still can't communicate with each other and become more and more wretched."

"Is the Royal Court Theatre at Buckingham Palace?"

"No, but it's only about ten minutes walk."

"I am most muddled," said Amaz with a deep sigh.

"Never mind. It's too complicated to explain with all this going on." Polly noticed out the corner of her eye that the sailors at the next table had been joined by two middle-aged Eurasian tarts, one of whom spoke Americanized English in a shrill metallic voice. The second tart, who had a wizened monkeylike face and no chin, was obviously a deaf mute because her companion and the sailors, rather lumberingly, were trying to converse with her by gestures. Their apparent lack of success in getting what they wanted to say across to her occasioned a great deal of hilarity. The vocal tart squealed more shrilly than ever and, on behalf of her silent friend, repeatedly held up four fingers of her right hand. One of the sailors, a snub-nosed, ginger-headed Yorkshireman, leant across and gave her an English ten shilling note. "Turn it oop luv," he said kindly, but with a note of impatience in his voice. "We don't feel like bedtime yet, we've only just got here. Get yourself a drink and piss off, there's a good girl." The tart grabbed the note with a little squeak, jumped to her feet, grabbed her friend and together they disappeared into the crowd. Polly laughed suddenly and the ginger-headed sailor favored her with a broad wink.

"Are you English?" he asked.

Polly nodded. "To the core," she said.

The sailor nudged a handsome, bearded giant sitting next to him whose arms were covered with intricate tattooing.

"What did I tell you," he said. "This young lady *is* English." He turned to Polly. "I thought as much when I first saw you. It's a small world and no error." He stood up, shook hands with Polly politely and sat down again. "Show her Percy," he said, turning once more to the bearded giant. "I have a feeling she'd appreciate our Percy."

The giant nodded laconically and went into the bar, reappearing a moment later with a small gray and pink parrot which was chained by its leg to a crosspiece of bamboo. He brought it proudly over to Polly.

"You're not afraid of parrots are you?" he asked anxiously.

"I don't really know," replied Polly. "I haven't actually met one before."

"I make an 'obby of them," said the giant. "I've got four on board as well as two monkeys and a bushbaby."

"The mess deck looks like bloody Whipsnade at meal times," interposed the Yorkshireman. Polly proffered her hand tentatively to the parrot, who stepped daintily from its bamboo perch onto her wrist and looked at her with its head on one side.

"Be most careful, Miss Polly," said Amaz unhappily. "It has a beak of great strength."

The parrot, with the utmost self-assurance, ruffled its feathers, fixed Polly with a beady eye and said clearly, "La-di-da!"

"There you are," said the giant with pride. "You see he likes you."

"Does he always say 'la-di-da' to people he likes?"

"That's all he ever says to me, but then I haven't had him very long."

425

"You should hear the other four," said the Yorkshireman. "They swear something horrible."

"Gladys don't swear," said the giant defensively. "She only says 'action stations' and 'My feet are killing me.'"

At this moment the parrot created a diversion by hopping onto the table with a loud squawk and plunging its beak into Polly's drink.

"'Ere now, none of that." The giant yanked him back onto his bamboo perch. "We can't 'ave you getting sozzled and making a beast of yourself in front of the young lady."

Percy gave a scream of frustration and, hopping nimbly back onto Polly's wrist, said "la-di-da" again three times in rapid succession. Polly, taking her courage in both hands, stroked its head, whereupon it made a cooing noise and proceeded to sway blissfully up and down.

"I've never known 'im take to anybody so quick before," said the giant in proud amazement. "You've just gone and won 'is little heart right off the bat, miss, that's what you've done."

"I'm glad," said Polly, gratified. "Because he's certainly won mine."

"Come on now, Perse." The giant gently detached him from Polly's wrist and put him back onto his perch. "We don't want to outstay our welcome do we? Just you come back into the bar and finish up that nice bit of lettuce I brought you." He transferred Percy to his left hand and shook Polly's hand solemnly with his right. "Nice to have known you, miss," he said. "It's been a real pleasure." He gave Amaz a friendly nod and disappeared into the bar. Percy, as they went, looked back heartrendingly at Polly and emitted one last plaintive "la-di-da."

"Oh!" Polly clasped her hands together ecstatically. "That is one of the sweetest things that has ever happened to me."

Amaz looked at her in wide-eyed astonishment. "You really liked that bird?"

"Like it?" said Polly. "I worshipped it. It loved me immediately and said 'la-di-da' to me on so short an acquaintance."

"I myself have no great affection for birds. They are most sudden in their movements."

"Let us be sudden in our movements and have another drink!"

"I like you when you make the jokes, even when I cannot quite understand them, because it means that you are happy." Amaz clapped his hands to attract the waiter's attention.

"I've never been so happy in my life—" She broke off. "Oh dear—there's Mr. Thingummy who did my hair."

Ambrose Wah Hai came up to the table and, with a hissing giggle, shook hands with them both.

"You've ruined it!" he cried, looking at Polly's smooth hair. "And after all that trouble I took. It's sacrilege!"

"I'm sorry." Polly laughed. "But it really did make my head look far too big."

"This is Gunther," said Ambrose, introducing a heavy, blond young man attired in brown Bermuda shorts, black stockings and a blue- and white-striped T-shirt. "He's the chief engineer on a German oil tanker and doesn't speak a word of English but we manage—*nicht var?*"

Gunther bowed and clicked his heels. *"Ya,"* he said, standing rigidly to attention.

"You will please perhaps join us for a drink?"

"Just a quickie then we must be on our way. Gunther's been at sea for two and a half weeks and it's all too fraught." He pulled over two chairs from the next table, which had been abandoned by the Chinese family. Gunther sat down and looked earnestly at Polly.

"Sprechen zie Deutsch?" he asked.

"Frankly, *nein,*" said Polly. "But I *can* say *'Ich habe mein herz in Heidelberg verloren.'*"

Gunther gave a loud guffaw. *"Aber das ist wunderschön!"* he cried, giving his immense thigh a resounding whack.

Ambrose scrutinized Polly intently. "I must say, bouffant or no bouffant, you look sensational."

Polly bowed demurely and the waiter appeared to take the order. Amaz asked what they would both drink.

"Gin on the rocks for me," said Ambrose. "And beer for Gunther. He drinks gallons of it." He said confidentially, "I can't think how he keeps his figure."

Polly, who wasn't quite sure that he had, smiled vaguely. Ambrose tilted his chair back and surveyed the milling crowds.

"Well," he said, "it sure is Amami night tonight. They're all out." A sinister-looking Arab came up to the table and whispered something lasciviously in his ear. Ambrose gave a high-pitched laugh. "Go away dear and don't be silly," he said. The Arab grinned and slunk away, whereupon a small Indian girl of about nine with large, lustrous eyes appeared suddenly at the table, slapped down a small blackboard, offered Ambrose a piece of chalk and waited expectantly. He handed it back to her at once. "Get lost, sweetheart. I've been caught like that before." The child looked at him without rancor and took the chalk and the board to another table.

"What did she want?" inquired Polly.

"Money of course. 'Noughts and Crosses.' It's a racket. They always win."

Suddenly a violent commotion broke out at a table on the other side of the pavement. There was a shrill scream and the crash of broken glass. A Negro sailor, bleeding profusely from a jagged cut on his forehead, fought his way, cursing, through the crowd which had concentrated with lightning speed round the scene of action. A

427

split second later he was followed by a fat Chinese woman, gibbering with fury and brandishing the broken half of a beer bottle. She was about to lunge it into the Negro's face when an English sailor standing nearby knocked her arm up with such force that the broken bottle was released from her grasp and went flying over the heads of the onlookers and fell with a crash behind one of the fruit stalls. The Negro, who was by now quite berserk, was grabbed by three husky sailors who pinioned his arms and proceeded to frog's-march him in the direction of the street. At this moment one of the Indian pedlars happened unfortunately to get in the way. The Negro, with a grunt of rage, executed a high kick that a ballet dancer would have envied, caught the pedlar's tray square in the middle, and shot it up into the air where it broke in half, scattering all its contents onto the heads of the crowd. There was an immediate scramble, a lot of shouting and complete pandemonium until the shrill note of a police whistle cut through the din and reduced it to a measure of silence. The Negro and his escorts disappeared. Two smartly dressed young Malay policemen proceeded with quiet authority to disperse the mob.

Amaz grasped Polly's arm. "Come away, Miss Polly," he said in an agitated voice.

"Certainly not," replied Polly, gently shaking him off. "I'm having a lovely time. It's making me quite homesick for Notting Hill Gate."

About a half an hour later when they were driving back to the Raffles Hotel in the car, Polly, with a little sigh, rested her head against Amaz's shoulder.

"Do you know what?" she said. "I believe I'm a tiny weeny bit drunk."

"I also am drunk," replied Amaz with a note of pride in his voice. "That is why I am with such excessive care driving the motor car. Tuan Bob says it is good to be drunk every once in a way."

"Once in a while," corrected Polly sleepily.

"He explains," went on Amaz, ignoring the interruption, "that it releases the exhibitions."

"Darling Uncle Bob," murmured Polly. "I shouldn't think he really had many exhibitions to release."

"Tuan Bob is surely a most lovely man."

"Baa baa black sheep," said Polly.

"What exactly is the meaning of that?"

Polly kissed his ear and then sat up again. "It's a nursery rhyme. We're taught them in England when we are children. There's another one about a cow jumping over the moon, but I don't suppose that would be popular in India because of cows being sacred. They aren't they?" She turned her face to him. "I mean they're allowed to wander about the streets and walk into shops?"

Amaz swerved violently to avoid a lonely cyclist who was wobbling along on the wrong side of the road. "I still am not knowing what we are talking about," he said. "But I do know that I most fondly love you."

"La-di-da," said Polly, as he parked the car in the drive of the hotel.

12

On Monday morning Polly woke with first light and knew beyond doubt that she was not going to be able to go to sleep again. Her brain seemed to be clattering in her head, leaping back and forth between past and present happenings and future possibilities with neither direction nor relevance. She lay still with her eyes shut, wondering whether or not to take an aspirin, decided against the aspirin and got quietly out of bed so as not to wake Amaz. . . . She put on her glasses and stood for a moment looking down at him. He looked trusting and young and vulnerable. He couldn't be more than twenty-seven, or at the outside, thirty, but still with Asiatics it was difficult to tell. The sheet only partially covered his body. He was breathing evenly. His chest, with its cross of silky black hair, rose and fell gently and his beautifully molded lips were parted a fraction as though he were secretly smiling. Polly bent down and drew the covers over him, then she tiptoed to the window, opened it noiselessly and stepped out onto the small balcony. After the coolness of the air-conditioned room, the damp, equatorial heat outside enveloped her like a warm eiderdown. There was not a breath of air: the sky was still gray, but lightening perceptibly, and the ships of all shapes and sizes riding at anchor in the roads looked as if they had been sketched in charcoal on the luminous sea.

The wide boulevard in front of the hotel was empty of traffic except for an occasional car or truck speeding by, creating a sudden harsh clamor for a brief moment which swiftly receded into the distance leaving undisturbed the unearthly stillness of the morning.

In the corner of the balcony was a rather dilapidated rattan chair and a small wooden table. Polly sat down on the chair and, resting both her elbows on the table, cupped her face in her hands and stared at a bank of heavy, gunmetal-colored storm clouds which moved with slow, ominous dignity across the horizon.

Three days ago, only three short days ago, she had stepped with her aunt out of the dim Customs shed into the blazing sunshine; resigned and correctly docile, and without the faintest premonition that within a very few hours the whole pattern of her life would violently change. In her mind's eye she saw again with dreadful clarity the gross, ungainly figure of Mrs. Innes-Hook propped up

429

against the side of the bed in her gaping mauve taffeta dressing gown, her skin already gray with the humiliation of approaching death. Later, the bare white hospital room with the Indian nurse and Dr. Renshaw bending over the bed and then standing aside to allow her to look for the last time at her aunt's face which, even with the spark of life extinguished, still managed to achieve a disagreeable expression. "It's no use," reflected Polly with a guilty sigh. "With the best will in the world I can't feel sorry. I know that there should be at least a shred of pity inside me somewhere but there just isn't. She didn't love me or even like me particularly. Actually I don't believe she ever loved or liked anyone. I owe her a little gratitude I suppose for having brought me on the cruise, but as I know perfectly well that it wasn't kindness that prompted her to bring me but only her need of an insignificant dogsbody to fetch and carry for her and be bullied by her, even that little gratitude is more than her due. Whatever I owe I owe to circumstances and my own capacity for taking advantage of them." She sighed again and watched a coolie in a circular straw hat pedaling a bicycle rickshaw slowly along the road. She lifted her eyes and looked again at the sea. "One of those ships," she thought, with a slight tremor, "is the S.S. *Alcona*, and a few hours from now I shall be up and away and sailing in it to Hong Kong!" Her heart gave a little thump of excitement. Uncle Bob had described Hong Kong enthusiastically to her yesterday while they were lunching in the cool, Sunday emptiness of the grillroom. He had advised her to stay in Kowloon on the mainland and had given her the names of three reasonable hotels. He had also given her several letters of introduction, one to the diamond merchant as he had promised, and the others to certain friends of his who, he said, might come in handy if she felt lonely. Dear Uncle Bob. He had certainly turned out to be a most comforting surprise. To some perhaps his moral values might appear to be a trifle haphazard but, she reflected with a giggle, she could scarcely be described as a pillar of moral rectitude herself. Yesterday before lunch they had both of them spent an interesting two hours discussing the practical aspects of her situation. Apart from the unitemized jewelry, she had the three wads of Aunt Eva's secretly hoarded bank notes, which amounted to one thousand, five hundred pounds. Her own fifty pounds worth of traveler's cheques which she had brought from London had mostly gone to pay Mrs. Ackbar Singh for the two dresses, Mr. Wing Foo for the contact lenses and Mr. Wah Hai for the hairdo and the cosmetics. She also had her aunt's transferred round-trip ticket and a paper from the shipping line which would enable her to get a refund on her own ticket when she ultimately got back to London. Uncle Bob had arranged to pay the Raffles Hotel bill and the hospital and funeral expenses, the total account of which he would send to Aunt Eva's lawyers. After a lot of paper and pencil work and head scratching they had finally assessed her jewelry assets to be somewhere in the neighborhood of seven thousand pounds. This intimate little board meeting had been interrupted by the promised telephone call from Rick Barlow. Uncle Bob had taken the call and with charm, slightly tinged with avuncular pomposity, had explained that his niece was heavily occupied with making final arrangements and packing and one thing and another, and sent him her kindest regards. Upon hanging up the receiver he had winked at Polly and said, "A little calculated suspense is very salutary, particularly to Texan oil magnates."

After lunch he tactfully left her to spend the rest of the day and evening with Amaz. Lorelei Chang apparently, after a blazing quarrel with Bob the night before, had repented and invited him to a party with some dubious but possibly entertaining friends of hers who owned a Chinese gothic palazzo near the Seleta airbase.

Amaz and Polly had had a happy day on the whole, shadowed only occasionally by Amaz lapsing into sudden moods of depression at the thought of their imminent parting. Being a creature of naturally resilient temperament, however, he permitted himself to be coaxed out of them. They had driven through the dusty, colored streets in rickshaws. They had wandered hand in hand through the Botanical Gardens. They had even, for a brief half an hour, gone to a movie, but it happened to be a very slow English picture which had won several critical awards, so they had come out again.

After a nostalgic sukiyaki dinner at Aki Soo's, during which Polly had managed her chopsticks with flamboyant success, they had driven out to the deserted beach where they had first made love. They had sat for a while leaning against the wall and looking out over the lagoon, but there were no stars and when some heavy drops of rain began to fall they had gone back to the car and driven silently, and a little sadly, home to the hotel.

As the first rays of the rising sun streamed up into the sky Polly rose and went back into the bedroom. A clock in the town struck six strokes as she closed the window behind her. Amaz, she knew, must be up and out of the hotel by eight-thirty because he was due to drive a party of American tourists on a sightseeing tour to the Straits of Johore at nine o'clock. This meant that he would be unable to come to the ship to see her off. She looked at him again, still sleeping peacefully, and her eyes, without warning, filled with tears. She put her glasses down on the table, slipped out of her nightgown and, lying down on the bed, tenderly wrapped her arms round him and pressed herself with sudden fierceness against his warm body.

13

Conspicuous in Polly's cabin on A Deck was an immense basket of vivid tropical fruits swathed in cellophane and looped with red satin ribbon. Uncle Bob's immediate reaction to it was to sit down on the bed and roar with laughter. Polly frowned at him a little self-consciously and searched among the acres of cellophane until she found an envelope.

"It wouldn't take a clairvoyant to foretell who *that* came from," said Bob. "Those little ole Texan oil wells must be fairly spouting."

Polly took a card out of the envelope and read it. The handwriting was large and rather undisciplined. "Happy Voyage," she read. "If you are not too tired and would like to dine with me quietly tonight, meet me in the bar at seven o'clock. Cordially, Rick."

She handed the card to Bob without comment. He read it and handed it back to her. "Cordially hits just the right note," he said. "Not exactly effusive but openhearted and friendly. Good old Rick."

"Don't laugh at me, Uncle Bob. I feel rather embarrassed."

"Nonsense. Play it cool. Grasp the nettle danger. As you said yourself the other night, 'The race is to the swift.'"

"You're an immoral old gentleman and I'm ashamed of you," said Polly, sitting on the bed next to him.

"I had a cable from your mother this morning. I kept it to give you as a farewell present."

"Oh dear!"

"Would you like me to read it to you? It's in answer to the one I sent her on Saturday."

"Is she in a state?"

"Of course. She's been in a state ever since she was born." He produced a cable from his inner pocket. "Here goes. 'Dreadfully worried by tragic news. Please tell Polly contact Mrs. Dowling our vicar's sister care of Y.W.C.A. Singapore immediately. Stop. She will arrange homeward passage as soon as possible. Stop. Trust dear Polly bearing up. Affectionately, Nell.'"

"What on earth are you going to reply?"

"I already have," Bob chuckled. "I sent it from the hotel this morning before I came to fetch you."

"What did you say?"

"I have a copy here." Bob produced a piece of paper. "'Polly already sailed for Hong Kong.'" he read. "'In charge of two sisters of mercy. Her courage has been magnificent we should all be proud of her. Writing. Love, Bob.'"

"Oh, Uncle Bob how *could* you!" Polly started to laugh.

"You'd better cable her yourself when you land. Say you're slowly getting over the shock and recuperating in a convent or something."

"Are there convents in Hong Kong?"

"There are convents everywhere. The Roman Catholic religion is tremendously efficient."

"But I'm not a Roman Catholic."

"That's mere hairsplitting," said Uncle Bob.

At this moment there was a loud banging of gongs and a peremptory, amplified voice shouting "All visitors ashore." Bob got up.

"I'd better be going." He hugged her affectionately and kissed her on both cheeks. "Enjoy yourself and try to remember that life is real, life is earnest and the grave is not the goal."

"Sometimes it is," said Polly. "Oh just one minute—I'd almost forgotten." She fumbled in her handbag and produced a package done up in brown paper. "Will you please give this to Amaz with my love. It's Aunt Eva's cigarette case and lighter. He's been so very sweet and . . ." Her voice faltered a little. "I want him to have something to remember me by."

Bob took the package and looked at her quizzically for a moment. Then he patted her cheek. "No regrets are worth a tear," he said and went out of the cabin.

Polly, left alone, went over and sat on the bed again. She took a cigarette out of a packet she had bought before leaving the hotel and lit it. She felt suddenly desolate and noticed that her hand was trembling. A discreet knock on the door startled her. She went to the door and opened it. Amaz was standing in the passage carrying an enormous bundle wrapped in newspaper.

"Oh, Amaz!"

He put the bundle on the floor, flung his arms round her and kissed her lingeringly. There was a renewed banging of gongs and further calls of "All visitors ashore."

"It is something by which you will perhaps remember me, Miss Polly. I must go. There is no more time."

He kissed her again and, with a little strangled sob, fled out of the cabin. Polly stood dumbly staring after him for a moment, then, kneeling down on the floor, she undid the newspaper wrappings disclosing a large bamboo bird cage. Inside it was a small gray and pink parrot.

"Percy!"

The parrot, at the sound of her voice, bounced up and down with great excitement. She opened the door of the cage and put her hand in. It stepped gingerly onto her wrist like an elderly matron approaching a moving escalator, then fluffed out its feathers. "La-di-da," it said cheerfully.

Polly bent and kissed the soft, downy feathers on its head. "Oh, la-di-da!" she murmured. "A thousand times la-di-da." Suddenly it fluttered away from her wrist and perched on the bed rail, from which it regarded her critically, with its head on one side.

"Oh, Percy. Dear sweet Percy."

"Pretty Polly," said Percy.

Polly buried her face in her hands, and it was hard to tell whether she was laughing or crying.

MRS. CAPPER'S BIRTHDAY

On the morning of Mrs. Capper's fiftieth birthday the alarm clock on the table by her bed went off at seven o'clock just as it always did and Mrs. Capper, dragged from the depths of early morning sleep, moaned and tried to bury herself in the warm pillow to escape from the dreadful sound. But it was no good and she knew it. Once that bloody bell had gone off she was awake and done for and the dream she was enjoying, whatever it was, was smashed beyond recall and the responsibilities of the day started queuing up. She sat up in bed and stretched and had a look at Fred's photo in the leather frame, just as she always did. It was an enlarged snapshot really, not a studio portrait like the one on the dressing table. Dorrie had taken it with her new Kodak on the day of the picnic at Box Hill. It was the last day of Fred's embarkation leave before he went to Burma. She preferred it to the one on the dressing table because it was more cheerful and relaxed. There he sat, set forever in time, with his back against a tree, grinning from ear to ear with a bottle of beer in one hand and Blitzie in the other. He was called Blitzie because Fred had rescued him from the rubble of a bombed house three doors down when they were living in Arlington Road in 1940. He was only a tiny puppy then and scared out of his wits. He lived until he was thirteen years old and blind in one eye, but he was never quite the same dog after Fred went away that summer in 1942, the day after Dorrie took the snap as a matter of fact.

Mrs. Capper took her lower plate out of the tumbler and slipped it in with a slight grunt of pain; she had been sleeping without it for the last few nights because it had been rubbing and it always hurt a bit when she put it back in, but it wore off after a while. She got out of bed, pulled up the blind and closed the window, which had been open a crack at the top. The sun was shining although it was none too warm, but it wasn't worth while lighting the gas-fire because she'd be down in the kitchen in a few minutes. She shared the kitchen with Mrs. Loft, who lived in the basement, and to do Mrs. Loft justice she nearly always kept the stove going.

When she was dressed and went downstairs Mrs. Loft was already up and about wearing her pink, padded dressing gown as per usual and made up to kill, beauty spot and all. Mrs. Capper often wondered why she took so much trouble in the early morning with no one to impress but herself, but Mrs. Loft was one of those gallant or foolish women—whichever way you care to regard them—who prefer to fight the bitterly encroaching years tooth and claw rather than to surrender gracefully to the inevitable and allow nature to take over. Her hair was a lyrical yellow but unfortunately rather dry and fuzzy. She massaged her face and neck assiduously with skin foods and astringents; no effort was spared to keep time at bay.

This morning as Mrs. Capper came into the kitchen she gave a little yelp and began singing "Happy Birthday to You" in a breathy voice, at the same time going to the dresser from which she took a small parcel wrapped in mauve paper which she pressed into Mrs. Capper's hand. While Mrs. Capper undid the parcel, flushing slightly with embarrassment, she stood watching her anxiously with her head a little on one side.

"You shouldn't have, Alice, you really shouldn't have," murmured Mrs. Capper automatically, finally getting the ribbon and paper undone and disclosing a pink box with a small bottle of Elizabeth Arden's "Blue Grass" nestling luxuriously inside it. She sniffed at the bottle without taking the stopper out. "It's lovely, it really is," she said. "So fresh, like spring flowers." She gave Mrs. Loft an awkward peck on the cheek and put the bottle carefully back into its box. It was kind of Mrs. Loft to have bought her a birthday present, but somehow she wished she hadn't. It wasn't that she was ungrateful exactly, it was just some quirk in her character that rebelled at the idea of being beholden to anyone for anything. She had always been like that ever since she was a little kiddie. She poured herself out a cup of tea and sat down at the table, oppressed with the thought that by some devious means she would have to find out when Mrs. Loft's birthday was and repay her in kind. Handkerchiefs were the safest bet, handkerchiefs with a nice monogram on them. She stirred her tea meditatively while she waited for the toast to jump up out of the electric toaster.

Later, jogging along in the Number 11, which she had got onto opposite the Chelsea Town Hall, she reflected that, on the whole, she was better off sharing a house with Alice Loft than with some people she knew. Alice, with all her silly affectations, was friendly and well disposed and certainly nobody could accuse her of lack of refinement: refinement was her middle name, indeed there were moments when it reached such a pitch that Mrs. Capper wanted to laugh out loud. But still it was better than drinking like a fish or using the word "fuck" in every sentence like Arlene Dunlop. Arlene was all right to go to the Tender Shepherd with occasionally and have a good laugh with but she wouldn't share a house with her for all the tea in China. Mrs. Capper reached for her bag, found a packet of Players in it and lit one. She enjoyed her morning cigarette on top of the bus every day although she was far from being a heavy smoker. It usually lasted her until it was time to get off at the Air Terminal.

She let herself into Number Seven with a latchkey which she kept on a chain next to her own. The hall was dark and the house silent. She switched on the light and went into the sitting room to draw the curtains: it smelt of stale smoke and there were used glasses and overflowing ashtrays all over the place. She surveyed the shambles confronting her, pursed her lips, murmured "Oh dear" to herself and went down into the kitchen to take off her hat and coat.

The kitchen was also a shambles: the sink was piled with dirty crockery, there was a saucepan coated with the remains of scrambled eggs and someone had let a cigarette burn out on the deal table, leaving an ugly brown scar. Mrs. Capper opened the window to let a little fresh air in, filled the kettle at the tap and put it on the gas-ring, rolled up her sleeves, put on her apron and went to work.

Toby and Audrey Nash had moved into Number Seven four years ago on their return from their honeymoon. It was a small house, furnished comfortably enough but without much imagination. The few good pieces of furniture in it belonged to Toby's mother who lived at Abingdon and made sporadic excursions to London, often appearing without warning which infuriated Audrey, who, not unnaturally, hated being taken unawares. On one occasion the formidable Mrs. Nash had arrived to discover her posing for Elmo Whitlock, who was doing a charcoal drawing of her in the nude as a Christmas present for Toby. There had been a grand drama over this and no amount of explaining that any woman would be just as safe stark naked with Elmo Whitlock as fully dressed with the Archbishop of Canterbury could persuade her outraged mother-in-law that the whole affair was entirely devoid of sexual implications.

The first three years of Toby's and Audrey's married life had been, apart from the usual trivial quarrels and reconciliations experienced by the newly wed, as smooth as silk. Then Toby, who worked in the family firm of Nash, Jevons and Mildmay, a real estate company, was made a partner. This change of status entailed a great deal of foreign travel; flying trips to European capitals and, indeed, on one occasion, three months in Australia with a fortnight's stopover in Tahiti on the way home. There was no doubt in Audrey's mind that those two weeks in Tahiti had been the beginning of all the trouble. In the weeks immediately following his return from this notoriously uninhibited island paradise it became increasingly apparent that something had happened. Once convinced of this it didn't take her long to worm the truth out of him. Toby was a transparent liar anyhow. The truth when it was finally extracted and lay quivering between them proved her suspicions to have been discouragingly accurate. He had been unfaithful to her. He had, in fact, spent ten days of his Tahitian fortnight living in a grass hut on the edge of a lagoon with a lady called Alina, her mother, two lesbians and an American marine. Audrey had been so fascinated at first by Toby's descriptions of this curious menage that she almost forgot to be upset; later, however, when she had gone through the motions of being a good sport, a fine understanding wife, and had kissed and forgiven him, she began to seethe and had been inwardly seething ever since. Her heart was not broken because she, although fond of him, was no longer, in the fullest sense, in love with him. She was thus spared the humiliating desolation of devouring jealousy. Her pride however was bitterly hurt and although she proceeded to behave outwardly as though nothing had occurred, there was a change in their relationship. Toby, less subtle than she, was puzzled and uneasy. She, feeding on her wounded vanity, was overvivacious and unhappy. In fact, they loved each other less.

On the morning of Mrs. Capper's birthday Audrey awoke at twenty minutes to ten and staggered into the bathroom with a searing headache. She popped two Alka-Seltzer tablets into the tooth glass and watched them fizz and jump about as though, in some dreadful, convulsive way, they were dying. When their last agonies were over she swallowed the contents of the glass in one gulp and sat down on the side of the bath feeling slightly sick. Then, as memories of last night's idiotic party began to seep into her consciousness, she started to her feet with a horrified gasp and went swiftly back into the bedroom. The sleeping form on the far side of the vast double bed gave a little grunt and turned on its face. Audrey stared with rising panic and stumbled over to the window to pull up the blind; the blind cord escaped her and the blind went flying up on its own with a tremendous rattle. A voice from the bed said "Christ!" and Audrey sat down helplessly on the stool in front of the dressing table; her face in the looking glass looked ghastly and she dabbed at it automatically with a powder puff and put on some lipstick. With the cool daylight the events of the night before dropped into place with merciless clarity. Laura's cocktail party, the drunken dinner at the White Elephant, then coming back to the house squashed into Bobby's car with Laura, Valerie, Cheepy, Elmo and Elmo's boyfriend, followed by the others in a taxi. Then there was the row in the kitchen about the Common Market while Elmo, in a white apron, scrambled eggs, and then the final humiliating scene with Toby upstairs culminating in her slapping his face and him slamming out of the house with Laura. After that, as far as she could remember, everyone drifted off except Bobby. . . . At this moment Bobby's voice cut huskily across her reflections.

"If there isn't any Alka-Seltzer in the house," it said, "I shall die here and now without any further fuss and there will be an inquest and you will have to attend and tell the truth, the whole truth and nothing but the truth."

"It's in the bathroom—the Alka-Seltzer."

Bobby got out of bed with a groan and went into the bathroom. She noticed as he passed that Toby's pajama jacket was far too small for him and then, suddenly envisaging Toby in the jacket instead of Bobby, her throat contracted, she put her aching head down on her outstretched arms and started to cry. When Bobby came out of the bathroom a little later, having brushed his hair, she had recovered herself, put on her dressing gown and slippers and was standing glumly looking out of the window. Mrs. Bertram came out of the house opposite with her awful dog on a lead. The dog dragged back and Mrs. Bertram waited while it lifted its leg against the area railings and looked up directly at Audrey, disapprovingly, as though it were fully aware of her wicked circumstances.

Bobby sat down heavily on the bed. "Well," he said, "this comes under the heading of the morning after the night before, doesn't it?"

Audrey looked at him miserably. "Yes—I suppose it does."

"I can't remember much on account of the demon alcohol, but I assume we are illicit lovers?"

"Yes—I suppose we are." Audrey went over to the bedside table, took a cigarette out of a box and lit it. He put out his hand, she gave it to him mechanically and lit another. "I suppose I'd better go and make some coffee."

"Let me help."

"No. You stay here. Mrs. Thing's probably here by now and she'd better not know that—" She broke off. "She'd better not know that it's you and not Toby—I mean she's used to seeing Toby in his pajamas but not you in Toby's pajamas—" She broke off again and then went on with a slight catch in her voice, "You'd better dress I think. I'll bring the coffee up when it's ready." She went swiftly out of the room and downstairs. Bobby, heaving a deep sigh, went back into the bathroom and turned on the taps.

Mrs. Capper had finished washing up and was just preparing to sit down and have a cup of tea and a breather when the telephone rang in the sitting room. She listened for a moment or two, then, realizing from its constant ringing that it had not been switched up to the bedroom, she went hurriedly upstairs and answered it. "Is that you, Mrs. Capper?" Toby's voice sounded rather hoarse. Slightly surprised at him being out so early on a Sunday morning, she replied, "Yes."

"Is my wife still asleep?"

"She hasn't rung yet, sir."

"Well, when she does tell her I'll be round in about half an hour and tell her to try not to be in a state and that I'll explain everything when I see her."

"Okay, sir." Mrs. Capper hung up the receiver and went slowly back to the kitchen feeling uneasy and a little shocked. She was fond of her employers. Their relationship, although it could not exactly be described as intimate, had been cheerful and friendly during the eighteen months she had worked for them. One or the other of them often had a little chat with her about nothing in particular, and once when Billy, her nephew, had come to the house with a message from Maureen to say she was going into the hospital right away as her pains had started, Mr. Nash had met him coming out of the front door and tipped him five bob.

Judging by the mess the whole place was in there'd been a beano last night and no mistake, and now here was Mr. Nash telephoning from outside at ten o'clock on a Sunday morning to say that he'd be round in about half an hour and that she was to tell his wife to try not to be in a state! Mrs. Capper frowned, shook her head, clicked her tongue against her teeth disapprovingly and sat down to her tea. There was something fishy going on, she felt it with every bone in her body. She had been aware, intuitively, of the change in the atmosphere of the house during the last few months, ever since Mr. Nash got back from Australia. They had always quarreled a bit of course, like all young people, but lately it had felt different.

She gave a wry smile and cast her mind back to herself and Fred during their first years together. They'd had terrible rows, but funny, now you came to look back on them. Fred had actually hit her once! The night they got back from their summer holiday at Ramsgate when Maureen was quite tiny. She'd just come down from putting her in her cot, she remembered, and Fred, who'd had a couple anyway, started off on Charlie Pritchard again, just because he'd taken her on the pier one evening while Fred was playing billiards in the Wheatsheaf. Charlie Pritchard indeed! She could hardly remember what he looked like.

The Nashes' rows had been more frequent lately, more frequent and rather more shrill. One day she'd come back with a loaf of bread from Mrs. Lockwood round the corner and found Mrs. Nash sitting on the stairs and crying her eyes out. That was about three months ago. Mrs. Capper shrugged her shoulders and gave a little sigh. It was none of her business of course, but it was a pity all the same. Two nicer young people you couldn't find in a day's march and they have to go and get at odds with one another and make one another miserable. Her mind went back to Fred and she sighed again. As a matter of fact her mind usually went back to Fred when she was suddenly depressed about something. She could still hardly believe that it was twenty years ago that that telegram came. She had been upstairs doing the bedroom when the front door bell rang: Maureen was on the floor playing with Blitzie, trying to make him sit up and beg, she could see her now—her reflections were interrupted by Audrey Nash coming into the kitchen. She looked pale and her eyes were a bit pink. Mrs. Capper got up.

"Don't get up, Mrs. Capper." Audrey forced a cheerful smile. "I just wondered if you'd be a dear and make us some coffee. Mr. Nash's feeling a bit under the weather this morning, there was a party last night and we got to bed far too late."

Mrs. Capper opened her mouth to speak and then shut it again. Audrey drifted over to the Frigidaire, took out a carton of orange juice and poured some into one of the newly washed glasses. She shot an anxious look at Mrs. Capper's face, perched herself on the edge of the table and sipped it. Mrs. Capper set about putting coffee into the Cona and filling the pot with water from the tap. Conscious that the silence was becoming oppressive, Audrey spoke again.

"I'll wait until it's ready," she said, "and take it up to Mr. Nash myself." She went absently over to the dresser and proceeded to put two cups and saucers and a sugar bowl onto a tray. She glanced at Mrs. Capper again and gave an unconvincing little laugh. "You're very silent this morning! Is anything the matter?"

"I don't rightly know," said Mrs. Capper after a slight pause, plugging the Cona into the wall bracket. "I couldn't say I'm sure."

This time Audrey looked her straight in the eye: her expression was definitely apprehensive. "Was that the telephone ringing just now? I forgot to switch it up."

"Yes," replied Mrs. Capper grimly, "it was."

"Anyone important?"

"It was Mr. Nash, Mrs. Nash." Mrs. Capper spoke with an effort.

"He said he would be round in about half an hour and I was to ask you not to get into a state and that he'd explain everything when he saw you."

"Oh." Audrey bit her lip. "Oh I see—" She sat down abruptly on a chair by the table. "This is rather embarrassing isn't it? I'm not quite sure that I know how to cope with it. I see now why you were looking so glum." She made a valiant effort to smile, but it wasn't very successful.

"It's no business of mine," said Mrs. Capper. "Hear no evil, speak no evil, think no evil. That's my motto. Like the three wise monkeys," she added redundantly.

"Mr. Nash and I had a row last night." Audrey spoke in an expressionless voice. "He slammed out of the house in a rage. I think he stayed with Mrs. Cartwright. Mr. Macmichael stayed here with me. It wasn't anything planned, it just happened like that. We'd all had a good deal to drink—it's all perfectly bloody and I wish it hadn't happened—" Her voice faltered and she began to cry. Mrs. Capper went over and patted her shoulder distractedly.

"There there, dear," she said in a worried tone. "There's no use crying over spilt milk. Mr. Nash will be here in a couple of shakes and you don't want him to see you with red eyes now do you?"

"I don't want him to see me with a lover in my bedroom either," said Audrey, half laughing under her tears, "but he might as well face the lot while he's at it, lover, red eyes and all." She started to cry again, this time with a definite note of hysteria.

"Sip some more of this nice orange juice," said Mrs. Capper practically. "And try to pull yourself together. Weeping and wailing won't get us anywhere." She patted Audrey's shoulder again, slightly harder than before, and handed her the glass. Audrey gulped some down and became calmer.

"How long did he say he'd be?"

"Within half an hour."

"Oh God!" She jumped to her feet. "Bobby must go at once."

"So I should think," said Mrs. Capper. "And the sooner the better. Pop up quick and get him out of the house."

"Thank you, Mrs. Capper." Audrey gave her a sudden hug and ran out of the kitchen. Mrs. Capper sat down at the table again and stirred her tea, which was by now stone cold. The coffee pot snored and grunted as though it were dreaming some dreadful dream. Mrs. Capper clicked her tongue against her teeth again and, with a spoon, absentmindedly pursued a tea leaf round the inside of her cup.

Toby arrived at the house precisely four and a half minutes after Bobby Macmichael had left it. Mrs. Capper came out of the sitting room and met him in the hall. He looked at her anxiously.

"Is she all right?"

441

Mrs. Capper looked blandly astonished. "I don't know I'm sure, sir. She hasn't rung yet."

Toby flung his hat on the hall chair, his coat over the banister, and went upstairs two at a time. Mrs. Capper returned to the kitchen and about half an hour later the bell rang sharply three times, the usual signal for coffee. She put the finishing touches to the tray, toast in toast rack, two pats of butter, no milk because they took their coffee black and marmalade in the jar.

When she went into the bedroom with the tray Audrey was sitting up in bed looking considerably more cheerful and filing her nails with an emery board. Toby was lying back in an armchair by the window; he had taken off his jacket and shoes and was smoking a cigarette. Mrs. Capper, immediately aware that all was well for the time being, permitted herself a crafty little smile as she carefully placed the breakfast tray across Audrey's legs. At this moment the telephone rang downstairs. Audrey stretched out, turned on a switch and lifted the receiver. She said, in an elaborately disguised cockney voice:

"Hallew—whew is it speaking?"

Mrs. Capper, realizing, without umbrage, that this was apparently supposed to be an imitation of herself, was about to go out of the room when she heard, to her horror, the unmistakable voice of Arlene Dunlop singing very loudly:

"Happy birthday to you—Happy birthday to you. Happy birthday Hilda Capper. Happy birthday to you." Audrey listened in astonishment for a moment, holding the receiver away from her ear, then handed it to Mrs. Capper.

"It must be for you."

Mrs. Capper grabbed it from her, said hurriedly, "Thanks Arlene, thanks a lot, I'll call you later," and hung up.

"I never knew your name was Hilda," said Audrey.

"Hilda Capper." Toby pronounced the two words very slowly twice. "It sounds like a letter in the Greek alphabet."

"Is it really your birthday?" inquired Audrey.

Mrs. Capper looked embarrassed. "Yes, Mrs. Nash. It's my fiftieth as a matter of fact."

"I've been meaning to give you a present for a long time. This is a marvelous opportunity." Audrey put aside the breakfast tray, got out of bed, went over to the dressing table and opened the top drawer, from which she took a small leather jewel case. She rummaged about in this for a minute and finally produced a quite beautiful amethyst and diamond brooch. "It's Victorian," she said, bringing it to Mrs. Capper with a smile. "It belonged to my great-aunt Marion. I hardly ever wear it and I'd love you to have it."

Mrs. Capper backed away. "Oh, Mrs. Nash, I couldn't—I couldn't really—"

"Nonsense. I insist. Let me pin it on for you." Audrey pinned it carefully onto Mrs. Capper's old green cardigan. While doing so she looked smilingly into her face and, with her back safely to Toby, gave a brazen and thoroughly conspiratorial wink. Mrs. Capper, in spite of herself, suddenly giggled and fled from the room.

When she had gone Audrey climbed back into bed and lifted the breakfast tray back onto her knees.

"Have you gone out of your mind?" Toby said. "That's quite a valuable brooch."

"Mrs. Capper is quite a valuable person," replied Audrey, pouring out the coffee.

Mrs. Capper took the brooch off and put it carefully into her pocket while she did the sitting room, but she put it on again before she went out, which was about one o'clock. Mr. Nash had called down at about twelve-thirty to tell her not to wait to do the bedroom because they were going to have a lazy day and would make the bed themselves later on. She said that she could come back in the afternoon if they liked, but he said not to trouble. Then he had appeared down the stairs in a dressing gown just as she was going out of the front door and pressed three pound notes into her hand.

"Happy birthday, Mrs. Capper," he had said. "Have yourself a ball!"

She had gone out into the street feeling pleased and a little flustered. Mr. Nash was ever so nice and so was she. Fancy her carrying on like that with Mr. Macmichael the moment his back was turned. People were funny all right, many of them just didn't seem to know when they was well off. She'd been properly upset though, no mistake about that. It would have been a nice to-do if she'd been caught out. Divorce as likely as not, and her, Mrs. Capper, having to appear in court and give evidence. Mrs. Capper shuddered and turned into the Queen's Head for a nice toasted sandwich and a glass of mild.

When she had finished her snack Mrs. Capper walked slowly back to Fulham through the quiet Sunday streets. The one thing she always looked forward to was her Sunday afternoon lay-down. On weekdays she wasn't always able to manage it because the Nashes sometimes required her to stay after washing up the lunch things and be there to answer the door if there were any afternoon callers and help if people dropped in for drinks. Every so often it was as late as half-past seven or eight before she could get away. But it varied: Toby and Audrey were neither of them creatures of routine and you could never be sure what was going to happen from one day to the next. Sundays, however, were different. It was only after a great deal of coaxing from Mrs. N. that she had agreed to work on Sundays at all; after all, most daily helps insisted on having the whole day off, but Mrs. Capper, as she often told herself, was a pushover. Anyway,

Mrs. N. was very persuasive and there was something appealing about her.

Mrs. Loft was out when she let herself into the house and she breathed a sigh of relief. Pussikins was sitting on the stairs washing herself as she came into the hall. Pussikins had had a litter of five kittens some weeks back, four of which Mrs. Loft had resolutely drowned. Mrs. Capper's sentimental heart had been lacerated by the whole business, but Pussikins had displayed little emotion. Now Twinkle, the last remaining one, had been wrested from her and given to Mrs. Turner at Number Five, who had mice. Pussikins still maintained a stoic indifference and minced through her bereaved days without sadness. Mrs. Capper murmured "Puss Puss" sympathetically as she stepped past her on the way to her room.

Mrs. Capper took off her hat and coat and glanced proudly at her lovely new brooch in the dressing-table mirror before she set about making the bed and tidying the room. There was one thing she couldn't stand at any price and that was the sight of an unmade bed and everything looking slummocky. She usually managed to make it in the morning before she went, but every now and again she'd let it lie and invariably, as now, regret it. However, it wasn't a long job as she didn't trouble to turn the mattress and the room was fairly neat otherwise. She could give it a good do-out later in the week. When the bed was done and she'd put aside two pairs of stockings for washing, she sat down in her chair and looked out of the window. It wasn't much of a view really, just the backs of the houses in Granger Street with their neatly segregated little yards. Through the window of one of the houses she could see a young man, stripped to the waist, shaving. A fine time to be shaving at three o'clock on Sunday afternoon! The picture of Fred shaving on the morning after their wedding night at the Marine Hotel, Bognor-Regis, slipped into her mind and she let it stay there for a little without pain while she examined it. Fred was taller than the boy opposite and Fred had had hair on his chest whereas the boy had none, and yet somehow there was a fleeting resemblance. The Marine Hotel had been all right as hotels go, but she hadn't really cared for it one way and another. In fact she hadn't really cared for her wedding night at all. Too much strain and fuss. They had both had too many drinks to start with, not only at the reception at Fred's mother's, but in the train going down and in the hotel bar when they arrived. She could never rightly remember what they had for dinner; all she could recall vaguely was that when they finally did get to bed it was all rather muddled and uncomfortable and nothing much happened.

The boy opposite wiped his face energetically with a wash flannel just like Fred used to. On that particular, faraway morning Fred had cut himself a bit on the chin. She remembered getting out of bed and dabbing some of her new eau-de-cologne on it; he had winced violently and then suddenly kissed her even more violently and after that everything that should have happened the night before seemed to happen at once and she remembered wondering at the back of her mind what they would do if the hotel maid came in and found them carrying on like that in broad daylight and finally not caring whether she did or whether she didn't.

While she was sitting there beginning to feel drowsy and trying to make up her mind whether to lie down on the newly made bed and give up to it or stay where she was and just doze, there was suddenly a loud peal at the front door bell. The shock of it startled her into full consciousness and although she was not as a general rule given to swearing, she said "Bugger" out loud and went irritably downstairs. When she opened the door who should it be but Mr. Godsall, and her exasperation increased. Not that she didn't quite like Mr. Godsall up to a point, but there was something apologetic about him that always got on her nerves. He was wearing a dark gray suit and a very bright, patterned tie and was holding a largish brown paper parcel in his left hand; her heart sank.

"I was hoping to find you in," he said, and his voice sounded even more apologetic than usual. "I just popped round to wish you many happy returns of the day." He pushed the parcel at her suddenly as though it were scalding his hand and she nearly as anything dropped it on the step.

"Well," she said, forcing a smile, "that's very nice of you I'm sure, but you really shouldn't have."

"It's my pleasure," he replied gallantly, at which moment Pussikins suddenly shot between her legs from behind and vanished down the area steps.

"That cat," she said, "will be the death of me one of these days. Won't you come in? Alice will be back soon I shouldn't wonder."

Mr. Godsall removed his bowler and walked past her into the hall. "It's you I came to see," he said with a self-conscious little whinny, "not Alice."

Mrs. Capper ignored this and ushered him into the front room. The front room was Alice Loft's pride and joy, but there was something about its determined refinement that Mrs. Capper always found faintly aggravating. There were a number of occasional tables with little mats on them, and on the little mats were little ornaments and photographs in frames. On the mantelpiece there were further ornaments and photograph frames and a Copenhagen china Pierrot and Columbine who stood, with relentless daintiness, one at each end.

Mrs. Capper indicated an armchair to Mr. Godsall in which he sat obediently, carefully hitching up his trousers as he did so so as not to destroy the crease. Mrs. Capper sat opposite him on the sofa and began to undo the parcel while he watched her anxiously. When unwrapped the parcel turned out to be a cut-glass vase. Mrs. Capper placed it with care on a table and surveyed it.

"It's really ever so pretty," she said. "It'll look lovely with flowers in it."

Mr. Godsall nodded as though completely carried away by this bizarre idea. "That's what I thought," he volunteered boldly.

"I still say you shouldn't have," said Mrs. Capper with perhaps a trace of archness. "But I love it all the same. Will you be all right here for a minute while I go and put the kettle on? There's an ashtray just by you if you want to smoke."

"Thanks," said Mr. Godsall. "I don't mind if I do."

Mrs. Capper went down to the kitchen, put the kettle on and hurriedly arranged the tea things on a tray. There was the remainder of a sponge sandwich in the larder; for a moment she toyed with the idea of making some toast but abandoned it because it would take too long. She placed the sponge sandwich on a large plate and arranged some petit beurre biscuits symmetrically round it. While she was thus occupied Pussikins started meowing outside the area door. Mrs. Capper let her in. "You're a spoiled cat," she said. "First you want to go out, then you want to come in, and now I suppose you're after some milk?" She poured some into a saucer and put it down by the dresser; Pussikins began lapping it noisily. She had to open a new packet of Brooke Bond's because there wasn't quite enough left in the old one. She wondered, a trifle apprehensively, what time Mrs. Loft would be back. She'd probably gone to the Christian Science church near Sloane Square. Mr. Godsall, who owned a small tobacconist's shop in Fortesque Street, had originally been what Mrs. Loft skittishly referred to as "One of my Bewes" and it was not without a certain dismay that Mrs. Capper had observed him unmistakably transferring his affections to herself. Whether or not Mrs. Loft had noticed she had no idea, the subject had never been mentioned; but the situation was disquieting none the less. Not that Alice Loft was the kind of woman to make ugly scenes, but she was on the touchy side and it was no good pretending she wasn't. Her preoccupation with the gospels of Mrs. Baker Eddy had not hitherto dampened her still vibrant enthusiasm for the opposite sex: indeed on certain occasions when she and Mrs. Capper had achieved a transient intimacy over a cup of tea or a small whiskey and water, she had given more than a hint that there had been other men in her life both before and since the late Mr. Loft. These intimations of overt sexuality, although couched in terms of the utmost refinement, always made Mrs. Capper feel a little awkward. Being by nature reticent herself, she had no particular interest in the confidences of others and would infinitely prefer it if they would keep them to themselves. Whether or not Mrs. Loft had any genuine feelings for Mr. Godsall, she had no idea, but her instincts warned her to look out for squalls when she came home and found her entertaining him alone in her own front sitting room. However, there was nothing to be done about it. She couldn't very well *not* have asked him in and offered him a cup of tea after he'd taken the trouble to buy her a cut-glass vase. She banged the teapot onto the tray with a muttered imprecation. The major mistake, of course, had been her answering the door in the first place.

Mr. Godsall chivalrously rose to his feet when she came in with the tea tray. He relieved her of it and placed it on a mauve pouf in front of the fire-screen ornament.

While she was pouring out she glanced at him out of the corner of her eye. He wasn't bad-looking really, although there was something wishy-washy about his personality. He had a bit of a paunch of course, but in all fairness you couldn't hold that against him at his age. His eyes were the giveaway really. They looked as though they were permanently scared of being separated from one another and seemed to be edging closer and closer together. He refused a petit beurre but accepted a bit of the sponge sandwich.

"I'm afraid it's yesterday's," said Mrs. Capper as she cut it for him. "Neither Alice or me expected company otherwise we'd have got something in. She ought to be back at any moment now," she added, aware of Mr. Godsall's eyes upon her and feeling a trifle flurried.

"As I said before, it's you I want to see, not Alice."

"Well it's very nice of you I'm sure." Mrs. Capper, ignoring all implications, laughed cheerfully and cut a bit of sponge sandwich for herself.

Mr. Godsall cleared his throat and a tiny crumb flew out of his mouth and onto the knee of his trousers, which Mrs. Capper saw and he didn't. "I've been wanting to talk to you alone for quite a long time." He looked at her intently and added "Hilda" rather breathlessly.

"Oh!" said Mrs. Capper blankly, aware of acute embarrassment and at the same time controlling an insane desire to laugh.

"As you know"—Mr. Godsall again cleared his throat—"I have been a widower for some years now and I've managed all right one way and another but it does get a bit monotonous being all by yourself all the time. After all Ethel passed over in 1952 and that's quite a while ago whichever way you look at it—" He paused. "What I mean to say is—"

"I know what you mean to say Mr. Godsall." Mrs. Capper spoke a little loudly. "And it's ever so kind of you and I do appreciate it—but it wouldn't work—really it wouldn't."

Mr. Godsall looked at her glumly. "How do you know it wouldn't?" The confidence had left his voice and the old apologetic note was back again; instead of being irritated by it as she generally was, Mrs. Capper discovered that she suddenly felt sorry for him. "I

447

don't know exactly," she went on. "It's just the way I feel—I mean I'm sort of set in my ways and I've got used to being on my own, in fact I rather like it. It isn't that I don't like you, truly it isn't, I've always liked you and I hope we shall always be friends—" She broke off, no longer conscious of embarrassment or ridicule but suddenly desolate. Fred had asked her to marry him on the top of a bus coming back from Wembley on June the seventh, 1936. It had come as a complete surprise to her because up to then she had always thought it was Dorrie he was after. That was twenty-six years ago and now Fred was gone and Dorrie was gone and Maureen was grown up and married, and here she was, an elderly woman with false teeth and graying hair, being proposed to again in a house that wasn't hers, by a man she hardly knew. She opened her mouth to go on with what she was meaning to say, but found she couldn't utter a word, and there she sat staring helplessly at the blurred, wobbling face of Mr. Godsall, because, against her will and to her dreadful shame, her eyes had filled with tears. There was complete silence for a moment and then Mr. Godsall got up and very gently put his arm round her shoulders.

"I didn't mean to upset you," he said. "Really I didn't—"

At this moment there was the sound of a key in the front door and they both started apart guiltily. Mr. Godsall went back to his chair and Mrs. Capper dabbed her eyes frantically with her handkerchief.

"Well, well, well, what a surprise!—I do hope I'm not intruding?" Mrs. Loft stood in the doorway smiling merrily at them. She was dressed almost entirely in pink and white and Mrs. Capper was irresistibly reminded of a bar of nougat; her guilty ear detected beneath Mrs. Loft's genial words a slight note of acrimony. Mr. Godsall rose and said, "What ho, Alice," rather self-consciously.

Alice, in reply, wagged her finger archly at him. "When the cat's away the mice will play!" she said, and sat down on the sofa with a sigh. "My poor feet," she went on. "I've walked all the way from Sloane Square. I'd love some tea if there's any left."

"I'll get another cup." Mrs. Capper got up and went swiftly from the room. When she came back she found Mr. Godsall and Mrs. Loft sitting side by side on the sofa discussing a film that Mrs. Loft had seen at the Classic the day before yesterday. "Don't go near it," she was saying. "It's all about common people and goes on for two hours and a half."

"Would you like me to make some fresh?" asked Mrs. Capper. "It won't take a minute."

"No thank you, dear, this will suffice," replied Mrs. Loft brightly, a little too brightly Mrs. Capper thought as she added some hot water to the pot and stirred it. Anyhow outwardly all appeared to be well and the conversation continued without any obvious indications of strain. Mrs. Capper, aware that Mr. Godsall was looking at her covertly whenever he possibly could, resolutely averted her eyes. When finally he got up to say good-bye he held her hand a fraction longer than was necessary and, on a wave of exhortations from Mrs. Loft to "Pop round any evening he felt like it," he collected his hat and went out. Mrs. Loft, who had seen him into the hall, came back into the sitting room. Her face was a trifle flushed.

"Well," she said. "We *are* a sly boots aren't we?"

"How do you mean?" inquired Mrs. Capper evenly.

Mrs. Loft gave a brittle laugh. "I wouldn't have intruded on your little teet-a-teet if only I'd known."

"If only you'd known what?"

"That you'd arranged a private rendezvous with poor Willie Godsall."

"I didn't arrange nothing," said Mrs. Capper. "I was just going to lay down and have my afternoon snooze when the front door bell rang and it was him. He brought me that vase," she added, pointing to it where it stood gleaming proudly on a side table. "It's pretty isn't it?"

Mrs. Loft, slightly nonplussed by Mrs. Capper's obviously unforced nonchalance, conceded that it was sweetly pretty and heaved a sigh. "He must be quite smitten with you," she said. "I must say I thought he had his eye on you the other night at the Tender Shepherd. Ah well . . ." She sighed again as though valiantly bidding farewell to a long cherished hope. "I can only say I wish you the best of luck, dear, now and always."

"Don't talk so silly." Mrs. Capper collected Mr. Godsall's cup and plate and put them back on the tray. "You're making a mountain out of a molehill."

"I like that I *must* say," cried Mrs. Loft. "I come back unexpectedly from church and find—"

"Alice," Mrs. Capper interrupted her firmly, "you're talking silly and working yourself up about nothing. In the first place you didn't come home unexpectedly from church, I was expecting you every minute. In the second place I had to ask the poor man in for a cuppa after he'd brought me the vase and all, I couldn't very well have sent him away with a flea in his ear. In the third place I don't care if he's smitten with me or not; I'm certainly not smitten with him. His eyes are too close together for one thing and his hands are sweaty to be going on with."

Mrs. Loft gave a little cry. "Sweaty! Really, dear, you do say the most awful things."

"I can do worse than that when roused," replied Mrs. Capper laconically, hoisting up the tray. "I'm now going to wash up these tea things and then I'm going to grab the forty winks I missed this afternoon on account of Marlon Brando Godsall dropping round to seduce

449

me. Don't forget we've got to be at Maureen's at six-thirty." She kicked the door wider open with her foot and went down to the kitchen with the tray.

Maureen and Jack's flat was in a new apartment building that looked like a gigantic gray matchbox standing on its end. The building was called Elsworth Court and, although the name had an Elizabethan ring to it, the edifice itself was aggressively contemporary. Maureen and Jack's flat was also contemporary. It was Jack's taste more than Maureen's. Jack had advanced ideas on house decoration and had once, before he went into insurance, actually done a course at the Polytechnic. The fruits of the knowledge he had gained there struck you in the eye the moment you entered the living room. In the first place each wall was distempered a different color, which Mrs. Capper said made her giddy. In the second place the furniture was what is described in catalogues and magazine advertisements as functional, which meant that it was ugly to look at and uncomfortable to sit on. On the variegated walls were hung four large reproductions of famous Impressionists. There was "The Bridge at Arles" by Van Gogh, a Tahitian Gauguin in rich reds and purples, an "Odalisque" by Matisse, which looked to Mrs. Capper as though it had been painted by a mad child of five, and a Raoul Dufy of the Promenade des Anglais at Nice, which looked as though it had been painted by an even madder child of four. There were no photograph frames or ornaments about and only one gray vase on the utility desk with a clump of gladioli in it. The vase was actually a little too small for them and they looked as though they could only prevent themselves from falling out by standing to attention.

At a quarter past six on the evening of Mrs. Capper's fiftieth birthday Maureen, her daughter, was kneeling on an oatmeal-colored rug changing the baby's nappies. Jack, her son-in-law, was lying on the sofa in his shirt sleeves reading the *Sunday Express*. The baby, Marylin, was lying docilely on its back staring up at its mother with round expressionless eyes like blue marbles. It was also dribbling.

"Who's a dirty girl?" murmured Maureen fondly, wiping the child's chin.

"Who isn't?" Jack said from the sofa.

"Trying to be funny now I see." She shot him a look of disdain. "Having made all those nasty cracks about mum you think you can make little jokes as though nothing had happened. Excuse me while I split my sides."

"I didn't make cracks about mum. I only said that if we had to go through this birthday dinner lark it would be a bloody sight better if she'd come on her own and not have to drag that simpering cow along with her."

"Mrs. Loft's a very nice woman underneath," said Maureen without conviction.

"It's on top that I'm worried about."

"Anyway, mum shares the place and it's very reasonable whatever you may say. It's only right that she should include her in when there's a bit of fun going."

"Bit of fun—Christ!" Jack noisily turned over a page of the paper and straightened it. "If it's your idea of fun to have to listen to that affected old bitch airing her views and giving her opinions on this, that and the other thing, you can have my share."

"I think you're mean to go on grumbling." Maureen lifted the baby onto her lap and turned it over onto its stomach. "It's mum's treat anyhow and if she wants to bring Mrs. Loft along with her that's her lookout and the least we can do is grin and bear it."

"All right—all right—have it your own way. We'll take them both to the Tender Shepherd afterward and get 'em pissed."

"Jack how *can* you?" At this moment there was a ring at the door bell. "That's either them or Mrs. Burgess, let them in there's a dear while I finish off baby."

Jack got up from the sofa and went into the hall. Maureen made some clucking sounds at the baby, but it continued to stare at her without interest. There was the sound of voices in the hall and a moment later Mrs. Capper and Mrs. Loft came in together. Mrs. Capper was wearing her new dark blue "two-piece" with the amethyst brooch prominent on the lapel of her jacket. Mrs. Loft was resplendent in mauve taffeta; she had left her shantung dust coat in the hall; the beauty spot on her dry white cheek stood out aggressively and her hair seemed brighter than ever. "We thought we'd *never* get here," she cried brilliantly. "We had to wait nearly *twenty* minutes for a bus!—Oh isn't she *sweet*—" She advanced upon the baby, who regarded her sternly and blew out a bubble swiftly followed by a staccato belch. Mrs. Loft, discouraged by this reception, drew back a little. Maureen patted the baby gently on the back. "It's wind," she said. "She's had it on and off all day."

"Everybody sit down and make themselves comfortable," cried Jack breezily. "We can't go anyhow until Mrs. Burgess comes to look after baby so we'd better while away the time with a little of what we fancy. What's your tipple, Mrs. Loft?"

Mrs. Loft smiled superciliously and shook her head. "I never drink spirits," she said. "I'll wait until later and maybe have a tiny sip of wine at dinner."

"Same as usual for you, mum?"

"Yes, please dear—gin and it and more it than gin."

"Righto."

Mrs. Capper, having kissed Maureen, bent still lower to kiss the baby. For the first time it betrayed some animation, suddenly sawing the air with its arms and gurgling with pleasure.

"She knows her old granny," said Mrs. Capper with pride, taking her up in her arms. "Doesn't she then?"

"Keep her a minute, mum," said Maureen. "I'll be back in two shakes." She got up from the rug and ran out of the room. Mrs. Capper, carefully holding the baby, settled herself on the sofa. Mrs. Loft scrutinized the Gauguin critically. "Fancy mixing that pink with that red," she said. "You'd think he'd have known better than to have two colors that clash like that right close to each other wouldn't you?"

"I don't suppose he thought they *did* clash," said Jack patiently, opening a bottle of vermouth.

Mrs. Loft sat down in an armchair without any arms. "Each one to his own taste," she said with a merry laugh, "that's what I always say."

After a slight pause, during which the baby belched again, Maureen came back carrying a brown paper parcel elaborately done up with red ribbon. She placed it on Mrs. Capper's lap, gave her a hurried kiss and relieved her of the baby.

"This is from Jack and me with our best love," she said all in one breath as though she had learnt the phrase recently by heart and was afraid of forgetting it. Mrs. Capper, with a slight contraction of the throat, looked at her standing there in front of her; a mature, chestnut-haired young woman with pretty gray eyes and a rather prominent chin, and twenty years flicked away and there was Maureen as a little girl standing just as she was standing now having given her, with pride, a birthday present of two iron holders, one with a white rose worked on it, the other with a red. She still had them tucked away somewhere. She opened the parcel carefully. Inside the brown paper was some tissue paper and inside that was a dove gray cardigan made of the softest wool. She held it up to her face ecstatically. "You shouldn't have," she said. "You really shouldn't have!" She jumped up and kissed Maureen and then went over to Jack, who was mixing drinks at the sideboard, and kissed him, too. "It's gorgeous, simply gorgeous, but you didn't ought to have spent so much money—look, Alice—" She held it up in front of Mrs. Loft, who fingered it admiringly.

"It'll keep the cold out," said Jack. "And here's something else to keep the cold out." He handed Mrs. Capper a brimming glass of gin and vermouth. "Between the two of them you'll be so hot we shall have to send for the fire brigade."

Mrs. Capper giggled, took a sip from the glass so that it

wouldn't spill over and returned to the sofa. It was then that Maureen noticed the amethyst brooch.

"Wherever in the world did you get that?" she cried. "It's the prettiest thing I ever saw—Jack come over here and look."

Jack came over and scrutinized it. "Smashing!" he said.

Mrs. Capper glowed with pleasure and took another sip of her gin and it. "It was Mrs. Nash," she said. "She give it to me this morning just after I'd taken the breakfast up. She said she'd been meaning to give me a present for ever so long and this being my birthday was a marvelous opportunity."

"How did she know it was your birthday?"

Mrs. Capper started to laugh. "It was that Arlene. She called up and Mrs. N. answered in a funny voice and Arlene must have thought it was me because she started singing 'Happy Birthday to You' at the top of her lungs. Mrs. N. nearly had a fit. So did I—I can tell you."

At this moment the door bell rang. "Mrs. Burgess," said Jack. "Now we can get cracking. Let mother hold the baby, Maureen, while you put on your hat and coat. I'll let her in."

"What's the panic?" Maureen handed the baby back to Mrs. Capper. "Anyone would think we'd got a train to catch." She went into the hall to greet Mrs. Burgess, who after a moment came into the room followed by Jack. She was a short, dumpy woman dressed in a brown coat and skirt and a salmon pink blouse which gave her the look of a fat little robin. Jack introduced her jovially to Mrs. Loft as "our lifesaver." Mrs. Burgess laughed and Mrs. Loft shook hands with her regally as though in course of her busy social existence she was accustomed to greeting all sorts and kinds of people with impartial graciousness.

Mrs. Burgess, apparently oblivious of any particular honor bestowed, sank down onto her haunches in front of the sofa, nodded affably to Mrs. Capper and chucked the baby under the chin. "There she is the little love-a-ducks," she exclaimed. The baby turned its head away in distaste and gave a hiccup. Mrs. Capper patted it gently on the back. "Wind," she explained. "Maureen says she's had it on and off all day."

"Would you like me to take her now?"

"Perhaps it would be better. I've got to tidy myself." She deposited the baby in Mrs. Burgess's arms and rose to her feet. The baby screamed gratifyingly at being taken from her and Mrs. Burgess admonished it with a playful little shake.

"Naughty—naughty," she said. "That's no way to behave."

Mrs. Capper went through the hall and into the bedroom. Maureen was sitting at the dressing table powdering her nose. Mrs. Capper stood behind her and stroked her shoulder affectionately. "I hope you and Jack didn't mind me bringing Alice Loft along," she said.

"She'd been dropping so many hints and going on about how dull Sunday evenings were in London, I felt I just had to ask her. After all she does let me have the room very cheap—with the use of the rest of the house thrown in—" Mrs. Capper, with a guilty pang, remembered her "teet-a-teet" in the front living room with Mr. Godsall and debated in her mind whether or not to tell Maureen about it. Then the picture of the crumb of sponge sandwich shooting from his mouth onto the knee of his trousers suddenly recurred in her mind and her mouth twitched.

"What's up?" inquired Maureen. "You look like a cat that's swallowed the cream."

"It's that Mr. Godsall . . . " Mrs. Capper hesitated and gave a little laugh. "He come to see me this afternoon when Alice was out and brought me a vase."

"Good for him," said Maureen. "Although I think he's a bit wet if you ask me."

"He tried to ask me to marry him but I stopped him," said Mrs. Capper with a rush. Maureen looked at her blankly.

"Marry you!" She gave a little frown. "Well—would you believe it?"

"He's not a bad sort really you know. I mean he's respectable and nicely spoken and he makes quite a lot out of that shop, he must do."

"Mum—are you seriously thinking of getting married again? I mean do you really feel you'd like to?"

"I don't know," replied Mrs. Capper soberly. "I don't rightly know and that's a fact."

"You could always come and live with us if you get fed up with living on your own, you know that."

Mrs. Capper patted her hand. "Yes I know it, but I wouldn't do it, not in a thousand years. I couldn't bear the thought of being a burden and it's no use pretending I wouldn't be because I would. Mothers-in-law always cause trouble."

"I never sort of thought of you as being married again." Maureen looked pensive. "I mean there's no earthly reason why you shouldn't if you want to, it's just that the idea never occurred to me. Do you mean to say he really proposed to you?"

"No. I nipped it in the bud like I just told you. But he was working up to it all right."

"Why didn't you let him get on with it—get it out of his system? At least you'd have known where you were."

"I know where I am anyway thanks very much," said Mrs. Capper. "And I didn't let him get on with it because in the middle of what he was saying I suddenly remembered your dad popping the question to me on a bus and I suddenly started to get all weepy and then Alice came in and that was that."

"You still miss dad don't you?" Maureen looked at her wonderingly. "After all these years you still miss him?"

"Yes, dear, and I expect I always shall," said Mrs. Capper in a matter-of-fact voice and, leaning forward, dabbed her nose with Maureen's powder puff because it looked shiny. "Don't say anything to Jack about Mr. Godsall, there's a dear. It makes me feel sort of silly."

Maureen laughed. "You're a dark horse and no mistake," she said.

Mrs. Capper regarded herself quizzically in the mirror. "Alice Loft said I was a sly boots and now you call me a dark horse—sly boots or dark horse—pay your money and take your choice." She laughed too and they went out of the room arm in arm.

The Chez Maurice was in Chelsea, in a turning off the King's Road. It had been open only a few months and was doing quite well in a modest way. Maurice Downes, the proprietor, when on the threshold of middle-age, had had the good fortune to meet a wealthy cotton broker from the Midlands. It was the cotton broker's money that financed the Chez Maurice but it was Maurice's own intelligence, industry and business acumen that enabled him to show a small profit after only three months. It was inexpensive compared with most of the other restaurants in the district and the food, although not exactly lavish so far as portions went, was of excellent quality and reasonably well cooked. The "decor" was earnestly Provençal, with nets and strings of garlic and onions hanging from a false beam. On each table was a red- and white-check cloth and a red candle in a beer bottle. The three waiters, Nicky, Michael and David, were dressed picturesquely in blue French sailor pants, fishnet shirts and red cotton scarves tied piratically round their heads. David indeed had appeared one evening sporting a large gold earring, but Maurice had had it off in a flash. "We can't have you clanking round the tables like Zaida, the Gypsy Queen," he said. "It's going *much* too far."

Maureen and Jack had been first taken there one evening some months back by a friend of Jack's from the Polytechnic who had taken up interior decoration as a business and was working for a private firm in Finsbury, and they had been back several times since. Neither Mrs. Loft nor Mrs. Capper had ever been before and they were both agreeably impressed. Maurice, having welcomed them with great urbanity and handed them each a scarlet menu, took their orders personally. Actually there was not a very wide choice. Mrs. Capper, Mrs. Loft and Maureen all plumped for shrimp soup and chicken à la Maryland while Jack chose melon and a grilled steak. Red or white wine was served by the glass. The ladies chose white, Jack, red. "You could have a bottle of rosé if you liked," said Maurice a trifle sibilantly, overemphasizing the accent on rosé. "We've just got some in and it's dreamy."

455

"I think we'll stick with the white and the red," said Jack. "Better the devil you know!" He winked at Mrs. Loft, who turned her head to one side in a refined manner while David placed a glass of *soi-disant* sauterne before her. Maurice bowed and went away. David, after he had served them all with wine, also went away. Jack handed round his cigarette case. Mrs. Loft accepted a cigarette exquisitely and held it in front of her with a slightly pouting expression until Michael, the more masculine-looking of the three waiters, approached her with a lighter and said, in a very high voice, "Allow me, madame."

Mrs. Capper looked round with interest. She wasn't used to dining in restaurants as a general rule. For lunch she usually went to the Queen's Head or to a snack bar near Victoria Station. In the evenings when she got home from work she was accustomed to frying herself a steak or chop with some potato chips, after which she'd make herself some tea and sit chatting for a while with Mrs. Loft if she felt like it, or else go straight upstairs to bed with a magazine. She actually preferred the evenings when Mrs. Loft was out visiting friends and she could have the kitchen to herself. On these occasions she sometimes, after her meal, went up and sat in the front room if it was warm enough and watched the telly for a bit. Mrs. Loft's set was very small and sometimes it wouldn't work properly however much she fiddled with the knobs, but it was all right for a change.

The clientele of the Chez Maurice was a mixed lot to say the least. The place consisted of a small room with another one opening out of it. There were not more than a dozen tables in all. Over by the window was an elderly man, quite respectable-looking, with a heavily made up woman in black. Her bosoms seemed to be on the point of bursting out of her dress and she occasionally laughed desperately and then bent over her plate as though the effort had exhausted her. On the other side of the room was a table with six people squashed round it. They were all quite young and a bit noisy. One of the girls had a dead-white face with no lipstick and hair that looked as if it hadn't been washed for weeks. The whole lot of them, Mrs. Capper reflected, could do with a bit of dusting and some soap and water. At the table next to their own were two men, one considerably older than the other. The elder one talked incessantly in a careful, educated voice while the younger one devoted himself doggedly to his food, occasionally looking up with a puzzled expression on his handsome face as though he were being suddenly recalled from a dream that he couldn't quite remember.

Mrs. Loft was bubbling with enthusiasm. "They've made it most picturesque I *must* say." She took in the whole restaurant with one patronizingly comprehensive glance. "You'd really think you were abroad wouldn't you instead of being only a stone's throw from the Albert Bridge?" She sighed nostalgically. "When Mr. Loft was alive we used to go abroad at least three times a year. He was in textiles you know and spoke French like a native. I remember once going to a place very like this in Amsterdam and—"

"I thought they spoke Dutch in Amsterdam," said Jack. Maureen shot him a warning look, but Mrs. Loft ignored the interruption and pressed on undeterred.

"It wasn't exactly like this of course because it was much bigger and there was a large stove made of colored tiles that jutted right out into the room." She took a sip of white wine. "I remember on that particular evening the gentleman who was with us kept on filling up my glass when I wasn't looking and believe it or not I got quite tipsy!" She gave a tinkling laugh. "Wasn't it *awful?*—Mr. Loft was furious—I often wonder—" She assumed a pensive expression. "I often wonder what would have happened to me if Mr. Loft had not passed over when he did." She paused and looked at Mrs. Capper and Maureen in turn as though expecting some dramatic surmises. Failing to get them she gave another little laugh, this time tinged with a note of bitterness. "One thing I *do* know and that is that I shouldn't be a lonely widow having to take in lodgers to make ends meet."

Mrs. Capper, who had heard variations on this particular theme several times before, spoke up quite sharply. "Come off it, Alice," she said, aware that Maureen and Jack were exchanging amused glances. "You've only got one lodger and that happens to be me and we don't have such a bad time together taken by and large. To hear you talk anyone'd think you spent every day of your life crying your eyes out. And you've told me a hundred times if you've told me once that Mr. Loft was a holy terror and that you was sick to death of him!"

"Hilda how *can* you!—I never said any such thing—I—"

At this point a diversion was caused by Maurice coming to the table. "I bring ghastly tidings," he said. "There's been a lash-up in the kitchen and the shrimp soup's off. I've ordered you some vichyssoise instead, but if you don't like it we'll dream up something else."

"I don't know what it is," said Mrs. Capper.

Maurice gave a titter. "It's out of a tin the same as the shrimp," he said disarmingly. "But we tidge it up with a little extra cream and chives. Try it anyway—it can't hurt you. Live dangerously." He motioned to David, who appeared with a tray and placed bowls of soup in front of Mrs. Capper, Mrs. Loft and Maureen and half a cantaloupe melon in front of Jack. "The melon's sensational tonight, dear," he said. "And there's sugar and dry ginger on the side of the plate if you fancy them."

Maurice frowned at David and dismissed him with a wave of the hand. "I'm forever telling that boy not to call the customers 'dear,'" he said. "But there's no stopping him. He says it's a mental block. As a matter of fact I'm liable to do it myself every now and then, it's sort of habit forming."

Jack laughed. "I'm broad-minded," he said. "Let's have some more vino all round."

The dinner slowly progressed. Mrs. Capper enjoyed the vichyssoise and the chicken Maryland was delicious, although the fried banana had given her a bit of a shock as she had expected it to be a potato; but it was all very tasty. The white wine, on top of the gin and it she had had at the flat had induced a pleasurable glow. In fact the whole evening was going all right and she was aware that she should be enjoying it thoroughly, but somehow, in her heart, there was unease. Not being given to lucid introspection, she tried to puzzle out in her mind why this should be. It could of course be put down to the vivacious presence of Mrs. Loft. She knew, with all her instincts, that Jack and Maureen didn't care for her and she cursed herself for having been soft enough to give in to her obvious hints. But it wasn't only Mrs. Loft. It was something deeper, more fundamental. It dawned on her suddenly while she was eating a pineapple ring that had been soaked in some sweet liqueur. Maureen was discussing with Mrs. Loft the merits and defects of certain current television programs, with occasional laconic interpolations from Jack, who had had another glass of red wine and was beginning to look rather flushed. The sly, incontestable truth that dropped into Mrs. Capper's mind was the sudden realization that she was lonely. She knew perfectly well that she had no right to be. She loved Maureen and Maureen loved her. She knew that Jack was reasonably fond of her too. They had both gone to the trouble and expense of giving her this birthday treat and buying her the lovely cardigan into the bargain. Everything was all right. Everything was more than all right, it was fine, and yet the grim little fact had to be faced; she wasn't particularly needed. Maureen had the baby and Jack had the baby and Maureen and his job; they had their own lives to live. If she, Mrs. Capper, suddenly took ill and died, Maureen would cry and wear black and come to the funeral and miss her for a little, but not more than that, not nearly so much as she still missed Fred and, for that matter, missed Maureen, too. Not the nice, sensible young woman sitting next to her, but the other Maureen, the young, growing, dependent Maureen who had to be fretted over and looked after and protected from all possible hazards and dangers. Mrs. Capper, with a small, desolate sigh, finished her pineapple ring and heard her own voice, a trifle louder than she intended it to be, ask Jack if she could have another glass of wine. Jack laughed. "Good for you, mother!" He snapped his fingers to attract attention. "Hold on to your hats boys—ma's on the booze again—hoo-bloody-ray!"

Maureen giggled. "Turn it up, dear, we don't want the whole place staring at us."

"I wouldn't say 'no' to another little sip myself," said Mrs. Loft. "It's got such a nice nutty flavor."

Michael, the stocky waiter, came up. Mrs. Capper, observing his hirsute torso largely exposed through the mesh of his vest, thought to herself how much nicer he would have looked in a clean white shirt.

"The same again all round," said Jack. Maureen made a half-hearted gesture of protest which he ignored. "This is a special occasion," he said. "Bring on the dancing girls." He winked at Maurice, who was hovering nearby. Maurice winked back, nodded and disappeared. A few moments later when Michael had brought the wine and David had placed four thick little cups and a coffee percolator on the table, there was a slight commotion at the head of the stairs leading down to the kitchen. Maurice then appeared bearing proudly a pink birthday cake with one candle on it which he placed ceremoniously in front of Mrs. Capper. The other waiters, Nicky, David and Michael, and Maurice himself, gathered round the table and sang rather self-consciously, "Happy birthday to you, happy birthday to you, happy birthday, Hilda Capper, happy birthday to you." There was a sudden silence and a spatter of applause from one of the other tables. Mrs. Capper, unable to speak, sat staring at the cake and feeling her neck and face flushing.

"Blow out the candle in one breath," said Jack. Maureen, noticing Mrs. Capper's expression, leant forward and patted her arm. Mrs. Capper, controlling her emotion with a valiant effort, blew out the candle, whereupon Jack, Maurice and the three waiters clapped their hands loudly. Mrs. Capper felt as though her heart was about to jump clean out of her chest; a wave of sentiment mixed with panic assailed her for a moment, but she held on to herself and managed to smile more or less ordinarily. "You shouldn't have, you really shouldn't have." Her voice sounded hoarse as though she were going to have one of her colds.

Maurice, sympathetically aware of her tension, broke it by offering her a silver knife. "Cut it, dear," he said, "and make yourself a lovely wish." Mrs. Capper carefully cut four slices and placed them on plates proferred by Michael, who proceeded to hand them round the table. Maurice then took the cake away. "I'll put it in a box for you," he said, "so that it won't get battered to pieces on the way home."

"Thanks, pal," said Jack.

Maurice looked at him with rather a strange expression. "Anything for you, dear," he said. "It's my pleasure."

Maureen glanced quickly from one to the other of them and laughed. As Maurice departed with the cake Jack looked at her inquiringly.

"What's the joke?"

"Nothing," Maureen replied. "It's just that he *does* talk a bit funny doesn't he?"

Saturday night was considered to be the big night at the Tender Shepherd. Sunday nights were a bit quieter as a rule and less

459

crowded; however it was fairly full when Mrs. Capper, Maureen, Jack and Mrs. Loft arrived. Maud and Dolly were on the dais, Maud banging away at the piano while Dolly, with a cigarette hanging from her mouth, banged away at the drums. A very small Jewess in a magenta jumper was screaming "Night and Day" into the mike. Lil and Ted greeted them from behind the bar as they passed through into the inner room where the music was. Vera, who was serving two youths in "glad-neck" shirts and a burly Jamaican, shouted "Cheerio" shrilly as they went by. Poor Vera was looking better Mrs. Capper thought, less peaky and her face had filled out a bit. Vera was Lil and Ted's daughter and had recently been in the Middlesex Hospital with some sort of kidney complaint. She was a nice enough girl, although inclined to be lackadaisical.

Arlene Dunlop rose from a table in the inner room and hailed them enthusiastically. "I thought you were never coming," she cried. "We can all squash round this table—move over, dear," she said to a morose-looking man in a navy blue suit. "You've got your arse on my handbag." The man looked startled and moved as close to the wall as he could.

Arlene was fiftyish and plump: her hair was vividly hennaed and she was wearing a black lace dress over a pink satin slip; it was cut low in front and her large breasts could be clearly seen huddling together. Arlene was what Mrs. Capper described as "a character" which meant that she was someone a little out of the usual run, someone whose behavior was unpredictable or at any rate predictably unpredictable. According to this view Arlene was certainly "a character" all right. In her earlier years she had been a soubrette, appearing in touring revues and provincial pantomimes and, during the war, had covered most of the Far East and Middle East with an E.N.S.A. troupe. Her descriptions of the excursions were uninhibited to say the least. For the last decade or so she had been the proprietress of a small milk bar in the Fulham Road. Actually it had originally begun as a café and developed into a milk bar later. She had had two or three husbands here and there along the line and was currently sharing a minute flat above the milk bar with a theatrical electrician a few years younger than herself. This love life, if her occasional forthright revelations were to be believed, had its ups and downs. Mrs. Capper was fond of her because she was good-hearted and made her laugh. Mrs. Loft didn't care for her at all and made no secret of it. "She's such a common thing," she said. "And her language!—well really—"

"She's all right in small doses," said Mrs. Capper equably. "And once she likes you she'd do anything in the world for you."

Anyway, here she was, more ebullient than ever and Mrs. Loft would just have to lump it. Mrs. Capper settled herself on the inside of the table with her back to the wall and smiled contentedly to herself. She always enjoyed an evening at "the Shepherd." The atmosphere of the place was cheerful and noisy without being rowdy and she loved watching the different types spring up onto the dais and sing. You just couldn't stop them. Some of them were quite good, but others—oh, dear—you'd never believe that people could be willing to make such fools of themselves in public. Dolly and Maud of course were wonderful. Maud could play anything by ear; someone would only have to hum her a few bars and off she'd go with Dolly keeping time on the drums. Mrs. Capper liked it best when Dolly marked the rhythm with the whisk only. This had a pleasing sound and wasn't quite so deafening.

"What's everyone going to have?" asked Jack.

"This is my lot," cried Arlene. "I was here first. As a matter of fact I came specially tonight on account of it being Hilda's birthday. I was pretty sure you'd all be in. What's it to be Hil? Veuve-bloody-Cliquot or mild-and-bitter?"

"Mild-and-bitter if it's all the same to you." Mrs. Capper gave a little laugh. "I wish everyone would stop going on about it being my birthday now. It's been lovely while it lasted, but between you and I I'm beginning to get a bit fed up with it."

"Relax, dear," said Arlene. "You're only middle-aged once. Personally I gave up counting birthdays years ago, too bloody depressing. I looked at myself in the glass this morning and gave a cry like a wounded animal. 'What's happened to that gorgeous little heart-shaped face?' I said. 'Gone with the wind!'—'And what about those lines round that old rosebud mouth?'—Clapham-bloody-Junction! Nearly fifty years of this and that and here and there and what have you got to show for it?' I said. 'Nothing, but an electrician who works nights and a fucking milk bar!'"

Mrs. Loft gave a muted scream. "Arlene!" she hissed. "People will hear you!"

"Natch," said Arlene cheerfully. "Unless they happen to be deaf fucking mutes."

At this Maureen went off into a fit of laughter and Vera came up to take the orders for drinks.

"You're looking better, dear," said Mrs. Capper. "Do you still have to go to the hospital?"

"Only once a week now for an injection," replied Vera.

"When I was with E.N.S.A.," said Arlene reminiscently, "I had so many injections that my arse looked like a bloody pincushion."

Vera giggled, took the orders and went away. Mrs. Loft scrutinized her face anxiously in her compact as though she feared that the vulgarity of her immediate surroundings might have left some indelible scar. She dabbed some powder on her nose, sighed heavily, snapped the compact shut and put it back into her bag.

Jimmy Bowdler, a curly-haired young man in a green turtle-

461

necked sweater and corduroy trousers, jumped up onto the stage and seized the mike. "Quiet everybody," he bellowed. "We are now going to 'ave the privilege and pleasure of 'earing the Tender Shepherd's favorite—one and only—Doreen Carter! Come on up Doreen—" He beckoned to a girl in a tight skirt and a blue blouse who was sitting at a table in the corner with two other girls and a middle-aged man. Jimmy, who had established himself in the Tender Shepherd with little opposition as a sort of permanent master of ceremonies, was tirelessly cheerful and unfailingly popular with all comers. He worked in a furniture shop in Earl's Court but it was obvious that his true aspirations were for The Theater.

Doreen Carter rose from her table and, amidst loud applause started firmly by Jimmy, minced up onto the stage and whispered to Maud with a professional air. Maud nodded sagely, took a swig of beer, placed the glass on the top of the piano and embarked on a spirited introduction. Doreen Carter took up an authoritative stance and, having adjusted the mike to her satisfaction, proceeded to sing, in a piercing and entirely toneless soprano, "Begin the Beguine." Her enormous bouffant hairdo diminished her sharp little face so that she resembled a marmoset wearing a busby.

Having finished "Begin the Beguine," the last notes of which made Mrs. Capper's ears ache, she sang, with complete confidence and absolutely no expression, "Smoke Gets in Your Eyes," and "Over the Rainbow," after which she stepped down from the stage to vociferous applause augmented by whistles and the stamping of feet from the bar.

Ernie, the bar boy, brought a tray of drinks. Arlene waved her hand regally.

"Put it all on my bill, Ernie," she said. "The Duke will pay when he gets here from Buckingham Palace. The saucy sod's late as it is."

At this moment there was a slight commotion. Ted came in hurriedly from the bar and went over to a group of young men who were sitting at a table next to Arlene's. After he had whispered to them urgently for a moment they got up and moved over to the wall.

"Jesus!" exclaimed Arlene. "It's either visitors from outer space or Princess Margaret."

After an expectant pause Ted ushered in an incredibly handsome young man wearing a sports coat, gray flannel trousers, a white silk shirt and a colored scarf, accompanied by two other young men dressed with equally careful nonchalance and a tall, blond woman in a scarlet hat and a chic white raincoat. The general buzz of conversation continued, but a lot of furtive and admiring glances were turned toward the newcomers.

"It's Gloria May and Kenny Blake—imagine!" whispered Maureen.

"Fancy them coming to a place like this on a Sunday night,"

said Mrs. Loft in awe-stricken tones. "You'd never credit it would you?"

"I don't see why they shouldn't," said Arlene. "They're liable to have as good a time here as anywhere else, if not better."

Jack took a swig of beer. "Slumming," he said contemptuously.

"It's nothing of the sort." Mrs. Capper was up in arms. "Kenny Blake used to come here ever so often in the old days."

"Sorry, Ma—I'd forgotten you used to work for him."

"I certainly did, and a nicer boy you couldn't find in a day's march." She looked past Arlene at Kenny Blake and his party who were arranging themselves at the table. He looked a bit older, more mature, but aside from that he hadn't changed much since she'd "done" for him in his two-roomed flat in Ebury Street eight years ago. He'd been playing a small part in a show in the West End. She remembered he'd given her two tickets to go and see him in it. She and Dorrie had gone together, it must have been about a year before Dorrie died. They hadn't thought much of the play, but they'd both agreed that he was wonderful; so boyish and sort of natural. Then of course he'd had this offer to act in a film in Hollywood and had sold up the flat and gone off to America all inside of a week. She remembered missing him very much, and Eddie, his friend who used to share the flat with him, he was heartbroken and no exaggeration. She remembered meeting him accidentally in the street a few weeks after Kenny had gone and he had thrown his arms around her and hugged her and taken her into the Dragon for a drink and talked about Kenny without drawing breath for an hour and a quarter. It didn't seem so very long ago really and yet here he was *the* Kenny Blake, one of the biggest movie stars in the world. She recollected now reading in the *Mail* only the other day that he was over here to act in a film with Gloria May. There had been a picture of them both getting out of an airplane. Mrs. Capper, watching out of the corner of her eye, saw Gloria slip off her raincoat and hang it over the back of her chair. She was wearing a plain black dress and a string of pearls. Kenny leant over and lit a cigarette for her.

"Christ, honey!" she said in her famous, husky voice, "this place is sheer heaven! I want to live here for the rest of my life."

Jimmy bounded up onto the stage again and sang a duet with a tall, red-headed young man who had a surprisingly deep voice and an immense Adam's apple, which seemed to be bobbing up and down in a frantic attempt to keep time. Kenny Blake and his group watched the proceedings with obvious enjoyment. A tray of drinks was brought to them by Ernie, who stared at Gloria May with his mouth open and his eyes bolting out of his head. Kenny called Ted over and asked him to sit down and have a drink. The two unnamed young men of the party occasionally nudged each other and giggled when they noticed some particular type who amused them. Gloria

May kept up a running commentary but the noise was too great for Mrs. Capper to be able to catch more than a word here and there. Two girls approached Kenny's table with two bits of grubby paper to be signed. He and Gloria obliged graciously, but Jimmy was up at the mike again in a flash.

Having yelled for silence and got it to a certain degree, he waved his hands in the air. "Listen boys and girls," he shouted. "We have the pleasure to have with us tonight our old friend Kenny Blake and his lovely star Gloria May—" The applause was deafening but after a moment or two he managed to quiet it. "They have come here," he went on, "just as we all have, to have a couple of drinks and enjoy themselves. They have *not* come here to wear their fingers to the bone signing autographs. So let's all wish 'em all the best and bloody well leave 'em alone!" He jumped down again amid loud cheering and laughter. Kenny got up and shook hands with him and introduced him to Gloria May, who flashed him a radiant smile and offered him a cigarette out of a heavily embossed gold cigarette case. The performance proceeded. The Jewess in the magenta jumper sang again and a slightly drunk young man in tight black trousers and a T-shirt sang "My Heart Belongs to Daddy" to loud and prolonged applause.

It was drawing near to closing time and the noise seemed to be growing correspondingly louder. Once more Jimmy jumped up and silenced it. As the buzz died down and Jimmy began to speak, Mrs. Capper was suddenly seized with a dread sense of premonition. "I have an announcement to make"—Jimmy was shouting—"to all you habitués and sons of habitués—pause for laugh—thanks very much—of this distinguished old joint. We have with us tonight one of the good old Shepherd's favorite customers, and it just happens to be her birthday—" Mrs. Capper's heart sank like a stone. "So I am going to ask you to raise your glasses one and all and drink to the health, wealth and happiness of our old friend—Hilda Capper!" Upon this everyone cheered enthusiastically, Jimmy made a sign to Maud, who bashed out the opening chords of "Happy Birthday," and when he started to sing it everybody joined in. Mrs. Capper sat stunned. She was smiling but she knew the smile to be false. It felt as though it had been pressed onto her face like a poultice. When the ordeal was over she waved her hand blindly and fumbled in her bag for her handkerchief. Maureen squeezed her arm affectionately, Jack raised his glass to her, Arlene bestowed another moist kiss on her cheek and Mrs. Loft mowed and becked with vicarious pleasure like an elderly parrot on a perch. Mrs. Capper, still too overwhelmed to speak or even to think, dumbly took out her packet of Players and lit one with a trembling hand. Ted came in and shouted "Time Gentlemen Please" several times. Maud played "God Save the Queen" with a final flourish and an extra drum roll from Dolly. Everyone stood up.

Suddenly Mrs. Capper, who was about to move away from the table after Maureen and Jack, felt two arms catch her from behind and swing her round.

"It *is* you!—after all these years!" Kenny Blake kissed her firmly on both cheeks. "Gloria—" He dragged Mrs. Capper over to Gloria May, who was putting on her raincoat. "This is one of my oldest friends, she used to look after me like a mother." Gloria smiled at her and put out her hand, which Mrs. Capper took a trifle uncertainly. "Pleased to meet you I am sure," she said. Kenny went on to introduce her to the two boys, but she was far too flustered to hear their names. Kenny rattled on about the old days in the flat and told her that Eddie had come out to join him in Hollywood a few years back and was now a successful agent. Mrs. Capper was glad about Eddie, he'd been a sweet boy and very sensitive, but she found it difficult to concentrate on much that Kenny said because the whole episode seemed to be a jumble of emotion, excitement, old memory and acute embarrassment. At long last Kenny kissed her again and wrung her hand affectionately and she was able to join Maureen and Jack, who were hovering in the background. Jack took one arm and Maureen took the other as though she had just fainted or had an accident, and they led her out through the bar and into the street.

Mrs. Loft and Arlene were already on the pavement. There was a fairly prolonged argument as to whether or not Arlene could be squeezed into the Mini and dropped off in the Fulham Road. It was finally decided that it could be managed if Maureen sat in the front with Jack and Mrs. Capper. Mrs. Loft and Arlene squashed into the back.

They were just about to drive off when Ernie came flying out of the pub and banged on the car window. Mrs. Capper, who happened to be on that side, let the window down. Ernie pushed a bottle of Three Star Martell into her hands. "It's from His Nibs," he said breathlessly. There was bit of folded paper with the bottle. Mrs. Capper opened it and read it in the light of a streetlamp. "Happy birthday, my dear," it said. "In memory of old times and with my love. Kenny."

When Mrs. Capper finally got into her bedroom she was too tired to try on the new gray cardigan as she had intended to do, so she took it out of its brown paper and laid it carefully in the top drawer of her chest of drawers to wait until the morning. She put the bottle of brandy on the wash-hand stand for the time being and took her lower plate out with a sigh of relief. It had been paining her badly for the last few hours although so much had been happening that she hadn't really paid much heed to it. She rubbed some of the stuff the chemist had given her onto her gum; it stung a bit and tasted sharp and tinny, but it did the trick. She undressed slowly and climbed into bed. She lay still for a few moments looking up at the ceiling and back over the day. Quite a day it had been, too, what with

465

one thing and another. She thought of her amethyst brooch and Audrey and Toby Nash bickering and squabbling and deceiving one another and wondered whether things would go from bad to worse and finish up in the divorce courts or whether they'd have the sense to stop acting silly and buckle down and try to make a go of it. It seemed a pity really, all that cocktail drinking and carrying on and upsetting each other for no particular reason. She sighed because she was fond of them both and wished them well. Then her mind switched to Mr. Godsall and the cut-glass vase and that awful crumb of sponge sandwich. For a moment or two she entertained a vision of being married to Mr. Godsall; living with him day after day, sleeping with him night after night. The picture of Mr. Godsall undressing apologetically, climbing into bed with her and pawing her about suddenly became too much for her and she started to laugh. It wouldn't do, and that's all there was to it. It just wouldn't do. Then she thought of Maureen and Jack and the dinner at the restaurant and the birthday cake, the remainder of which, still in its cardboard box, she had put in the larder before coming up to bed. Her heart swelled with love and gratitude for Maureen and Jack, taking all that trouble to give her such a good time. They'd be all right those two. Maureen was sensible and Jack was steady and they had a baby. She hoped they'd have another sooner or later, a boy for preference. It would be nice to have a little grandson. Then she started to laugh again at the thought of Alice Loft and Arlene. Alice being so refined and piss-elegant and Arlene shocking the daylights out of her. It was a scream, it really was, to see them together. Then that Jimmy jumping up to the mike and making everybody sing "Happy Birthday" to her! She felt herself blushing all over again. She still wished he hadn't and yet she was glad that he had. If he hadn't, ten to one Kenny Blake wouldn't have noticed she was there, and it had been nice, him being so nice and kissing her and giving her the bottle of Three Star. He was a nice boy and deserved everything he got and good luck to him. She closed her eyes for a moment feeling the beginnings of sleep creeping over her, the sense of loneliness she had suddenly felt in the restaurant seemed to have evaporated completely. You couldn't be lonely with everybody laying themselves out to take such a lot of trouble could you? She opened her eyes again, picked up the frame with Fred's photo in it and looked at it for quite a while. Mr. Godsall indeed! Mr. Anybody for the matter of that. She gave an indignant little snort and put the frame back in its place.

"Good night, Fred," she said out loud, and pulled the string that switched off the light.

ME
AND THE
GIRLS

Tuesday

I like looking at mountains because they keep changing, if you know what I mean; not only the colors change at different times of the day but the shapes seem to alter too. I see them first when I wake up in the morning and Sister Dominique pulls up the blind. She's a dear old camp and makes clicking noises with her teeth. The blind rattles up and there they are—the mountains I mean. There was fresh snow on them this morning, that is on the highest peaks, and they looked very near in the clear air, blue and pink as if someone had painted them, rather like those pictures you see in frame shops in the King's Road, bright and a bit common but pretty.

Today was the day when they all came in: Dr. Pierre and Sister Françoise and the other professor with the blue chin and a gleam in his eye, quite a dish really he is, hairy wrists but lovely long slim hands. He was the one who actually did the operation. I could go for him in a big way if I was well enough, but I'm not and that's that, nor am I likely to be for a long time. It's going to be a slow business. Dr. Pierre explained it carefully and very very gently, not at all like his usual manner which is apt to be a bit offish. While I was listening to him I looked at the professor's face: he was staring out at the mountains and I thought he looked sad. Sister Françoise and Sister Dominique stood quite still except that Sister Françoise was fiddling with her rosary. I got the message all right but I didn't let on that I did. They think I'm going to die and as they've had a good dekko inside me and I haven't, they probably know. I've thought of all this before of course before the operation, actually long before when I was in the other hospital. I don't know yet how I feel about it quite, but then I've had a bit of a bashing about and I'm tired. It's not going to matter to anyone but me anyway and I suppose when it does happen I shan't care, what with being dopey and one thing and another. The girls will be sorry, especially Mavis, but she'll get over it. Ronnie will have a crying jag and get pissed and wish he'd been a bit nicer, but that won't last long either. I know him too well. Poor old Ron. I expect there were faults on both sides, there always are, but he was a little shit and no two ways about it. Still I brought it all on myself so I mustn't complain. It all seems far away now anyhow. Nothing seems very near except the mountains and they look as if they wanted to move into the room.

When they had all filed out and left me alone Sister D came back because she'd forgotten my temperature chart and wanted to fill it in or something, at least that was what she said, but she didn't fool me: what she really came back for was to see if I was all right. She did a lot of teeth clicking and fussed about with my pillows and when she'd finally buggered off I gave way a bit and had a good cry, then I dropped off and had a snooze and woke up feeling quite spry. Maybe the whole thing's in my imagination anyhow. You never know really do you?—I mean when you're weak and kind of low generally you have all sorts of thoughts that you wouldn't have if you were up and about. All the same there *was* something in the way Dr. Pierre talked. The professor squeezed my hand when he left and smiled but his eyes still looked sad. It must be funny to be a doctor and always be coping with ill people and cheering them up even if you have to tell them a few lies while you're at it. Not that he said much. He just stood there most of the time like I said, looking at the mountains.

This is quite a nice room as hospital rooms go. There is a chintzy armchair for visitors and the walls are off-white so as not to be too glarey. Rather like the flat in the rue Brochet which Ronnie and I did over just after we'd first met. If you mix a tiny bit of pink with the white it takes the coldness out of it but you have to be careful that it doesn't go streaky. I can hardly believe that all that was only three years ago, it seems like a lifetime.

All the girls sent me flowers except Mavis and she sent me a bottle of Mitsouko toilet water which is better than flowers really because it lasts longer and it's nice to dab on at night when you wake up feeling hot and sweaty. She said she'd pop in and see me this afternoon just for a few minutes to tell me how the act's getting on. I expect it's a bit of a shambles really without me there to bound on and off and keep it on the tracks. They've had to change the running order. Mavis does her single now right after the parasol dance so as to give the others time to get into their kimonos for the Japanese number. I must remember to ask her about Sally. She was overdue when I left and that's ten days ago. She's a silly little cow that girl if ever there was one, always getting carried away and losing her head. A couple of drinks and she's gone. Well if she's clicked again she'll just have to get on with it and maybe it'll teach her to be more careful in the future. Anyway Mavis will know what to do, Mavis always knows what to do except when she gets what she calls "emotionally disturbed," then she's hell. She ought to get out of the act and marry somebody and settle down and have children, she's still pretty but it won't last and she'll never be a star if she lives to be a hundred, she just hasn't got that extra something. Her dancing's okay and she can put over a number all right but that dear little *je ne sais quoi* just isn't there poor bitch and it's no good pretending it is. I know it's me that stands in her way up to a point but I can't do anything about it. She knows all about me. I've explained everything until I'm blue in the face but it doesn't make any difference. She's got this "thing" about me not really being queer but only having caught it like a bad habit. Would you mind! Of course I should never have gone to bed with her in the first place. That sparked off the whole business. Poor old Mavis. These girls really do drive me round the bend sometimes. I will say one thing though, they *do* behave like ladies, outwardly at least. I've never let them get off a plane or a train without lipstick and the proper clothes and shoes. None of those ponytails and tatty slacks for George Banks Esq.: not on your Nelly. My girls have got to look dignified whether they like it or not. To do them justice they generally do. There have been one or two slip-ups like that awful Maureen. She was a slut from the word go. I was forever after her about one thing or another. She always tried to dodge shaving under the arms because some silly bitch had told her that the men liked it. Imagine! I told her that that lark went out when the Moulin Rouge first opened in eighteen-whatever it was but as she'd never heard of the Moulin Rouge anyway it didn't make much impression on her. This lot are very good on the whole. Apart from Mavis there's Sally, blond and rather bouncy; Irma, skin a bit sluggish but comes up a treat under the lights; Lily-May, the best dancer of the lot but calves a bit on the heavy side; and Beryl and Sylvia Martin. They're our twins and they're planning to work up a sister act later on. They're both quite pretty but that ole debbil talent has failed to touch either of them with his fairy wings so I shouldn't think the sister act will get much further than the Poland Rehearsal Rooms. The whole show closes here next Saturday week then God knows what will happen. I wrote off to Ted before my operation telling him that the act would have to be disbanded and asking him what he could do for them, but you know what agents are, all talk and no do as a rule. Still he's not a bad little sod taken by and large so we shall see.

Wednesday

Mavis came yesterday as promised. I didn't feel up to talking for long but I did my best. She started off all right, a bit overcheerful and taking the "Don't worry everything's going to be all right" line, but I could see she was in a bit of a state and trying not to show it. I don't know if she'd been talking to any of the Sisters or whether they'd told her anything or not. I don't suppose they did, and her French isn't very good anyhow. She said the act was going as well as could be expected and that Monsieur Philippe had come backstage last night and been quite nice. She also asked if I'd like her to write to Ronnie and tell him about me being ill but I jumped on that double-quick pronto. It's awful when women get too understanding. I don't want her writing to Ronnie any more than I want Ronnie writing to me. He's got his ghastly Algerian *and* the flat so he can bloody well get on with it. I don't mind anymore anyway. I did at first, of course, I couldn't help myself, it wasn't the Algerian so much, it was all the lies and scenes. Fortunately I was rehearsing all through that month and had a lot to keep my mind occupied. It was bad I must admit but not so bad that it couldn't have been worse. No more being in love for me thank you very much. Not I expect that I shall have much chance. But if I do get out of this place all alive-o there's going to be no more of that caper. I've had it, once and for all. Sex is all very well in its way and I'm all for it but the next time I begin to feel that old black magic that I know so well I'll streak off like a bloody greyhound.

When Mavis had gone Sister Clothilde brought me my tea. Sister Clothilde's usually on in the afternoons. She's small and tubby and has a bit of a guttural accent having been born in Alsace-Lorraine; she also has bright, bright red cheeks which look as if someone had pinched them hard just before she came into the room. She must have been quite pretty in a dumpy way when she was a girl before she took the veil or whatever it is you have to take before you give yourself to Jesus. She has quite a knowing look in her eye too as though she wasn't quite so far away from the wicked world as she pretended to be. She brought me a madeleine with my tea but it was a bit dry. When she'd gone and I'd had the tea and half the madeleine I settled back against the pillows and relaxed. It's surprising what funny things pop into your mind when you're lying snug in bed and feeling a bit drowsy.

I started to try to remember everything I could from the very beginning like playing a game, but I couldn't keep dead on the beam: I'd suddenly jump from something that happened fifteen years ago to something that happened two weeks back. That was when the pain had begun to get pretty bad and Monsieur Philippe came into the dressing room with Dr. Pierre and there was I writhing about with nothing but a jockstrap on and sweating like a pig. That wasn't so good that bit because I didn't know what was going to happen to me and I felt frightened. I don't feel frightened now, just a bit numb as though some part of me was hypnotized. I suppose that's the result of having had the operation. My inside must be a bit startled at all that's gone on and I expect the shock has made my mind tired. When I try to think clearly and remember things I don't seem able to hold on to any subject for long. The thing is to give up to the tiredness and not worry. They're all very kind, the Sisters and the doctors, even the maid who does the room every morning gives me a cheery smile as if she wanted to let me know she was on my side. She's a swarthy type with rather projecting eyes like a pug. I bet she'll finish up as a concierge with those regulation black stockings and a market basket. There's a male orderly who pops in and out from time to time and very sprightly he is too, you'd think he was about to take off any minute. He's the one who shaved me before the operation and that was a carry-on if ever there was one. I wasn't in any pain because they'd given me an injection but woozy as I was I managed to make a few jokes. When he pushed my old man aside almost caressingly with his hand I said *"Pas ce soir Josephine, demain peutêtre"* and he giggled. It can't be much fun being an orderly in a hospital and have to shave people's privates and give them enemas and sit them on bedpans from morning till night, but I suppose they must find it interesting otherwise they'd choose some other profession. When he'd finished he gave my packet a friendly little pat and said, *"Vive le sport."* *Would* you mind! Now whenever he comes in he winks at me as though we shared a secret and I have a sort of feeling he's dead right. I suppose if I didn't feel so weak and seedy I'd encourage him a bit just for the hell of it. Perhaps when I'm a little stronger I'll ask him to give me a massage or something just to see what happens—as if I didn't know! On the other hand of course if what I suspect is true, I shan't get strong again so the question won't come up. Actually he reminds me a bit of Peter when we first met at Miss Llewellyn's Dancing Academy, stocky and fair with short legs and a high color. Peter was the one that did the Pas de Deux from "Giselle" with Coralie Hancock and dropped her on her head during one of the lifts and she had concussion and had to go to St. George's Hospital. It's strange to think of those early days. I can see myself now getting off the bus at Marble Arch with my ballet shoes in that tatty old bag of Aunt Isobel's. I had to walk down Edgeware Road and then turn to the left and the dancing academy was down some steps under a public house called the Swan. There was a mirror all along the one wall with a *barre* in front of it and Miss Adler used to thump away at the upright while we did our bends and kicks and positions. Miss Llewellyn was a character and no mistake. She had frizzed-up hair, very black at the parting; a heavy stage makeup with a beauty spot under her left eye if you please and a black velvet band around her neck. She always wore this rain or shine. Peter said it was to hide the scar where someone had tried to cut her throat. She wasn't a bad old tart really and she did get me my first job in a Christmas play called *Mr. Birdie.* I did an audition for it at the Garrick Theatre. Lots of other kids had been sent for and there we were all huddled at the side of the stage in practice clothes waiting to be called out. When my turn came I pranced on followed by Miss Adler, who made a beeline for the piano, which sounded as if someone had dropped a lot of tin ashtrays inside it, you know, one of those diabolical old uprights that you only get at auditions. Anyhow I sang "I Hear You Calling Me"—it was before the poor darlings dropped so I was still a soprano—and then I did the standard sailor's hornpipe as taught at the academy, a lot of hopping about and hauling at imaginary ropes and finishing with a few quick turns and a leap off. Mr. Alec Sanderson, who was producing *Mr. Birdie,* then sent for me to go and speak to him in the stalls. Miss Adler came with me and he told me I could play the heroine's little brother in the first act, a gnome in the second and a frog in the third, and that he'd arrange the business side with Miss Llewellyn. Miss Adler and I fairly flew out into Charing Cross Road and on wings of song to Lyon's Corner House where she stood me tea and we had an éclair each. I really can't think about *Mr. Birdie* without laughing and when I laugh it hurts my stitches. It really was a fair bugger, whimsical as all get-out. Mr. Birdie, played by Mr. Sanderson himself, was a lovable old professor who suddenly inherited a family of merry little kiddos of which I was one. We were all jolly and ever so mischievous in act one and then we all went to sleep in a magic garden and became elves and gnomes and what have you for acts two and three. Some of us have remained fairies to this day. The music was by Oliver Bakewell, a ripsnorting old queen who used to pinch our bottoms when we were standing round the piano learning his gruesome little songs. Years later when I knew what was what I reminded him of this and he whinnied like a horse.

Those were the days all right, days of glory for child actors. I think the boys had a better time than the girls on account of not being so well protected. I shall never forget those jovial wet-handed clergymen queuing up outside the stage door to take us out to tea and stroke our knees under the table. Bobby Clews and I used to have bets as to how much we could get without going too far. I once got a box of Fuller's soft-centers and a gramophone record of *Casse Noisette* for no more than a quick grope in a taxi. After my voice broke I got pleurisy and a touch of T.B. and had to be sent to a sanatorium near Buxton. I was cured and sent home to Auntie Iso after six months but it gave me a fright I can tell you. I was miserable for the first few weeks and cried my eyes out, but I got used to it and quite enjoyed the last part when I was moved into a small room at the top of the house with a boy called Digby Lawson. He was two years older than me, round about seventeen and a half. He died a short time later and I really wasn't surprised. It's a miracle that I'm alive to tell the tale, but I must say we had a lot of laughs.

It wasn't until I was nineteen that I got into the chorus at the Palladium and that's where I really learnt my job. I was there two and a half years in all and during the second year I was given the understudy of Jackie Foal. He was a sensational dancer and I've never worked so hard in my life. I only went on for him three times but one of the times was for a whole week and it was a thrill I can tell you when I got over the panic. One night I got round Mr. Lewis to let me have two house seats for Aunt Iso and Emma, who's her sort of maid-companion, and they dressed themselves up to the nines and had a ball. Emma wore her best black with a bead necklace she borrowed from Clara two doors down and Auntie Iso looked as though she were ready for tiara night at the opera: a full evening dress made of crimson taffeta with a sort of lace overskirt of the same color; a dramatic headdress that looked like a coronet with pince-nez attached and the Chinese coat Uncle Fred had brought her years ago when he was in the merchant navy. I took them both out to supper afterward at Giovanni's in Greek Street. He runs the restaurant with a boy friend of his, a sulky-looking little sod as a rule but he played up that night and both he and Giovanni laid on the full V.I.P. treatment, cocktails on the house, a bunch of flowers for the old girls and a lot of hand kissing. It all knocked me back a few quid but it was worth it to see how they enjoyed themselves. They both got a bit pissed on Chianti and Emma laughed so much that her upper plate fell into the zabaglione and she had to fish it out with a spoon. Actually it wasn't long after that that Auntie Iso died and Emma went off to live with her sister in Lowestoft. I hated it when Auntie Iso died and even now after all these years it still upsets me to think of it. After all she was all I'd got in the way of relations and she'd brought me up and looked after me ever since I was five. After she'd gone I shared a flat with Bunny Granger for a bit in Longacre which was better than nothing but I'd rather have been on my own. Bunny was all right in his way; he came to the funeral with me and did his best to cheer me up but he didn't stay the course very long really if you know what I mean and that flat was a shambles, it really was. Nobody minds fun and games within reason but you can have too much of a good thing. There was hardly a night he didn't bring someone or other home and one night if you please I nipped out of my room to go to the bathroom which was up one flight and there was a policeman scuffling back into his uniform. I nearly had a fit but actually he turned out to be quite nice. Anyway I didn't stay with Bunny long because I met Harry and that was that. Harry was the first time it ever happened to me seriously. Of course I'd hopped in and out of bed with people every now and again and never thought about it much one way or another. I never was one to go off into a great production about being queer and work myself up into a state like some people I know. I can't think why they waste their time. I mean it just doesn't make sense does it? You're born either hetero, bi or homo and whichever way it goes there you are stuck with it. Mind you people are getting a good deal more hep about it than they used to be but the laws still exist that make it a crime and poor bastards still get hauled off to the clink just for doing what comes naturally as the song says. Of course this is what upsets some of the old magistrates more than anything, the fact that it *is* as natural as any other way of having sex, leaving aside the strange ones who get excited over old boots or used knickers or having themselves walloped with straps. Even so I don't see that it's anybody's business but your own what you do with your old man providing that you don't make a beeline for the dear little kiddies, not, I am here to tell you, that quite a lot of the aforesaid dear little kiddies don't enjoy it tiptop. I was one myself and I know. But I digress as the bride said when she got up in the middle of her honeymoon night and baked a cake. That's what I mean really about the brain not hanging on to one thing when you're tired. It keeps wandering off. I was trying to put down about Harry and what I felt about it and got sidetracked. All right—all right—let's concentrate on Harry-boy and remember what he looked like and not only what he looked like, but him, him himself. To begin with he was inclined to be moody and when we first moved into the maisonette in Swiss Cottage together he was always fussing about whether Mrs. Fingal suspected anything or not, but as I kept explaining to him, Mrs. Fingal wouldn't have minded if we poked Chinese mice providing that we paid the rent regularly and didn't make a noise after twelve o'clock at night. As a matter of fact she was quite a nice old bag and I don't think nor ever did think that she suspected for a moment, she bloody well knew. I don't mean to say that she thought about it much or went on about it to herself. She just accepted the situation and minded her own business and if a few more people I know had as much sense the world would be a far happier place. Anyway, Harry-boy got over being worried about her or about himself and about us after a few months and we settled down, loved each other good and true for two and a half years until the accident happened and he was killed. I'm not going to think about that because even now it still makes me feel sick and want to cry my heart out. I always hated that fucking motorbike anyhow but he was mad for it, forever tinkering with it and rubbing it down with oily rags and fiddling about with its engine. But that was part of his character really. He loved machinery and engineering and football matches and all the things I didn't give a bugger about. We hadn't a thing in common actually except the one thing you can't explain. He wasn't even all that good-looking now I come to think of it. His eyes were nice but his face wasn't anything out of the ordinary: his body was wonderful, a bit thick-set but he was very proud of it and never stopped doing exercises and keeping himself fit. He never cared what the maisonette looked like and once when I'd bought a whole new set of loose covers for the divan and the two armchairs, he never even noticed until I pointed them out to him. He used to laugh at me too and send me up rotten when I fussed about the place and tried to keep things tidy. But he loved me. That's the shining thing I like to remember. He loved me more than anyone has ever loved me before or since. He used to have affairs with girls every now and again, just to keep his hand in, as he used to say. I got upset about this at first and made a few scenes but he wouldn't stand for any of that nonsense and let me know it in no uncertain terms. He loved me true did Harry-boy and I loved him true, and if the happiness we gave each other was wicked and wrong in the eyes of the Law and the Church and God Almighty, then the Law and the Church and God Almighty can go dig a hole and fall down it.

Thursday

I had a bad night and at about two in the morning Sister Jeanne-Marie gave me a pill and I got off to sleep all right and didn't wake until seven. I couldn't see the mountains at all because the clouds had come down and wiped them away. My friend the orderly came in at eight o'clock and gave me an enema on account of I hadn't been since the day before yesterday and then only a few goat's balls. He was very cheery and kiss-me-arse and kept on saying "Soyez courageux" and "Tenez le" until I could have throttled him. After it was all over he gave me a bath and soaped me and then, when he was drying me, I suddenly felt sort of weak and despairing and burst into tears. He at once stopped being happy-chappy and good-time-Charlie and put both his arms round me tight. He'd taken his white coat off to bath me and he had a stringy kind of vest and I could feel the hairs on his chest against my face while he held me. Presently he sat down on the loo seat and took me on to his lap as though I were a child. I went on crying for a bit and he let me get on with it without saying a word or trying to cheer me up. He just patted me occasionally with the hand that wasn't holding me and kept quite still. After a while the tears stopped

475

and I got hold of myself. He dabbed my face gently with a damp towel, slipped me into my pajama jacket, carried me along the passage and put me back into bed. It was already made, cool and fresh and the flowers the girls had sent me had been brought back in their vases and put about the room. I leant back against the pillows and closed my eyes because I was feeling fairly whacked, what with the enema and the crying jag and one thing and another. When I opened them he had gone.

I dozed on and off most of the morning and in the afternoon Sally came to see me. She brought me last week's *Tatler* and this week's *Paris Match,* which was full of Brigitte Bardot as usual. If you ask me, what that poor girl needs is less publicity and more discipline. Sally was wearing her beige two-piece with a camp little red hat. She looked very pretty and was in high spirits having come on after all nearly ten days late. She said the Hungarian had come to the show the night before and given her a bottle of Bellodgia. I asked her if she'd been to bed with him again and she giggled and said, "Of course not, for obvious reasons." Then I asked her if she really had a "thing" about him and she giggled some more and said that in a way she had because he was so aristocratic and had lovely muscular legs but that it wasn't serious and that anyhow he was going back to his wife in Vienna. She said he went into quite an act about this and swore that she would be for ever in his heart but that she didn't believe a word of it. I told her that she'd better be more careful in the future and see to it that another time she got more out of a love affair than a near miss and a bottle of Bellodgia. She's a nice enough kid really, our Sally, but she just doesn't think or reason things out. I asked her what she was going to do when the act folds on Saturday week and she said she wasn't sure but that she'd put a phone call through to London to a friend of hers who thinks he can get some modeling for her, to fill in for the time being. She said that all the girls sent me their love and that one or other of them was coming to see me every day, but Mavis had told them not more than one at a time and not to stay long at that. Good old Mavis. Bossy to the last.

Sally had brought me a packet of mentholated filter-tip cigarettes and when she'd gone I smoked one just for a treat and it made me quite dizzy because I've not been smoking at all for the last few days, I somehow didn't feel like it. During the dizziness the late afternoon sun came out and suddenly there were the mountains again, wobbling a bit but as good as new. I suppose I've always had a "thing" about mountains ever since I first saw any, which was a great many too many years ago as the crow flies and I'd just got my first "girl" act together and we had a booking on the ever so gay continent. Actually it was in Zurich in a scruffy little dive called Die Kleine Maus or something. There were only four girls and me and we shared a second-class compartment on the night train from Paris. I remember we all got nicely thank you on a bottle of red wine I bought at the station buffet and when we woke up from our communal coma in the early hours of the morning there were the mountains with the first glow of sunrise on them and everyone did a lot of ooh-ing and aah-ing and I felt as though suddenly something wonderful had happened to me. We all took it in turns to dart down the corridor to the lav and when we'd furbished ourselves up and I'd shaved and the girls had put some slap on, we staggered along to the restaurant car and had large bowls of coffee and croissants with butter and jam. The mountains were brighter then, parading past the wide windows and covered in snow and I wished we weren't going to a large city but could stay off for a few days and wander about and look at the waterfalls. However we *did* go to a large city and when we got there we laid a great big gorgeous egg and nobody came to see us after the first performance. It was a dank little room we had to perform in with a stage at one end, then a lot of tables and then a bar with a looking glass behind it so we could see our reflections, which wasn't any too encouraging I can tell you. A handful of square-looking Swiss gentlemen used to sit at the tables with their girl friends and they were so busy doing footy-footy and gropey-gropey that they never paid any attention to us at all. One night we finished the Punch and Judy number without a hand except from one oaf in the corner on the right, and he was only calling the waiter. There were generally a few poufs clustered round the bar hissing at each other like snakes, apart from them that was it. The manager came round after the third performance and told us we'd have to finish at the end of the week. He was lovely he was, bright red in the face and shaped like a pear. I had a grand upper and downer with him because we'd been engaged on a two weeks' contract. His English wasn't up to much and in those days I couldn't speak a word of German or French so the scene didn't exactly flow. There was a lot of arm waving and banging on the dressing table and the girls sat round giggling, but I finally made him agree to pay us half our next week's salary as compensation. The next morning I had another upper and downer with Monsieur Huber, who was the man who had booked the act through Ted Bentley, my agent in London. Monsieur Huber was small and sharp as a needle with a slight cast in his eye like Norma Shearer only not so pretty. As a matter of fact he wasn't so bad. At least he took our part and called up the red pear and there was a lot of palava in Switzer-Deutsch which to my mind is not a pretty language at all and sounds as if you'd got a nasty bit of phlegm in your throat and were trying to get rid of it. At any rate the upshot of the whole business was that he, Monsieur Huber, finally got us another booking in a small casino on the Swiss side of Lake Lugano and we all drove there in a bus on the Sunday and opened on the Monday night without a band call or even a dress rehearsal. I can't truthfully say that we tore the place up but we didn't do badly, anyway we stayed there for the two weeks we'd been booked for. We lived in a pension, if you'll excuse the expression, up a steep hill at the back of the town which was run by a false blond Italian lady who looked like an all-in wrestler in drag. She wasn't a bad sort and we weren't worried by the other boarders on account of there weren't any. The girls shared two rooms on the first floor and I had a sort of attic at the top like *La Bohème*, which had a view, between two houses, of the lake and the mountains. I used to watch them, the mountains, sticking up out of the mist in the early mornings, rather like these I'm looking at now. Madame Corelli, the all-in wrestler, took quite a fancy to us and came to see the show several times with her lover, who was a friend of the man who ran the casino. I wish you could have seen the lover. He was thick and short and bald as a coot and liked wearing very tight trousers to prove he had an enormous packet which indeed he had: it looked like an entire Rockingham tea service, milk jug and all. His name was Guido Mezzoni and he could speak a little English because he'd been a waiter in Soho in the dear dead days before the War. He asked us all to his place one night after the show and put on a chef's hat and made spaghetti Bolognese and we all got high as kites on vino rosso and a good time was had by *tutti* until just before we were about to leave when he takes Babs Mortimer, our youngest, into the bathroom, where she wanted to go and instead of leaving her alone to have her Jimmy Riddle in peace and quiet, he whisked her inside, locked the door and showed her all he'd got. Of course the silly little cow lost her head and screamed bloody murder whereupon Madame Corelli went charging down the passage baying like a bloodhound. That was a nice ending to a jolly evening I must say. Nice clean fun and no questions asked. You've never heard such a carry-on. After a lot of banging on the bathroom door and screaming he finally opened it and Babs came flying into the room in hysterics and I had to give her a sharp slap in the face to quiet her, meanwhile the noise from the passage sounded as though the Mau Maus had got in. We all had another swig all round at the vino while the battle was going on and I couldn't make up my mind whether to grab all the girls and bugger off home or wait and see what happened, then I remembered that Madame Corelli had the front-door key anyhow so there wouldn't be much point in going back and just sitting on the curb. Presently the row subsided a bit and poor old Guido came back into the room looking very hangdog with a nasty red scratch all down one side of his face. Madame followed him wearing what they call in novels a "set expression" which means that her mouth was in a straight line and her eyes looked like black beads.

We all stood about and looked at each other for a minute or two because nobody could think of anything to say. Finally Madame hissed something to Guido in Italian and he went up miserably to Babs and said, "I am sawry, so sawry and I wish beg your pardon." Babs shot me a look and I nodded irritably and she said "Granted I'm sure" in a very grand voice and minced over to look out of the window which was fairly silly because it looked out on a warehouse and it was pitch dark anyway. Madame Corelli then took charge of the situation. Her English wasn't any too hot at the best of times and now that she was in the grip of strong emotion it was more dodgy than ever, however she made a long speech most of which I couldn't understand a word of, and gave me the key of the front door, from which I gathered that she was going to stay with Guido and that we were expected to get the hell out and leave them to it. I took the key, thanked Guido for the evening and off we went. It was a long drag up the hill and there was no taxi in sight at that time of the morning so we had to hoof it. When we got to the house the dawn was coming up over the lake. I stopped to look at it for a moment, the air was fresh and cool and behind the mountains the sky was pale green and pink and yellow like a Neapolitan ice, but the girls were grumbling about being tired and their feet hurting so we all went in and went to bed.

The next day I had a little set-to with Babs because I thought it was necessary. I took her down to a café on the lakefront and gave her an iced coffee and explained a few of the facts of life to her. Among other things I told her that you can't go through life shrieking and making scenes just because somebody makes a pass at you. There are always ways of getting out of a situation like that without going off into the second act of *Tosca*. In any case Guido hadn't really made a pass at her at all, he was obviously the type who's overproud of his great big gorgeous how-do-you-do and can't resist showing it to people. If he'd grabbed her and tried to rape her it would have been different, but all the poor little sod wanted was a little honest appreciation and probably if she'd just said something ordinary like "Fancy" or "What a whopper!" he wouldn't have wanted to go any further and all would have ended happily. She listened to me rather sullenly and mumbled something about it having been a shock and that she wasn't used to that sort of thing having been brought up like a lady, to which I replied that having been brought up like a lady was no help in cabaret and that if she was all that refined she shouldn't have shoved her delicate nose into show business in the first place. Really these girls make me tired sometimes. They prance about in bikinis showing practically all they've got and then get hoity-toity when anyone makes a little pounce. What's so silly about it really is that that very thing is what they want more than anything only they won't admit it. Anyway she had another iced coffee and got off her high horse and confessed, to my great relief, that she wasn't a virgin and had had several love affairs only none of them had led to anything. I told her that it was lucky for her that they hadn't and that if at any time she got herself into trouble of any sort that she was to come straight to me. After that little fireside chat we became quite good friends and when she left the act, which was about three months later, I missed her a lot. She finally got into the chorus of a musical at the Coliseum and then got married. I sometimes get a postcard from her but not very often. She must be quite middle-aged now. Good old Babs.

The other three were not so pretty as Babs but they danced better. Moira Finch was the eldest, about twenty-six, then there were Doreen March and Elsie Pendleton. Moira was tall and dark with nice legs and no tits to speak of. Doreen was mousy, mouse-colored hair, mouse-colored eyes and a mouse-colored character, she also had a squeaky voice just to make the whole thing flawless. I must say one thing for her though, she *could* dance. Her kicks were wonderful, straight up with both legs and no faking and her turns were quick as lightning. Elsie was the sexiest of the bunch, rather pallid and languorous with the sort of skin that takes makeup a treat and looks terrible without it. They were none of them very interesting really, but they were my first lot and I can remember them kindly on the whole. We were together on and off for nearly a year and played different dance halls and casinos all over Italy, Spain, Switzerland and France. I learnt a lot during that tour and managed to pick up enough of the various languages to make myself understood. Nothing much happened over and above a few rows. Elsie got herself pregnant in Lyons, where we were appearing in a sort of nightclub-cum-knocking-shop called Le Perroquet Vert. A lot of moaning and wailing went on but fortunately the old tart who ran the joint knew a character who could do the old crochet hook routine and so she and I took Elsie along to see him and waited in a sitting room with a large chandelier, a table with a knitted peacock blue cloth on it and a clanking old clock on the mantelpiece set between two pink china swans, the neck of one of them was broken and the head had been stuck on again crooked. After quite a long while during which Violette Whatever-her-name-was told me a long saga about how she'd first been seduced at the age of thirteen by an uncle by marriage, Elsie came back with the doctor. He was a nasty piece of work if ever I saw one. He wore a greasy alpaca jacket with suspicious-looking stains on it and his eyes seemed to be struggling to get at each other over one of the biggest bonks since Cyrano de Bergerac. Anyway I paid him what he wanted, which was a bloody sight more than I could afford, and we took Elsie back to the hotel in a taxi and put her to bed. She looked pale and a bit tearful but I suppose that was only to be expected. Violette said she'd better not dance that night so as to give her inside time to settle down after having been prodded about and so I had to cut the pony quartet which couldn't be done as a trio and sing "The Darktown Strutters' Ball" with a faked-up dance routine that I invented as I went along. Nobody seemed to care anyway.

When we finally got back to London I broke up the act and shopped around to see if I could get a job on my own. I had one or two chorus offers but I turned them down. A small part, yes, even if it was only a few lines, but not the chorus again. I had a long talk with Ted Bentley and he advised me to scratch another act together, this time with better material. I must say he really did his best to help and we finally fetched up with quite a production. There was a lot of argle-bargle about how the act should be billed and we finally decided on "Georgie Banks and His Six Bombshells." Finding the six bombshells wasn't quite so easy. We auditioned hundreds of girls of all sorts and kinds until at long last we settled on what we thought were the best six with an extra one as a standby. In all fairness I must admit they were a bright little lot, all good dancers and pretty snappy to look at. Avice Bennet was the eldest, about twenty-seven with enormous blue eyes and a treacherous little gold filling which only showed when she laughed. Then there was Sue Mortlock, the sort of bouncy little blonde that the tired businessmen are supposed to go for. Jill Kenny came next on the scroll of honor, she was a real smasher, Irish with black hair and violet blue eyes and a temper of a fiend. Ivy Baker was a redhead just for those who like that sort of thing, she ponged a bit when she got overheated like so many redheads do and I was always after her with the Odorono, but she was a good worker and her quick spins were sensational. Gloria Day was the languid, sensuous type, there always has to be one of those, big charlies and hair like kapok, but she could move when she had to. (Her real name was Betty Mott but her dear old whiteheaded mum who was an ex-Tiller girl thought Gloria Day would look better on the bills.) The last, but by no means the least, was Bonny Macintyre—if you please—she was the personality kid of the whole troupe, not exactly pretty but cute—God help us all—and so vivacious that you wanted to strangle her, however she was good for eccentric numbers and the audiences always liked her. The standby, Myrtle Kennedy, was a bit horsey to look at but thoroughly efficient and capable of going on for anyone which after all was what she was engaged for. This was the little lot that I traipsed around the great big glorious world with for several years on and off, four and a half to be exact. Oh dear! On looking back I can hardly believe it. I can hardly believe that *Io stesso—Io mismo—Je, moi-même, Il signore—El señor—* Monsieur George Banks Esq.: lying here rotting in a hospital bed really went through all that I did go through with that merry little bunch of egomaniacs. I suppose I enjoyed quite a lot of it but I'm here to say I wouldn't take it on again, not for all the rice in Ram Singh's Indian restuarant in the Brompton Road.

Friday

The loveliest things happen to yours truly and no mistake. I'm starting a bedsore! Isn't that sweet? Dr. Pierre came in to see me this morning and Sister Dominique put some ointment and lint on my fanny and here I am sitting up on a hot little rubber ring and feeling I ought to bow to people like royalty.

There was quite a to-do in the middle of the night because somebody died in number eleven, which is two doors down the passage. I wouldn't have known anything about it except that I happened to be awake and having a cup of Ovaltine and heard a lot of murmuring and sobbing going on outside the door. It was an Italian man who died and the murmuring and sobbing was being done by his relatives. Latins aren't exactly tight-lipped when it comes to grief or pain are they? I mean they really let go and no holds barred. You've never heard such a commotion. It kind of depressed me all the same, not that it was all that sad. According to Sister Jeanne-Marie the man who died was very old indeed and a disagreeable old bastard into the bargain, but it started me off thinking about dying myself and wondering what it would feel like, if it feels like anything at all. Of course death's got to come sometime or other so it's no use getting morbid about it but I can't quite imagine not being here anymore. It's funny to think there's going to be a last time for everything: the last time I shall go to the loo, the last time I shall eat a four-minute egg, the last time I shall arrive in Paris in the early morning and see waiters in shirtsleeves setting up the tables outside cafés, the last time I shall ever feel anybody's arms round me. I suppose I can count myself lucky in a way not to have anybody too close to worry about. At least when it happens I shall be on my own with no red-eyed loved ones clustered round the bed and carrying on alarming. I sometimes wish I was deeply religious and could believe that the moment I conked out I should be whisked off to some lovely place where all the people I'd been fond of and who had died would be waiting for me, but as a matter of fact this sort of wishing doesn't last very long. I suppose I'd like to see Auntie Iso again and Harry-boy but I'm not dead sure. I've got sort of used to being without them and they might have changed or I might have changed and it wouldn't be the same. After all nothing stays the same in life does it? And I can't help feeling that it's a bit silly to expect that everything's going to be absolutely perfect in the afterlife, always providing that there is such a thing. Some people of course are plumb certain of this and make their plans accordingly, but I haven't got any plans to make and I never have had for the matter of that, anyway not those sort of plans. Perhaps there is something lacking in me. Perhaps this is one of the reasons I've never quite made the grade, in my career I mean. Not that I've done badly, far from it. I've worked hard and had fun and enjoyed myself most of the time and you can't ask much more than that can you? But I never really got to the top and became a great big glamorous star which after all is what I started out to be. I'm not such a clot as not to realize that I missed out somewhere along the line. Then comes the question of whether I should have had such a good time if I *had* pulled it off and been up there in lights. You never really know do you? And I'm buggered if I'm going to sit here on my rubber ring sobbing my heart out about what might have been. To hell with what might have been. What *has* been is quite enough for me, and what *will* be will have to be coped with when the time comes.

Another scrumptious thing happened to me today which was more upsetting than the bedsore and it was all Mavis's fault and if I had the strength I'd wallop the shit out of her. Just after I'd had my tea there was a knock on the door and in came Ronnie! He looked very pale and was wearing a new camel's-hair overcoat and needed a haircut. He stood still for a moment in the doorway and then came over and kissed me and I could tell from his breath that he'd had a snifter round the corner to fortify himself before coming in. He had a bunch of roses in his hand and the paper they were wrapped in looked crinkled and crushed as though he'd been holding them too tightly. I was so taken by surprise that I couldn't think of anything to say for a minute then I pulled myself together and told him to drag the chintz armchair nearer the bed and sit down. He did what I told him after laying the flowers down very carefully on the bed table as though they were breakable and said, in an uncertain voice, "Surprise—surprise!" I said "It certainly is" a little more sharply than I meant to and then suddenly I felt as if I was going to cry, which was plain silly when you come to analyze it because I don't love him anymore, not really, anyhow not like I used to at first. Fortunately at this moment Sister Françoise came in and asked if Ronnie would like a cup of tea and when he said he didn't want anything at all thank you she frigged about with my pillows for a moment and then took the roses and went off to find a vase for them. This gave me time to get over being emotional and I was grateful for it I can tell you. I asked after the Algerian and Ronnie looked sheepish and said he wasn't with him anymore, then he told me about the flat and having to have the bathroom repainted because the steam from the geyser had made the walls peel. We went on talking about this and that and all the time the feeling of emptiness seemed to grow between us. I don't know if he felt this as strongly as I did, the words came tumbling out easily enough and he even told me a funny story that somebody had told him about a nun and a parrot and we both laughed. Then suddenly we both seemed to realize at the same moment that it wasn't any good going on like that. He stood up and I held out my arms to him and he buried his head on my chest and started to cry. He was clutching my left hand tightly so I stroked his hair with my right hand and cried too and hoped to Christ Sister Françoise wouldn't come flouncing in again with the roses. When we'd recovered from this little scene he blew his nose and went over to the window and there wasn't any more strain. He stayed over an hour and said he'd come and see me again next weekend. He couldn't make it before because he was starting rehearsals for a French T.V. show in which he had a small part of an English sailor. I told him he'd better have a haircut before he began squeezing himself into a Tiddley suit and he laughed and said he'd meant to have it done ages ago but somehow or other something always seemed to get in the way. He left at about five-thirty because he was going to have a drink with Mavis at the L'Éscale and then catch the seven forty-five back to Paris. When he'd gone I felt somehow more alone than I had felt before he came so I had another of Sally's mentholated cigarettes just to make me nonchalant but it didn't really. Him coming in like that so unexpectedly had given me a shock and it was no good pretending it hadn't. I wriggled myself into a more comfortable position on the rubber ring, looked out at the view and tried to get me and Ronnie and everything straight in my mind but it wasn't any use because suddenly seeing him again had started up a whole lot of feelings that I thought weren't there anymore. I cursed Mavis of course for being so bloody bossy and interfering and yet in a way I was glad she had been. The sly little bitch had kept her promise not to write to him but had telephoned instead. I suppose it was nice of her really considering that she'd been jealous as hell of him in the past and really hated his guts. You'd have thought that from her point of view it would have been better to let sleeping dogs lie. She obviously thought that deep down inside I wanted to see him in spite of the way I'd carried on about him and the Algerian and sworn I never wanted to clap eyes on him again. After all she *had* been with me all through the bad time and I *had* let my hair down and told her much more than I should have. I don't believe as a rule in taking women too much into your confidence about that sort of thing. It isn't exactly that they're not to be trusted but it's hard for them to understand really, however much they try, and it's more difficult still if they happen to have a "thing" about you into the bargain. I never pretended to be in love with Mavis. I went to bed with her every now and again mainly because she wanted me to and because it's always a good thing to lay one member of the troupe on account of it stops the others gabbing too much and sending you up rotten. I leant back against the pillows which had slipped down a bit like they always do and stared out across the lake at the evening light on the mountains and for the first time I found myself hating them and wishing they weren't there standing between me and Paris and the flat and Ronnie and the way I used to live when I was up and about. I pictured Mavis and Ronnie sitting at L'Éscale and discussing whether I was going to die or not and her asking him how he thought I looked and him asking her what the doctor had said and then of course I got myself as low as a snake's arse and started getting weepy again and wished to Christ I *could* die, nice and comfortably in my sleep, and have done with it.

I must have dropped off because the next thing I knew was Sister Françoise clattering in with my supper tray and the glow had gone from the fucking mountains and the lights were out on the other side of the lake and one more day was over.

Saturday

Georgie Banks and his six bombshells I am here to tell you began their merry career together by opening a brand new night spot in Montevideo which is in Uruguay or Paraguay or one of the guays and not very attractive whichever it is. The name of the joint was La Cumparsita and it smelt of fresh paint and piddle on account of the lavatories not working properly. We'd had one hell of a voyage tourist class in a so-called luxury liner which finished up in a blaze of misery with a jolly ship's concert in the first-class lounge. We did our act in its entirety with me flashing on and off every few minutes in my new silver lamé tail suit which split across the bottom in the middle of "Embraceable You." The girls were nervous and Jill Kenny caught her foot in the hem of her skirt in the Edwardian quartet and fell arse over apple cart into a tub of azaleas which the purser had been watering with his own fair hands for weeks. She let out a stream of four-letter words in a strong Irish brogue and the first-class passengers left in droves. The purser made a speech at the end thanking us all very much indeed but it didn't exactly ring with sincerity. Anyhow our opening at La Cumparsita went better and we got a rave notice in one local paper and a stinker in the other which sort of leveled things out. The Latin Americanos were very friendly on the whole if a bit lecherous and the girls had quite a struggle not to be laid every night rain or shine. Bonny Macintyre, vivacious to the last, was the first to get herself pregnant. This fascinating piece of news was broken to me two weeks after we'd left Montevideo and moved on to Buenos Aires. Fortunately I was able to get her fixed up all right but it took a few days to find the right doctor to do it and those few days were a proper nightmare. She never stopped weeping and wailing and saying it was all my fault for not seeing that she was sufficiently protected. *Would you mind!* When it was all over bar the shouting she got cuter than ever and a bit cocky into the bargain and I knew then and there that out of the whole lot our Bonny was the only one who was going to cause me the most trouble, and baby was I right! The others behaved fairly well taken by and large. Jill was a bit of a troublemaker and liable to get pissed unless carefully watched. Ivy Baker got herself into a brawl with one of the local tarts when we were working in the Casino at Viña del Mar. The tart accused her of giving the come-on to her boy friend and slapped her in the face in the ladies' john, but she got as good as she gave. Ivy wasn't a redhead for nothing. The manager came and complained to me but I told him to stuff it and the whole thing died away like a summer breeze.

On looking back on that first year with the bombshells I find it difficult to remember clearly, out of all the scenes and dramas and carry-ons, what happened where and who did what to who. It's all become a bit of a jumble in my mind like one of those montages you see in films when people jump from place to place very quickly and there are shots of pages flying off a calendar. This is not to be surprised at really because we did cover a lot of territory. It took us over seven months to squeeze Latin America dry and then we got a tour booked through Australia and New Zealand. By this time all the costumes looked as though we'd been to bed in them for years and so they had to be redone. We had a lay-off for a week in Panama City and we shopped around for materials in the blazing heat and then went to work with our needles and thread. Avice was the best at this lark. I know I nearly went blind sewing sequins onto a velvet bodice for Sue Mortlock, who had to do a single while we were all changing for "The Darktown Strutters' Ball" which we had to do in homemade masks because there wasn't any time to black up.

The voyage from Panama City to Australia was wonderful. The ship was quite small, a sort of freighter, but we had nice cabins and the food wasn't bad. It was the first time we'd had a real rest for months and we stopped off at various islands in the South Seas and bathed in coral lagoons and got ourselves tanned to a crisp all except poor Ivy, who got blistered and had to be put to bed with poultices of soda-bicarb plastered all over her. She ran a temperature poor bitch and her skin peeled off her like tissue paper. All the girls behaved well nearly all the time and there were hardly any rows. There was a slight drama when Bonny was found naked in one of the lifeboats with the chief engineer. It would have been all right if it hadn't been the captain who found them. The captain was half-Norwegian and very religious and he sent for me to his cabin and thumped the table and said I ought to be ashamed of myself for traipsing round the world with a lot of harlots. I explained as patiently as I could that my girls were not harlots but professional artistes and that in any case I was not responsible for their private goings-on and, I added, that harlots were bloody well paid for what they did in the hay whereas all Bonny got out of the chief engineer was a native necklace made of red seeds and a couple of conch shells which were too big to pack. After a while he calmed down and we had two beers sitting side by side on his bunk. When he'd knocked back his second one he rested his hand a little too casually on my thigh and I thought to myself "'Allo 'allo! Religious or not religious we now know where we are!" From then on we lived happily ever after as you might say. It all got a bit boring but anything for a quiet life.

The Australian tour believe it or not was a wow particularly in Sydney, where we were booked for four weeks and had to stay, by popular demand, for another two. It was in Sydney that Gloria Day fell in love with a lifeguard she met on the beach, really in love too, not just an in and out and thank you very much. I must say I saw her point because he had a body like a Greek god. Unfortunately he also had a wife and two bouncing little kiddies tucked away somewhere in the bush and so there was no future in it for poor Gloria, and when we went away finally there was a lot of wailing and gnashing of teeth and threats of suicide. I gave her hell about this and reeled off a lot of fancy phrases like life being the most precious gift and time being a great healer, etc., etc., and by the time we'd got to Singapore, which was our next date, she'd forgotten all about him and was working herself up into a state about the ship's doctor who, apart from being an alcoholic, was quite attractive in a battered sort of way.

It was on that particular hop that things came to a head between me and Avice. We'd been in and out of bed together on and off for quite a long while but more as a sort of convenience than anything else. Then suddenly she took it into her head that I was the one great big gorgeous love of her life and that she couldn't live without me and that when we got back home to England we'd get married and have children and life would blossom like a rose. Now all this was cock and I told her so. In the first place I had explained, not in detail but generally, what I was really like and that although I liked girls as girls and found them lovely to be with that they didn't really send me physically, anyway not enough to think of hitching myself up forever. Then of course there was a big dramatic scene during which she trotted out all the old arguments about me not really being like that at all and that once I'd persevered and got myself into the habit of sleeping with her regularly that I'd never want to do the other thing again. After that snappy little conversation I need hardly say that there was a slight strain between us for the rest of the tour.

487

Poor old Avice. I still hear from her occasionally. She finally married an electrician and went to Canada. She sent me a snapshot of herself and her family about a year ago. I could hardly recognize her. She looked as though she'd been blown up with a bicycle pump.

After Singapore we played various joints in Burma and Siam and one in Sumatra which was a bugger. It was there that Myrtle Kennedy, the standby, got amoebic dysentery and had to be left behind in a Dutch hospital where she stayed for nearly four weeks. She ultimately rejoined us in Bombay looking very thin and more like a horse than ever.

Bonny Macintyre's big moment came in Calcutta. She'd been getting more and more cock-a-hoop and pleased with herself mainly I think because her balloon dance always went better than anything else. It was our one unfailing showstopper and even when there was hardly anyone in front she always got the biggest hand of the evening with it. In Calcutta she started ritzing the other girls and complaining about her hotel accommodation and asking for new dresses. She also had a brawl in the dressing room with Jill and bashed her on the head so hard with her hairbrush that the poor kid had concussion and had to miss two performances. This was when I stepped in and gave our Bonny a proper walloping. I usually don't approve of hitting women but this was one of those times when it had to be done. She shrieked bloody murder and all the waiters in the joint came crowding into the room to see what was going on. The next day all was calm again, or outwardly so at least. That night however when I arrived at the club in time to put my slap on I was met by Avice wearing her tragedy queen expression. She went off into a long rigmarole which I couldn't help feeling she was enjoying a good deal more than she pretended to. There was always a certain self-righteous streak in Avice. Anyway what had happened was that Bonny had bolted with a Parsee radio announcer who she'd been going with for the last ten days. She'd left me a nasty little note which she had put into Avice's box in the hotel explaining that she was never coming back again because I wasn't a gentleman and that she'd cabled home to her mother in High Wycombe to say she was going to be married. She didn't say where she and the Parsee had bolted to and so that was that. There wasn't really anything to be done. I knew she couldn't possibly leave India because I'd got her passport—one of the first rules of traveling around with a bunch of female artistes is to hang on to their passports—however, we were all due to leave India in a few weeks' time and I couldn't see myself setting off to search the entire bloody continent for Bonny Macintyre. Nor could I very well leave her behind. I was after all responsible for her. It was a fair bitch of a situation I can tell you. Anyhow there I was stuck with it and the first thing to do was to get the show reorganized for that night's performance. I sent Avice haring off to get Sue into the balloon dance dress; sent for the band leader to tell him we were altering the running order; told Myrtle to be ready to go on in all the concerted numbers. I then did a thing I never never do before a performance. I had myself a zonking great whiskey and soda and pranced out gallantly onto the dance floor ready to face with a stiff upper lip whatever further blows destiny had in store for me.

The next week was terrible. No word from Bonny and frantic cables arriving every day from her old mum. Avice I must say was a Rock of Gibraltar. She kept her head and came with me to the broadcasting station where we tried to trace the Parsee. We interviewed lots of little hairy men with green faces and high sibilant voices and finally discovered that Bonny's fiancé—to coin a phrase—had been given two weeks off to go up to the hills on account of he'd had a bad cough. Nobody seemed to know or care what part of the hills he'd gone to. We sat about for a further few days worrying ourselves silly and wondering what to do. Our closing date was drawing nearer and we had all been booked tourist class on the homeward-bound P. and O. Finally, to cut a dull story short, our little roving will-o'-the-wisp returned to us with a bang. That is to say she burst into my room in the middle of the night and proceeded to have hysterics. All the other girls came flocking in to see what the fuss was about and stood around in their nightgowns and dressing gowns and pajamas with grease on their faces looking like Christmas night in the whorehouse. I gave Bonny some Three Star Martell in a tooth glass which gave her hiccups but calmed her down a bit. Presently, when Jill had made her drink some water backward and we'd all thumped her on the back she managed to sob out the garbled story of her star-crossed romance, and it was good and star-crossed believe me. Apparently the Parsee had taken her in an old Ford convertible which broke down three times to visit his family, a happy little group consisting of about thirty souls in all, including goats, who lived in a small town seventy miles away. The house they lived in was not so much a house as a tenement and Bonny was forced to share a room with two of the Parsee's female cousins and a baby that was the teeniest bit spastic. She didn't seem to have exactly hit it off with the Parsee's dear old mother who snarled at her in Hindustani whenever she came within spitting distance. There was obviously no room for fun and games indoors so whatever sex they had had to take place on a bit of wasteland behind the railway station. She didn't enjoy any of this very much on account of being scared of snakes but being so near the railway station often *did* actually give her the idea of making a getaway. Finally after one of the usual cozy evenings *en famille* with mum cursing away in one corner and the spastic baby having convulsions in the other, she managed to slip out of the house without her loved one noticing and run like a stag to the station. It was a dark night but she knew the way all right having been in that direction so frequently. After waiting four hours in a sort of shed a train arrived and she got onto it and here she was more dead than alive.

By the time she'd finished telling us all this the dawn had come up like thunder and she began to get hysterical again so Avice forced a couple of aspirins down her throat and put her to bed. Three days after this, having given our last triumphant performance to a quarter-full house, we set sail for England, home and what have you, and that was really the end of Georgie Banks and his six bombshells.

Sunday

It's Sunday and all the church bells are ringing and I wish they wouldn't because I had a bad night and feel a bit edgy and the noise is driving me crackers.

It wasn't a bad night from the pain point of view although I felt a little uncomfortable between two and three and Sister Clothilde came in and gave me an injection which was a new departure really because I usually get a pill. Anyway it sent me off to sleep all right but it wasn't really sleep exactly, more like a sort of trance. I wasn't quite off and I wasn't quite on if you know what I mean and every so often I'd wake up completely for a few minutes feeling like I'd had a bad dream and couldn't remember what it was. Then I'd float off again and all sorts of strange things came into my mind. I suppose it was thinking yesterday so much about me and the bombshells that I'd got myself kind of overexcited. I woke up at about eight-thirty with a hangover but I felt better when I'd had a cup of tea. The orderly came in and carried me to the bathroom and then brought me back and put me in the armchair with an eiderdown wrapped round me while the bed was being made and the room done. One of the nicest things about being ill is when you're put back into a freshly made bed and can lie back against cool pillows before they get hot and crumpled and start slipping. The orderly stayed and chatted with me for a bit. He's quite sweet really. He told me he'd got the afternoon and evening off and that a friend of his was arriving from Munich who was a swimming champion and had won a lot of cups. He said this friend was very "costaud" and had a wonderfully developed chest but his legs were on the short side. They were going to have dinner in a restaurant by the lake and then go to a movie. I wished him luck and winked at him and wished to God I was going with them.

Later. It's still Sunday but the bells have stopped ringing and it's started to rain. The professor with the blue chin came to see me after I'd had my afternoon snooze. He looked different from usual because he was wearing quite a snappy sports coat and gray flannel trousers. He told me he'd had lunch in a little restaurant in the country and had only just got back. I watched him looking at me carefully while he was talking to me as though he wanted to find out something. I told him about having had the injection and how it made me feel funny and he smiled and nodded and lit a cigarette. He then asked me whether I had any particular religion and when I said I hadn't he laughed and said that he hadn't either but he supposed it was a good thing for some people who needed something to hang on to. Then he asked me if I had ever talked to Father Lucien who was a Catholic priest who was sort of attached to the *clinique*. I said he'd come in to see me a couple of times and had been quite nice but that he gave me the creeps. Then he laughed again and started wandering about the room sort of absentmindedly as though he was thinking of something else, then he came back, stubbed his cigarette out in the ashtray on my bedtable and sat down again, this time on the side of the bed. I moved my legs to give him a bit more room. There was a fly buzzing about and a long way off one of those bloody church bells started ringing again. I looked at him sitting there so nonchalantly swinging his legs ever so little but frowning as though something were puzzling him. He was a good-looking man all right, somewhere between forty and fifty I should say, his figure was slim and elegant and his face thin with a lot of lines on it and his dark hair had gone gray at the side. I wondered if he had a nice sincere wife to go home to in the evenings after a busy day cutting things out of people, or whether he lived alone with a faithful retainer and a lot of medical books and kept a tiny vivacious mistress in a flashy little apartment somewhere or other or even whether he was queer as a coot and head over heels in love with a sun-tanned ski instructor and spent madly healthy weekends with him in cozy wooden chalets up in the mountains. He looked at me suddenly as though he had a half guess at what I was thinking and I giggled. He smiled when I giggled and very gently took my hand in his and gave it a squeeze, not in the least a sexy squeeze but a sympathetic one and all at once I realized, with a sudden sinking of the heart, what the whole production was in aid of, why he had come in so casually to see me on a Sunday afternoon, why he had been drifting about the room looking ill at ease and why he had asked me about whether I was religious or not. It was because he knew that I was never going to get well again and was trying to make up his mind whether to let me know the worst or just let me go on from day to day hoping for the best. I knew then, in a sort of panic, that I didn't want him to tell me anything, not in so many words, because once he said them there I'd be stuck with them

491

in my mind and wake up in the night and remember them. What I mean is that although I knew that I knew and had actually known, on and off, for a long time, I didn't want it settled and signed and sealed and done up, gift wrapped, with a bow on top. I still wanted not to be quite sure so that I could get through the days without counting. That was a bad moment all right, me lying there with him still holding my hand and all those thoughts going through my head and trying to think of a way to head him off. I knew that unless I did something quickly he'd blurt it out that I'd be up shit creek without a paddle and with nothing to hang on to and no hope left and so I did the brassiest thing I've ever done in my life and I still blush when I think of it. I suddenly reared myself up on my pillows, pulled him toward me and gave him a smacking kiss. He jumped back as if he'd been shot. I've never seen anyone so surprised. Then before he could say anything, I went off into a long spiel—I was a bit hysterical by then and I can't remember exactly what I said—but it was all about me having a "thing" about him ever since I'd first seen him and that that was the way I was and there was nothing to be done about it and that as he was a doctor I hoped he would understand and not be too shocked and that anyway being as attractive as he was he had no right to squeeze people's hands when they were helpless in bed and not expect them to lose control and make a pounce at him and that I'd obeyed an impulse too strong to be resisted—yes I actually said that if you please—and that I hoped he would forgive me but that if he didn't he'd just have to get on with it. I said a lot more than this and it was all pretty garbled because I'd worked myself into a proper state, but that was the gist of it. He sat there quite still while I was carrying on, staring at me and biting his lip. I didn't quite know how to finish the scene so I fell back on the old ham standby and burst into tears and what was so awful was that once I'd started I couldn't stop until he took out his cigarette case, shoved a cigarette into my mouth and lit it for me. This calmed me down and I was able to notice that he had stopped looking startled and was looking at me with one of his eyebrows a little higher than the other, quizzically as you might say, and that his lips were twitching as though he was trying not to laugh. Then he got up and said in a perfectly ordinary voice that he'd have to be getting along now as he had a couple more patients to see but that he'd come back and have a look at me later. I didn't say anything because I didn't feel I could really without starting to blub again, so I just lay puffing away like crazy at the cigarette and trying not to look too like Little Orphan Annie. He went to the door, paused for a moment, and then did one of the kindest things I've ever known. He came back to the bed, put both his arms round me and kissed me very gently, not on the mouth but on the cheek as though he were really fond of me. Then he went out and closed the door quietly after him.

Monday

I woke up very early this morning having slept like a top for nearly nine hours. I rang the bell and when Sister Dominique came clattering in and pulled back the curtains it was a clear, bright morning again, not a bit like yesterday. When she'd popped off to get me my tea I lay quite still watching a couple of jet planes flying back and forth over the mountains and making long trails of white smoke in the pale blue sky. They went terribly quickly and kept on disappearing and coming back into view again. I tried to imagine what the pilots flying them looked like and what they were thinking about. It must be a wonderful feeling whizzing through the air at that tremendous speed and looking down at the whole world. Every now and then the sun caught one of the planes and it glittered like silver. I had some honey with my toast but it was a bit too runny. When the usual routine had been gone through and I was back in bed again I began to think of the professor yesterday afternoon and what I'd done and I felt hot with shame for a minute or two and then started to laugh. Poor love, it must have been a shock and no mistake. And then I got to wondering if after all it had been quite such a surprise to him as all that. Being a doctor he must be pretty hep about the so dainty facts of life and, being as dishy as he is, he can't have arrived at his present age without someone having made the teeniest weensiest pass at him at some time or other. Anyway by doing what I did I at least stopped him from spilling those gloomy little beans, if of course there were any beans to spill. Now, this morning, after a good night, I'm feeling that it was probably all in my imagination. You never know do you? I mean it might have been something quite silly and unimportant that upset me, like those bloody church bells for instance. They'd been enough to get anybody down. Anyway there's no sense in getting morbid and letting the goblins get you. Maybe I'll surprise them all and be springing about like a mountain goat in a few weeks from now. All the same I shan't be able to help feeling a bit embarrassed when the professor comes popping in again. Oh dear—oh dear!

Here it is only half past eight and I've got the whole morning until they bring me my lunch at twelve-thirty to think about things and scribble my oh so glamorous memories on this pad which by the way is getting nearly used up so I must remember to ask Mavis to bring me another one. She'll probably be coming in this afternoon. It's funny this wanting to get things down on paper. I suppose quite a lot of people do if you only knew, not only professional writers but more or less ordinary people, only as a rule of course they don't usually have the time, whereas I have all the time in the world—or have I? Now then, now then none of that. At any rate I've at least had what you might call an *interesting life* what with flouncing about all over the globe with those girls and having a close-up of the mysterious Orient and sailing the seven seas and one thing and another. Perhaps when I've finished it I shall be able to sell it to the *Daily Express* for thousands and thousands of pounds and live in luxury to the end of my days. What a hope! All the same it just might be possible if they cut out the bits about my sex life and some of the four-letter words were changed. Up to now I've just been writing down whatever came into my mind without worrying much about the words themselves. After all it's the thought that counts as the actress said to the bishop after he'd been bashing away at her for three hours and a half.

When I got back to London after that first tour with the bomb-shells I let them all go their own sweet ways and had a long talk to Ted about either working up an act on my own or trying to get into a West End show. Not a lead mind you. I wasn't so silly as to think I'd get more than a bit part, but if I happened to hit lucky and got a *good* bit part and was noticed in it then I'd be on the up and up and nothing could stop me. All this unfortunately came under the head-ing of wishful thinking. As a matter of fact I *did* get into a show and it *was* a good part with a duet in act one and a short solo dance at the beginning of act two, but the whole production was so diabolical that Fred Astaire couldn't have saved it and we closed after two weeks and a half. Then I decided that what I really needed was acting experience. After all nobody can go on belting out numbers and kick-ing their legs in the air forever whereas acting, legitimate acting that is, can last you a lifetime providing you're any good at it. Anyhow Ted managed to get me a few odd jobs in reps dotted over England's green and pleasant land and for two whole years, on and off, I slogged away at it. I had a bang at everything. Young juveniles—"Anyone for tennis"—old gentlemen, dope addicts, drunks. I even played a Japanese prisoner-of-war once in a ghastly triple bill at Dun-dee. My bit came in the first of the three plays and I was on and off so quickly that by the end of the evening none of the audience could remember having seen me at all. Somewhere along the line during those two years it began to dawn on me that I was on the wrong track. Once or twice I did manage to get a good notice in the local paper but I knew that didn't count for much and finally I found myself back in London again with two hundred and ten pounds in the bank, no prospects and a cold. That was a bad time all right and I can't imagine now, looking back on it, how I ever lived through it. Fi-nally, when I was practically on the bread line and had borrowed forty pounds from Ted, I had to pocket my pride and take a chorus job in a big American musical at the Coliseum which ran for eighteen months and there I was, stuck with it. Not that I didn't manage to have quite a good time one way or another. I had a nice little "combined" in Pimlico—Lupus Street to be exact—and it had a small kitchenette which I shared with a medical student on the next floor. He was quite sweet really but he had a birthmark all down one side of his neck which was a bit off-putting, however one must take the rough with the smooth is what I always say. When the show closed I'd paid back Ted and got a bit put by but not enough for a rainy day by any manner of means, so back I went into the chorus again and did another stretch. This time it lasted two years and I knew that if I didn't get out and do something on my own again I'd lose every bit of ambition I'd ever had and just give up. Once you really get into a rut in show business you've had it. All this was nearly five years ago and I will say one thing for myself, I *did* get out of the rut and although I nearly starved in the process and spent all I'd saved, I was at least free again and my own boss. I owe a great deal to Ted really. Without him I could never have got these girls together and now of course, just as we were beginning to do really nicely I have to get ill and bugger up the whole thing. This is where I come to a full stop and I know it and it's no good pretending any more to myself or anybody else. Even if I do get out of this *clinique* it'll take me months and months to get well enough to work again and by that time all the girls will have got other jobs and I shall have to shop around and find some new ones and redo the act from the beginning, and, while we're at it, I should like to know how I'm going to live during those jolly months of languid convalescence! This place and the operation and the treatment must be costing a bloody fortune. Ted and Mavis are the only ones who know exactly what I've got saved and they're coping, but it can't go on for much longer because there just won't be anything left. I tried to say something to Mavis about this the other day but she said that everything was all right and that I wasn't to worry and refused to discuss it any further. I've never had much money sense I'm afraid, Ted's always nagging me about it, but it's no use. When I've got it I spend it and when I haven't I don't because I bloody well can't and that's that. All the same I have been careful during the last few years, more careful than I ever was before, and there must still be quite a bit in the bank, even with all this extra expense. I must make Mavis write to Ted and find out just exactly how things are. He's got power of attorney anyhow. Now you see I've gone and got myself low again. It's always the same, whenever I begin to think about money and what I've got saved and what's going to happen in the future, down I go into the depths. I suppose this is another lack in me like not having had just that extra something which would have made me a great big glamorous star. I must say I'm not one to complain much as a rule. I've had my ups and downs and it's all part of life's rich pattern as some silly bitch said when we'd just been booed off the stage by some visiting marines in Port Said. All the same one can't go on being a cheery chappie forever can one? I mean there are moments when you have to look facts in the face and not go on kidding yourself, and this, as far as I'm concerned, is one of them. I wish to Christ I hadn't started to write at all this morning, I was feeling fine when I woke up, and now, by doing all this thinking back and remembering and wondering, I've got myself into a state of black depression and it's no use pretending I haven't. As a matter of fact it's no use pretending ever, about anything, about getting to the top, or your luck turning, or living, or dying. It always catches up with you in the end. I don't even feel like crying which is funny because I am a great crier as a rule when things get bad. It's a sort of relief and eases the nerves. Now I couldn't squeeze a tear out if you paid me. That really is funny. Sort of frightening. That's the lot for today anyway. The *Daily Express* must wait.

Tuesday

Mavis came yesterday as promised and I forgot to ask her about getting another writing pad, but it doesn't matter really as there's still quite a lot of this one left. I didn't feel up to talking much so I just lay still and listened while she told me all the gossip. Lily-May had sprained her ankle, fortunately in the last number, not a bad sprain really, not bad enough that is for her to have to stay off. She put on cold compresses last night and it had practically gone down by this morning. Beryl and Sylvia were taken out after the show on Saturday night by a very rich banking gentleman from Basel who Monsieur Philippe had brought backstage. He took them and gave them a couple of drinks somewhere or other and then on to an apartment of a friend of his which was luxuriously furnished and overlooked the lake except that they couldn't see much of it on account of it being pitch dark and there being no moon. Anyway the banker and his friend opened a bottle of champagne and sat Beryl and Sylvia down as polite as you please on a sofa with satin cushions on it and while they were sipping the champagne and being thoroughly piss-elegant, which they're inclined to be at the best of times, the banker, who'd gone out of the room for a minute, suddenly came in again stark naked carrying a leather whip in one hand and playing with himself with the other. The girls both jumped up and started screaming and there was a grand old hullabaloo for a few minutes until the friend managed to calm them down and made the banker go back and put on a dressing gown. While he was out of the room he gave the girls a hundred francs each and apologized for the banker saying that he was a weeny bit eccentric but very nice really and that the whip was not to whack them with but for them to whack him, the banker, with, which just happened to be his way of having fun. Then the twins stopped screaming and got grand as all get-out and said that they were used to being treated like ladies. They didn't happen to mention who by. Then the banker came back in a fur coat not having been able to find a dressing gown and said he was sorry if he had frightened them and would they please not say a word to Monsieur Philippe. They all had some more champagne and the banker passed out cold and the friend brought them home in a taxi without so much as groping them. Anticlimax department the whole thing. Anyway they got a hundred francs each whichever way you look at it and that's eight pounds a head for doing fuck all. I must say I couldn't help laughing when Mavis told me all this but she wasn't amused at all, oh dear me no. There's a strong governessy streak in our Mavis. She went straight to Monsieur Philippe and carried on as if she were a mother superior in a convent. This made me laugh still more and when she went she looked quite cross.

Friday

I haven't felt up to writing anything for the last few days and I don't feel too good now but I suppose I'd better make an effort and get on with it. I began having terrible pains in my back and legs last Tuesday night I think it was, anyway it was the same day that Mavis came, and Dr. Pierre was sent for and gave me an injection and I've felt sort of half asleep ever since, so much so that I didn't even know what day it was. I've just asked Sister Dominique and she told me it was Friday. Imagine! That's two whole days gone floating by with my hardly knowing anything about it. I've been feeling better all day today, a bit weak I must admit, but no more pain. The professor came in to see me this afternoon and brought me a bunch of flowers and Mavis brought me a little pot of pâté-de-foie-gras, or maybe it was the other way round, anyway I know that they both came. Not at the same time of course but at different times, perhaps it was the day before yesterday that the professor came. I know he held my hand for quite a long time so he can't have really been upset about me behaving like that. He's a wonderful man the professor is, a gentle and loving character and I wish, I wish I could really tell him why I did what I did and make him understand that it wasn't just silly camping but because I was frightened. I expect he knows anyhow. He's the sort of man who knows everything that goes on in people's minds and you don't have to keep on saying you're sorry and making excuses to him any more than you'd have to to God if God is anything like what he's supposed to be. The act closes tomorrow night if today really is Friday and all the girls have promised to come to say good-bye to me on Sunday before they catch the train, at least that's what Mavis said. I had the funniest experience last night. I saw Harry-boy. He was standing at the end of the bed as clear as daylight wearing his blue dungarees and holding up a pair of diabolical old socks which he wanted me to wash out for him. Of course I know I didn't really see him and that I was dreaming, but it did seem real as anything at the time and it still does in a way. Harry never could do a thing for himself, like washing socks I mean, or anything useful in the house. I'm not being quite fair because he did fix the tap in the lavatory basin once when it wouldn't stop running, but then he was always all right with anything to do with machinery, not that the tap in the lavatory basin can really be called machinery but it's the same sort of thing if you know what I mean. All the girls are coming to say good-bye to me on Sunday before they catch the train, at least that's what Mavis said. Good old Mavis. I suppose I'm fonder of her than anybody actually, anybody that's alive I mean. If she doesn't come before Sunday I can tell her then. The weather's changed with a vengeance and it's raining to beat the band which is a shame really because I can't see the mountains anymore except every now and then for a moment or two when it lifts. I wonder whatever became of Bonny Macintyre. I haven't had so much as a postcard from her in all these years. She was a tiresome little bitch but she had talent and there's no doubt about it and nobody else ever did the balloon dance quite the way she did it. It wasn't that she danced all that brilliantly, in fact Jill could wipe her eye any day of the week when it came to speed and technique. But she had something that girl.

Sister Clothilde pulled the blinds down a few minutes ago just before Dr. Pierre and Father Lucien came in. Dr. Pierre gave me an injection which hurt a bit when it went in but felt lovely a few seconds later, a sweet warm feeling coming up from my toes and covering me all over like eiderdown. Father Lucien leant over me and said something or other I don't remember what it was. He's quite nice really but there *is* something about him that gives me the creeps. I mean I wouldn't want him to hold my hand like the professor does. The act closes on Saturday and the girls are all coming to say good-bye to me on Sunday before they catch the train. I do hope Mavis gets a job or meets someone nice and marries him and settles down. That's what she ought to do really. It isn't that she's no good. She dances well and her voice is passable, but the real thing is lacking. Hark at me! I should talk. I wish Sister Clothilde hadn't pulled the blinds down, not that it really matters because it's dark by now and I shouldn't be able to see them anyhow.

SOLALI

Davina Lavenham, as usual, had her breakfast early on the verandah. Early, in the Samolan Archipelago, meant six forty-five, just after sun-up. The well-worn cliché that early morning in the tropics is the best time of day, like most clichés, is disarmingly accurate. Twilight, those few brief minutes after sunset before the stars appear, runs it a close second but early morning is the best, almost a full hour of changing sky and sea. From the moment she threw open her shutters when lights were still palely twinkling in the village, the magic began. First the line of luminous green above the horizon, merging, as the light strengthened, into scarlet and orange until, with startling swiftness, the vast red sun seemed to leap out of the sea; a flock of white parakeets clattered in the coco palms and the banana leaves on Dod Fawcett's plantation at the other side of the valley glinted like emeralds.

Agana, her houseboy, tiny and immaculate in his white drill coat and multicolored sarong, placed before her the inevitable slice of pawpaw flanked by the equally inevitable fresh limes, cut neatly in half. Davina, with automatic resignation, squeezed the limes onto the terracotta fruit and added a sprinkling of sugar. She had never, in all her years in the tropics, really worked up any enthusiasm for pawpaw. It was watery and, even with the embellishment of lime juice, flavorless, but as it was supposed to be saturated with admirable health-giving properties, she ate it dutifully but without joy.

Across the bay the silhouette of the main island stood against the brightening sky; the highest of its volcanic peaks, still swathed in flimsy white cloud, would emerge later in the morning, grim and unadorned with an ominous wisp of smoke spiraling from its crater. There hadn't been a major eruption for many years, actually since the devastating one of 1915 when all the villages on the south side of the island had been destroyed and thousands of lives lost, but it still rumbled occasionally, shaking the house and making the shutters rattle, as though to prove that it was far from being as demure as it looked. When this happened natives would stop whatever they were doing and look anxiously first at the mountain itself then at the sea, for a tidal wave was the usual concomitant of even a minor eruption.

Davina, in her late forties, was still an attractive woman. Even in the early morning, without makeup and dressed in an old housecoat with a scarf tied round her head, she looked surprisingly young for her age. Her body was slim and well proportioned, her skin clear and lightly tanned. Her eyes, wide and gray with a deceptively trusting expression, were her best feature: her worst was her mouth which was thin lipped and drooped at the corners, betraying perhaps a certain ruthlessness, a meagerness of heart. That particular organ on this particular morning was gayer than usual for the adequate reason that her husband, Roy, was away on a visit to the main island. It was not that she disliked Roy for any specific incompatibility. One couldn't dislike Roy because he was too uncomplicated and easygoing; it was merely that he bored her, and had bored her amiably and monotonously for nearly twenty years. Ordinarily he would be sitting there opposite to her at the table, pink, healthy and a little too plump, reading her extracts from the *Daily Reaper* and regaling her with his unremarkable views on the state of the world in general and the state of the Samolan Islands in particular. He was the archetype of those conservative Englishmen who in earlier years assiduously dug white man's graves in far-off places and then proceeded gallantly to administer them. He was in fact honest, sober, reliable, industrious and, almost triumphantly, dull. Davina, exulting in her unaccustomed solitude, watched a small green lizard snap up a fly and sighed luxuriously. She looked idly across the sloping lawn to the hibiscus hedge which Solali was trimming with languid concentration. Samolans were racially incapable of executing any task, however urgent, with speed. It was probably the warm, always temperate, climate that encouraged them to be so lackadaisical. This consistently unhurried tempo occasionally exasperated her. Solali had been pruning that damned hibiscus hedge for at least three days. She watched him straighten up for a moment and stretch. The sweat glistened on his muscular brown torso. He was wearing a battered old straw hat and a pair of ragged, faded blue jeans, probably a gift to his father from the Americans when they occupied the island during World War Two. He glanced up and seeing that she was looking at him, ceremoniously doffed his hat and bowed. Davina on an impulse beckoned to him, whereupon he dropped his machete and came loping toward her across the patchy grass. It was one of Davina's constant annoyances, that sparse, mangy-looking lawn, but there was nothing to be done about it. She had had grass seed specially flown from England which had been carefully sown under her supervision and watered and mowed and cosseted but all to no avail. The smooth velvety turf she had envisaged failed to materialize. Apparently the soil was too thin or the sun too strong or something. Ella Corbett over on the other side of the island had, after years of effort, managed to produce a reasonable-looking croquet-lawn, but that, after all, was high in the mountains where there was more moisture than down here on the coast. Solali bounded up the verandah steps and stood before her exposing his dazzlingly white teeth in an inquiring smile.

"Good morning, Solali," she said briskly. "I see that you are still cutting back the hibiscus hedge." Solali, still smiling, nodded. "Yes, Mistress. It is most quick growing and has become thick."

"Surely not thick enough to necessitate wasting three whole days on it?" The tone of chill displeasure in her voice vanquished his smile, he shuffled his feet and looked stricken. "If Mistress is discontented I am most sorry."

Davina bit her lip, repressing an impulse to laugh. The unexpected formality of Samolan English always amused her. "I am more irritated than discontented, Solali. There is a great deal to be done in the garden before the rains come. The hibiscus can wait. Where is Kekoa this morning? I haven't seen him about."

Kekoa, a barrel-chested youth of seventeen with very short legs, was Solali's assistant.

"Kekoa is in much distress because his aunt from the far islands has come home."

"Doesn't he like her?"

"I do not think that he knows her very clearly, but she is old and sick and is in the Nalikowa hospital, with grave swellings of her body. The doctors will perhaps cut her, but there is strong fear that she will die."

"When is he coming back?"

"He has promised to return to us on the evening bus but if she should pass away he will rest with his uncle until she is buried."

"I see. Thank you, Solali."

Solali, having registered dismissal with another polite bow, retreated down the verandah steps. Davina watched him as he sauntered across the lawn; as though he was aware that she was looking at him he stopped suddenly, turned, and with a sly grin which might almost have been construed as a wink, changed his course and ostentatiously avoiding the hibiscus hedge disappeared in the direction of the kitchen garden.

Late in the afternoon of that same day, Davina, still reveling in her solitude but beginning to feel a trifle oppressed by it, decided to drive over to the Fawcetts' for a drink. Dod and Mabel Fawcett were middle-aged Americans from Cleveland, Ohio. Friendly, hospitable and ostentatiously wealthy, they had resolved, after marrying off both their daughters, to realize a mutual dream, cherished for many years, which was to visit the islands of the Southern Pacific. This seductive, adventurous dream, far from being unique in the United States, has become, since World War Two, less a dream than a national institution. Travel agencies and shipping lines having cashed in on it with such commercial fervor that there is now scarcely a remote coral atoll in that vast ocean which has not shuddered at the impact of shiploads of enthusiastic tourists. In the early nineteen-fifties, however, although cruise ships appeared fairly regularly, the rising wind had not yet achieved its present hurricane force. There were still certain islands or groups of islands which remained comparatively isolated. One of these happier groups was the Samolan Archipelago. The *Matsonia,* in which the Fawcetts arrived in nineteen fifty-three, had paused in the Grand Harbor at Pendarla for a full day, from six-thirty A.M. until eleven-thirty P.M. Dod and Mabel, with a crowd of their fellow passengers, were conveyed from ship to shore in a tender with a bent funnel which belched acrid smoke and covered everyone with greasy black smuts. A fleet of limousines, organized by the Samolan Tourist Board, waited at the dock to drive them to the routine beauty spots of the island and return them in good order for reembarkation in the evening. Dod and Mabel stepped ashore, bemused by the dazzling light, the general dockside din and the conflicting smells: frangipani, peokoka, gasoline, hot tar and the overall sweet-sick stink of copra drying in the sun. They had barely set foot on shore when a handsome young Samolan of about seventeen placed two "leis" of scented white flowers round their necks. In that moment Mabel Fawcett's heart lurched in her breast, a lurch in no way symptomatic of any cardiac affliction; a lurch of sudden, almost intolerable joy. She clutched Dod's arm and, looking at her, he was startled to see tears in her eyes.

"This is it," she murmured breathlessly. "This is the place for us." It *was* it. It *was* the place for them and that evening the *Matsonia* set off across the Pacific without them.

They welcomed Davina with their usual uninhibited enthusiasm, forced her into the most comfortable chair on the verandah and gave her an ice cold rum punch. Sitting there, listening with only half an ear to their gossip, her nerves soothed by the pleasant Ohio burr in their voices, she looked across at her own house nestling into the side of the opposite mountain with its familiar protective Royal Palm swaying almost imperceptibly against the darkening sky. She noticed irritably that Agana, as usual, had switched on the lights in the sitting room far too early, which was not only waste of electricity but attracted the insects. As she had expected, both Dod and Mabel urged her to stay to dinner. She sensed in this attitude an unspoken compassion for her inevitable loneliness with Roy away, but she refused their pressing invitation and finally got up to go. They both came out, looking a little crestfallen, to see her into her car, still obviously hoping that she might change her mind. It was curious, she reflected, after she had waved to them and driven smartly off down the drive, how the majority of people she knew seemed to crave casual companionship. Solitude, to so many of her friends, appeared to be a state of dread, to be avoided at all costs. It was inconceivable to both Dod and Mabel that she was genuinely looking forward to her long evening alone. They probably imagined that she was being socially overconsiderate, or proud, or perhaps a trifle eccentric. She stopped the car at the end of the long curve of Lalua beach where the road turned inland toward the mountains, and lit a cigarette. The night was still and she could hear, above the incessant clatter of the cicadas, the rumbling of the surf on the distant reef. A few yards to the right of her the small waves of the lagoon flopped onto the wet sand; the coco palms on the headland were motionless and a streak of light on the horizon heralded the rising moon.

Davina accepted the night's enchantment without emotion; she was too accustomed to such spectacularly romantic displays to derive any particular pleasure from them. The lights of Piccadilly Circus viewed through the window of a comfortable limousine would, at the moment, have entranced her far more than this monotonous panorama of the eternal stars. She was one of those unfortunate characters who are temperamentally doomed to discontent. Although neither insensitive nor unintelligent, her view of the world and the people she encountered in it was tarnished by an inherent petulance of spirit. There was no apparent environmental justification for this basic irascibility. Her life, from her christening in St. Paul's, Knightsbridge, to her marriage in St. George's, Hanover

Square, had been set in pleasant ways. No grinding genteel poverty or neurotic frustrations had darkened her early years. The most painstaking psychiatrist would be at a loss to discover any far-back, sinister justification for her adult dissatisfactions. At most he could only observe that she was the sort of woman who could be agreeable so long as she got her own way, and extremely disagreeable when she didn't. The psychiatrist might however, if he happened to be astute as well as painstaking, have deduced from the way she spoke, the way she moved and the sensual manner in which she inhaled a cigarette, that sexually she was both unsatisfied and omnivorous. Like most women of her class and upbringing, Davina when she married Roy had been technically a virgin. She had of course fallen in and out of love, been passionately kissed and, on occasion, amorously mauled but usually, alas, by young men who were almost as inexperienced as she was. Her bridal night with Roy in the Hotel Lancaster in Paris had been, as such occasions frequently are, both painful and disillusioning. Roy was an athlete and a "Physical Fitness before Everything" fanatic which meant that his virginity had been as reverently guarded as The Holy Grail. No sophisticated friend of either sex had ever explained to him that successful physical lovemaking demands a certain amount of finesse from at least one of the participants, if not both. Even in the mid-twentieth century, when many shuttered windows have been flung wide open and many outmoded taboos vanquished, the stubborn Puritan belief that sexual dalliance is sinful and immoral still persists in England's green and pleasant land.

Davina, even now after nearly twenty-five years, could still shudder at the recollection of her honeymoon. Poor Roy, so kind and considerate and so very much in love, and yet so ignorantly, brutally clumsy. During her early married years she had gradually resigned herself to the inevitable. It was not until the Blaydons' house party in Kent during the summer of 1945 that Barry had strolled across the tennis court and sat himself down beside her. It was a swing seat she remembered; striped blue and white canvas with a canopy. He had propelled it gently backward and forward by the pressure of his foot on the grass while he talked to her. Having just played two energetic sets without a pause he was sweaty and a little breathless. Undeniably handsome, tall and well proportioned, with the suspicion of a brogue in his voice, he was perhaps a shade too consciously charming but his masculine "allure" was definite and unmistakable. A few days later she met him again by chance in Kensington Gardens, just near the Peter Pan statue. They sat together on two uncomfortable green chairs and fell in love.

Davina sighed and lit another cigarette. A strange seabird with thin pedantic legs minced through the shadows darting its head to right and left furtively as though it thought it was being followed.

Barry, she reflected, was probably the only man in her life with whom she had been genuinely in love. Even now, with so many years between, she could still vividly remember the miseries and ecstasies of those two turbulent years. Oddly enough she had seen Barry only eighteen months ago just a couple of days before she sailed back with Roy at the end of their leave. She had been lunching with two other people in a restaurant in Soho when she looked across the room and saw Barry sitting on a banquette against the opposite wall. He was with a pallid girl of about twenty-four whose skin looked unhealthy, as though she had lived most of her life in a cellar. Barry had put on weight and his hair had thinned on top and at the sides, leaving only a thin brilliantined wedge in the middle. He lifted his glass to her with an urbane, almost conspiratorial smirk. She smiled back at him, a remote smile without warmth and was aware of a sudden pang of distaste. The snows of yesteryear wherever they were had evidently not diminished their capacity to chill. Barry had been the first man in her life to arouse her latent sensuality but now even he, whose ardent hands had guided her so adroitly through the intricacies of sexual pleasure, seemed to have suffered a sea change and taken his place among the other unsatisfactory shadows. She flicked her half-finished cigarette out of the car window, let in the clutch, switched on the ignition and was about to drive away when she was startled to see a figure gesticulating in the beam of the headlights and limping toward her. As he drew nearer she recognized Solali and a second later she observed that his left leg was bleeding.

"Solali! What on earth has happened?"

Solali managed to produce a painful grin. "It is of no great matter, Mistress, but I fell on the reef when I was fishing. It was great fortune for me to see the car lights. To walk all the way back would be most hurtful."

"It certainly would." Davina opened the car door. "Get in at once and try to keep your leg as still as possible."

Solali climbed in and flopped onto the seat by her side. "There is much bleeding, I fear the car will be made nasty."

"Never mind about that for the moment. The first thing is to find out how badly you've been cut."

On arrival at the house ten minutes later she managed with the help of Agana to get Solali onto one of the beds in the spare room. He lay still and disconsolate while she and Agana washed his wound with Dettol and warm water. Fortunately it was a good deal less serious than it looked, merely a rather jagged but superficial cut to the left of the shinbone. Agana produced bandages and lint from the medicine cupboard and presently when the leg had been bound up, Solali made an effort to rise. Davina gently pushed him back onto the bed.

"You'd better stay where you are for the night, Solali. Agana will bring you anything you need. Perhaps you'd like a cup of tea or a glass of milk? I don't advise anything stronger because of the bleeding."

"Mistress is most gentle and kind."

Davina smiled and as she turned to go he seized her hand and kissed it. His lips felt hot and dry on the back of her hand and when he looked up she saw that his fine brown eyes were filled with tears. She also noted, with a curious sensation of embarrassment, the scuptural magnificence of his dark body lying there on the white counterpane. She withdrew her hand abruptly, said "Good night, Solali," and went out of the room.

The next morning she awoke later than usual after a night of disturbing dreams. Not nightmares exactly but a series of wildly improbable happenings which, in the strange hinterland between half sleeping and half waking, her mind accepted without question. One instance she could still recapture clearly: she and Roy and Barry were standing in a sort of Roman Forum. Roy was attired in a flowing toga with a laurel wreath on his head. Barry was stark naked except for a solar-topi. Roy had a whip in his hand with which he was lashing the strong back of a young Negro who crouched at his feet. The shiny satin skin of the Negro quivered under the blows and thin scarlet weals appeared between his shoulder blades. Roy finally flung the whip on the ground whereupon it immediately turned into a long brown snake and wriggled into a hole in the rocks. "That will teach you," he screamed in a strange high-pitched voice, "to have ideas above your station." The Negro rose slowly to his feet and with a lightning stroke severed Roy's head from his shoulders with a machete and turning to Davina, said, in the pedantic tone of an Oxford Don, "Perhaps Mistress would like a cup of tea or a glass of milk? I do not advise anything stronger because of the bleeding." At this moment Davina woke up and lay trembling in the half-darkened room trying to remember where she was: sunshine seeping through the closed shutters made stripes of light across the floor and far away in the distance she could hear the shrill cries of the beach boys riding the surf. She got up and without waiting to put on her dressing gown went out onto the verandah. The bright morning greeted her as usual, no clouds or portents stained the empty sky. The bland lagoon, vivid blue streaked with jade in the shallows, lay on the shore without a ripple and across the deeper blue beyond the reef a tall-masted fishing boat sailed into the sun. It was not until Agana brought her breakfast tray that she remembered that Solali was in the spare room.

"What happened to your visitor, Agana, is he still with us?"

Agana, assuming a disapproving expression, nodded. "He is

still sleeping, Mistress. I went with a cup of tea to him an hour ago but he made no movement. You would wish that I wake him?"

"No, let the poor boy sleep on, I'll go in later and have a look at his leg."

"His leg will swiftly heal, Mistress; of that there is no doubt but—" he paused.

"But what?"

"If Mistress will excuse me the spare room is for Mistress's special private friends. It is not fitting that a garden boy should rest in it."

"There was nowhere else to put him," she cried sharply. "I couldn't very well leave him to bleed to death on the beach."

"Mistress is most kind and charitable, but it would not be good if Solali should boast to his family of his splendid adventure."

"I didn't know he had a family."

"He has four sisters and three brothers and a father who drinks kala-kala every night until he falls to the ground."

"I can't see that that is sufficient reason not to take care of him when he has hurt himself. In any case Solali doesn't strike me as being a boastful type. On the contrary he seems rather shy and self-effacing."

"He is very young, and the young are easily made foolish."

"So, it seems, are the middle-aged," she replied tartly. "That will be all for the moment, Agana."

Agana bowed and withdrew. Davina bit her lip and poured herself out another cup of coffee. She sipped it for a moment then, banging the cup down with such force that some of its contents slopped over into the saucer, she got up and walked across the verandah into the spare room. The shuttered dimness after the blazing sunlight outside made her pause for a moment. She closed the door behind her and tiptoed to the bed. Solali was lying as she had left him, his bandaged leg propped up on a pillow. He stirred as she came in and opened his eyes. She stood staring down at him. Still looking into her eyes he reached for her hand and pulled her toward him. For a split second she resisted; with his other hand he tugged at the cord of her dressing gown; almost irritably she slipped it off and with a quiet sigh, pressed her mouth onto his.

On the twenty-fifth of June in the year 1814 the *Good Samaritan*, a trading vessel of roughly 450 tons, ran into a bad storm in the Samolan Straits and was wrecked on the reef just off Gakhua Point. Twenty-one survivors including seven of the crew managed to get ashore in a boat. Unhappily for the Samolans, among those who escaped were three missionaries en route for Australia and New Zealand respectively. Two of them, Josiah Healy and Gavin Sitton, were grim, humorless men accompanied by their wives and children. The third, Esther Brunstock, was a spinster of twenty-eight, traveling with the Healys. It is difficult to assess which of them did the most damage to the Samolans but according to contemporary accounts it would seem that the militant Miss Brunstock won hands down. She was a pallid, thin young woman burning with religious fervor and convinced beyond shadow of doubt that she had been specially selected by the Almighty to bring the boon of Christianity to the un-regenerate heathen. Her spiritual conceit being only equaled by her fanatical energy, she contrived to wreak a considerable amount of havoc and confusion in a remarkably short space of time. The reasons that her efforts seemed to be more immediately effective than the quieter, less hysterical methods of her male colleagues, could be attributed primarily to her personality, which was formida-ble; secondly to her sex, which although rigorously repressed was clearly recognizable; and thirdly because she made a great deal of noise. The histrionic abandon with which she exhorted her bewil-dered listeners to come to Jesus appealed to their innate sense of drama. She shrieked and gesticulated and pounded her flat breasts with such force that she occasionally made herself cough and had to pause to sip a glass of water. The Samolans, fascinated by such unaccountable bravura, played up with enthusiasm, proceeded to beat their own breasts and were converted in droves. Later, when the excitement of the moment had died down and they found them-selves encased to the neck in hot cotton Mother Hubbards and were forbidden on pain of hellfire to indulge in the sexual pleasures they had hitherto so casually enjoyed, their ardor diminished. A few remained loyal to the Christian revelation but the majority slipped back to the less demanding worship of their painted wooden idols. However, the damage had been done, the maggot had burrowed into the apple. A sense of imported sexual guilt permeated the islands and they were never to be the same again.

Later, when Davina had regained the privacy of her own room, she lay down on the bed and buried her face in the pillow. Panic-stricken and seared with bitter self-contempt, she lay there quiver-ing with humiliation for nearly an hour until Agana tapped on the door and inquired whether he should run her bath for her. She re-plied in a muffled voice that she had a bad headache and would do it for herself later on. She heard the thud of his feet disappearing down the passage and jerked herself up to a sitting posture. Her face felt as though it were flaming red but when she dragged herself to the looking glass on the dressing table she was surprised to see that it looked as pale as usual. She sat for a while staring at herself with frowning intensity then, with a shaking hand, she reached for a cig-arette and lit it. She had committed, according to all the social and moral tenets of the island colony, an unforgivable sin. To have an affair with someone else's husband, with the Airport manager, with poor Jamie Ferguson of the Tourist Board who had been pestering her for ages, would have been all right; scandalous, perhaps, and an unwise indiscretion . . . but to have gone to bed with a native, her own garden boy! She took a long draw at her cigarette and suddenly started to laugh uncontrollably until, detecting in her laugh a note of rising hysteria, she jumped up and poured herself a glass of cold water from the Thermos jug by her bed.

Sitting on the bed, sipping the water, she managed with a commendable effort of will to control her hysteria and face calmly the implications of the situation in which she had so idiotically placed herself. Her brain, feverishly considering and rejecting various possibilities, finally concentrated on what seemed to be the most sensible and practical solution: Escape. At all costs she must get away from the island immediately, either to the mainland where she could stay with the Carters for a few weeks or even England where she could go to Monica in Sussex or find a reasonable hotel in London and look for a job of some sort. She stubbed out her cigarette and repressed an impulse to laugh again. The idea of uprooting her whole life, disrupting her marriage, involving herself in a tangle of confused explanations and pretenses just because she had weakly surrendered to a trivial sexual temptation was grotesque and utterly lacking in common sense. It was also cowardly. There was no reason for anybody to know that she had spent the night with Solali, unless of course he was indiscreet enough to boast about it to his cronies in the village, which she instinctively felt he was unlikely to do. Even if he did, it was still more unlikely that anyone would believe him. Her position as Roy's wife, the owner of one of the largest banana plantations in the island, was fairly impregnable and certainly too high in the social hierarchy to be easily tarnished by kitchen gossip, in addition to which her own reputation for being rather stiff-necked and unbending, of which she was perfectly aware, was so well known that the idea of her committing adultery with one of her husband's employees would be received with blank incredulity. Feeling calmer and more in command of herself, she got up, went into the bathroom and turned on the shower.

For the next three days she hardly saw Solali at all, on one occasion as she turned the Buick into the drive she thought she saw him cutting bamboos in the thicket by the tennis court but when she came level with it he had disappeared. On the evening of the third day she dined with the Fergusons in Lanialu Valley which was about nineteen miles away on the Northern Coast of the island. Jamie as usual was a trifle overassiduous. Ingrid, his wife, a formidable blonde with a thick Swedish accent, spent the three-quarters of an hour before dinner rushing into the kitchen and reappearing with very hot plates of various Smörgåsbord, which she proudly slapped down on the long coffee table on the verandah. It was a small party, only Bimbo and Lucy Chalmers, Maisie Coffrington, Hugh Tremlett and herself. The dinner was excellent as it invariably was at the Fergusons because they had a vast Samolan cook who had been painstakingly trained by Ingrid. It was one of the accepted rules of the house that he should be sent for and thanked and complimented on his prowess after dinner. This ceremony over, the guests retired to an arbor at the bottom of the garden overlooking the sea. While they were drinking their coffee and sipping some delicious old brandy that Jamie had produced from the much-vaunted cellar which was his pride and joy, Bimbo Chalmers, who was in the act of lighting a cigarette for Davina, said casually: "I caught that romantic-looking garden boy of yours red-handed the other evening."

Davina's heart jerked with sudden panic but her face remained bland. "Red-handed! How do you mean?"

Bimbo laughed. "Practically in *flagrante delicto* with that voluptuous cashier from Wong's Emporium. I fear my unexpected appearance on the beach with a couple of dogs may have spoiled their fun."

"Really?" Davina managed a disinterested smile. "When did this happen?"

"A couple of nights ago. I was driving back along the coast road and had stopped the car and got out for a practical reason that we need not go into at the moment and there they were, tucked away behind a rock in what could only be described as a compromising position."

"Dear Solali." Davina, still smiling, took a sip of coffee. "I'm afraid he has quite a reputation as a ladykiller."

"Judging by the discreet but ecstatic sounds she was emitting, he didn't seem to be actually killing her."

"You really are an incorrigible gossip, Bimbo. You ought to write a social column for the *Reaper*."

"I do," he replied complacently, "under a series of assumed names. All those glutinous little comments about dinner parties at Government House and those pert interviews with visiting celebrities which dear old Hilda is supposed to churn out are actually written by me. One day I am 'A Little Bird,' another I am 'Miss Mouse'; once when that heavy-bosomed Hollywood starlet arrived with her dubious Arabian prince I was 'A Fly on the Ceiling'!"

"Do stop talking nonsense, Bimbo," said Lucy. "It's terribly unkind to try to filch dear old Hilda's crown away from her. Without her wildly inaccurate tidbits in the *Reaper* we should have nothing to read in the hairdresser's. Also somebody might believe you."

"Nobody has so far," Bimbo sighed. "Not even you, my chosen mate in the eyes of Heaven."

"One could hardly describe that squalid little Registry Office in Paddington as Heaven."

Bimbo sighed again. "She has never forgiven my irreligious refusal to lead her to the altar. All her ghastly sisters were planning to be bridesmaids in mauve lace when I whisked her into the marriage bed before they'd had time for a first fitting."

During this routine interchange between the passionately devoted Chalmerses Davina sat, outwardly composed but inwardly quivering with an emotion which her realistic mind humiliatingly identified as the one human weakness she most despised—jealousy. She felt as though her whole body was shaking with it. The picture Bimbo's casual words had conjured up of Solali and the blond cashier erotically entwined on the beach branded itself on her mind with such horrifying clarity that she felt physically sick. Her coffee cup rattled in its saucer and with an effort she managed to put it down on the table without upsetting it. Fortunately the general conversation switched to a rather ribald discussion of the imminent Charity Fête to be given in aid of the English Church, which allowed Davina time to get a grip on herself. Presently to her relief, Maisie and Hugh got up to leave, apologizing profusely for breaking up the party but explaining reasonably enough that they had twenty-seven miles of twisting mountain road to negotiate and wouldn't get home much before midnight anyway. Amid a flood of protests from Jamie and Ingrid, imploring her to stay at least a quarter of an hour longer, Davina also managed to make her departure. She too had a long drive home and her confused and tormented mind welcomed the prospect of it. An hour alone in her open convertible under the quiet stars would give her time to think and soothe her jangled nerves. She stopped the car at the far end of Lalua beach, almost at the identical spot where only three nights ago she had seen Solali staggering toward her in the beam of the headlights. The realization that it was actually only three nights ago seemed incredible. She spread the rug from the car on the sand high up on the beach and settled herself against the stump of an ancient kailayia tree. There were streaks of bright green phosphorus in the shallows of the lagoon and all round her in the sea scrub sounded the incessant trilling of the cicadas mingled with the deeper, raucous note of the tree frogs in the ironwood grove which separated the road from the shore. She reached in her evening bag for her cigarette case which, to her dismay, was empty. She delved again and with a sigh of relief found an extra packet put there by the ever-efficient Agana. Having torn it open, taken a cigarette and lit it, she buried the burnt match in the powdery sand and stared absently at the sea and the stars and the gleaming white spray of the rollers as they broke on the outer reef.

Bimbo had said "A couple of nights ago." He had caught "that romantic-looking" garden boy of hers red-handed, a couple of nights ago. Only three nights ago, she, Davina Lavenham, had lain naked in the arms of that same romantic-looking garden boy. She gave a little shudder of distaste and felt the sudden sting of humiliating tears. With an exasperated gesture she brushed her eyes with the back of her hand, pulled her handkerchief from her bag and blew her nose. This was no moment for tears, for weak hysterical abandon. This was no moment even for regret. What was done was done.

After she had sat there for a little while the mental turmoil into which Bimbo's casual, gossiping words had so unexpectedly, so humiliatingly plunged her, began gradually to evaporate. The remote, lonely little beach and the vast quietness of the sky eased the tension of her strained nerves as an injection of some soporific drug eases physical pain. She remembered many years ago lying in a hospital bed and wondering in panic how much more she could bear. The matron had come into her room followed by a young intern in a long white coat and pushing a trolley rattling with bottles and instruments. He had rolled up the sleeve of her nightgown and with gentle efficiency inserted a fearsome-looking needle into a vein on the inner side of her elbow. She had winced at the sting of the hypodermic then, having wiped away a tiny crimson bead of blood, he had asked her to hold on the spot a small wad of alcohol-soaked lint. After he had patted her hand reassuringly he and the matron went out, leaving her lying there still pressing the piece of lint and waiting for the expected miracle. Unlike most expected miracles it began to work almost immediately. First of all a prickling drowsiness beginning at her feet crept blissfully upward until her whole body was relaxed. The pain was still there, she could feel it, almost watch it with detachment, but the sharp anguish of it was fading, second by second, as though the drug was actually pushing it out of her consciousness. Finally it disappeared entirely. She remembered stretching her arms and legs gingerly for fear the least movement might bring it back, but it didn't and she lay still, smiling in incredulous relief.

For more than an hour Davina sat, until her legs began to feel cramped and she became aware of a chill in the air. She got up, shook the rug free of sand and drove slowly home. Agana had left the lights on in the sitting room and on the patio but the rest of the house was dark. Having switched them all off, leaving only the lights in the passage she opened her bedroom door and, with a sudden start of terror, stopped dead in her tracks. The verandah windows were wide open and in the glow from the night outside she saw a dark figure stretched on the white counterpane of her bed. Putting her hand to her mouth instinctively to repress a scream she stood in the doorway for a moment without moving. Then, realizing with a sharp pang of irritation who the intruder must obviously be, she switched on the light and walked over to the bed. Solali was lying stark naked with his face buried in the pillow, his left arm dangling over the side of the bed with fingers almost touching the floor. The muscles on his strong back gleamed faintly in the light as though they had been oiled.

"Solali." She spat out his name in a venomous whisper. "Sola-li." He moved in his sleep and gave a little grunt.

"Solali." She seized his shoulder and shook him furiously. After a moment or two he grunted again, turned over almost petulantly onto his back and opened his eyes. He stared up at her, momentarily dazed with sleep, then seizing her hand he pressed it to his face, she snatched it away and moved back from the bed.

"Please get up immediately and go away." She spoke with icy authority, the mistress to the servant, the superior to the inferior, the white to the black, the sharpness of her tone startled him into full wakefulness, he sat up and looked at her in bewilderment.

"Kindly get out of my room please—now—at once. I will speak to you in the morning."

He muttered something in Samolan and rose slowly to his feet. She stood facing him, her body taut with anger and her eyes blazing.

"Please, Mistress. I meant no trouble, no harm for you by what I did. I was waiting for you to come back from Lailanu to say you a sweet good night. I waited in the drive, then on the verandah and then my eyes became heavy with sleep." He put out his hand and touched her arm, she brushed it away violently and slapped his face. He stepped back and stared at her incredulously, stroking his cheek where she had struck it as if to wipe away the shame and misery of the blow.

"I have no way to make head nor tail of this great anger." His voice was husky as though he was trying not to cry. "I have done no evil bad thing to earn such displeasure. I have only waited for my lady to come back."

"You were not waiting for your lady to come back two nights ago when you were seen rolling on the beach with your blond fancy-girl." Davina stopped short and looked away, appalled by the vulgarity of what she had just said. She felt stifled, as if she were struggling through some macabre nightmare. Solali continued to stare at her in bewilderment, a small frown puckered his forehead and he looked utterly woebegone.

"Two nights ago I was in Nalikowa where Mistress had dispatched me to collect the spare parts for the new tractor. I was on no beach rolling with someone. Perhaps some stranger has spoken of me untruthfully to cause this dreadful happening?"

Davina turned back and looked at him blankly. What he had

just said was unquestionably true. She had completely forgotten that two nights ago she *had* sent him into Nalikowa to fetch the spare parts. Bimbo had obviously made a mistake. It had not been Solali whom he had seen on the beach. A wave of relief surged over her, she repressed an impulse to throw her arms round Solali's neck. Instead she smiled, an apologetic smile, and put out her hand. Solali, still confused, took it in his and pressed it ardently.

"It was all a mistake, a silly mistake. It was Mr. Chalmers who told me at dinner that he had seen you with the girl from Wong's Emporium."

A broad smile spread across Solali's face. He clapped his hands gleefully. "I see it now most clearly. My brother Kyana, the fisherman who is two years my elder, has been the sweetheart of Miss Potter since Easter Monday. He has a strong likeness to me. It was he who Mr. Chalmers saw rolling."

Davina started to laugh helplessly and sank down onto the bed. Immediately Solali was beside her, his arms wound round her and his head nuzzling her neck. With only a slight struggle of protest she submitted and let him press her gently back onto the pillow, his hand caressing her neck rhythmically as if he were soothing a scared animal, soon it left her throat and slid down into the hollow of her breasts, with an almost imperceptible sigh she drew him closer.

For the next three weeks he was with her almost every night. She never again found him on her bed, usually he would be waiting in the darkest corner of the verandah, or in the shadows on the other side of the lawn. She would stand sometimes looking at the lagoon in the moonlight. Then out of the corner of her eye she would detect a sight movement among the ironwoods, and, smiling to herself, go swiftly into her bedroom leaving the door ajar so that he could see the ribbon of yellow light beckoning him through the darkness. The emotional conflict which her original surrender to him had created in her mind died away and troubled her no more. It was as though a shutter in her brain had silently closed down between her emotions and her conscience. She gave herself up to the almost animal urgency of his lovemaking with a sexual abandon which hitherto she could never have imagined herself capable of feeling. When she was not with him, when she was occupied with the normal routines of her daily life, a surge of physical longing for him would suddenly come over her, making her whole body trembled. Had she been a weaker character given to easy tears and able to find relief in self-indulgent hysteria, had she been less prone to dissect and analyze her feelings, had she in fact been less intelligent, her dismayed self-contempt could probably have been rationalized out of existence, but her will was strong and her mind too clear to accept any compromise. She was, she admitted grimly to herself, in the grip of a sexual obsession,

514

an "expense of spirit in a waste of shame." To pretend, even for a moment, that it was anything else would be idiotic. The immediate problem was how to cope with it. Roy was returning from the main island in a few days' time and although she had previously rejected flight as the best solution it now seemed to her to be the only possible way out. She would cable him at once, telling him to stay where he was and that she was flying out to join him. She would add that she had been feeling unwell lately and that Dr. Newman had advised her to go into the main hospital for a checkup. Having made this decision and aware of a lightening of her spirits, she walked to the bureau and took a cable form from the top drawer. The P.S.A.S. (Pan Samolan Air Service) she knew made thrice-weekly flights to the main island. On telephoning the main office in Nalikowa she discovered that one was leaving that same afternoon. She reserved a seat on it and went into her bedroom to pack a suitcase. An hour or so later, when she was backing her car out of the garage she saw Solali leaning against a tree trunk watching her. The sudden sight of him startled her but she managed to smile casually and wave her hand. He raised his hand to wave back and then, as if he instinctively realized that something was wrong, he lowered it and forlornly turned away.

When the plane had touched down, turned with a deafening roar of its engines and lumbered bumpily along the runway to the reception building, Davina saw Roy talking to the Airport manager, a brick-red, tubby little man wearing white shorts which were too long and a khaki solar-topi which was too big. Roy, bareheaded, looked cool and unruffled as usual. When she stepped out of the air-conditioned coolness of the plane, the dazzling heat struck at her viciously and she felt suddenly weak. She rested her hand for a moment on the gangway rail to steady herself but it was so searingly hot that she quickly withdrew it. Roy relieved her of her small dressing case, bestowed a perfunctory kiss on her cheek and introduced her to the Airport manager, who shook her hand as though he were pumping water from a well. In the car, driving through the interminable sugar plantations which lay between Pendarla and the sea, she heaved a deep sigh of relief. Roy gave her an anxious look and she smiled and patted his hand. "There's nothing to worry about," she said; "it's just that my insides have been acting up again, probably only a hangover from that bout of fever I had in April. Old Newman thought it would be sensible to have a thorough examination. There are no indications of anything sinister, but I've been having occasional dizzy spells and feeling generally run-down so I thought I'd better do something about it. I suppose Dr. Cardew is here? I mean he isn't away on leave or anything?"

"No, he's here all right. He and the Matron have everything organized, they've got a quiet room for you at the far corner with a verandah overlooking the sea."

Davina looked at Roy out of the corner of her eye. His face was expressionless but a slight, preoccupied frown puckered his forehead, as though his thoughts were far away concentrated on some private problem which had nothing to do with her being ill and having to go into hospital, conceivably nothing to do with her at all, probably some minor irritation arising from the banana conference. Whatever it was she had neither the inclination nor the energy to question him about it at the moment. She felt flat and faintly apprehensive, as though the story she had cooked up about her imaginary illness was actually true. The memory of Solali leaning so disconsolately against the tree by the garage flashed into her mind for a moment, but she resolutely pushed it away. She had escaped, that was the most important thing; she had managed, in the nick of time, to extricate herself from a situation which might have become infinitely dangerous. She was conscious of an uprush of gratitude for Roy, for the fact of him being her husband, even for his placid, unromantic reliability. His solid, masculine obtuseness, which she had so often stigmatized in her mind as dull and boring, now seemed suddenly reassuring, something eternally valid which she could hang on to and trust. She again glanced furtively at his face. It was still inscrutable and he was still frowning.

Dr. Cardew and the Matron received them at the hospital and after she had unpacked her overnight case, undressed and settled herself in the cool fresh bed, Roy, who had been talking to Dr. Cardew in the corridor, came back into the room and stood looking down at her.

"Feeling all right?"

"Of course. I'm absolutely certain there's nothing really the matter with me. I'll be up and about again in a day or two. You can leave me now without a care in the world and go and have a nice lunch at the Club."

He bent down and kissed her on the forehead. "That remark was plain silly," he said. "The idea of having a nice lunch at the Club belongs in the realms of fantasy. I shall have a slice of leathery cold beef, two very old baked potatoes and a pawpaw and lettuce salad that tastes of ammonia."

"Try something else. What about a plain omelet?"

"That suggestion was even sillier. You must be running a high temperature." He went out and left her alone. She lay back on the pillows staring at the painfully vivid watercolor of Lalua Beach at sunset in a wooden frame facing her bed, and wearily closed her eyes.

After a week in the hospital in course of which she endured

with fortitude all the crude indignities of what is lightly described as a routine checkup, she and Roy flew back to Olinawa. Agana met them with the Buick and they drove home along the coast road. It was suffocatingly hot and a bank of menacing thunderclouds lay on the horizon. It was the beginning of the monsoon season and the sea was flat, metallic and without life. In the evening when Roy had driven off to the other end of the plantation in the Jeep, she lay in her "Planter's chair" on the verandah and watched listlessly the light fade from the distant mountains. Agana brought her a glass of iced fresh lime and soda.

"Mistress would like some kraki nuts or perhaps a small biscuit?"

"No, thank you. Nothing to eat."

He bowed and was about to go when she called him back. "Where's Solali? I haven't seen a sign of him since I arrived this morning."

Agana shuffled his feet and looked embarrassed. "Solali is no more here, Mistress."

"No more here? What on earth do you mean?"

"He behaved with most ugly insolence to the Master and so he was sent sharply away bag and baggage."

Davina felt a sudden pang of fear. "Insolence? In what way was he insolent? What did he do?"

"I cannot exactly say but the Master was angry and there were loud words spoken."

"Had he been drinking?" As she asked this question she knew that the answer would be No. Samolans very rarely drink spirits except on ceremonial occasions when kala-kala, a fearsome concoction distilled from a particular mountain shrub, is consumed in large quantities.

"No, Mistress, he had not been drinking. What he had been doing was more bad then drinking."

"Stop being so mysterious, Agana. What *had* he been doing?"

"The Master will tell the sad story I am sure if Mistress would ask him."

"Never mind about the Master for the moment. I am asking you. Please tell me the truth."

Agana stared at the ground for a little and then, still without meeting her eyes, said mournfully, "Solali is a foolish boy. He had been taking oaaki."

"Oaaki?" Davina's heart sank. Oaaki, a local herb which in early times had been widely used on the island as an aphrodisiac, had since British colonization been ruthlessly stamped out. Any Samolan found with a leaf of it in his garden was liable to a stiff term of imprisonment. Oaaki could either be chewed like betel nut or

517

powdered into a paste which, after being dried in the sun, was mixed with tobacco and smoked like opium. The latter method was usually employed by the Samolans, for the root in its natural state was tough and stringy and left a pungent telltale smell on the breath. Its effects, unlike opium, were far from soporific. Genuine oaaki addicts, and there were many more of them than the government cared to admit, were liable to lose all sense of responsibility and certainly every vestige of the Christian morality so painstakingly instilled into them by the missionaries. They could, in fact, be exceedingly dangerous. The Samolans, although by nature gentle, indolent and well disposed toward their white-skinned overlords, concealed beneath their eternally smiling friendliness a strain of cruelty which was all the more startling on the rare occasions when it rose to the surface. The early history of the enchanted islands had been bloody in the extreme but there were no recorded instances of actual cannibalism, possibly because the Samolans were vegetarians and disliked the taste of meat in any form. Sociological research in the nineteenth century had unearthed evidence that their expertise in various most complicated forms of physical torture had been, to put it mildly, imaginative. Any excess of alcohol or stimulative drugs was likely to unleash their latent barbarism and although the crime rate in the islands was comparatively low, whenever a murder occurred or an outbreak of hooliganism in the slums of Okilawa, the perpetrators were usually discovered to have been either drunk or under the influence of oaaki.

When Agana had gone back into the house, Davina lay back in her chair and gazed up at the sky. Night had closed down with its usual tropical abruptness, its usual swift theatrical transition from daylight to darkness. She remembered once during their last leave in England going to the Odeon in Leicester Square on a Sunday evening. After a documentary short and the newsreel there was an interval before the main picture and while an organist pounded away at the Wurlitzer, changing colors were projected onto the wide screen. She had giggled nostalgically and when Roy had asked her what she was laughing at she replied that it was so exactly like any evening on their own verandah in Samolo that she felt quite homesick. When Agana had told her that Solali had gone she had felt a momentary stab of dismay, followed quickly by a surge of relief. Her impulse to fly to the main island had obviously been the right one. Even the unpleasantness of her week in the hospital had been well worthwhile for it had given her the opportunity to think things out, time to rationalize the insane folly she had committed and, with comforting sophistry, dismiss it as no more than a casual indiscretion. Unfortunately however such facile rationalizations were beyond Solali's mental capacity. He was an uncomplicated sensual young animal, not given to analyzing and dissecting his emotions. Having conceived a romantic, reverent adoration for Davina who, apart from being his employer's wife, represented a world which to him, a native garden boy, was as remote as another planet, he was astonished and even shocked at her willingness to accept him as her lover. Never, during the most abandoned moments of their lovemaking, was he able entirely to overcome a secret amazement that such a situation could exist. When she had left to fly to the main island and he had watched her backing the car out of the garage he had been inconsolable, almost suicidal. He had driven the banana truck into the town and had drunk himself into a stupor. A few days later, weak and shaken after his protracted orgy, he had taken refuge in a wooden shack on the beach belonging to old Naliava, with whom, when he was a boy, he had learned spear fishing on the reef. Naliava, his wife and three stalwart sons had accepted him without comment and asked no questions. He went out with the boys in a dugout canoe and swam and fished not only from dawn until dusk but often in the night as well, hoping that by physically exhausting himself he could rid his mind of the image of Davina, but it was no good. The memory of her refused to be banished; he would wake in the night, stumble miserably out onto the beach and wander along the edge of the lagoon, aimlessly kicking the little hermit crabs out of his way and wishing he could die. He went back to the town, found himself a cheap room in a lodging house down by the harbor in which he lay day after day, emerging only at night to prowl about in the streets or sit, sullen and unapproachable, in the cafés and bars of the waterfront. The savings he had accumulated, which didn't amount to much, began to run out and he realized, in his more lucid moments, that he would soon have to get a job of some sort or starve. It was in one of these waterfront dives that he met "Ginger" Macleary. Ginger, a half-breed, was a well-known figure in the underworld of Olikawa; the son of an Irish seaman and a Samolan prostitute, he had achieved a certain affluence by pimping for visiting sailors and, as a lucrative sideline, peddling dope. He had observed Solali in various bars and his sharp eyes had assessed his potentialities. Young men of Solali's physique were in much demand either for private enterprise or for the town brothels where they could be induced to perform sexually with the local inmates for the edification of the visiting tourists. In order to stimulate enthusiam for such endeavors a small measure of powdered oaaki dropped into a glass of kala-kala was well known to achieve satisfactory results. It was Ginger Macleary therefore who, after a long lascivious preamble, most of which Solali didn't understand, finally persuaded him to try the drug, just for the hell of it. To Solali, the hell of it was not immediately apparent, he was aware only of an overwhelming sensation of sensual excitement.

Ginger watched his reactions with clinical satisfaction and after tucking a small white envelope into Solali's jacket, tactfully withdrew.

The weeks slid by and the summer came. The Samolan summer varied very little in temperature from the other seasons. It was seldom unbearably hot but there was an increase in humidity and in July and August, the typhoon season, demonic thunderstorms occurred when the rain fell like sheets of glass and the minor dirt roads became impassable. One evening, after a day of lowering clouds and unusual heat, Roy brought home a strange young man to dinner. He had landed that morning from the inter-island cargo steamer and was a replacement for Ken Morrisson, the administrator of the N.R.P. (Nalikowa Rubber Plantation), who was about to retire to the chillier but less enervating climate of the Kentish marshes. The young man's name was Colin Marshall. He was tall, athletic-looking and, although not conspicuously handsome, had charm. The sort of casual English charm which foreigners occasionally find deceptive. He was affable, well-mannered and one felt instinctively on first meeting him that he ought to be permanently dressed in yellowing white flannels and a blazer. Beneath this overtypical exterior however he was shrewd, efficient and surprisingly well read. Davina, on that evening when he made his first fateful entrance into her life, found him agreeable to talk to if perhaps a trifle suburban, and having thus summarily assigned him his role as a pleasant unattached male who could be relied on for dinner parties and tennis tournaments, paid no particular attention to him. A week or so later, however, when she had encountered him at a lunch party given by the Fawcetts and at the Saturday night dance at the Club, she decided that he was attractive enough to be asked to dinner. He accepted her telephoned invitation with obvious alacrity and in due course arrived, impeccably dressed in the routine white jacket and dark trousers and wearing a scarlet paraina flower in his buttonhole. She laughingly told him during dinner that in the Samolan Islands the wearing of a paraina flower implied immediate amorous availability. He accepted this information with a quizzical smile and said that that was the exact reason that he was wearing it. After dinner when they were all drinking coffee on the verandah he got up unobtrusively, went back into the house and began to play the piano. Davina, slightly puzzled by such unconventional insouciance, listened with increasing surprise. The piano, like all pianos in the tropics, was tinny and out of tune but he played it with such brio and delicacy that its usual metallic harshness was muted. After a little while she rose and, half-concealed by the curtains of the French window, stood silently watching him. He looked up and, without losing the rhythm of what he was playing, beckoned her to come closer to the piano. She glanced at the others who were engrossed in a discussion of the new airport which was to be built alongside the golf course, went in, drew up a chair and sat down. She watched Colin's hands as he played. They were slim, muscular hands and appeared to be effortlessly in command of the keyboard. For as far back as she could remember Davina had longed to be able to play the piano. At school she had doggedly practiced scales until her fingers ached and later when she was eighteen she had persuaded her parents to let her have lessons from a Professor Paliani who had a studio in Conduit Street and smelt of garlic. Unfortunately both her own efforts and Professor Paliani's were of no avail. She did manage, after weeks of concentrated anguish, to master the first movement of a skittish little composition by Chaminade, but the second movement proved too andante for her uncooperative fingers and defeated her. She could still remember crying in a bus all the way from Bond Street to Sloane Square after the irascible old professor had told her bluntly that to continue her lessons would be sheer waste of time and money. He explained to her with mounting vehemence, probably the result of weeks of accumulated frustration, that a desire to play the piano was not enough, that application, industry and determination were not enough either, that in order to perform on any musical instrument from a penny whistle to a double bass, a certain amount of natural talent was essential. The fact that he clearly considered her to be without even a vestige of this basic necessity was too obvious to be ignored and her romantic visions of herself, dressed austerely in either plain black or white, brilliantly rattling off Chopin polonaises and intricate Mozart arpeggios to enraptured audiences in the Aeolian Hall, faded and died for ever. However, her appreciation of music, which was emotional rather than academic, remained. When she drew the chair up to the piano to listen more attentively to Colin's playing it was because she recognized immediately that his talent was above the ordinary. She wondered vaguely why, being fortunate enough to possess such an unmistakable gift, he seemed content to use it merely as a social asset, a drawing-room accomplishment, and had decided to become a rubber planter on a remote tropical island on the other side of the world? Perhaps he had quarreled with his family or been involved in some sort of scandal? Perhaps he was escaping from the toils of some disastrous love affair? Looking at him sitting there so cheerfully on the piano stool she was forced to dismiss the last possibility as unlikely. He didn't appear to be the type to be easily plagued by secret sorrows. As though aware that she was assessing him, sizing him up, he winked at her and laughed.

"Why are you laughing?"

"I don't know, because I'm happy I suppose. I'm always happy when I find an attentive audience."

"Well I'm certainly that. You play beautifully."

He shook his head. "Not really. I'm an awful fake. I could have been good one day perhaps, if I'd concentrated."

"Why didn't you concentrate?"

"Because I was bone lazy I suppose." He picked out with one finger a few bars of the Irving Berlin song "I want to live out in the sun—with no work to be done."

"I don't quite believe that."

"The wanting to live out in the sun bit is true enough," he laughed. "I've always been a sun worshipper. When I was at school I was discovered stark naked on the roof of the cricket pavilion by my housemaster."

"Did he punish you?"

"Judging by the look in his eyes that was not his intention. I had to run for my life."

"Please don't stop playing," cried Maisie Coffrington. "We were so enjoying it."

"Certainly," he winked at Davina. "Background music is my speciality." He twisted round on the piano stool and concentrated on the opening phrases of Debussy's "Clair de Lune."

Davina gave a sigh of pleasure. Myra Hess had played "Clair de Lune" at the first piano recital she had ever been to, when she was fourteen years old. The preliminary descending chords, definite and evocative, had moved her then as they moved her now. She closed her eyes.

Dod Fawcett's voice grated harshly behind her. "I bid 'No Trumps' partner."

A few evenings later, returning from a large cocktail party given by some American business friends of Roy's at the Royal Samolan Hotel Davina, feeling tired and irritable because large cocktail parties always bored her, left Roy to put the car away in the garage and groped her way up the steps onto the verandah. For once, Agana had not left every light in the house blazing and the darkness was so thick as to be almost tangible. She had her torch but the battery was running out and it shed only a feeble oval of light wobbling before her feet. On the first step she paused in astonishment; somebody, very softly, was playing the piano. After the first shock of surprise she realized that it must be Colin, nobody else in the Colony would be likely to creep into somebody else's house and play "Rosenkavalier" in the pitch dark. Hearing her footsteps Colin stopped playing and came out onto the verandah.

"Please don't call the police until you've heard my story." He kissed her hand with exaggerated courtesy and grinned at her.

"It would be useless to call the police anyhow at this time of the evening. They have a tea break from five to ten-thirty."

"I came on a bread-and-butter visit to thank you for the other night. Nobody was about, the windows were wide open and the Steinway invited me in."

"The Steinway knows when it's well off. It has few sympathetic friends on this damned island. If I mixed you a nice drink would you play a little more? You've no idea how much pleasure it would give me."

He smiled again and without saying another word went back to the piano.

From then onward it became an accepted fact that he could come in after office hours and practice on the Steinway whenever he felt inclined. He usually felt inclined about three times a week. It no longer came as a surprise to Davina to return from an afternoon's shopping and hear music issuing from the house as she turned into the garage. Sometimes, with unwonted punctiliousness he would call up during the day and ask if he could come; usually, however, he just came trusting to luck that the coast would be clear and he could practice uninterrupted. Roy, who frequently found him, on returning from the office, strumming away in the drawing room, greeted him affably, offered him a drink and on several occasions invited him breezily to stay on to dinner but Colin politely refused. During these agreeable uneventful weeks Davina felt happier and more relaxed than she had felt for a long time. Only one thing worried her, a strange recurrent suspicion that she was being watched. The first intimation of this occurred one afternoon when she had just washed her hair and was sitting in the garden under the shade of the giant kaikoya reading a book with her head bound up in a towel. A movement in the shrubbery behind her made her turn sharply but there was nothing to be seen. It was probably only a chek-chek lizard or perhaps a mongoose. A few days later, she went out, in the early evening, for a short stroll along the beach and sat for a while with her back against a rock watching the pale sand crabs skittering along the water's edge on their long spidery legs. When she got up and began to walk back she happened to notice her own recent footprints on the wet sand and saw with a shock of surprise that there were other, larger footprints immediately behind them. Seized with sudden panic she stopped and looked round. The beach was completely deserted; nothing moved except a white heronlike bird which fluttered up from a half-submerged rock and uttered a raucous squawk. She turned back to go home and found, to her irritation, that she was almost running. When she reached the house she found Roy on the verandah entertaining two heavily perspiring Dutchmen who were apparently on a three-day visit to the island. After Roy had introduced them and they had resettled themselves heavily in the Planters' chairs, Davina managed to escape with the plea that she was hot and sticky and had to have a bath. Having turned it on she undressed slowly, unable to rid her mind of the curious, undefined fear that had assailed her on the beach. The warm bath soothed her however and by the time she had dressed and come down back to the verandah her nerves had returned to normal. The next morning Roy went off after breakfast in the jeep to collect the Dutchmen from the Royal Samolan and take them on a two-day expedition to the southernmost point of the island to visit the Carmichaels' cocoa plantation which, owing to old Gyp Carmichael's recent death, was shortly to be put up for sale. Roy's almost obsessive concern with economic development frequently irritated Davina. In her view, which was the reverse of gregarious, the island was already overcrowded, not only with tea planters, coffee planters and other overoptimistic fortune seekers, but with their wives and children as well. Americans of course were predominant, importing all kinds of gadgets and laborsaving devices which encouraged the native Samolans to be more lackadaisical and laissez-faire than they were by nature.

When Roy had gone, Davina settled herself on the verandah with the *Daily Reaper* which although sparsely informative on world affairs redeemed itself by carrying the *Daily Telegraph* crossword puzzle. True, owing to smudged printing, it was often impossible to make out the clues, but every morning Davina persevered stubbornly until she finally, with a feeling of triumph, managed to finish it. While she was frowning in perplexity at a word which looked surprisingly like "syphilitic" but couldn't possibly be, Agana came out of the house and stood for a moment without saying anything, shuffling his feet with gloomy embarrassment.

"What is the matter, Agana? Is anything wrong?"

"I have received Mistress most sad news on the telephone."

"I'm sorry. What sort of sad news?"

Agana looked down. "My nephew, from the sister of my first wife, has been drowned under the water when he was spear fishing. His foot became clasped by the shell of a conch and he was unable to make it free."

"How perfectly horrible. Was he fishing alone?"

"No, his friends were in a boat above. They dived down but could not pull him away."

"Oh dear." Davina shuddered.

"He is to be buried at sundown and his mother wishes me to be with her."

"Where is he to be buried?"

"Alas, a long way away, in Bakhua, near the village where he was born. That is why I have come to ask if I may be away for the night. Cook Anala can move over from the bungalow and sleep in my room if Mistress fears to be alone in the house.

"Nonsense, Agana, Cook Anala can stay where he is. I am not in the least afraid of being alone. You'd better get off now, as soon as possible if you have to go all the way to Bakhua. Have you enough money for the journey?"

"Mistress is deeply understanding. I am humbly grateful for such kindness."

"Never mind about that, Agana. Just tell Cook Anala that I shall be alone for lunch and dinner and I don't want much to eat anyhow."

Agana bowed sadly and withdrew. Davina, suppressing an unworthy pang of irritation, returned to her crossword.

At about nine-thirty that evening when she had finished a light meal which Cook Anala had brought her on a tray and was sitting reading on the verandah she was momentarily startled to see a figure coming toward her across the moonlit lawn. As it drew nearer she recognized Colin and when he came up the steps she was surprised and a little shocked to see that he was slightly drunk. He sat down heavily in a chair and giggled.

"I am, as your sharp eye has obviously discerned, what could be described as 'in my cups.' Not very deeply in you understand, but enough to betray my social principles to the extent of coming to your house uninvited, intruding on your privacy and in fact making a bloody nuisance of myself. Do you think you could forgive me?"

Davina laughed. "There's nothing to forgive. Ordinarily my natural impulse would be to offer you a drink but I think in the particular circumstances it would be unwise. Can I get you a glass of milk?"

"I was dreading you'd say that but I suppose there's no alternative."

"There is Alka-Seltzer. I'm sure Roy has some in his medicine cupboard."

"I don't approve of these newfangled miracle drugs, you never know where they may lead. It had better be milk."

"Very well. I shan't be a minute. Why don't you lie down on the swing seat?"

"I bet you say that to every man you meet." Colin giggled and Davina went into the house. When she came back a few seconds later he was lying flat on his back on the floor of the verandah. For a moment she was startled, thinking he had passed out, but he raised his head and waved to her reassuringly.

"Don't be alarmed. The swing seat was too wobbly, also the canopy prevented me from seeing the stars. They look marvelous from here, all rushing about the sky like illuminated ants."

"Here, drink some milk and you'll feel better."

"I remember my dear old white-haired mother saying that to me the day I was born." He giggled again. She knelt down beside him, slipping her arm around his shoulders and hoisted him into a half-sitting position.

"I can't believe she can have been all that white-haired the day you were born."

"All my family matured early. My cousin Eileen was lint-white and stone-deaf at the age of fourteen."

"Stop talking nonsense and drink some milk." She held the glass to his lips, he swallowed a little and then turned his head away.

"Milk is a wonderful invention but one can have too much of a good thing," he shifted himself so that he could lean against a rattan chair. "You are a very kind and gentle lady. You could knock spots off Florence Nightingale any day of the week." He took her hand and pressed it against his cheek. She put the half-empty glass down and looked at him. His skin was deeply tanned and his open shirt exposed a dark shadow of hair on his chest. The grip of his hand strengthened and he pulled her toward him.

"The stars are no longer whizzing about in the sky," he said softly. "They've now got into my head."

A few hours later Davina was awakened from a light sleep by the sound of footsteps on the verandah. Colin, stretched beside her, was breathing rhythmically, his arm curved behind his head and his knee pressing against her thigh. In the stillness before dawn the noise of the cicadas and tree frogs sounded unnaturally loud. The feeling of panic which had seized her on the lonely beach suddenly struck at her again. She lay trembling, staring at the stripes of moonlight shining through the slats of the closed shutters. Wide-eyed with terror she watched them slowly open; silhouetted against the outside glow she saw for a moment a dark figure step noiselessly into the room, then the shutters closed again and she was in the darkness. She tried to scream but her throat was so contracted with fear that she could make no sound. She fumbled wildly for the bedside lamp and managed to switch it on. Then the scream came; she heard it remotely as though the sound was coming from somebody else. Colin woke up, and still dazed with sleep, stumbled out of bed and rushed toward Solali. Davina heard herself cry "Look out!—he has a machete" but the warning was too late. Solali seized Colin's upraised arm and with one blow severed his hand from his wrist. Colin, with a shriek of agony, fell to the ground where he lay twitching convulsively in a swelling pool of blood. Davina had no time to be aware of anything more beyond the insane glare in Solali's bloodshot eyes and the sickeningly sweet smell of oaaki. She had staggered to her feet but the force of his first blow knocked her half across the room. She crashed against the wall and slid unconscious to the floor. Her nightgown had slipped up uncovering her knees and on the side of her face and neck where Solali had struck her was a pink stain like a summer rash. Solali, with a little whimpering sigh, walked toward her.

The two mutilated bodies were discovered at seven o'clock the next morning by Cook Anala who, in Agana's absence, went into Davina's bedroom with her early tea. Roy, returning from his trip to Lanialu with the two Dutchmen, was met at the drive gates by the chief of police who broke the news to him and suggested that it would be sensible not to go inside the house until the coroner had made his examination, the place had been tidied up and the bodies removed. Roy, stunned and bewildered, protested at first but finally allowed himself to be taken to the inspector's office in the police station where he was given brandy and the not entirely welcome company of a Roman Catholic priest who appeared out of the blue as though lured by professional instinct to be on the spot in a moment of emergency. Roy, too bemused at first to pay any attention to him, finally with a note of exasperation in his voice, persuaded him to go away and leave him alone. The two Dutchmen, shocked and unprotesting, were bundled into a police van and driven back to the Royal Samolan Hotel.

The gruesome story of the double murder which produced, not surprisingly, glaring headlines in the *Reaper* for several days, shocked the whole colony. Nothing else was discussed in the offices, shops, restaurants and hotels. Wildly inaccurate rumors were invented and elaborated and the stormy affairs of the larger world outside the Samolan Islands were relegated to half-columns on the back pages of both the *Reaper* and the *Evening Star.*

The double funeral took place on the evening following the crime. Colin and Davina were buried in the British cemetery on the hills behind Government House. Most of the British colony came and Agana, having returned precipitately from his own family funeral in Bakhua stood, conscience-stricken and forlorn, weeping into a large peacock blue handkerchief.

Mrs. Elsworth-Sutton, an aging relic of the more select and imperial years of Anglo-Samolan society, drove back from the cemetery encased in deep mourning with her niece Fiona, a sallow spinster of fifty-three.

"You know, Fiona," she announced portentously as the car turned at the corner by the giant cottonwood tree and headed toward the coast road, "I never did trust that garden boy of Lavenham's. I always thought he had a shifty look in his eye."

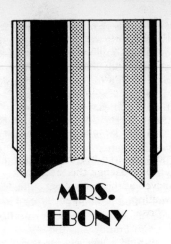

MRS.
EBONY

Mrs. Ebony stood on the steps of the hospital in the glare of the afternoon sun and shaded her eyes with her hand. Ricardo saw her immediately and began to back the Rolls out of the parking lot. A nurse bustled through the glass entrance doors and was on her way down the steps when she stood for a moment and looked at Mrs. Ebony solicitously. Mrs. Ebony recognized her as the fattish one who had come into the room with the doctor. She had a square, peasant face, with high cheekbones and kind eyes. Mrs. Ebony made an effort to smile at her, but the effort wasn't very successful. The nurse hurried on down the steps, and Mrs. Ebony took her dark glasses from her bag, put them on, and the sharp colors of the day softened. A man and woman and a little boy came up the steps, talking in whispers, as though they were about to enter a church. The little boy was clutching a bunch of yellow roses wrapped in mauve paper. Ricardo arrived with the car, sprang out of the driver's seat and held open the door for her. She answered the anxious question in his eyes with a brief nod and got in.

On their arrival at the hotel, Monsieur Ernest came out from behind the reception desk to greet her. His professional smile faded as he saw the expression on her face. "What is the news, madame?"

"The worst, I'm afraid. It's all over." She took off her glasses and put them back in the bag.

Monsieur Ernest raised his chubby white hand high, with fingers outstretched, as though evil tidings could be manually prevented from coming any closer, then dropped them to his side with a little thud. His round eyes glimmered with sympathy. "Is there anything I can do?"

"No, thank you, Monsieur Ernest." Mrs. Ebony's voice was even and without a tremor. "Dr. Benoist is taking care of everything. He has been most kind."

Monsieur Ernest ushered her into the lift, and they stood side by side in silence until it reached the third floor.

When they arrived at the door of her suite, Mathilde, the *femme de chambre*, was waiting. She stepped forward eagerly. *"Madame a besoin de quelque chose?"*

"Rien pour le moment, merci, Mathilde."

Monsieur Ernest waved Mathilde out of the way.

Mrs. Ebony turned to Monsieur Ernest. "Thank you so much, Monsieur Ernest. I shall be perfectly all right, I assure you; but as I have a great deal to think about, I would be grateful if you would tell them downstairs that I don't wish to be disturbed. No messages or telephone calls; nothing—until I let you know."

"Certainly, madame."

"If by any chance anyone should telephone me from the hospital, would you be very kind and take the call for me? It can no more be anything urgent." She felt her voice break a little.

Monsieur Ernest bowed and withdrew, gently closing the door behind him.

Mrs. Ebony took off her hat and gloves in front of the long looking glass in her bedroom and stared at herself. Quite remarkable! Everything in place. The pink two-piece Chanel sports dress, the pearls, the perfect makeup, the shady white straw hat in her hand: a slim and erect woman, possibly in her late fifties, at most her early sixties. She gave a wry smile, flung her hat and gloves on the bed, took a cigarette out of a blue malachite box on the bedside table and lighted it with the gold and sapphire lighter Lorry had given her in 1946. "Late fifties or early sixties, nonsense!" she reflected. I shall be seventy-six years old on September the fourteenth."

She wandered out onto the balcony and settled herself in the cane armchair. The awning was lowered, and it was pleasantly cool. The mountains on the opposite side of the lake were gray against the vivid sky, and the white steamer bound for Évian gave a petulant hoot and glided away from the pier; the tightly packed people crowding the decks looked like colored bonbons. A speedboat swerved

529

dangerously across the bows, dragging a slim, tanned young man on water skis in its wake.

No tears cooled the intolerable dryness of her eyes as she stared across the bright water. She put on her dark glasses again and waited for them to come; but no gentle rain from heaven, no quality of mercy came to her aid. She felt like an Egyptian mummy tightly swaddled in arid misery. She stubbed out her cigarette in an ashtray and lighted another. She had been a compulsive smoker for the past fifty years of her life, against all doctors' advice and ominous warnings of lung cancer, heart failure, respiratory troubles and eye trouble. Occasionally, she had permitted herself to be bullied into submission and gone in for filters and ghastly cigarette holders containing little glassy bullets of crystals, which, in a few hours, became dark brown and slimy and smelled most disgusting. Once she had forced herself to stop entirely for four months; but the frustration and irritation became unbearable; added to which, she began to put on weight, so back she went with infinite relief, gradually at first—two after breakfast, one before lunch, three after lunch and so on—until she had arrived at her normal twenty-five to thirty a day. Now, happily, it was too late to worry; only a few more years to go, so she might just as well enjoy them as much as possible. Her heart lurched suddenly. Without Ellen, it would be more a question of endurance than enjoyment.

Ellen had first come to her in the summer of 1924, forty-one years ago. She remembered interviewing her rather absentmindedly under the stern eye of Palmer, Nicky's valet, who had obtained her from a registry office in Kensington. In those days, Ellen was a wispy girl of twenty-one, with dark, untidy hair, bright eyes and a sort of fox-terrier alertness. You felt that she might jump up and bark if you opened the front door.

At that time, there had been no question of Ellen's being a personal maid; she was far too raw and inexperienced; she had merely been engaged to help Mrs. Bartlet in the kitchen. That was at the house in Chester Street, when Nicky was still at the Foreign Office. Two years—no, three years before the accident. The "accident." It is odd how one blanket word can be used to cover so much shock and violent change and despair. Nicky's accident had been the first crushing, unbelievable sorrow of her life.

She and Nicky had been married—brilliantly, ecstatically married—in January, 1919, just after he had been demobilized. They had moved into the Chester Street house in 1921. It was a bit cramped, of course; Palmer had to sleep in a tiny room behind the kitchen, while Mrs. Bartlet and Ellen shared a room at the top. Curiously enough, it was Ellen who broke the news to her about Nicky's being killed. She had come back after a matinee, Mrs. Bartlet was out for the afternoon and there was nobody in the house when the telegram came. Palmer had been with Nicky, killed instantly, as he was.

Ellen greeted her in the hall and followed her into the drawing room. It was a hot summer afternoon, and she remembered opening the window at the far end of the L-shaped room because it smelled stuffy. Ellen stood just inside the door and said in a stifled voice, "If you please, ma'am, there's been a telegram." In that swift instant, premonition of disaster crashed into the room.

Ellen gave her the telegram she had been holding behind her back. "I hope I did right to open it. Mr. Palmer always told me to open any telegram that came to the house just in—just in—" Her voice faltered to a stop, while Mrs. Ebony slowly read the telegram and sat down on the sofa. Ellen shifted about uncertainly for a minute, and then, with a little sob, she went to Mrs. Ebony and put her arms around her.

Now Mrs. Ebony sighed, looked at the lake and the brown young man, still skiing backward and forward behind the speedboat, and leaned her head back against the chair. All that had been almost forty years ago, that dreadful, frozen moment of grief. Suddenly, with a surge of relief, she felt her throat contracting. "I'm going to cry!" she murmured to herself. "I really believe I'm going to cry at last."

The luncheon party had been very successful. Hilary Bland had been as amusing as ever; Lucinda had just sat still, as usual, looking lovely and saying little; the two Barringtons had obviously been thrilled to meet Hilary and had thanked her effusively when they'd left. They were an agreeable couple; he very handsome and she a bit mousy, but worth cultivating. Mrs. Ebony was proud of her little luncheon parties. They were really the only form of entertaining she indulged in anymore, but they were invariably successful, and she always took pride in ordering the wine and food with care. Today had been no exception.

Hilary was the last to go, having lingered behind the others to stay on the terrace with her, sipping Grand Marnier and telling her some of the latest London gossip. He was a sweet old friend, entirely unaffected by his literary success, always pleasant to see again, always ready to pick up the threads wherever they had been dropped, without strain or effort. Dear Hilary. When he finally drove away in his new Mercedes, of which he was so proud, she went upstairs as usual for her afternoon rest. She called to Ellen from the sitting room to let her know she was back and then, after putting her bag and gloves on the desk and glancing at the pad to see if there had been any telephone messages, she walked into the bedroom.

It was in that moment that normal reality ceased and the nightmare began. Ellen was lying on the floor at the foot of the bed.

Her body was twisted, and her head was pressed back on the rug at an unnatural angle; her mouth was slightly open, her face was ashen gray and she was dreadfully still. Mrs. Ebony stumbled onto the floor beside her and felt for her heart, which was still beating but almost imperceptibly. She then rose, helping herself up by the bed, as the shock had unsteadied her, and reached for the telephone.

From then on, the nightmare had completely taken charge and whirled her along, helpless and unresisting, until the ultimate moment in the small, green-painted room in the emergency ward in the hospital when Ellen, without opening her eyes, without for one instant regaining consciousness, gave a strange, defeated little gasp and died.

Mrs. Ebony, who had been kneeling by the bed with her arm around Ellen's thin shoulders, gently withdrew it, laid her back on the pillow, moved across to the window and sat down on a wooden chair. She took a cigarette from the cigarette case in her bag, and the doctor's assistant, a red-haired young man in a white coat, stepped forward and lighted it for her. Everyone was very kind. People are always kind in moments of personal loss: the faces of complete strangers automatically assume expressions of routine sympathy; their mouths go down at the corners, their foreheads pucker, and their voices become muted with solicitude.

Mrs. Ebony, high on her little balcony, looking mistily at the changing colors of the mountains and the lake, stopped crying and dabbed her eyes with a piece of tissue. The brown young man had finally abandoned his skiing and was now clambering into the boat. The chugging of its engine sounded very loud, as though it were much nearer than it actually was. The white Évian steamer had diminished in the distance and looked like a small swan gliding away across the green glass water.

Frowning and blinking her eyes, which were cooler now, she made an effort to concentrate, to discipline her thoughts sensibly and reasonably, and decide, without emotion or sentiment, what was to be done. She felt suddenly utterly helpless. "Sola, perduta, abbandonata"—the phrase dropped into her mind, the words that tiresome woman sang in the last act of Manon Lescaut. A musically lovely aria, but riddled with self-pity. Mrs. Ebony permitted herself a fleeting smile and lighted another cigarette. This was no moment for self-pity. No moment, in fact, was the moment for self-pity; it was a contemptibly self-indulgent emotion. The fact that Manon found herself alone, lost and abandoned was entirely the result of her own feckless silliness; it was also inaccurate, because Des Grieux was hovering about nearby in that unlikely Louisiana desert, ready and willing for her to bellow her dying words to him.

"I fear," reflected Mrs. Ebony, "that I lack Manon's effortless facility for dying. My old bones are hard and my constitution strong. Alone, lost and abandoned certainly, but not through my own folly and selfishness—just by the inevitability of death. Nobody's fault; nobody to blame except, perhaps, God for being so inconsiderate and unmannerly to a rich old woman of seventy-five, who, after all, has had most of what she wanted out of life and is therefore really in no position to complain. Ellen, my beloved friend, my loyal servant, is dead. There is nothing whatever to be done about it. Thirteen years younger than I am, and dead, gone far away into the distant land beyond hope of recall, the only human being left from all my crowded years of friendships and loves who cared deeply about my day's happiness. Never to be seen again. Over and done with, snuffed out into nothingness. It can matter only to me; no one else is involved. There's an old sister of Ellen's somewhere in Canada, I believe, but they never cared for each other, even when they were young, and hadn't corresponded for years. It can matter only to me, and I cannot possibly have so many years left. I shall have to grin and bear it, to behave well and calmly, because there is absolutely nothing else for me to do."

Like the air raids in the War: "The bravery of the English!" She had heard those words so often in furry, friendly American voices. "I can't imagine how you *endured* it—I mean, night after night. I'd have gone crazy. I *know* I would!" What nonsense people talked. How could we have done anything else but endure it? There wasn't anything else to do. How could she now do anything but endure the loss of Ellen? There was no way out. The days and months and years must be got through somehow or other. She must try to find a replacement as soon as possible—as though there could ever be a replacement for Ellen—but there must be somebody, a middle-aged woman, for preference, between forty and fifty, who could press her clothes, do her hair and look after her daily needs up to a point.

Perhaps Monsieur Ernest would help. Monsieur Ernest was, in a remote way, an old friend; he knew her ways, the pattern of her life. She had known him since she had first come to the hotel many years before, when he was merely the assistant concierge, affable and well disposed, with a pink face and curly dark hair. Now the curly hair had vanished, and the pink had drained away; but the affability was still there, together with an ingrained instinct to serve, to be of use to people. Good hotel managers could be as dedicated as concert pianists and ballet dancers and doctors. It was a definite *métier*, outwardly subservient, perhaps, but not necessarily humiliating. There could be pride and dignity behind the professional bowing and smiling.

She would talk to him tomorrow. Tomorrow! She put her hand

up to her mouth, as though to prevent herself from crying out, and closed her eyes wearily. She would have to deal with tomorrow when tomorrow came. In the meantime, she must set her abruptly bereft world to rights as efficiently as she possibly could.

First, a certain amount of trivia must be disposed of; the Salvertes' dinner tonight, poor old Melanie's bridge party tomorrow afternoon, the opening night of the Bologna Opera Company on Thursday. She had been going to take Ellen to that. Monsieur Ernest had got her the tickets, and they were at this moment propped against a vase on the mantelpiece in her sitting room. She would have to think of someone to give them to. Ellen had always loved opera—more than she did herself, actually. Once, three years ago, they had gone to Milan and stayed at a noisy hotel near the Duomo, just for a four-night operatic orgy. *La Bohème, Rigoletto, Norma* and a curious production of *Lucia di Lammermoor*, well sung but hideous to look at, with too much brocade and velvet and a lot of black-and-white-check kilts in the third act. She and Ellen had started to laugh and been unable to stop, and the people behind had leaned forward to shush them. Mrs. Ebony sighed and wondered if even the efficient Monsieur Ernest would be able to find her a personal maid who was capable of giggling at *Lucia di Lammermoor*.

Her reflections were interrupted by a violent screeching of brakes in the road beyond the gardens, followed by a grinding crash. She rose and went to the balcony rail. A white sports car, reversing carelessly out of a parking space, had been hit by an approaching van. It was obviously not a serious accident, nobody appeared to be hurt; but a crowd collected immediately, and there was a good deal of shouting and the shrill sound of a police whistle.

Her heart had jumped for a moment, nevertheless; there was an unnerving twist of memory in that ghastly noise of metal grinding against metal. How many years ago? Seven, at least, when she and Ellen had been driving from Monte Carlo into Nice to see a film that Mariette had said was the best thing she'd seen since *Casque d'Or*. The small Peugeot had come careering around the corner on the wrong side of the road just before Cap-d'Ail. It had all happened in a split second. The Peugeot had struck the left wing of the Rolls, ricocheted off it, skidded across the road to the low stone wall on the opposite side, and as though it had been lifted by a gust of wind, jumped the wall and disappeared from view. There had been an eternity of silence and then the sickening crash of the little car hitting the rocks far below.

She and Ellen had sat still, numb with shock. Then had come the shouting and the police and the lines of cars halting one behind the other in the glittering sunshine. Ellen had produced a bottle of smelling salts from her bag and forced her to sniff it; the sudden pungency had pulled her together enough to control her trembling. Ellen had quietly got a cigarette out of her case and lighted it for her.

Half an hour later, when the questioning was over and she had agreed to appear as a witness the following day, Gaston had managed to turn the car around and drive them slowly back to the Hôtel de Paris, where Ellen had put her to bed, dosed her with aspirin and sat beside her, stroking her hand almost hypnotically until, oddly enough, she had dropped off to sleep.

That must have been eight years ago, not seven, because Henri and Solange had dined that night, and Henri died in 1958. She remembered clearly that she had had to leave them in the middle of dinner to go back to bed again, because she felt sick. Actually, she had stayed in bed for three days, on the orders of Dr. Michel, who had diagnosed her condition as shock and delayed reaction. Ellen had appeared before the police the following day, in her place, and had given her account of the accident. Nobody had troubled to inquire whether or not Ellen might also be suffering from shock and delayed reaction, perhaps because she was merely a lady's maid and therefore less fragile, less vulnerable to such delicate nervous disorders.

Now the crowd in the road began to disperse, and Mrs. Ebony returned to her chair. "I was a pampered and spoiled old woman then," she said to herself, "and I am a pampered and spoiled old woman still. At least, I was until two forty-five this afternoon. From now onward, there will be no more of it. I shall have to fend for myself." A wave of self-pity engulfed her, and her eyes filled with tears again. She looked up at the empty sky, and her lip trembled. "It isn't fair," she said aloud, with sudden vehemence, and frowned at the harshness of her voice. "I'm too old to be struck down into such cruel loneliness. Ellen was thirteen years younger than I, strong as a horse, hardly a day's illness in her life. Why should it have been *her* heart that failed and stopped? How could that particular, loving, self-effacing heart be so unexpectedly disloyal?" Again she fumbled in her bag for a tissue and blew her nose.

"It must be done now," she decided bleakly. The dreaded moment had been hovering nearer and nearer, like a growing shadow. "I must go now, this very moment, to her room and sort out her things, look through her papers, whatever letters she has kept, and stack the little remains of her private life in order and decency. Nobody else must be allowed to intrude. I owe her that, at least." She got up from her chair with a firm step, walked through the sitting room and into the corridor.

Ellen's room, number 356, was on the same floor but on the other side of the hotel. As she passed the lift, the doors clanged open, and a very old man in a gray suit was wheeled out in an invalid chair by a startlingly handsome young man of about twenty-four. The old man's head was nodding forward, as though too many years had made the weight of it intolerable. The young man glanced at her as she passed by. Shining black hair, brilliant brown eyes and an olive skin; probably Italian. There was the suspicion of a smile in his glance, a little arrogance, too, as though he felt his youth to be a special accolade. He patted the old man's shoulder with a swift gesture of affection; the old man looked up briefly and then nodded again. Mrs. Ebony felt an impulse to grab the young man's arm and whisper urgently, "Take care of yourself. Don't be too sure of your young immortality. See to it that you stay alive longer than he does. He mustn't be left old and alone." Youth and age trundled along the passage and disappeared around the corner.

Ellen's door was unlocked, so there was no necessity to call Mathilde to open it. Mrs. Ebony had shrunk from the thought of having to face Mathilde's chocolate-brown eyes brimming with exuberant sympathy. This was an undertaking that must be carried through alone and unobserved, a personal business concerning only Ellen and herself. No extraneous emotion, however kindly intentioned, must be allowed to intrude on its private melancholy.

Ellen's room was dim, because the shutters were closed against the glare of the afternoon sun. Mrs. Ebony opened them and then sat down on the bed. On the bedside table were a crocodile-leather traveling clock, a bottle of aspirin and a small silver photograph frame. On the shelf underneath, a glass jar of acid drops stood on a pile of magazines. She picked up the frame and looked at the photograph in it. It was an enlarged snapshot, taken years ago, of Ellen and herself sitting side by side in steamer chairs. They were swathed in plaid rugs and balancing tea trays on their knees. Mrs. Ebony looked closely at it for a moment or two and then put it down on the table. It must have been taken on the voyage back from New York in 1949. They had been staying with Chloe van Hoyt, on Long Island, and Ellen had been given an elaborate bedroom with a marble bathroom, which she had said made her feel like the Queen of Sheba.

Sixteen years ago! Mrs. Ebony sighed. Just after her divorce from Lorry. Her last love, really; no one had twisted her heart since Lorry. Lorrimer Ebony. The fascinating, rich, debonair Lorrimer Ebony. Drinking away his handsome looks, his charm, his bright mind and finally, just a few years ago, his life. She remembered reading of his death in a newsmagazine's ghoulish little weekly list. "Died, four times married, three times divorced, ex-Virginian playboy Lorrimer Ebony, 51, leaving widow twenty-two-year-old film starlet Marcia Gage, and one daughter, Gloria, born 1953—of liver cancer."

It was Ellen who had brought her that particular magazine in this very hotel, her grimly set mouth betraying drama before she had spoken. "It's him, madame. He's dead."

Mrs. Ebony had read the gruesome announcement with little emotion beyond a vague feeling of sadness.

That evening, she and Ellen had gone across to Évian on the steamer, to have dinner at the casino and gamble a little. Mrs. Ebony had enjoyed playing chemin de fer, while Ellen, eyes gleaming with excitement, would sit on a chair just behind her. Occasionally, she would get up and go to the roulette table to have a flutter of her own; but she seldom would vanish for long. That particular evening, Mrs. Ebony had done rather well, and she and Ellen had had a glass of champagne each in the bar, just to celebrate, before going to the steamer.

When they sailed back to Lausanne over the moonlit lake and Ellen had finally settled her in bed with her Ovaltine and her book-rest, Mrs. Ebony had suddenly sighed. "Poor Lorry. What a waste!" Ellen had turned at the door; she had never cared for Lorry, which was not surprising, considering the number of times she had had to help undress him and get him, sodden, into bed. "Good riddance to bad rubbish, if you ask me," she had said, and gone out.

Ellen's room overlooked the drive and front entrance of the hotel. The sudden honk of a horn shattered the afternoon stillness and brought Mrs. Ebony abruptly back to the dismal present. She got up from the bed and opened the built-in clothes cupboard. Ellen's dresses, neat on their hangers, swayed slightly in the draft from the open window. Mrs. Ebony stared at them blankly: The familiar black evening dress, one of her own originally, a Balenciaga model made over years ago by Ellen's expert fingers. Next to it, the dark gray day dress and the brown tweed two-piece traveling suit, with which Ellen always wore her beige straw hat with the brown velvet bow. The hat was on the shelf above. Also on the shelf above was a small suitcase.

Mrs. Ebony reached up for it and managed to get it down and onto the bed. It was locked. She bit her lip irritably, looked helplessly around the room. On the dressing table stood Ellen's handbag. She went to it with an effort and foraged about in it until she found a bunch of keys on a little keyring shaped like a horseshoe. When she had tried several keys, found the right one and unlocked the case, she paused before opening it and sat down weakly in an armchair by the window, noticing with annoyance that her hands were trembling. She lighted a cigarette to steady herself and stared at a colored picture on the wall. It was an eighteenth-century lithograph, but she couldn't seem to distinguish it very clearly.

Outside, there was a burst of laughter. She glanced down without interest and watched a blond girl and a young man drive off in an open car that looked like a scarlet bullet. Presently she stubbed out her cigarette in an ashtray, went swiftly to the bed and opened the suitcase. It was, of course, neatly packed. Ellen was incapable of untidiness. There were some bundles of papers on the top and a small leather case. On the envelope was written, in Ellen's rather childish writing, "For Madame." Mrs. Ebony slit open the envelope and took out the letter. It was dated January 17, eighteen months before.

> *My very dear Madame,*
>
> *I do hope that you will never have to read this letter. I am only writing it in case anything should happen to me. I have been having dizzy spells lately on and off and feeling not too good one way and another, so last month I went to see Dr. Lawson. He was very kind as always and examined me carefully, and then he told me that my heart was a bit dickey and that I should have to take things easy. He gave me some pills to take whenever I felt a bad spell coming on. I made him promise not to say anything to you, because I didn't want you to be worried. I'm sure there isn't anything to worry about really, because I'm perfectly all right now, but you never know, do you?*
>
> *Anyhow, if by chance anything did happen and I suddenly got bad or died, I wouldn't like to think of you being fussed and bothered and have to sort everything out and tidy things up. There isn't much to tidy up, really. Everything to do with me is in this suitcase. My taxes and insurances are all paid to date. Mr. Finch knows all about it, because I went to see him, too, before writing this.*
>
> *The packet of letters in the rubber band are from Ron. You remember I told you all about Ron years ago, when we were driving back from Aix les Bains and you had the bad foot. Anyhow, he got through the war all right and married that Belgian girl. I'd be grateful if you would send the letters back to him. I haven't heard from him for years, but I know he still lives in the same place—Ronald Birch, Esq., 43 Elkins Road, Leeds, Yorkshire. He must be a bit long in the tooth by now, and getting the letters will give him a shock, I expect; but that's his lookout, isn't it? I mean, he shouldn't have written them in the first place if he didn't really mean them, so it will serve him right.*
>
> *I've got eighteen hundred and twenty-nine pounds in Barclay's Bank. Mr. Finch knows all about this, too. I'd like it to go to my cousin Doris's boy, Stanley Booker. He's about fourteen now and very bright for his age. He wants to be an architect, and I thought the money might give him a start. Anyhow,*

he's the only relation I've got that I care about. There's nothing you need to do about this, because it's all written down in the will Mr. Finch and I drew up together.

There are some odds and ends in the leather box, which I suppose my sister had better have. I haven't had so much as a Christmas card from her since 1960, but her address is—Mrs. Larkin, Care of C.C.R.C. (Canadian Cement and Rubber Corporation), Winnipeg, Canada. But please don't worry your head about this. Just send the lot to Mr. Finch and let him cope with it.

Now I must come to the difficult part of the letter, which is to say good-bye to you. I can't go on much about this, because it makes me feel too miserable. Serving you has been my whole life, and I couldn't have wished for a happier one. Thank you for everything, dearest Madame. For all the fun and gallivanting about we've enjoyed together, and for all the ups and downs we've been through, too. I've never been one to pay much mind to the idea of people's meeting again in another life; but if I have to go before you do, I have a sort of feeling that some little bit of me will stay near you somehow or other. Please try not to fret for me more than you can help. Your obedient servant and ever-loving Ellen.

P.S. If I should happen to die, I would like the amethyst brooch you gave me to be buried with me. I know this may sound silly, but there it is. If I'm not wearing it, you'll find it in the little leather case.

Some hours later, Mrs. Ebony sat once more on her balcony overlooking the lake. Utter weariness had induced a curious detachment. Her brain was alert, but her nervous system seemed to have atrophied; she felt immune, invulnerable and devoid of sensitivity. If someone fired off a pistol close to her, she doubted if she would even turn her head.

Night lay over the lake and the mountains. The sky was brilliant with stars, but there was no moon. The lights of Évian glittered in the distance, and from the lakeside café nearby came the sound, filtered by distance, of a small orchestra playing the theme song from *Around the World in 80 Days*. The treacly tune, recognizable only intermittently against the traffic noises in the square, rose and fell and faded into a thin spatter of applause.

Monsieur Ernest had been kindness itself. He had dealt with all her social telephone calls. He had sent a telegram to Mr. Finch, to fly out from London tomorrow and take charge of all the formalities and arrangements that sudden death inevitably creates. She had dined frugally in her sitting room, served by a new floor waiter because, fortunately, it was Giovanni's day off, so there had been no sympathetic glances to be evaded and no kindly intended condolences to ward off. Monsieur Ernest had also busied himself with the task of finding her a temporary maid and had contacted three applicants, who were to come to see her in the morning.

The memory of Ellen emerged from the shadows and sat down next to her on the balcony, knitting away diligently at that dark blue cardigan she had been engaged on for the past two months. Mrs. Ebony leaned her head back and gazed up at the stars. A meteor flashed across the sky in an arc of pale sparks. "I should have thought of a wish," she reflected, "but it's too late now to think of wishes. Only one, perhaps. That the years I have left will not be too long."

The orchestra struck up again, an aria from *Lucia di Lammermoor*. Mrs. Ebony smiled the ghost of a smile and closed her eyes.

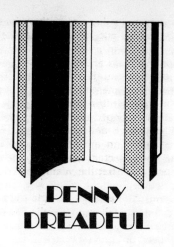

PENNY
DREADFUL

The last day of Edwin Pendleton's life began with a heavy shower soon after sunrise as though the heavens, with celestial prescience, were unable to control their tears. Unaware of this sad augury he slept until eight-thirty when Bruiser called him, as usual, with a cup of tea and a glass of lemon juice and hot water. Edwin Pendleton, "Mr. Penny," at the age of fifty-six showed remarkably few signs of his advancing years. Even in the cold gray light of a London morning his face retained a certain chubby innocence: his curly reddish hair, discreetly bleached at the sides as a gesture to eminence, still had a lively sheen and his body, although not so svelte as it once had been, still remained trim.

Bruiser shook him gently by the shoulder until he opened his eyes. . . . Even when clouded by fretful surprise at being dragged from deep, warm sleep, Mr. Penny's eyes were unquestionably his most important attribute: round, blue and wide they stared up at Bruiser through a haze of semi-consciousness. Bruiser gave his shoulder a little extra shake. "Time to wake up, dear," he said, "I've brought your tea and lemon." The early morning innocence faded from Mr. Penny's face, the lambent eyes hardened and the mouth drew down at the corners.

"For God's sake, shut the window, the room's like a Frigidaire." He heaved himself up onto the pillows and sipped his hot water and lemon. Bruiser shut the window and turned. "Your bath's ready," he said, "but we're out of 'Roman Hyacinth,' you'll have to make do with 'Rose Geranium' and there's only a drop left of that." He went out, closing the door behind him. Mr. Penny, with an irritable expression, watched him go and sighed. The day, outside the windows, looked unpromising. The trees stood about the square like embarrassed strangers at the beginning of a dull party: it wasn't actually raining but the day was leaden. Mr. Penny sighed again and stirred his tea. To some people the beginning of each new day is a recurrently fascinating adventure, a glowing moment in time rich with unfulfilled promise and anticipatory delight. Mr. Penny, alas, was not one of those fortunate beings. The morning to him was invariably a misery: not until he had drunk his tea and lemon, smoked without enthusiasm his first cigarette, dragged himself anxiously to the loo, bathed and shaved, not indeed until he was back in bed and waiting for his breakfast tray did his customary resilience begin to reassert itself. Sometimes even then, propped up against his pillows, shining and clean and smelling of some new masculine eau-de-cologne, clouds of discontent still shrouded his spirit. It wasn't, he reflected, as though he were a drunkard inured by long habit to the agonies of a hangover. As a matter of fact, he was a creature of abstemious tastes; a cocktail before dinner (*never* before lunch), a little wine during dinner and perhaps, if occasion demanded it, a couple of whiskeys and sodas later on, was his maximum intake. The exigencies of his public life, as he frequently reminded himself, were too pressing, too demanding to allow any margin for folly.

Mr. Penny's consciousness of his own importance, not only to himself but to the hundreds of thousands of his readers, provided a sturdy bulwark against frivolous temptations. Sometimes, when he allowed his mind to dwell on the position he had created for himself, the image he had created *of* himself in the hearts of so many ardent, trusting followers, he felt suddenly humble, overwhelmed by a surge of grateful humility, and his eyes filled with tears. On one or two occasions when in the grip of one of these moods of reverent self-analysis, he found himself muttering an incoherent little prayer of gratitude to The One Above. Apart from these especially poignant moments, his communications with The One Above were infrequent. He attended church, of course, on public occasions such as weddings and funerals, and when staying in what remained of the Houses of the Great; the charm of village worship, particularly when in the company of titled hosts and hostesses, appealed to him strongly. In fact one of his most popular pieces in *The Ladies' Own* had dealt winningly with this most touching aspect of English county life. The piece had been called "Through a Stained Glass Window" and had caused a brisk increase of fan mail for several weeks.

In spite of all this, however, it must frankly be admitted that God, to Mr. Penny, remained little more than an emotional abstraction. It wasn't that he lacked religious feeling, he was conscious of vast reserves of it bubbling away in his subconscious mind, it was just that he seemed to have so little time. Once, it is true, many years ago when he had just been demobilized from the R.A.F., he had toyed with the idea of becoming a Roman Catholic but then Father Rafferty had been recalled to County Cork and spiritual radiance faded from the immediate horizon. He was glad now of course that he had remained unobtrusively Protestant, a sudden flight to Rome might have alienated many of his most ardent fans. He still, however, a trifle coquettishly perhaps, corresponded with Father Rafferty.

Bruiser kicked open the door and came in with the breakfast. Mr. Penny winced as he always did and looked at Bruiser reproachfully.

"It's no use looking like that, dear," said Bruiser, "I've only got one pair of hands and if I have to keep putting the tray down on the floor and picking it up my back will go again." Bruiser's back "going" was a recurrent threat and Mr. Penny, recognizing it as such, ignored it.

"Is Miss Mac here yet?"

"Yes, she's in the office sorting mail. She'll be up in a minute." Bruiser walked over to the built-in wardrobe and flung open the door dramatically. "What sort of mood are we in today, dear? Gray, brown or black? If we're in a blue pin-stripe mood we're out of luck because it's being pressed."

"Black," said Mr. Penny absently. "I'm lunching with the Chatterworths. But I shan't dress yet. When I've been through the letters I've got to finish my piece for Sunday. Is there a fire in the library?"

"Not yet, dear. Mrs. Black's in there prancing about with that bloody Hoover, but I'll light it the moment she's gone. Drink up your coffee while it's hot."

Bruiser laid out a black suit carefully on a chair, selected a white shirt from the chest of drawers, placed shoes, socks, tie, handerkerchief neatly in a position and went out humming, "I Could Have Danced All Night."

Mr. Penny, left alone, poured himself a cup of coffee and wished, not for the first time, that Bruiser had acquired over his years of devoted service a little more polish. It was obviously too late to do anything about it now, although Mr. Penny regretted that in the early days he had encouraged him quite so unheedingly to become a "character," for with the passing of time Bruiser's erstwhile lovable outspoken eccentricity had set into a rigid pattern. He was like a comedian who scores an initial triumph on a first night and gradually deteriorates in subtlety as the play continues to run. Refreshing candor is only acceptable in small doses. Bruiser's candor had long lost its original sparkle and become automatic and a trifle stale. Unfortunately, Mr. Penny reflected, he had nothing but his own generous heart to blame. Years ago when he had just started writing his daily column for *The Trumpet* he had immortalized Bruiser on several occasions. The keynote of those early articles had been unaffected boyish simplicity. The series had been published every morning under an overall heading "Mr. Penny's Day" and in each article Mr. Penny frankly and openly had discussed his own domestic life, his early struggles with cooking and housekeeping, his problems with Arethusa, his Siamese cat, now, alas, passed over, and his devotion to Auntie Min (now an advanced alcoholic), and Miss Mac and Bruiser.

All these small and occasionally winsome intimacies encouraged his readers to identify themselves with him: his fan mail increased by thousands a week. In fact, "Mr. Penny's Day" remained for two solid years the most widely read column in any newspaper in the British Isles. Mr. Penny could never look back upon those first years of burgeoning fame without a surge of emotion. How wonderful they had been, with all their ups and downs, with all their soul-destroying hard work, they had been the first two golden rungs on his ladder to fame. He could afford now to smile whimsically at some of those long ago dramas and despairs, the arguments with the subeditor, the threatened libel suits, for he had been then as he was still entirely fearless in stating his views on any contemporary issue or scandal that happened to outrage his principles. There were few episodes in the passing show of life during that period that he did not comment upon, sometimes boldly going against the tide of popular opinion in order to prove his points. He had for instance on one occasion defended a play by an author he happened to admire personally, and which had been all but destroyed by the critics. Miraculously, after four consecutive boosts in "Mr. Penny's Day" the business had picked up and the play had run for seventeen months.

Then there was his courageous apologia for a clergyman from Beaconsfield who, it later transpired, had been wrongfully accused of curious behavior on the towpath at Richmond. Mr. Penny had sifted this unsavory story to the dregs and ultimately published his findings. To this very day he received a card each Christmas from the clergyman, now discreetly retired. These and many other excitements punctuated those two glorious years, culminating in 1948 with the famous Doreen Snipe Story, which for all time sanctified his name in the hearts of millions of British mothers. Mr. Penny, in course of a trip to Manchester for *The Trumpet*, had interviewed a working-class family in a slum not far from the Canal. This family, the Snipes, consisted of a drunken father, a tubercular mother and seven children, the youngest of which, little Doreen, had been stricken with polio. Without pausing to think of the expense or the difficulties Mr. Penny and his accompanying photographer flew "Little Doreen Snipe" in a chartered plane to London, where she was installed in one of the major hospitals. For weeks little Doreen hovered between life and death, her daily progress, almost her every heartbeat, was faithfully recorded in *The Daily Trumpet*. Mr. Penny, in addition to visiting her every other day and loading her with dolls and teddybears, made a spirited appeal on the wireless which resulted in subscriptions amounting to seventy-nine thousand pounds in ten days. Little Doreen ultimately recovered sufficiently to be moved to a convalescent home for retarded children in Bexhill, where, a few months later, she died of pneumonia. For this anticlimactic tragedy *The Daily Trumpet* sounded no Requiem.

Altogether those early years had indeed been richly rewarding, but their rewards, although gratifying, were as nothing compared with those that were to follow. It was as though a benign Destiny, eternally smiling, was beckoning him on to further heights, to even more shining vistas. "Mr. Penny's Day," the "Open Sesame" to so much future glory, was ultimately published in two hardback volumes later on to descend with unimpaired dignity to a paperback edition in one volume which had sold hundreds of thousands of copies in the first few months of its issue. Later had followed other more mature works, an autobiography entitled *Myself When Young* and two more volumes of collected and revised newspaper articles under the respective titles of *Trumpet Calls* and *More Trumpet Calls*. Then had emerged the first of the "Mr. Penny Goes" series, a series which was destined to assure its author of a fixed place on the bestseller list for many years to come.

The first of these, *Mr. Penny Goes to America* caused a mild sensation. It was not a long book but it was packed with dynamite. Dynamite to the extent of causing a number of violent explosions from certain United States citizens who resented Mr. Penny's outspoken criticisms of their country's mores and institutions. They were perhaps justified in their complaints, considering that Mr. Penny's invasion of their territory, although fairly comprehensive, had lasted for no longer than a brief two months. Those two months however had been enough to implant in the author's observant mind a number of prejudices which, injudiciously perhaps, he had stated with his usual fearless candor. He had been received, as all visitors of importance are received in America, with gratifying publicity and overwhelming hospitality. This however had failed to blind him to certain aspects of the American Way of Life which quite frankly saddened him. He had interviewed leading citizens, movie stars, taxi drivers, housewives (of course) and one or two emancipated Negro intellectuals. He had taken tea with Father Divine (one of the more enthusiastic chapters in the book) and visited the Grand Canyon, Niagara Falls (disappointing), a Dude Ranch in Wyoming, the Lincoln Memorial in Washington and Greenwich Village. Mr. Penny's main criticisms of America were concerned with commercialism, overadvertising and vulgarity. To Mr. Penny, vulgarity was "anathema." He couldn't stand it. It affected him at times almost physically. He hotly resented, as what patriotic Englishman would not, references to our own British Royal Family by their Christian names. His spirit squirmed when faced with such headlines as "Liz and Phil Start Goodwill Tour," "Meg and Tony Take the Plunge" (a holiday snapshot), and to do him justice he shuddered impartially at a photograph of Mrs. J. F. Kennedy listening with a strained expression to a pop singer at a charity benefit with the headline "Jackie Winces at Warbler." To Mr. Penny, Royal Personages or heads of state and those immediately connected with them were by their rank alone entitled to outward respect at least. Movie stars and eminent politicians, he was willing to concede, had lesser claims. All of which was perfectly understandable; the point of view of an average middle-class Englishman, who, although he had achieved more than average celebrity himself, remained at heart simple, unaffected and true to the traditions in which he had been brought up to believe.

The reception of *Mr. Penny Goes to America* in America itself was, as he had stated, unenthusiastic. In England, however, it was an immediate success and ran through a series of editions in a short space of time. The successive accounts of Mr. Penny's peregrinations entitled respectively *Mr. Penny Goes to Paris, Mr. Penny Goes to Rome* and *Mr. Penny Goes to Sea* (the latter a delightful account of a yachting trip in the Mediterranean with two Indian undergraduates) were, although filled to overflowing with his customary wit and observation, less controversial. It is true that one cynical critic suggested that the next of the series should be entitled *Mr. Penny Goes Too Far,* but Mr. Penny, conscious of mounting sales, could well afford to shrug off this trivial witticism with his customary sangfroid. He had long ago faced without undue chagrin, that his writing would never be accepted by the literati; in fact, he was frequently known to make wry little jokes about this to his more intimate friends. He was aware, however, in his heart of hearts, of a small pang of disappointment. It would be so gratifying, just once in a way, to be praised for his style, to be taken seriously as the eminent writer he knew himself to be, but he was far too resilient by nature to be seriously disturbed. Time would tell, he reflected philosophically, and it was obviously too much for a writer of his overwhelming popularity, to say nothing of his growing acclaim as a famous television personality, to expect immediately more portentous accolades. They would come later, perhaps even after he was dead, but that they would ultimately come he had no doubts whatever.

Mr. Penny's reflections were interrupted by Miss Mac coming in bearing an orange cardboard folder containing the more personal letters of the morning's mail. Fan letters, except those which were outstandingly adulatory, requests for autographs or money, official invitations and various business communications had all been left downstairs on her desk to be dealt with later. Miss Naomi Mackerel at the age of fifty-eight was one of those women from whom Nature had callously withheld the gift of personal charm. She was thin and gray; efficient, industrious and did her job with almost aggressive conscientiousness. She had been Mr. Penny's personal secretary for fifteen years and her devotion to him was the bright and shining heaven of her life. Her relationship with Bruiser was outwardly serene. She tolerated him, laughed primly at his jokes and wished ardently that he was dead and at the bottom of the sea. His exaggerated cockneyisms offended her and his familiarity with Mr. Penny set her teeth on edge. To Bruiser, his employer's occasional outbursts of temperament were of little significance, no more than foolish little flurries to be dismissed with cynical indulgence. To Miss Mac they were an active personal misery even when she herself was in no way responsible for them. The frown on his brow, the sudden hardening of his round blue eyes, the rising inflection of his voice lacerated her spirit. To do Mr. Penny justice these choleric outbursts were rare, although of late they had become more frequent; as a general rule he was amiably disposed and his philosophical detachment in the face of unexpected irritations or disappointments was nothing short of remarkable. But just every now and then his iron control snapped and the sunniest day was abruptly plunged into dreadful darkness and no birds sang. The causes of these sudden furies were superficially various but they usually stemmed from the same baleful source, an outrage of some kind to his ego. For even the most adoring and slavish admirers of his public consequence and private grace could not fail to deny that his Ego was a force—albeit an expanding force—to be reckoned with. In fact it had to be admitted bravely and unequivocally, even by his closest friends, that Mr. Penny was "touchy," and the increasing evidences of this "touchiness" during recent years were beginning to cause grave concern. Even Bruiser, whose carapace of self-assurance seldom dented, was worried. "Some of us are working ourselves up into one of our tantrums," he would report gloomily to Miss Mac, having descried the first indications of stormy weather when he had delivered the morning tea. "Some of us have been dreaming something that didn't agree with us, and it's soon going to be lower the boats, and each man for himself." Miss Mac was accustomed to greeting these racy prognostications with outward calm but inner panic, and on the occasions when the portents were bad, she ascended to the bedroom with a heavy heart. On this particular day however there were no significant gale warnings. Bruiser popped his head round the corner of her office on his way down to the kitchen. "Nothing more than a freshening northwesterly breeze this morning," he cried. "There may be a few squalls later but there's no call to batten down the hatches yet at any rate." Bruiser's brief but highly colored career in the Merchant Navy during the war had bequeathed a salty tang to his vocabulary.

On arrival in Mr. Penny's room, she drew up a chair to the side of the bed as she usually did. Mr. Penny looked at her critically.

"Why don't you ever wear the brooch I gave you for Christmas?"

Miss Mac fingered her mulberry-colored cardigan helplessly. "It doesn't go with this," she said.

"Nonsense," said Mr. Penny, "it would go with anything. It's just that you will not take the trouble to tart yourself up a bit. You haven't had your hair done for weeks," he added, buttering a piece of toast. "You're just allowing yourself to go to seed, that's what you're doing."

"There's a very nice letter from that Mrs. Bartock," she said appeasingly.

"What Mrs. Bartock?" Mr. Penny's voice was still unmollified.

"The one you interviewed on 'Ordinary People.' She says that the fact that you picked her out of all those hundreds to talk to has made the whole difference to her life and that she's got a job at Whiteley's."

"Let me see." Mr. Penny stretched out his hand and Miss Mac gave him the letter. He read it through with obvious gratification.

Miss Mac, aware that the sun had burst through the clouds, produced a large gilt-edged card. "Here's your invitation for the Gala Première of *Love and More Love* on Thursday. It says you're to be there sharp at eight-fifteen on account of Princess Margaret arriving at eight-thirty."

"I shall be there at eight twenty-five," said Mr. Penny.

She greeted this harmless braggadocio with an appreciative whinny, and produced a mauve letter from her folder. "This is rather tiresome I'm afraid," she said, handing it to him. "It's from Miss Baxter, as you can see from the writing paper. Auntie Min has fallen down again. It's not serious, she's only bruised her hip, but Miss Baxter is in a state as usual."

"She ought to watch her more carefully." Mr. Penny read the letter irritably. "She doesn't say she was drunk, but I suppose she was." He sighed. Miss Baxter was an ex-hospital matron whom he had engaged to look after Auntie Min in 1959. She was a brusque, efficient woman but a born grumbler. Not that he could altogether blame her; looking after Auntie Min was a full-time job as well as a fairly exasperating one, as he knew to his own cost. Auntie Min had been the mainstay of his life since she had taken charge of him when he was four years old just after his mother and father were killed in a railway accident. It was she who had brought him up and it was she who had played an important role in his essays in journalism. In fact his earliest series of articles for an insignificant weekly magazine had appeared under the heading "Auntie Min and Me." It was this series which had originally attracted the attention of *The Daily Trumpet*. Auntie Min, like Bruiser, had expanded over the years in the agreeable glow of notoriety shed upon her by her nephew's enthusiastic prose. She had put on weight with alarming rapidity and along with the weight an increasing sense of her own importance. Mr. Penny had done his work almost too well and he was forced to watch with some dismay his cozy Frankenstein poaching with cheerful ebullience on his own cherished preserves. It had gradually become more and more irritating when attending some opening night or gala performance with Auntie Min to discover that she was almost as enthusiastically received by the curbside lookers-on as he was. Bruiser at least was never seen in public. Happily, in the mid-fifties when the situation was become really tense, Aunt Min had the first of her falls and was confined to hospital for eight months with a fractured pelvis, and during those eight months Mr. Penny firmly erased her name and personality from the public consciousness. When she finally emerged from her plaster casts, thinner, deflated and a trifle querulous, he dispatched her to a pension in Menton for a further two months and by the time she returned from there her star had set and she retired into well-nourished oblivion. This enforced withdrawal, although irksome at first, she gradually learned to accept, but resignation was not achieved without scenes and tears. The transition from the former Auntie Min, purveyor of bromidic advices and recipes for stuffed eggs and coconut cakes, to an anonymous old lady living in South Kensington took time, and the time it took was a considerable strain on Mr. Penny. He visited her dutifully once or twice a week and endured with admirable stoicism lachrymose outbursts alternating with veiled reproaches and embittered martyrdom. "I'm an old woman and no one cares what happens to me anymore. There was a time when you came to me with all your problems; now of course, when you have so many fine friends to turn to, I don't count." However finally, she ceased to mourn quite so poignantly the warmth of vicarious limelight and settled down contentedly to queen it over her immediate neighbors and enjoy the continual ups and downs of a love-hate relationship with Miss Baxter. Miss Baxter, herself no stranger to the joys of tight-lipped martyrdom, palpably enjoyed the situation as much as she did. Mr. Penny's weekly or bi-weekly visits were high spots to be looked forward to. He came and departed like an invigorating breeze laden with heady fragrances from a larger, more exotic world. He regaled them generously with news of the latest plays and parties and social junketings; he discussed with his usual disarming frankness, leading figures of society and the stage, all of whom he appeared to know intimately, and he invariably left the flat exhilarated by the conviction of a duty done and a good deed accomplished. Only during the last two years had a slight cloud shadowed the gentle glow of these conscientious visits. He had noticed on several occasions that Auntie Min's speech sounded a trifle fuddled and the natural pinkness of her complexion had deepened to a richer hue. Worried by this phenomenon he had questioned Miss Baxter privately and elicited from her, after many anguished evasions, the fact that Auntie Min had of late been drinking a good deal more than was good for her. The shock of this revelation was very painful to Mr. Penny. His first instinct was to berate Miss Baxter for not having told him before and for permitting such a situation to have continued for so long; but, after a few moments of reflection, his anger evaporated and was replaced by a surge of compassion. Miss Baxter vowed that she would never forget until the day she died the expression on his face when, having conquered his immediate rage, he said, with a sad little smile, "Let her drink as much as she wants to. She has little enough pleasure in her life." He had turned away after this pronouncement and she could see by the droop of his shoulders and the clenching and unclenching of his hands that he was profoundly moved.

Bruiser, some time later, when the news inevitably leaked out that Auntie Min was hitting the bottle, had taken a more cynical view.

"The sooner that clacking old mare drinks herself to death the better it will be for His Nibs, and all of us," he remarked to Miss Mac, who, with pursed lips, shuddered at such uncompromising realism.

Mr. Penny handed Miss Baxter's letter back to Miss Mac. "You'd better call up and find out how she is and say I'll be round tomorrow as usual. Today is Thursday, isn't it?" Miss Mac nodded. "Let's have a look at the book." She gave him his engagement book from the bedside table and he looked at it pensively. "Lunch—Chatterworths. Three o'clock Bainbridge Studio 'Hats for Men' photograph. Four o'clock interview Hilary Blair—Savoy Hotel. Six o'clock, rest. Seven o'clock pick up Myfanwy at her flat—Seven-thirty First night *Oh, Mr. Porter.* Ten o'clock dinner—Caprice. Eleven onward Mumble's party." He sighed and put the book back on the bedside table. "I don't know how I get through it all, really I don't." He gave a resigned smile as though chiding himself for his own reckless vitality.

Miss Mac rose. "I'll be in the office if you want me." She looked at him for a moment, lying propped up against the pillows, his russet hair tousled and the blue smoke from his cigarette spiraling up into the air. There was no doubt about it, he did look a little tired. She went out, closing the door quietly behind her, little dreaming that that was the last time she would see him alive.

The first Baron Acton's cynical but accurate statement that "Power tends to corrupt and absolute power corrupts absolutely" is becoming more and more apparent in these overcharged years. In earlier days power was circumscribed by geographical distance and slowness of communication. Napoleon could perhaps sway an audience of several hundred or even several thousand people. Today, however, with the help of television, the radio and the press, he could have impressed the strength of his personality upon several million in a few minutes. We have all watched and listened to political dictators growing more and more inflamed with the sense of their own importance until circumstances combine to rout them or the assassin's weapon strikes them down. In the arts as well as in international politics outstanding egos follow, to a lesser extent, the same timeworn patterns. First the early struggles for recognition, then the first sweet moments of success, then the growing avalanche of publicity and then, except in rare cases, the inevitable decay of humility and common sense. Mr. Penny, in whose character introspection and self-criticism existed in only a minor degree, was, even to those intimates who loved him dearly, gradually approaching the borderline. The symptoms were only too evident; a marked increase of irritability when disagreed with in minor arguments; a tendency to be more sharply critical of his contemporaries than he had ever been before; increasingly recurrent references to the inviolability of his own position and his impromptu triumphs on television and, above all, the growing frequency of his sudden rages. These rages when in full spate were a frightening spectacle. His face went scarlet, his eyes suffused, his voice rose several tones and he developed a violent stammer. Fortunately they were, as a general rule, short-lived, and a little while afterward it was as though they had never been. But both Miss Mac and Bruiser knew that whatever had struck the initial spark, a caustic remark or a real or imagined slight, it would continue to rankle for some time to come, sometimes indefinitely.

Mr. Penny's feuds were unhappily becoming quite famous. He was not on speaking terms with many of his former friends and acquaintances and was liable to become bitter at the mere mention of their names. There was Cedric Blake for instance. Cedric Blake was a successful stage designer and although he and Mr. Penny could never have been described as intimate friends, they were amiable enough to each other when they met at parties or first nights. Then had occurred the dreadful evening at Bobo Montague's when Cedric, possibly under the influence of several dry Martinis, had taunted Mr. Penny in front of a roomful of people with the Marylyn Prosser story. There had been a scene of some violence after which Mr. Penny, scarlet with fury, had stormed out of the house. The Marylyn Prosser story happened to be one of Mr. Penny's rare journalistic errors. It had all begun with a piece in one of the evening papers accompanied with a photograph of a smiling child of thirteen. The headline was "Little Marylyn Interfered with on Wimbledon Common." Mr. Penny, all his trained newspaper instincts tingling, had been hot on the scent and contrived in the short space of an hour to obtain a personal interview with little Marylyn and her parents. This interview he wrote up at length for the second page of *The Sunday Trumpet*. The article, in its way, was a masterpiece and the moral indignation underlying the simple homely description of the wronged little girl and her honest hardworking Mum and Dad, was profoundly moving. Unfortunately however, in course of the domestic interview, he elicited from little Marylyn a detailed description of the fiend who attacked her. He was apparently of medium height, wearing a bottle-green Norfolk jacket, corduroy trousers and brown leather sandals. He also had a small pointed beard. On the strength of Mr. Penny's heartstirring article the man was immediately traced and questioned and turned out to be a perfectly respectable married tobacconist who remembered distinctly seeing little Marylyn in the company of three other children and a cocker spaniel. The three other children were then rounded up and questioned and it transpired that they had been with little Marylyn all the time and that no one had come near her. Then as a final bonne-bouche, little Marylyn had hysterics and confessed that she had made up the whole story inspired by an item she had read several weeks ago in, of all papers, *The Daily Trumpet*. To say that Mr. Penny had been shocked would be an understatement. He had been bitterly disillusioned and made to look ridiculous, added to which he had been further upset by certain snide comments in the press and sharply criticized in certain letters he received in his fan mail.

After a few weeks the Marylyn Prosser scandal faded inevitably from the public consciousness, but on Mr. Penny's vulnerable ego it had left a scar which would take a long, long time to heal completely. Miss Mac indeed privately considered that this perceptible decline in the equability of Mr. Penny's disposition had been set in motion by the perfidy of little Marylyn Prosser. From that base betrayal had stemmed much evil, and it was only since then that

Dr. Maddox had discovered in course of one of his usual checkups a faint but ominous flutter of the heart that had not been apparent before, and had implored him to do less than he was accustomed to doing per day, and to force himself to longer periods of relaxation. Unfortunately however, Mr. Penny's sense of duty, to his legend, his public and to himself was stubborn; he refused to alter, to any marked degree, the stimulating tempo of his life. A public figure has no time to waste on mollycoddling himself. He must press on regardless. Mr. Penny pressed on regardless.

2

Morton, Lady George Chatterworth's butler, flung open the drawing-room door and announced "Mr. Edwin Pendleton" in a stentorian voice and retired. Amy Chatterworth, who was lying on the sofa with a telephone clamped to her ear, waved to Mr. Penny. "You must forgive Morton," she said, putting her hand over the receiver, "he was a famous toastmaster at City banquets for years and I cannot get him out of the habit of bellowing like a bull moose. There's a Martini in that jug, so help yourself. I shan't be a minute."

Mr. Penny, although he didn't as a rule drink in the middle of the day, went to the drink table and poured himself a Martini as ordered. After all, he had finished his Sunday piece only a quarter of an hour ago and felt a bit depleted. His hostess resumed her telephone conversation.

"No, darling, we weren't cut off, it was only Morton roaring as usual—Well if you can't come on Friday, come on Saturday. Donald is driving down and he can bring you. . . . Nonsense, he's a brilliant driver and anyhow he's got a new Jaguar with seat belts. No, dear, that wasn't his fault in the least, the idiotic man with the milk cart came shooting out of a side-turning on the wrong side of the road. It was all settled in the police court and Donald only got a five-pound fine and that was only because the magistrate took against him on sight. Of course nobody was hurt. The milkman had slight concussion, and the High Street was flooded with 'Grade A'—Anyhow, you can't go through life timorously. All right, all right—come on the twelve forty-three from St. Pancras. You'll have to face one of those ghastly railway lunches with gray plaice and hunks of leathery mutton and serve you right. All right, Pugsie will meet you if I can't. See you Saturday." She hung up and swung herself into a sitting position. "That was poor Elspeth, she's always a prey to dreadful fears. I once flew to Rome with her and she never stopped crossing herself from the Air Terminal to the Excelsior. Do sit down and try one of those wild-looking crisps, I believe they're made of Chinese fish. I can't bear them myself but everyone else seems to adore them. You were an angel to come. Lunch is likely to be a bit gruesome, I had to ask old Dora because she's the chairman of the committee and that Mrs. What's-her-name with pince-nez who organizes everything. Apart from them there's only Charlie and Vickie Cartwright, Pugsie, if he gets back in time, Cedric and you and me."

"Cedric Blake?" Mr. Penny swallowed a sharp bit of Chinese crisp and nearly choked.

"Yes, he's been a perfect darling and designed the program cover. I haven't seen it yet but it's to be dotted with colored stars with a *cinque-cento* medallion in the middle held up by two cherubim." She either failed to notice or decided to ignore the expression of displeasure on Mr. Penny's face and went on gaily. "He's also tarting up the Royal Box with toile de Jouy and plastered the private loo with a Nattier wallpaper covered with dainty ladies in swings."

Mr. Penny, with highly commendable savoir faire, managed to smile appreciatively. Nobody would have guessed, after the first shock of dismay at the news that Cedric was coming to lunch, that his heart was leaden in his bosom and his day ruined. Obviously Amy Chatterworth had no idea that he and Cedric were not on speaking terms and, equally obviously, there was nothing he could do about it beyond feigning sudden illness and leaving the house immediately before his enemy entered it. It was a dreadful dilemma and also a crushing disappointment. Mr. Penny always enjoyed lunching or dining with the Chatterworths. They represented the crème de la crème of the younger aristocracy. Lord George Chatterworth (Pugsie) was the third son of the Duke of Lulworth; his wife, *née* The Honorable Amy Melford, had been the most publicized debutante of 1958. Their marriage at St. Margaret's, Westminster, had been the great wedding of the year in 1959. In fact it was because of a romantic description he had written of the ceremony that he had first come to know them. Lord George (Pugsie) followed his wife's lead in encouraging Mr. Penny and quite liking him. This liking, however, was qualified by an embarrassment which he tried valiantly to overcome.

The elderly Duchess to whom Amy Chatterworth had referred so irreverently as "Old Dora" was announced by Morton in a voice of thunder. She was an agreeable, untidy-looking woman whose clothes seemed to be kept together by clips and brooches. She kissed Amy and shook hands with Mr. Penny.

"How nice to meet you at last," she said. "I've heard so much about you from my niece, Jessica."

Mr. Penny glowed with pleasure. The Duchess's niece Jessica was one of his later social conquests.

Lady Jessica was one of those young society matrons whose determination to be "with-it" was almost as strong as Mr. Penny's determination to be "with-it" with her; a mutual sympathy was swiftly established and he had been invited to lunch twice and dinner once in the short space of two months.

The Duchess settled herself in an armchair, her bracelets and brooches clinking gently like Japanese windflowers. Mr. Penny sprang forward with a dry Martini. "I can't imagine," she said, accepting it gratefully, "why I was ever asked to be chairman of this particular committee. I've only been to two meetings in the last three years and nobody ever tells me anything about anything."

"You don't have to worry, darling," said Amy. "Mrs. Broomhead's coming to lunch and she has the whole business cut and dried."

"Oh, dear," the Duchess sipped her Martini and sighed, "I've tried so hard to like her but in vain. I think it's her energy that puts me off. She seems to vibrate all the time like one of those things you plug into the wall."

At this moment Charlie and Vickie Cartwright came into the room. Charlie Cartwright was a dim-looking young man with an undecided chin; Vickie, his wife, was exquisitely dressed and blond with all the assurance of a pretty woman who realizes that her husband is dull and intends to compensate for it with the utmost vivacity. She kissed Amy and the Duchess affectionately, accorded Mr. Penny a ravishing smile and sat next to Amy on the sofa.

"We refused to let Morton announce us," she said, "because Charlie had a mastoid operation only last month and we were afraid the noise might start it up again."

"Be a darling and deal with the drinks," said Amy to Mr. Penny. "I know I ought to do it myself but I'm far too lazy to move. Pugsie always says I have the manners of a warthog."

Mr. Penny, agreeably sensible of the implied intimacy of Amy's request, went to the drink table where he mixed a Bloody Mary for Vickie and a whiskey and soda for Charlie. Beneath his outward suavity his heart was thudding with apprehension. At any moment now Cedric would appear and he had not yet had time to decide on his manner of greeting him. He might be in one of his bitchy, sneering moods. On the other hand of course he might be completely charming, which he could be when he chose. There was just no knowing. Mr. Penny, tormented by his inward dilemma, decided to keep his head and remain poised and calm whatever happened. Mrs. Broomhead arrived, bearing an armful of papers and apologizing profusely for being late. Pugsie strolled in, acknowledged everyone with agreeable casualness and helped himself to a gin and tonic. Still no sign of Cedric. Mr. Penny's spirits began to rise. Perhaps he wasn't coming after all, but this of course was too good to be true. He was just about to embark on a conversation with Vickie Cartwright when Morton's voice crashed through the room. "Mr. Cedric Blake." Cedric stood in the doorway for a moment and surveyed the assembled company. "I know I'm late," he said, "and I expect the soufflé's ruined but you will have to forgive me because I've had the most shattering morning of my life." He kissed Amy, Vickie and the Duchess, shook hands with Charlie and Mrs. Broomhead, patted Pugsie affectionately on the face and turned to Mr. Penny. "Well," he said, "this is a very very tricky moment, isn't it? What are we going to do about it?" Mr. Penny, with a frozen smile put out his hand. "Hallo, Cedric," he said, aware that to any extraperceptive listeners the strain in his voice would be apparent. "Amy's been telling me about the cover you've designed for the program. It sounds marvelous."

"Well done." Cedric shook his hand. "Mistress of herself when china falls." Before anything further could be said a deafening roar from Morton announced that luncheon was served.

There could be no question that from Mr. Penny's point of view the lunch party was an unqualified success. Cedric, the dreaded potential, the hooded cobra in the undergrowth, seemed determined to erase all traces of former unpleasantness. His attitude to Mr. Penny throughout was one of easy camaraderie unblemished by the slightest suggestion of sarcasm. He spoke glowingly of a recent television interview in which Mr. Penny had courageously defended a young unmarried mother from Huddersfield who had refused to marry the father of her child in spite of much religious and paternal pressure, and had accordingly been expelled on the grounds of moral turpitude from the button factory in which she worked. Through Mr. Penny's advocacy and a succession of blasts from *The Daily Trumpet* the girl had been presented with enough money to emigrate to Australia, where also through the influence of *The Daily Trumpet* a suitable job had been procured for her. The Duchess, on whose left Mr. Penny was sitting, had been deeply impressed by the story. "I know one *reads* a lot about the power of the press," she said, "but a case like this really brings it home to one most forcibly. And how fortunate for the poor creature," she continued, recklessly helping herself to more chocolate soufflé, "to have someone like you to stand by her in her time of need. When one thinks of the amount of young unmarried mothers there are all over the place nowadays, it's comforting to know that at least one has had the luck to be whisked overseas where she can start a new life."

"*Another* new life," interpolated Cedric. "She'd already started one."

Mr. Penny joined in the general laughter. He had had two glasses of Moselle as well as the dry Martini and all dormant "touchiness" was buried deep beneath his shining consciousness of social well-being. Before lunch was over he had consented to write a stirring piece about the imminent film première and had also agreed to be one of the reception committee who were to be lined up in the foyer to greet Princess Margaret.

In the drawing room after lunch Cedric, with a cup of coffee in his hand, sidled up to Mr. Penny. "I'm afraid you're hooked," he said in an agreeably conspiratorial whisper, "but it's your own fault for being so radiantly cooperative. You'll just have to squeeze yourself into your best bib and tucker and take it on the jaw." Mr. Penny giggled benignly. On other less harmonious occasions the word "squeeze" might have been a little suspect, but today all was golden.

The photographic session at the Bainbridge studio passed off without incident. The editor of *The Trumpet* was planning to launch a campaign for the brightening of male attire and Mr. Penny had agreed to start the ball rolling with a full-page article for the Sunday edition. He had already typed out some notes on the brilliant satins and silks and brocades of eighteenth-century masculine adornment as compared with the drab tweeds and alpacas of the present day and, using Mother Nature as a valid supporter of his argument, had pointed out that since the beginning of Time male animals, birds and insects were well known to be more gaily colored and resplendent than their female counterparts. He had not extended his analogy to include fish because his knowledge of marine activities was insecure and he found fish dull anyway. *The Trumpet* campaign had started with a bang with an article by Penelope Larch who had suggested saxe-blue or scarlet velvet for evening wear and knee breeches, silver buckles and flowing cloaks of various colors for the daytime. This initial onslaught was to be topped by photographs of Mr. Penny in a series of hats of original design with a further article written in his own inimitable style on the same revolutionary subject. Mr. Penny had been dubious about the idea at first but the large check involved, over and above his normal salary, together with a promise of commission from all the principal hatters in London, had finally quelled his doubts. Paul Bainbridge, the proprietor of the studio, greeted the project with enthusiasm. He was a tall, thin gray man with a pronounced Adam's apple and abnormally long arms. He treated Mr. Penny with tactful, almost servile deference and only made a small moue of dismay when he rejected three of the various hats assembled as being too chi-chi. After the sitting tea was served and Paul Bainbridge, with furtive pride, showed Mr. Penny some private photographs which he kept locked away in a suitcase under the divan. Looking at them passed half an hour agreeably and Mr. Penny finally left glowing with the conviction that he had been democratic, charming and unspoiled and had unquestionably added one more fervent admirer to his collection.

From the Bainbridge studio he drove directly to the Savoy

Hotel for a preliminary interview with Hilary Blair, on whose weekly television series he was scheduled to appear the following Sunday evening. Hilary Blair, whom Mr. Penny had hitherto never met, had a reputation, fully earned, of being a dangerous man to cross swords with. His weekly "hour" was eagerly viewed by several million people. And it was only this fact, coupled with the blandishments of his editor, that had persuaded Mr. Penny reluctantly to submit himself to the experience. It was therefore with some inner trepidation that he was ushered into Blair's river suite at the Savoy. The room was empty when the floor waiter let him in and he sat on the window seat watching the barges and the traffic tearing along the Embankment, irritably aware that his customary sangfroid had temporarily deserted him. The one thing Mr. Penny couldn't stand was being made a mock of and, as Hilary Blair's principal attribute as a TV interviewer was his talent for polite but sardonic mockery, it was not surprising that Mr. Penny should feel ill at ease. However when Blair at last emerged from the adjoining bedroom clad in a blue silk dressing gown and red leather slippers, his immediate affability swept Mr. Penny's apprehensions away and he accepted a gin and tonic and a filter-tipped American cigarette, settled himself in a deep armchair and relaxed. Hilary Blair's technique was carefully calculated and irresistible and before he knew it Mr. Penny was chatting away to him about Auntie Min and Miss Mac and Bruiser and his early struggles as though they had been intimate friends for years. It was not until nearly an hour had passed that catastrophe struck. Whether Mr. Penny's sentimental effusiveness exasperated Hilary Blair beyond endurance or he decided that the interview had gone on too long and wished to get rid of his guest will never be quite clear; at all events he asked a question that cut through the atmosphere of easy camaraderie like a wire through cheese. Still deceptively amiable, still polite, he leant forward with a conspiratorial glint in his eye and said, "But tell me, Edwin—I may call you Edwin, mayn't I?—what do you privately think of all that God-awful hogwash that those idiotic women write to you? Doesn't it sometimes make you want to vomit?"

Mr. Penny sat stunned for a moment feeling the blood suffusing his face and neck and a surge of scalding anger rising from the pit of his stomach. He sprang to his feet and faced Hilary with blazing eyes. Conscious that his legs were trembling he clutched the back of an armchair to steady himself. "How dare you say such a thing? How dare you?!" On the second "how dare you" his voice rose to almost a screech.

"Calm down, old boy," said Hilary equably. "It was a perfectly reasonable question, there's no necessity to work yourself into a tizzy. I merely wondered, that's all."

"It was *not* a reasonable question, it was vulgar and insulting and I see now, only too clearly, that it was also quite typical."

"Hoity-toity!" Hilary looked up at him with a bland smile. "I *have* put my foot in it, haven't I? Come off your perch, there's a dear, and sit down and relax. You'll have a heart attack in a minute. Your eyes are sticking out like prawns. I'm sorry if I offended you, I honestly didn't mean to. There now. I've apologized, so accept it in the spirit in which it was offered and have another drink."

"I will *not* accept your apology. I will *not* have another drink and what's more I shall never speak to you again until the day I die."

"That will be sooner than you think unless you learn to control your schoolgirl tantrums."

"I have met enough envy and jealousy in my life to be able to recognize it when I see it." Mr. Penny spoke with quivering disdain. "What you said just now stamps you as the mean, frustrated, unsuccessful journalistic hack I've always suspected you to be."

"There's a reply to that I couldn't bring myself to utter in the presence of ladies."

Mr. Penny walked to the door and turned. "Good-bye Hilary." He spoke in a tone of withering grandeur. "I'm sorry our friendship should have to end like this."

"Nonsense," replied Hilary. "It hasn't ended at all, for the simple reason that it never existed."

Mr. Penny went out, slamming the door with such force that a china shepherdess fell off the mantelpiece and shattered to pieces in the fireplace.

Mr. Penny drove home to his house in Egerton Mews in a state verging on hysteria. Before he had time to get out his latchkey Bruiser opened the front door and looked at him in dismay. "Goodness gracious me," he said. "Whatever in the world has happened? You look white as a fish's belly."

Mr. Penny pushed past him and walked upstairs to his bedroom. "I've had a very unpleasant experience," he said over his shoulder, "so I'm going to lie down for a little. Get me a couple of aspirin and a glass of water and tell Miss Mac I shan't need her anymore. You can also tell her that if Mr. Hilary Blair rings up at any time of the day or night, that I am not in."

Bruiser, on his way to get the iced water, paused at the open door of the office. Miss Mac, with the inevitable cup of tea beside her, was typing a letter. "There's been a tiff, dear," he said *sotto voce*. "His Nibs and our Hilary have had a proper upper and downer. Keep your fingers crossed and pray for a change of wind."

A little later, when Bruiser had brought Mr. Penny the aspirin and he had swallowed it, his accumulated emotions became too much for him, and he burst into sobs. "There there, dear," said Bruiser, automatically, being well accustomed to such outbursts.

"Lie down on the bed like a good boy and let me do your neck and back. We can't have you going to the theater tonight all tensed up with red eyes, can we?"

Mr. Penny lay obediently on the bed face downward and allowed Bruiser's experienced hands to relax his muscles. He continued to weep quietly for a little but after a while the rhythmic massage soothed him and he managed to go off to sleep.

Mr. Penny, after his nap and the aspirin, woke feeling calmer. The hateful image of Hilary Blair's cynical leer slipped into his consciousness for a moment but with commendable willpower he dismissed it with the contempt it deserved. He shared his bath, as usual, with a large pink celluloid duck called Mrs. Siddons, which he had cherished sentimentally for many years. Once indeed he had referred to it in one of his Sunday articles, but the editor had tactfully persuaded him to cut it on the grounds that it might appear, to some of his more unimaginative readers, a thought too whimsical.

"I'm afraid there's something a bit dodgy about Mrs. Siddons," said Bruiser as he helped him off with his dressing gown. "She keeps falling over on her side. She must have sprung a leak somewhere. We can't very well send her to the vet, can we?"

Mr. Penny acknowledged this callous witticism with a thin smile and got into the bath.

Later, sipping a dry Martini at Myfanwy Jessel's flat, the afternoon's unpleasantness receded still further. Myfanwy was one of his most devoted adorers. She was a bulky, enthusiastic spinster in her mid-fifties who accorded to everything Mr. Penny wrote an uncritical, almost Biblical reverence. She had a small private income augmented by an occasional check for proofreading for a publisher friend of hers who specialized in children's books. Mr. Penny frequently asked her to go to First Nights with him, firstly because he liked to "give the poor old girl a treat" and, more important, because she was no trouble and could be bundled off home in a taxi directly after the play, leaving him free to sup quietly with a few special cronies or go, when invited, to the routine First Night party given either by the star of the show or by the management. On this fateful evening, having consumed two cocktails and some pungent little canapés which Myfanwy had concocted from a recipe in *Paris Match*, they set forth in the hired limousine that Mr. Penny always rented for such occasions. Myfanwy was wearing a simple black dinner dress which Mr. Penny approved of and a Chinese mandarin coat which he did not. Owing to a press of traffic in Piccadilly they arrived at the theater a few minutes after the curtain had risen, which put Mr. Penny in a bad mood to start with. He was always punctilious about being on time at a theater because, as he said with his usual forthright realism, a writer of his reputation had to set a good example. Having hurriedly collected his tickets from the box office without glancing at them, they went down the stairs and were ushered into two aisle seats in the last row but one.

Mr. Penny, shocked beyond measure, hissed at the program girl, "I think there's been some mistake."

She produced an electric torch and shone it onto the ticket stubs in his hand. "That's right," she said briskly. "Row O, numbers Fourteen and Fifteen."

With a tremendous effort at self-control Mr. Penny said, this time a little above a whisper, "I have never sat in Row O in my life and I have no intention of doing so now."

By then however she had left him to look after another group of latecomers.

He stood dazed for a moment clutching Myfanwy's hand, then, conscious of a sharp pain in his left arm and a thunderous pounding of blood in his ears, he stumbled forward to a vacant stall in the second row on the aisle, collapsed into it and died.

A monumental lady next to him swathed in emerald green taffeta shrank back, imagining him to be drunk.

"Really," she said in a voice of outraged disgust. "The West End Theatre is certainly not what it used to be."

The funeral, which took place three days later, attracted such vast crowds that special police had to be sent for to maintain order. This was far from easy because many of the anonymous mourners were in a state of shrieking hysteria. One diminutive woman wearing pince-nez and a pink nylon raincoat pushed through the cordon and tried to fling herself into the grave but was hauled back and sent home in an ambulance.

Bruiser, standing with Miss Mac, blew his nose vigorously. "Think what a story His Nibs could have made out of this," he said.

They turned and walked slowly toward the cemetery gates.

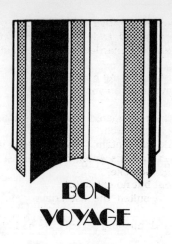

BON
VOYAGE

Captain Berringer glanced through the list of names that the purser laid before him, said, "Oh, Christ!" and buried his head in his hands.

Outside, in the gathering dusk, the myriad lights of San Francisco receded against the darkening sky while through the porthole the plaintive shrieks of seagulls wheeling and squabbling over the wake sounded melancholy, almost valedictory, as though they were bidding the ship good-bye for ever. Olaf Hansen, the purser, whose professional cheerfulness had been enhanced by four straight vodkas in the doctor's cabin, gave a slight snigger. Captain Berringer looked at him balefully.

"What's so funny?"

"Mrs. Kaplan sent you her best regards."

"Well you can wipe that grin off your face or I'll have her transferred to your table."

"She wouldn't stand for it. Nothing but the best for that old meat-axe. After all this is her third cruise with us, we've got to give her the full treatment."

"Yes, Goddamnit, I know we have." The captain sighed and looked at the list again. "What about the others?"

The purser, breathing rather heavily, leaned over the captain's shoulder. "Sir Roderick and Lady Bland. He's an ex-governor of Singapore. Their daughter married out there and they're visiting her."

"Leaving the ship at Hong Kong?"

"Yes. She'll have to be on your right."

"What about Mrs. K?"

"Left." The purser sniggered again. "I explained the situation to her and she took it quite well."

"Big deal!" said the captain. "Why's this one underlined?"

"Lola Widmeyer. Famous writer. Bestseller list twice running."

"What does she look like?"

"Well turned out but no chicken."

The captain consulted the list again. "Mr. and Mrs. Teitelbaum?"

"No trouble. Both pushing seventy. He had his gallbladder out a couple of months ago."

The captain groaned. "Special diet I suppose?"

"That's all taken care of." The purser spoke soothingly. "I talked to Peppo and he's got everything taped."

"Anybody *under* seventy?"

"Those two." The purser pointed with a nicotine-stained finger. "Honeymoon couple. He's the son of Senator Wendle. She's quite a dish."

"If she's on her honeymoon it doesn't matter if she's a dish or not. Couldn't you have found me *one* reasonably unattached female in the whole damned passenger list? Just someone I could look at without wanting to shoot myself?"

"The list's made up in the head office. It's not my fault."

"Who's this?" The captain pointed to the last name on the list.

"Bad news, I'm afraid." The purser sighed. "Eldrich Trumbull the Third. Son of General Trumbull. Mid-thirties, stinking rich, married and divorced three times and looks to me like an alcoholic. Anyway he was loaded when he came on board."

"Thanks a million, Hansen." The captain rose wearily to his feet. "I don't know what I should do without you"

2

Mrs. Irma Z. Kaplan, having unpacked, sat on a stool in front of her dressing table and contemplated her reflection in the looking glass. Her hair, which had been washed, set, permed and blue-rinsed that very morning in the beauty parlor of the Fairmount Hotel, retreated from her rather protruding forehead and gleamed with a sophisticated sheen. Her pearls also gleamed satisfactorily against the ocher of her neck. Her wrapper was periwinkle blue and edged with mara-bou. She had had her doubts about it in the shop on account of the color being a bit harsh, but these doubts now were dispelled. She scrutinized her face with loving thoroughness and tentatively ap-plied a little of the mauve eyeshadow which Madame Renee had forced upon her as a parting gift. She put her head a little on one side and observed the result, then, with a nod of satisfaction, put on a little more. The face she was examining with such meticulous care looked back at her with smiling complacency. There were compara-tively few lines imposed by the ravaging years. Irma Kaplan, née Schultz, even in the days of her youth in Springfield, Illinois, had never been a beauty in the strictly classical sense. Her nose was too small for one thing and her chin too large, but there was "some-thing," a glint of animation in her small gray eyes, a certain style in her bearing which had marked her out from her contemporaries. Even in those far-off days, she reflected with a nostalgic sigh, at picnics, barbecues, weeny-roasts and poor Sybil Huberman's coming-out dance, it was always she who had the local young men clamoring for her favors. She remembered her mother saying to her on that very occasion in a tone of semi-humorous reproof: "You must re-member dear that this is *Sybil's* night!"

With a rueful little laugh she glanced at a photograph of her late husband framed in red leather which, at the moment, was half obscured by a pot of vanishing cream. She removed the pot and looked at the photograph gravely. It was an enlarged snapshot origi-nally taken on a golf course in Bermuda on their silver wedding an-niversary. The camera had caught the late Howard Z. Kaplan in a rare moment of genial abandon. He was wearing tartan Bermuda shorts, an open-necked shirt and a raffia hat and was waving a golf club in the air obviously having just completed a successful drive. His legs, which were none too long at the best of times, looked foreshortened owing to the angle of the camera and he was notice-ably overweight, nevertheless the photograph was a gay memento of one of their happier vacations. The slight blur on the right of the pic-ture was the foot of Mr. Eberhart, the manager of the Coral Strand Hotel. Poor old Howard. Irma's serene forehead puckered into a wist-ful frown. Those two weeks in Bermuda in 1955, although they had both naturally been unaware of it at the time, had been the begin-ning of the end. Only three days after they had returned to Scarsdale he had had a stroke in the men's room at the country club and been rushed off in an ambulance to the Gottlieb Memorial Hospital where, twenty-four hours later, he had died. Irma, who was with him at the end, could recall vividly the small green-painted room and the high white bed on which Howard lay breathing stertorously with his eyes closed. Before lapsing into his final coma he had regained consciousness for a few minutes, opened his eyes and stared at her. Irma had always been puzzled by the expression on his face. He mumbled something and she had leant forward to catch what he was trying to say; he made another attempt and with a supreme effort reared himself up onto his pillow; she patted his hand. This time his words were clear. He said, "Okay Irma—you win!" After which he had fallen back with his eyes shut and his mouth open and, even now, nine years later, she still wondered what he could possibly have meant. She transferred her gaze from Howard's photograph back to her own reflection in the mirror and tried to decide whether to retire to bed and have the steward bring her a light dinner on a tray or whether to put on her plain black, have a cocktail at the bar and go down to the saloon. Captain Berringer wouldn't be down of course, he never dined in the saloon on the first night at sea, but she was curious to see his other privileged guests, particularly the British governor's lady who, for reasons of pure protocol, so Hansen had assured her, had superseded her on the captain's right hand. Whatever she was like, Irma certainly had the edge on her, having already made two trips on the ship and being on familiar but dignified terms with Peppo, the maître d', Mr. Reiner, the chief steward, and most of the rest of the ship's personnel. She decided, after a few more moments' consideration, to have a bath, redo her face, put on her Balmain-via-Bergdorf Goodman cocktail gown instead of the plain black and see what adventures and encounters the evening had in store.

3

Lisa Wendle lay on one of the twin beds in A178 wearing a diaphanous négligée and smoking a cigarette. She had large gray eyes set wide apart, blond hair, a generous mouth, a slim, well-proportioned figure and superb legs. Orford, her bridegroom, aged twenty-three, was still fussing about putting socks in drawers and suits on hangers.

"I see that I have married a neat and tidy man," said Lisa. "I've always been warned about neat and tidy men, they're liable to be frigid."

"The hell they are."

"Who are all those carnations from? The yellow ones."

Orford glanced at the card attached to them. "Peggy and Grover."

"Why don't you take off your shirt? You look much nicer without it."

"According to the traditions of my family, which as you know is pure Beacon Hill, a virgin bride shouldn't have the faintest idea what her husband looks like without his shirt."

"Bride I may be, but virgin comes under the heading of wishful thinking."

"I don't know what the younger generation is coming to."

"I do," said Lisa, stubbing out her cigarette, "and it's lovely."

"I'll take my shirt off if you'll promise to lay off me until I've sorted out these ties."

"After all we *are* on our honeymoon—Ah—that's better." Orford took off his shirt, bent over and kissed her austerely on the forehead. "Not exactly carnal, but better." She ran her fingers lightly over his chest. "Do you suppose you are going to get hairier and hairier as you grow older and older?"

"I expect so. " Orford returned to his ties. "It runs in the family. The first time I saw my father, the senator, in the shower, I thought he was wearing an astrakhan coat."

"Give me another swig of that tepid champagne."

Orford poured out a glass of champagne and brought it to her. She sat up and sipped it, looking thoughtfully at him over the rim of the glass. "Little did I think" she said, "when I first saw you in that 'Hasty Pudding Club show' wearing falsies and a blond wig that I should one day be the mother of your children!"

"You're not yet."

"We haven't really concentrated up to now."

"I was planning to surprise you after dinner."

"I'd rather you surprised me before dinner."

"What if the steward comes in with some merry goodwill telegrams?"

"Lock the door."

"What if I'm timid and nervous and too overcome by the tensions and stresses of this sacred day to be able to make the grade?"

"That," said Lisa placing her champagne glass carefully on the bedside table and pulling him down onto her, "would surprise me very much indeed!"

Orford buried his face in her neck and slipped his hand inside her négligée.

"What about the door?" she murmured.

"It's already locked."

"You think of everything."

"I love you my darling."

4

Mrs. Henry Teitelbaum, encased in Bois de Rose taffeta, rubbed some Mary Chess's "Gardenia"·behind her tiny pink ears and, seating herself on the small sofa beneath the porthole, waited placidly for her husband to come out of the bathroom. She gazed happily round the cabin. There was a large, cellophane-wrapped basket of fruit from the Kindlers; a mauve two-pound box of Sherry's candies from Clara and George and a pretty pot of azaleas from dear Dr. Weatherfield. In addition to these tributes there was a pile of opened telegrams on the end of the dressing table. She reached for them and read them through again. "BON VOYAGE LAURA"—"HAVE A GOOD TRIP HILDA AND DIETER"—"COME BACK SOON WE MISS YOU ALREADY PEACHIE AND JOE"—Mrs. Teitelbaum felt almost teary. She was always inclined to become a little emotional whenever she thought of Peachie and Joe. Peachie was her recently acquired niece; Joe, her sister Louise's boy, had met Peachie at the Chicago Institute of Technology where he was doing a course and they had fallen in love and got married all in a minute. At least it seemed all in a minute although actually three months had elapsed between their first encounter and the wedding. But there was no keeping up with Time nowadays, it went in a flash. It seemed only yesterday that Joe, in swaddling clothes, had been brought to the house in Mayfield Street, but it wasn't only yesterday, it was twenty-two years ago. At this moment Mrs. Teitelbaum's reflections were interrupted by Henry coming out of the bathroom. He still looked a little drawn after his operation poor darling, but he was gaining weight and some of his old sparkle was gradually returning. He was wearing a white shirt and the pants of his tuxedo. On his face was an expression of frustration and in his hand, a dark purple evening tie.

"It's no good, honey," he said. "You'll have to fix it for me. I can't manage the darned thing."

Mrs. Teitelbaum rose with alacrity and, standing him in front of her facing the dressing-table mirror, she adroitly tied the tie into a neat bow and then helped him on with his madras dinner jacket. A steward passed along the passage striking a series of musical chimes for a gong.

"Does that mean that we have to go down right now?"

Mr. Teitelbaum pondered the question for a moment while his wife looked at him in wild surmise.

"It's probably only the first call. We'll have a drink in the bar anyway."

"Oh, Henry—do you think you *should?*"

"The Doc said I could have a whiskey sour before dinner."

"We *are* at the captain's table owing to that letter Mr. Edelston wrote. It wouldn't do to be late."

"To hell with it," Henry patted her cheek reassuringly. "We're paying for the trip ain't we?"

Mrs. Teitelbaum smiled. Henry's indomitable spirit of independence had impressed her for fifty years.

5

Eldrich Trumbull the Third lay stark naked on the bed in A121 and watched his cabin steward finish unpacking his suitcases. On the table at his side stood a double Scotch and soda from which he took an occasional sip. The cabin steward, a Japanese boy, shot his nude passenger a furtive glance from time to time accompanied by a slight hissing sound. Eldrich lit a cigarette.

"Where you allee samee come from?" he enquired in a labored attempt at pidgin English.

The steward smiled exposing a great number of teeth. "My birth was in Yokohama," he replied; "but now my home is San Francisco."

"What's your name?"

"Kito."

"Married?"

"No, sir. Not married, but plenty fliends," Kito laughed hilariously.

"Very sensible," said Eldrich. "You look after me allee samee chop-chop and I give you good present at the end of trip. Now put out the gray suit and one of those blue shirts. I've got to get myself down to the captain's table before I die."

"Yes sir." Kito took a gray suit on a hanger from the closet and hooked it over the door, then he laid out a blue shirt on a chair and selected shoes and socks which he placed neatly by the bed. Eldrich, who had by now polished off what was left of his Scotch highball, rose a little unsteadily and patted him on the shoulder.

"You are a lovely boy, Kito," he said; "and we are all set for a fascinating relationship, providing that you never forget that under this gay, cynical exterior I am a profoundly tragic figure. I am also"— he added—"an enthusiastic and dedicated lush." Observing a bewildered expression on Kito's face, he placed both hands on his shoulders and shook him gently. "Do you know what a lush is?"

"No sir." Kito blinked and made an effort to break away but Eldrich held him firmly.

"A lush," went on Eldrich, shaking Kito rhythmically backward and forward, "is a drunk—an alcoholic—a poor wretched victim of life's hurlyburly who seeks escape from the exhausting attentions of women, men, dogs, children, horses, parrots and what all. At least that's the sort of lush I am. There are other varieties of course, gray, defeated men with sagging bellies and very very narrow shoulders. These fly to the demon alcohol for other reasons. I have not yet, as you observe, developed a sagging belly and my shoulders are magnificent." He paused and held Kito still for a moment staring intently into his face. "But my problem, as you have possibly also observed, is that I am too Goddamned physically attractive. This radiant shaft of self-revelation illumined my mind only after I had been victimized, devoured and rejected by a series of predatory bitches, to three of whom I am forced to pay heavy alimony. You Kito, born in Yokohama and at present domiciled in San Francisco, are hereby charged with protecting me not only from the blood-sucking vampires who undoubtedly infest this ungainly vessel, but from my own psychological despair. You are hereby also charged with the heavenly task of cosseting me, mothering me, massaging me, procuring heady firewater for me at any moment of the day or night and, in general, worshipping me. This last injunction, I may add, must be carried out with discretion. I am in no mood at the moment for emotional involvements. Owing to the rarefied circumstances of my life I am forced into the position of being a V.I.P. which in turn forces me to be a guest at the captain's table and for which my father, who was a famous general, a man of iron and fire and flame and a cracking bore, is entirely responsible."

Eldrich, suddenly letting go of Kito who staggered slightly and retreated toward the bathroom, went to his wallet which was lying on the dressing table, extracted a hundred-dollar bill from it and waved it in the air like a flag.

"This," he said, "is a material token of our newly born spiritual affinity. You may now vanish in a cloud of smoke and indulge in any shady occupations that your devious mind can devise." He pressed the hundred-dollar bill into Kito's hand. Kito stared at it incredulously for a moment and then, with a prolonged hiss, bowed low.

"You are indeed a most beautiful and wonderful man." He stared at him adoringly for a moment and then backed out of the cabin.

"Jesus!" muttered Eldrich, sitting down on the bed. "I've done it again!"

6

In M152, Lady Bland, attired in a two-piece gray traveling suit, screwed a small pearl earring into her right ear. Her husband, Sir Roderick, a pale man in the early sixties, was standing by the porthole gloomily scanning the passenger list.

"No hope of anyone we know I suppose?" said Lady Bland over her shoulder.

Sir Roderick grunted. "No, and very little hope of anyone we'd want to know. I've never seen such a lot of ghastly names in my life. I can't think where they get them from. Eldrich Trumbull the Third! Can you beat that!"

"Trumbull's quite a well-known American name. There was a

Harriet Trumbull at school in Lausanne during Sarah's last term. She was quite a nice girl as far as I can remember, but noisy."

"They're all noisy," said Sir Roderick.

"I'm dreading the captain's table but I suppose we'd better go down and get it over and done with."

"It'll be a mixed bag I expect."

"I know there's a honeymoon couple and a woman novelist," Lady Bland sighed. "The purser told me some of the other names but I've forgotten them. I'm not sure that one of them wasn't your Trumbull the Third."

She rose from the dressing table, a tall, distinguished-looking woman with only slightly projecting teeth. Her skin was good and her figure well preserved for her age. It was not difficult to imagine her presiding with gracious austerity at shining mahogany dinner tables in remote Government Houses. She wore a string of genuine but unremarkable pearls, a diamond and sapphire brooch and excellent rings. Her hair, ash brown in its heyday, had been discreetly touched up and was now ash gray.

"I met what they call the 'Cruise Hostess' on the promenade deck just after we had sailed," said Sir Roderick. "She rushed at me suddenly out of a doorway, wrung my hand like a pump handle and said that it was just wonderful having me on board and that if there was anything I wanted she would arrange it for me. I can't think what she meant."

"I met her too outside the purser's office when I was putting away my valuables. The poor thing looked raving mad to me. I must say I don't envy her job. Imagine what it must be like ricocheting back and forth across the Pacific and having to cope with all those ghastly tourists?"

"Shall we find out where the bar is and have a stengah or something?"

"By all means. I feel absolutely exhausted. Three days with the Lorrimers, kind as they are, were really too much of a good thing, and that suffocatingly overheated house gave me claustrophobia."

They left the cabin and proceeded along the shining, hygienic corridor in the direction of the lift.

7

Lola Widmeyer, an experienced traveler, had insisted on a cabin on the sun deck. It had its disadvantages of course. People were apt to stamp up and down in the early mornings and there was usually a preponderance of children, but taken by and large it was, for her purposes, more convenient. She suffered from insomnia and often during the night she became oppressed by the air-conditioned stuffiness of her cabin and had to get out into the open air to soothe her nerves. Many a dawn on many a ship had discovered her, warmly clad in a sweater, skirt and scarf, staring out over the monotonous sea to the newly glowing sky. In her early life Lola had been a newspaper woman and the training had stood her in good stead later when she decided to renounce journalism and become a writer of novels. She wrote economically and well and the habit of writing was ingrained in her. No newly acquired fame or money or luxurious circumstances could prize her away from her typewriter for any length of time. Every morning, ill or well, rain or shine, she sat herself automatically before her portable Olivetti and tapped away for three or four hours. To say that she was either happy or unhappy would be too easy a simplification. She was certainly lonely, but loneliness and solitude were necessary adjuncts to her trade. Now that she was fifty she began to realize, a trifle ruefully perhaps, that social relations were only valuable to her insofar as they contributed to her work. She had acquired over the years a handful of genuine friends who were precious to her. She was reasonably famous, sought-after, intelligent, didactic, vital and, on the whole, content.

When the steward passed her door banging out the musically harmonious chimes to announce dinner, she rose from the bed on which she had been lying fully dressed, pitched the paperback thriller she had been reading with growing irritation into the wastepaper basket and went over to her dressing table to set her face in order. Unlike Mrs. Irma Z. Kaplan she looked at her reflection without enthusiasm. She was willing to concede that her eyes and eyelashes were good and that the bone structure of her face had so far resisted the interference of Time. There were as yet no signs of sagging flabbiness and her skin, although a trifle sallow, was smooth. Her dark brown hair had had some telltale streaks of gray discreetly removed and her well cared for teeth had been capped and reorganized whenever her dentist had considered it necessary. She smiled at herself rather grimly. The years already seemed to be passing with increasing speed and when another ten of them had gone she would be sixty. She applied a little dry rouge to her high cheekbones, rubbed it in with her forefinger and powdered over it, filled her cigarette case and put it in her bag with her lighter and lipstick and went out of the cabin.

8

Adolph Reiner, the chief steward, surveyed the half-empty dining saloon with a cold eye. He looked at his wristwatch and glanced disdainfully at the few tables that *were* occupied. A crummy-looking lot, chiefly family groups, most of whom had already reached the dessert course. There were, he noted, too many children as usual. He beckoned to Peppo Vega, the maître d'hôtel, a swarthy, perpetually smiling Venezuelan, and nodded toward the captain's table, which was situated at the opposite end of the saloon from the glass entrance doors and was now unoccupied.

"Have you checked how many of them are coming down?"

"They're all coming down."

"Where the hell are they then?"

"In the bar."

"You'd better go up and winkle them out. We don't want to be here all night."

At this moment Mr. and Mrs. Teitelbaum stepped apologetically out of the elevator.

"The name is Teitelbaum," said Mr. Teitelbaum. "The captain's table."

The chief steward smiled remotely, noting from their manner and the fact that they were in evening dress, that they were inexperienced travelers, obviously ill at ease and of no account whatsoever.

"Mr. Vega will take care of you."

Peppo bowed, flashed them a dazzling smile and set off through the sea of tables. They followed him, Mrs. Teitelbaum gripping her husband's arm. She was suddenly aware that everyone but themselves was in day clothes. When Peppo had left them forlornly seated side by side and gone to fetch the menu, she shot Henry a look of anguish.

"We're the only ones dressed," she whispered. "We ought to have asked somebody."

"Who cares!" He spoke with defiance although beneath his outward bravado he was conscious of embarrassment. "We've got a right to doll ourselves up if we feel like it. It's a free country ain't it?"

"Oh, Henry!" Mrs. Teitelbaum gave an unconvincing little giggle and jumped as Peppo suddenly appeared from behind her with the menu. Before she had time to look at it Sir Roderick and Lady Bland arrived at the table escorted by the chief steward himself.

"The captain sends his compliments and regrets that he will not be coming down to dinner this evening. He always remains on the bridge on the first night at sea."

"How reassuring," murmured Lady Bland vaguely.

"I don't suppose it matters much how we are placed does it?" said Sir Roderick. "The captain can rearrange us tomorrow if he sees fit."

"You are welcome to sit wherever it pleases Your Excellency." The chief steward bowed, smiled and retreated to his point of vantage by the entrance doors.

Lady Bland turned to the Teitelbaums. "How do you do?" she

said. "As there is nobody here to introduce us I suppose we had better introduce ourselves."

Mr. and Mrs. Teitelbaum rose to their feet as though summoned by some piercing trumpet call.

"The name is Teitelbaum," they said almost in unison.

"Fancy!" said Lady Bland before she could stop herself. "Roddy, this is Mr. and Mrs. Teitelbaum—I am Lady Bland and this is my husband, Sir Roderick." She leant forward and shook hands while Sir Roderick bowed. Lady Bland, noting Mrs. Teitelbaum's pink face, seized, with commendable intuition, on the cause of it. "How sensible of you to change for dinner. So few people do nowadays and it's such a pity. Personally I hate this idiotic convention of not dressing on the first night at sea. One has to have a bath and freshen up anyhow so one might just as well put on an evening frock while one's at it. I would have myself only my husband was too lazy to put on a dinner jacket."

"Actually we didn't know what we ought to do," said Mrs. Teitelbaum, responding to the kindness of Lady Bland's tone with an outburst of frankness. "You see, this is the first time we've been on a cruise, either of us. As a matter of fact it's the first time we've ever been out of the United States—Imagine! My husband's been sick and the doctor said he must have a rest and a change of air."

"Very sound advice," grunted Sir Roderick devoting himself to a menu that Peppo had flicked before him.

At this moment Lola Widmeyer came up to the table and pulled out a chair for herself facing the Teitelbaums. She nodded briskly to them and to the Blands as she seated herself.

"I always find the first evening of a voyage rather demoralizing," she said, looking round at the, by now, almost empty dining room. "I had half a mind to stay in my cabin and order something from room service but I thought better of it. My name is Lola Widmeyer."

Mrs. Teitelbaum gave a subdued squeak of satisfaction. "Well of all things!" she exclaimed. "This is indeed an unexpected pleasure. There was a debate in our local literary club only last week on your new novel. Mrs. Larch, our president, who's really a brilliant woman, said it was the finest book she had read since *The Grapes of Wrath*."

"In that case," replied Lola with a smile, "I fear her literary intake must be fairly meager."

"I am Lady Bland and this is my husband Sir Roderick." Lady Bland leant forward. "And these are Mr. and Mrs. Teitelbaum."

Lola bowed perfunctorily all round and accepted a menu from Peppo, who was hovering at her elbow. "Now that we all know who we are I suppose the next thing is to decide what we're going to eat."

"The sole Amandine is very good," suggested Peppo.

"Amandine means nuts doesn't it?" inquired Mrs. Teitelbaum. When Peppo nodded assent she shook her head. "No nuts for you Henry. You know what Doc Weatherfield said."

"I could scrape them off," said Henry wistfully.

"Better not risk it."

"What's fried chicken Southern style?" asked Sir Roderick.

"It is really Chicken Maryland, sautéed in butter with corn fritters, fried banana and pommes croquettes."

"You know you can't stand fried bananas," said Lady Bland. "Why don't we both go in for a small steak?"

"All right."

"Rare or medium, madame?"

"Medium, please. And would you be very kind and cut off any fat? Sir Roderick detests fat."

"Certainly, madame."

"I'll have marinated herring and a plain omelet," said Lola in a tone that brooked no argument.

Mrs. Teitelbaum, after a whispered conversation with her husband, ordered chicken à la king, green salad with Roquefort dressing and apple pie à la mode for them both.

"I do hope," said Lady Bland, filling in a pause, "that the weather stays pleasant for the first few days at least. It's so tiresome when everything starts falling about—personally I always . . ."

The rest of her sentence died away owing to the arrival of Irma Z. Kaplan, followed, a trifle unsteadily, by Eldrich Trumbull the Third. General introductions were exchanged while Irma bowed, with ostentatious recognition, to Peppo and every steward within sight. "They're all old friends of mine," she said. "I've been on this ship so often that I'm almost one of the family."

"Perhaps you can explain to me, then," said Sir Roderick, "why it is impossible to get one's cabin steward without telephoning somebody called a bell captain?"

"I'm afraid that's the usual system on American ships," Irma Kaplan gave an indulgent laugh.

"It seems like a waste of time to me. Leaving aside the fact that the chap's line is liable to be engaged it would surely be far simpler to ring an ordinary bell in an ordinary way like everybody else does."

"*Autres tempes, autres moeurs,*" murmured Lady Bland conciliatively.

At this moment Lisa and Orford Wendle arrived at the table. "I'm afraid we're the last!" Lisa included everyone in a wide, guileless smile. "It's all my husband's fault. He took ages over his unpacking. He has a passion for neatness, like an old spinster in a boardinghouse. Everything has to be smoothed and folded and put in the right place."

"I took a course in valeting at Harvard," said Orford.

Lisa sat down next to Sir Roderick and smiled at him. "I know you're Sir Roderick Bland because the chief steward told me, but I should have known you were British anyway from your manner. Only the British have that particular sort of 'something' about them."

"An ambiguous statement if ever I heard one," said Lola.

Orford, who was sitting next to her, turned to her with a grin. "I'm afraid my girl bride's determination to be fascinating is sometimes a little heavy-handed. At the moment she is overexcited and the teeniest bit 'high'—we must all make allowances."

"Well!" exclaimed Irma Kaplan. "What a thing to say!"

"Harvard is well known to produce the finest type of aristocratic manhood in America," said Lisa. "My husband, as you see, is an outstanding example of the system."

Lady Bland gave a polite little laugh and bit cautiously into an olive.

"I presume," said Eldrich Trumbull, gripping the edge of the table with one hand and signaling to the wine waiter with the other, "that our esteemed host the chief, the old man, the captain and commander of this floating caravanserai is busy coping with marine perils on the bridge?"

"The captain *never* comes down to dinner on the first night out of port," said Irma with the patronizing air of one well accustomed to the vagaries of nautical behavior.

"If I were the captain I wouldn't come down at all." Eldrich beamed round the table. "No offense intended to any of the distinguished company here assembled." He turned to the wine waiter who had appeared at his elbow. "A double Rob Roy on the rocks." He looked round the table again. "Will anyone join me?"

"Thank you," said Lola. "I will. I didn't have a drink before I came down and I am feeling depleted."

"God bless you Mr. Copperfield," said Eldrich. "I hate drinking alone."

"I find that difficult to believe but we'll let it go for the moment."

"*Touché,*" said Eldrich blandly and turned to the wine waiter. "Two double Rob Roys on the rocks."

"Before committing myself irrevocably," said Lola, "I should like to know what a Rob Roy is."

"A heady mixture of whiskey and vermouth. Actually it's a Manhattan only made with Scotch instead of bourbon."

"I seldom drink cocktails," volunteered Irma Kaplan. "I much prefer a nice glass of dry sherry."

575

"Then have one." Eldrich clawed the wine waiter by the sleeve as he was about to move away. "A glass of the driest possible sherry for the lady in the pretty blue dress."

"My name is Irma Z. Kaplan," said Irma.

"What does the Z stand for?" enquired Eldrich.

"My late husband's middle name was Zaccariah."

"I knew a chap at Harvard whose middle name was Nebuchadnezzar," said Eldrich. "He used to play the oboe."

"I didn't mean when I said I liked a glass of dry sherry that I wanted one now," said Irma, slightly flustered.

"Nonsense! Grasp the nettle danger. This may be our only chance to carouse. After tonight we shall be writhing under the steely eye of the captain who is probably a militant prohibitionist."

"He most certainly isn't anything of the sort." Irma spoke with some heat. "He's a very convivial and charming man." She turned to Lady Bland. "This is my third cruise on this ship you know. I make a trip every year."

"How nice," replied Lady Bland.

"This is the first time Henry, my husband, and I have ever been on a ship at all!" announced Mrs. Teitelbaum. "Would you believe it?"

Upon this there was a momentary silence during which everyone stared at a bowl of celery, olives, carrots, gherkins and spring onions which stood in the center of the table.

"I'll have a spring onion if you will," said Lisa to Orford.

"I see that I must steel myself to take the rough with the rough," said Orford, doling out two spring onions onto her plate and two onto his. Emboldened by this, Mrs. Teitelbaum selected an ungainly stick of celery, tore it apart with an effort and regarded it doubtfully.

"Watch out, honey," said Mr. Teitelbaum. "It looks a bit stringy."

His wife gave him a grateful smile and embarked on the thinner of the two stalks.

Irma Kaplan caught Lady Bland's eye and leaned forward. "Have you been in America long?"

"Alas, no." The plaintive note Lady Bland injected into her voice lacked complete sincerity. "My husband and I left England only three weeks ago. We spent a couple of nights in New York, a week in Washington and the last few days with friends in San Francisco."

"I always say that San Francisco is the most stimulating city in the United States."

"I'm afraid we haven't had the opportunity to visit enough of the other cities to be able to compare them. It certainly is very beautiful."

"The Gateway to the East," said Mr. Teitelbaum with authority, biting into a crescent-shaped roll covered with small black seeds.

"An aunt of mine once fell off a cable car in San Francisco," said Eldrich.

"Poor thing—how dreadful!" murmured Lady Bland.

"She rolled over and over and over for three blocks until she was stopped by traffic lights."

"How did the traffic lights stop her?" inquired Lola.

"By changing from green to red of course."

Mrs. Teitelbaum put down her stick of celery and stared at him. Irma Kaplan frowned. Lady Bland screwed up her eyes at the corners and stared into the middle distance as though she were trying to work out some abstruse mathematical formula. Lisa Wendle laughed.

"That's my kind of joke," she said.

At this moment the wine waiter with the drinks and the two table stewards with the food arrived simultaneously.

9

The dinner meandered on and the general conversation meandered on with it. Sir Roderick contributed little beyond an occasional grunt of approval or disapproval. Mrs. Teitelbaum turned her head expectantly toward anyone who spoke as though fearful of missing some sophisticated witticism which she could recount later in a letter to Peachie and Joe. Mr. Teitelbaum devoted himself to his chicken à la king, which had been sent away and returned without the powdering of paprika that had originally adorned it. Lady Bland wrestled with her "small steak" which turned out to be the size of an average bedroom slipper and protruded at least an inch on either side of her plate. It was embellished with a mound of thick French fried potatoes, several large mushrooms, two balls of beetroot cowering on a crimson-stained lettuce leaf and a vast tomato stuffed with a dubious gray substance. Lisa and Orford, after one or two attempts at conversation, gave up and contented themselves with mutual glances of ill-concealed impatience. Eldrich Trumbull, having knocked back a second and then a third Rob Roy, lapsed into a state of benign euphoria, fiddled about with whatever food happened to be placed before him and occasionally, having muttered something incomprehensible, indulged in a private giggle. Lola Widmeyer, having disposed of her marinated herring and a solid-looking yellow omelet, lit a cigarette, after a gracious interchange of glances with Lady Bland, and silently observed her fellow guests in general and Eldrich Trumbull in particular. Over and above his drunkenness, which irritated her, there was something about him, almost a touching quality, that intrigued her. Good-looking, obviously wealthy, equally obviously the playboy, ne'er-do-well type she instinctively despised, she nevertheless felt vaguely sorry for him. Whenever he giggled at his own mumbled witticisms his eyes crinkled at the corners and assumed a curious expression of innocence like a small boy who knows perfectly well that he is being badly behaved but also knows that, after the inevitable punishment, he will be forgiven and comforted and allowed to have a piece of chocolate. Being a conscientious newspaper reader Lola was acquainted with his background and his flamboyant marital exploits. Also, being a professional novelist, her acquisitive brain examined him, assessed him, docketed him and filed him away for future reference. Irma Kaplan was the only member of the party who seemed to be unaffected by the prevailing lassitude. She was naturally conscious of it but her highly developed social sense, upon which she had frequently been congratulated by her admiring clique in Scarsdale, could, she knew, always be relied on to rise supreme when occasion demanded it and this occasion, in her opinion, most certainly did. A group of strangers collected round a captain's dinner table, without even the presence of the captain himself to ease the situation, was a challenge that she accepted as a matter of course. To be a "giver" rather than a "taker" was an axiom to which Irma had clung tenaciously since the age of eighteen, when this remarkable quality had been explained to her by a visiting cousin of her mother's who traveled in electrical equipment. True, he had rather vitiated the compliment a few moments later by slipping a warm, be-ringed hand under her skirt and squeezing her thigh, but she had always been grateful to him in a way for having had the wit to observe, even at that early age, one of her most important natural assets. Tonight, after a long and wearying day including hours spent in the Fairmount beauty parlor and the various complications of embarkation and unpacking, she was still capable, she reflected whimsically, of stepping into the social breach and, to coin a phrase, "get the evening off the ground!" Her method of achieving this was quite simple. She just talked incessantly. A spate of anecdotes, experiences and shipboard reminiscences cascaded from her lips, interlarded every now and then with shrewd observations on world affairs culled principally from the *Reader's Digest* and the glossy pages of *Look* magazine. The fact that by the end of the meal her stunned listeners had been reduced to almost total silence was to her a shining tribute to her success and when finally she had retired to her cabin, kicked her shoes off and sunk wearily down before her dressing-table mirror, the small eyes that looked back at her held in their shallow depths a glint of congratulatory triumph.

The rest of the party went its various ways. Lola walked out onto the promenade deck, which was deserted with the exception of a stout, elderly man in a yellow check sports jacket and plum-colored pants, who was lying, snoring gently, in a steamer chair. In the abandonment of sleep his upper plate had slipped down and lay trembling on his lower lip, giving him a haughty expression. Lola pushed open the heavy glass door aft and strolled out onto an open part of the deck in the center of which was a lighted swimming pool. There wasn't much water in the pool because the ship was rolling slightly and she could hear what little there was smashing back and forth against the tiled sides. Most of the deck chairs were stacked against the ship's rail and secured with ropes; however, there were a few unattached ones dotted about. Lola sat down in one of them, lit a cigarette and reviewed in her mind the encounters of the evening. The Blands. Mr. and Mrs. Teitelbaum. Lola smiled indulgently. The United States of America were crowded with Mr. and Mrs. Teitelbaums. The honeymooners, Orford and Lisa Wendle. Lola smiled again. Young, happily situated financially, attractive, newly married and in love. To be envied or pitied? She shrugged her shoulders. It seemed to her that there was little to be envied nowadays in the fact of being young. The future was too menacing and the present too hectic. Mrs. Irma Z. Kaplan. She shuddered with the realization that, owing to her own folly in accepting the invitation to the captain's table, she was doomed to listen to Irma Z. Kaplan's insistent voice for the forthcoming three weeks. Her thoughts had turned with relief to the contemplation of Eldrich Trumbull the Third when she was startled to see him at that very moment emerge from the quarter-filled swimming pool in a pair of abbreviated blue swimming trunks. He shook himself like a retriever, spraying the decks around him with drops of water and approached her with an engaging smile.

"I am sure you will be fascinated to hear that I am now stone cold sober. At any rate I am, beyond the shadow of a doubt, stone cold."

"Haven't you got anything to put on?"

"Certainly I have," replied Eldrich. "It's in the lifeboat immediately behind you. It's a hideous terry-toweling bathrobe presented to me by my last wife exactly eleven days before she retired to Reno, Nevada, with her lawyer and a hangover. I put it in the lifeboat because I didn't want it to blow away. If you will be kind enough to veil your eyes, which I have already noted are uncannily observant, I will slip it on and, with due consideration of the decencies, slip off these wet trunks under it. I will also"—he added—"bum a cigarette off you if you have by now forgiven me for my oafish behavior at dinner."

"There's nothing to forgive."

"I was drunk and repulsive."

"You were certainly drunk but I don't remember you being particularly repulsive."

"Don't look round till I tell you to." He scuffled about in the shadows behind her. "And even then it would be advisable to count slowly up to seventeen."

"I feel no overwhelming urge to look round at all."

"That can only mean that your sense of adventure and derring-do is becoming atrophied." After some further scuffling she heard him jump heavily on the deck obviously to rid himself of the wet trunks, then he drew up an adjacent chair and sat down next to her.

"Where's that cigarette you promised me?"

"Here." Lola handed him her case and a box of matches. "You'd better light it yourself, the wind is rather strong."

"You're a living doll." Eldrich lit a cigarette expertly and handed her back her case and the matches.

"I think, on the whole, that you were lucky to be loaded at dinner. It must at least have deadened the impact of Mrs. Kaplan's monologue."

"You're quite right. I was conscious of a continuous rasping sound but I attributed it to some busybody sawing off the funnel."

After a slight pause, Lola looked at him thoughtfully.

"What are you running away from?"

"The Past, the Present and the Future."

Lola sighed. "I suppose I deserved that sort of answer for asking that sort of question."

Eldrich took a drag at his cigarette. "The question was reasonable enough in the circumstances and the answer, although admittedly a bit pompous, wasn't so far out. The Past depresses me, the Present bores me and the Future scares me to death."

"Too glib," said Lola. "Try again."

"You're a formidable lady. Why don't you put away your scalpel, relax and contemplate the Goddamned stars?"

"You called me a 'living doll' just now. Can 'living dolls' be formidable?"

"You bet your sweet life they can."

"Seriously, what on earth induced you to come on this cruise?" She held up her hand warningly. "Please don't say 'to get away from it all' or I shall leave you immediately and go to bed."

Eldrich laughed. "I'm actually going to Hong Kong to have some new shirts and suits made. I have a tailor there called Ah Fing. He's crazy about me."

"Isn't everybody?"

"Don't be snappy." Eldrich laughed. "Every butterfly, when pinned down, is entitled to a last despairing flutter of wings."

Lola rose. "I think I'll go to bed now anyway," she said. "It's getting a bit chilly."

"I've offended you or irritated you in some way, haven't I?"

"Not in the least." She forced a smile.

"Please don't go. Please sit down again for just a few more minutes, or I shall have to go and find Mrs. Kaplan and talk to her."

"People don't talk to Mrs. Kaplan. She talks to them."

"Sit down again—please—"

Lola looked at him undecidedly for a moment. "Very well," she said. She sat down again and opened her cigarette case. "We'll have one more cigarette each. There are only two left anyway!" After a pause during which he lit two cigarettes and handed her one of them, she looked at him again and lowered her eyes. "I think perhaps I owe you an apology, or at least an explanation."

"Good God! Whatever for?"

"For being inquisitive and firing leading questions at you. Curiosity is my besetting sin, curiosity about people I mean. It is also part of my stock in trade. Small talk bores me but finding out about human behavior fascinates me, not only because I happen to be a writer, but because I really am genuinely interested, particularly when I run across someone like you for instance, someone who so obviously conforms to type that I become suspicious."

"Suspicious, hey?"

"Yes." Lola nodded. "You seem to be more intelligent than your average prototype."

"All this talk of types and prototypes. Am I so cut and dried?"

"Outwardly yes. Mind you, my assessment of you is colored by my having read about you from time to time in the newspaper columns."

"Oh, Lord!"

"The pattern, you must admit, is stereotyped to say the least. Enough money, more than enough marriages, an assured social position and sufficient personal charm to keep you in constant trouble."

Eldrich laughed. "So far so good. Your crystal ball is working overtime."

"Unfortunately it's far from infallible. It leaves whole areas cloudy and unexplained."

"Perhaps that's just as well."

"Was that one more despairing flutter of wings?"

"No. I decided to surrender a few moments ago, when you threatened to leave me alone. I don't like being left alone."

"It's one of the greatest blessings in the world," said Lola vehemently. "You should learn to appreciate it."

"All very fine for you with your pens and pencils and notebooks and butterfly collections. You always have something to do, a purpose in life. I haven't any particular talent or any particular purpose."

"I see your problem, but I'm not very impressed with it."

Eldrich got up suddenly, strolled over to the ship's rail, flicked his cigarette into the sea, came back and sat down next to her again.

"Okay Salvation Nell," he said. "Let's get down to cases. You asked me what induced me to come on this cruise and at the same time you warned me, under threat of walking out on me, not to say, 'To get away from it all!' Well, like it or not, the exact and accurate reason for me flying from New York to San Francisco and embarking on this ship was just that—to get away from it all! My father, the general, has announced, in no uncertain terms that my 'way of life' as he calls it, appalls him. My stepmother's response to my vintage personal charm is negative to the point of fanaticism. In fact she can't stand the sight of me. The three women I was foolish enough to marry turned out, after the first fine physical careless rapture had been merrily exhausted, to be noisy, ill-mannered, predatory and dull. One of them indeed added promiscuous nymphomania to her already impressive list of conjugal defects. They all of them however, in spite of sharing an average level of intelligence that an Aboriginal herdsman would despise, contrived, by dint of some basic, primeval shrewdness, to procure for themselves the most brilliant and unscrupulous lawyers in the United States. These legal vultures succeeded in extorting from me more than three-quarters of the income left in trust for me by my mad maternal grandmother who lived in a Gothic mausoleum in Gloucester, Massachusetts, and, in her declining years, was given to feeding seagulls with imported Beluga caviar spread on triangular pieces of hot buttered toast."

"You're making my head reel."

"I'm making my own head reel," admitted Eldrich. "But it must be getting accustomed to it by now what with one thing and another."

"What do you hope to achieve by this 'getting away from it all'?"

"Peace and quiet and time to think. The moment has come for me to take stock of myself, face my manifold weaknesses squarely in the eye and see if I can discover the faintest glimmer of hope in the shadowed future."

"It sounds all right on the surface, but I'm still not really impressed."

"I didn't expect you to be," Eldrich sighed.

"Are you planning to become a genuine alcoholic or is this merely a passing phase?"

"I thought we'd get to that sooner or later."

"That isn't exactly an answer to my question."

"If my alcoholism is a passing phase, it's sure taking a hell of a long time to pass."

"Neither is that." Lola rose. Eldrich got up too and looked at her inquiringly.

"Do I look like an alcoholic? I mean did you recognize me as one the first moment you saw me?"

582

"No—not exactly. You seemed to me to drink with a little too much bravado for that, as though it still amused you to shock people."

"Did I shock you?"

"Yes, a little. Waste of time and life and intelligence always shocks me."

"Have you never wasted a moment? Has every hour of every day of your busy successful life been neatly and satisfactorily accounted for?"

"Of course not." Lola made an impatient movement to go but he restrained her by putting his hand on her arm.

"You've been kinder than you know this evening. I wouldn't like you to think that it had been entirely in vain, or too casually taken for granted."

"You've already explained about your personal charm, there's really no necessity to labor the point."

"Was that meant to be as unkind as it sounded?"

"Please let go my arm."

Eldrich let her arm drop, leaned forward and kissed her lightly on the mouth.

Lola stepped back. "That was silly," she said icily.

"Not at all. I kissed you because I wanted to."

"I'm old enough to be your mother."

"Only if you were careless enough to be raped at the age of thirteen."

"Good night, Mr. Trumbull."

"Good night, Miss Widmeyer. And thank you for the cigarettes."

She turned abruptly and walked away from him. He watched her disappear through the glass doors and then wandered over to the ship's rail and stared out over the gently moving sea. There was no moon but the sky glittered with stars.

10

At ten o'clock the next morning Lola Widmeyer was lying in bed with her arms behind her head staring into space, when the stewardess came in bearing a case of red roses from the ship's florist and a note. She waited until the stewardess had left the cabin before she read the note which was brief and to the point. "Please don't be angry with me. Please don't despise me and please forgive me. Eldrich." She put it down, reached for a cigarette, lit it and lay back against her pillows. She had had a troubled night, sleeping only for brief spells and it was not until after sunrise, when she had walked round the sun deck three times, that she had returned to her darkened cabin and finally drifted off. "Please don't be angry with me. Please don't despise me and please forgive me." She picked up the note again and was about to throw it into the wastepaper basket when she changed her mind and stuffed it far back in the drawer of her bedside table. "Nice manners anyway," she reflected wryly. "Better than mine I think on the whole." She tried unsuccessfully to dismiss what had occurred between Eldrich and herself from her mind. It had been after all nothing more than a trivial, casual incident, and it was idiotic to attach the slightest importance to it, but the memory of it persisted and she reproached herself for having allowed herself to become involved in such a foolish and humiliating situation. It mortified her to realize that with all her self-sufficiency, age and experience she could still, without even being aware of it at the time, indulge in the sort of banal flirtatiousness she most despised. She recalled, with a groan of embarrassment, the intense, rather arch questions she had asked him. "What are you running away from?" "You called me a living doll just now, can living dolls be formidable?" Oh, God! She got up and looked out of the porthole. The sea was gray and forbidding and flecked with white horses and she felt the floor of the cabin moving unpleasantly under her feet. She was never afflicted by seasickness, but a rolling and pitching ship exacerbated her nerves as well as making it impossible for her to use her typewriter with any degree of comfort. She gave it a baleful look as it sat, almost expectantly, on the dressing table, clambered back into bed again crossly and lit another cigarette.

11

On the second evening out neither the "Welcome Aboard" gathering presided over by Mavis Whittaker, the cruise hostess, in the Winter Garden Lounge, nor Captain Berringer's "Get Together" cocktail party in his cabin, could be described as entirely successful. The reason for this was the freakish behavior of the elements. At noon a stiffening breeze had sprung up which by two-thirty had developed into a steady gale. Over sixty percent of the passengers, being unprepared for the hazards of ocean travel and not having had enough time to acquire their sea legs, were flung into dreadful disarray. Stewards and stewardesses staggered back and forth along the slippery passages bearing basins. The ship's doctor, accompanied by two sullen assistants, lurched from cabin to cabin administering Dramamine, Miltown, aspirin, Seconal, Nembutal, Tuinal, Sodium Amytal and codeine. Wailing matrons were discovered lying on the floors of their cabins amid a swirling sea of mixed fruit, nuts, Blum's candies and broken bottles of Revlon's "Intimate" toilet water. Bruised, vomiting children were carried moaning to sick bay with grazed knees and bumps on their heads. A retired dentist and his wife, both wearing life jackets, were found lying clasped in each other's arms in an alcoholic coma, while two empty vodka bottles assaulted them viciously with every movement of the ship.

In the captain's cabin Sir Roderick and Lady Bland majestically rocked from side to side and pitched backward and forward balancing their drinks in their hands. Facing them on the sofa sat Irma Kaplan wearing a Russian pink hostess gown. Eldrich Trumbull, in an armchair, peered sardonically over the rim of his highball glass, while Captain Berringer, perched higher than the others in the swing chair facing his desk, apologized repeatedly for the weather and made unsuccessful efforts to stem the ceaseless flow of Irma Kaplan's conversation. For the last twenty minutes she had been explaining, with detailed analysis, her own miraculous immunity from seasickness. It seemed that from her earliest nautical experience on a Lake Erie steamboat at the age of seven she had never suffered so much as a qualm. And on one occasion, which she could remember as clearly as if it were yesterday, she had been traveling to Europe for the first time on the old *Île de France* and the whole ship had virtually to be battened down. She could recall even now the expression of amazement on the face of the chief steward when she appeared as usual for breakfast, on the dot of nine-thirty. "There's no doubt about it." She gave a merry laugh. "I am one of the fortunate ones."

"Indeed you must be," said Lady Bland and turned to Eldrich. "I believe we had the pleasure of meeting your father once. He dined with us in Mombasa just after the war. He was General Trumbull, wasn't he?"

"He still is," replied Eldrich.

"At least I think it was Mombasa but I can't be sure. We were on the move so much during those post-War years it's hard to remember. I know we were on the way to somewhere or other."

"My father's a man of incredible gallantry," said Eldrich. "Not only did he lead an entire division onto a wrong beach in Sicily during the War, but he married my stepmother."

"Oh," said Lady Bland blankly.

"I remember having a terrible experience once in Sicily," said Irma. "I had just gone ashore with some friends of mine, Alma and Vincent Kringle, who came from Saint Paul and had never been to Europe before, and we hadn't been on dry land for more than half an hour when suddenly there was an awful rumbling sound and the ground began to shake beneath our feet . . ."

"Probably the Mafia," said Eldrich. "The Mafia are enormously powerful in Sicily, in fact it was there that they started the whole thing. When I was a boy of seven in Portsmouth, New Hampshire, we had an Italian cook who was completely under the thumb of the Mafia. She was also covered in warts and used to sing Neapolitan sea chanties. Do you know any Neapolitan sea chanties?"

"No I don't," said Irma.

"Well take my advice and give them a wide berth."

At this moment a diversion was caused by the ship giving a more prolonged and violent roll than usual. There was the sound of crashing crockery from the officers' galley and Lady Bland's cocktail shot out of her hand and landed in the captain's lap.

"Oh dear!" she cried. "I *am* so sorry."

"It's nothing," said the captain, dabbing at his sodden flies with a paper napkin.

"What happens," inquired Eldrich, "if we roll over so far that water gets into the funnels?"

"Really, Mr. Trumbull, you are too absurd." Lady Bland rose to her feet with a harrassed smile and steadied herself by holding on to the back of her chair. "I'm afraid we must leave you now, Captain Berringer. It was so kind of you to invite us. I am so sorry for having been so clumsy. I presume you won't be coming down to dinner yourself?"

"No, Ma'am," replied the captain. "I'll have to be getting back to the bridge."

Sir Roderick rose, muttered "Good evening" gruffly to the captain and followed his wife unsteadily out of the cabin. Irma Kaplan also rose with a sigh.

"Well. I suppose all good things come to an end," she said. "Are you coming down to dinner, Mr. Trumbull?"

"Later on," said Eldrich. "I have a pressing appointment in the bar. But I will accompany you to the elevator with pleasure."

"Thank you," said Irma coldly.

Eldrich turned to the captain and shook hands. "God bless this ship," he said. "And nearly all who sail in her."

12

By noon on the following day the wind had dropped and the sea had quieted down. Mr. and Mrs. Teitelbaum struggled wanly onto the promenade deck where a steward tucked them into two steamer chairs, wrapped rugs round their legs and brought them some hot consommé.

Orford and Lisa disentangled themselves from each other's arms at approximately twelve-fifteen. Lisa got out of bed and slipped on her négligée while Orford lay, still naked, puffing a cigarette.

"If I don't have some coffee I shall die," said Lisa. "You'd better dial that fresh bell captain and ask him to send the steward or stewardess or somebody. You'd also better put on your pajama top at least."

"You're wearying of me," said Orford sadly, reaching for the telephone. "You are beginning already to find me physically repellent. What's going to happen by the time we get to Honolulu?"

"With any luck I'll have got my second wind," said Lisa.

Eldrich lay on his bed face downward while Kito, the cabin steward, reverently massaged his back. The ship was still rolling but the weather had improved and shafts of watery sunlight pierced the gray morning sky.

"You'll have to do better than that, Kito," murmured Eldrich into the pillow. "That fluttering, butterfly touch would be appropriate in a geisha but I require a stronger, more masculine approach. You will discover, if you dig deeper with those dainty yellow fingers, horrible knots of constricted muscle under my shoulder blades and at the base of my spine. These are caused by too much alcohol and emotional tension and it is your honor and privilege to dissipate them with all the virile strength at your command."

"Yes, sir." Kito hissed and exerted a little more pressure.

"Better," said Eldrich, "but still too tentative. Bash away until I shriek for mercy."

"Very good, sir." Kito, with an apologetic sigh, obediently dug his fingers into a soft spot beneath Eldrich's collarbone. Eldrich groaned with pain.

"Good," he grunted. "Don't mind me crying, just press on."

There was silence for a few minutes broken only by Kito's heavy breathing and an occasional moan from Eldrich who presently pushed him gently away and turned over on his back.

"You may now hand me a cigarette," he said. "And if you're a good boy I'll let you break my neck later."

"Yes, sir." Kito handed him a cigarette, lit it for him and stood gazing at him with an expression of unabashed adoration.

"I always understood that Orientals were supposed to be impassive," said Eldrich. "I am beginning to suspect that I have been misinformed."

At this moment there was a knock on the door. Kito, galvanized into swift action, pulled the sheet up over Eldrich and went to open it. He returned an instant later with a note.

"It is from Sun Deck Twenty-three," he said handing it to him. "The stewardess say there is to be no answer."

Eldrich slit open the envelope, took out the note and read it with a slight frown. "Dear Mr. Trumbull, How kind of you to send me those roses. They are quite lovely. Thank you so much. Yours Sincerely Lola Widmeyer."

"The stewardess was quite right," said Eldrich. "There is certainly to be no answer. At any rate for the time being." He tore the note into small pieces which he handed to Kito to put in the waste-paper basket. "You see lying before you, Kito, the unnecessarily shrouded figure of a pampered professional charmer who has received what is known as The Brush-Off."

Kito grinned anxiously.

"It is only, I trust, a temporary setback," Eldrich went on. "But curiously enough it has saddened me. There is something about this strange, well-groomed, intelligent lady, who, let's face it, is no ingénue, that has kindled new fires in my ancient bones. Apart from having an excellent figure and a swift mind there is a quality in her which, for me, has a most definite allure. She is far removed from the oversexed, rapacious, petulant little tramps whom I am accustomed to find, in the grim light of morning, scuffling about in bed beside me. She has in fact what might vulgarly be described as 'class' and class, Kito, in this era of proletarian infiltration, mindless nymphomania and commercial television, is becoming rarer and rarer. In the course of one short conversation she managed to see through me, undermine my self-confidence and finally dismiss me with well-bred contempt. Only the romantic stars witnessed my dire humiliation but I couldn't look at them anymore because I felt they were laughing. Now then—" His voice assumed a more practical tone. "In order to dispel this dark cloud of disenchantment which has suddenly enveloped me, I will take—if you will be kind enough to hand it to me—a swig from that bottle of vodka on the dressing table."

"It is not yet noon, sir." Kito reluctantly handed him the bottle.

"Yours not to reason why, my little Japanese Sandman," said Eldrich. "Yours but to do and die. You may now bugger off and leave me to my somber meditations."

Kito bowed, and with a reproachful hiss, went out of the cabin.

13

By late afternoon on the third day at sea, the *Mara*, all passion spent, had settled into a languid roll which was too slow and rhythmical to upset any but the most vulnerable stomachs. The Winter Garden Lounge, the smoking room and the "Lanai" bar were all crowded. The dining saloon began to fill up as early as seven o'clock. At eight o'clock Captain Berringer appeared, resplendent in a white mess jacket, and presided at his table, from which the only guest missing was Lola Widmeyer, who had sent a message via the chief steward explaining that she had a slight headache and was having a light dinner in her cabin. Conversation was general whenever Irma Kaplan allowed it to be. Eldrich Trumbull insisted upon ordering three bottles of imported champagne to celebrate, he said, their miraculous escape from the perils of the deep. Lady Bland, who had formed a private resolution to head off Irma Kaplan as often as she possibly could, embarked on a series of gentle anecdotes about the British Royal family with whom, it appeared, she had been on agreeable although not intimate terms for many years. The Teitelbaums listened wide-eyed to these mild reminiscences; Lisa and Orford Wendle glanced at each other from time to time repressing surreptitious giggles and Captain Berringer occasionally interposed a respectful guffaw. Irma Kaplan, none too pleased that the ball of conversation should be so purposefully dribbled away from her, made a misguided effort to compete.

"I remember once," she said, "sitting at the next table to the Duke and Duchess of Windsor at a charity ball at the Waldorf Astoria."

"I'm not at all surprised," said Lady Bland with an empty smile. "I believe they go in a great deal for that sort of thing. As I was saying . . ." She turned to the captain and continued her explanation of the difference between Trooping the Colour and the Changing of the Guard. "You see, Trooping the Colour takes place only once a year in honor of the Queen's birthday, whereas the Guard is changed outside Buckingham Palace every day."

"London must be just wonderful," said Mrs. Teitelbaum enthusiastically. "With so much going on all the time."

"We have St. Patrick's Day and the Shriners," said Eldrich with a hint of patriotic reproach in his voice. "So we really can't complain."

"What on earth are Shriners?" inquired Sir Roderick.

"A lot of elderly men wearing funny hats who walk about a great deal."

"What for?"

"I'm not quite sure. Some sort of atavistic compulsion I suppose. They also get out of hand later in the day and goose people in elevators."

"My late husband was a Shriner," said Irma angrily. "And proud to be one."

"In which case," replied Eldrich, "I can only offer you my apologies and my heartfelt sympathy."

"I do not require either, thank you." Irma got up and turned to the captain. "I do hope you will excuse me not waiting for coffee. I have an appointment to play bridge in the smoking room at nine o'clock." She smiled sourly at everybody, shot Eldrich a glance of hatred and flounced away from the table.

"Oh dear!" said Lady Bland with palpable lack of conviction. "*How* unfortunate!"

"I'm afraid I put my foot in it," said Eldrich.

"You certainly did and it was splendid," Lisa laughed.

"I'm sorry, captain, for causing a fracas at your smoothly conducted table."

"That's okay," said the captain. "Mrs. Kaplan often gets into snits like that. We've had her with us before, you know."

"I still don't know what a Shriner is," said Sir Roderick plaintively.

"Never mind now, my dear," said Lady Bland. "I think we should all talk about something entirely different."

"Perhaps you will all do me the honor of taking a liqueur with me in the main lounge?" Captain Berringer rose to his feet. "We can have our coffee up there."

"That will be delightful." Lady Bland also rose. "Sir Roderick and I thought of going to the movie at nine-thirty. It's called *Swinging All the Way Home*. Has anybody seen it?"

"Yes," said Eldrich with a shudder. "It's about a colored trumpet player who falls in love with a nun. It has a strong social message and I shouldn't advise it."

"Good Heavens!" murmured Lady Bland as they moved away from the table. "What will they think of next?"

"The end is particularly impressive," said Eldrich. "As the convent gates clang to behind the vanishing nun, the colored trumpeter sinks to his knees in the dust and plays 'Ave Maria.'"

"I must say that doesn't sound like Sir Roderick's cup of tea." Lady Bland sighed. "Perhaps we'd better go to bed after all."

14

The following morning Lola, after a restless night, rose early, had her breakfast and sat down at her typewriter dismally conscious that she was in no mood to be either detached or objective. The episode with Eldrich Trumbull on the promenade deck two evenings ago had disturbed her more than she had, at first, been prepared to admit. Now, however, with two virtually sleepless and overintrospective nights behind her, she was forced to the uncomfortable conclusion that she was behaving like an idiot. To refuse to go down to the saloon for meals and remain in her cabin was not only ill-mannered but humorless and dull. It was also a course that could not be pursued indefinitely. She intended in any event to leave the ship at Hong Kong, linger there perhaps for a while and then fly back to the States. But Hong Kong was three weeks away and in the meantime she would have to pull herself together and stop exaggerating in her mind a situation which was really of no significance whatsoever. She regretted sending Eldrich that curt little note thanking him for the roses. He had behaved foolishly, perhaps a trifle arrogantly but that was no excuse for *her* to behave with such humorless petulance. The only thing to do in the circumstances, she reflected, was to make every effort to remedy her ungraciousness as soon as possible. She began to laugh, took a cigarette out of a pack, lighted it and took the lid off the typewriter.

Four hours later she went out on deck for a little fresh air before going to the bar for a cocktail before lunch. She was wearing an emerald-colored wool sports dress and white jacket with gold buttons which looked vaguely nautical. She had wound a green chiffon scarf round her head to prevent her hair blowing about and felt suddenly cheerful, with that cheerfulness only writers know when they have successfully completed a morning's work. After a rather sticky beginning she had managed to do just over her average of three pages, which, with double spacing, amounted to nearly eight hundred words. The sky was a cloudless blue and there was a new softness in the air. She bowed and smiled to Mr. and Mrs. Teitelbaum who were wrapped up in their steamer chairs. They smiled back and Mrs. Teitelbaum waved a fat little hand. In the Winter Garden Lounge she found Sir Roderick and Lady Bland sitting at a table by the window with two bright pink drinks before them. Lady Bland was knitting an unidentifiable garment in navy blue wool while Sir Roderick stared, with knotted brows, at a crossword puzzle that had been cut out of a back number of the London *Times*. Lady Bland, on seeing Lola, put down her knitting.

"We haven't met since the first evening," she said. "Won't you have a drink with us? Roddy dear, you remember Miss Widmeyer."

Sir Roderick rose, shook hands and pulled up a vacant chair. "What can I order for you?"

Lola looked at the pink drinks. "What are those?"

"Alas!" sighed Lady Bland. "They're supposed to be Singapore gin slings, but I fear they are not entirely successful. My husband tried to explain to the barman how they should be made but I don't think he quite understood."

"I'll try one anyway."

Sir Roderick signaled to the barman. Lady Bland bowed austerely to Irma Kaplan who happened to pass by, chatting, with her usual animation, to a red-faced, elderly man wearing a vivid yellow sports shirt on which scarlet and blue hula maidens in emerald green grass skirts disported themselves.

"I'm so glad she found a friend," said Lady Bland. "I do hope it will last." She looked after Irma. "I'm afraid she's rather a trial. There was quite a little scene at dinner last night between her and Mr. Trumbull. He really was naughty but I think she deserved it."

"What happened?"

"He made a joke about 'Shiners' or something and it turned out that her late husband happened to be one."

"Shriners?" suggested Lola.

"That's the word. I knew I'd got it muddled. At any rate she went quite red in the face and flew at him, then of course he made everything much worse by pretending to apologize and giving her another dig at the same time. I know he drinks far too much and is apt to say rather unpredictable things, but I can't help liking him. He has charm, don't you think?"

"Yes." Lola nodded with a slight smile. "He has a great deal of charm."

"Does anybody know what he *does* in life? Apart from keeping on getting married and divorced, the captain told me all about that when we were having coffee in the lounge."

"I don't think he does anything very much."

"What a pity! It seems such a waste, somehow, doesn't it? I mean he really is intelligent and surprisingly well read. It's strange to find an American in his sort of circumstances who really loves Jane Austen, isn't it?"

"I don't know," replied Lola dryly. "She has acquired quite an international reputation lately, having got into the paperbacks."

"Got it!" announced Sir Roderick with a note of triumph in his voice. "Got the damned thing at last."

"Got what, dear?"

"That anagram. It's been holding me up."

"What's the clue?"

"'Sour Taste Pal.' Seven and five."

"Parlous State," said Lady Bland, putting her knitting away in her bag.

"Why on earth didn't you say so before?"

"You never asked me, dear."

"I'm really very impressed," said Lola. "I've looked at your English crosswords and I can never understand them."

"It's only a knack you know. If you go on doing them you soon begin to twig. We always bring a number of them with us when we travel although I must say *The Times* has been getting increasingly complicated lately. Ah—here's your drink. If you don't like it, please have something else."

Lola sipped the long pink drink the steward brought her. "It's delicious."

"It should really have fresh limes, of course. That's actually what's the matter with it."

At this moment Eldrich strolled up to the table. "May I join you?"

"Of course. Pull up a chair," said Lady Bland.

"Good morning, Miss Widmeyer." He looked at Lola with a twinkle in his eye. "We've missed you. Not only have we missed you but you, although you may not realize it, have missed a great deal of quiet, clean fun. Dinner last night was the occasion of a famous victory. Lady Bland and I between us succeeded in routing the redoubtable Mrs. Irma Z. Kaplan hook line and sinker."

"You behaved very badly, Mr. Trumbull, you know you did. I had nothing whatever to do with it," said Lady Bland.

"Nonsense," said Eldrich. "You mowed her down like a machine gun. I only administered the final *coup de grace*. What on earth is that you're all drinking? It looks like cough mixture."

"It also tastes rather like cough mixture, I'm afraid," said Lady Bland. "Roddy dear, do let's have something normal and safe like a gin fizz or a dry Martini. Mr. Trumbull?"

"Just tomato juice for me," said Eldrich. "I've decided to go on the wagon for several hours. My liver is in a state of seething rebellion. I know all the symptoms. Intense dissatisfaction with myself, maudlin regret for all my past misdemeanors." He shot a sidelong glance at Lola. "And sudden uncontrollable outbursts of weeping."

"How absurd you are," said Lady Bland summoning a steward. "Put that tiresome crossword away now, Roddy, there's a dear, and be sociable."

Sir Roderick obediently folded the puzzle and put it in his pocket. "Dry Martinis for everybody?"

"Yes please," said Lola.

"I really meant what I said about the tomato juice but . . ." he added to the steward, "please fill it to the brim with salt, pepper, tabasco, Worcestershire sauce and lemon so as to mitigate the dullness of the tomato."

Lola looked at Eldrich, casually dressed in a sleeveless white shirt, well-cut gray Dacron trousers and a blue patterned scarf knotted carelessly round his neck: she noted the brownness of his arms, the small flecks of gray at his temples, the blue of his eyes, enhanced by the colored scarf, his long, slim hands and his firm but sensual mouth, and knew, suddenly and incredulously, what it was that had been destroying her sleep and tormenting her mind. She had, beyond all shadow of a doubt, fallen in love.

15

The *Mara* tied up alongside the dock at six-thirty A.M. The day was clear and the air sweet with the scent of flowers. Little coffee-colored native boys dived repeatedly into the oily water for pennies thrown by the passengers who lined the ship's rails; a group of white-clad Hawaiians ground out the routine "Aloha" on their ukuleles; colored paper streamers were flung from ship to shore and from shore to ship; the sun shone with all its might and presently an endless stream of clamorous tourists stepped off the gangway to be duly festooned with "leis" of carnations, frangipani, pekoke and other local blooms, most of which became oppressively hot after a little while and had to be furtively discarded when nobody was looking. The Hawaiian islands in earlier days were among the most beautiful islands in the world. Lately, much of their intrinsic loveliness has been inevitably commercialized and spoiled, but there is still a magic in the air and a sweetness in the people.

The *Mara* was not due to sail until midnight and all shore-going passengers were requested to be on board not later than eleven o'clock. Sir Roderick and Lady Bland were met by a smart black Cadillac and whisked off to some gracious home on Diamond Head. Mr. and Mrs. Teitelbaum produced a hired car and drove, rather timorously, to the Royal Hawaiian Hotel which they had been told was the most famous and the best. Irma Kaplan, having invited Captain Berringer to lunch at the Royal Hawaiian and been refused with the utmost regret, accepted, without enthusiasm, an invitation to drive out to Pearl Harbor with her newly found friend, Mr. Pitoski, and a wealthy married couple called Klotz, who happened to be Mr. Pitoski's neighbors at the purser's table.

Orford and Lisa Wendle went ashore a good deal later than anyone else and were taken, by a hired chauffeur, to a restaurant on top of a skyscraper which very slowly revolved while they ate their lunch.

"I'm glad we didn't come here on our honeymoon aren't you?" said Lisa.

"We *are* on our honeymoon."

"I mean I'm glad we didn't come straight here by air. I think I should have committed suicide."

"Am I boring you?"

"Of course not. Don't be cute."

"The Hawaiian islands are supposed to be the Paradises of the Pacific."

"Well if the others are anything like this I'll settle for Miami Beach."

"You wouldn't be allowed in. You've got Arab blood."

"Only on Daddy's side. His grandfather went to Persia for Standard Oil when he was still in his teens. He got into all sorts of trouble."

"Shall we go for a swim later on Waikiki beach?"

"It would be like swimming in the subway."

"There's no pleasing some people."

"Do get the check, darling, this place going round and round is driving me mad."

"We could always go back to the ship, after all, it *is* air-conditioned."

"That's just what I was thinking."

"You're sure you wouldn't like to see some hula dancers in grass skirts?"

"No, thank you."

"What would you like to do?"

"Don't be *silly*, darling."

Orford signaled to the waiter to bring the check. Lisa scrutinized her face in the mirror of her compact. "Oh, God!" she said. "The wear and tear is beginning to show."

16

Lola sat in an armchair in the lobby of the Royal Hawaiian Hotel waiting for Eldrich and decided, with an irrepressible uplift of her heart, that she had gone raving mad. Her eyes, usually so sharply observant, stared vaguely at the chattering throng of tourists milling about in front of her, almost without seeing them. Arrivals and departures; perspiring men in Palm Beach suits; equally perspiring women dressed for traveling but wearing native-made raffia hats and carrying native-woven handbags; family groups; sparsely clad teenagers; uniformed bellboys scurrying to and from the elevators weighed down with baggage of all shapes and sizes. She didn't even recognize Mr. and Mrs. Teitelbaum until they came right up to her.

"Good morning," said Mrs. Teitelbaum. "How nice to see a friendly face. Are you all alone?"

"At the moment, yes. Actually I'm waiting for some friends to call for me and take me to see some of the island."

"I expect you must have friends everywhere, being a famous person and having written all those wonderful books. Henry and I were wondering whether to go out and have a look at the Waikiki beach or just sit down somewhere and have some iced tea. He's not supposed to do much, you know, after his operation. I promised the doctor not to let hm overtire himself. Miss Whittaker invited us to go on a tour of all the beauty spots. She's taking about thirty people, but I thought that might be a little too much of a good thing."

"I think you're very wise," said Lola. "Organized tours can be very exhausting."

"If you'll excuse me saying so that is the most darling hat I've ever seen, but then you always seem to wear just the right things. Henry and I were talking about it only this morning. That dress you wore at the captain's dinner last night was just perfect."

"Thank you." Lola smiled. "It's very sweet of you to say so."

"We were watching you and Mr. Trumbull dancing in the lounge afterward," Mrs. Teitelbaum went on with growing enthusiasm. "I remember whispering to Henry that if I hadn't known you both I would have sworn you were professionals. Didn't I, Henry?"

"Yes, honey," replied Mr. Teitelbaum.

"I'm afraid you're exaggerating. Mr. Trumbull is certainly a beautiful dancer but I fear I'm not in his class. I used to be good when I was younger but that was a long time ago. Actually I haven't danced for years."

"It's a question of knack," said Mrs. Teitelbaum with finality. "You either can or can't. Personally, I've always been clumsy. Henry always used to laugh at me when we were first married."

"That was very unkind of him."

"He was quite right." Mrs. Teitelbaum looked lovingly at her husband. "That's been the trouble all our married life. Henry is always quite right."

"You just button your lip, honey, and stop boring the hell out of Miss Widmeyer." He slipped his arm affectionately through his wife's. "She's a born natterer," he said to Lola with a wink. "If I didn't put my foot down every now and again, she'd talk us all into the ground. Come on now"—he gave Mrs. Teitelbaum's arm a little tug—"let's you and me go and grab ourselves that iced tea we've been talking about and leave Miss Widmeyer in peace." He raised his hat politely to Lola. "Maybe we'll all meet up again later in the day."

"I hope so," said Lola. "Enjoy yourselves."

She watched them wander away together arm in arm and felt a sudden stab of sentimental envy. Two old people, still, after fifty years of married life, serene and innocently happy in each other's company. A rare achievement indeed. So many couples she had known of that age had failed to find the secret of such curious, undemanding content. Life for most of them had degenerated into a state of resigned acceptance of each other, a chilly vacuum of slow years unwarmed by genuine affection and even the remnants of vanished love, in which nothing more was likely to happen beyond an occasional outburst of suppressed resentment or mutual acrimony. The Teitelbaums, mused Lola, were in no danger of such a bleak aftermath. Fate had been kind to them in endowing them both with cheerful and giving dispositions. No embittered, minor anticlimax threatened their last days; they were safe from everything but the cleaner, major tragedy of separation by death. Innocence, she reflected, even ignorance to a certain degree, had more advantages than were generally recognized by more sophisticated minds. There was a lot to be said for going through life without asking too many questions or knowing too many answers. True, such a process could not be exactly described as progressive, but then, progressiveness was a question of degree like anything else. Perhaps, in the final analysis, it was more progressive to be happy than unhappy. Here she was, a woman of fifty years old, intelligent, introspective, critical and without, she hoped, too many illusions either about herself or the world around her, about to embark on a love affair with a man many years younger than herself. How could this, the greatest illusion of all, bring her ultimately anything but misery? She had been in love, really in love, three times in her life, and not one of those strained, overecstatic, overcolored episodes could be said to have been really successful. There had been moments of course, unforgettable moments of sudden enchantment, but those, lovely though they had undoubtedly been, had never really compensated for the pain and self-recrimination that had come later. She was far too honest with herself not to acknowledge the fact that in each case the final disillusionment had been almost entirely her own fault. She was no good at love, or rather at "being in love." She was too concentrated, too inherently suspicious, perhaps too egocentric ever to be able to sustain an intimate relationship with any other human being. She remembered the agonizing pangs of jealousy she had endured, most of them entirely unfounded: the quarrels, the accusations, the tears, those humiliating tears she had shed when the conflict between her intelligence and her emotions had become too intolerable to be borne. "If I had one scrap of common sense," she said to herself, almost out loud, "instead of sitting here tremulous as a silly schoolgirl waiting for her first beau, I'd get a taxi, drive back to the ship, pack everything up and take the next plane to the mainland. I swore to myself over twelve years ago that I would never allow such a thing to happen to me again. I have my work to do and my life to live and I wish neither to be twisted out of shape nor disrupted by any extraneous and, at my age, ridiculous, emotional tensions. I know that my age itself is really the cause of it. I'm going through, I suppose, what is called 'the dangerous time.' I have been celibate too long and this is my damned female sexual urge rearing its ugly head again at a moment when I least want it to. There can be no doubt that I am about to make a complete and absolute fool of myself."

17

At twelve-fifteen Eldrich reappeared in an open Chevrolet convertible. Lola, with a suddenly pounding heart, saw him come into the lobby. He was wearing pale gray slacks, sandals and a blue open-necked shirt. In the back of the car was a large hamper and an ice bucket.

"I was longer than I intended to be. It was getting the lunch organized that took the time. Are you all right?"

"Yes," replied Lola, settling herself into the seat next to him. "I'm quite all right." She threw her hat onto the backseat, took the scarf she had brought out of her bag and tied it round her head. "Where are we going?"

"I had thought first of taking you up to the Pali."

"What's that?"

"It's a gap in the mountains with a fabulous view. Then I suddenly realized that Miss Mavis Whittaker would also be at the Pali yelping superlatives at at least half of the passenger list, so I changed my mind and I'm taking you in another direction entirely, to somewhere that I hope is still beyond the reach of our merry shipmates. It's a small, crescent-shaped coral beach hidden from prying eyes by a grove of palms and ironwood trees. We may of course find a chromium-plated motel sitting in the middle of it, but I don't really think that that is likely because, as far as I know, it's still private property."

"That sounds wonderful," said Lola. "How is it that you know this island so well? Did you bring any of your wives here?"

"Only the second one. Actually it was here, during our honeymoon, that I observed the first telltale symptoms of her incipient nymphomania."

"It couldn't have been a very happy honeymoon."

"It wasn't," said Eldrich. "To have to keep on hauling one's bride out of other people's beds becomes tedious after a while."

"Were you in love with her?"

"I suppose I thought I was. I enjoyed sleeping with her, but the communal aspect of the whole business began to get me down, so we flew back to New York where she divorced me for mental cruelty."

"What about the first and third?"

"The first was a proper Bostonian, a lady to her fingertips. That happy union was organized with calculated efficiency by my father and the family. We had a grand and most impressive wedding followed by a doleful week in Bermuda during which it rained incessantly and she fell off a bicycle and broke her collarbone. If she had broken her neck it would have saved me a lot of time and a lot of money."

"I gather that you were not in love with her?"

"It's difficult to be passionately in love with a woman who shuts her eyes, clenches her fists and moans with terror before you've even got into bed with her."

"What did she divorce you for?"

"Incompatibility of temperament, desertion and promiscuous fornication. And she was dead right."

"And the third?"

"Why, Miss Widmeyer. I do believe you're planning to put me into one of your clever novels!"

"Could be," said Lola. "Writers are notoriously unscrupulous."

"How would you write about me, I wonder. Sympathetically? Or with a sort of arid, clinical detachment?"

"A little of both I expect. Go on about the third."

"All right—all right—don't rush me. The third was even more disastrous than the other two."

"In what way?"

"She was a professional waif; one of nature's rebels, what is known colloquially as a 'kook.'"

"Oh dear!" sighed Lola. "I know the type. No lipstick, no hair-brush and the wrong stockings."

"Exactly. She was also a small-part actress, which I am happy to say she still is. She played in incomprehensible, avant-garde, off-Broadway productions and lived in a cold-water apartment in Green-wich Village."

"What on earth induced you to marry her?"

"I don't know really. Perhaps the fact that she was so vastly different from the others. She had enormous eyes, an attractive little body and gave the impression of being a great deal more intelligent than she actually was. In addition to which she was in love with me for at least seven months. I was also influenced by the knowledge that both my father and my stepmother had taken an instant dislike to her on sight. I took her to lunch with them at the Plaza where they were staying for a few days. She had three double dry Martinis, told a couple of extremely dirty stories, then gave a long dissertation on Brecht and explained that her brother had served a prison sentence for un-American activities. As she omitted to explain that her brother's un-American activities had merely consisted of indecent exposure on the corner of Lexington Avenue and Forty-ninth Street, they not unnaturally concluded that I was marrying into a family of dyed-in-the-wool communists."

"What nonsense you do talk," said Lola. "I don't believe a word of it."

"What is truth?" Eldrich laughed. "Poor Amanda." He sighed. "After our divorce she returned to experimental drama and is now living with the stage manager of a theater-in-the-round just outside Pittsburgh."

After about half an hour's driving, first of all through cane fields and banana plantations, then over a ridge of hills and down the other side, Eldrich turned the car off a straight white road, jumped out to open a rickety wooden gate and then drove on through a grove of trees to the edge of a little bluff overlooking the sea.

"There's the crescent-shaped coral beach I promised you," he said. "And there, nestling in the fold of those shallow hills are the ranches of the High and the Mighty. In other words the aristocracy of

599

Honolulu. They are all very wealthy indeed, principally because they are the descendants of the first missionaries who came to these islands. These men of God, I am here to tell you, apart from spreading the light, stamping out sin and forcing everybody to wear Mother Hubbards, happened to be very smart cookies. They combined business with pleasure by buying acres and acres of all the valuable land they could lay their Christian hands on. This beach for instance. This private and exclusive Robinson Crusoe hideaway would fetch today at least a million times more than its original price, which was probably no more than one dollar, seventy-five cents and a string of colored beads."

"If it's so private and exclusive what shall we do if some of the High and Mighty happen to come down and find us trespassing on it?"

"Personally," said Eldrich, "I shall wring them warmly by their various hands and remind them that we met at a dinner party given by the late Vincent Astor."

"What happens if they didn't know the late Vincent Astor?"

"Nobody in that money bracket could have failed to know the late Vincent Astor. Let's have no more of this quibbling now and take a swim before lunch. You shall undress behind that clump of wild bananas and I shall undress behind the car and when we meet again in the far future, it will be with a sudden, mutual cry of incredulous recognition."

"All right," said Lola. She smiled at him, took the bag containing her bathing things out of the back of the car and disappeared into the shadow of the ironwood trees. She was aware suddenly of uninhibited, blissful contentment. The pounding of the surf on the reef two miles away sounded like gentle thunder. A small green lizard ran up the bole of a tree and looked at her with its head on one side puffing an orange fan out of the middle of its tiny body. Vaguely, in the distance, she heard the sound of a car on the main road.

When they had swum lazily in the clear water, they unpacked the hamper. Eldrich had selected the lunch with discrimination. There was cold roast chicken, potato salad, fresh tomatoes, hard boiled eggs, half a papaya, bananas, pears and, in the ice bucket, two bottles of vin rosé. He had also brought plastic plates and cups, knives and a corkscrew. There was even pepper and salt and a pot of French mustard.

"No caviar?" said Lola. "*How* disappointing!"

"Caviar is no good in bright sunshine. It needs chopped egg, seductive lighting and vodka. You must be patient. All that comes later. I am taking you to dine in a classy little restaurant where only the very best people go."

"What happens if we've quarreled by then and aren't speaking?"

"I shall eat the caviar by myself and you can go to a cinema. There are quite a lot of good movies in the town. All with Peter Sellers in them."

"Fancy remembering pepper and salt. You really are very well organized."

"I aim to please," said Eldrich.

When they had finished lunch they packed the remains in the hamper. Lola had put on her dress again and Eldrich his slacks and they lay side by side in the shade leaning against the hamper, smoking and looking up at the feathery tufts of the casuarinas swinging gently in the breeze. The muffled booming of the Pacific rollers on the reef sounded suddenly louder. Lola, intensely aware of the tanned, naked torso nearly touching her, closed her eyes and gave an involuntary sigh. Eldrich rested his hand lightly on hers.

"Was that a happy sigh, darling?"

"Yes." She turned her hand and twisted her fingers through his. "A very happy sigh."

"Life may not be all beer and skittles, as someone romantically put it, but it does provide a few moments to remember if you allow it to."

"Permission must be obtained though to enjoy them completely. Not necessarily permission from one's conscience, but from one's common sense."

"Has your common sense given you the go-ahead? Are the lights green?"

"Yes. The lights are green. As a matter of fact my common sense washed its hands of the whole business two days ago. In the Winter Garden Lounge before lunch."

"I wonder why they called it the Winter Garden Lounge? It's such a cold, forbidding name for such an enchanted place."

Eldrich turned his body, leaned over her and looked searchingly into her face.

"You should be very proud of your eyes," he said. "I know they're bright and clear and don't miss a trick, but they've still somehow kept their innocence."

"Oh my sad young love. Don't talk such foolishness." She pulled his head down and pressed his mouth onto hers.

18

On the run from Honolulu to Yokohama the date line is crossed and a whole day disappears. This invariably causes a great deal of bewildered discussion among the passengers. Pencils and paper are produced. Arguments take place. Jocular references to age are made. Also, from the scenic point of view, the voyage is apt to become a little monotonous. There is nothing to be seen but the illimitable blue of the ocean. No misty islands float provocatively on the horizon and if, rarely, a passing ship is seen in the distance, excitement reaches fever pitch and people crowd to the ship's rails with binoculars. This was always the part of the trip that poor Mavis Whittaker particularly dreaded. Her inventiveness was strained to the utmost. Shuffleboard contests, deck tennis matches and tournaments, orgies of bingo, bridge and canasta, even pen and pencil games and dancing competitions were mercilessly organized. In addition to which there were the children to be considered. There was an elaborate nursery of course, decorated whimsically with Walt Disney animal characters. In this were playpens, toys of every description and a depressed woman in white called Mrs. Bagel, who sat in it from early morning until late afternoon trying to prevent the smaller tots from wetting themselves and bashing each other on the head. Mavis Whittaker occasionally dashed in and out with a frantic expression in her pale blue eyes. Among the many unalluring chores laid down in her official directive as cruise hostess was the arranging of a gay young folks musical entertainment which usually took place in the Winter Garden Lounge on the fifth day out from Honolulu. For this children of all shapes and sizes under the age of fifteen were recruited. Rehearsals took place daily; Mrs. Bagel banged away at the piano, the keyboard of which she always had to scrub with moistened Kleenex before she set to work; Mavis, quivering with synthetic goodwill coaxed, cajoled and marshaled her reluctant and frequently sullen little artistes into learning concerted and solo vocal numbers and simplified dance routines. There were squabbles, tears and often outbursts of hysteria from the infant performers as well as acrimonious disputes among the mothers present who watched their progeny with proud and jealous eyes. On the day of the actual performance the atmosphere of the whole ship was tremulous with expectation.

"I suppose we really ought to put in an appearance," said Lady Bland at lunch. "If only for the sake of that poor wretched woman. I do feel so dreadfully sorry for her."

"On the last cruise," volunteered Irma, "there was the most talented child I ever saw in my whole life. There's a star in the making, I said to the friend who was with me, if ever I saw one. She couldn't have been more than seven and she was cute as a June bug. She sang 'Over the Rainbow' and did a dance with an enormous mauve teddybear almost as big as herself. She got quite an ovation, she really did."

"Be careful, Mrs. Kaplan," said Eldrich. "You're sending our good intentions whistling down the wind."

"Perhaps you don't care for children, Mr. Trumbull," said Irma waspishly. "After all you've never had any of your own have you?"

"No, thank God, but I've had a few near misses."

"You really are disgraceful," murmured Lady Bland with a suppressed titter.

"I think" said Lola, "that the time has come to change the subject completely. Does anyone know if we arrive in Yokohama in the morning or the evening?"

"That all depends upon whether or not the harbor has been swept clear of mines," replied Eldrich. "The Japs are notoriously treacherous you know. We mustn't let ourselves be deceived by the fact that they've just produced *My Fair Lady* in a Tokyo dialect. That may only have been part of their overall plan to undermine the West and lull us into a sense of false security."

"Personally," said Sir Roderick, "I don't care for the Japanese any more than I care for the Germans. I never have and I never will."

"If we all thought like that the world would be in a terrible state," said Irma. "I mean we have to learn to forgive and forget, don't we? I mean no civilization can continue to exist if it's based on bitterness and hatred, can it?"

"More than one rhetorical question in one sentence always bewilders me," said Eldrich. "Are we going to have coffee here or up aloft?"

"Up aloft," said Lady Bland, rising with alacrity. "Come Roddy dear. I must stop at our cabin on the way up to fetch my scarf. The children's thing doesn't start until two-thirty does it?"

"No," said Eldrich. "But it's liable to go on for a very long time. Would you like me to go ahead and keep places for you?"

"That would be very kind. Not too near the front though. Just in case we feel like creeping away before it's finished."

"I'm quite sure," whispered Eldrich to Lola as they walked out of the saloon, "that if I hadn't fallen in love with you, I should have fallen in love with Lady Bland."

"There's not too much difference in the age group anyhow."

"Now then. None of that."

They crowded, with the others, into the waiting elevator.

Miss Mavis Whittaker's Children's Follies started nearly twenty minutes late owing to the fact that two of the more prominent Braves in the Indian number couldn't be found. They were finally discovered by one of the deck stewards hiding in a lifeboat from which they were dragged shrieking and brandishing their tomahawks. The performance, when at last it began, was received at first with delighted and indulgent applause. After an hour or so, however, the enthusiasm of the audience began to wilt. The children wandered on and off untidily displaying no discernible talent or even interest in the proceedings. They hopped and skipped through their dances dressed variously as Indians, cowboys, gnomes, butterflies and spacemen. Two of them, aged about nine, attired as nigger minstrels with blacked-up faces, staggered through a half-hearted double-shuffle. A hideous little girl of fourteen with projecting teeth and rimless glasses sang "I'm in Love with a Wonderful Guy" with misdirected bravura and dried up dead in the middle of it. There was an agonized pause during which she stood first on one leg and then the other while Mrs. Bagel and Mavis Whittaker hissed the words at her from the sidelines. Finally she burst into tears and ran screaming out of the lounge followed, at a brisk trot, by her mother and the purser.

"Poor child," said Lady Bland wearily, "I wonder why they let her keep her glasses on."

The Grand Finale, which was Mavis Whittaker's version of an old-fashioned square dance, was reduced to a shambles by a very small boy who kept on jumping up and down in the same spot, waving a rattle in one hand and holding his genitals firmly with the other.

After Lady Bland had said a few gracious words of congratulation to Mavis Whittaker and Mrs. Bagel, everybody drifted out onto the deck. There was a cloudless sky and flying fish skittered away from the bows with their fins glittering in the late afternoon sunshine. Eldrich and Lola walked along to the swimming pool where they found Orford and Lisa in bathing suits, playing Scrabble.

"How was it?" inquired Lisa.

"Perfectly ghastly, and unrelieved by the faintest glimmer of potential talent."

"What did I tell you, Orford?" Lisa giggled. "We had quite an argument as to whether we should go or not. Orford said it might be funny, but my instincts knew better."

"Have you heard the dreadful tidings?" Orford said cheerfully to Lola.

"No. What are they?"

"The captain's fancy-dress dinner has been put forward two days owing to uncertain weather off the Japanese coast."

"Oh dear. I do wish they'd leave us alone."

"Personally, I can't wait." said Eldrich. "I love all kinds of organized communal gaiety."

"Are you going to contribute to the general fun by wearing something comical?"

"Frankly, no. I prefer to be an observer rather than a participant."

"Lady Bland is going to present the prizes."

"You two are full of information today. Where do you get it from?"

"We went to a cocktail party in the doctor's cabin last night. He told us lots of tidbits about what goes on in the ship. He's a gossipy old soak."

"I'm glad you've both decided to circulate a bit anyway," said Eldrich. "You've been fairly exclusive up to now."

"You must remember we're on our honeymoon," replied Lisa. "You, of all people, should know what honeymoons are."

"Come away, Eldrich, and leave them to their Scrabble." Lola slipped her arm through his. "You've been vanquished."

They walked away along the deck. Lisa looked after them thoughtfully.

"That's a shipboard romance if ever I saw one," she said.

"Well if it is, all I can say is good luck to them."

"She's years older than he is."

"What difference does that make? Look at Ninon de L'Enclos!"

"Who's she?"

"A sexy old French broad who went on having affairs until she was over eighty."

"I wish I'd been to Harvard," said Lisa wistfully. "They never taught us things like that at Bryn Mawr."

19

Although she refused to admit it to herself in so many words, Irma Kaplan was not enjoying the trip quite so much as she had expected to. It was not that she resented Lady Bland occupying the seat of honor on the captain's right. Hers, heaven knew, was not the sort of nature to be affected by anything so trivial, but it had struck her that Captain Berringer himself had been a little less cordial to her than he had been on her previous voyages in the *Mara*. It might be, of course, that he was harassed by the presence of British stuffed shirts like the Blands. Irma had nothing, so to speak, against the British as a race. In course of her various travels she had always got on with them very well, although there was no denying that they were inclined to give themselves airs and imagine that they were superior to everyone else. Lady Bland was a case in point. Irma didn't actually dislike Lady Bland. There was nothing about her to dislike really: she just sat there and talked in that high-pitched affected voice and appeared to take it for granted that everything she said or did was right. At the end of meals for instance, it was always Lady Bland who rose from the table first and expected everybody else to follow suit as a matter of course. Really the gall of some people! She laughed to herself.

Taken by and large she wasn't too impressed with any of her fellow passengers at the captain's table. Those awful, common Teitelbaums! She laughed again. She couldn't imagine how they had ever got themselves to the captain's table in the first place. There must have been some string-pulling behind the scenes. Orford and Lisa Wendle made no claim on her interest. She had tried, politely, to get into conversation with them on one or two occasions but without much success. They were obviously too pleased with themselves and too wrapped up in each other to make the faintest social effort. Lola Widmeyer was one of those hard types she knew only too well: "career women" was what they were called. Irma frankly didn't feel that she could ever be really relaxed and cozy with Lola Widmeyer. There remained Eldrich Trumbull. She was forced to admit to herself fairly and squarely that she just couldn't stand Eldrich Trumbull at any price. He was fresh to begin with and forever trying to be funny. You only had to read the newspaper columns to know the sort of life he led. Too much money, no sense of responsibility and no morals; always having affairs with women and getting drunk. He was the kind of wealthy ne'er-do-well who gave America a bad name abroad. Before the trip was over, Irma promised herself, she was going to give herself the pleasure of telling Mr. Eldrich Trumbull the Third exactly what she thought of him. It had not escaped her vigilant eye however that he had been drinking a great deal less than he had at the beginning of the trip, and it had occurred to her that maybe Lola Widmeyer might have been somehow influential in bringing this about. They were certainly becoming increasingly friendly. She had dismissed as foolish any idea of a romance between them. The disparity in their ages was too great to permit of such a possibility; even so, she wasn't quite sure. She had happened to be leaning on the ship's rail on the evening the ship sailed from Honolulu, watching the remainder of the shore-going passengers staggering on board, and she *had* happened to notice that among the last were Eldrich and Lola. She couldn't actually swear that he had his arm round her as they came up the gangway because she had stupidly left her long-distance glasses in her cabin, but it had certainly looked suspiciously like it. If her suspicions were correct and they were indulging in an illicit love affair, all she could say was that it was disgusting. A woman of Lola Widmeyer's name and reputation carrying on with a man half her age. Irma was conscious of a longing to discuss it with someone or other. Neither Mr. Pitoski nor the Klotzes would be any good and anyway she had had quite enough of them on that dreadful drive out to Pearl Harbor. She finished dressing thoughtfully, picked up a novel she had borrowed from the ship's library and sauntered out onto the promenade deck.

Every day, from approximately ten o'clock until twelve-thirty,

Sir Roderick and Lady Bland sat side by side in two steamer chairs sheltered from the noise and activity of the swimming pool by a glass partition. When Irma came up to them Sir Roderick, as usual, was working on a crossword puzzle while Lady Bland was engrossed in one of the earlier novels of Anthony Trollope.

"Isn't it the most wonderful morning?" said Irma, plumping herself down on the vacant chair next to Lady Bland.

Lady Bland looked up with a slight start. "Yes," she said. "It is indeed."

Sir Roderick looked up from his crossword and acknowledged Irma's vivacious "Good morning" with a brief nod.

"What are you reading?" Irma peered at the book in Lady Bland's hand.

"A novel by Trollope that I've never happened to read before. It's called *Is He Popenjoy?*"

"What a funny title."

"Yes, it is, isn't it?"

"Is it a funny book?"

"Very," said Lady Bland. "He was a witty writer."

"I got this from the library," said Irma indicating the immense volume she was carrying. "It's been on the bestseller list for months but I don't think I am going to like it very much."

"What a pity." Lady Bland closed *Is He Popenjoy?* with a sigh of resignation and looked out to sea.

"Too much sex in it for my taste," went on Irma undeterred. "Most modern novels have too much sex in them, don't you think?"

"I don't know really. I read so few of them."

"Sex is all very well in its place but when it's overdone it can become too much of a good thing can't it?" Irma gave a conspiratorial little laugh. "Did you read *The Carpetbaggers*?"

"No, I'm afraid I didn't."

"My dear!" Irma looked up to heaven as though invoking celestial accord. "I just couldn't believe my eyes—I couldn't really."

"If you'll excuse me," said Sir Roderick, rising to his feet, "I must go to my cabin and fetch my pipe."

"Come back soon, dear." There was an unmistakable note of supplication in Lady Bland's voice which Sir Roderick heartlessly ignored. "We shall meet at luncheon," he said to Irma and strode off along the deck. Lady Bland, bereft of hope, settled back in her chair.

"What a darling man he is," said Irma enthusiastically. "And so distinguished. I'm afraid that particular type of British gentleman is dying out."

"We still have a few of them left in England."

"I just adore England. There's a sort of something about it that no other country in the world has got."

"I'm glad you like it. I'm rather attached to it myself," said Lady Bland.

"I went on a wonderful motor trip just after the War with some friends of mine called Vogel. We started from Edinburgh and drove all the way to John o'Groats."

"It's a little difficult to capture the real essence of England in the Scottish Highlands."

Irma gave a self-deprecatory cackle. "That's me all over," she said. "I'm always getting things wrong. But after all it is more or less the same country, if you know what I mean, isn't it?"

"There are still quite a number of people on either side of the border who wouldn't agree with you."

"Have you got any Scotch blood?"

"A great deal. My family came from Perthshire."

"Isn't that fascinating! Mrs. Vogel's grandmother on her father's side was Scotch."

"Scottish," corrected Lady Bland gently.

"What do you think of Lola Widmeyer?" said Irma, abandoning further small talk and getting down to brass tacks.

"I like her very much. Why?" Lady Bland looked slightly puzzled at the abrupt change of subject.

"She's got such a *clever* face, hasn't she? And she really is wonderfully well preserved for her age."

"I have no idea what her age is."

"She'll never see fifty again," said Irma.

"Perhaps she doesn't want to." A note of irritation was discernible in Lady Bland's voice. Irma either didn't notice it or decided to ignore it.

"I always find people fascinating, don't you? That's why I'm never bored for a single minute. My late husband always used to say: 'Put Irma down in an hotel lobby and she'll be happy for hours.'"

"And did he?" inquired Lady Bland.

"What I mean to say is—" Irma pressed on. "If you're really interested in your fellow creatures and what they say and what they do you need never feel really alone."

"Being alone is sometimes a blessing," replied Lady Bland pointedly.

"Have you noticed the budding romance between Lola Widmeyer and that Eldrich Trumbull?" Irma gave a tinkling laugh.

"Which Eldrich Trumbull? I was not aware that there was more than one on board."

"Thank heaven for that at any rate. He's the sort of wealthy American playboy type that I just have no use for at all." Irma unwisely allowed her resentment of Eldrich to outweigh her discretion. "He has much too good an opinion of himself and is always trying to be funny at other people's expense."

"How odd that you should think that. I find him most charming and very amusing."

"I don't think it's charming or amusing to carry on with a woman old enough to be your mother."

"Really, Mrs. Kaplan." Lady Bland looked at her with icy distaste. "I cannot feel that either Mr. Trumbull's or Miss Widmeyer's private affairs are any concern of yours or mine. If your interest in your fellow creatures leads you to make malicious innuendos about them behind their backs, I can only suggest that you curb it, at least in my presence." Without a further glance at her, she gathered up her book and her knitting bag and walked away. Irma, tight-lipped and quivering with rage, watched her go. Her blood rising to her cheeks beneath her Elizabeth Arden foundation cream imparted a sickly mauvish tint to her round, plump face. She sat where she was for a moment in order to give herself time to control her expression. Then with an effort, she got up and went out onto the after-deck which, as usual at this time in the morning, was crowded with people sitting round the swimming pool. Mr. and Mrs. Teitelbaum, walking arm in arm, came face to face with her.

"Mr. Teitelbaum and I were wondering if you'd care to join us for cocktails in the smoking room this evening? Sir Roderick and Lady Bland have promised to come."

"No," said Irma curtly. "I would not." She walked away leaving them staring after her in blank amazement.

20

The absence of Irma Kaplan from the Teitelbaums' cocktail party in the smoking room in no way impaired the success of the occasion. In addition to their captain's table-mates they had invited an agreeable young couple called Markel who, with their three small children, were on their way to take up residence in Tokyo, where Mr. Markel was to be attached to the American Embassy, and two young men in their middle thirties named respectively Bill Heisinger and Dennis Carp who, it transpired, ran an antique shop in Bridgeport, Connecticut, and were making an extensive tour in search of bizarre Oriental knickknacks. Both of them appeared to be exceedingly fond of Mrs. Teitelbaum, whom they had made friends with during a canasta tournament. In fact Dennis Carp, the more sibilant of the two, nudged Eldrich confidentially after having knocked back three dry Martinis in quick succession and said, "Isn't she the most divine old camp you ever saw?" Eldrich agreed that she most certainly was. Mrs. Teitelbaum, unaware of this affectionate compliment, was engrossed in a cozy chat with Lady Bland in course of which she told her all about Peachie and Joe and showed her a snapshot of them taken on their wedding day. They were standing in front of a gargantuan wedding cake and laughing uncontrollably. Lady Bland peered at the snapshot through her lorgnette.

"They look sweet," she said. "And what an enormous cake!"

A succession of stewards passed to and fro among the guests bearing dishes of highly colored canapés; Lola got into rather an intense discussion with Bill Heisinger about the merits of James Baldwin as a novelist and kept on giving Eldrich imploring looks in the hope that he would extract her from it; however he ignored her pleas, winked at her maddeningly and went on with his conversation with Dennis Carp, who giggled a great deal and occasionally tossed his head as though his hair was getting in his eyes. As he happened to have a close crewcut, this gesture was unnecessary.

"You must admit—" Bill Heisinger was saying, "*Another Country* was dreamy."

"'Dreamy' is not exactly the word I should have chosen," replied Lola. "But parts of it are certainly very well-written."

In spite of mild protests from Lady Bland, Mr. Teitelbaum insisted on ordering another round of drinks for everyone. Mrs. Teitelbaum looked at him anxiously. He had already had two old-fashioneds and his face was looking rather pink, however in spite of what Doc Weatherfield had said, probably just one extra once in a way wouldn't do him any harm and he was so evidently enjoying himself, that she didn't want to be a spoilsport.

While the final round was being consumed, Dennis Carp, emboldened by his fifth Martini, edged a little closer to Eldrich.

"I'll tell you something," he said. "You're *simpatico,* that's what you are, *molto simpatico.*"

"Thank you very much," said Eldrich. "Or perhaps I should say '*Grazie tante.*'"

"Oh, la bella bella Italia," sighed Dennis nostalgically. *"Mi chiammano Mimi!"*

"I'm not entirely surprised."

"I knew you'd be dishy," went on Dennis. "After all you couldn't very well not be dishy with your reputation and all those wives and one thing and another, but what I didn't know was that you'd be so—shall we say *gemütlich?*"

"By all means. *Danke schön.*"

"I shall get hell from Bill for monopolizing you like this. Bill's perfectly okay until he gets a few drinks inside him, then he's apt to get ugly."

"Aren't we all?"

610

Dennis went into peals of laughter. "You slay me you know. You really do."

"I'm so glad."

"Isn't this the most diabolical ship you've ever been on? Just look at those murals!—And the food! *Dio mio!* As my old grandmother used to say."

"Mine always said *'Madonna mia.'*"

"Bill and I are getting off in Yokohama and joining the ship again in Kobe, that is if we don't get caught up in Tokyo."

"Un bel di vedremo," said Eldrich gratefully as he saw Lady Bland rise with a graceful air of finality. "*'Ciao* for now,' as my other old grandmother used to say." He got up. "We're bound to meet again soon. *Hasta la vista.*"

"I can't wait," said Dennis fervently.

"How sweet of you to give us such a delightful party," said Lady Bland to Mr. and Mrs. Teitelbaum as they all went down in the elevator. Mrs. Teitelbaum bridled.

"It was our pleasure," she said.

When they arrived at the table they discovered the captain and Irma Kaplan sitting alone. Irma, wearing a black dress and an electric blue stole, was picking at a slice of smoked salmon that looked like orange felt. The captain rose to greet them.

"We really must apologize for being so late," said Lady Bland, taking her seat beside him, "but we were having such fun at Mr. and Mrs. Teitelbaum's cocktail party that we lost all track of the time."

"That's perfectly okay, Ma'am," said the captain reseating himself. "As a matter of fact I've only just got down myself. Mrs. Kaplan was just telling me how she once got fish poisoning in a hotel in Casablanca."

"How interesting," said Lady Bland.

"Let's hope you don't get it again." Eldrich looked pointedly at Irma's smoked salmon and then at the menu. "Personally I'm going to lead off with some Vichyssoise and go recklessly on to a broiled double French lamb chop."

"You'd better have that too, Henry," said Mrs. Teitelbaum. "Only don't have it too rare."

They all ordered what they wanted and the conversation became general. Irma Kaplan made one or two half-hearted efforts to force whatever subject was under discussion to coincide with some personal experience of her own, but it was obvious to everyone that her shrill persistence had lost its impetus. Whenever she opened her mouth to speak Lady Bland put down her knife and fork and leaned forward with an expression of steely politeness which would have silenced the chatter of a cageful of orangutans. After a while even Irma's iron self-esteem had to admit defeat and, with her mouth set

611

in a sullen line, she lapsed into silence for the rest of the meal.

A couple of hours later, Eldrich and Lola, having walked out in the middle of an inane Hollywood movie, which dealt with the wholesomely erotic adventures of a group of "teenagers" in a summer camp, went up onto the boat deck. Eldrich unfolded two chairs which had been stacked against one of the ventilators, and they sat, side by side, looking up at the swaying stars.

Eldrich rested his hand lightly on Lola's.

"Will you be at home tonight if I should happen to be passing by?"

"Of course."

"What's the matter?"

"The matter?—Nothing's the matter."

"Yes there is. I know there is. Something's upset you. I felt it at lunch today and I've felt it ever since."

"Nonsense. You're imagining things. I admit I was in an irritable mood at lunch because I'd done a bad morning's work. I couldn't concentrate. Everything I wrote was banal, laborious and dull."

"Was I to blame in any way?"

"Don't let's go on about it. It really isn't important. All writers have to go through that particular sort of frustration every once in a while, it's part of the process."

"Am I getting in the way?"

"Of course you are. But it isn't your fault. Being in love always gets in the way. You're in my mind and heart and thoughts every minute of the day. I can't even get rid of you for a few brief hours. I wonder what you're doing; whether you're awake or asleep; who you're talking to. I stare at the telephone and long to call you up, just to hear your voice."

"You certainly haven't succumbed to that temptation to any marked degree." Eldrich laughed dryly. "Has it ever struck you that I might be thinking of you too, and also staring at the Goddamned telephone."

Lola lifted his hand and pressed it against her face. "Don't be cross with me, my love. I know I'm behaving like a whimpering idiot. But it isn't only that."

"What do you mean?"

"Your instincts were right. There is something upsetting me. But I was absolutely determined not to mention it to you. It's tiresome and trivial and quite irrelevant really."

"Give, darling. Don't hoard up miserable little worries all by yourself."

There was silence for a moment, then Lola said with an effort, "I'm afraid we haven't been quite so discreet as we thought we were. Our secret is out."

"How do you know?"

"My stewardess. She hovered about when I was having my breakfast this morning and made a few pointed remarks about how nice you were and didn't I think it a shame about you having been so unlucky in love, etc.; then, smelling a rat, I began to question her casually. She's a garrulous old thing from Saint Paul, Minnesota, and, as a rule, I discourage her from talking, but today I let her have her head. It appears that her greatest friend on board is one of the women who works in the Beauty Salon, and this friend sets and washes Irma Kaplan's hair every other day. Need I say more?"

"How did the old bitch find out?"

"I don't think she has actually found out anything, but she apparently saw us coming on board that night in Honolulu and has noticed that we are together quite a lot. She has noticed that you are not drinking so much as you were and attributes it to my dominance over you."

"She's not so far out at that."

"She has also been fairly vitriolic about the disparity in our ages."

"Aha!" Eldrich gave a low whistle. "That explains it."

"Explains what?"

"Lady Bland's reply when I commented on Irma not being at the cocktail party."

"Lady Bland?—Oh dear!"

"She said, 'So much the better. That woman's a perfect horror.' She said it with such venom that I was quite startled."

"Do you suppose Irma told *her*?"

"Probably, and got put smartly in her place. I wouldn't like to incur the wrath of that redoubtable governor's lady."

"Oh, God!" Lola shuddered. "It's really too humiliating."

"Are you sure it matters as much as you think it does? After all, it's nobody else's business but ours."

"Of course it matters. It's sort of—of—degrading. I hate it."

"I don't see that it's all that degrading."

"Of course you don't. It's different for you anyway, you're a man and after all you're more or less accustomed to have your private affairs discussed. I'm not."

"You're really angry, aren't you?"

"Yes, I am—I am. I'm bitterly angry, not with you but with myself."

"Thank you for absolving me from all responsibility so generously. It's restored my self-confidence which, as you know, is notoriously vulnerable."

"Now it's you who are angry."

"You bet the hell I'm angry. Nobody exactly enjoys being told that they're a degrading influence."

"I didn't say that at all."

"In any case I think you're making a great drama out of nothing."

"I am *not* making a great drama. I just can't tolerate the idea of everybody on the ship whispering behind their fans and gossiping about us. I don't like my conduct having to be defended by Lady Bland either."

"I've no proof that Lady Bland defended you, or that she knows anything about it at all. It was merely a guess."

"Don't let's talk about it anymore. I'm sorry I was idiotic enough to mention it in the first place."

"Okay by me." Eldrich got up. "This particular enchanted evening seems to have got a bit brown at the edges. What I need is a drink. Do you want one?"

"No, thank you. I don't indulge in that form of escape."

"Hoity toity!" said Eldrich "Perhaps you'd be a little less scratchy if you did. Call me when you feel like seeing me. I promise to wear dark glasses and a false beard."

He walked away along the deck. Lola watched him go and clenched her hands together to stop them trembling. She sat still for a while listening to the noise of the waves slapping against the hull of the ship and an occasional snatch of dance music coming from the main lounge. A man and woman, laughing and talking, came round the corner. They looked at her curiously as they passed and disappeared down the ladder leading to the deck below. Presently she got up and wandered along toward the bow. The wind assaulted her burning face and tore at her hair. She leaned on the rail and stared into the darkness. The noise of the sea was louder here and a little light on the foremast bobbed and swayed against the sky. Here it was, the old familiar pattern, starting all over again. The misery and the doubt and the self-recrimination, pointless quarrels, overstrained nerves, the awareness that other people, strangers, were watching, commenting, gossiping about her heart's private secrets. In this particular instance they were probably laughing as well. There was always something ridiculous in the spectacle of an elderly woman besotted over a man years younger than herself. She was perfectly conscious that she had behaved unkindly to Eldrich, but her anger over the situation in which she had so idiotically placed herself was still stronger than her regret. Eldrich was in no way to blame for what had happened. She had lashed out at him and hurt him because her own personal pride had been humiliated. That she would suffer for this she had no doubt, but now she was still too furious to care whether she had hurt him or not. She left the forward deck and walked through the almost deserted writing room on the way down to her cabin. She paused for a moment to comb her hair into a semblance of tidiness. As she was about to pass the entrance to the

"Lanai" bar, she saw Eldrich come out of it. He was obviously drunk and holding on to the arm of a pretty red-haired young woman in a tight-fitting silver lamé evening gown which could leave no doubts in anyone's mind of the excellence of her figure. Lola stood back in the doorway of the closed florist's shop and watched them as they weaved their way down the main staircase. Then, numb with unhappiness, she made her way to her cabin, shut the door and locked it and flung herself, face downward, onto her bed. She lay there, still and dry-eyed, for more than an hour. Finally she dragged herself up with an effort and began to undress. It wasn't until she had brushed her teeth, put on her nightgown and sat in front of the dressing-table mirror to cream her face that she started to cry. She stared at the tears coursing down her cheeks without making any effort to stop them. She wasn't even aware of any particular pain. The weeping was just a process that she observed dully without thought. Suddenly she heard a very gentle knock on her door. She grabbed a piece of Kleenex and dabbed frantically at her eyes. "Who is it?" Her voice sounded as though it belonged to someone else. There was no answer, then the knock was repeated, this time a little louder. Lola snatched her dressing gown from the bed, threw it on and opened the door. Eldrich was standing in the passage. He was wearing a pajama jacket and gray flannel trousers; his feet were bare. He stumbled past her into the room and sat down heavily on the bed. She shut the door again and locked it, then came over and stood looking down at him. He suddenly put his arms round her, pulled her to him and buried his face in her breast.

"I'm drunk," he muttered, almost inaudibly.

"Yes. I know you are."

"I am in no condition to be in charge of a car. I should be arrested and fined heavily for driving when under the influence of alcohol."

"Fortunately you're not driving a car."

"That's just where you're wrong," he said. He released her, took both her hands in his and looked up at her appealingly. "I *am* driving a car. I'm driving a rented Chevrolet convertible. The sun is bright in the sky and the weather is smiling and beside me is sitting a lady whom I love very much. She has a tender mouth, sharp, observant eyes and a colored scarf tied round her snow-white hair, because you see she is very very very much older than me, so old in fact that I have to slow down at every curve in case she should lurch forward and bash her poor wrinkled old kisser into the windscreen."

"This is no moment for whimsical charm, Eldrich. It's too easy." She tried to break away from him but he held on to her hands. "Please let go of me."

"Not until you let go of me."

615

"Please Eldrich . . ." She felt tears starting to fill her eyes again and turned her face away. He lifted her right hand and pressed his lips into the palm of it.

"Don't be angry with me anymore. I know I behaved badly and made you unhappy, but don't be angry with me anymore. It's such a waste of time."

"Getting drunk is also a waste of time."

"You said that to me once before, a long time ago. We were sitting on the deck of some ship or other, we didn't know each other very well."

"We don't know each other very well now." She wrenched her hands away from his and went over to the dressing table. There was a packet of cigarettes lying by her handbag. She took one, lit it unsteadily and sat down with her back to him. After a moment or two he got up from the bed and came over to her. He stood behind her and rested his hands on her shoulders. She looked up at him in the mirror and saw that his eyes were brimming with tears, then she leant forward and buried her head in her arms.

"This is intolerable," she said in a muffled voice. "Please go away, Eldrich. I can't bear any more."

"Can I have a cigarette?"

"Yes." She pushed the packet toward him. "If you'll only go back to your cabin and leave me alone. We'll talk in the morning."

"That will be too late, the moment will have gone." He tried unsuccessfully to light his cigarette. "This damned lighter doesn't work."

She took the lighter from his hand and lit his cigarette for him. He took a long drag at it and then knelt on the floor beside her. "Please look at me, darling. Don't turn away from me anymore. I'm not going back to my cabin and we're not going to talk in the morning, we're going to talk now. I know I'm drunk, but however drunk I am I can still make a little sense. That's always been one of my most notorious social assets. Loaded to the gills but overarticulate to the last drop." He gave the ghost of a smile and then resolutely turned her round until she was forced to look at him. "We had a quarrel up on the boat deck, right? Not a very important one really. Then I went and got stinking drunk because I was ashamed of myself. That was all that happened then, not really enough to justify what's happening now—right?" He gave her a little shake. After a moment she nodded reluctantly and bit her lip. "What's happened since to upset you so deeply?" He looked at her intently. "That's what I want to know."

"I think you can answer that question better than I can."

"What do you mean?"

"It doesn't matter."

"The hell it doesn't matter! It matters a great deal. What do you mean?"

"I saw you come out of the bar. I was on my way down to my cabin."

"Oh—so that's it."

"Yes. That *is* it." Lola's lip trembled. "Who was she? The red-haired woman who so considerately took you to bed."

"Her name, believe it or not, is Marybelle Goldstein, pronounced 'Steen' to rhyme with Listerine, rather than 'Stine' to rhyme with Einstein. She is married to a gentleman in the textile business who doesn't understand her, and she did *not* take me to bed. I admit she made every effort to do so but we finally parted outside my cabin door with every expression of mutual esteem. To rhyme with scream!"

"Oh, Eldrich." Lola lowered her head. Eldrich rose to his feet, lifted her up and put his arms round her.

"I'll go back to my cabin now if you want me to, but if I do you'll have to come with me. Marybelle may have staggered back in a drunken stupor and be lying there waiting for me. I didn't lock the door."

Lola murmured something inaudibly in a choked voice and clung tightly to him.

A few hours later when the first light of early dawn shone through the porthole Lola awoke from a dreamless sleep. Eldrich's left arm was stretched protectively across her naked body and his head was resting on her breast. She lay very still so as not to wake him. Overhead she heard the familiar early morning sound of seamen swabbing down the boat deck. She glanced at her traveling clock on the table beside her and noted that the time was ten minutes to six. In a half an hour it would be full daylight. Memories of the evening before flooded into her mind and she closed her eyes again, reliving for a moment all the foolish misery. Eldrich gave a little grunt and she felt his arm tighten round her. She stroked his hair gently. "Wake up my darling," she whispered. "You really must wake up now. The day is beginning."

Presently, when he had finally put on his pajama jacket and gray trousers and she had peeped out of the door to see if the coast was clear, she watched him padding away on his bare feet along the deserted corridor, closed the door after him, walked over to the porthole and looked out at the morning. The sea was a pinkish-mauve color and looked translucent under the radiant sky. She stayed there for some time, staring at the changing light.

21

The only members of the captain's party who deigned to put on fancy dress for the Gala Dinner and Dance were Mr. and Mrs. Teitelbaum and Irma Kaplan. Lady Bland, it is true, had wound a purple silk bandeau round her ash gray hair because, as she confessed to Lola on the way down from the smoking room, it would at least prevent her from having to wear a paper hat. Mrs. Teitelbaum, with great ingenuity and the assistance of Mavis Whittaker, had disguised herself as an early Roman matron. Her tubby little body was swathed in a white sheet; on her head was a wreath of gold leaves (sewn together by Mrs. Bagel on Mavis Whittaker's sewing machine) and on her feet a pair of gold sandals with rather unromanesque high heels which she usually wore with her pink taffeta evening dress. Her only other ornaments were a gold lamé belt, two slave bangles and a pair of enormous gold drop earrings, kindly lent by Miss Gimbell from the Beauty Salon. The total effect of all this was slightly spoiled by her rimless glasses, but without them she was unable to read the menu. Mr. Teitelbaum, after much heated discussion, had succumbed to his wife's coaxing and borrowed from Mavis Whittaker's fancy dress store a complete Mephistopheles outfit including a pointed black beard which he laid by his plate during dinner because it got in his way. Irma Kaplan, who arrived late, received a round of applause from the other tables. She was dressed expensively, elaborately and inaccurately as Madame Butterfly. Her reception at the captain's table was tepid. The captain himself made a gallant effort and mumbled something archly about Lieut. Pinkerton and putting the cherry blossoms to shame, Lady Bland raised her eyes briefly from her plate, surveyed her with an expressionless smile, then lowered them again and continued to eat her fileted sole.

After dinner the "Grand Parade" took place in the main lounge. The captain's party occupied the table of honor in the center and the procession, to the accompaniment of "The March of the Wooden Soldiers" played by the ship's band, ambled slowly by them. Mavis Whittaker attired as an Alice-blue Pierrette, Mrs. Bagel, impressive in gray lace, and Olaf Hansen, the purser, wearing a comical fireman's helmet, acted in the capacity of sheepdogs, herding the competitors through one door and out of the other and trying to persuade them to keep some semblance of a line. This was none too easy for many of them had had a great deal to drink at dinner and were inclined to stop in their tracks and exchange jokes with admiring friends. When it was all over and the band at last stopped playing "The March of the Wooden Soldiers" and switched to a selection from *Oklahoma*, they were all herded back again and arranged, by the indefatigable sheepdogs, in a ring, while a large table bearing the prizes was carried in by two stewards. The captain rose and made a jocular speech at the end of which he introduced Lady Bland, who went and stood by his side. When she had acknowledged the polite applause with a gracious inclination of the head, she produced her lorgnette from her evening bag and consulted a piece of paper she was holding in her left hand. Then, in a clear, incisive voice she announced unfalteringly the long list of prizewinners. (It was laid down emphatically in Mavis Whittaker's directive from the head office that never less than twenty-five prizes were to be awarded on gala nights, otherwise passengers were apt to consider themselves unfairly treated and write bitter letters of complaint.) Mrs. Teitelbaum, suffused with blushes and deafened with applause, waddled up to receive the first prize, which was a large package done up in a shiny pink paper with a blue bow on the top. The second prize went to a Mr. Stack who was dressed humorously as a barrel of beer. Mr. Stack was a tall man and his long, thin head and long, hairy legs protruding from either end of his cardboard carapace caused much boisterous merriment. Irma Kaplan sullenly received the third prize. Lady Bland, with the most admirable finesse, just contrived to be smiling over her shoulder at the captain as she handed it to her. One by one the long line of happy contestants shuffled up to the table, received their gifts and backed away again. Lady Bland, with an unflagging smile, managed to murmur a brief congratulatory word or two to each one of them. Among the minor winners were Bill Heisinger and Dennis Carp as gladiators attired only in silver paper helmets and sequined bathing trunks. They carried long nets and spears and Bill Heisinger had palpably shaved his chest in honor of the occasion. Another proud winner was Marybelle Goldstein. (Lady Bland pronounced it firmly to rhyme with wine.) She was wearing a number of colored balloons, several of which had been burst by merry friends with cigarette ends. Her bosom and legs were only sparsely covered and her back was virtually bare.

"I don't believe," whispered Lola to Eldrich, "that her husband doesn't understand her. My theory is that he understands her only too well."

At long last the ritual came to an end and Lady Bland was able to return gratefully to her chair.

"Thank goodness that's over," she said as she sat down between Lola and Orford Wendle. "I thought it was going on for ever. Did you ever see such extraordinary getups?"

"You did it beautifully, Lady Bland," said Lola. "You were perfectly charming to everybody."

"Not quite everybody." Lady Bland gave a little laugh. "Wasn't it lovely that our Mrs. Teitelbaum won the first prize?"

"Did you fix that?" inquired Orford.

"Hush, Mr. Wendle." Lady Bland tapped him reprovingly with her lorgnette. "You mustn't ask indiscreet questions."

22

Orford and Lisa Wendle were leaving the ship at Yokohama because part of their honeymoon itinerary was to visit the Japanese countryside in cherry-blossom time. They gave a small farewell cocktail party in the "Lanai" bar the night before the ship was due to arrive. Apart from their own little group which consisted of Sir Roderick and Lady Bland, Lola, Eldrich and the Teitelbaums, there were very few people in the bar. The weather had been fairly rough and the ship was still rolling and pitching quite a lot. The Blands and the Teitelbaums were staying on the ship and going on to Kobe by sea. Eldrich and Lola however had decided to stay a night in Tokyo, visit Kyoto the next day and rejoin the ship at Kobe the day after that.

Neither of them made the slightest attempt to disguise the fact that they were making this little excursion alone together and Lady Bland made no comment beyond saying that Kyoto was still beautiful and comparatively unspoiled and that if they ran into an old French professor there called Benoist, that they were to give him her love without fail and ask him to explain the historical background of the place and show them the sacred carp.

At about nine o'clock the next morning the *Mara* sailed into the bay of Yokohama. The weather had cleared and the water was glittering in the sunshine. By noon everyone had passed through customs and immigration and been allowed ashore. Eldrich had ordered a hired limousine by radio and, driven by an affable chauffeur whose mouth gleamed with gold fillings, he and Lola set off through the crowded streets for the Okura Hotel in Tokyo.

They were both aware of a slight feeling of self-consciousness at being alone together away from the confines of the ship. Eldrich gave her hand a squeeze.

"Our bonnets are now floating down the mill stream and our boats are blazing behind us. How do you feel about it?"

"I think it's a windmill that one throws one's bonnet over, not a water-mill."

"I apologize for the sublime hideousness of this drive. The Japanese have embraced Western industrialism with excessive zeal."

"I've at last seen a woman in a kimono," said Lola.

"I'm going to buy you the most gorgeous kimono in Tokyo this very afternoon and the next time there's a captain's gala dinner you can knock everybody's eye out."

"What shall I buy you?"

"You shall buy me a wonderful pencil that lights up at the end. You can get them anywhere in Japan."

"Isn't it glorious to think that we're not going to have ship's food for two whole days and nights? What shall we have for lunch?"

"Japanese or European?"

"European, please, darling. Don't let's be too experimental too soon."

"I see your point," said Eldrich. "I also love you very much."

23

Forty-eight hours later the *Mara* sailed out of Kobe harbor. It was a warm spring day but the sky was overcast. An hour earlier Eldrich and Lola had come on board. Irma, wearing a rust red two-piece suit and a sour expression, watched them get out of a black Cadillac and walk to the gangway followed by a chauffeur carrying their luggage and some large parcels.

At luncheon Lady Bland, perfectly aware of Irma's pursed lips and silent disapproval, questioned Lola and Eldrich about their stay in Kyoto and enquired whether or not they had run into her old friend Professor Benoist.

"We asked for him at the hotel," said Lola, "but they said he was away in Korea for a few weeks. However, the mere fact that we asked for him seemed to impress the hotel manager very much. He was tremendously polite to us."

"He also hissed a great deal and had more teeth than are usual," said Eldrich.

"The temples were lovely and we stared for hours at the sacred carp, they looked so relaxed."

"One of them winked at us," said Eldrich, "as though he knew that it was spring and that we were having a good time."

"That's the cutest thing I've ever heard," cried Mrs. Teitelbaum.

Irma Kaplan looked at her disdainfully and concentrated on her tomato salad.

Later, when Lola and Eldrich were sitting in a corner of the Winter Garden Lounge having coffee, Lola suddenly laughed.

"You were certainly brazen about the carp!"

"I felt brazen. There's something about our Irma that brings out the 'devil-may-care' in me. I wanted to rush round the table to her and say 'Why do you walk through the fields in gloves—O fat white woman whom nobody loves.'"

"Fancy you knowing that," said Lola. "You really are full of surprises."

"I did a course of English poetry at Harvard. 'The grass is soft as the breast of doves—and shivering-sweet to the touch—O why do you walk through the fields in gloves—missing so much and so much?'"

"It was written by Frances something-or-other."

"Cornford. I loved it immediately I read it. There are so many fat white women who walk through so many many fields in gloves. It's a sad thought, isn't it?"

"Have some more coffee," said Lola.

"On the whole," Eldrich pushed his cup toward her, "I should say that these last forty-eight hours have been the happiest I have ever known."

Lola's hand shook a little as she poured the coffee. "You say that so surely, and so sweetly, that I almost believe it."

"Why shouldn't you believe it? It was the same for you, wasn't it?"

"Of course." She closed her eyes for a moment. "I shall relive every single minute—long after . . ." she stopped.

"Long after what?"

"I was going to say 'long after it's all over' but it would have sounded crude and ungrateful."

"'And yonder all before us lie—deserts of vast eternity.' Mr. Marvell wrote that when he was irritated by his coy mistress."

"Are you irritated with yours?"

"My dear." He rested his hand lightly on hers. "You couldn't be coy if you tried." He smiled, but there was a hint of sadness in it. "However you could be, and frequently are, painfully distrustful. Stop trying to see the whole wood, just relax and enjoy the trees."

"I'm used to constructing my stories technically in advance. I always know, before I start, exactly what the end is going to be."

"Surely not quite always. Doesn't it sometimes happen that a certain character suddenly takes charge and begins to push you around?"

"Very very rarely. I usually manage to keep cool."

"But there have been one or two occasions when you have been defeated?"

"Only by truth, never by fiction."

"And what sad truth are you trying to inject into our little love affair?"

"Just that, that is all it is, all it can ever be." She bent her head and fumbled in her bag for her cigarette case.

"Why shouldn't it last for ever and a day?"

"Because nothing ever does." She kept her head down and her voice sounded muffled.

"I see I've been foolish enough to get myself involved with a whiner! A terrified creature who's scared of shadows and covers her heart with her hands."

"I've never whined in my life." Lola looked up indignantly. Eldrich laughed.

"I thought that word would snap you out of it."

Lola rose to her feet. "Let's go out on deck," she said, "and watch the sea go by."

24

In course of every long sea voyage there are certain days that feel as thoough they had been ringed in black on some Olympian calendar; days that seem to be taken over and gleefully disorganized by unkind gods. Just such a day dawned when the *Mara* was steaming in innocence through the gray-green waves thirty-six hours away from the island of Hong Kong. It began with Captain Berringer, at seven-fifteen A.M., cutting a sizable hunk of flesh from his chin with a new razor blade. At nine-forty, in the main dining saloon, a Mrs. Reubens of Spokane, Washington, hitherto unnoted and unsung, caused a sensation by upsetting a pot of scalding coffee into her lap and being carried shrieking to the sick bay by two stewards. Lady Bland, while strolling with Lola Widmeyer along the boat deck, got a smut from the funnel in her eye which tormented her for an hour and a half until, in desperation, she went to the doctor who, with an unsteady hand, rolled her eyelid back on a match stick and extracted it. Luncheon proceeded uneventfully until Peppo, the maître d'hôtel, made a dramatic entrance bearing a flaming *soufflé en surprise*, tripped over a large tin truck which a little boy had left beside his chair and deposited the soufflé upside down in the center of a table for which it was not intended. The afternoon was punctuated by further disasters: a lady from Salt Lake City with uncontrollable blue hair inadvertently dropped her raffia handbag containing her passport, her traveler's cheques and three colored snapshots of her late husband into the sea, gave a loud cry and collapsed unconscious on the deck. A small boy of four, with fiendish ingenuity, managed to prize loose a colored bead from his playpen and swallow it and had to be held upside down by Mavis Whittaker and struck repeatedly by Mrs. Bagel until he was sick and the bead reappeared decorated with some half-digested lettuce.

Lola, lying on her bed in her cabin, awoke from a light sleep to find herself, unaccountably, in tears. She searched her mind in vain to try to recapture whatever sad dream it was that had so depressed her but could remember nothing. She sat up, dabbed her eyes, lit a cigarette and then lay back again staring up at the moving reflections of the water making patterns on the deck-head above her. In two days' time she would be in Hong Kong and the romantic fantasy in which she had allowed herself to drift so irresponsibly for the last two weeks would come to an end. It would have to come to an end. Of this she was convinced. She also knew that it must be she herself who would have to summon up the courage and resolution to break the spell. Eldrich would be no help. He would fight her every step of the way. He would be unhappy too—her heart contracted at the thought of this—but less unhappy in the long run if she had the strength to make a clean cut rather than subject them both to the slow miseries of mutual disillusionment and anticlimax. She had no doubts that he loved her, or at least imagined that he did; but the love of a charming, slightly dissolute man of thirty-seven for a woman of fifty could surely offer very very little hope of survival. When *he* was fifty, in the prime of life, she would be sixty-three, and when he was sixty, still, she was sure, elegant and energetic, she would be an old woman of seventy-three and probably a fairly snappish and querulous old woman at that. At this point of her reflections her sense of humor reasserted itself and she began to laugh; however, there was a slight note of hysteria in her laughter that her sharp, introspective ear did not fail to register.

She finally decided, lying there in the slowly darkening cabin, for it was almost time to dress for dinner and the warning chimes had already tinkled along the ship's corridors, that the present, the gay, enchanting present must remain blindly and lovingly as it was, unsullied by useless foreboding, until the moment came, and come it would, when the word "farewell" relegated it to the past.

On this particular evening it was the turn of Sir Roderick and Lady Bland to give a cocktail party in the smoking room. The captain, his face decorated with a large ring of plaster, descended a half an hour earlier than usual to grace the occasion. Much to everyone's surprise Irma Kaplan was present, resplendent in a cerise velvet "hostess gown." Her manner was subdued but there was an unmistakable glint in her eye which might have signified either triumph or relief that the redoubtable Lady Bland had at last seen fit to release her from the doghouse.

Mrs. Teitelbaum, swathed in pink tulle, was in a state of high excitement having received a mother-of-pearl compact that very afternoon from the quivering hands of Mavis Whittaker in grateful acknowledgment of her prowess at canasta. The compact was passed reverently from hand to hand and suitably admired. Mr. Teitelbaum watched the proceedings with shining eyes.

When they all rose to go down to dinner the captain detained them for a few moments by toasting Sir Roderick and Lady Bland and wishing them a happy time in Hong Kong and a pleasant journey to Singapore where they were to be met by their married daughter and no less than three grandchildren, none of whom they had yet seen. He extended the scope of this little peroration by bidding an affectionate adieu to Eldrich and Lola, who were also leaving the ship at Hong Kong, and adding tactfully how happy he was that Mr. and Mrs. Teitelbaum and Mrs. Kaplan would be still gracing his table on the voyage home to the States. As he concluded, Mr. Teitelbaum said "Hear Hear" with sudden fervence and they all made their way down to the saloon.

It was not a "Captain's Gala Dinner" in the accepted sense. That is to say there were neither paper hats, colored balls to throw nor favors of any kind. There was, however, an air of tingling, valedictory excitement in the dining saloon and a decorated menu of elaborate design which drew forth appropriate murmurs of appreciation. The dishes listed, however, although ornamented with tritons, fishes and curlicues, remained as uninspired as usual. The captain announced, with a self-conscious guffaw, that the wine of the evening was "on him." When it arrived, it turned out to be a sparkling Californian burgundy, at the first sip of which Sir Roderick muttered something incomprehensible and choked.

It was toward the end of the meal that the various petty stresses and strains of the tiresome day culminated in abrupt and intolerable tragedy. Mr. Teitelbaum, who had not spoken for some time, which in itself was not unusual, suddenly gave a pitiful little cry, clutched his right arm just below the shoulder and fell forward onto the table. There was a horrified silence for a moment. Eldrich jumped up and lifted him back into the chair; the captain also rose and ran to the doctor's table which was nearby. Mrs. Teitelbaum leant forward and touched her husband's face with her hand, delicately, as though she were soothing a frightened kitten, then she said, in a small voice, almost inaudibly, "Oh no—Oh no!" and putting both her arms round him, pressed her face against his cheek. Some people at the next table stood up to see what was happening. The captain returned with the doctor who immediately undid Mr. Teitelbaum's collar and felt his pulse. Lady Bland gently but firmly disengaged Mrs. Teitelbaum's arms from her husband's body and pulled her back into her chair. Mrs. Teitelbaum gave a little moan and, for a moment, her head nodded as though she were about to drop off to sleep. Lady Bland dipped a napkin into a tumbler of water and bathed her forehead. The doctor signed to two stewards who hoisted up the inert figure of Mr. Teitelbaum and carried him out of the saloon followed by the doctor and the captain. People stood up as they passed and there was a subdued buzz of conversation. Mrs. Teitelbaum struggled to her feet. Lady Bland signed to Eldrich and between them they managed to guide her through the tables to the elevator.

"I think," said Sir Roderick in a tired voice, "we'd better go up to the smoking room. My wife will know what to do."

Lola and Irma followed him out in silence.

25

The Peak of Hong Kong Island stood darkly against the bright morning sky. The ship threaded her way slowly through the crowded harbor and the echo of her siren ricocheted back and forth between the mainland and the Peninsula.

Mrs. Teitelbaum, having packed all Henry's things and her own, sat on her bed and stared at her hands which were clasped tranquilly on her lap: they were fat and pink as usual, secure in their own detached efficiency and untouched by grief. They had neatly folded Henry's suits and shirts and handkerchiefs, as they had done for fifty years, and were now at liberty to relax. They had completed their last task for Henry; they would no more have to pour out a drink for him, tie his evening bow, fit a new blade into his safety razor or gently massage his neck and shoulders when he had a touch of bursitis. Mrs. Teitelbaum, no longer plagued by sorrow, no longer touched by any emotion whatsoever, remained entirely still; a plump old woman in a beige two-piece traveling suit with a white hat, sitting on a bed looking forward to nothing and waiting, without interest, for what was going to happen to her next. The steward appeared and took away the luggage and then Lady Bland came and led her off the ship, down the gangway and into a waiting taxi. The taxi drove them briefly through noisy, crowded streets and deposited them at a hotel. Presently she was in a quiet room shuttered against the strong sunlight, sitting on another bed.

Later a tray of food was brought to her, after which a gray-haired man with an English accent came in and gave her an injection in her arm which made her more drowsy than ever. Later still, it might have been hours or days or centuries, she was sitting in a comfortable chair and a young woman in blue with bright lips was fastening a belt across her body. She struggled instinctively for a moment and heard herself mutter, in an unfamiliar voice, "Where is he?" The girl in blue patted her approvingly as though she were a talented dog who had just managed to balance of lump of sugar on its nose. "It's all right," she said with professional kindness. "Your relatives are meeting you in San Francisco. Just relax."

"Where is he?" Mrs. Teitelbaum's forehead puckered into a frown and she bit her lip as though she might be going to cry.

"Your husband is on the plane with you," said the girl. "Everything has been arranged."

"He can't be," said Mrs. Teitelbaum, "because he's dead." The girl pressed a knob and tilted her seat back; there was suddenly a thunderous noise and a feeling of swift movement, and she went to sleep.

On the following evening, Eldrich, Lola and Sir Roderick and Lady Bland were dining in the Marco Polo room at the Peninsular Hotel. The Marco Polo room was discreetly decorated, discreetly lit and the small orchestra which supplied "background music" was so gentle so as to be almost self-effacing. The Blands were sailing the next morning on a P. & O. ship bound for Singapore. Sir Roderick scrutinized the menu with affectionate concentration. "I believe in making hay while the sun shines!" he said, with an uncharacteristic chuckle, then he patted his wife's hand. "You look a bit peaky, my dear. I'm afraid looking after that poor old girl has tired you."

Lady Bland sighed. "Yes—it has a little."

"You'd better choose something light. Personally I'm going to start with some smoked salmon just for the relief of seeing it without lettuce."

"We shan't have to worry about lettuce on the P. & O." said Lady Bland. "It's a British ship and we don't go in for lettuce so much as the Americans do."

"It isn't a question of 'going in for it,'" said Eldrich. "It's part of our way of life. We revere and worship it. For us it is a status symbol representing refinement and daintiness. No self-respecting American housewife would dream of serving even a simple sandwich, unless it was stuffed with lettuce. We regard it as a sort of spiritual gas station on our rocky road to sophistication."

"You're being unpatriotic and I'm ashamed of you," said Lola.

When they had all ordered what they wanted and Sir Roderick had conducted a solemn discussion with the wine waiter, Lady Bland turned to Lola.

"I can hardly believe that that long voyage is over. At moments I must admit it seemed interminable, but now it seems to have gone like a flash." She looked at Lola quizzically and there was the ghost of a smile in her eyes. "Are you going to stay here long before going back to America?"

"I don't know"—Lola hesitated—"I expect . . ."

"We're staying here until next Tuesday," interrupted Eldrich, helping himself to a salted almond. "Then we're flying on to Fiji and Tahiti to have a look at the islands before they become really over-run . . ." Ignoring Lola's exasperated gasp of amazement he continued, "I believe Bora Bora is still comparatively unspoiled. It is about an hour by air from Tahiti and the hotel is apparently first-rate."

"It sounds lovely," said Lady Bland.

"Of course we shall have to stop off at Manila for a few days," went on Eldrich, "because it's American territory and, both of us being Americans, it will be simpler to be married there than anywhere else."

627

"I say!" said Sir Roderick with slightly overdone heartiness. "What a delightful surprise. This calls for a toast. Where's the damned wine waiter?" He snapped his fingers briskly like a Spanish dancer.

"It doesn't really call for a toast," said Lola ominously, "because it isn't true."

"How disappointing," murmured Lady Bland. "It sounds such a pleasant program."

"After Bora Bora," continued Eldrich, "our plans are uncertain."

"Not nearly so uncertain as they are before Bora Bora," said Lola.

Eldrich patted her hand soothingly and smiled at Lady Bland. "My future wife is many many years older than I am," he said. "And she is apt, at moments, to become rather irascible and argumentative, but underneath her harsh, professional exterior I assure you she is gentle as a lamb."

Lady Bland looked shrewdly at Lola and then back again to Eldrich. "I decided when we first met at the captain's table that you were a peculiar young man," she said. "And I am bound to admit that I have since seen no reason to change my opinion."

"I was drunk then," replied Eldrich cheerfully. "I am now sober as a judge."

"In that case," said Lola, "I can only conclude that you are out of your mind."

"Of course I'm out of my mind. People who are in love are always out of their minds. Don't you agree, Lady Bland?"

"For God's sake be quiet, Eldrich," said Lola, with a slight catch in her voice. "You're being hideously embarrassing."

"Do you agree with that statement, sir?" Eldrich leant across the table and addressed Sir Roderick.

"I'm damned if I know where the conversation's got to," said Sir Roderick. "Or the wine waiter either for the matter of that." He clapped his hands sharply. "Ah—here comes the fellow now. Please bring the wine I ordered immediately. If it happens to be the wrong temperature, it can be corrected later. The moment is urgent."

The wine waiter bowed and withdrew hurriedly. Lola lit a cigarette with a trembling hand and turned to Lady Bland. "I apologize, Lady Bland, really I do. This whole situation is ridiculous."

"On the contrary," Lady Bland began to laugh, "I'm finding it most entertaining."

"By the way, I almost forgot." Eldrich abruptly lifted Lola's left hand and kissed it. "Will you do me the honor of becoming my wife in Manila on the fourteenth of April?"

"Certainly not."

Eldrich shrugged his shoulders. "In that case we shall have to go on living in sin, which is morally reprehensible and socially untidy."

"Please stop—please, please stop."

"One more question—just one. Do you love me?"

Lola made an effort to rise from the table and then sat down again.

"You'd better say 'yes,'" said Lady Bland gently. "It will save time in the long run."

Aware that she was on the verge of tears Lola made a supreme effort to control herself. "Yes," she said, rather more loudly than she had intended.

"And will you do me the honor of becoming my wife in Manila on the fourteenth of April?"

"Have it your own way," said Lola, searching irritably in her bag for her handkerchief.

"Good," said Lady Bland. "Then that's settled.

26

The *Mara* sailed out of Hong Kong harbor at six P.M. on her homeward voyage to San Francisco. In the captain's cabin Olaf Hansen, the purser, in the grip of a painful hangover, stood uneasily to attention while the captain scanned the list he had handed to him.

"Who's that?"

The purser looked at the name at which the captain's finger was pointing.

"Sigmund Larsen. He's a movie director."

"Oh, God!"

"Mr. and Mrs. Elmer Schulberg."

"What's their line?"

"Something to do with leather goods, I think. They're on a stop-off—round-the-world trip. She's fat and he's thin."

"Miss Celia Addison." The captain looked up. "Any hope?"

The purser sadly shook his head. "Early sixties, slightly lame and a Christian Scientist."

"She's no right to be lame if she's a Christian Scientist."

"Mrs. Lynden looks a bit more snazzy, sir." The purser pointed to the fourth on the list. "Late thirties, well dressed and has good luggage."

"Who's this last one—Buck Lester?"

"Beefcake, sir. A friend of Mr. Larsen's."

"What sort of friend?"

"Your guess is as good as mine, sir."

"Thanks, Hansen. You'd better put Mrs. Kaplan on my right."

"I've already done so, sir."

At eight o'clock the musical chimes were sounded for dinner. At a quarter-past eight, Irma Kaplan, having treated herself to a dry Martini in the bar because she felt a little depressed, descended in the elevator and walked to the captain's table. Peppo showed her, smilingly, to her place on the captain's right. She bowed graciously and sat down.

"I'm afraid you'll be all alone tonight, Mrs. Kaplan. No one else is coming down." He shrugged his shoulders, a gesture of commiseration. "Can I bring you a cocktail?"

"I've already had one Martini in the bar," she said with a bright, disappointed smile. "But I'll have another small one just to celebrate going home."